D0592179

EPOCH

E 69

EPOCH

Edited by

ROBERT SILVERBERG
and
ROGER ELWOOD

Published by
Berkley Publishing Corporation
Distributed by G. P. Putnam's Sons, New York

Upsala College
Library
East Orange, N. J. 07019

808.83
E64

COPYRIGHT © 1975
BY ROBERT SILVERBERG AND ROGER ELWOOD

*All rights reserved. This book, or parts thereof,
may not be reproduced in any form without permission
in writing from the publisher. Published simultaneously
in Canada by Longman Canada Limited, Toronto.*

166309

PRINTED IN THE UNITED STATES OF AMERICA

CONTENTS

INTRODUCTION

"Science fiction" is one of those catch-all terms that one finds so hard to pin down to an exact definition. Once, thirty or forty or fifty years ago, it was *fiction about science*—fiction about technology, really, fiction that demonstrated man's interaction with the products of science; and to a certain degree, that is still what science fiction mostly is. The pure item is not yet extinct. There are writers whose idea of science fiction is a story that rigorously explores the consequences (social, economic, environmental, or whatever) of a single technological or scientific innovation—some new means of transportation, say, or synthetic human beings, or an antigravity device. When done with skill, this classic kind of science fiction is a marvelously stimulating intellectual exercise.

But the Buddha probably would not recognize contemporary Buddhism, Orville Wright would be baffled by the cockpit of a Boeing 747, and modern science fiction has undergone evolutions that have carried it very far indeed from the pioneering concepts of Hugo Gernsback and other science popularizers of yore. Like many third-generation phenomena, science fiction today tends to carry its original purpose and method submerged in the deeper strata. For example, a story such as Alexei and Cory Panshin's "Lady Sunshine and the Magoon of Beatus" is only indirectly a study of the effects of technology on man; the events of the narrative depend for their entire existence on certain technological developments, such as the development of workable interstellar travel, but that whole universe of scientific advance is taken for granted by the authors, who say, in effect: Let's imagine a time in which we can travel freely between the stars. *What then?* An earlier science-fictionist might have concentrated totally on the development of interstellar travel, the invention of a space drive, the early test flights, first contact with the denizens of an extrasolar planet, and so on and on. The Panshin story, like most other science-fiction stories of today, sweeps all that into the background and goes on to look at the quality of life in a society where such far-ranging travel is commonplace.

So too with most of the stories in *Epoch*. Some of them are science fiction to satisfy the most rigorous purist, as, for example, Gregory Benford's "Cambridge 1:58 A.M.," but the majority are concerned with the consequences of consequences rather than directly with specific scientific events. We have tried, in assembling this volume— one of the largest collections of previously unpublished science-fiction stories ever put together—to illustrate the enormous scope and range of modern-day science fiction, displaying the astoundingly rich vitality and inventiveness and *variety* of this exciting literary field. Somehow all these stories qualify as science fiction, all of them reflect in some way the impact of technology on man; but they fit themselves into that expansive category in strange and wondrous ways. One would hardly expect such ferociously independent writers as Joanna Russ, R. A. Lafferty, Brian W. Aldiss, Frederik Pohl, Ursula K. Le Guin, and the others that crowd the Contents pages with such distinction, to settle for yesterday's outworn formulas, nor have they disappointed us with stale goods. *Epoch* will, we think, amaze and surprise and give delight.

ROBERT SILVERBERG
ROGER ELWOOD

EPOCH

ARM

by Larry Niven

The ARM building had been abnormally quiet for some months now.

We'd needed the rest—at first. But these last few mornings the silence had had an edgy quality. We waved at each other on our paths to our respective desks, but our heads were elsewhere. Some of us had a restless look. Others were visibly, determinedly busy.

Nobody wanted to join a mother hunt.

This past year we'd managed to cut deep into the organlegging activities in the West Coast area. Pats on the back all around, but the results were predictable: other activities were going to increase. Sooner or later the newstapers would start screaming about stricter enforcement of the Fertility Laws, and then we'd all be out hunting down illegitimate parents—all of us who were not involved in something else.

It was high time I got involved in something else.

This morning I walked to my office through the usual edgy silence. I ran coffee from the spigot, carried it to my desk, punched for messages at the computer terminal. A slender file slid from the slot. A hopeful sign. I picked it up—one-handed, so that I could sip coffee as I went through it—and let it fall open in the middle.

Color holographs jumped out at me. I *was* looking down through a pair of windows over two morgue tables.

Stomach to brain: LURCH! What a hell of an hour to be looking at people with their faces burned off! Get eyes to look somewhere else, and don't try to swallow that coffee. Why don't you change jobs?

They were hideous. Two of them, a man and a woman. Something had burned their faces away, down to the skulls and beyond—bones and teeth charred, brain tissue cooked.

I swallowed and kept looking. I'd seen the dead before. These had just hit me at the wrong time.

Not a laser weapon, I thought . . . though that was chancy. There are thousands of jobs for lasers, and thousands of varieties to do the jobs. Not a hand laser, anyway. The pencil-thin beam of a hand laser would have chewed channels in the flesh. This had been a wide, steady beam of some kind.

I flipped back to the beginning and skimmed.

Details: They'd been found on the Wilshire slidewalk in West Los Angeles around 4:30 A.M. People don't use the slidewalks that late. They're afraid of organleggers. The bodies could have traveled up to a couple of miles before anyone saw them.

Preliminary autopsy: they'd been dead three or four days. No signs of drugs or poisons or puncture marks. Apparently the burns had been the only cause of death.

It must have been quick, then—a single flash of energy. Otherwise they'd have tried to dodge, and there'd be burns elsewhere. There were none. Just the faces, and char marks around the collars.

There was a memo from Bates, the coroner. From the looks of them, they might have been killed by some new weapon. So he'd sent the file over to us. Could we find anything in the ARM files that would fire a blast of heat or light a foot across?

I sat back and stared into the holos and thought about it.

A light weapon with a beam a foot across? They make lasers in that size, but as war weapons, used from orbit. One of those would have vaporized the heads, not charred them.

There were other possibilities. Death by torture, with the heads held in clamps in the blast from a commercial attitude jet. Or some kind of weird industrial accident—a flash explosion that had caught them both looking over a desk or something. Or even a laser beam reflected from a convex mirror.

Forget about its being an accident. The way the bodies were abandoned reeked of guilt, of something to be covered up. Maybe Bates was right. A new, illegal weapon.

And I could be deeply involved in searching for it when the mother hunt started.

The ARM, the police branch of the United Nations, has three basic functions. We hunt organleggers—dealers in illicit transplants, who get their raw material through murder. We monitor world technology—new developments that might create new weapons or that might affect the world economy or the balance of power among nations. And we enforce the Fertility Laws.

Come, let us be honest with ourselves. Of the three, protecting the Fertility Laws is probably the most important.

Organleggers don't aggravate the population problem.

Monitoring of technology is necessary enough, but it may have happened too late. There are enough fusion power plants and fusion rocket motors and fusion crematoriums and fusion seawater distilleries around to let any madman or group thereof blow up the Earth or any selected part of it.

But if a lot of people in one region started having illegal babies, the rest of the world would scream. Some nations might even get mad enough to abandon population control. Then what? We've got eighteen billion on Earth now. We couldn't handle more.

So the mother hunts are necessary. But I hate them. It's no fun hunting down some poor sick woman so desperate to have children that she'll go through hell to avoid her six-month contraceptive shots. I'll get out of it if I can.

I did some obvious things. I sent a note to Bates at the coroner's office: "Send all further details on the autopsies, and let me know if the corpses are identified." Retina prints and brain-wave patterns were obviously out, but they might get something on gene patterns and fingerprints.

I spent some time wondering where two bodies had been kept for three to four days, and why, before being abandoned in a way that could have been used three days earlier. But that was a problem for the LAPD detectives. Our concern was with the weapon.

So I started writing a search pattern for the computer: find me a widget that will fire a beam of a given description. From the pattern of penetration into skin and bone and brain tissue, there was probably a way to express the frequency of the light as a function of the duration of the blast, but I didn't fool with that. I'd pay for my laziness later, when the computer handed me a foot-thick list of light-emitting machinery and I had to wade through it.

I had punched in the instructions and was relaxing with more coffee and a cigarette, when Ordaz called.

Julio Ordaz was a slender, dark-skinned man with straight black hair and soft black eyes. He was a detective inspector of homicide in the Los Angeles Police. The first time I saw him in a phone screen, he had been telling me of a good friend's murder. Two years later I still flinched when I saw him.

"Hello, Julio. Business or pleasure?"

"Business, Gil. It is to be regretted."

"Yours or mine?"

"Both. There is murder involved, but there is also a machine. . . . Look, can you see it behind me?" Ordaz stepped out of the field of view, then reached invisibly to turn the phone camera.

I looked into somebody's living room. There was a wide circle of discoloration in the green indoor-grass rug. In the center of the circle, a machine and a man's body.

Was Julio putting me on? The body was old, half-mummified. The machine was big and cryptic in shape, and it glowed with a subdued eerie blue light.

Ordaz sounded serious enough. "Have you ever seen anything like this?"

"No. That's some machine." Unmistakably an experimental device —no neat plastic case, no compactness, no assembly-line welding. Too complex to examine through a phone camera, I decided. "Yah, that looks like something for us. Can you send it over?"

Ordaz came back on. He was smiling, barely. "I'm afraid we cannot do that. Perhaps you should send someone here to look at it."

"Where are you now?"

"In Raymond Sinclair's apartment on the top floor of the Rodewald Building in Santa Monica."

"I'll come myself," I said. My tongue suddenly felt thick.

"Please land on the roof. We are holding the elevator for examination."

"Sure." I hung up.

Raymond Sinclair!

I'd never met Raymond Sinclair. He was something of a recluse. But the ARM had dealt with him once, in connection with one of his inventions, the FyreStop device. And everyone knew that he had lately been working on an interstellar drive. It was only a rumor, of course, but if someone had killed the brain that held that secret . . .

I went.

The Rodewald Building was forty stories of triangular prism with a row of triangular balconies going up each side. The balconies stopped at the thirty-eighth floor.

The roof was a garden. There were rosebushes in bloom along one edge, full-grown elms nestled in ivy along another, and a miniature forest of bonsai trees along the third. The landing pad and carport were in the center. A squad car was floating down ahead of my taxi. It landed, then slid under the carport to give me room to land.

A cop in vivid orange uniform came out to watch me come down. I couldn't tell what he was carrying until I had stepped out. It was a deep-sea fishing pole, still in its kit.

He said, "May I see some ID, please?"

I had my ARM ident in my hand. He checked it in the console in the squad car, then handed it back. "The inspector's waiting downstairs," he said.

"What's the pole for?"

He smiled suddenly, almost secretively. "You'll see."

We left the garden smells via a flight of concrete stairs. They led down into a small room half full of gardening tools, on the far side of which was a heavy door with a spy-eye in it. Ordaz opened the door for us. He shook my hand briskly, glanced at the cop. "You found something? Good."

The cop said, "There's a sporting-goods store six blocks from here. The manager let me borrow it. He made sure I knew the name of the store."

"Yes, there will certainly be publicity on this matter. Come, Gil . . ." Ordaz took my arm. "You should examine this before we turn it off."

No garden smells here, but there was something—a whiff of something long dead—that the air-conditioning hadn't quite cleared away. Ordaz walked me into the living room.

It looked like somebody's idea of a practical joke.

The indoor grass covered Sinclair's living-room floor, wall-to-wall. In a perfect fourteen-foot circle between the sofa and the fireplace, the rug was brown and dead. Elsewhere it was green and thriving.

A man's mummy, dressed in stained slacks and turtleneck, lay on its back in the center of the circle. At a guess, it had been about six months dead. It wore a big digital wristwatch with extra dials on the face and a fine mesh platinum band, loose now around a wrist of bones and brown skin. The back of the skull had been smashed open, possibly by the classic blunt instrument lying next to it.

If the fireplace was false—and it almost had to be; nobody burns wood—the fireplace instruments were genuine nineteenth- or twentieth-century antiques. The rack was missing a poker. A poker lay inside the circle, in the dead grass next to the disintegrating mummy.

The glowing goldberg device sat just in the center of the magic circle.

I stepped forward, and a man's voice spoke sharply. "Don't go inside that circle of rug. It's more dangerous than it looks."

It was a man I knew—Officer-One Valpredo, a tall man with a small, straight mouth and a long, narrow Italian face.

"Looks dangerous enough to me," I said.

"It is. I reached in there myself," Valpredo told me, "right after we got here. I thought I could flip the switch off. My whole arm went numb. Instantly. No feeling at all. I yanked it away fast, but for a minute or so after that, my whole arm was dead meat. I thought I'd lost it. Then it was all pins and needles, like I'd slept on it."

The cop who had brought me in had almost finished assembling the deep-sea fishing pole.

Ordaz waved into the circle. "Well? Have you ever seen anything like this?"

I shook my head, studying the violet-glowing machinery. "Whatever it is, it's brand-new. Sinclair's really done it this time."

An uneven line of solenoids was attached to a plastic frame with homemade joins. Blistered spots on the plastic showed where other objects had been attached and later removed. A breadboard bore masses of heavy wiring. There were six big batteries hooked in parallel, and a strange, heavy piece of sculpture in what looked like pure silver, with wiring attached at three curving points. The silver was tarnished almost black, and there were old file marks at the edges.

Near the center of the arrangement, just in front of the silver sculpture, were two concentric solenoids embedded in a block of clear plastic. They glowed blue, shading to violet. So did the batteries. A less perceptible violet glow radiated from everywhere on the machine, more intensely in the interior parts.

That glow bothered me more than anything else. It was too theatrical. It was like something a special-effects man might add to a cheap late-night thriller to suggest a mad scientist's laboratory.

I moved around to get a closer look at the dead man's watch.

"Keep your head out of the field!" Valpredo said sharply.

I nodded. I squatted on my heels outside the borderline of dead grass.

The dead man's watch was going like crazy. The minute hand was circling the dial every seven seconds or so. I couldn't find the second hand at all.

I backed away from the arc of dead grass and stood up. Interstellar drive, hell. This blue-glowing monstrosity looked more like a time machine gone wrong.

I studied the single throw switch welded to the plastic frame next to the batteries. A length of nylon line dangled from the horizontal handle. It looked like someone had tugged the switch *on* from outside the field by using the line; but he'd have had to hang from the ceiling to tug it *off* that way.

"I see why you couldn't send it over to ARM headquarters. You can't even touch it. You stick your arm or your head in there for a second, and that's ten minutes without a blood supply."

Ordaz said, "Exactly."

"It looks like you could reach in there with a stick and flip that switch off."

"Perhaps. We are about to try that." He waved at the man with the fishing pole. "There was nothing in this room long enough to reach the switch. We had to send—"

"Wait a minute. There's a problem."

He looked at me. So did the cop with the fishing pole.

"That switch could be a self-destruct. Sinclair was supposed to be a secretive bastard. Or the . . . field might hold considerable potential energy. Something might go blooey."

Ordaz sighed. "We must risk it. Gil, we have measured the rotation of the dead man's wristwatch. One hour per seven seconds. Fingerprints, footprints, laundry marks, residual body odor, stray eyelashes—all disappearing at an hour per seven seconds." He gestured, and the cop moved in and began trying to hook the switch.

"Already we may never know just when he was killed," said Ordaz.

The tip of the pole wobbled in large circles, steadied beneath the switch, made contact. I held my breath. The pole bowed. The switch snapped up, and suddenly the violet glow was gone. Valpredo reached into the field warily, as if the air might be red-hot. Nothing happened, and he relaxed.

Then Ordaz began giving orders, and quite a lot happened. Two men in lab coats drew a chalk outline around the mummy and the poker. They moved the mummy onto a stretcher, put the poker in a plastic bag, and put it next to the mummy.

I said, "Have you identified that?"

"I'm afraid so," said Ordaz. "Raymond Sinclair had his own autodoc."

"*Did* he? Those things are expensive."

"Yes. Raymond Sinclair was a wealthy man. He owned the top two floors of this building, and the roof. According to records in his 'doc, he had a new set of bud teeth implanted two months ago." Ordaz pointed to the mummy, to the skinned-back dry lips and the buds of new teeth that were just coming in.

Right. That was Sinclair.

That brain had made miracles, and someone had smashed it with a wrought-iron rod. The intersteller drive—that glowing goldberg device? Or had it been still inside his head?

I said, "We'll have to get whoever did it. We'll *have* to. Even so . . ." Even so. No more miracles.

"We may have her already," Julio said.

I looked at him.

"There is a girl in the autodoc. We think she is Dr. Sinclair's great-niece."

It was a standard drugstore autodoc, a thing like a giant coffin with walls a foot thick and a headboard covered with dials and red and green lights. The girl lay face-up, her face calm, her breathing shallow. Sleeping Beauty. Her arms were in the guts of the 'doc, hidden by bulky rubbery sleeves.

She was lovely enough to stop my breath. Soft brown hair showing around the electrode cap; small, perfect nose and mouth; smooth pale-blue skin shot with silver threads.

That last was an evening dye job. Without it the impact of her would have been much lessened. The blue shade varied slightly to emphasize the shape of her body and the curve of her cheekbones. The silver lines varied too, being denser in certain areas, guiding the eye in certain directions—to the tips of her breasts, or across the slight swell of abdominal muscle to a lovely oval navel.

She'd paid high for that dye job. But she would be beautiful without it.

Some of the headboard lights were red. I punched for a readout, and was jolted. The 'doc had been forced to amputate her right arm. Gangrene.

She was in for a hell of a shock when she woke up.

"All right," I said. "She's lost her arm. That doesn't make her a killer."

Ordaz asked, "If she were homely, would it help?"

I laughed. "You question my dispassionate judgment? Men have died for less!" Even so, I thought he could be right. There was good reason to think that the killer was now missing an arm.

"What do you think happened here, Gil?"

"Well . . . any way you look at it, the killer had to want to take Sinclair's . . . ah . . . time machine with him. It's priceless, for one thing. For another, it looks like he tried to set it up as an alibi. Which means that he knew about it before he came here." I'd been thinking this through. "Say he made sure some people knew where he was a few hours before he got here. He killed Sinclair within range of the . . . call it a generator. Turned it on. He figured Sinclair's own watch would tell him how much time he was gaining. Afterward he could set the watch back and leave with the generator. There'd be no way the police could tell that Sinclair wasn't killed six hours earlier, or any number you like."

"Yes. But he did not do that."

"There was that line hanging from the switch. He must have turned it on from outside the field—probably because he didn't want to sit with the body for six hours. If he tried to step outside the field after he'd turned it on, he'd bump his nose. It'd be like trying to walk through a wall, going from field time to normal time. So he turned it off, stepped out of range, and used that nylon line to turn it on again. He probably made the same mistake Valpredo did: he thought he could step back in and turn it off."

Ordaz nodded in satisfaction. "Exactly. It was very important for him—or her—to do that. Otherwise he would have no alibi and no profit. If he continued to try to reach into the field—"

"Yah, he could lose the arm to gangrene. That'd be convenient for us, wouldn't it? He'd be easy to find. But, look, Julio, the girl could have done the same thing to herself trying to *help* Sinclair. He might not have been that obviously dead when she got home."

"He might even have been alive," Ordaz pointed out.

I shrugged.

"In point of fact, she came home at one-ten, in her own car, which is still in the carport. There are cameras mounted to cover the landing pad and carport. Dr. Sinclair's security was thorough. This girl was the only arrival last night. There were no departures."

"From the roof, you mean."

"Gil, there are only two ways to leave these apartments. One is from the roof, and the other is by elevator, from the lobby. The elevator is on this floor, and it was turned off. It was that way when we arrived. There is no way to override that control from elsewhere in this building."

"So someone could have taken it up here and turned it off afterward . . . or Sinclair could have turned it off before he was killed. . . . I see what you mean. Either way, the killer has to be still here." I thought about that. I didn't like its taste. "No, it doesn't fit. How could she be bright enough to work out that alibi, then dumb enough to lock herself in with the body?"

Ordaz shrugged. "She locked the elevator before killing her great-uncle. She did not want to be interrupted. Surely that was sensible? After she hurt her arm, she must have been in a great hurry to reach the 'doc."

One of the red lights turned green. I was glad for that. She didn't look like a killer. I said, half to myself, "Nobody looks like a killer when he's asleep."

"No. But she is where a killer ought to be. *Qué lástima.*"

We went back to the living room. I called ARM headquarters and had them send a truck.

The machine hadn't been touched. While we waited I borrowed a camera from Valpredo and took pictures of the setup *in situ*. Relative positions of the components might be important.

The lab men were in the brown grass using aerosol sprays to turn fingerprints white and give a vivid yellow glow to faint traces of blood. They got plenty of fingerprints on the machine, none at all on the poker. There was a puddle of yellow in the grass where the mummy's head had been, and a long yellow snail track ending at the business end of the poker. It looked like someone had tried to drag the poker out of the field after it had fallen.

Sinclair's apartments were roomy and comfortable and occupied the entire top floor. The lower floor was the laboratory where Sinclair had produced his miracles. I went through it with Valpredo. It wasn't that impressive. It looked like an expensive hobby setup. These tools would assemble components already fabricated, but they would not build anything complex.

Except for the computer terminal. That was like a little womb, with a recline chair inside a 360-degree wraparound holovision screen and enough banked controls to fly the damn thing to Alpha Centaurus.

The secrets there must be in that computer! But I didn't try to use it. We'd have to send an ARM programmer to break whatever fail-safe codes Sinclair had put in the memory banks.

The truck arrived. We dragged Sinclair's legacy up the stairs to the roof in one piece. The parts were sturdily mounted on their frame, and the stairs were wide and not too steep.

I rode home in the back of the truck. Studying the generator. That massive piece of silver had something of the look of *Bird in Flight*—a triangle operated on by a topology student, with wires at what were still the corners. I wondered if it was the heart of the machine, or just a piece of misdirection. Was I really riding with an interstellar drive? Sinclair could have started that rumor himself, to cover . . . whatever this was. Or . . . there was no law against his working two projects simultaneously.

I was looking forward to Bera's reaction.

Jackson Bera came upon us moving it through the halls of ARM headquarters. He trailed along behind us. Nonchalant. We pulled the machine into the main laboratory and started checking it against the holos I'd taken, in case something had been jarred loose. Bera leaned against the doorjamb, watching us, his eyes gradually losing interest, until he seemed about to go to sleep.

Jackson Bera was a big dark man crowned with a carefully tended sphere of puffy black hair. I'd met him three years ago when I returned from the asteroids and joined the ARM. Maybe he'd wondered why I kept staring at his hair. But a Belter who wore his hair in that fashion would have needed a spacesuit helmet the size of a cannibal's cooking pot.

He'd been twenty then, and two years an ARM; but his father and grandfather had both been ARMs. Much of my training had come from Bera. And as I learned to hunt men who hunt other men, I had watched what it was doing to him.

An ARM needs empathy. He needs the ability to piece together a picture of the mind of his prey. But Bera had too much empathy. I remember his reaction when Kenneth Graham suicided with a battery-operated droud—a single killing surge of current through the plug in his skull and down the wire to the pleasure center of his brain. Bera had been twitchy for weeks. And the Anubis case, early last year. When we realized what the man had done, Bera had been close to killing him on the spot. I wouldn't have blamed him.

Last year Bera had had enough. He'd gone into the technical end of the business. His days of hunting organleggers were finished. He was now running the ARM laboratory.

He *had* to want to know what this oddball contraption was. I kept waiting for him to ask, and he watched, faintly smiling. Finally it dawned on me. He thought it was a practical joke, something I'd cobbled together for his own discomfiture.

I said, "Bera . . ."

And he looked at me brightly and said, "Hey, man, what is it?"

"You ask the most embarrassing questions."

"Right, I can understand your feeling that way, but what *is* it? I love it, it's neat, but what is this that you have brought me?"

I told him all I knew, such as it was. When I finished, he said, "It doesn't sound much like a new space drive."

"Oho, you heard that too, did you? No, it doesn't. Unless . . ." I'd been wondering since I first saw it. "Maybe it's supposed to accelerate a fusion explosion. You'd get greater efficiency in a fusion drive."

"Nope. They get better than ninety percent now, and that widget looks *heavy*." He reached to touch the bent silver triangle, gently, with long, tapering fingers. "Huh. Well, we'll dig out the answers."

"Good luck. I'm going back to Sinclair's place."

"Why? The action is here." Often enough he'd heard me talking wistfully of joining an interstellar colony. He must know how I'd feel about a better drive for the interstellar slowboats.

"It's like this," I said. "We've got the generator, but we don't know anything about it. We might wreck it. I'm going to have a whack at finding someone who knows something about Sinclair's generator."

"Meaning?"

"Whoever tried to steal it. Sinclair's killer."

"If you say so." But he looked dubious. He knew me too well. He said, "I understand there's a mother hunt in the offing."

"Oh?"

He smiled. "Just a rumor. You guys are lucky. When my dad first joined, the business of the ARM was *mostly* mother hunts. The organleggers hadn't really got organized yet, and the Fertility Laws were new. If we hadn't enforced them, nobody would have obeyed them at all."

"Sure, and people threw rocks at your father. Bera, those days are *gone.*"

"They could come back. Having children is basic."

"Bera, I did not join the ARM to hunt unlicensed parents." I waved and left before he could answer. I could do without the call to duty from Bera, who was through with hunting men and mothers.

* * *

I'd had a good view of the Rodewald Building, dropping toward the roof this morning. I had a good view now from my commandeered taxi. This time I was looking for escape paths.

There were no balconies on Sinclair's floors, and the windows were flush to the side of the building. A cat burglar would have trouble with them. They didn't look like they'd open.

I tried to spot the cameras Ordaz had mentioned as the taxi dropped toward the roof. I couldn't find them. Maybe they were mounted in the elms.

Why was I bothering? I hadn't joined the ARM to chase mothers or machinery or common murderers. I'd joined to pay for my arm—my right arm, after it had been sheared clean to the shoulder in an industrial accident in the Belt.

I hadn't had the money to buy a new arm from the Belt organ banks. I'd come back to Earth because my citizens' medical insurance would pay for it there. Later I'd found that my new arm was not part of some condemned criminal. It had reached the World Organ Bank Facility via a captured organlegger's cache. Some honest citizen had died unwillingly on a city slidewalk, and now his arm was part of me.

I'd joined the ARM to hunt organleggers.

The ARM doesn't deal in murder *per se*. The machine was out of my hands now. A murder investigation wouldn't keep me out of a mother hunt. And I'd never met the girl. I knew nothing of her, beyond the fact that she was where a killer ought to be.

Was it just that she was pretty?

Poor Janice. When she woke up . . . For a solid month I'd wakened to that same stunning shock, the knowledge that my right arm was gone.

The taxi settled. Valpredo was waiting below.

I speculated. Cars weren't the only things that flew. But anyone flying one of those tricky ducted-fan flycycles over a city, where he could fall on a pedestrian, wouldn't have to worry about a murder charge. They'd feed him to the organ banks regardless. And anything that flew would have left traces anywhere but on the landing pad itself. It would crush a rosebush or a bonsai tree or be flipped over by an elm.

The taxi took off in a whisper of air.

Valpredo was grinning at me. "The Thinker. What's on your mind?"

"I was wondering if the killer could have come down on the carport roof."

He turned to study the situation. "There are two cameras mounted on the edge of the roof. If his vehicle was light enough, sure, he could land there, and the cameras wouldn't spot him. Roof wouldn't hold a car, though. Anyway, nobody did it."

"How do you know?"

"I'll show you. By the way, we inspected the camera system. We're pretty sure the cameras weren't tampered with."

"And nobody came down from the roof last night except the girl?"

"Nobody. Nobody even landed here until seven this morning. Look here." We had reached the concrete stairs that led down into Sinclair's apartments. Valpredo pointed at a glint of light in the sloping ceiling, at heart level. "This is the only way down. The camera would get anyone coming in or out. It might not catch his face, but it'd show if someone had passed. It takes sixty frames a minute."

I went on down. A cop let me in.

Ordaz was on the phone. The screen showed a young man with a deep tan, with shock showing through the tan. Ordaz waved at me, a shushing motion, and went on talking. "Then you'll be here in fifteen minutes? That will be a great help to us. Please land on the roof. We are still working on the elevator."

He hung up and turned to me. "That was Andrew Porter, Janice Sinclair's lover. He tells us that he and Janice spent the evening at a party. She dropped him off at his home around one o'clock."

"Then she came straight home, if that's her in the 'doc."

"I think it must be. Mr. Porter says she was wearing a blue skin dye job." Ordaz was frowning. "He put on a most convincing act, if it was that. I think he really was not expecting any kind of trouble. He was surprised that a stranger answered, shocked when he learned of Dr. Sinclair's death, and horrified when he learned that Janice had been hurt."

With the mummy and the generator removed, the murder scene had become an empty circle of brown grass marked with random streaks of yellow chemical and outlines of white chalk.

"We had some luck," said Ordaz. "Today's date is June 4, 2124. Dr. Sinclair was wearing a date watch. It registered January 17, 2125. If we switched the machine off at ten minutes to ten—which we did—and if it was registering an hour for every seven seconds that passed outside the field, then the field must have gone on around one o'clock last night, give or take a margin of error."

"Then if the girl didn't do it, she must have just missed the killer."

"Exactly."

"What about the elevator? Could it have been jiggered?"

"No. We took the workings apart. It was on this floor, and locked by hand. Nobody could have left by elevator . . ."

"Why did you trail off like that?"

Ordaz shrugged, embarrassed. "This peculiar machine really does bother me, Gil. I found myself thinking: Suppose it can reverse time? Then the killer could have gone down in an elevator that was going up."

He laughed with me. I said, "In the first place, I don't believe a word of it. In the second place, he didn't have the machine to do it with. Unless . . . he made his escape before the murder. Damnit, now you've got me doing it."

"I would like to know more about the machine."

"Bera's investigating it now. I'll let you know as soon as we learn anything. And *I'd* like to know more about how the killer couldn't possibly have left."

He looked at me. "Details?"

"Could someone have opened a window?"

"No. These apartments are forty years old. The smog was still bad when they were built. Dr. Sinclair apparently preferred to depend on his air-conditioning."

"How about the apartment below? I presume it has a different set of elevators. . . ."

"Yes, of course. It belongs to Howard Rodewald, the owner of this building—of this chain of buildings, in fact. At the moment, he is in Europe. His apartment has been lent to friends."

"There are no stairs down to there?"

"No. We searched these apartments thoroughly."

"All right. We know the killer had a nylon line, because he left a strand of it on the generator. Could he have climbed down to Rodewald's balcony from the roof?"

"Thirty feet? Yes, I suppose so." Ordaz's eyes sparked. "We must look into that. There is still the matter of how he got past the camera, and whether he could have gotten inside, once he was on the balcony."

"Yah."

"Try this, Mr. Hamilton. Another question. How did he *expect* to get away?" He watched for my reaction, which must have been satisfying, because it *was* a damn good question. "You see, if Janice

Sinclair murdered her great-uncle, then neither question applies. If we are looking for someone else, we have to assume that his plans misfired. He had to improvise."

"Uh-huh. He could still have been planning to use Rodewald's balcony. And that would mean he had a way past the camera. . . ."

"Of course he did. The generator."

"Right. If he came to steal the generator . . . and he'd have to steal it regardless, because if we found it here, it would shoot his alibi sky-high. So he'd leave it on while he trundled it up the stairs. Say it took him a minute; that's only an eighth of a second of normal time. One chance in eight that the camera would fire, and it would catch nothing but a streak. . . . Uh-oh."

"What is it?"

"He had to be planning to steal the machine. Is he really going to lower it to Rodewald's balcony by *rope?*"

"I think it unlikely," said Ordaz. "It weighed more than eighty pounds. He could have moved it upstairs. The frame would make it portable. But to lower it by rope . . ."

"We'd be looking for one hell of an athlete."

"At least you will not have to search far to find him. We assume that your hypothetical killer came by elevator, do we not?"

"Yah." Nobody but Janice Sinclair had arrived by the roof last night.

"The elevator was programmed to allow a number of people to enter it, and to turn away all others. The list is short. Dr. Sinclair was not a gregarious man."

"You're checking them out? Whereabouts, alibis, and so forth?"

"Of course."

"There's something else you might check on," I said. But Drew Porter came in, and I had to postpone it.

Porter came casual, in a well-worn one-piece jumpsuit he must have pulled on while running for a taxi. The muscles rolled like boulders beneath the loose fabric, and his belly muscles showed like the plates on an armadillo. Surfing muscles. The sun had bleached his hair nearly white and burned him as brown as Jackson Bera. You'd think a tan that dark would cover for blood draining out of a face, but it doesn't.

"Where is she?" he demanded. He didn't wait for an answer. He knew where the 'doc was, and he went there. We trailed in his wake.

Ordaz didn't push. He waited while Porter looked down at Janice, then punched for a readout and went through it in detail. Porter seemed calmer then, and his color was back. He turned to Ordaz and said, "What happened?"

"Mr. Porter, did you know anything of Dr. Sinclair's latest project?"

"The time-compressor thing? Yah. He had it set up in the living room when I got here yesterday evening. Right in the middle of that circle of dead grass. Any connection?"

"When did you arrive?"

"Oh, about . . . six. We had some drinks, and Uncle Ray showed off his machine. He didn't tell us much about it. Just showed what it could do." Porter showed us flashing white teeth. "It *worked*. That thing can compress time! You could live your whole life in there in two months! Watching him move around inside the field was like trying to keep track of a hummingbird. Worse. He struck a match—"

"When did you leave?"

"About eight. We had dinner at Cziller's, and . . . listen, what *happened* here?"

"There are some things we need to know first, Mr. Porter. Were you and Janice together for all of last evening? Were there others with you?"

"Sure. We had dinner alone, but afterward we went to a kind of party. On the beach at Santa Monica. Friend of mine has a house there. I'll give you the address. Some of us wound up at Cziller's House of Irish Coffee around midnight. Then Janice flew me home."

"You have said that you are Janice's lover. Doesn't she live with you?"

"No. I'm her steady lover, you might say, but I don't have any strings on her." He seemed embarrassed. "She lives here, with Uncle Ray. Lived. Oh, *hell*." He glanced into the 'doc. "Look, the readout said she'll be waking up any minute. Can I get her a robe?"

"Of course."

We followed Porter to Janice's bedroom, where he picked out a peach-colored negligee for her. I was beginning to like the guy. He had good instincts. An evening dye job was not the thing to wear on the morning of a murder. And he'd picked one with long, loose sleeves. Her missing arm wouldn't show so much.

"You call him Uncle Ray," said Ordaz.

"Yah. Because Janice did."

"He did not object? Was he gregarious?"

"Gregarious? Well, no, but *we* liked each other. We both liked puzzles, you understand. We traded murder mysteries and jigsaw puzzles. Listen, this may sound silly, but are you sure he's dead?"

"Regrettably, yes. He is dead, and murdered. Was he expecting someone to arrive after you left?"

"Yes."

"He said so?"

"No. But he was wearing a shirt and pants. When it was just us, he usually went naked."

"Ah."

"Older people don't do that much," Porter said. "But Uncle Ray was in good shape. He took care of himself."

"Have you any idea whom he might have been expecting?"

"No. Not a woman; not a date, I mean. Maybe someone in the same business."

Behind him, Janice moaned.

Porter was hovering over her in a flash. He put a hand on her shoulder and urged her back. "Lie still, love. We'll have you out of there in a jiffy."

She waited while he disconnected the sleeves and other paraphernalia. She said, "What happened?"

"They haven't told me yet," Porter said with a flash of anger. "Be careful sitting up. You've had an accident."

"What kind of . . . ? *Oh!*"

"It'll be all right."

"My *arm!*"

Porter helped her out of the 'doc. Her arm ended in pink flesh two inches below the shoulder. She let Porter drape the robe around her. She tried to fasten the sash, quit when she realized she was trying to do it with one hand.

I said, "Listen, I lost my arm once."

She looked at me. So did Porter.

"I'm Gil Hamilton. With the UN Police. You really don't have anything to worry about. See?" I raised my right arm, opened and closed the fingers. "The organ banks don't get much call for arms, as compared to kidneys, for instance. You probably won't even have to wait. I didn't. It feels just like the arm I was born with, and it works just as well."

"How did you lose it?" she asked.

"Ripped away by a meteor," I said, not without pride. "While I was asteroid mining in the Belt." I didn't have to tell her that we'd caused the meteor cluster ourselves, by setting the bomb wrong on an asteroid we wanted to move.

Ordaz said to her, "Do you remember how you lost your own arm?"

"Yes." She shivered. "Could we go somewhere where I could sit down? I feel a bit weak."

We moved to the living room. Janice dropped onto the couch a bit too hard. It might have been shock, or the missing arm might be throwing her balance off. I remembered. She said, "Uncle Ray's dead, isn't he?"

"Yes."

"I came home and found him that way. Lying next to that time machine of his, and the back of his head all bloody. I thought maybe he was still alive, but I could see the machine was going; it had that violet glow. I tried to get hold of the poker. I wanted to use it to switch the machine off, but I couldn't get a grip. My arm wasn't just numb, it wouldn't move. You know, you can wiggle your toes when your foot's asleep, but . . . I could get my hand on the handle of the damn poker, but when I tried to pull, it just slid off."

"You kept trying?"

"For a while. Then . . . I backed away to think it over. I wasn't about to waste any time, with Uncle Ray maybe dying in there. My arm felt stone dead. . . . I guess it was, wasn't it?" She shuddered. "Rotting meat. It smelled that way. And all of a sudden I felt so weak and dizzy, like I was dying myself. I barely made it into the 'doc."

"Good thing you did," I said. The blood was leaving Porter's face again as he realized what a close thing it had been.

Ordaz said, "Was your great-uncle expecting visitors last night?"

"I think so."

"Why do you think so?"

"I don't know. He just . . . acted that way."

"We are told that you and some friends reached Cziller's House of Irish Coffee around midnight. Is that true?"

"I guess so. We had some drinks, then I took Drew home and came home myself."

"Straight home?"

"Yes." She shivered. "I put the car away and went downstairs. I knew something was wrong. The door was open. Then, there was Uncle Ray lying next to that machine! I knew better than to just run up to him. He'd told us not to step into the field."

"Oh? Then you should have known better than to reach for the poker."

"Well, yes. I could have used the tongs," she said, as if the idea had just occurred to her. "It's just as long. I didn't think of it. There wasn't *time*. Don't you understand, he was dying in there, or dead!"

"Yes, of course. Did you interfere with the murder scene in any way?"

She laughed bitterly. "I suppose I moved the poker about two inches. Then, when I felt what was happening to me, I just ran for the 'doc. It was awful. Like dying."

"Instant gangrene," said Porter.

Ordaz said, "You did not, for example, lock the elevator?"

Damn! I should have thought of that.

"No. We usually do when we lock up for the night, but I didn't have time."

Porter said, "Why?"

"The elevator was locked when we arrived," Ordaz told him.

Porter ruminated that. "Then the killer must have left by the roof. You'll have pictures of him."

Ordaz smiled apologetically. "That is our problem. No cars left the roof last night. Only one car arrived. That was yours, Miss Sinclair."

"But," said Porter, and he stopped. He thought it through again. "Did the police turn on the elevator again after they got here?"

"No. The killer could not have left after we got here."

"Oh."

"What happened was this," said Ordaz. "Around five-thirty this morning, the tenants in . . ." He stopped to remember. ". . . In 36A called the building maintenance man about a smell like rotting meat coming through the air-conditioning system. He spent some time looking for the source, but once he reached the roof, it was obvious. He—"

Porter pounced. "He reached the roof in what kind of vehicle?"

"Mr. Steeves says that he took a taxi from the street. There is no other way to reach Dr. Sinclair's private landing pad, is there?"

"No. But why would he do that?"

"Perhaps there have been other times when strange smells came from Dr. Sinclair's laboratory. We will ask him."

"Do that."

"Mr. Steeves followed the smell through the doctor's open door. He called us. He waited for us on the roof."

"What about his taxi?" Porter was hot on the scent. "Maybe the killer just waited till that taxi got here, then took it somewhere else when Steeves finished with it."

"It left immediately after Steeves had stepped out. He had a taxi clicker if he wanted another. The cameras were on it the entire time it was on the roof." Ordaz paused. "You see the problem?"

Apparently Porter did. He ran both hands through his white-blond hair. "I think we ought to put off discussing it until we know more."

He meant Janice. Janice looked puzzled; she hadn't caught on. But Ordaz nodded at once and stood up. "Very well. There is no reason Miss Sinclair cannot go on living here. We may have to bother you again," he told her. "For now, our condolences."

He made his exit. I trailed along. So, unexpectedly, did Drew Porter. At the top of the stairs he stopped Ordaz with a big hand around the inspector's upper arm. "You're thinking Janice did it, aren't you?"

Ordaz sighed. "What choice have I? I must consider the possibility."

"She didn't have any reason. She loved Uncle Ray. She's lived with him on and off these past twelve years. She hasn't got the slightest reason to kill him."

"Is there no inheritance?"

His expression went sour. "All right, *yes*, she'll have some money coming. But Janice wouldn't care about anything like that!"

"Ye-ess. Still, what choice have I? Everything we now know tells us that the killer could not have left the scene of the killing. We searched the premises immediately. There was only Janice Sinclair and her murdered uncle."

Porter bit back an answer, chewed it. . . . He must have been tempted. Amateur detective, one step ahead of the police all the way. Yes, Watson, these *gendarmes* have a talent for missing the obvious. . . . But he had too much to lose. Porter said, "And the maintenance man. Steeves."

Ordaz lifted one eyebrow. "Yes, of course. We shall have to investigate Mr. Steeves."

"How did he get that call from . . . uh . . . 36A? Bedside phone or pocket phone? Maybe he was already on the roof."

"I don't remember that he said. But we have pictures of his taxi landing."

"He had a taxi clicker. He could have just called it down."

"One more thing," I said, and Porter looked at me hopefully.

Upsala College
Library
East Orange, ı. . .   ˙ ˙ ˙ ˘

"Porter, what about the elevator? It had a brain in it, didn't it? It wouldn't take anyone up unless they were on its list."

"Or unless Uncle Ray buzzed down. There's an intercom in the lobby. But at that time of night he probably wouldn't let anyone up unless he was expecting him."

"So if Sinclair was expecting a business associate, he or she was probably in the tape. How about going down? Would the elevator take you down to the lobby if you weren't in the tape?"

"I'd . . . think so."

"It would," said Ordaz. "The elevator screens entrances, not departures."

"Then why didn't the killer use it? I don't mean Steeves, necessarily. I mean *anyone,* whoever it might have been. Why didn't he just go down in the elevator? Whatever he did do, that had to be easier."

They looked at each other, but they didn't say anything.

"Okay." I turned to Ordaz. "When you check out the people in the tape, see if any of them shows a damaged arm. The killer might have pulled the same stunt Janice did—ruined her arm trying to turn off the generator. . . . And I'd like a look at who's in that tape."

"Very well," said Ordaz, and we moved toward the squad car under the carport. We were out of earshot when he added, "How does the ARM come into this, Mr. Hamilton? Why your interest in the murder aspect of this case?"

I told him what I'd told Bera—that Sinclair's killer might be the only living expert on Sinclair's time machine. Ordaz nodded. What he'd really wanted to know was: could I justify giving orders to the Los Angeles Police Department in a local matter? And I had answered: yes.

The rather simple-minded security system in Sinclair's elevator had been built to remember the thumbprints and the facial bone structures (which it scanned by deep radar, thus avoiding the problems raised by changing beard styles and masquerade parties) of up to one hundred people. Most people know about a hundred people, plus or minus ten or so. But Sinclair had listed only a dozen, including himself: Raymond Sinclair; Andrew Porter; Janice Sinclair; Edward Sinclair, Sr.; Edward Sinclair, III; Hans Drucker; George Steeves; Pauline Urthiel; Bernath Peterfi; Lawrence Muhammad Ecks; Bertha Hall; and Muriel Sandusky.

Valpredo had been busy. He'd been using the police car and its phone setup as an office while he guarded the roof. "We know who some of these are," he said. "Edward Sinclair III, for instance, is Edward Senior's grandson, Janice's brother. He's in the Belt, in Ceres, making something of a name for himself as an industrial designer. Edward Senior is Raymond's brother. He lives in Kansas City. Hans Drucker and Bertha Hall and Muriel Sandusky all live in the Greater Los Angeles area; we don't know what their connection with Sinclair is. Pauline Urthiel and Bernath Peterfi are technicians of sorts. Ecks is Sinclair's patent attorney."

"I suppose we can interview Edward III by phone." Ordaz made a face. A phone call to the Belt wasn't cheap. "These others . . ."

I said, "May I make a suggestion?"

"Of course."

"Send me along with whoever interviews Ecks and Peterfi and Urthiel. They probably knew Sinclair in a business sense, and having an ARM along will give you a little more clout to ask a little more detailed questions."

"I could take those assignments," Valpredo volunteered.

"Very well." Ordaz still looked unhappy. "If this list were exhaustive, I would be grateful. Unfortunately, we must consider the risk that Dr. Sinclair's visitor simply used the intercom in the lobby and asked to be let in."

Bernath Peterfi wasn't answering his phone.

We got Pauline Urthiel via her pocket phone. A brusque contralto voice, no picture. We'd like to talk to her in connection with a murder investigation; would she be at home this afternoon? No. She was lecturing that afternoon, but would be home around six.

Ecks answered dripping wet and not smiling. So sorry to get you out of a shower, Mr. Ecks. We'd like to talk to you in connection with a murder investigation. . . .

"Sure, come on over. Who's dead?"

Valpredo told him.

"Sinclair? *Ray* Sinclair? You're sure?"

We were.

"Oh, lord. Listen, he was working on something important. An interstellar drive, if it works out. If there's any possibility of salvaging the hardware . . ."

I reassured him and hung up. If Sinclair's patent attorney thought it was a star drive, maybe it was.

"Doesn't sound like he's trying to steal it," said Valpredo.

"No. And even if he'd got the thing, he couldn't have claimed it was his. If he's the killer, that's not what he was after."

We were moving at high speed, police-car speed. The car was on automatic, of course, but it could need manual override at any instant. Valpredo concentrated on the passing scenery and spoke without looking at me.

"You know, you and the detective inspector aren't looking for the same thing."

"I know. I'm looking for a hypothetical killer. Julio's looking for a hypothetical visitor. It could be tough to prove there wasn't one, but if Porter and the girl were telling the truth, maybe Julio can prove the visitor didn't do it."

"Which would leave the girl," he said.

"Whose side are you on?"

"Nobody's. All I've got is interesting questions." He looked at me sideways. "But you're pretty sure the girl didn't do it."

"Yah."

"Why?"

"I don't know. Maybe because I don't think she's got the brains. It wasn't a simple killing."

"She's Sinclair's niece. She can't be a complete idiot."

"Heredity doesn't work that way. . . . Maybe I'm kidding myself. Maybe it's her arm. She's lost an arm; she's got enough to worry about. I know." And I borrowed the car phone to dig into records in the ARM computer.

PAULINE URTHIEL. Born Paul Urthiel. Ph.D. in plasma physics, University of California at Ervine. Sex change and legal name change, 2111. Six years ago she'd been in competition for a Nobel prize, for research into the charge suppression effect in the Slaver disintegrator. Height: 5'9". Weight: 135. Married Lawrence Muhammad Ecks, 2117. Had kept her (loosely speaking) maiden name. Separate residences.

BERNATH PETERFI. Ph.D. in subatomics and related fields, MIT. Diabetic. Height: 5'8". Weight: 145. Application for exemption to the Fertility Laws denied, 2119. Married 2118, divorced 2122. Lives alone.

LAWRENCE MUHAMMAD ECKS. Master's degree in physics. Member of the bar. Height: 6'1". Weight: 190. Artificial left arm. Vicepresident CET (Committee to End Transplants).

Valpredo said, "Funny how the human arm keeps cropping up in this case."

"Yah." Including one human ARM who didn't really belong there. "Ecks has a master's. Maybe he could have talked people into thinking the generator was his. Or maybe he thought he could."

"He didn't try to snow *us*."

"Suppose he blew it last night? He wouldn't necessarily want the generator lost to humanity, now, would he?"

"How did he get out?"

I didn't answer.

Ecks lived in a tapering tower almost a mile high. At one time Lindstetter's Needle must have been the biggest thing ever built, before they started with the arcologies. We landed on a pad a third of the way up, then took a drop shaft ten floors down.

He was dressed when he answered the door, in blazing yellow pants and a net shirt. His skin was very dark, and his hair was a puffy black dandelion with threads of gray in it. On the phone screen I hadn't been able to tell which arm was which, and I couldn't now. He invited us in, sat down, and waited for the questions.

Where was he last night? Could he produce an alibi? It would help us considerably.

"Sorry, nope. I spent the night going through a rather tricky case. You wouldn't appreciate the details."

I told him I would. He said, "Actually, it involves Edward Sinclair —Ray's great-nephew. He's a Belt immigrant, and he's done an industrial design that could be adapted to Earth. Swivel for a chemical rocket motor. The trouble is, it's not *that* different from existing designs, it's just *better*. His Belt patent is good, but the UN laws are different. You wouldn't believe the legal tangles."

"Is he likely to lose out?"

"No, it just might get sticky if a firm called FireStorm decides to fight the case. I want to be ready for that. In a pinch I might even have to call the kid back to Earth. I'd hate to do that, though. He's got a heart condition."

Had he made any phone calls, say, to a computer, during his night of research?

Ecks brightened instantly. "Oh, sure. Constantly, all night. Okay, I've got an alibi."

No point in telling him that such calls could have been made from anywhere. Valpredo asked, "Do you have any idea where your wife was last night?"

"No, we don't live together. She lives three hundred stories over my head. We've got an open marriage. Maybe too open," he added wistfully.

There seemed a good chance that Raymond Sinclair was expecting a visitor last night. Did Ecks have any idea . . . ?

"He knew a couple of women," said Ecks. "You might ask them. Bertha Hall is about eighty, about Ray's age. She's not too bright, not by Ray's standards, but she's as much of a physical-fitness nut as he is. They go backpacking, play tennis, maybe sleep together, maybe not. I can give you her address. Then, there's Muriel something. He had a crush on her a few years ago. She'd be thirty now. I don't know if they still see each other or not."

Did Sinclair know other women?

Ecks shrugged.

Whom did he know professionally?

"Oh, lord, that's an endless list. Do you know anything about the way Ray worked?" He didn't wait for an answer. "He used computer setups mostly. Any experiment in his field was likely to cost millions, or more. What he was good at was setting up a computer analogue of an experiment that would tell him what he wanted to know. Take, oh . . . I'm sure you've heard of Sinclair molecule chain."

Hell, yes. We'd used it for towing in the Belt; nothing else was light enough and strong enough. A loop of it was nearly invisibly fine, but it would cut steel.

"He didn't start working with chemicals until he was practically finished. He told me he spent four years doing molecular designs by computer analogue. The tough part was the ends of the molecule chain. Until he got that, the chain would start disintegrating from the endpoints the minute you finished making it. When he finally had what he wanted, he hired an industrial chemical lab to make it for him.

"That's what I'm getting at," Ecks continued. "He hired other people to do the concrete stuff, once he knew what he had. And the people he hired had to know what they were doing. He knew the top physicists and chemists and field theorists everywhere on Earth and in the Belt."

Like Pauline? Like Bernath Peterfi?

"Yah, Pauline did some work for him once. I don't think she'd do it again. She didn't like having to give him all the credit. She'd rather work for herself. I don't blame her."

Could he think of anyone who might want to murder Raymond Sinclair?

Ecks shrugged. "I'd say that was your job. Ray never liked splitting the credit with anyone. Maybe someone he worked with nursed a grudge. Or maybe someone was trying to steal this latest project of his. Mind you, I don't know much about what he was trying to do, but if it worked, it would have been fantastically valuable, and not just in money."

Valpredo was making noises like he was about finished. I said, "Do you mind if I ask a personal question?"

"Go ahead."

"Your arm. How'd you lose it?"

"Born without it. Nothing in my genes, just a bad prenatal situation. I came out with an arm and a turkey wishbone. By the time I was old enough for a transplant, I knew I didn't want one. You want the standard speech?"

"No thanks, but I'm wondering how good your artificial arm is. I'm carrying a transplant myself."

Ecks looked me over carefully for signs of moral degeneration. "I suppose you're also one of those people who keep voting the death penalty for more and more trivial offenses?"

"No, I—"

"After all, if the organ banks ran out of criminals, you'd be in trouble. You might have to live with your mistakes."

"No. I'm one of those people who blocked the Second Corpsicle Law, kept that group from going into the organ banks. And I hunt organleggers for a living. But I don't have an artificial arm, and I suppose the reason is that I'm squeamish."

"Squeamish about being part mechanical? I've heard of that," Ecks said. "But you can be squeamish the other way, too. What there is of me is all me, not part of a dead man. I'll admit the sense of touch isn't quite the same, but it's just as good. And . . . look."

He put a hand on my upper forearm and squeezed.

It felt like the bones were about to give. I didn't scream, but it took an effort. "That isn't all my strength," he said. "And I could keep it up all day. This arm doesn't get tired."

He let go.

I asked if he would mind my examining his arms. He didn't. But then, Ecks didn't know about my imaginary hand.

My imaginary hand was a side effect of the accident that had cost me my own right arm. It turned out that I had latent psi powers—esper and PK. They were weak. The heaviest thing I could lift in Earth's gravity was a shot glass half full. They were further restricted by my imagination. I couldn't sense anything farther away than the reach of a missing right arm.

But with the real arm missing, I had developed a ghost arm; and when I replaced the real arm with a transplant, the imaginary arm had remained. It could reach through solid matter.

I probed the advanced plastics of Ecks's false arm, the bone and muscle structure of the other. It was the real arm I was interested in.

When we were back in the car, Valpredo said, "Well?"

"Nothing wrong with his real arm," I said. "No scars."

Valpredo nodded.

But the bubble of accelerated time wouldn't hurt plastic and batteries, I thought. And if he'd been planning to lower eighty pounds of generator two stories down on a nylon line, his artificial arm had the strength for it.

We called Peterfi from the car. He was in. He was a small man, dark-complexioned, mild of face, his hair straight and shiny black around a receding hairline. His eyes blinked and squinted as if the light were too bright, and he had the scruffy look of a man who has slept in his clothes. I wondered if we had interrupted an afternoon nap.

Yes, he would be glad to help the police in a murder investigation.

Peterfi's condominium was a slab of glass and concrete set on a Santa Monica cliff face. His apartment faced the sea. "Expensive, but worth it for the view," he said, showing us to chairs in the living room. The draperies were closed against the afternoon sun. Peterfi had changed clothes. I noticed the bulge in his upper left sleeve, where an insulin capsule and automatic feeder had been anchored to the bone of the arm.

"Well, what can I do for you? I don't believe you mentioned who had been murdered."

Valpredo told him.

He was shocked. "Oh, my. Ray Sinclair. But there's no telling how this will affect . . ." And he stopped suddenly.

"Please go on," said Valpredo.

"We were working on something together. Something . . . revolutionary."

An interstellar drive?

He was startled. He debated with himself; then: "Yes. It was supposed to be secret."

We admitted having seen the machine in action. How did a time-compression field serve as an interstellar drive?

"That's not exactly what it is," Peterfi said. Again he debated with himself. Then: "There have always been a few optimists around who thought that just because mass and inertia have always been associated in human experience, it need not be a universal law. What Ray and I have done is to create a condition of low inertia. You see—"

"An inertialess drive!"

Peterfi nodded vigorously at me. "Essentially, yes. Is the machine intact? If not . . ."

I reassured him on that point.

"That's good. I was about to say that if it had been destroyed, I could re-create it. I did most of the work of building it. Ray preferred to work with his mind, not with his hands."

Had Peterfi visited Sinclair last night?

"No. I had dinner at a restaurant down the coast, then came home and watched the holo wall. What times do I need alibis for?" he asked jokingly.

Valpredo told him. The joking look turned into a nervous grimace. No, he'd left the Mail Shirt just after nine; he couldn't prove his whereabouts after that time.

Had he any idea who might have wanted to murder Raymond Sinclair?

Peterfi was reluctant to make outright accusations. Surely we understood. It might be someone he had worked with in the past, or someone he'd insulted. Ray thought most of humanity were fools. Or . . . we might look into the matter of Ray's brother's exemption.

Valpredo said, "Edward Sinclair's exemption? What about it?"

"I'd really prefer that you get the story from someone else. You may know that Edward Sinclair was refused the right to have children because of an inherited heart condition. His grandson has it too. There is some question as to whether he really did the work that earned him the exemption."

"But that must have been forty to fifty years ago. How could it figure in a murder now?"

Peterfi explained patiently. "Edward had a child by virtue of an exemption to the Fertility Laws. Now there are two grandchildren. Suppose the matter came up for review? His grandchildren would lose the right to have children. They'd be illegitimate. They might even lose the right to inherit."

Valpredo was nodding. "Yah. We'll look into that, all right."

I said, "You applied for an exemption yourself not long ago. I suppose your . . . uh . . ."

"Yes, my diabetes. It doesn't interfere with my life at all. Do you know how long we've been using insulin to handle diabetes? Almost two hundred years! What does it matter if I'm a diabetic? If my children are?"

He glared at us, demanding an answer. He got none.

"But the Fertility Laws refuse me children. Do you know that I lost my wife because the board refused me an exemption? I deserved it. My work on plasma flow in the solar photosphere . . . Well, I'd hardly lecture you on the subject, would I? But my work can be used to predict the patterns of proton storms near any G-type star. Every colony world owes something to my work!"

That was an exaggeration, I thought. Proton storms affected mainly asteroidal mining operations. "Why don't you move to the Belt?" I asked. "They'd honor you for your work, and they don't have Fertility Laws."

"I get sick off Earth. It's biorhythms; it has nothing to do with diabetes. Half of humanity suffers from biorhythm upset."

I felt sorry for the guy. "You could still get the exemption. For your work on the inertialess drive. Wouldn't that get you your wife back?"

"I . . . don't know. I doubt it. It's been two years. In any case, there's no telling which way the board will jump. I thought I'd have the exemption last time."

"Do you mind if I examine your arms?"

He looked at me. "What?"

"I'd like to examine your arms."

"That seems a most curious request. Why?"

"There seems a good chance that Sinclair's killer damaged his arm last night. Now, I'll remind you that I'm acting in the name of the UN Police. If you've been hurt by the side effects of a possible space drive, one that might be used by human colonists, then you're concealing evidence in a . . ." I stopped, because Peterfi had stood up and was taking off his tunic.

He wasn't happy, but he stood still for it. His arms looked all right. I ran my hands along each arm, bent the joints, massaged the knuckles. Inside the flesh I ran my imaginary fingertips along the bones.

Three inches below the shoulder joint the bone was knotted. I probed the muscles and tendons.

"Your right arm is a transplant," I said. "It must have happened about six months ago."

He bridled. "You may not be aware of it, but surgery to reattach my own arm would show the same scars."

"Is that what happened?"

Anger made his speech more precise. "Yes. I was performing an experiment, and there was an explosion. The arm was nearly severed. I tied a tourniquet and got to a 'doc before I collapsed."

"Any proof of this?"

"I doubt it. I never told anyone of this accident, and the 'doc wouldn't keep records. In any case, I think the burden of proof would be on you."

"Uh-huh."

Peterfi was putting his tunic back on. "Are you quite finished here? I'm deeply sorry for Ray Sinclair's death, but I don't see what it could possibly have to do with my stupidity of six months ago."

I didn't either. We left.

Back in the car. It was five-twenty; we could pick up a snack on the way to Pauline Urthiel's place. I told Valpredo, "I think it was a transplant. And he didn't want to admit it. He must have gone to an organlegger."

"Why would he do that?" Valpredo wondered. "It's not that tough to get an arm from the public organ banks."

I chewed that. "You're right. But if it was a normal transplant, there'll be a record. Well, it could have happened the way he said it did."

"Uh-huh."

"How about this? He was doing an experiment, and it was illegal. Something that might cause pollution in a city, or even something to do with radiation. He picked up radiation burns in his arm. If he'd gone to the public organ banks, he'd have been arrested."

"That would fit too. Can we prove it on him?"

"I don't know. I'd like to. He might tell us how to find whomever he dealt with. Let's do some digging. Maybe we can find out what he was working on six months ago."

Pauline Urthiel opened the door the instant we rang. "Hi! I just got in myself. Can I make you drinks?"

We refused. She ushered us into a smallish apartment with a lot of fold-into-the-ceiling furniture. A sofa and coffee table were showing now; the rest existed as outlines on the ceiling. The view through the picture window was breathtaking. She lived near the top of Lindstetter's Needle, some three hundred stories up from her husband.

She was tall and slender, with a facial structure that would have been effeminate on a man. On a woman it was a touch masculine. The well-formed breasts might be flesh or plastic, but surgically implanted in either case.

She finished making a large drink and joined us on the couch. And the questions started.

Had she any idea who might have wanted Raymond Sinclair dead?

"Not really. How did he die?"

"Someone smashed in his skull with a poker," Valpredo said. If he wasn't going to mention the generator, neither was I.

"How quaint." Her contralto turned acid. "His own poker, too, I presume. Out of his own fireplace rack. What you're looking for is a traditionalist." She peered at us over the rim of her glass. Her eyes were large, the lids decorated in semipermanent tattoo as a pair of flapping UN flags. "That doesn't help much, does it? You might try whoever was working with him on whatever his latest project was."

That sounded like Peterfi, I thought. But Valpredo said, "Would he necessarily have a collaborator?"

"He generally works alone at the beginning. But somewhere along the line he brings in people to figure out how to make the hardware, and make it. He never made anything real by himself. It was all just something in a computer bank. It took someone else to make it real. And he never gave credit to anyone."

Then his hypothetical collaborator might have found out how little credit he was getting for his work, and . . . But Urthiel was shaking her head. "I'm talking about a psychotic, not someone who's really been cheated. Sinclair never *offered* anyone a share in anything he did. He always made it damn plain what was happening. I knew what I was doing when I set up the FyreStop prototype for him, and I knew what I was doing when I quit. It was all him. He was using my training, not my brain. I wanted to do something original, something *me*."

Did she have any idea what Sinclair's present project was?

"My husband would know. Larry Ecks, lives in this same building. He's been dropping cryptic hints, and when I want more details, he has this grin . . ." She grinned herself suddenly. "You'll gather I'm interested. But he won't say."

Time for me to take over, or we'd never get certain questions asked. "I'm an ARM. What I'm about to tell you is secret," I said.

And I told her what we knew of Sinclair's generator. Maybe Valpredo was looking at me disapprovingly; maybe not.

"We know that the field can damage a human arm in a few seconds. What we want to know," I said, "is whether the killer is now wandering around with a half-decayed hand or arm—or foot, for that . . ."

She stood and pulled the upper half of her body stocking down around her waist.

She looked very much a real woman. If I hadn't known . . . And why would it matter? These days, the sex-change operation is elaborate and perfect. Hell with it; I was on duty. Valpredo was looking nonchalant, waiting for me.

I examined both her arms with my eyes and my three hands. There was nothing. Not even a bruise.

"My legs too?"

I said, "Not if you can stand on them."

Next question. Could an artificial arm operate within the field?

"Larry? You mean *Larry?* You're out of your teeny mind."

"Take it as a hypothetical question."

She shrugged. "Your guess is as good as mine. There aren't any experts on inertialess fields."

"There was one. He's dead," I reminded her.

"All I know is what I learned watching the Gray Lensman show in the holo wall when I was a kid." She smiled suddenly. "That old space opera . . ."

Valpredo laughed. "You too? I used to watch that show in study hall on a little pocket phone. One day the principal caught me at it."

"Sure. And then we outgrew it. Too bad. Those inertialess ships . . . I'm sure an inertialess ship wouldn't behave like those did. You couldn't possibly get rid of the time-compression effect." She took a long pull on her drink, set it down, and said, "Yes and no. He could reach in, but . . . You see the problem? The nerve impulses that move the motors in Larry's arm—they're coming into the field too slowly."

"Sure."

"But if Larry closed his fist on something, say, and reached into the field with it, it would probably stay closed. He could have brained Ray with . . . No, he couldn't. The poker wouldn't be moving any faster than a glacier. Ray would just dodge."

And he couldn't pull a poker out of the field, either. His fist wouldn't close on it after it was inside. But he could have tried, and still left with his arm intact, I thought.

Did Urthiel know anything of the circumstances surrounding Edward Sinclair's exemption?

"Oh, that's an old story," she said. "Sure, I heard about it. How could it possibly have anything to do with . . . with Ray's murder?"

"I don't know," I confessed. "I'm just thrashing around."

"Well, you'll probably get it more accurately from the UN files. Edward Sinclair did some mathematics on the fields that scoop up interstellar hydrogen for the cargo ramrobots. He was a shoo-in for the exemption. That's the surest way of getting it: make a breakthrough in anything that has anything to do with the interstellar colonies. Every time you move one man away from Earth, the population drops by one."

"What was wrong with it?"

"Nothing anyone could prove. Remember, the Fertility Restriction Laws were new then. They couldn't stand a real test. But Edward Sinclair's a pure math man. He works with number theory, not practical applications. I've seen Edward's equations, and they're closer to something Ray would come up with. And Ray didn't need the exemption. He never wanted children."

"So you think—"

"I don't *care* which of them redesigned the ramscoops. Diddling the Fertility Board like that, that takes *brains*." She swallowed the rest of her drink, set the glass down. "Breeding for brains is never a mistake. It's no challenge to the Fertility Board, either. The people who do the damage are the ones who go into hiding when their shots come due, have their babies, then scream to high heaven when the board has to sterilize them. Too many of those, and we won't have Fertility Laws anymore. And *that* . . ." She didn't have to finish.

Had Sinclair known that Pauline Urthiel was once Paul?

She stared. "Now, just what the bleep has that got to do with anything?"

I'd been toying with the idea that Sinclair might have been blackmailing Urthiel with that information. Not for money, but for credit in some discovery they'd made together. "Just thrashing around," I said.

"Well . . . all right. I don't know if Ray knew or not. He never raised the subject, but he never made a pass, either, and he must have researched me before he hired me. And, say, listen, Larry doesn't know. I'd appreciate it if you wouldn't blurt it out."

"Okay."

"See, he had his children by his first wife. I'm not denying him children. . . . Maybe he married me because I had a touch of . . . um . . . masculine insight. Maybe. But he doesn't know it, and he doesn't want to. I don't know whether he'd laugh it off or kill me."

I had Valpredo drop me off at ARM headquarters.

This peculiar machine really does bother me, Gil. . . . Well it should, Julio. The Los Angeles Police were not trained to deal with a mad scientist's nightmare running quietly in the middle of a murder scene.

Granted that Janice wasn't the type. Not for this murder. But Drew Porter was precisely the type to evolve a perfect murder around Sinclair's generator, purely as an intellectual exercise. He might have guided her through it; he might even have been there, and used the elevator before she shut it off. It was the one thing he forgot to tell her—not to shut off the elevator.

Or: he outlined a perfect murder to her, purely as a puzzle, never dreaming she'd go through with it—badly.

Or: one of them had killed Janice's uncle on impulse. No telling what he'd said that one of them couldn't tolerate. But the machine had been right there in the living room, and Drew had wrapped his big arm around Janice and said, *Wait, don't do anything yet, let's think this out.* . . .

Take any of these as the true state of affairs, and a prosecutor could have a hell of a time proving it. He could show that no killer could possibly have left the scene of the crime without Janice Sinclair's help, and therefore . . . But what about that glowing thing, that time machine built by the dead man? *Could* it have freed a killer from an effectively locked room? How could a judge know its power?

Well, could it?

Bera might know.

The machine was running. I caught the faint violet glow as I stepped into the laboratory, and a flickering next to it; and then it was off, and Jackson Bera stood suddenly beside it, grinning, silent, waiting.

I wasn't about to spoil his fun. I said, "Well? Is it an interstellar drive?"

"Yes!"

A warm glow spread through me. I said, "Okay."

"It's a low-inertia field," said Bera. "Things inside lose most of their inertia . . . not their mass, just the resistance to movement. Ratio of about five hundred to one. The interface is sharp as a razor. We think there are quantum levels involved."

"Uh-huh. The field doesn't affect time directly?"

"No, it . . . I shouldn't say that. Who the hell knows what time really is? It affects chemical and nuclear reactions, energy release of all kinds, but it doesn't affect the speed of light. You know, it's kind of kicky to be measuring the speed of light at three hundred and seventy miles per second with honest instruments."

Damnit. I'd been half-hoping it was an FTL drive. I said, "Did you ever find out what was causing that blue glow?"

Bera laughed at me. "Watch." He'd rigged a remote switch to turn the machine on. He used it, then struck a match and flipped it toward the blue glow. As it crossed an invisible barrier, the match flared violet-white for something less than an eyeblink. I blinked. It had been like a flashbulb going off.

I said, "Oh, *sure*. The machinery's warm."

"Right. The blue glow is just infrared radiation being boosted to violet when it enters normal time."

Bera shouldn't have had to tell me that. Embarrassed, I changed the subject. "But you said it was an interstellar drive."

"Yah. It's got drawbacks," said Bera. "We can't just put a field around a whole starship. The crew would think they'd lowered the speed of light, but so what? A slowboat doesn't get that close to light speed anyway. They'd save a little trip time, but they'd have to live through it five hundred times as fast."

"How about if you just put the field around your fuel tanks?"

Bera nodded. "That's what they'll probably do. Leave the motor and the life-support system outside. You could carry a godawful amount of fuel that way. . . . Well, it's not our department. Someone else'll be designing the starships," he said a bit wistfully.

"Have you thought of this thing in relation to robbing banks? Or espionage?"

"If a gang could afford to build one of these jobs, they wouldn't need to rob banks." He ruminated. "I hate making anything this big a UN secret. But I guess you're right. The average government could afford a whole stable of the things."

"Thus combining James Bond and the Flash."

He rapped on the plastic frame. "Want to try it?"

"Sure," I said.

Heart to brain: THUD! What're you doing? You'll get us all killed! I knew we should never have put you in charge of things. . . . I stepped up to the generator, waited for Bera to scamper beyond range, then pulled the switch.

Everything turned deep red. Bera became as a statue.

Well, here I was. The second hand on the wall clock had stopped moving. I took two steps forward and rapped with my knuckles. Rapped, hell; it was like rapping on contact cement. The invisible wall was tacky.

I tried leaning on it for a minute or so. That worked fine until I tried to pull away, and then I knew I'd done something stupid. I was embedded in the interface. It took me another minute to pull loose, and then I went sprawling backward; I'd picked up too much inward velocity, and it all came into the field with me.

At that, I'd been lucky. If I'd leaned there a little longer, I'd have lost my leverage. I'd have been sinking deeper and deeper into the interface, unable to yell to Bera, building up more and more velocity outside the field.

I picked myself up and tried something safer. I took out my pen and dropped it. It fell normally—32 ft/sec/sec, field time. Which scratched one theory as to how the killer had thought he would be leaving.

I switched the machine off. "Something I'd like to try," I told Bera. "Can you hang the machine in the air, say, by a cable around the frame?"

"What have you got in mind?"

"I want to try standing on the bottom of the field."

Bera looked dubious.

It took us twenty minutes to set it up. Bera took no chances. He lifted the generator about five feet. Since the field seemed to center on that oddly shaped piece of silver, that put the bottom of the field just a foot in the air. We moved a stepladder into range, and I stood on the stepladder and turned on the generator.

I stepped off.

Walking down the side of the field was like walking in progressively stickier taffy. When I stood on the bottom, I could just reach the switch.

My shoes were stuck solid. I could pull my feet out of them, but there was no place to stand except in my own shoes. A minute later my feet were stuck too; I could pull one loose, but only by fixing the other ever more deeply in the interface. I sank deeper, and all sensation left the soles of my feet. It was scary, though I knew nothing terrible could happen to me. My feet wouldn't die out there; they wouldn't have time.

But the interface was up to my ankles now, and I started to wonder what kind of velocity they were building up out there. I pushed the switch up. The lights flashed bright, and my feet slapped the floor hard.

Bera said, "Well? Learn anything?"

"Yah. I don't want to try a real test; I might wreck the machine."

"What kind of real test?"

"Dropping it forty stories with the field on. Quit worrying, I'm not going to do it."

"Right. You aren't."

"You know, this time-compression effect would work for more than just spacecraft. After you're on the colony world you could raise full-grown cattle from frozen fertilized eggs in just a few minutes."

"Mmm. . . . Yah." The happy smile flashing white against darkness, the infinity look in Bera's eyes: Bera liked playing with ideas. "Think of one of these mounted on a truck, say, on Jinx. You could explore the shoreline regions without ever worrying about the bandersnatchi attacking. They'd never move fast enough. You could drive across any alien world and catch the whole ecology laid out around you, none of it running from the truck. Predators in mid-leap, birds in mid-flight, couples in courtship."

"Or larger groups."

"I . . . think that habit is unique to humans." He looked at me sideways. "You wouldn't spy on *people,* would you? Or shouldn't I ask?"

"That five-hundred-to-one ratio. Is that constant?"

He came back to here and now. "We don't know. Our theory hasn't caught up to the hardware it's supposed to fit. I wish to hell we had Sinclair's notes."

"You were supposed to send a programmer out there. . . ."

"He came back," Bera said viciously. "Clayton Wolfe. Clay says the tapes in Sinclair's computer were all wiped before he got there. I don't know whether to believe him or not. Sinclair was a secretive bastard, wasn't he?"

"Yah. One false move on Clay's part and the computer might have wiped everything. But he says different, hmmm?"

"He says the computer was blank, a newborn mind all ready to be taught. Gil, is that possible? Could whoever killed Sinclair have wiped the tapes?"

"Sure, why not? What he couldn't have done is left afterward." I told him a little about the problem. "It's even worse than that, because as Ordaz keeps pointing out, he thought he'd be leaving with the machine. I thought he might have been planning to roll the generator off the roof, step off with it, and float down. But that wouldn't work. Not if it falls five hundred times as fast. He'd have been killed."

"Losing the machine maybe saved his life."

"But *how did he get out?*"

Bera laughed at my frustration. "Couldn't his niece be the one?"

"Sure, she could have killed her great-uncle for the money. But I can't see how she'd have a motive to wipe the computer. Unless . . ."

"Something?"

"Maybe. Never mind." Did Bera ever miss this kind of manhunting? But I wasn't ready to discuss this yet; I didn't know enough. "Tell me more about the machine. Can you vary that five-hundred-to-one ratio?"

He shrugged. "We tried adding more batteries. We thought it might boost the field strength. We were wrong; it just expanded the boundary a little. And using one less battery turns it off completely. So the ratio seems to be constant, and there do seem to be quantum levels involved. We'll know better when we build another machine."

"How so?"

"Well, there are all kinds of good questions," said Bera. "What happens when the fields of two generators intersect? They might just add, but maybe not. That quantum effect . . . And what happens if the generators are right next to each other, operating in each other's accelerated time? The speed of light could drop to a few feet per second. Throw a punch, and your hand gets shorter!"

"That'd be kicky, all right."

"Dangerous, too. Man, we'd better try that one on the Moon!"

"I don't see that."

"Look, with one machine going, infrared light comes out violet. If two machines were boosting each other's performance, what kind of radiation would they put out? Anything from X rays to antimatter particles."

"An expensive way to build a bomb."

"Well, but it's a bomb you can use over and over again."

I laughed. "We did find you an expert," I said. "You may not need Sinclair's tapes. Bernath Peterfi says he was working with

Sinclair. He could be lying—more likely he was working *for* him, under contract—but at least he knows what the machine does."

Bera seemed relieved at that. He took down Peterfi's address. I left him there in the laboratory playing with his new toy.

The file from City Morgue was sitting on my desk, open, waiting for me since this morning. Two dead ones looked up at me through sockets of blackened bone, but not accusingly. They had patience. They could wait.

The computer had processed my search pattern. I braced myself with a cup of coffee, then started leafing through the thick stack of printout. When I knew what had burned away two human faces, I'd be close to knowing who. Find the tool, find the killer. And the tool must be unique, or close to it.

Lasers, lasers—more than half the machine's suggestions seemed to be lasers. Incredible, the way lasers seemed to breed and mutate throughout human industry. Laser radar. The laser guidance system on a tunneling machine. Some suggestions were obviously unworkable, and one was a lot too workable.

A standard hunting laser fires in pulses, which is what makes it "sporting." But it can be jiggered for a much longer pulse or even a continuous burst. Assassins have been doing it for years.

Set a hunting laser for a long pulse, and put a grid over the lens. The mesh has to be optically fine, on the order of angstroms. Now the beam will spread as it leaves the grid. A second of pulse will vaporize the grid, leaving no evidence. The grid would be no bigger than a contact lens; if you didn't trust your aim, you could carry a pocketful of them.

The grid-equipped laser would be less efficient, as a rifle with a silencer is less efficient. But the grid would make the laser impossible to identify.

I thought about it and got cold chills. Assassination is already a recognized branch of politics. If this got out . . . But that was the trouble; someone seemed to have thought of it already. If not, someone would. Someone always did.

I wrote up a memo for Lucas Garner. Aside from his being my boss, I couldn't think of anyone better qualified to deal with this kind of sociological problem.

Nothing else in the stack of printout caught my eye. Later I'd have to go through it in detail. For now, I pushed it aside and punched for messages.

Bates had sent me another report. They'd finished the autopsies on the two dead ones. Nothing new. But Records had identified the fingerprints. Two missing persons, disappeared six and eight months ago. Aha!

I knew that pattern. I didn't even look at the names; I just skipped on to the gene coding.

Right. The fingerprints did not match the genes. All twenty fingertips must be transplants. And the man's scalp was a transplant; his own hair had been blond.

I leaned back in my chair, gazing fondly at the corpses.

Organleggers, both of them. With all that raw material available, most organleggers change their fingerprints constantly, and their retina prints; but we'd never get prints from those charred eyeballs. So, weird weapon or no, they were ARM business.

And we still didn't know what had killed them, or who.

It could hardly have been a rival gang. For one thing, there was no competition: plenty of business for everyone left alive after the ARM had swept through them last year. For another, why had they been dumped on a city slidewalk? Rival organleggers would have taken them apart for their own organ banks. Waste not, want not.

On that same philosophy, I had something to be deeply involved in when the mother hunt broke. Sinclair's death wasn't ARM business, and his time-compression field wasn't in *my* field. This was both.

I wondered what end of the business they had been in. The file gave their estimated ages—forty for the man, forty-three for the woman, two years' margin of error. Too old to be raiding the city streets for donors. That takes youth and muscle. I billed them as doctors, culturing the transplants and doing the operations; or salesmen, charged with quietly letting prospective clients know where they could get an operation without waiting two years for the public organ banks to come up with the material.

So, they'd tried to sell someone a new kidney and been killed for their impudence. That would make the killer a hero. So why hide them for three days, then drag them out onto a city slidewalk in the dead of night?

Because they'd been killed with a fearsome new weapon?

I looked at the burned faces and thought: Fearsome, right. Whatever did that *had* to be strictly a murder weapon, just as the optical grid over a laser lens would be strictly a murder technique.

So, a secretive scientist and his deformed assistant, fearful of rousing the wrath of the villagers, had dithered over the bodies for three days, then disposed of them in that clumsy fashion because they panicked when the bodies started to smell. Maybe.

But a prospective client needn't have used his shiny new terror weapon. He had only to call the cops after they were gone. It read better if the killer was a prospective *donor;* he'd fight with anything he could get his hands on.

I flipped back to full shots of the bodies. They looked to be in good condition. Not much flab. You don't collect a donor by putting an armlock on him; you use a needle gun. But you still need muscle to pick up the body and move it to your car, and you have to do that damn quick. Hmmm. . . .

Someone knocked at my door.

I shouted, "Come on in!"

Drew Porter came in. He was big enough to fill the office, and he moved with a grace he must have learned on a board. "Mr. Hamilton? I'd like to talk to you."

"Sure. What about?"

He didn't seem to know what to do with his hands. He looked grimly determined. "You're an ARM," he said. "You're not actually investigating Uncle Ray's murder. That's right, isn't it?"

"That's right. Our concern is with the generator. Coffee?"

"Yes, thanks. But you know all about the killing. I thought I'd like to talk to you, straighten out some of my own ideas."

"Go ahead." I punched for two coffees.

"Ordaz thinks Janice did it, doesn't he?"

"Probably. I'm not good at reading Ordaz's mind. But it seems to narrow down to two distinct groups of possible killers. Janice, and everyone else. Here's your coffee."

"Janice didn't do it." He took the cup from me, gulped at it, set it down on my desk, and forgot about it.

"Janice and X," I said. "But X couldn't have left. In fact, X couldn't have left even if he'd had the machine he came for. And we still don't know why he didn't just take the elevator."

He scowled as he thought that through. "Say he had a way to leave," he said. "He wanted to take the machine—he *had* to want that, because he tried to use the machine to set up an alibi. But even if he couldn't take the machine, he'd still use his alternate way out."

"Why?"

"It'd leave Janice holding the bag, if he knew Janice was coming home. If he didn't, he'd be leaving the police with a locked-room mystery."

"Locked-room mysteries are good clean fun, but I never heard of one happening in real life. In fiction they usually happen by accident." I waved aside his protest. "Never mind. You argue well. But what was his alternate escape route?"

Porter didn't answer.

"Would you care to look at the case against Janice Sinclair?"

"She's the only one who could have done it," he said bitterly. "But she didn't. She couldn't kill anyone, not that cold-blooded, prepackaged way, with an alibi all set up and a weird machine at the heart of it. Look, that machine is too *complicated* for Janice."

"No, she isn't the type. But—no offense intended—you are."

He grinned at that. "Me? Well, maybe I am. But why would I want to?"

"You're in love with her. I think you'd do anything for her. Aside from that, you might enjoy setting up a perfect murder. And there's the money."

"You've got a funny idea of a perfect murder."

"Say I was being tactful."

He laughed at that. "All right. Say I set up a murder for the love of Janice. Damn it, if she had that much hate in her, I wouldn't love her! Why would she want to kill Uncle Ray?"

I dithered as to whether to drop that on him. Decided *yes*. "Do you know anything about Edward Sinclair's exemption?"

"Yah, Janice told me something about . . ." He trailed off.

"Just what did she tell you?"

"I don't have to say."

That was probably intelligent. "All right," I said. "For the sake of argument, let's assume it was Raymond Sinclair who worked out the math for the new ramrobot scoops, and Edward took the credit, with Raymond's connivance. It was probably Raymond's idea. How would that sit with Edward?"

"I'd think he'd be grateful forever," said Porter. "Janice says he is."

"Maybe. But people are funny, aren't they? Being grateful for fifty years could get on a man's nerves. It's not a natural emotion."

"You're so young to be so cynical," Porter said pityingly.

"I'm trying to think this out like a prosecution lawyer. If these brothers saw each other too often, Edward might get to feeling embarrassed around Raymond. He'd have a hard time relaxing with him. The rumors wouldn't help. . . . Oh, yes, there are rumors. I've been told that Edward couldn't have worked out those equations, because he doesn't have the ability. If that kind of thing got back to Edward, how would he like it? He might even start avoiding his brother. Then Ray might remind brother Edward of just how much he owed him . . . and that's the kiss of death."

"Janice says no."

"Janice could have picked up the hate from her father. Or she might have started worrying about what would happen if Uncle Ray changed his mind one day. It could happen anytime, if things were getting strained between the elder Sinclairs. So one day she shut his mouth—"

Porter snarled in his throat.

"I'm just trying to show you what you're up against. One more thing: the killer may have wiped the tapes in Sinclair's computer."

"Oh?" Porter thought that over. "Yah. Janice could have done that just in case there were some notes in there, notes on Ed Sinclair's ramscoop field equations. But, look, X could have wiped those tapes too. Stealing the generator doesn't do him any good unless he wipes it out of Uncle Ray's computer."

"True enough. Shall we get back to the case against X?"

"With pleasure." He dropped into a chair. Watching his face smooth out, I added, *and with great relief.*

I said, "Let's not call him X. Call him K, for 'killer.'" We already had an Ecks involved, and his family name probably *had* been X, once upon a time. "We've been assuming K set up Sinclair's time-compression effect as an alibi."

Porter smiled. "It's a lovely idea. 'Elegant,' as a mathematician would say. Remember, I never saw the actual murder scene. Just chalk marks."

"It was . . . macabre. Like a piece of surrealism. A very bloody practical joke. K could have deliberately set it up that way, if his mind is twisted enough."

"If he's that twisted, he probably escaped by running himself down the garbage disposal."

"Pauline Urthiel thought he might be a psychotic. Someone who worked with Sinclair, who thought he wasn't getting enough credit." Like Peterfi, I thought, or Pauline herself.

"I like the alibi theory."

"It bothers me. Too many people knew about the machine. How did he expect to get away with it? Lawrence Ecks knew about it. Peterfi knew enough about the machine to rebuild it from scratch. Or so he says. You and Janice saw it in action."

"Say he's crazy, then. Say he hated Uncle Ray enough to kill him and then set him up in a makeshift Dali painting. He'd still have to get *out*." Porter was working his hands together. The muscles bulged and rippled in his arms. "This whole thing depends on the elevator, doesn't it? If the elevator hadn't been locked, and on Uncle Ray's floor, there wouldn't be a problem."

"So?"

"So. Say he did leave by elevator. Then Janice came home, and she automatically called the elevator up and locked it. She does that without thinking. She had a bad shock last night. This morning she didn't remember."

"And this evening it could come back to her."

Porter looked up sharply. "I wouldn't—"

"You'd better think long and hard before you do. If Ordaz is sixty percent sure of her now, he'll be a hundred percent sure when she lays that on him."

Porter was working his muscles again. In a low voice he said, "It's possible, isn't it?"

"Sure. It'd make things a lot simpler, too. But if Janice said it now, she'd sound like a liar."

"But it's *possible*."

"I give up. Sure, it's possible."

"Then who's our killer?"

There wasn't any reason I shouldn't consider the question. It wasn't my case at all. I did, and presently I laughed. "Did I say it'd make things simpler? Man, it throws the case wide open! *Anyone* could have done it. Uh, anyone but Steeves. Steeves wouldn't have had any reason to come back this morning."

Porter looked glum. "Steeves wouldn't have done it anyway."

"He was your suggestion."

"Oh, in pure mechanical terms, he's the only one left who didn't need a way out. But you don't know Steeves. He's a big, brawny guy with a beer belly and no brains. A nice guy, you understand, I *like* him, but if he ever killed anyone, it'd be with a beer bottle. And he was proud of Uncle Ray. He liked having Raymond Sinclair in his building."

"Okay, forget Steeves. Is there anyone you'd particularly like to pin it on? Bearing in mind that now *anyone* could get in to do it."

"Not anyone. Anyone in the elevator computer, plus anyone Uncle Ray might have let up."

"Well?"

He shook his head.

"You make a hell of an amateur detective. You're afraid to accuse anyone."

He shrugged, smiling, embarrassed.

"What about Peterfi? Now that Sinclair's dead, he can claim they were equal partners in the . . . uh . . . time machine. And he tumbled to it awfully fast. The moment Valpredo told him Sinclair was dead, Peterfi was his partner."

"Sounds typical."

"Could he be telling the truth?"

"I'd say he's lying. Doesn't make him a killer, though."

"No. What about Ecks? If he didn't know Peterfi was involved, he might have tried the same thing. Does he need money?"

"Hardly. And he's been with Uncle Ray for longer than I've been alive."

"Maybe he was after the immunity. He's had kids, but not by his present wife. He may not know she can't have children."

"Pauline *likes* children. I've seen her with them." Porter looked at me curiously. "I don't see having children as that big a motive."

"You're young. Then, there's Pauline herself. Sinclair knew something about her. Or Sinclair might have told Ecks, and Ecks blew up and killed him for it."

Porter shook his head. "In red rage? I can't think of anything that'd make Larry do that. Pauline, maybe. Larry, no."

But, I thought, there are men who would kill if they learned that their wives had gone through a sex change. I said, "Whoever killed Sinclair, if he wasn't crazy, he had to want to take the machine. One way might have been to lower it by rope . . ." I trailed off. Eighty pounds, lowered two stories by nylon line. Ecks's steel and plastic arm . . . or the muscles now rolling like boulders in Porter's arms. I thought Porter could have managed it.

Or maybe he'd thought he could. He hadn't actually had to go through with it.

My phone rang.

It was Ordaz. "Have you made any progress on the time machine? I'm told that Dr. Sinclair's computer—"

"Was wiped, yah. But that's all right. We're learning quite a lot about it. If we run into trouble, Bernath Peterfi can help us. He helped build it. Where are you now?"

"At Dr. Sinclair's apartment. We had some further questions for Janice Sinclair."

Porter twitched. I said, "All right, we'll be right over. Drew Porter's with me." I hung up and turned to Porter. "Does Janice know she's a suspect?"

"No. Please don't tell her unless you have to. I'm not sure she could take it."

I had the taxi drop us at the lobby level of the Rodewald Building. When I told Porter I wanted a ride in the elevator, he just nodded.

The elevator to Raymond Sinclair's penthouse was a box with a seat in it. It would have been comfortable for one, cozy for two good friends. With me and Porter in it, it was crowded. Porter hunched his knees and tried to fold into himself. He seemed used to it.

He probably was. Most apartment elevators are like that. Why waste room on an elevator shaft when the same space can go into apartments?

It was a fast ride. The seat was necessary; it was two gee going up and a longer period at half a gee slowing down, while lighted numbers flickered past. Numbers, but no doors.

"Hey, Porter. If this elevator jammed, would there be a door to let us out?"

He gave me a funny look and said he didn't know. "Why worry about it? If it jammed at this speed, it'd come apart like a handful of shredded lettuce."

It was just claustrophobic enough to make me wonder. K hadn't left by elevator. Why not? Because the ride up had terrified him? *Brain to memory: dig into the medical records of that list of suspects. See if any of them have records of claustrophobia.* Too bad the elevator brain didn't keep records. We could find out which of them had used the boxlike elevator once or not at all.

In which case we'd be looking for K_2. By now I was thinking in terms of three groups. K_1 had killed Sinclair, then tried to use the low-inertia field as both loot and alibi. K_2 was crazy; he hadn't wanted the generator at all, except as a way to set up his macabre tableau. K_3 was Janice and Drew Porter.

Janice was there when the doors slid open. She was wan, and her shoulders slumped. But when she saw Porter she smiled like sunlight and ran to him. Her run was wobbly, thrown off by the missing weight of her arm.

I stepped past them, shook hands with Ordaz and Valpredo, and looked around.

The wide brown circle was still there in the grass, marked with white chalk and the yellow chemical that picks up bloodstains. White outlines to mark the vanished body, the generator, the poker.

Something knocked at the back door of my mind. I looked from the chalk outlines, to the open elevator, to the chalk . . . and a third of the puzzle fell into place.

So simple. We were looking for K₁, and I had a pretty good idea of who he was.

Ordaz was asking, "How did you happen to arrive with Mr. Porter?"

"He came to my office. We were talking about a hypothetical killer"—I lowered my voice slightly—"a killer who isn't Janice."

"Very good. Did you reason out how he must have left?"

"Not yet. But play the game with me. Say there was a way."

Porter and Janice joined us, their arms about each other's waists. Ordaz said, "Very well. We assume there was a way out. Did he improvise it? And why did he not use the elevator?"

"He must have had it in mind when he got here. He didn't use the elevator because he was planning to take the machine. It wouldn't have fit."

They all stared at the chalk outline of the generator. So simple. Porter said, "Yah! Then he used it anyway, and left you a locked-room mystery!"

"That may have been his mistake," Ordaz said grimly. "When we know his escape route, we may find that only one man could have used it. But of course we do not even know that the route exists."

I changed the subject. "Have you got everyone on the elevator tape identified?"

Valpredo dug out his spiral notebook and flipped to the jotted names of those people permitted to use Sinclair's elevator. He showed it to Porter. "Have you seen this?"

Porter studied it. "No, but I can guess what it is. Let's see . . . Hans Drucker was Janice's lover before I came along. We still see him. In fact, he was at that beach party last night at the Randalls'."

"He flopped on the Randalls' rug last night," said Valpredo. "Him and four others. One of the better alibis."

"Oh, *Hans* wouldn't have anything to do with this!" Janice exclaimed. The idea horrified her.

Porter was still looking at the list. "You know about most of these people already. Bertha Hall and Muriel Sandusky were lady friends of Uncle Ray's. Bertha goes backpacking with him."

"We interviewed them too," Valpredo told me. "You can hear the tapes if you like."

"No, just give me the gist. I already know who the killer is."

Ordaz raised his eyebrows at that, and Janice said, "Oh, good! Who?" which question I answered with a secretive smile. Nobody actually called me a liar.

Valpredo said, "Muriel Sandusky's been living in England for almost a year. Married. Hasn't seen Sinclair in years. Big, beautiful redhead."

"She had a crush on Uncle Ray once," said Janice. "And vice versa. I think his lasted longer."

"Bertha Hall is something else again," Valpredo continued. "Sinclair's age, and in good shape. Wiry. She says that when Sinclair was on the home stretch of a project he gave up everything friends, social life, exercise. Afterward he'd call Bertha and go backpacking with her to catch up with himself. He called her two nights ago and set a date for next Monday."

I said, "Alibi?"

"Nope."

"Really!" Janice was indignant. "Why, we've known Bertha since I was that high! If you know who killed Uncle Ray, why don't you just say so?"

"Out of this list, I sure do, given certain assumptions. But I don't know how he got out, or how he expected to, or whether we can prove it on him. I can't accuse anyone *now*. It's a damn shame he didn't lose his arm reaching for that poker."

Porter looked frustrated. So did Janice.

"You would not want to face a lawsuit," Ordaz suggested delicately. "What of Sinclair's machine?"

"It's an inertialess drive, sort of. Lower the inertia, time speeds up. Bera's already learned a lot about it, but it'll be a while before he can really . . ."

"You were saying?" Ordaz asked when I trailed off.

"Sinclair was *finished* with the damn thing."

"Sure he was," said Porter. "He wouldn't have been showing it around otherwise."

"Or calling Bertha for a backpacking expedition. Or spreading rumors about what he had. Yah. Sure, he knew everything he could learn about that machine. Julio, you were cheated. It all depends on the machine. And the bastard did wrack up his arm, and we can prove it on him."

* * *

We were piled into Ordaz's police car—me and Ordaz and Valpredo and Porter. Valpredo had set the thing for conventional speeds so he wouldn't have to worry about driving. We'd turned the interior chairs to face each other.

"This is the part I won't guarantee," I said, sketching rapidly in Valpredo's borrowed notebook. "But remember, he had a length of line with him. He must have expected to use it. Here's how he planned to get out."

I sketched in a box to represent Sinclair's generator, a stick figure clinging to the frame. A circle around them to represent the field. A bow knot tied to the machine, with one end trailing up through the field.

"See it? He goes up the stairs with the field on. The camera has about one chance in eight of catching him while he's moving at that speed. He wheels the machine to the edge of the roof, ties the line to it, throws the line a good distance away, pushes the generator off the roof, and steps off with it. The line falls at thirty-two feet per second squared, normal time, plus a little more because the machine and the killer are tugging down on it. Not hard, because they're in a low-inertia field. By the time the killer reaches the ground, he's moving at something more than . . . uh . . . twelve hundred feet per second over five hundred . . . uh, say three feet per second internal time, and he's got to pull the machine out of the way fast, because the rope is going to hit like a bomb."

"It looks like it would work," said Porter.

"Yah. I thought for a while that he could just stand on the bottom of the field. A little fooling with the machine cured me of that. He'd smash both legs. But he could hang onto the frame; it's strong enough."

"But he didn't have the machine," Valpredo pointed out.

"That's where you got cheated. What happens when two fields intersect?"

They looked blank.

"It's not a trivial question. Nobody knows the answer yet. *But Sinclair did*. He had to, he was *finished*. He must have had two machines. The killer took the second machine."

Ordaz said, "Ahh."

Porter said, "Who's K?"

We were settling on the carport. Valpredo knew where we were, but he didn't say anything. We left the taxi and headed for the elevators.

"That's a lot easier," I said. "He expected to use the machine as an alibi. That's silly, considering how many people knew it existed. But if he didn't know that Sinclair was ready to start showing it to people—specifically to you and Janice—who's left? Ecks knew only that it was some kind of interstellar drive."

The elevator was uncommonly large. We piled into it.

"And," said Valpredo, "there's the matter of the arm. I think I've got that figured too."

"I gave you enough clues," I told him.

Peterfi was a long time answering our buzz. He may have studied us through the door camera, wondering why a parade was marching through his hallway. Then he spoke through the grid. "Yes? What is it?"

"Police. Open up," said Valpredo.

"Do you have a warrant?"

I stepped forward and showed my ident to the camera. "I'm an ARM. I don't need a warrant. Open up. We won't keep you long." *One way or another*.

He opened the door. He looked neater now than he had this afternoon, despite informal brown indoor pajamas. "Just you," he said. He let me in, then started to close the door on the others.

Valpredo put his hand against the door. "Hey . . ."

"It's okay," I said. Peterfi was smaller than I was, and I had a needle gun. Valpredo shrugged and let him close the door.

My mistake. I had two-thirds of the puzzle, and I thought I had it all.

Peterfi folded his arms and said, "Well? What is it you want to search this time? Would you like to examine my legs?"

"No, let's start with the insulin feeder on your upper arm."

"Certainly," he said, and startled hell out of me.

I waited while he took off his shirt—unnecessary, but he needn't know that—then ran my imaginary fingers through the insulin feed. The reserve was nearly full. "I should have known," I said. "Damnit. You got six months' worth of insulin from the organlegger."

His eyebrows went up. "Organlegger?" He pulled loose. "Is this an accusation, Mr. Hamilton? I'm taping this for my attorney."

And I was setting myself up for a lawsuit. The hell with it. "Yah, it's an accusation. You killed Sinclair. Nobody else could have tried that alibi stunt."

He looked puzzled—honestly, I thought. "Why not?"

"If anyone else had tried to set up an alibi with Sinclair's generator, Bernath Peterfi would have told the police all about what it was and how it worked. But you were the only one who knew that, until last night, when he started showing it around."

There was only one thing he could say to that kind of logic, and he said it. "Still recording, Mr. Hamilton."

"Record and be damned. There are other things we can check. Your grocery-delivery service. Your water bill."

He didn't flinch. He was smiling. Was it a bluff? I sniffed the air. Six months' worth of body odor emitted in one night? By a man who hadn't taken more than four or five baths in six months? But his air-conditioning was too good.

The curtains were open now to the night and the ocean. They'd been closed this afternoon, and he'd been squinting. But it wasn't evidence. The lights: he had only one light burning now, and so what?

The big, powerful camp-out flashlight sitting on a small table against a wall. I hadn't even noticed it this afternoon. Now I was sure I knew what he'd used it for. . . . But how to prove it?

Groceries. . . . "If you didn't buy six months' worth of groceries last night, you must have stolen them. Sinclair's generator's perfect for thefts. We'll check the local supermarkets."

"And link the thefts to me? How?"

He was too bright to have kept the generator. But come to think of it, where could he abandon it? He was *guilty*. He couldn't have covered *all* his tracks.

"Peterfi? I've got it."

He believed me. I saw it in the way he braced himself. Maybe he'd worked it out before I did. I said, "Your contraceptive shots must have worn off six months early. Your organlegger couldn't get you that; he's got no reason to keep contraceptives around. You're dead, Peterfi."

"I might as well be. Damn you, Hamilton! You've cost me the exemption!"

"They won't try you right away. We can't afford to lose what's in your head. You know too much about Sinclair's generator."

"Our generator! We built it together!"

"Yah."

"You won't try me at all," he said more calmly. "Are you going to tell a court how the killer left Ray's apartment?"

I dug out my sketch and handed it to him. While he was studying it, I said, "How did you like going off the roof? You couldn't have *known* it would work."

He looked up. His words came slowly, reluctantly. I guess he had to tell someone, and it didn't matter now. "By then I didn't care. My arm hung like a dead rabbit, and it stank. It took me three minutes to reach the ground. I thought I'd die on the way."

"Where'd you dig up an organlegger that fast?"

His eyes called me a fool. "Can't you guess? Three years ago. I was hoping diabetes could be cured by a transplant. When the government hospitals couldn't help me, I went to an organlegger. I was lucky he was still in business last night."

He drooped. It seemed that all the anger went out of him. "Then it was six months in the field, waiting for the scars to heal. In the dark. I tried taking that big camp-out flashlight in with me." He laughed bitterly. "I gave up after I noticed that the walls were smoldering."

The wall above that little table had a scorched look. I should have wondered about that earlier.

"No baths," he was saying. "I was afraid to use up that much water. No exercise, practically. But I had to eat, didn't I? And all for nothing."

"Will you tell us how to find the organlegger you dealt with?"

"This is your big day, isn't it, Hamilton? All right, why not. It won't do you any good."

"Why not?"

He looked up at me very strangely.

Then he spun about and ran.

He caught me flatfooted. I jumped after him. I didn't know what he had in mind; there was only one exit to the apartment, excluding the balcony, and he wasn't headed there. He seemed to be trying to reach a blank wall with a small table set against it, a camp-out flashlight on it and a drawer in it. I saw the drawer and thought, *gun!* And I surged after him and got him by the wrist just as he reached the wall switch above the table.

I threw my weight backward and yanked him away from there, and then the field came on.

I held a hand and arm up to the elbow. Beyond was a fluttering of violet light—Peterfi thrashing frantically in a low-inertia field. I hung on while I tried to figure out what was happening.

The second generator was here somewhere. In the wall? The switch seemed to have been recently plastered in, now that I saw it close. Figure a closet on the other side, and the generator in it. Peterfi must have drilled through the wall and fixed that switch. Sure, what else did he have to do with six months of spare time?

No point in yelling for help. Peterfi's soundproofing was too modern. And if I didn't let go, Peterfi would die of thirst in a few minutes.

Peterfi's feet came straight at my jaw. I threw myself down, and the edge of a boot sole nearly tore my ear off. I rolled forward in time to grab his ankle. There was more violet fluttering, and his other leg thrashed wildly outside the field. Too many conflicting nerve impulses were pouring into the muscles. The leg flopped about like something dying. If I didn't let go, he'd break it in a dozen places.

He'd knocked the table over. I didn't see it fall, but suddenly it was lying on its side. The part with the drawer must have been well beyond the field. The flashlight lay just beyond the violet fluttering of his hand.

Okay. He couldn't reach the drawer; his hand wouldn't get coherent signals if it left the field. I could let go of his ankle. He'd turn off the field when he got thirsty enough.

I almost did.

Then something jarred together in my head, and: *Brain to hand: Hang on, for our lives! Don't you understand? He's trying to reach the flashlight!*

I hung on.

Peterfi suddenly stopped thrashing about in there. He lay on his side, his face and hands glowing blue. I was trying to decide whether he was playing possum when the blue light behind his face quietly went out.

I let them in. They looked it over. Valpredo went off to search for a pole to reach the light switch. Ordaz asked, "Was it necessary to kill him?"

I pointed to the flashlight. He didn't get it.

"I was overconfident," I said. "I shouldn't have come in alone. He's already killed two people with that flashlight. The organleggers who gave him his new arm. He didn't want them talking, so he burned their faces off and then dragged them out onto a slidewalk. He probably tied them to the generator and then used the line to pull it. With the field on, the whole setup wouldn't weigh more than a couple of pounds."

"With a flashlight?" Ordaz pondered. "Of course. It would have been putting out five hundred times as much light. A good thing you thought of that in time."

"Well, I do spend more time dealing with these oddball science-fiction devices than you do."

"And welcome to them," said Ordaz.

Larry Niven writes:

The science-fiction detective story is a rare and difficult form. It requires the author to follow two sets of rules: the world-constructing disciplines of science fiction, plus the obligation to present a fair puzzle to the reader. The reader too faces a difficulty: he must learn to think in new terms (the obligation of the science-fiction reader) before he can attempt to solve the whodunit.

Difficult, but I knew it had been done. I'd read Needle, The Caves of Steel, The Naked Sun, *and other successful SF detective novels. I decided to try it myself, way back at the beginning of my career, eleven years ago.*

I came a cropper. I have a long letter from John W. Campbell, and the memory of a conversation with Fred Pohl, to tell me what was wrong with the original version of "ARM."

Only the kernel of that story survives in this, the third of the tales of Gil (the Arm) Hamilton of the United Nations Police. I think that the delineated future is believable and the puzzle fair.

ANGEL OF TRUTH

by Gordon Eklund

Stanley, fast asleep, dreamed of a place where the ocean was pale yellow, where he was sitting in the middle of a drifting rowboat, searching the surrounding sea, seeking a thing of the utmost significance, whose identity he had—if only temporarily—forgotten.

Then he saw something out there, far away—a pair of black circles, unequal in size, bobbing in the yellow waves. Bending his back, Stanley drove the oars into the water, forcing the frail craft forward, dashing across the surging waves. Strangely, as he approached, the circles failed to assume a more positive identity, remaining shadowy, ambiguous—carefully obscured debris floating upon the pale water. But he was nearly there.

Something stank.

Pausing, Stanley cautiously sniffed the air. Bending nearly in half, he clutched the big pot of his belly, gagging, retching. The odor was dreadful, as thick as sulfur, as bitter as garlic.

He couldn't understand; this wasn't fair.

Never before had such a thing risen to desecrate the ritual of his dream. Bending his back, he drove the boat savagely in a wide circle, seeking the source of the odor. His eyes burned. Tears leaked down. He could barely breathe. At last, gazing down, he spotted something in the water. He stopped. It was a living creature, moving faintly, just beneath the surface.

Without a moment's hesitation, he dived. His head pierced the high surface of the sea. His fingers closed around something very soft. Shutting his eyes against the salt water, struggling to contain his breath, he squeezed and squeezed and squeezed. After a time, he did not even have to think about it. A single moment more, and . . .

The dream faded.

Shouting in anguish, Stanley leaped to his feet. The yellow ocean was gone, replaced by a blank metallic floor. Suddenly, standing motionlessly, Stanley realized his hands were full.

He looked down. His hands enclosed the thick, soft neck of a three-legged lopsided beast. The creature had tufts of bright-red hair growing in the most unexpected places, and bare pink skin everywhere else. Three huge eyes bulged in the center of a square head. Whatever it was, the thing was dead. And Stanley had killed it.

He heard a noise. Tottering in a circle, he struggled to turn.

Behind, standing beside a gray wall, staring straight at him, were a dozen creatures belonging to the same race as the thing he had just killed. Deliberately, with subdued defiance, he let the dead beast slip from his hands. Tentatively, he risked a smile. The creatures stood mutely frozen, regarding him coldly. Pointing to himself, Stanley said, "Friend." There was no response.

"If that's the way you want it," he said. Lifting his fists, adjusting his elbows, he prepared to defend his vulnerable middle.

In sharp clicking tones, the creatures began speaking among themselves. Stanley lowered his hands and tried to appear relaxed. He hummed a light ditty, something he had picked up somewhere in his endless wanderings. One of the creatures waved a hand, pointing at Stanley, then spoke excitedly to the group. Once more, Stanley prepared to fight. He tensed his knees and tried to do the same with his slack belly muscles. He shuffled his feet in a vague imitation of grace. Two of the creatures turned to watch. One attempted to duplicate his motions but fell in a heap to the floor. Stanley skidded to a halt. Clearly, some decision was being formed.

Finally, one stepped forward, approaching Stanley, who chose to hold his ground, elbows protecting his kidneys, fists clenched like steel hammers. The creature was slightly larger than the others and, alone among them, wore clothing, a bright rainbow sash circling hairless hips. Reaching into the sash, the creature removed a long knife. Stanley gulped as the blade reflected the dull interior light. The sight was enough to send him to his knees. Locking his fists together, he prayed deeply.

The creature ignored him. Instead, with dazzling speed, it knelt beside the carcass of its comrade and cut a neat square hole in the chest. Dropping his hands, Stanley waddled over to where he could observe the operation more closely. "It smelled up my dreams," he explained. The odor still infected the air, but seemed remote and tepid now. Again the knife flashed. Then, standing, the creature recognized Stanley for the first time, gesturing at him to stand too. In one hand it held a bloody, puffy, pink-and-white mass of tissue.

Stanley glanced at the extended hand. "Ugh," he said with feeling.

The creature made an impatient motion, as if expecting Stanley to accept an offered gift.

"Get that thing away from me," Stanley said.

"But you must consume the vessel." The creature spoke the common tongue with barely a trace of accent.

"You don't mean eat it?"

"It is known and accepted."

"But that's a heart."

"And spirit," the creature said reverently. "Many thousands of spirits. Within this organ—alone among a manklin's particles—the true being resides."

"So what?" Stanley asked.

"Exactly." Nodding, the creature flashed an ugly smile. "If the blessed vessel remains unconsumed, then the spirits shall dangle eternally in the void. Because you are the slayer of the living flesh, the vast responsibility of salvation is yours."

"Mine?"

"It is known and accepted."

"Well, not by me."

"You will do it, of course."

Disgusted by the sight of the heart, Stanley turned his back. Staring at the cold metallic walls, he thought of the vanished yellow sea. With that gone, what else was there? Finally he turned back. "I won't do it," he said firmly, spreading his arms. "Kill me instead."

The manklin's name was Kelwainn. It turned out he was chieftain, high priest, physician, confessor, tribal elder of the flock. Stanley gladly explained the circumstances surrounding the murder, neglecting to detail the content of the dream but dwelling patiently upon the ordeal of the invading stink. Kelwainn refused to express a judgment. Once more he asked, "You will do it, of course?" The heart remained in his outstretched hand.

"Hell, no," Stanley said, turning his back.

Returning to his comrades—Stanley counted, there were twelve—Kelwainn issued a series of clicks. Immediately the others expanded their huge chests and emitted an awful wailing. Wincing painfully, Stanley covered his ears. Now what was up? He bustled over, shouting at Kelwainn to explain.

"Among us," Kelwainn shouted, "it is known and accepted that certain denizens of the shadowland—the charma—will now approach. It is their desire to attempt to claim the voided spirit that dangles alone, and our responsibility to protect him until proper consumption can be performed. The wailing of living spirits combats the designs of those whose very life is death. They cannot stand the racket."

"Me, too," Stanley said. The wailing was slipping through his hands. Hastily he scurried to inspect the cloistered chamber in which he had found himself. The only exit was a high door at the far end of the room. He pounded his fists frantically against the steel, but, with the wailing, could barely hear himself.

Coming back to Kelwainn, he pointed at the wailers.

"How long is this going to last?"

"The wailing shall continue until the spirit is consumed." He pointed at the heart, which now rested on the floor.

"That's blackmail," Stanley said. "It isn't even fair. What kind of savage are you?"

"It is our responsibility," Kelwainn said.

"Oh, feathers," said Stanley. "You're a civilized creature. You speak the common tongue. Hasn't that taught you enough to know?"

"I have learned nothing that conflicts with the ancient faith of my race."

"Then you ought to listen to me. I used to be a missionary. I could name you a dozen planets where the natives rate me next to God Himself. Stanleyism, it's called. If anyone knows the whole truth, it's got to be me."

Kelwainn attempted to reply, but his words were drowned in a suddenly rising tide of wails. Sighing, Stanley went back to his inspecting. The ship appeared to be a freighter of the type commonly used for intrasystem cargo hops. Strangely, the hold was empty except for a single crate of processed food. He sat down against the wall and lifted his hands from his ears long enough to fill a battered briar pipe with a thick milky substance. He found a match in the pocket of his trousers. The odor of the smoke was strong enough to drive away the last of the stink. He gripped the pipe stem between his teeth. He held his ears again. The wailing grew louder and louder, until the vibrations seemed to rattle his bones. The pipe provided scant relaxation. It was a weird, uncomfortable feeling. Finally he had to stand.

Kelwainn, joining the other twelve, had added his wails to theirs. Putting a finger to his lips, Stanley drew Kelwainn aside to a relatively quiet pocket of the hold.

"Okay," he said. "But"—gesturing back toward the heart—"I've got to demand a fork."

In the center of Kelwainn's square face, the triangle of red eyes flashed triumphantly. Wordlessly he shoved a hand into his sash and, with a flourish, removed two thin sticks.

"Good God," said Stanley, accepting the gift. "Chopsticks," he murmured, bemused. He approached the heart. Around him, the room fell obediently silent.

While he ate—Kelwainn had kindly lent a knife—Stanley attempted to justify his presence aboard the ship. Since he could not exactly recollect boarding the craft, the attempt proved a flat failure. Kelwainn loomed dangerously near, as though feeling a personal responsibility to ensure that every last particle of the heart was consumed.

"Back there," Stanley said, pointing at the floor, "I ran into the usual bloody hell." He sighed. "What did you say was the name of the place?"

"Manklin."

"Ah, your home world. Mine is Earth. It's been ages, ages since I've last seen those green, dazzling hills." He managed a bite. But gagged. Standing, clutching his throat, he roared for water. Kelwainn fetched a pint flask. The water was foul, but Stanley gulped. "I never made it out of the spaceport," he said, dropping back to his haunches.

Kelwainn nodded.

Stanley raised another bite toward his lips. Swallowing hastily, he felt the old familiar rage welling up. "Who do they think they are? There are places in the galaxy where my name is mentioned in the same breath with Christ and Muhammad. Yet, around here, they call me a criminal. As soon as my notorious face is spotted on a planet, they tell me to go away. I imagine being a religious figure yourself—that you can sympathize." He peered down at the half-eaten heart, then raised both hands, weaving the fingers into a single solid knot. He shook the great fist beneath Kelwainn's jaw. "It's like this. The martyr . . . the saint. Entwined. Merged. Fused. And there's no way of splitting"—his hands flew apart—"the two."

Kelwainn nodded.

"The trouble with me," Stanley confided between bites, "is that I've seen the truth. I've seen more worlds and people than any man's mind ought to be able to comprehend. I suppose you ought to seem weird to me, but compared to some of the races I've known—and not just known, I mean lived, slept, prayed with—you are no more alien than my own left hand." Deep in his belly, the heart lay. He seemed to feel it pulsating down there. Quickly he swallowed a gulp of brackish water.

"What was it you saw?" Kelwainn asked politely, his eyes firmly fixed to the remaining fragments of the heart.

Stanley ate again. "Nothing."

"I thought you mentioned—"

"Nothing!" Quickly Stanley calmed himself. "Can I explain how it happened? I cannot. I traveled and traveled, stealing rides like this, sometimes paying my way, occasionally even crewing. I got farther and farther out, till for years, I met no other human being. It was a lonely time. At last, unexpectedly, I reached the very edge of the universe. I looked straight out, too. There was nothing—just emptiness . . . the void . . . a black hole. So I looked back. And there was nothing there, either. It was the same. I had seen the truth—as blunt and ugly as can be. Sure, I was scared. I ran all the way back here, trying to forget. Alas, who could? When you know, really know, that there's nothing"—his voice dropped to a confidential whisper—"then you're utterly free. You've got to do damn well what you want. I fell into an enormous mess of trouble. Being free got me hated, loathed, spat upon. On numerous planets my name was substituted for traditional curses. I violated their laws and customs, laughed in the face of their taboos. They drove me away, banished me to a half-life of eternal wandering. But I don't care." The final bite lay upon the floor. With a great speed denying his bulk, Stanley gripped the piece between the sticks and rammed it down his throat. "Free," he said, sighing. He wiped his lips, belched. "Where did you say we were bound?"

"To the Jakla," Kelwainn said reverently.

Smiling, Stanley stood and waved a finger at the moist spot on the floor. "I didn't have to do that. I could have given my word, and then, when your pals shut up, raised a ruckus and fetched the crew. So, in return for that favor, I expect you people to remember the name. Late at night, when you're crouched around the blazing tribal campfires, when you're gazing up at the twinkling mysteries of the nighttime sky, moaning or praying or doing whatever it is you do when confronting the vast unknown, I want you to recollect the only free man you've ever met." He hastened toward the door, calling back, "Stanley!"

He banged his fists against rigid steel. "Okay, okay! Open up!

You've got a stowaway! Come on!" But the door failed to budge. Puzzled, Stanley dropped his hands and listened.

A gentle hand touched his shoulder. Kelwainn stood, holding a silver key to the door and grinned. The key fit snugly. The door popped open. Stanley stepped through into the crew quarters.

The room was empty. "Ready or not, here I come," he called, stepping ahead into the control room.

And that was empty too.

They were hiding. Bastards. Bending down, he peeked beneath chairs, cots, stove, toilet, sink, control panel. There was nobody there. "How the hell?" he murmured. Kelwainn had followed him forward. Glancing back, Stanley saw a half-dozen three-eyed faces peering past the edge of the open door. He faced the control panel directly, hands on hips. It had been smashed. Wires, levers, dials, glass, chrome—everything lay everywhere. He approached the broken frame of the pilot's chair and leaned forward, gazing down into the transparent rectangle of the observation window. The topmost layer of glass had been shattered. Through an intricate pattern of exploding lines, he saw the blackness of space. Here and there, like twinkling bugs captured in an enormous web, the stars shone through. One was huge, bright, a giant.

"The Jakla," said Kelwainn, leaning over and stroking the screen softly.

Stanley gasped, then stood upright, hands trembling. "You're joking."

Kelwainn shook his head.

"That's where we're going? To that star?"

"It is the resting place."

"In this ship? At this speed? Why, it'll take"—he made rapid computations in his head—"forever."

"But it is known," Kelwainn said, "and accepted."

"You idiots!" Stanley cried.

Stanley sat slumped against the wall, munching on a handful of processed grain, while across from him, huddled in an indistinguishable mass, the manklins slept. Stanley was smoking, too. The thick fumes provided a measure of relief, but already his supply had dwindled dangerously low.

Finishing his dinner, he resumed toying with the shells and seed. He had picked them up someplace in his wanderings and would never travel without them. With dazzling speed he moved the shells across the slick floor. Stopping, he arranged them in a neat line. There were three shells—identical from the outside—painted midnight black. He tapped one with a fingernail, causing it to perform a neat half-flip. Beneath—worn smooth by years of traveling—the seed lay bluntly revealed. Stanley clapped his hands, smiling. "I win," he said.

"Excuse me."

Stanley glanced up. Standing above was a manklin—not Kelwainn, but, with a trio of tiny breasts, a female.

"You speak the common tongue," Stanley said.

"We are required to learn."

Stanley pushed the shells and seed aside. "Care to sit?"

The manklin dropped down. "My name is Darjinn," she said. "There is a thing I wish to ask you. It is a thing I heard you tell Kelwainn. About the edge—the edge of the universe."

"Oh, that," said Stanley.

"Yes. I am . . . I find it difficult to conceive. It is a thing far surpassing what we know—even the most advanced."

"Is that you?"

"I am young but"—proudly—"a very rapid learner. My spirit consumption is very great."

"But you won't make it. That star is light-years away."

"In olden times, before your race came to our world with ships capable of sailing the sky, we placed our dead beneath the stars and tried to drive their spirits up and away. This way is much better."

"You'll die."

"Perhaps. But the ship—"

"And more expensive." Stanley calculated rapidly. The cost of purchasing the ship, paying the crew, the automatic equipment. "Tell me, Darjinn, do you people carry money—federation credits?" He reached into his pocket and revealed a single worn tin coin.

Darjinn nodded. "We work in the port. Kelwainn carries them in his sash."

"The money belongs to him?"

"It is as much mine as his," Darjinn said, plainly offended. "We share all things."

Stanley took a moment to consider the possibilities. Abruptly, deciding, he tucked the coin away and then motioned with the other hand, indicating the shells and seed. "Do you enjoy games?"

"But—"

"Here—I'll demonstrate." Keeping the seed separate, he arranged the shells in a line. "Now, here," he said, placing the seed beneath the center shell, "this is our trick. You've got to watch closely. Don't blink an eye." With his usual dazzling speed, Stanley rearranged the shells. "Well?"

Darjinn tapped the center shell. "There."

"You think the seed is there?"

"It is."

"We'll see." Stanley flipped the shell. Nothing. "You lose," he said.

"Then it is this one," Darjinn said, pointing to the shell on the right.

"And, again, you lose." Stanley flipped the final shell, revealing the seed.

"But how. . . ?"

"All in the hand." Stanley gave his fingers a shake. "Quicker than the eye, two eyes, even three. But my idea is, we bet."

"Bet?"

"Wager, gamble. You can use a few of your community coins. I'll stake my"—he removed the tin coin—"fortune. Three-to-one odds."

"But," Darjinn said, watching the shells as they formed a line, "what about the edge?"

"Oh, that." Bowing his head, Stanley searched the floor for his missing pipe. "A lie. A means of attracting attention. A silly, childish foible of mine. I do apologize. Nothing more."

"A lie?"

"Completely. Choose."

Sitting in a corner of the cargo hold, back facing the room, Stanley diligently counted his coins, arranging each batch of ten into a neat pile. From behind, he heard a dreadful thump, and turning, observed, stretched out on the floor, the unmoving body of a manklin. Kelwainn stood about his fallen companion, gazing remotely ahead, muttering in a series of quick, high-pitched clicks and growls. The others —including Darjinn—were fast asleep.

Stanley counted the last of the coins, then stuck the lot in a pocket and crossed over. "That was damn quick," he said, when Kelwainn ceased clicking. He pointed down. "Heart attack? Brain fever?"

"No, this." Kelwainn opened a fist, revealing several small pink capsules. "A simple poison."

"You killed him, huh?"

Kelwainn bent down. Quick as a flash, the knife glinted in his hand. Stanley observed the slicing. Within a moment the dead heart lay cradled in Kelwainn's hands.

"You intend to eat all of it?" Stanley asked.

Kelwainn placed the heart on the floor and carefully, using the sharp tip of the knife, began to divide the organ into equal portions. "We will share. There are many thousands of spirits here. Sharing is the best method."

"It is known," Stanley intoned. "It is accepted."

"It is."

"But what about me?"

"You will not be forced. The slayer of the living flesh is required to consume those spirits he has set free. But this being died by his own hand."

Stanley shook his head. "Afraid not. I want my share." He pointed at the heart as if calling upon it to testify in his behalf. "I'm here—right?—I didn't ask to be here, but it's too late now. I want to do my part."

"And why is that?"

"I'm hungry. Tired of eating processed food. Besides, the food'll last longer this way. Do I need a reason?"

Kelwainn paused to consider. "You may eat only the heart," he warned. "Among us, it is taboo to consume the flesh. The body will be ejected into space."

"I'm no cannibal. Except for heart."

"And you are willing to bear the burden of the spirits?"

"I've done all right so far. Sure. I'm brimming over with spirits. In fact, right this minute I can feel them hopping and popping inside me."

"If it is your desire . . ." Kelwainn stood and went to wake the others. His gaze never wholly left Stanley. On the floor, the heart lay neatly severed into equal portions. Stanley counted, ensuring that there were thirteen. Then he grinned. "Hey . . . forget the chopsticks." He picked up one portion of the heart in his fingertips. "I can manage this little bit."

Darjinn pointed at the center shell. "That one," she said with certainty.

Stanley cut off another slice of the heart. Chewing, he flipped the indicated shell. "Too bad," he murmured through a full mouth.

Darjinn passed over the final three coins that lay in front of her. "That is all," she said with finality.

"You're not quitting?"

"You have taken all my coins," Darjinn, too, was eating a portion of the heart, but more slowly, painstakingly, as though each additional bite was an event of vast consequence.

Stanley waved vaguely toward the corner where the manklins slept. "Go borrow someone else's share. Kelwainn won't need the money. Not till we reach the Jakla."

"But he has no share. The coins belonged to all of us in common. I used them all."

"I see," said Stanley. Continuing to chew, he considered. Looking down at the trio of shells, the exposed seed, he envisioned the long hours that would follow, devoid of even this bare amusement, the hollow sense of victory. Oh, hell, he thought, even though it went against his principles. "Here." He passed a stack of ten coins to Darjinn. "Consider these a loan."

"I thank you," she said stiffly.

Stanley inserted the seed beneath a shell and began the ritual of rearrangement. "Do you happen to remember what you wanted to know the first time we talked?"

"I remember," Darjinn said, refusing to allow her gaze to move from the shells. When the rearrangement was complete, she looked up and tapped the center shell. "There."

Stanley flipped the shell. "Well. How about that?" He passed three coins to Darjinn, enlarging her meager fortune. "I lied to you. About the edge. I have seen it."

"I don't understand. I thought we agreed—"

"I spoke metaphorically. The human race—that's me—started out on a planet called Earth. What I saw was the end of that beginning, and, it seems to me, that is the real subjective end of everything. I drifted in my youth, wandering the romantic spacelanes, the same as you heard me tell Kelwainn. I had a fine time, meeting a certain woman, falling in love, producing a child. We settled on a colonial world and built a cabin. On an island. A few miles offshore from the main colony. This world was a young planet, still in the process of forming, in search of a real identity, totally devoid of intelligent life. The island was small enough that I could hike around it between breakfast and lunch. It teemed with wild game, huge dumb beasts possessed of the richest, most divine meat and juice. One would step up and eat out of your hand, and then, when you released the gas, fall over—*kerplop*—with a big smile. The regular colonists wanted to form a government and petition the federation for recognition. They said I had to attend the meeting, so I rowed to the mainland. The meeting was long and dull, and somewhere in the middle, the building twitched. I slept. In the morning, when I rowed back to the island, it wasn't there. Three days I searched those wild, raging waters. Okay, I finally had to admit. That twitch had been an earthquake. The little island had sunk. With it—naturally—my woman, my child, my teeming game. I left the planet as soon as the annual freighter came. Soon enough, I reached Earth. A freak of fate had brought me there—a curious twitch in the lifeline. A blasted, burned, ugly, desolate world. I established camp. That first night, in spite of a roaring fire, a pack of filthy, hairy, two-legged beasts attacked me. Squatting down, I unloosed a dreadful barrage. The bastards fell but wouldn't stop. I killed them all. Chowtime, I thought, with some satisfaction, but when I went to skin the first, I realized that the eyes were too damn familiar. Humans. People. Men. The sons of the fathers of my race. I got out of there, too. I had seen enough: the end—where we're all going. We started out beasts, and we're ending the same damn way. I kept drifting. Choose."

"That one," Darjinn said, pointing to a shell.

Stanley flipped. "Right again." He shook his head in astonishment and passed the requisite coins. "I learned one thing: never believe in nothing. That's how you get—like me—to be free."

"But I know differently," Darjinn said. She struck her chest with two fists. "Here, I know."

Stanley leaned back. "You feel the spirits?"

"I do."

"Then," Stanley asked, "how come I don't?"

"You don't?"

"Not a damn thing. And I've consumed an entire heart. Remember? I'm afraid old Kelwainn is fooling you."

"But I can feel . . ."

"Are you sure? I wouldn't lie to you. All I ask is that you think about it." He shook his head. "But let's play."

Stanley was reaching out to turn the indicated shell when someone screamed. He glanced up hastily. In the corner where the manklins slept, one had come awake. The creature stood on tiptoe, face painfully contorted by some tremendous emotion, fists clenched and waving violently in the air.

"Oh, no!" Darjinn cried, bolting upright. "He has fallen!"

But the enraged manklin had found a knife and dived into the sleeping mass of his companions. Rhythmically, the blade went up and down. Blood flowed everywhere. At last Darjinn reached the scene of the slaughter and grabbed the manklin by the throat, hauling him back. He let out a howl of frustration, struggled, then broke free, holding the knife high, prepared to strike at Darjinn. Stanley, who had come running, reached high and slapped the knife away. He scooped it up, and in a single fluid motion, leaped, driving the knife cleanly into the manklin's throat.

By this time the others had come awake. Kelwainn danced to his feet and began clicking angrily at Darjinn. Stanley waited patiently for the excitement to die down, but when it didn't, he shouted, "Shut up!"

The manklins, unaccustomed to such blunt commands, fell immediately silent.

"What's the problem here?" Stanley said. "If it's all these loose spirits, then don't worry. The slayer of the living flesh must consume the freed spirits. It is known and—"

"But—" said Kelwainn.

"I killed him," Stanley said. "He killed them. So that makes me responsible for everybody."

"But you cannot bear that great burden," Darjinn said.

Stanley came over and patted her head. "Sure, I can. It won't mean a thing to me. Remember what I told you." Then he faced Kelwainn, pointing down. "Cut," he commanded.

"But—" Kelwainn said.

"It is known," said Stanley. "It is accepted. So"—he giggled brightly—"cut."

Fat and bloated, Stanley lay against the wall, burping gently. Glancing up at last, he noticed Darjinn standing above. "I'm king of the spirits," Stanley told her.

"You feel them?" she asked hopefully.

"Nope."

"Nothing?"

"Not a thing." He added, "Absolutely."

"I . . ." Darjinn began, but stopped.

"Go on," Stanley said, sitting up, suddenly alert.

"I can't feel them anymore either."

"You're sure?" he asked.

"I . . . Yes."

"Not even this much?" Stanley made a sign with his fingers—a bare, faint inch.

Darjinn shook her head weakly.

"Nothing?"

"Nothing," she said. "Absolutely."

"Good golly!" Stanley clapped his hands and smiled hugely. He bounded to his feet and spread his arms. Rushing forward, he hugged Darjinn in his wide embrace and drew her face down to his. He kissed her lips, then pushed her back. Genuine tears formed in his eyes and spilled down flushed cheeks. "I'm so glad," he said. "It's been so long. I haven't had a convert since . . . since . . ." Unable to remember, he kissed Darjinn again, patted her head. "Oh, I don't know when." He fell to his knees and gladly remained there, weeping without restraint.

Alone in the control room, Stanley sat with his back braced against the bare wire skeleton of the pilot's seat. Gazing through the shattered rectangle of the observation window, he observed below the twinkling sphere of the Jakla. The sight both moved and confused him. Although he knew the Jakla could be only minutely closer than before, the white star seemed strangely more vast, larger, but it wasn't so much a matter of size as one of power and dominance. The Jakla had assumed a significance, a mastery, a place in the sky it had not previously possessed. The phenomenon frankly puzzled Stanley. He thought he ought to try to work it out. There was a solution, he was convinced, yet it had so far eluded him.

"Stanley?"

"Huh?" He turned, the chair swiveling with him. "Oh . . . you."

"I must speak with you," Kelwainn said.

Stanley smiled, folding his hands on his belly. "Still mad about how I stole your dinner?"

"I must speak to you of Darjinn. I must ask—implore—that you not see her again."

"Are you kidding?" Stanley waved a hand, indicating the ship. "In here?"

"You must refuse to speak to her."

"Uh-uh." Stanley staggered to his feet, intending to deprive Kelwainn of the advantage of height, but the meal he had so recently consumed made him feel weak and dizzy. His belly felt as if it were filled with bricks, not spirits. He burped and fell back in the chair. "Darjinn's my friend," he managed.

"A lie," said Kelwainn.

"Hey," Stanley said. "Watch that."

"A liar," Kelwainn continued fervently. "I knew the moment you awoke. You are a thief, Stanley, a murderer, a mongrel. But most of all, you are a liar. You have caused Darjinn to doubt. She told me what you have asserted. I was forced to listen to your lies. It is common knowledge among your people that the Earth was destroyed ages past. You have no more seen that world than I have visited the Jakla."

"I spoke metaphorically," Stanley said.

"You spoke as a liar. Devil."

"Angel." Stanley touched his heart. "Angel of truth."

"Prince of lies."

"Me?" Stanley said, managing a tired laugh. At last, tottering freely, he reached his feet. "The devil has horns, a barbed tail, hooves. He is not a fat, talkative, doped-up old man like me . . . like Stanley."

"The devil may appear in whatever fancy he desires."

"I said that was enough. I said shut up." Turning, Stanley fell against the shattered remains of the control panel, barely supporting himself.

"She believes you, Stanley. She cannot feel the spirits anymore. You have taken her sacred existence and made it meaningless. You have—"

"Oh, come off it," Stanley murmured. "I saved her."

"You will learn," Kelwainn said.

For a long moment after Kelwainn left, Stanley remained where he was. At last he fell, landing in the pilot's seat, tilting forward. Beneath him, the expansive vista of the observation window lay revealed. "Oh, no," he whispered, drawing in his breath. "Oh, God." It was the white star—the Jakla.

It had grown again.

Stanley forced the last bit of bread between his swollen lips and chewed furiously. The bread was stale, penetrated by mold, as hard as stone—the fragment of some half-consumed sandwich left behind by a neglectful crew member. The processed food was gone. Hardly enough water remained for a half-dozen swallows each.

Choking on the bread, Stanley struggled to force the dry crust down his throat. At last, succeeding, he could face his companions. Darjinn was gazing down at the floor, her face hidden from view.

Kelwainn smiled meagerly, then also looked away. Between the three of them, the shells and seed were waiting.

"I don't like this," Stanley said. "I think we ought to wait. A ship might find us. We might all be saved."

"Do we want to be saved?" Darjinn asked.

Kelwainn nodded slowly in agreement and pointed at the shells. "Explain your game to me."

"But this isn't the way to handle it," Stanley said. "We're talking about one of us dying. This way is just silly."

"Explain."

"But—"

"Tell him," Darjinn said.

"Oh, all right." Stanley carefully told Kelwainn how the shell game was played.

"And the one drawing the seed," Darjinn said, "will be the winner. He must swallow the capsule. If neither of us draws, then Stanley will be declared the winner. Are we agreed?"

"No," Stanley said.

"Yes," Kelwainn said.

"The capsule, please," said Darjinn.

Kelwainn removed one of the pale-pink capsules from his sash and laid it on the floor beside the shells. Darjinn signaled Stanley to begin.

"I won't," he said. "But—all right—I will." He planted the seed beneath the center shell and commenced the pattern of arrangement. At first his hands moved slowly, hesitantly, then faster, gaining speed and momentum as he juggled the shells with graceful proficiency, shifting them beneath and between his hands. He soon forgot everything except this art that he knew so well. Like miniature planets, the shells streaked across the floor, crisscrossing paths, darting chaotically, like particles in a universe gone haywire.

He stopped, fixing the shells in a neat line.

"Kelwainn?"

"Yes." Kelwainn reached boldly out, clearly intending to tap the center shell.

Darjinn grabbed his hand.

"No . . . me." She reached for the same shell.

"I am the elder," Kelwainn said, preventing her in turn.

"It can make no difference," she said. "I am the one who no longer believes, so it is proper that I should lead."

"In that case," Kelwainn said, "Stanley should precede us both."

"Stanley is an alien. It must be me."

"Don't be silly," Stanley broke in. "Kelwainn is right. Let him go first."

"No . . . me." Again Darjinn reached out.

Stanley slapped her hand aside. "Kelwainn," he said.

"Me." Desperately Darjinn tried to reach the shell. Stanley could see no other choice. Turning his hand into a tight fist, he cracked her solidly on the jaw. Her eyes dropped shut. She toppled forward. Stanley caught her arms, and standing, laid her carefully down.

"She'll be all right," he told Kelwainn. "But I couldn't—"

"I know."

"So I guess you'll have to go first." Stanley hurried back to his place. "If we need her, we can wake her."

"Of course," said Kelwainn.

Swearing, Stanley dug deeply with the knife, trying to free the heart from the gentle embrace of the dead creature's chest. But it wouldn't come loose. Pausing, he wiped his face with the back of a bloody hand, and glancing around, noticed that Darjinn was awake and looking at him.

"Kelwainn," he informed her, "lost."

She nodded. "You mean he won?"

"It wasn't my idea," he said. "Didn't I tell you to wait? You were the one who had to go ahead. Stubborn, senseless, stupid . . ."

He waited for her reply, and when it failed to come, returned to his work. The knife caught against a rib and refused to budge. Angrily Stanley tried to force it loose, but lost his grip instead, and the knife flew out of the open chest, bounding across the floor. "Damn it." He went to retrieve the tool. When he returned, he stopped in front of Darjinn.

"You're going to have to help me."

"I cannot." But she did stand, going to Kelwainn's body, kneeling down beside it. Quickly she removed the rainbow sash from around his hips and tied it around her own.

"Look, you have to help me," Stanley said. "I can't do this all alone."

"Then don't."

"And not eat the heart?"

"Who cares?"

"He does," Stanley said, pointing down.

"But he's dead."

"Well, yes." Stanley crouched down, inserting the knife. "But we do have to eat something. Spirits or no spirits, food is food."

"I cannot."

"Oh, stop saying that." He laughed derisively, pausing in his work. "Don't tell me you've fallen back. You're not afraid of Kelwainn's spirit?"

"It is not a matter of fear," she said, maintaining the same tone she had assumed since waking. "I do not choose to violate the ancient law unless it is necessary."

"What law?" Stanley held the bloody knife under her eyes. "Doesn't the law command you to share?"

"Not him. The law forbids that."

"Because he was your chief?"

"No, because he was my father."

"I was wrong," Stanley said, the newly transformed heart beating firmly inside him. He held Darjinn tightly by the shoulders so that she could not avoid him. "I can feel them now. I can. When I told you I couldn't, it was a lie."

Easily she slipped away from him. "Liar," she said. In her hands she held the shells and seed. Carefully she placed them on the floor, then inserted the seed. Her motions were slow, tentative, lacking in grace.

Stanley kicked the shells across the room. "Forget that . . . listen to me." He opened his shirt, revealing a bald chest. "I can feel them in here. I can hear them. They want out. Isn't that right? They want to reach the resting place. I'm not lying. You have to believe me."

Darjinn stood and went to fetch the scattered shells.

Stanley chased after her. "I can," he said. "I swear it. I really can. I can feel the Jakla and . . . and . . ."

"I don't care," Darjinn said. Bending down, she retrieved the seed. "I can feel nothing. And that is what matters to me."

When the chorus of voices deep inside him grew too loud to be easily ignored, Stanley tossed the half-eaten chunk of raw meat aside and sprang to his feet. He screamed.

But no one heard. On the opposite side of the hold, Darjinn was sound asleep. Asleep? Why wasn't she dead? It had been weeks since she had eaten a bite. The water was long since gone.

But hunger and thirst were things Stanley could bear, and the voices were not. It wasn't the tiny, shrill, piping one that bothered him; it was that one big loud one. Kelwainn, of course. Having his revenge. It wasn't fair. Stanley was the one who didn't even believe. Why wouldn't they let him alone? Why should he have to suffer so much?

Again he screamed.

Calming himself, he whispered, "No, no, no." It was all up there, in his head—pure imagination. Laughing fitfully he stumbled forward, his legs barely agreeing to carry him. He wanted to walk one way, but there was something else, a spirit, that wanted to go the other way, while another one said turn left, and yet another said turn right, and one more—the biggest of all, Kelwainn—said stop.

Stanley tripped and fell in a graceless heap.

Lying there, hands covering his ears, he fought them down, chased them back to the place where they belonged—the heart. At last, firmly in control, he crawled forward on his belly, giggling in triumph. The door to the forward compartment was open, so he crawled through, pausing at the edge of the control room to gather his strength before making the final plunge. He tried to stand and walk, but his legs refused to budge, lying uselessly below like pounds of dead meat. It wasn't lack of food and water; it was the spirits. They weren't even going to allow him this much. He had sinned, refusing to recognize their existence. They were there—he knew that now—and they had won.

"Please," he murmured. "Let me up. Let me see."

He tottered to his feet. Dimly, far ahead, he spied the battered frame of the pilot's chair. Here we go, he thought, lunging, tripping, falling, twisting his body at the last possible moment so that it landed upright in the chair.

Then he let his head fall forward.

His forehead struck the observation window. Bouncing. When the motion ceased, he opened his eyes, straining to see what lay ahead.

Through the intricate design of exploding lines, he saw the stars shining within the void. He stared, as if unable to accept the testimony of his own eyes, and in a blink, the stars vanished. Then he could see only one: the white star—the Jakla. He shivered. It was so close. If he wanted, he was certain, he could simply reach out and touch that star. Deep inside, the spirits also heard. They demanded to be set free. He laughed, pitching forward, then fell, tumbling out, passing effortlessly through myriad layers of impenetrable glass and plastic. Unhindered, as free as a particle suddenly cut loose from the laws of the physical universe, Stanley rushed through the vastness of interstellar space. All sensations of direction and motion, mass and velocity, fled from him. All he knew was the Jakla, the resting place, which approached, drawing closer and closer, until he was sure he felt its dry, scorching heat. The light burned his eyes. He drove onward, stretching his hands in front of him, awaiting that final answering touch, the merger, the cosmic fusion, the end.

Then he was falling back. He screamed, wanting to remain, but he was falling. Darkness swallowed him. Then he glimpsed the pattern of the stars. The Jakla dwindled to a bare pinpoint of light. He fell up . . . and out. The dull silence of the control room embraced him. For a moment he could only sit and wonder. Then his head fell. His forehead struck the observation window. He stayed there.

On silent, naked feet, Stanley entered the cargo hold. Darjinn knelt on the floor. Seeing her, Stanley could not contain himself. He rushed forward, shouting, "I felt it! I saw it! It's real!"

Slowly Darjinn raised her eyes, meeting his. "Is it?" she asked coldly. Shifting slightly, she revealed the shells and seed. "Let's play."

Stanley dropped down beside her, observing carefully as her hands moved tentatively, inserting the seed, arranging the shells. Suddenly, breaking off, she laughed.

"What is it?" he asked, lifting his gaze.

"You lied to me."

"I never denied it," he said. "Lying is . . . I've always lied."

"Me too," she said.

"No!"

"So now we're even." Reaching across, she patted his head tenderly. "Now, choose."

He did, expecting that, this time, he couldn't lose.

Gordon Eklund writes:

If the golden age of science fiction, as Peter Graham once remarked, is twelve, then I was especially fortunate in having my own chronological years coincide exactly with that green, rich, fertile moment in literary history: when Gordon Eklund turned twelve, in

1957, he was reading his first science-fiction story, Clifford Simak's remarkable "Desertion." That same year also saw, powerfully, the launching of man's first artificial satellite, and I recall how the science-fiction magazines of the time made a great fuss over this event. Their pages were soon inundated with faintly scientific articles and learned discussions of the dawning of the Space Age. Infinite speculations ran like mountain brooks: when will man (presumably Russian) first set foot on the Moon? How about 1970? 1975? 2010? Hell, no, I thought at the time, why not, in fact, July 1969?

That gift of prophecy soon deserted me. So, similarly, did most of the faintly scientific articles involved: these left me cold. Who could be riled by gray visions of the dawning of a secular Space Age, when that age, in all its beatific glory, already existed fullborn in the holy (fictional) pages of these very same science-fiction magazines? Not me, at twelve, for one.

But that was 1957, and let's see what we've lost since. I've already alluded to my private gift of prophecy, and innocence always goes, but what about those scientific speculations? Gone, I'll tell you, gone. And most of the magazines, too, though that's more a matter of publishing trends than cosmic connections.

The Space Age, too. The one that had been dawning, that is. I can no more guess what may happen tomorrow than you or Chairman Mao, but it's entirely feasible that man's moment in space may be finished for our lifetimes, and do you know what that leaves? Well, the fiction, for one thing, the stories. That's right where it began, in the pages of the remaining magazines, in this book and many others, in my work and that of the other men and women of the field. It began there; it may end there. I think that's grand.

Science fiction is often accused (by those who do not like it) of being unnecessarily esoteric. You can't understand the stuff, we are told, unless you've already read a fat pile of it. SF writers use devices not readily comprehensible to an outside reader. Take faster-than-light travel, hyperspace, fourth and fifth dimensions.

Well, um, I say. The truth is that anything worth knowing demands effort, and the science fiction understandable only to science-fiction readers is almost invariably the very best kind written. What we've done (we, the people of science fiction—writers, readers, editors, fans) is create our own mutual space age. To hell with that other dying thing. Ours is there for anyone to visit: it exists, like concrete. Though often raped by trivialities and triteness, this age endures, perseveres, goes on. We live in a remarkable time that permits us the existence of a future as firm and real as our so-called present. Men have often chosen to live in better (or worser) pasts, but only with science fiction has the range of human temporal consciousness been extended beyond tomorrow. If this story here gives you a taste or tickle of that, it will have succeeded way beyond its author's sometimes modest expectations. Thank you.

MAZES

by Ursula K. Le Guin

I have tried hard to use my wits and keep up my courage, but I know now that I will not be able to withstand the torture any longer. My perceptions of time are confused, but I think it has been several days since I realized that I could no longer keep my emotions under aesthetic control, and now the physical breakdown is also nearly complete. I cannot accomplish any of the greater motions. I cannot speak. Breathing, in this heavy foreign air, grows more difficult. When the paralysis reaches my chest, I shall die—probably tonight.

The alien's cruelty is refined, yet irrational. If it intended all along to starve me, why not simply withhold food? But instead of that, it gave me plenty of food, mountains of food, all the greenbud leaves I could possibly want. Only they were not fresh. They had been picked; they were dead; the element that makes them digestible to us was gone, and one might as well eat gravel. Yet there they were, with all the scent and shape of greenbud, irresistible to my craving appetite. Not at first, of course. I told myself: I am not a child, to eat picked leaves! But the belly gets the better of the mind. After a while it seemed better to be chewing something, anything, that might still the pain and craving in the gut. So I ate, and ate, and starved. It is a relief, now, to be so weak I cannot eat.

The same elaborately perverse cruelty marks all its behavior. And the worst thing of all is just the one I welcomed with such relief and delight at first: the maze. I was badly disoriented at first, after the trapping, being handled by a giant, being dropped into a prison; and this place around the prison is disorienting, spatially disquieting; the strange, smooth, curved wall-ceiling is of an alien substance, and its lines are meaningless to me. So, when I was taken up and put down, amidst all this strangeness, in a maze, a recognizable, even familiar maze, it was a moment of strength and hope after great distress. It seemed pretty clear that I had been put in the maze as a kind of test or investigation, that a first approach toward communication was being attempted. I tried to cooperate in every way. But it was not possible to believe for very long that the creature's purpose was to achieve communication.

It is intelligent, highly intelligent; that is clear from a thousand evidences. We are both intelligent creatures, we are both maze builders; surely it would be quite easy to learn to talk together! If that were what the alien wanted. But it is not. I do not know what kind of mazes it builds for itself. The ones it made for me were instruments of torture.

The mazes were, as I said, of basically familiar types, though the walls were of that foreign material much colder and smoother than packed clay. The alien left a pile of picked leaves in one extremity of each maze, I do not know why; it may be a ritual or superstition. The first maze it put me in was babyishly short and simple. Nothing expressive or even interesting could be worked out from it. The second, however, was a kind of simple version of the Ungated Affirmation, quite adequate for the kind of reassuring, outreaching statement I wanted to make. And the last, the long maze, with seven corridors and nineteen connections, lent itself surprisingly well to the Maluvian mode, and indeed to almost all the New Expressionist techniques. Adaptations had to be made to the alien spatial understanding, but a certain quality of creativity arose precisely from the adaptations. I worked hard at the problem of that maze, planning all night long, reimagining the links and spaces, the feints and pauses, the erratic, unfamiliar, and yet beautiful course of the True Run. Next day when I was placed in the long maze and the alien began to observe, I performed the Eighth Maluvian in its entirety.

It was not a polished performance. I was nervous, and the spatiotemporal parameters were only approximate. But the Eighth Maluvian survives the crudest performance in the poorest maze. The evolutions in the ninth encatenation, where the "cloud" theme recurs so strangely transposed into the ancient spiraling motif, are indestructibly beautiful. I have seen them performed by a very old person, so old and stiff-jointed that he could only suggest the movements, hint at them, a shadow gesture, a dim reflection of the themes; and all who watched were inexpressibly moved. There is no nobler statement of our being. Performing, I myself was carried away by the power of the motions and forgot that I was a prisoner, forgot the alien eyes watching me; I transcended the errors of the maze and my own weakness, and danced the Eighth Maluvian as I have never danced it before.

When it was done, the alien picked me up and set me down in the first maze—the short one, the maze for little children who have not yet learned how to talk.

Was the humiliation deliberate? Now that it is all past, I see that there is no way to know. But it remains very hard to ascribe its behavior to ignorance.

After all, it is not blind. It has eyes, recognizable eyes. They are enough like our eyes that it must see somewhat as we do. It has a mouth, four legs, can move bipedally, has grasping hands, etc.; for all its gigantism and strange looks, it seems less fundamentally different from us, physically, than a fish. And yet, fish school and dance and, in their own stupid way, communicate!

The alien has never once attempted to talk with me. It has been with me, watched me, touched me, handled me, for days; but all its motions have been purposeful, not communicative. It is evidently a solitary creature, totally self-absorbed.

This would go far to explain its cruelty.

I noticed early that from time to time it would move its curious horizontal mouth in a series of fairly delicate, repetitive gestures, a little like someone eating. At first I thought it was jeering at me; then I wondered if it was trying to urge me to eat the indigestible fodder; and then I wondered if it could be communicating *labially*. It seemed a limited and unhandy kind of language for one so well provided with hands, feet, limbs, flexible spine, and all; but that would be like the creature's perversity, I thought. I studied its lip motions and tried hard to imitate them. It did not respond. It stared at me briefly and then went away.

In fact, the only indubitable *response* I ever got from it was on a pitifully low level of interpersonal aesthetics. It was tormenting me with knob-pushing, as it did once a day. I had endured this grotesque routine pretty patiently for the first several days. If I pushed one knob, I got a nasty sensation in my feet; if I pushed a second, I got a nasty pellet of dried-up food; if I pushed a third, I got nothing whatever. Obviously, to demonstrate my intelligence, I was to push the third knob. But it appeared that my intelligence irritated my captor, because it removed the neutral knob after the second day. I could not imagine what it was trying to establish or accomplish, except the fact that I was its prisoner and a great deal smaller than it. When I tried to leave the knobs, it forced me physically to return. I must sit there pushing knobs for it, receiving punishment from one and mockery from the other. The deliberate outrageousness of the situation, the insufferable heaviness and thickness of this air, the feeling of being forever watched yet never understood, all combined to drive me into a condition for which we have no description at all. The nearest thing I can suggest is the last interlude of the Ten Gate Dream, when all the feintways are closed and the dance narrows in and in until it bursts terribly into the vertical. I cannot say what I felt, but it was a little like that. If I got my feet stung once more, or got pelted once more with a lump of rotten food, I would go vertical forever. . . . I took the knobs off the wall (they came off with a sharp tug, like flowerbuds), laid them in the middle of the floor, and defecated on them.

The alien took me up at once and returned me to my prison. He had got the message, and had acted on it. But how unbelievably primitive the message had to be! And the next day he put me back in the knob room, and there were the knobs, as good as new, and I was to choose alternate punishments for his amusement. . . . Until then I had told myself that the creature was alien, therefore incomprehensible and uncomprehending, perhaps not intelligent in the same *manner* as we, and so on. But since then I have known that, though all that may remain true, it is also unmistakably and grossly cruel.

When it put me into the baby maze yesterday, I could not move. The power of speech was all but gone (I am dancing all this, of course, in my mind; "the best maze is the mind," the old proverb goes), and I simply crouched there, silent. After a while it took me out again, gently enough. There is the ultimate perversity of its behavior: it has never once touched me cruelly.

It set me down in the prison, locked the gate, and filled up the trough with inedible food. Then it stood, two-legged, looking at me for a while.

Its face is very mobile, but if it speaks with its face, I cannot understand it; that is too foreign a language. And its body is always covered with bulky, binding mats, like an old widower who has taken the Vow of Silence. But I had become accustomed to its great size, and to the angular character of its limb positions, which at first had seemed to be saying a steady stream of incoherent and mispronounced phrases, a horrible nonsense dance like the motions of an imbecile, until I realized that they were strictly purposive movements. Now I saw something a little beyond that in its position. There were no words, yet there was communication. I saw, as it stood watching me, a clear signification of angry sadness—as clear as the Sembrian Stance. There was the same lax immobility, the bentness, the assertion of defeat. Never a word came clear, and yet it told me that it was filled with resentment, pity, impatience, and frustration. It told me it was sick of torturing me, and wanted me to help it. I am sure I understood it. I tried to answer. I tried to say, "What is it you want of me? Only tell me what it is you want." But I was too weak to speak clearly, and it did not understand. It has never understood.

And now I have to die. No doubt it will come in to watch me die; but it will not understand the dance I dance in dying.

Ursula K. Le Guin writes:

"Mazes" is a Clarion story. I have been writer-in-residence at the three Clarion West workshops in writing science fiction; each time, I used the afternoons of my week for in-class writing exercises, trying to give us all a workout on some particular problem or effect or bit of technique. The first time, in 1971, we did Aliens: description of aliens, taking the alien viewpoint, and so on. We got some lovely verbal sketches out of it, but I was bothered because most of the people continued to be jocular about their aliens—defensively, using humor as a distancing device, a safety device. I was trying to get them to live dangerously, to be aliens. So on the last afternoon I said, "Now, okay, write me a story on this theme: An alien creature is dying. A human being is present. You write from inside the alien, from its point of view, strictly." I figured they couldn't get too many har-hars out of that.

So we all hunched up around the room with our backs turned and scribbled for about an hour, in a silence punctuated only by deep sighs and murmured "Shits" and loud, angry sounds of scratching-out and erasing. Then we all turned slowly around and read our stories to each other. They were very rough, of course, but some of them were beautiful. The best one was by Lin Neilsen, about a bright, fierce creature that has been debeaked and declawed and treated as a child's pet, but I never could persuade her to revise and publish it; so here's the second-best one.

FOR ALL POOR FOLKS AT PICKETWIRE

by R. A. Lafferty

1

"We ought to have a bigger place for the children to play in the summertime," Lemuel said one day. "How many do we have now?" Lemuel was a bent young man with bright and slightly peering eyes.

"Five, Lem, five," Griselda said. This Griselda was something of a looker.

If Lemuel Windfall hadn't always seen so far ahead, he might have been one of the very top inventors of the world. But isn't foresight a good quality in an inventor or in anyone?

Sure it is, but it's not good if you rub it into the ground. It is possible to be too foresightly. Lemuel could see ahead both to the immediate and to the ultimate use of whatever gadget he might devise. And he could pretty well weigh it out in green money how much it could be turned for. It would have been wonderful if he'd let it go at that; if he'd gathered each harvest in as it came to season, and had put his bills of expectation on their proper spindle till they had realized themselves. But Lemuel always saw forward, past the use and application of a device. He saw forward to its obsolescence. And what is the use to activate a device or a potential or a condition if it is going to be obsolete in a decade or two?

"For the money, that's what's the use," the wife, Griselda, would say. "We can use the money right now, and I don't care whether it will be obsoleted next century."

"But why should we be bothered for money?" Lemuel would always ask. "Surely it's always an advantage in any circumstance to reduce the number of moving parts, and money in this life is made up entirely of moving parts. And didn't I invent instant money just a fortnight ago?"

"Indeed you did, Lem," good Griselda said, "but you didn't go into production on the stuff. You looked into the future, and you discovered that it would be a short-term (not over fifty years' duration) affair. You said that ethical backlash and other difficulties would blow the whistle on it by then. Look, Lem, I'm reasonable. I'm not even asking for instant money today. I'll settle for thirty-minute money. I'll give you just thirty minutes to raise some household cash, and that's the limit. Thirty minutes, Lem. Did you hear me?"

"Yes," he would always say. Then he would put a few working drawings of something under his arm and would go down the street to Conglomerate Enterprises or Wheeler-Heelers and sell them for whatever he could get in thirty minutes.

"I could get more for things if I had the time and fare to take them to Le Conglomerat in Paris," Lem would say wistfully. "They've written me that they'll pay well for any new thing of mine, and they say that their offer will stand forever, for a reasonable ever. I could always get more if I had fifteen years to deal instead of thirty minutes."

"Lem, everything that you've ever sold, you've already had it on the shelf for at least fifteen years," Griselda would say with weary patience.

"Yes, I guess so," Lem would admit.

"And remember that you've promised me a trip to Paris."

"Yes, and I'll give it to you yet, Grissie."

And there was a worse hitch in the Lemuel mental and fabricatory process. He didn't like to produce anything unless working conditions were just right. And he had the sad conviction that nowhere in the world were conditions ever just right.

"I should have a workshop that's in a total vacuum," he would say sometimes. "That's the least of the conditions."

"You should have your head a total vacuum," Griselda would counter.

"Why, such thing would implode my brains," Lem would state, "and what would be the compensating advantage?"

"You never know, dear. There might be useful side effects."

"Yes, I should have a workshop in total vacuum," he'd dream and beam, "and dust-free, and in a place completely without gravity. And it should be without the quality of temperature; neither medium, nor very high, nor very low temperature will serve; it must be without even the idea of temperature. And it should be beyond the power of hard radiation of every sort, beyond the fury of excessive ultraviolet rays or actinic rays or triatomic oxygen. 'And all baleful beams,' as the psalmist says. And my place of enterprise should be beyond the temporal cloud, and I do not mean anything so simple as time-standstill, no, nor eternity either. There must not be duration; there must be only moment. No duration is ever long enough to get anything done.

"And my workshop should be spared the effect of every magnetic field, of every voltage differential, of every solar wind. And it should not have any topography at all. Perhaps it shouldn't even have location, or shape, or size. Griselda, if I had a workshop or factory so situated and appointed, all processes would become easy, and there would be scarce a limit to what might be achieved. Hey, I could make coal then! Oh, but there's plenty of coal. But in this little workshop here, and in the bigger workshop whose name is World, with all their disabilities of gravity and magnetism and electrical field, and baleful rays and temperature and existence in time and space, and subject to indexing as to shape and size and color and aroma, why, it just doesn't seem worthwhile even to try to do any work here."

"But, Lem, if you hadn't gone tilt-brained and thought up all these objections, then you could believe that you had the finest place in the world, and you could do the finest work anywhere. Say, there's a title to a piece of land in Colorado that came in the mail today. A Mr. Jasher Halfhogan sent it to you. As far as I can tell, the little piece of land is on a small creek named Picketwire, and there isn't any town near it anywhere."

"What? What? Oh, how fortuitous can it get!" Lemuel cried with real enthusiasm. "On Picketwire Creek in Colorado, you say? Why, that's almost the same thing as having no topography at all. Nuggets of gold and orichalcum on my head! I guess that this is just my lucky day."

"But shouldn't this man have sent you money instead of a title to a no-good piece of land?"

"Of course he should have, Griselda. What luck he didn't! He should have sent me a great lot of money, and I suppose that there are persons who would prefer money. Oh, this is lucky! There is bound to be advantage come of it. One of the requirements of the ideal working place is that it should be unlocated and of no value. May the years teach me enough wisdom to find advantage in this thing! And in the meanwhile, it might be a nice place to turn the children loose in the summertime. How many of them do we have now?"

"Six, Lem, six. They are six of the reasons that I'm often after you for money. And remember that you've promised me a trip to Paris. That takes money too."

In a different year Griselda said, "Do you know how much taxes we got a bill for on that stupid piece of land in Colorado, Lem? Eighty-five cents. It must be *some* place."

"It makes one feel cheap, doesn't it, Grissie? I'll see what I can do about getting the taxes raised. Jasher Halfhogan goes out there pretty often. I guess that I should find out a little bit more about that piece of property."

"I guess that I should find out a little bit more about that man Jasher Halfhogan," Griselda said. "He has some kind of hook into you. Jasher Halfhogan sounds like a name that you'd invent. And that funny-looking old man looks like someone you'd invent, too. I'm asking you seriously, Lem: did you?"

"No, not consciously I didn't invent him, Grissie. And yet I did invent him a little bit, I suppose. And he me. We are all formed by feedback and interaction. We see more than there is in other people, and we ourselves are seen for more than we are. And we grow to match our seeming. Don't you like Jasher?"

"I've never met him, Lem. Every time I've seen him he was scurrying away like some night ghost that was afraid of being shone on by sunlight. Well, if he's a Halfhogan, what would a Wholehogan be?"

"You really don't know, Griselda? Sometimes you astonish me," Lemuel said. He was a bent man who had recently slipped into middle age without much noise. "But as to the Colorado land, Jasher says that it's a gateway to a whole new life. It has something to say to me in the future, I know. And meanwhile, it might be a nice place to take the children some summer. How many do we have now?"

"Seven, Lem, seven." Somehow Griselda had remained one of the really good-lookers.

There finally came a year when Lemuel thrived in his erratic discoveries and enterprises in spite of his being forced to work and invent in places and circumstances of matter and atmosphere and gravity and magnetism and electrical manifestation and temperature and baleful rays and time and space and shape. Money seemed approximately sufficient. But always Griselda had something to worry about.

"I won't say that I don't like your friend Jasher Halfhogan," she said once. "I'm sure that he means well. I have met him now, you know, just a few years ago. Once, I believe, I saw him attempt a smile. It didn't work. But I do believe that he's a bad omen for you, Lem. A little buzzard recently whispered to me that he'll be the death of you yet."

"No, he'll not cause my death, Grissie," Lemuel said seriously. "Though the neighborhood children of whatever age hoot at him and call him Mr. Deathman and Mr. Soul Broker, yet I believe that they misunderstand his role. He will not cause my death. 'Twill be a mere synchronicity. He wants me to locate by that entrance in Colorado some year soon, to go to that little property of ours. That's one of the entrances to the next step in living, he says. And it would be nice to visit it, Grissie, before we die, or soon after that, in any case. And it might be pleasant to take the children there for a little vacation. How many do we have now?"

"Eight, Lem, but they're all married and moved away. I believe that it's too late for us to arrange such a trip together. In the next life, maybe."

"Maybe so, Grissie. It's good to think about." Lem was a bent old man now, and he hadn't intended to let himself get into such a state. And Griselda was still a good-looker, now and forever. "Colorado seems to loom pretty big in the next life," Lem was saying. "I'm feeling a bit doddery lately. I may ask Jasher Halfhogan what he thinks about it all."

So the next season, when Jasher came through town again, Lemuel asked him about several things. "I'd like someday to visit that little Colorado property that you once deeded to me for services rendered," Lem said. "I have high expectations for it. And I'm reaching the age where I need something of value to concretize my expectations a little."

"Oh, the property itself is worthless, Lem," Jasher said. "Don't set any expectations on its value."

"But, Jash, you once said that it was a gateway to a whole new life."

"So I did, and so it is. But even a broken gate that's not worth half a dollar may be a gateway to a whole new life. It's the location that's important, Lem. There are a few other localities equally important, and they all give ingress to the same place. But it would be impossible to put any of them into right context without the services of a special informant such as myself. The place is analogous to a mail drop, Lem, in that it gives communication to places almost without limit. Rather think of it as a world drop or a life drop. It's better to take these things under guidance and control than to go at random and in ignorance. Besides, I get a commission on you. I work largely on commission."

"I never did know what you did, Jasher," Lemuel said. "I'm not one to wonder about a friend's occupation, but my wife often speculates out loud about yours. She says that you'll be the death of me yet."

"No death is foreordained, Lem. I'll collect a fee on yours when it does happen, but that's only because you're in my territory. Lemuel, do you have any particular later life desires or aspirations? We may be able to do something about them."

"Oh, yes. And what desires I have left do seem to get a little bit stronger with age. In particular, I've always believed that I could accomplish things almost without limit if I had the proper working conditions for discovering and processing and manufacturing. I have found, Jasher, quite a few things that *had to have been* fabricated in more nearly ideal circumstances than are found on Earth. Or at least they had to be patterned and triggered in more favorable circumstances. These things have been passed off by most persons as natural or quasi-natural phenomena. But they're not natural. I know manufactured things when I see them, and many of these things are manufactured. Aye, Jasher, but they're not made under the disabilities that afflict our local planet.

"I want to make such things also. I want to make them in such profusion that they will be mistaken for natural or quasi-natural phenomena. I want to make them so nearly perfect that they will be almost unnoticed in their excellence, and so tremendously large that they will escape scrutiny and stand like invisible and accepted giants. I do not want money or recognition for these services that I am burning to perform. But, Jasher, the sites and circumstances for such doings are simply not to be found on this world."

"It may be that they *are* to be found with one foot on this world, Lem," Jasher Halfhogan said, "or with one tentacle. The world puts out some very long and tricky tentacles, a few of them so tremendous that they *do* escape scrutiny. So I will bet that we can find good site and circumstances for your workshop or whatever. Just what specifications do you have in mind for it?"

So Lemuel Windfall explained to Jasher Halfhogan just what he would need for the minimum. And Jasher nodded from time to time and mumbled, "I think so. Yes, I think so." Lem listed the things that he had often poured into the erratic ears of his wife and into the stoppered ears of the world at large. All about the avoidance of atmosphere and magnetism and gravity and baleful rays. "And somehow Griselda must get a trip to Paris out of it," he said.

"You're making it easy for us, Lem," Jasher said. "You're going right down the line with all our specialities. Lem, I know just the place for it. When will you be ready to go?"

"I'd go quickly enough if I knew where I was going and what I'd find," Lemuel stated with the confidence of one who doesn't expect his hand to be called.

"You'll find just the conditions that you have been speaking of, Lem. But can you handle it, or will you go right past the place? I've never been certain that you have enough of the cantankerous metal in you, and without it you'll have too easy a passage to discover these conditions. Have you the need to be compensating enough that you must create things in such profusion and perfection? For it *does* go by need, and I simply don't believe that you have a strong enough need in you. Lem, I don't believe that you have been a bad enough man to be called to the extraordinary ransom and prodigy."

"Have I not been bad enough?" Lemuel crooked his voice at Jasher. "Let me tell you about it, low and into your ear here." And Lemuel talked into Jasher's ear in a serious and hushed voice until all the blood was drained out of Jasher's face.

"Stop, stop! Yes, you've been bad enough, Lem," Jasher croaked with distaste. "I was wrong to doubt you. How soon will you be ready to go? It's to your little land in Colorado. It's a better entrance than most places to the whole new circumstance and life."

"I'll be ready to go by nightfall, Jasher," Lemuel said.

And that was almost the last that anyone saw of Lemuel Windfall around the old place. He cashed in his chips, as they say. He lowered his flag, so the colloquialism has it. He had his ticket punched, as the phrase goes. He went West, as the older fellows say. He shipped off to Colorado, as the proverb has it.

His wife, Griselda, put on widow's weeds when he was gone. She had always been an impatient woman.

2

More energy has been spent in explaining the presence of coal deposits on our Earth, and more especially in explaining petroleum deposits, than in almost any other thing. Probably more energy has been spent in explaining them than in forming them. But it comes to nothing.

One authority insisted that the carboniferous gluts of our world came from the tails of comets that sideswiped the Earth. And this is one of the most nearly intelligent of all the explanations that have been put forward!

There is one geologist who says that petroleum is formed only between layers of bituminous shale, and that it is formed in such case by great pressure and heat. That is a little like using cheese for the jaws of a vise intended to exert tremendous pressure. Bituminous shale just isn't the rock for the job. And trying to explain the presence of petroleum is child's play compared with trying to explain the presence of bituminous shale.

There is another authority who maintains that petroleum and natural gas are largely due to the resinous spores of rhizocarps. Savor that opinion for a moment, reader, and you must conclude that there is at least one authority running loose who should be confined.

In every case, the temperatures sufficient to form coal or petroleum are somewhat higher than the temperature sufficient to vaporize the entire Earth. One exasperated authority stated that all such deposits must have been made by kobalds or gnomes laboring under the roots of mountains. He was righter than he knew. But the question remains: how could any circumstances on Earth serve to trigger such deposits and results? And the answer is an easy one: they couldn't.

—Arpad Arutinov, *The Back Door of History*

But there *is* a condition, neither on Earth nor off it, not in any place, really, where circumstances *could* trigger such results. This is a condition lacking the quality of location (Jews, close your ears! Greeks, harden your hearing! Covenanters, avert your senses lest you be affronted by it!), a realm of ransom and recompense and incredible self-assigned labor, a scene where such accumulations of carbonaceous matter are indeed patterned and planned and instigated.

—Arpad Arutinov, *The Back Door of History,*
Second Revised Edition

There were new cargoes and traffics appearing, new potentials and circumstances; but it was only Conglomerate Enterprises and Wheeler-Heelers and Le Conglomerat and such like firms that guessed that the new things weren't really natural or even quasi-natural. The new things were manufactured—these canny companies recognized this quickly enough—and they weren't exactly manufactured on this world.

The conditions here just weren't right for them. And, as it seemed to the men of the several discerning firms and conglomerates, the new cargoes and traffics and products had the signature of one man all over them.

So several gentlemen from Conglomerate Enterprises came to visit Griselda Windfall. They had been in the habit of taking advantage of Griselda's husband, Lemuel, and they didn't intend to get out of the habit just because he had left town.

"It is absolutely necessary that we locate your husband, Lemuel Windfall," they said in unison (there were three gentlemen).

"It isn't necessary to me, it isn't necessary to Lem, and I'm not sure that it's necessary at all," Griselda said. "If Lem had wanted to be located, he could have stayed here."

"He could have *what?*" the three Conglomerate gentlemen croaked in disbelief in their single voice. "Mrs. Windfall, your husband is making all the new things available free. There are millions of dollars in this if you can help us locate him, or simply tell us where he is, if you know. Then we can work out the double modification, and we will have everything on a paying basis."

"Millions in it for me, and tens of millions in it for you," Griselda said thoughtfully. "And what is in it for my husband, Lemuel, who apparently doesn't want to be found? Please explain to me about the double modification."

"We will take one example out of dozens," the three men spoke in their single voice. "Smithstone Clay has become edible, and we believe that Lemuel Windfall has made it so. In nine billion years, Smithstone Clay has never been edible before; and now it is. There were previous hints of it, of course. There were clay eaters in assorted boondocks. But real Smithstone Clay has never been found in abundance before. Now it is. And who can say when or how it happened? Who kept a running census of so worthless a thing as Smithstone Clay? But now it is no longer scarce and no longer worthless. That is good.

"But it comes free to everybody. That is bad.

"It would be simple to put a modification into it at the other end, at your husband Lemuel's end, so that it wouldn't become edible until we put the countering modification into it at this end. This is the double modification. By this we can control the products or traffics or cargoes or potentials or circumstances. And then we will be able to sell it, for a fair price, to the whole world, instead of having it go free. And people always appreciate a thing more when they have to pay for it."

"Oh, sure," Griselda said. "I will think about this, gentlemen. And I will ask Lemuel what to do about it, if I can find him with his ears standing open."

"And, Mrs. Windfall, there are dozens of other new and advantaged things besides Smithstone Clay," the three men tried to explain to Griselda in their unity talk.

"I know pretty much what the other new things would be," she said. "I watch the ripples, and I can guess what innovative rocks are being dropped into the pond. Particularly can I guess them when I've heard Lemuel talk about them for fifty years. I will let you know, gentlemen."

Griselda had a little talk with herself after the gentlemen of the Conglomerate had taken their leave.

"My Lem has succumbed to the devil's most transparent temptation," she said. "I wish that he wouldn't do things like that. He should never wander off from me and do things on his own. He hadn't left his first childhood, and now he's fallen into his second. 'Command that these stones be bread,' the devil must have told him. Why is it that nobody sees the heresy of the 'Feed-the-world-by-easy-device' proposal any longer? The devil got Lem in a weak place there. He always had a soft spot in his heart for the devil, and he always had a soft spot for the 'Feed-the-world-by-easy-device' ploy. I've told him that the devil will be the ruin of him yet."

Griselda went to visit a sibyl in a cave out on the Sand Springs road. It was one of those caves that run back into the bluffs just before you come to Union Street Hill. Once there was a restaurant and nightclub named the Cave in that block. Now the block was known as Sibyls' Row. There were half a dozen sibyl studios and one brake-lining shop in that block, and one empty cave with a For Rent sign.

"I would like your help in locating my husband," Griselda told the sibyl. "Here is his address."

"If you have his address, why do you need my help in locating him?" the sibyl asked. "Does he live at the address?"

"Yes, I suppose he does," Griselda said, "but I don't. I'm not sure that the address is real. I hardly know how to say this, but there is something very spooky about the place. I believe I could go there—and I intend to—and that my husband would be there. And yet I might not be able to see him or talk to him. And I might not be able to come back. There are things accumulating there. Things were accumulating long before my husband went there to work and live. And other things have been similarly accumulating in other places, or in other entrances to the same place, for long ages. I have this information but I don't know where I have it from."

"I will give the address to my python," the sibyl said. "He will get to the effective level of it." The sibyl went down into a lower room to give the assignment to the python. And, after a while, she came back.

"Rats, rats!" she said in an odd voice.

"Is that an expletive?" Griselda asked her.

"Not this time. It's just that I'm almost out of rats. You know, there isn't a single rat catcher listed in the phone book this year. Rats and rabbits are what the python eats. You were talking about accumulations, Mrs. Windfall. Yes, there have been these most spooky accumulations for ages. For long ages before men appeared, these accumulations are to be found, so the peculiarity of the addresses must go back before mankind. I wonder just who was living at those dubious addresses then. Whatever the species, they had affinity for mining and for well-digging: mythology tells us that much about them. They manufactured things by processes that seem impossible. There was always one element missing. I believe that there was bilocation involved. I believe that there still is. Ah, the python has the address analyzed."

The python's voice came through a sort of ventilator shaft in man-serpent accents: "The address is at one of the primary interchanges, though physically it is on a small creek in Colorado. The full name of this creek is El Río de las Ánimas Arrepentidas en Limbo, or the River of the Compensating Souls in the Borderland or Limes. But the early Spanish people did not *name* the creek so. With rare intuition, they *recognized* the site for what it was, and their name was the perfect translation of the primordial name, which is very old. The creek is also called Lost Souls Creek and Picketwire Creek. Sophia, ask the lady whether she happens to have a rat with her."

"Oh, no I don't have," Griselda said. "I never carry them."

"Nobody carries them anymore," the man-serpent complained. "Well, the creek rises at, nay, it falls down from Trinchera Peak in Las Ánimas County, and it ends in the John Martin Reservoir on the Arkansas River in Bent County. The lower hundred and fifty miles of the creek, from Hoene to the town of Las Ánimas, does not touch on inhabited region at all.

"The same creek, bearing the name of Las Ánimas, is also found hundreds of miles distant, in Sierra County, New Mexico. There is some mystery about this bilocation of the creek on Earth, but the fact of the bilocation hasn't been doubted. It is really a case of multilocation, as it is with every primary interchange place.

"Ah, there's lots of words and names welling up out of my depths, and all of them refer to this location. Some of them call it a dislocation; some of them say that it is one of the limbos or halfway places; or a half-mansion, or a half-house."

"How about a half-hogan?" Griselda asked the educated snake in the room below.

"I don't know," the python said. "But what seems to be the trouble? Why don't you go ahead and visit the place, lady?"

"Yes, I will, I'll do that," Griselda said. "Thank you, python. Thank you, sibyl."

3

... mineral as well as metal, and that which is now only a name, and was then something more than a name—orichalcum—was dug out of the earth. ... The red light of orichalcum.

—Plato

As Griselda came near the place, she was surprised to find what name the local people called the stream. It was startling; it was a name unbelieved by many; it was ironic.

"Jews, close your ears!" a prairie dog barked.

"Greeks, harden your hearing!" a rattlesnake voiced.

"Covenanters, avert your senses lest you be affronted by it!" a bull-bat spoke in a series of little booms.

"What I say is that Lem is lucky to have done even as well as this," Griselda said.

This was the evening of the following day after the conversation with the Conglomerate gentlemen and with the sibyl and the python. It was a few hundred miles distant from the previous scene, and Griselda Windfall, having found her way somehow to an interior place, was dining with a funny little creature in a funny little restaurant. They were set down to a fine compendium of the new edible clays and stones. It was a queer, refractory sort of place, but Griselda had adjusted to it in everything except her eyes and her mind. Her dinner date had been getting smaller, and the café-restaurant had been getting stranger and more intimate.

"I knew, of course, that Smithstone Clay had become edible," she said, "but I had no idea that one could now eat Dogtooth Rock or Ganister or Mealing Stone. I sure did not have any idea that they were so excellent."

"Ah, yes, we are about to rehabilitate very many of the rocks and ores and metals. We will adapt them to Earth," Griselda's dinner companion said. He was a bent sort of little gnome with bright and peering eyes. "We can find a dozen uses for every one of them. The folks here were needing some new ideas when I came along. Oh, coal and oil and gas are good enough, and they couldn't be had by regular people without the aid of folks who had fallen into my case. But people appreciate new benisons. Yes, and it is an act of charity and compensation to supply these new things, I believe. Stilbite, Amazonstone, Aztec Money—ah, they are wonderful stones, and we are finding wonderful uses for them."

"Toad's Eye Tin, Asparagus Stone, Dry-Bone Ore," Griselda murmured fondly. "My husband, Lemuel, thought he could do great things with them if ever he could find appropriate working place and conditions. Listen, bright eyes, what's good is that there can be money in these things. Somebody goofed at first and let Smithstone Clay become edible free of charge. Now that they have it in such exotic restaurants as this, though, there will be a profit in it somewhere."

"Do you not understand that all food was originally free food?" that little gnome said with his bent smile. "Do you not know that all shelter was originally free shelter, and that all property was originally free property?"

"Didn't work, did it? And all those free things will not add up to a

free trip to Paris for me. There has to be money generated somewhere. How did you become so bent, little bright eyes? You remind
me very much of someone. How did I get here, anyhow, since the
map had gone all haywire?"

"Or picketwire," the gnome said.

"Yes, but I got here. And then both you and the place got funnier
and funnier. However did you become so bent?"

"The first and second lumbar vertebrae are reversed. This
emphasizes the crook in the back. It bends the head forward and
down, to the ideal working and cogitational position. Really, the way
that humans have their heads tilted, I don't understand how they can
do any thinking or working at all. This reversing of the vertebrae
makes a change in the facial expression: one must always look up
and peer at another person. There are even cases where persons
aren't recognized by their familiars after the change. The reversing of
these spinal segments also brings a change in the thought pattern,
right down where it matters. Folks have spoken mistakenly of visceral thought, but that basic thing is really spinal thought. Spinal
thought is very big here. So is medical practice. The changes are all
made without surgery. They are made, in fact, without the . . . ah
. . . patient being touched in any way. All topographical inversions
are easy in a nontopographical ambience like this."

"And you've been topographically inverted, bright eyes?" Griselda
asked. "You weren't always a gnome?"

"Oh, God help us all, Grissie! Being a gnome is all in the mind
and in the shape."

"What is that moaning and groaning?" she asked. "It seems to be
in the background of everything in this dismal place. And why aren't
there any colors here?"

"Oh, one of the requirements for a good workshop is that it be
without distracting colors at all. And some folks moan and groan a
lot when they're at labor. They're carrying on now like a bunch of
ham actors because we've set them to work triggering easy-to-find deposits of orichalcum on Earth. We tell them that it's easier to make
than coal or oil, but they whimper about having to learn something
new."

"Orichalcum? You're arranging for it to be found on Earth? Not
for free, I hope?"

"You want it to be somehow otherwise, Grissie?"

"Certainly, Lem. Oh, I called you Lem—you remind me of him. I
want the trick that they call the double modification set into it. I want

it set in to my own gain. I'd like a few little fortunes to accrue to me, for a few little years."

"Oh, I suppose so, Grissie. I'll have them make out a Conveyance of Patent that you can take back to Earth with you. Yes, they are moaning and groaning quite a lot. They are the uncreative folks, so they must be set to simple tasks. And simple tasks do become groaningly tedious."

"What are the simple tasks, bright eyes?"

"Oh, mostly the old faithfuls. Consider all the coal and oil deposits that have been fabricated for Earth. Kobalds and goblins and gnomes, so long as they are in this place of tribulation and tribute, are forced to serve the people with these products. Yes, the legends of them working in mines and wells under the roots of mountains are true ones. The making of these things is the hard part. Transferring them from nontopographical ambience like this to Earth is easy. It's a law that all objects tend to locate themselves in the nearest topography. The great accumulations or deposits or gluts on Earth have been passed off as natural or quasi-natural occurrences. They aren't, Grissie. They are manufactured things, and they were manufactured here."

"I'm promised fortunes on the orichalcum intrusions," Griselda said. "Oh, what are some of the other things that you are making in new profusion and for new uses?"

"Oh, Mealing Stone, French Chalk, Cottonball Borax."

"Oh, yes, yes. Lemuel was projecting work on all of those. How about Horseflesh Ore and Iron Rose?"

"We'll be ready with them quite soon, Grissie. And Mispickel and Noselite."

"Two of Lemuel's favorites. Oh, how startling! I've been sitting here with you and not realizing that you were Lemuel. I thought you were some gnome. But at least we buried you for Lemuel, though somehow you didn't seem quite dead. If you had, I wouldn't have come here on this wild-goose ride. No wonder I got lost. The deed said Picketwire Creek, but the people in the area call it Purgatory Creek."

"No, I don't seem quite dead, Grissie. This dying makes quite a change in some persons, but it hardly touched me at all. It upset Jasher Halfhogan seriously, very early in his life; that's why he always seemed a little strange to you. But dozens of things have happened to me that seem more decisive than dying. Ah, here's the Conveyance of Patent. They do fine engraving here, do they not? And this agrees to the double modification and assigns you the benefits. You can take this to Conglomerate Enterprises, or to Wheeler-Heelers, or to Le Conglomerat in Paris, or to any of them; and you'll be paid handsomely."

"To Paris? Oh, if I could only get there, Lem! And with a fortune yet!"

"Oh, you can walk out of here and into any of a thousand different primary interchanges on Earth. *Think* Paris, and you will come out in Paris."

"Oh, Lem, Lem! Is there anything that you need here?"

"Why don't you send me my old red sweater? There's always been so much moaning and groaning about the heat here that they have overcompensated against it. It will be nice to have my old sweater here when I work late."

"I'll send it, Lem, I'll send it!" Griselda cried. She kissed him, or perhaps she missed him. She *thought* Paris. She rushed out of there. And she came out in Paris in the middle of . . .

. . . the Rue de Purgatoire. And right around the corner was Le Conglomerat, where she traded the Conveyance of Patent for a few of those fortunes. And all around every corner was Paris.

"Oh, the red light of orichalcum," she sang, "and Paris!" For Griselda was a good-looker, now and forever. And with the kind of fortunes that she had, a good-looker like Griselda could have her heart's desire in that place.

R. A. Lafferty writes:

Many fantasy worlds are so similar as to require a common origin. This common origin is now discovered to be a world of fact and not of fantasy. It is prosaic, it is common, it is earthy, and especially it is underearthy. The dislocated Picketwire world is fact, and the fantasies were only misunderstandings of it.

The world of the Picketwire syndrome is on the inside of mountains in an ambience that is null-everything, which is only to say that it is a world that has suffered topographic inversion. And the common workmen there, gnomes, kobalds, poor souls, trolls, are only humans who have suffered topographic inversion.

The handiwork done on Picketwire is superior to anything done on Earth, and it is done at a fraction of the cost (because of the null-everything ambience). Considering the potential for efficient production there, and the difficulties here, it seemed that a scientific study of the possibilities and advantages should be undertaken. "For All Poor Folks at Picketwire" is that scientific study.

Take one feasibility estimate: If the book Epoch were printed and produced at Picketwire instead of on surface Earth, it could be done, on glossy paper and with orichalcum cover, for less than three cents a copy. It's true that the transportation from Picketwire to surface Earth would be around seventeen thousand dollars a copy, but this might be halved or even quartered for very large tonnage shipments.

Lemuel Windfall will arrange for such production if everybody is willing.

GROWING UP IN
EDGE CITY

by Frederik Pohl

In the evenings after school Chandlie played private games. He was permitted to do so. His overall index of gregariousness was high enough to allow him to choose his own companions, or no companion at all but a Pal, when he wanted it that way. On Twoday and Fourthday he generally spent his time with a seven-year-old female named Marda, quick and bright, with a chiseled, demure little face that would have beseemed a pretty woman of twenty, apt at mathematical intuitions and the stringing of beads. The proctors logged in their private games under the heading of "sensuality sensitivity training," but they called them "You Show Me Yours and I'll Show You Mine." The proctors, in their abstract and deterministic way, approved of what Chandlie did. Even then he was marked for special challenge, having been evaluated as Councilman potential, and when on most other evenings Chandlie went down to the machine rooms and checked out a Pal, no objections were raised, no questions were asked, and no follow-up warnings were flagged in the magnetic cores of his record-fiche. He went off freely and openly, wherever he chose. This was so, even though there was a repeating anomaly in his log. Almost every evening, for an hour or two, Chandlie's personal transponder stopped broadcasting his location fix. They could not tell where he was in Edge City. They accepted this because of their own limitations. It was recorded in the proctors' basic memory file that there were certain areas of the city in which old electromagnetic effects interfered with the radio direction-finding signals. They were not strategically important areas. The records showed nothing dangerous or forbidden there. The proctors noted the gap in the log, but attached no importance to it. As a matter of routine they opened up the Pal's chrome-steel tamper-proof course-plot tapes from time to time, but it was only spot-checking. They did the same for everyone's Pal. They never found anything significantly wrong in Chandlie's. If they had been less limited they might have inquired further. A truly good program would have cross-referenced Chandlie's personality profile, learned from it that he was gifted in man-machine interactions, and deduced from this the possibility that he had bugged the Pal. If they had then checked the Pal's permanent record of instructions, they would have learned that it was so. They did not do that. The proctors were not particularly sophisticated computer programs. They saw in their inputs no reason to be suspicious. Chandlie's father and mother could have told the programs all about him, but they had been Dropouts since he was three.

At the edge of Edge City, past the school sections, near the hospital and body-disposal units, there was a dark and odorous place. Ancient steel beams showed scarred and discolored. They bore lingering radioactivity, souvenir of an old direct hit from a scrambler missile. It was no longer a dangerous place, but it was not an attractive one, either, and on the master location charts it was designated for storage. It was neither very useful nor very much used. What could be stored there was only what was not very much valued, and there were few such things kept in Edge City. If they were remembered. The air was dank. Spots of mildew and rust appeared and swelled on whatever was there. However often the Handys came in to scrub and burn and polish, the surfaces were never clean. It was environmentally interesting, in a city where there was no such thing as environment, for at times it was pervaded by a sound like a distant grumbling roar, and at times it grew quite cold or quite hot. These were the things that had first interested Chandlie in it. What capped his interest was discovering by accident, one evening when he had just returned from wandering in the strange smells and sounds, that the proctors had not known where he was. He determined to spend more time there. The thought of doing something the proctors did not know all about was both scary and irresistible. His personal independence index had always been very high, almost to the point of remedial action. On his second visit, or third, he discovered the interesting fact that some of the closed doors were not locked on a need-to-enter basis. They were merely closed and snapped. Turning a knob would open them. Anyone could do it. He opened every door he passed. Most of them led only to empty rooms, or to chambers that might as well be empty for all he could make of the gray metal cylinders or yellowed fiber cartons that were stacked forgotten inside them. Some of the doors, however, led to other places, and some of the places were not even marked on the city charts. With his Pal romping and humming its shrill electronic note by his side, Chandlie penetrated the passages and stairways he found right up to the point at which he became certain he was not permitted to be there. A buckled guide rail that gouged at his flesh told him that. These areas were dangerous. Having reached that conclusion, he returned to his studies and spent a week learning how to reprogram the Pal to go into sleep mode on voice command from himself. He then returned to the dangerous area, left the Pal curled up inside one of the uninteresting doors, and went on into the unknown, down a broad and dusty flight of stairs.

In the pits under Edge City the air was damper and danker even than in the deserted places above. It was not at all cold. Chandlie was astonished to discover that he was sweating. He had never known what it was like to sweat before in his life, except as a natural consequence of exercise or, once or twice, while experiencing an illness surrogate. It took some time for him to realize that the reason for this was that the air about him was quite warm, perhaps as much as ten degrees over the twenty-eight degrees Centigrade at which he had spent his life. Also the grumbling, roaring noise was sharper and nearer, although not as loud as he had sometimes heard it before. He looked about him wonderingly and uncertainly. There were many things here that were strange, unfamiliar, and, although he had not had enough of a background of experience to be sure of correctly identifying the sensation, frightening. For example, this part of the city was not very well lighted. Every other public place he had ever seen had been identically illuminated with the changing skeins of soft brilliance from their liquid crystal walls. Here it was not like that. Light came from discrete points. There was a bright spot enclosed in a glass sphere here, another there, another five meters away. Objects cast shadows. Chandlie spent some time experimenting with making shadows. Sometimes there were considerable gaps between the points of light, with identical glass spheres that looked like the others but contained no central glowing core, as though they had stopped working and for some reason the Handy machines had not made them work again. Where this happened the shadows merged to produce what he recognized as darkness. Sometimes, as a little boy, during the times when his room light was sleep-reduced, he had pulled the coverlid over his head to see what darkness was like. Warm and cozy. This was not cozy. Also there were distant thumping, creaking sounds. Also he remembered that not far above him and beyond him was the corpse-disposal area, and while he had no unhealthy fear of cadavers, he did not like them. Chandlie felt to some degree ill-at-ease. To some degree he wished that he had not countercommanded his Pal to stay behind. It was exciting to be all on his own, but it was also worrisome. It would have been a comfort to have it gamboling and humming beside him, to see its bright milky-blue eyes following him, to know that in the event of any unprogrammed event it would automatically relay a data pulse to the proctors for evaluation and, if need be, action. What action? he thought. Like rescuing a little boy from goblins, he joked to himself, remembering a story from his preprimary anthropology talk-times. Joking to himself helped him put aside the cobwebby fears. He still felt them, but he did not feel any of them strongly enough to turn back. His index of curiosity, also, was very high.

All of this was taking place on a Wonday, after scheduled hours, which meant that Chandlie had received his weekly therapies that day and was chock-full of hormones, vitamins, and confidence. Perhaps it was that which made him so bold. On such accidents of timing so many things depend. But he went on. After a time he discovered that the new world he was exploring was no longer getting darker. It was getting lighter. Simultaneously it was becoming even more hot. Sweat streamed from his unpracticed pores. Salty moisture drenched the long hair at his temples, dampened his chest, rolled in beads from his armpits and down his back. He became aware that he himself had an odor. The light was brighter before him than it was behind, and, rounding a corner, he saw a yellow radiance that made him squint. He stopped. He stared through his half-spread fingers. Then, heedless, he ran down a flight of ancient steps, almost falling as one slid loosely away beneath him, but righting himself and running on. He stopped on an uneven surface of grayish-yellowish gritty grains that he recognized, from Earth Sciences, as sand. The great distant noise was close now, grave and impersonal rather than threatening; he saw what it came from. Rolling hillocks of water humped themselves slowly up out of a flat blue that receded into infinity before him. They grew, peaked, bent forward, and crashed in white wet spray, and the noise was their serial collision with themselves and with the sand. The heat was unbearable, but Chandlie bore it. He was entranced, thrilled, consternated, delighted almost out of his skull. This was a "beach"! That was "sea"! He was "outdoors"! No such things had ever happened to any young person he had ever known or heard of. No such things happened to anyone but Dropouts. He had never expected any such thing to happen to him. It was not that he was unaware that there were places not in the cities. Earth Sciences had taught him all of that, as they taught him about the sluggishly molten iron core at the Earth's heart and the swinging distant bodies that were called "Moon" and "planets" and "stars." He had even known, by implication and omission rather than by ever hearing it stated as a fact, that somewhere in the world between the cities were places like the places where people had lived, generations and, oh, ages ago, when people were dull and cruel, and that it was at least in theory possible for a person from a city to stand in such a place and not at once become transformed into a Dropout, or physically changed, or killed. But he had never known that such places could be found near Edge City.

All of that very painful brightness came from one central brightness, which, as Chandlie knew, was the "Sun." It cost him some pain and several minutes of near-blindness to learn that it could not be looked at directly without penalty. Its height, he recalled, meant "midday," which was puzzling until he deduced and remembered enough to understand that city time was world time. He had known that solar time differed as one went east or west, but it had never mattered before. As he became able to see again, he looked about him. When he looked before him he saw the rolling sweep of the ocean, dizzyingly big. When he looked behind him he saw the skirted and stilted bulk of Edge City rising away like the Egyptian tetrahedral tombs for the royal dead. To his right was a stretch of irregular sand and sea that curved around out of sight under a corner of the city. But to his left there was something quite strange. There were buildings. Buildings, plural. Not one great polystructure like a proper city, buildings. People moved among them. He breathed deeply to generate courage and walked toward them. Plodding through the sand was new to him, difficult, like walking with five-kilogram anklets on a surface that slid and slipped and caved irregularly away under his footgloves. The people saw him long before he was close enough to speak or hear, even a shout, over the wind and the breaking waves. They spoke to each other, and then gestured toward him. He could see that they were smiling. He knew at once that they were Dropouts. As he came closer to them, and a few of them walked toward him, he could see that some of them were not very clean, and all of them were straggly-haired, the women just on their scalps, the men wherever men could grow hair, beards, sideburns, moustaches, one barrel of a man thatched front and back with a bear's pelt. They all seemed quite old. Surely not one was under twenty. Physically they were deviant in accidental and unwholesome ways. On school trips to the corpse-disposal areas Chandlie had been struck by the unkemptness of the dead, but these people were living and unkempt. Some were gray and balding. Some women's breasts hung like sucked-dry fruits. Some wore glass disks in frames before their eyes. The faces of some were seamed and darkened. Some stood stooped, or bent, or walked limping. The clothes they wore did not hug and constrain them as right clothing should. The things they wore were smocks or shorts or sweaters. Or anything at all. As Chandlie had never seen an ugly person, he did not recognize what he felt as revulsion; and as he did not recognize it, it was not that, it was only disquiet. He looked at them curiously and seekingly. It occurred to him that his father and mother might be among these people. He did not recognize them, but then, he had very little memory of what his father and mother looked like.

As a very little boy Chandlie had experienced a programming malfunction in one of his proctors. It had taken the form of giving him incomplete answers, and sometimes incomplete questions. The parts it left out were often the direct statements. The parts it gave him were then only the supplementary detail: "Proctor, what is the shape of the Earth?" ". . . which is why your transparency buildups show a ship disappearing from the bottom up as it reaches the horizon." He had required remedial confidence building after that. And may have had an overdose. It was a little like that with the Dropouts. They made him welcome, speaking to him from very close up, so that he turned his head to avoid their breaths. They offered him disgusting sorts of food, which he ate anyway, raw fruits and cooked meats. Some of them actually touched him, or tried to kiss him. "What we want to give you," they said, "is love." This troubled him. He did not want to conceive a child with any of them, and some of the speakers, also, were male. They said things like, "You are so young to come to us, and so pretty. We welcome you." They showed him everything they did, and offered him their pleasures. On a walkway made of wood with the beach below them and surf spraying up onto his face they took him into a round building with a round turntable. Some of the younger, stronger men pushed at poles and stanchions and got it revolving slowly and wobblingly. It bore animal figures that moved as it turned, and they invited him to ride them. "It is a merry-go-round," they cried. To oblige them he sat on one of the horses for a revolution or two, but it was nothing compared to a Sleeter or Jumping Pillows. "We live freely and without constraint," they said. "We take what the world gives us and harm no one. We have joys the city has forgotten." Causing him to detach the lower part of his day garment, so that his feet and legs were naked to the codpiece, they walked with him along the edge of the water. Waves came up and bathed his ankles and receded again. Grit lodged between his toes. His thighs itched from drying salt. They said to him, "See over here, where the walls have corroded away." They led him under the skirt of the city to an in-port. Great cargo carriers were rolling in from the agrocommunes, pouring grain and frozen foods into the hoppers, from which three of the youngest Dropouts were scooping the next day's meals into canvas pouches. "The city does not need all of this," they said, "but if they knew we took it, they would drive us away." They warmed berries between their grimy palms and gave them to Chandlie until he could eat no more. "Stay with us," they pleaded. "You are a human being, or you would not have come here alone! The city is not a life for human beings." He began to feel quite ill. He was conscious, too, of the passage of time. As the sun disappeared behind the gray pyramid and the wind from the sea became cold, they said, "If you must go back, go back. But come again. We do not have many children here ever. We like you. We want to love you." He allowed some of them to touch him, then turned and retraced his steps. He did not like the way he felt, and did not understand the way he smelled. It was the first time in his life that Chandlie had been dirty.

When he reactivated his Pal, the machine immediately went into receiving mode. It then turned to Chandlie with its milky-blue eyes gleaming and spoke. "Chandlie, you must report at once to the proctors." "All right," he said. He had been expecting it. Although he was good at reprogramming machines, he had not expected to be gone so long, and had not prepared for it.

The proctors received him in the smallest of the Interview Halls. He entered through a door that closed behind him and immediately became only one more square in a checkerboard of mirrors and gray metal panels. Behind some of the mirrors the proctors were scanning him. Behind others there might be members of the council, or apprentices, or interested citizens, anyone. He could not see them; he could see only himself reflected into infinity wherever he looked. He stood under the heatless bright lights, blinking stubbornly. The proctors did not ask him any questions. They did not make any threats, either. They merely made a series of statements as follows: "Chandlie. First, you have interfered with the operation of your Pal. Second, you have absented yourself without authorization. Third, you have visited an area of the city where you have no occasion to go. Fourth, you have failed to report your activities in the proper form." They were then silent for a time. It was at this time that he was permitted to offer any corrections or supplementary information if he wished to do so. He did not. He stood mute, and after the appropriate time had passed, the proctors instructed him to withdraw. One square of mirror swung forward and became a door again, and he left the room. He returned to his dormitory. His peers were all in their own rooms and presumably asleep; it was very late. Chandlie bathed carefully, attempted to vomit, failed, rinsed his mouth carefully, and put on a sleeping blouse. The food the Dropouts had given him did not satisfy him, but he was afraid to eat until it had gone through his system. All that night he tossed and turned, waking up enough to know where he was and remember where he had been, and then falling back to sleep again, unsatisfied and unresolved.

For some days Chandlie continued his normal life, but he was aware that the matter would not stop there. Prudence suggested to him that he should behave at least normally, if possible exemplarily. Curiosity overrode prudence. In free-study times he dialed for old books that were known to be of interest to Dropouts, *Das Kapital* and *Walden* and silly, sexy satires by people like Voltaire and Swift. He played old ballads by people like Dylan Thomas and Joan Baez. He read poetry: Wordsworth, Browning, Ginsberg. He studied old documents that, so said his books, had once been electrically important, and was baffled by contextural ignorance ("A well-regulated militia being necessary to the security of a free State, the right of the people to keep and bear arms shall not be infringed." "Militia"? "State"? "Bear"—in the sense of bearing a child, perhaps? But only the arm parts?), until he reached the decision to ask for clarification from the preceptors for social studies. Then he was baffled to understand why these things were important. They were gritty days for Chandlie. His age peers detected that something was wrong almost at once, deduced that he was in trouble with the proctors, and, naturally enough, anticipated the punishment of the proctors with punishments of their own. In Living Chess he was played only as a pawn, though usually he had been a bishop and once a rook. His Tai Chi movements were voted grotesque, and he was not invited to exercise with the rest of his group. They did not speak of his situation to him directly, except for Marda. She sat down next to him in free time and said, "I'll miss you if you go away, Chandlie." He pored mulishly over a series of layover transparency prints. "Why do you look at them when I'm here?" she cried. He said crushingly, "Your genitalia are juvenile. These are adult, much more interesting." She grew angry. "I don't think I want to conceive with you, ever," she said. He put down the cassette of transparencies, stood up, and rapped on the door of an older girl. It was the first time he had ever seen tears. The second time was the following Fiveday, when he was called before the council of decision-making persons and saw his own.

The council, which was charged with the responsibility for making decisions in all cases not covered by standing instructions to the proctors, met when it needed to, where it chose to. Chandlie was of some interest to them, for whatever personal reasons each of them had for concerning him/herself, and so there were nearly twenty-five persons present when he was admitted. The room they chose to use this time was rather like the drawing room of a gentlemen's club. There were small tables with inlaid chessboards; sideboards with coffee, candies, refreshments of all kinds; stereopaints of notables of the city's history squirming on the walls. The head of the council, as of that hour, indicated a comfortable seat for Chandlie and gave him a cup of chilly sweet foam that was flavored with fruits and mint. He was a man. He looked about thirty, with neat bangs, wide-spaced tawny eyes, diffraction-grating rings on his fingers that moved hypnotically as he gestured. "Chandlie," he said, "we have a full file of reports. Beach sand, bits of weathered wood, and caked salt have been found on your garments and on your skin, after evaporating wash water. Stool analysis shows consumption of nearly raw vegetable foods. We then ordered a spectral study of your skin, and found compensatory pigmentation of your arms, face, neck, and lower body compatible with exposure to unfiltered sunlight. There is no point in wasting our time, Chandlie. It is clear that you have been outside the city." The boy nodded and said, "Yes, I have been outside the city." He had thought carefully of what he should say when he was asked questions, for he was aware of the risks involved. Risks to himself, to some extent. His ambitions were not fully formed at that time, but they excluded being downgraded as a potential Dropout. Risks to the Dropouts themselves, in a much more immediate way, of course. "What did you see outside?" asked the head of the council in a friendly and curious way, and all of the twenty-five, or almost all, stopped talking or reading to listen. "I saw a beach," cried Chandlie. "It was very strange. The Sun was so hot, the wind so strong. There were waves a meter and a half high that came in and crashed on the sand. I walked in the water, I found berries. They did not taste very good, but I ate them. There were buildings made of wood and, I think, plaster? . . ." He was asked to describe the buildings; he did so. He was asked why he was there; he told them it was curiosity. Finally he was asked, very gently, "And did you see any people?" At once he replied, "Of course, there were some women in the corpse-disposal area. I think someone they knew had died. And a man adjusting some Handys." "No," said the head of the council, "we mean outside. Did you see anyone there?" Chandlie looked astonished. "How could anyone live there?" he asked. "No. I didn't see anyone." The head of the council, after a while, looked around at the others. He held up seven fingers inquiringly. Most of them nodded, some shrugged, a few were paying no attention at all. "You have seven demerits, Chandlie," he said, "and you will work them off as the proctors direct." At once Chandlie was enraged. "Seven!" he cried. "How unfair!" It was maddening that they should have believed him and still award so harsh a punishment, seven days without free time, or seven weeks with no optional-foods privileges, or seven of whatever the proctors judged would be most punitive, and therefore most likely to discourage repetition of the infractions, for him. Before he left, he was in tears, which only resulted in two additional demerits. He was then returned to his peer group, who gradually accepted him again as before.

For more than twenty years Chandlie kept the secret of the Dropout colony outside Edge City. He did not return there in all that time. But he did not speak of it, not even to Marda, by whom he did indeed conceive a child at the appropriate time. As a child he accumulated very few further demerits; and as a young adult, none. His conduct was a model to the entire city, and particularly, almost offensively, to his peer group, who reluctantly but inevitably elected him their age representative when he was almost thirty. It was then, with a seat on the council, that he achieved his attention. He disclosed the full truth of his expedition outside the city. He denounced the former councilpersons for their failure to recognize when a little boy was lying. He accused them of suspecting that there was indeed a Dropout colony at the edge of Edge City, and proposed that he himself be given the authority to deal with it. Angrily the ones he had denounced left, refusing to vote. Resentfully the ones who remained gave him the authority. He then, in person—in person, he himself— went outside, himself directing the armed Pals with their lasers and serrated steel fangs. The weathered buildings burned sullenly but surely, as the heat of the lasers drove out the long accumulation of brine. The Dropouts screamed and ran before the Pals snapping at them. Some escaped, but not very many. A crew of Handys was set to repairing and strengthening the walls around the food-input areas, so that in the event any Dropouts returned they would be unable to continue their pilferage. When Chandlie reentered the city there was nothing left outside that was alive or useful. The following year he was elected head of the council, years before his turn, and several times again. This had been his intention. He knew that he could not have achieved this so soon if it had not been for the Dropouts. In a sense he remained forever grateful to them. Sometimes he wondered if any of them were still alive in whatever part of the scarred and guarded Earth they had fled to. In a way, he hoped some had. It would have been useful to know of another Dropout colony, although he really had no particular interest in harrying them, unless, of course, he could see a way in which it would benefit his career.

Frederik Pohl writes:

I was spending a long weekend in "Edge City"—more conventionally known as Cape May, New Jersey—being shown around by old friends who had moved there, and speculating on what it had looked like centuries ago . . . and what it would look like centuries from now. The more I thought about it, the more real it began to look to me, and an idle typewriter turned up just when I needed it.

Then, to my surprise, the rhythms of the story took over, and I found that the proper way to write it seemed to be in isolated para-

graphs. As with most writers, the urge toward stylistic experimentation strikes me unpredictably and often. Usually the experiments fail, and I do the story over in more conventional ways. This time it seemed to work . . . and here it is.

DURANCE

by Ward Moore

With his marker Larry scratched "498" on the concrete-block walls of his cell, down low where no snooping fink would direct his flashlight—assuming he was privileged to possess a flashlight—looking for evidence of contraband, yet not so low that another snooping fink looking for signs of digging in the cracks of the ancient concrete floor would see it either. (He was not at all sure what constituted contraband, nor had he any evidence of his cell being searched for any reason.) Of course, 498 was practically an arbitrary figure, little more than a random guess, for he had no way of calculating how many days he had passed here before he discovered the fragment of metal on whose origin he had speculated often, sharpened to a fine point by rubbing it on the floor until it would make a mark in the wall deep enough for him to feel, even though there was no light in the cell for him to read the numbers he had scratched day after day, never free from the sinking fear that he had forgotten to scratch yesterday's number or that he was scratching today's for the second time. Undoubtedly there had been a period when the cell had been lit, for even now there was light in other parts of the institution—unreliable, flickering, dimming, brightening, dying, reviving light which could tease a man into relying on it, expecting it to keep on shining, only to go out without warning.

In one way, 498 was as preposterous a number as a tormented mind could have—as it might well have done in his case—conjured up. It was as out of the question for him to calculate how many days he had passed in here before he discovered the marker and scratched the first number as it would have been for Archbishop Ussher to speculate on what happened before October the whatever 4004 BC. Because the world, so far as he, Larry (who had once had a longer name and a proper name to go with it, both now only rarely remembered), was concerned, the world, the universe, the cosmos, had been tohu v'bohu, without form and void, before he had come to live in this place of dusk, agony, and unbelievable foetor.

Putting aside the indisputable fact that he and this tomb in which he existed must have been created simultaneously, 498 days was only a little more than a year and a third, and in a year and a third . . . His thought trailed off. Even if the count were exact from the moment he began using the marker—a dubious assumption indeed . . . Once again he lost his thought. The marker, oh, yes, the marker. He had no idea what it might have been before he found it—the tongue of a buckle, the tine of a fork, not a nail, no—he spent some time speculating on this; after all, it was at least as engrossing as the calculations of the learned archbishop.

He had picked it up on one of his daily excursions to the office. (He called it an office for lack of another term; perhaps it was no office after all. Examination room? Psychotherapy theater? Who knew?) It had been a lifelong habit to walk with his eyes trained downward; as a reward for all he missed in the world above knee-level he had discovered many pennies, nickels, dimes, quarters, one or two paper dollars, and once a twenty-dollar bill. Among other things of doubtful value.

Would he have been better advised if instead of scratching a number for each day he had arbitrarily called the first one January 1 and so on? Cumbersome. Better to have begun with the French Revolutionary calendar. If he could remember the initial month. Nivoise?

Of course, he had no way of telling time, but his body, his metabolism, had become adjusted to the routine of the prison. If prison it were, not a hospital, mental institution, veterans' home, experimental clinic of some kind. He wished—fleetingly—he knew. This adaptation warned him they would come for him, as they did daily, in a few minutes—what he guessed was between five and fifteen minutes from now.

Acclimated, yes. Yet there was something wrong. His eyes had never become properly habituated to the lack of light. By this time he should have developed night vision, at least to distinguishing more than just the difference between pitch dark and the looming outline of the guards, or whatever they were, who would be coming for him. Nor had he become hardened to the stench in the cell. The overwhelming stink that was made up of many other stinks blending together into one incredibly foul compound.

The excrement bucket, called for at a time he could only assume was early morning and emptied into some kind of tank on wheels in the corridor outside and returned without being washed or even rinsed. The pile of straw—wild grass?—constituting his bed, never changed or renewed. The smell of his body and his body's sweat, distinct (was it really?) from the smell of the sores rubbed raw to form fresh pockets of pus, which periodically broke open to discharge their effluvia around him. The putridity of his rotting, ill-tanned moccasins and fur clothing, and the lingering odor of the decaying raw meat that constituted his daily meal. And of course there was the stink of confinement itself, a stink that had bitten into the stone walls like acid, the corrosive odor of fear and despair.

He waited stoically, but with the faintest undercurrent of excitement, for this was one of the three breaks in the agonizing monotony of the day. Bucket-emptying time and feeding time could hardly compare with the experience of actually leaving his cell.

Although he knew, partly through logic and partly through instinct, that he wasn't supposed to speak aloud, he whispered, "My name is Larry . . . Larry Smith." The memory of the name of which "Larry" was only a part had slowly eroded, since he never had the chance to speak it aloud. As for "Smith"—was his name really Smith? How could he be sure? Why should he be sure? Some other—other what?—could easily have changed names with him, run off with Larry's distinctive last name, leaving the scuffed and worn Smith for Larry to pick up, as he had picked up his precious marker, or leave lying in the dirt as he chose. Who cared? Who could possibly care?

Four hundred and ninety-eight days. Plus. Oh, it would be nice to go on with the list beginning "My name is Larry Smith." "I have—had?—a wife whose name is . . ." Well, did he have a wife? Was her name Lucille? Did they have two children, Sandra and George?

When the fifteen minutes were nearly up, his ears, sensitized to the perpetual silence as his eyes had refused to be sensitized to the perpetual gloom, picked up the faint whisper of moccasins in the corridor. Another riddle to add to all the unsolved puzzles: what had happened to boots and shoes? Why had one skill, one raw material been lost instead of another? The electrical system for locking the cells had evidently gone, yet the flickering lights in the office worked—erratically. But there was no plumbing, and plumbing was simpler and older than electricity. Moccasin-making was surely no more primitive than shoemaking. Or was it?

He did not have to speculate at which cell they were going to stop. He had accumulated enough evidence in 498-plus days to convince him that he alone occupied this part of the institution, if not the entire building. The whole apparatus—building, guards, administrators, spies, might exist solely to keep him in custody. Solipsism gone mad.

The susurration of the moccasins stopped. He heard the manipulation of the big, awkward padlock that now did the work of the electrically manipulated bolts. The deputy's dead voice said, "All right."

He had no idea what would happen if he failed to step forward at this point. Would they lay hands on him, hit him, twist his arms as they dragged him out? He had no idea because he had never disobeyed them, never considered disobeying them. Even in his most secret thoughts he did not use the wording "never yet." He had become the ultimate nonresister.

As always, inexplicably, his night vision was better in the corridor. Was there some hidden source of light? Perhaps a wall had fallen into such disrepair, or the roof had holed to let some daylight seep through. He could discern the shape of his escort, large men with fur hoods over their heads and bulky, shapeless fur garments. Technology had deteriorated, as witness the padlock on his cell, but he was convinced from fleeting glimpses that they had cotton cloth; why furs in a temperate climate?

Docilely he went forward and stood between them. Long ago—498-plus days ago?—he would have asked: Where are we going? Or if in an especially daring mood: Great day for a stroll, isn't it? But he knew they would no more respond now than they had then. Almost certainly they were bound by no vow of silence, no disciplinary interdiction against all speech. He conjectured that they simply had nothing to say to him and couldn't conceive of his having anything to say to them worth the effort of listening to.

Larry—if his name were really Larry—walked at the customary pace between them. He could have covered the route blindfold without missing a turn or stumbling into a wall. He had been led along it daily for 498 days. He had long ago added to his sparse knowledge of "them" the fact that they had neither a four-, nor a seven-, nor a ten-day work week. Unless the personnel were rotated? He was convinced—mystically?—that these men (men?) were the same who had come for him every day.

And the interview at the end of the walk from his cell followed the same predictable pattern of its 498 forerunners. Except that there was always an unspoken, impalpable suggestion that perhaps today his interrogator—inquisitor, psychotherapist, jailer, warden, judge, executioner—would choose to vary the program, if only by an intonation here, an inflection there, to make it a confrontation, an exchange, a struggle, a descent (ascent?) to the human level.

The lights flared on just as they entered the office, and, painfully blinded, he shut his eyes tightly. The glimpse he caught of the room registered in incandescent lines on his retina as an afterimage. How could these people—"they"—have so quickly lost all knowledge of what was, after all, not so complicated a craft? Quickly? But had it really been quickly? His beard had grown, grown long even. He had no way of knowing if his hair had turned gray, if his muscles had relaxed and sagged, if his hands had become puffy, his knuckles enlarged. His teeth had not loosened and dropped out, but then, he had always had good teeth. His father had bragged . . . At what age? His father had had the advantage of calendars to consult; Larry hadn't even a mirror to see how nearly his throat was coming to resemble a turkey gobbler's.

Granted that "they" had lost the power to repair their electrical system, as the Arabs forgot how to repair the clocks their ancestors made, why was this place in darkness? "They" must have animal fats, since "they" tanned skins for footwear and wore furs, and much of the food shoved under the door seemed to be the flesh of seals or whales. Why hadn't "they" devised candles or oil lamps? Even more pertinently, why didn't "they" let the daylight in? Had some unbelievable catastrophe dimmed the sun? A volcanic cloud, like Krakatoa's? Unlikely? What could be more unlikely than to find himself imprisoned? Or to put it more genteelly, confined?

As soon as the retinal afterimage faded, he opened his eyes, blinked, endeavoring to adjust to the normal dusk after the blazing flash. Ahead of him loomed the shadowy desk, the hooded figure of the official—if official he were—seated behind it. "Good day," the passionless voice from the depths of the hood said.

Good day, never good morning, good evening, good afternoon. Not even that much of a scrap of information. Just good day, another indistinguishable one.

"Good day," he answered. What would happen if he shouted, cursed, yelled, became intransigent, insubordinate, uncooperative, militant, physically violent? Was it possible the hooded figure didn't know either, was waiting for his response to discover?

The hooded one was also gloved. Thin gloves, clearly, in case of a need to write or draw. What with the gloves and the hood, it was impossible to discover the color of the interrogator's skin. For that matter, it was impossible to find out the color of his own in the eternal twilight of the institution. A liter of water a day for all purposes didn't leave enough for washing off the long-accumulated ingrained grime. He had tried washing in urine, but the sting of it in his sores was unbearable. And even if he had managed to get rid of the dirt, would he have dared to strip off his prison jacket to inspect the underside of his arms in the presence of the warden—assuming the light was conveniently on? No one had ever told him any of the rules regulating the conduct of inmates; perhaps there were none, but if there were, written or unwritten, surely "Do nothing to irritate those in charge" must be fundamental. He had a feeling—intuition? hope for a less vulnerable status?—that he was a caucasian, but his fingers in his long hair gave him no certainty. His hair seemed wavy; many blacks with an admixture of "white" blood had wavy hair. Was his nose broad, nostrils round? He had no way of telling, and if he had, would it mean anything irrefutable? His ears were small, but this was debatable evidence. Was a long, tangled, tightly curled beard caucasian? Perhaps, perhaps not.

As he had been, ever since the first day in his cell, he was struck by the utter absence of sound. Beyond the quiet padding of his guards' moccasins on the concrete floor when they came for him, the creak of the honey cart's wheels, and the noise of his own movements, the place was utterly silent. Terrifyingly silent. Prisoners (patients?) didn't shout for guards (attendants?), rattle something (what? who had anything to rattle?) against the bars of cells; no one screamed in rage or anguish. There was no roar of planes overhead, or of cars outside the walls. Very well, this culture had no cars. But horses (donkeys, camels, oxen) made noises of their own, carts (wagons, vans, drags, buggies) creaked and clanked, squeaked and squealed. No typewriters clacked, no pens scratched, no one drank midmorning coffee with smacks or satisfied grunts, munched dry crackers, guzzled Cokes, belched, farted, blew their noses. If chunks of broken concrete were dislodged, they fell noiselessly, became dust before they landed; if rats, or mice scurried out of holes, their nails scratched silently; if an institutionally sanctioned cat pounced on and devoured them, they died without squealing, and their captors did not purr.

"Do you have something to tell me?"

As always, he struggled to understand what lay behind this question. "What do you want me to tell you? Do you want me to confess to crimes? Whatever they are, I'll admit to them. Any and all of them. I'll confess freely. Murder, robbery, rape, mayhem, kidnap-

ping, embezzlement, blackmail, commingling, espionage, compurga-
tion, conspiracy, forgery, slander, incest, perjury, bribery, extortion,
arson—anything you want. I'll give you details, name accomplices, expose plots. Swear I know anyone you like was implicated in whatever
you want. I'll write out confessions, repent in open court, on the
scaffold, beg for the harshest penalty—won't even ask for a trial—if
you'll just tell me what you want. I beg you, I beg you."

There was a heavy silence in the already silent room. In the same
level, dead tones, the hooded figure said (regretfully?—surely not),
"You have nothing to say to me."

Recklessly Larry shouted, "But I have, I have. I want to know
where I am and why I'm kept here. When will I be tried, and what is
the charge? I demand to know." There was no answer. In the stillness
he could hear his own breathing, but no one else's. "At least tell me
if I'm charged with a political offense."

Again there was no answer.

"Oh, you can say there's no difference. That killing someone is
treason to the regime—whatever regime is in power at the moment.
Murder is treason, treason is murder. Theft is a crime against the
state, sedition is a crime against the security of the citizen. I understand. But surely you have some form of arrest, or indictment, ar-
raignment, or charge—even in the most secretive of tyrannies one isn't
punished without some formality. I implore you to repeat that form
to me. I implore you."

The lights flickered on, just long enough for Larry to see the eyes
staring at him through the holes in the hood. They did not blink; neither did they move to the right or left.

He took a deep breath to control his rising hysteria. "Will you at
least tell me how long my sentence is?"

"I have no way of knowing."

"But you must know how long I've been incarcerated. You can tell
me that."

"You have no way of evaluating such information. It would be
useless to give you meaningless data. And surely you understand it
isn't the time you've been here, but the time you've yet to stay that's
vital."

"Very well. How much time do I have to serve?"

"I have no way of knowing."

"Is this some mystical thing? Will I wake one morning knowing
I've paid my debt to society and am about to be released? Or will you
get a directive in the mail to that effect?"

"It is impossible to say. There are too many factors. Do you sleep well?"

Briefly Larry had a tantalizing hint of the other's viewpoint. There were no yes or no answers: too many factors. Did he sleep well? In sleep he escaped into an oblivion, a refuge from the misery of being alive. In his sleep he endured new torments, new terrors. "I don't know."

"Take a handful of coca leaves."

Why not? The drug would give him new endurance for his misery. Why reject the soporific simply because it was offered by authority? As well refuse the food shoved under his cell door. Was this some masochistic puritan streak that urged him to cap inflicted suffering with voluntary hurt, affliction with self-denial, and, like the Christians, pay for the agony on the cross with mortification of the flesh? He shook his head.

His jailer was silent.

At this point, Larry knew, the interview was over. Desperately he cried out, "Can't I be allowed in the open air for a few minutes? I swear I'll not try to run away. Let me see the light, let me . . ." He felt the tears running down his cheeks, furrowing channels in the dirt. "I beg . . ." He stopped, knowing it was futile.

The hooded one maintained the ominous, inhuman silence. Larry thought of throwing himself upon the impassive figure, pressing his thumbs into the windpipe, strangling, hammering the concealed face with his fists, forcing the others in the room to rush forward and kill him. But would they? Perhaps there would be no interference, no overt action at all. They might not even shout for him to stop. Perhaps he could run out of this office without hindrance, find his way from the building, and go free, without anyone raising a hand to stop him. What inhibited him, prevented him from putting it to the test? Perhaps if there had been light . . .

He turned away from the desk, sensed his two wardens moving to either side of him. All three walked, out of step, through the door of the office (or whatever it was), into the corridor. Greatly tempted, he began, "What would happen if I . . . ?" but the knowledge that his words went unheard because of their complete lack of interest, their utter unconcern, forced him to let his voice trail off.

They progressed at an even pace, retracing their route. Without a word of direction or a pressure against his arm, all three turned at the proper corners and halted before the door of his cell. He had an impulse to say: Well, here we are, back at the old home; or: See ya tomorrow, boys. Instead he stepped quietly across the threshold and heard them slide the door closed behind him and snap the padlock. Home, he whispered voicelessly to himself, this is my home; I'll live and almost certainly die here. One day they'll come for me, unlock the door, and call: All right! and get no response. What then? Let the corpse lie here until the flies and rats pick it clean, throw a forkful of fresh straw on top of it, and there you are—all ready for the next man. Or woman.

Or woman. When he had first come here he had been bothered— plagued was too strong a word—by thoughts of women. Young girls particularly. Prenubile girls, almost ready, shrinking from the prospective defloration: Ah, no, please don't. Then oscillating to envision courtesans, call girls, the cheapest hookers, young, mature, overripe, having in common only facility, marble cold and lynx eyed, shrewdly alert, contemptuous of masculine weakness yet, perversely, giving more pleasure, since the hired bodies kept the bargain while the jaded minds stayed aloof.

But the preoccupation had faded away. He had become a *castrato*, a eunuch, without a knife ever touching his flesh. Perhaps he should be glad to escape the torments of desire, but he was neither glad nor sorry. He no longer saw visions of female bodies; he was that much poorer, but this poverty failed to make him rage at his loss. He did not even have the impulse to say: Too bad.

He lay down on the straw, shielding his eyes with his arms, even though the straw had become so limp with time that it didn't threaten to prick him. It was at such a pass that men were said to turn to matters of the spirit, to see visions and follow supernatural guidance. One would think the imprisoned seers and prophets ought to be grateful to their jailers for the mind-stretching experience, yet Cervantes had not dedicated a book to the Turks, nor John Bunyan one to the Stuarts.

Outside of the sores on his body, misery, boredom, and general discomfort, he had not been ill. What would happen if he were attacked by some disease—typhus, say, or some other filth-borne sickness? Would they simply leave him in the cell to die? Or would there be a whole new dispensation: orderlies, a stretcher trip, gentle, cautious, to an infirmary, white, antiseptic, hidden in the depths of the building, scrupulously clean, staffed with nurses in starched uniforms, glorious hair pinned up under perky white caps, crisply directing the lustful but cowed orderlies to strip off his filthy clothes and carefully lower his befouled naked body into a bath of exactly the proper temperature while they tenderly bathed him, not neglecting his private parts, and bending over him in frowning preoccupation to offer enchanting glimpses of rounded breasts and rosy nipples? Would they massage him with fragrant oils and healing unguents, being scrupulous not to irritate his dreadful sores, over which they exclaimed in pitying horror? Would they dress him in fresh cotton nightclothes, give him a sleeping pill, and sit beside his bed while he slept deeply, not waking till his fever broke and he was animated again?

Dozing off in the midst of his speculative daydream, he woke to an unchanged reality. Not quite unchanged, for now, in addition to the irritation of the straw and the pain of his sores, he had the aches, rapid pulse, and lapsing consciousness of fever. High fever, it seemed to him. He thrashed around on the straw and longed for a drink of cold, clear water. But he was conscious enough to know he would get no water for the rest of the day. He groaned.

The next time he woke, he was sure hours had passed. His fever was higher, and he thought he had the clue to his imprisonment. Eskimos—jailed by Eskimos. Revenge for bringing them smallpox and syphilis. To say nothing of Indian tea and refined flour. But why me? I was never north of Maine in my life. They must have been after another Larry Smith—like the Germans shooting the wrong Otto Schmidt. A thousand pardons; you understand, it was a perfectly natural mistake. Oh, quite. "The act says, 'encompassing the death of the heir apparent,' nothing about not meaning it." A policeman's lot is not a happy one. Why, I'm going to die. Right here in this filth. The wrong Smith.

He tried to drag himself off the straw, to stand up. His knees folded, his body collapsed. "Help," he groaned, "help me."

The cell, in which no sound had been audible, save for the terse command by his guards, now reverberated with a single "Thunk!" as of a great mallet hitting the concrete-block walls. But this was impossible; had anyone been put in the nearby cells, he would have heard them being led in. Yet the sound was indubitable.

"Thunk! Thunk!

"Thunk! Thunk! Thunk!"

Counting. Why? To establish that these were not random noises, but made purposefully by a sentient being?

"Thunk! Thunk! Thunk! Thunk!"

Four. Not Morse code. Simple counting. Would the authorities stop it? Was the thumper trying to communicate? Or was it a retarded intelligence merely showing off its ability to count? "Thunk! Thunk! Thunk! Thunk! Thunk! . . ." He lost count, began again. He counted sixteen thumps hazily, not sure. Making a feverish guess— was the full count twenty-six, for the letters of the alphabet? If so, then it would be the English, or rather the Latin, alphabet, not Cyrillic, German, Greek, or Arabic. If the thumps constituted a message, might it not be in the most elementary of all codes, with one thump for A, two for B, and so on? He willed his mind to concentrate, not to slip away on the tide of fever into the tempting drowsiness. One, two, three . . . The count was merely being repeated. He paid attention rigorously: nineteen, twenty . . . Yes, there was no doubt, twenty-five, twenty-six. Could this be some mechanical repetition, the effect of an electronic device set in place long ago and only now activated to count endlessly up to twenty-six, and then begin again? Despairing, he held off collapse while he kept on counting.

Long pause. One: A. Two: B. One: A. Fourteen: N. No question; he had the key. Four: D. Fifteen: O. Fourteen: N.

He could guess the rest, but he kept on counting intently. One, twelve, twelve. Pause. Eight, fifteen, sixteen, five. ALL HOPE. ABANDON ALL HOPE. Long pause. Four, five, nineteen, sixteen, one, nine, eighteen: DESPAIR.

After two years, someone or something had spoken to him. To him specifically, or to any inmate, to all humanity? What did it matter? But what—who—was sending (had sent) the messages? What did the words ultimately mean? *Why* should he abandon all hope, despair? Having conveyed so much, why not more? Why not explain the force that confined him, the reason for the confinement, the inevitability of despair? (Were the jailers as captive as the prisoners? Were both acting out a script from which no deviations were permitted?)

He fell back into another stupor, to be awakened by the clanging open of his cell door, and the ritual, "All right."

"I can't," he groaned. "I'm sick."

He was aware of them on either side of the door, waiting patiently, impatiently, implacably, for him to rouse himself, throw off the fever, stagger to the front of the cell, accompany them as always. He knew they would not invade the cell, grab his arms, pull him to his feet, drag him through the corridors to the office to endure the hooded commander's questioning, to plead with him vainly. Probably they couldn't hear what he was saying: they didn't expect him to talk, therefore he wasn't talking.

He rolled over, got to his hands and knees, crawled to the door.

He put out a hand, grasped the furred leg of the guard on his right. It was a measure of discipline—or inhumanity—that he didn't flinch but let Larry pull himself to his feet by holding onto the fur. Trembling, he stood erect at last. "I can't," he muttered, "I can't."

Both guards took a half-step forward. Rather than let go, Larry took the half-step with them. Shuffling and staggering, slowly, torturedly, they plodded toward the office. Several times he fell, clung to the luxury of withdrawal, resignation. Each time, the silent expectation of the guards, their perceptible conviction that he would eventually get to his feet, forced him to obey.

When they reached the inquisitorial desk, Larry collapsed again. No one urged him to rise; there was no unspoken exhortation in the air. He had fallen: so be it. The hooded one spoke. "Have you anything to tell me?"

"Yes," he whispered, knowing his voice could not carry. "Yes. No one is innocent. All are guilty."

"Do you sleep well?" pursued the voice behind the hood.

"I don't know what you mean," said Larry. "What is sleep, and what is waking? Where is the line dividing them?"

"You may have a handful of coca leaves."

"Why? So I'll be doped when your executioner does his work? No thanks." He tried to rise. He should have taken the coca; it would have supplied the hysterical energy to meet death with dignity. Ridiculous. One met death dignifiedly only to impress an audience. And what audience was there in figures with faces masked?

Despair. Could the carefully banged-out message to abandon hope have come directly from his captors to cow him into a final, absolute, unprotesting submission to his fate?

By some curious stimulation his fever momentarily receded. With an effort of will he rose from the floor, and swaying, stumbled away from the desk. He had no feeling the warders were accompanying him. He stumbled out into the corridor, came to the familiar spot where he was accustomed to turning right. Surely that was what they were expecting—that he had become so conditioned that he would return meekly to his cell. Of course, they must know about the painful enumeration of days, had almost surely put the marker where he was bound to find it. Yes, yes, everything had been preparation for his ultimate act of resignation.

He turned left and immediately fell into a panic at the unfamiliarity of the walls. He guided himself with his hand against the nearest one, resolved to turn right at the first opening and find his way to his cell.

But though it was inconceivable that he had missed it, the first opening was very far away. He must have walked, staggered, much farther than the distance to his barred sanctuary. And—unbelievably —he thought he felt a faint stirring of air on his cheek, replacing the noxious atmosphere of the prison.

Surely by this time "they" had summoned the killers, traced out his course, located his position, sent the executioner to do his work. He braced—tried to brace—his shoulders against the blow of the ax that would surely come any second now. Or the bludgeon crushing his skull. Or would they break their silence, discard their reversion to primitive means, and shoot him in the back of the head? He flinched. He would never hear the shot.

Incredibly, there seemed to be light ahead. Not a dim glow, but actual, blazing sunlight. Though it was constrained by an opening narrower than the corridor, it stabbed his eyes excruciatingly. He leaned against the wall with his eyes shut against the pain.

He tried to open his lids slightly. Impossible. He could either open them wide, closing them again instantly, or keep them shut. He blinked rapidly. This was less painful. Also, at the end of the blink, he could close the upper lid. Interesting knowledge: couldn't half-open, could half-shut.

No question—it was daylight ahead. What a refinement of torture to let him get so close to escape before stopping him, killing him, or returning him to his cell. What if he whirled around suddenly? No longer facing the light, he could open his eyes wide. But whirl around? It was all he could do to slump against the wall. They were cunning, too cunning for him.

If he put his hand over his face, he could tolerate the light let in between his fingers. He moved forward, still hunching his shoulders against the expected blow.

A few feet—yards—farther on he was in a large entranceway. No doors, no bars, just open space. He crept forward, still shielding his eyes, to what seemed to be an open courtyard. Ahead he saw a tree. A tree with green leaves. To see, to see *color*. He began weeping helplessly, mourning his imprisonment and imminent death, but most of all the chromatic world.

Putting his arms around the twisted shape of the tree, clinging to it, he stared back at the squat, grim building, standing there in a freedom as enigmatic as the captivity he had left behind.

Ward Moore writes:

I was walking along Fountain Avenue, which is one of the crummier streets in the tiny business district of Pacific Grove, a street which had distinct possibilities in, say, 1905, but which had unquestionably failed even to begin to fulfill them seventy years later. The November sun turned the cement sidewalk, the asbestos-shingled roofs, and the soapily washed windows into iridescent rainbows batting their vibgyors back and forth in a dazzling tennis volley. The fall sun is northern California's premature promise of the resurrection and the life; it is our belated, very belated summer, soon—any day—to be flooded and frosted to death. But while it endures, it is summer.

The sun's heat penetrates through the bones, into the marrow of old men. But they do not think forbidden thoughts—even the sun isn't that powerful. They think thoughts more proper to their senior citizenship.

So I walked along, nursing my thoughts like invalid gruel, reflecting on all the intimations of mortality which were crowding in on me, the soothing, damning, triumphant words: . . . not alarm you, but . . . medication . . . see . . . Well, one must face reality. Facts. Whatever.

After all, I thought, it is possible to resign oneself to reality. Seventy-second year, hearing gone to hell, eyesight going, hemmerods, gall bladder, all the disgusting ailments of aging. Resign oneself to decay, deterioration, desuetude. Even the unspeakable prospect. Another five, ten, even a miraculous fifteen years. Resignation, fortitude. Acceptance. Why not?

And then, coming toward me, one of the glorious natural wonders of the world. Sandals on unblemished tanned feet. Long, fine, tanned thighs in revealing white shorts, legs and thighs covered with fine, golden down. Above, a laced white bodice showing a sweet belly and a sweet bellybutton, the lacing strained apart by sturdy breasts, curved, the pink nipples just suggested rather than showing. . . .

No, I could not be resigned. Not this year.

THE GHOST OF A
MODEL T

by *Clifford D. Simak*

He was walking home when he heard the Model T again. It was not a sound that he could well mistake, and it was not the first time he had heard it running, in the distance, on the road. Although it puzzled him considerably, for so far as he knew, no one in the country had a Model T. He'd read somewhere, in a paper more than likely, that old cars, such as Model T's, were fetching a good price, although why this should be, he couldn't figure out. With all the smooth, sleek cars that there were today, who in their right mind would want a Model T? But there was no accounting, in these crazy times, for what people did. It wasn't like the old days, but the old days were long gone, and a man had to get along the best he could with the way that things were now.

Brad had closed up the beer joint early, and there was no place to go but home, although since Old Bounce had died he rather dreaded to go home. He certainly did miss Bounce, he told himself; they'd got along just fine, the two of them, for more than twenty years, but now, with the old dog gone, the house was a lonely place and had an empty sound.

He walked along the dirt road out at the edge of town, his feet scuffing in the dust and kicking at the clods. The night was almost as light as day, with a full moon above the treetops. Lonely cricket noises were heralding summer's end. Walking along, he got to remembering the Model T he'd had when he'd been a young sprout, and how he'd spent hours out in the old machine shed tuning it up, although, God knows, no Model T ever really needed tuning. It was about as simple a piece of mechanism as anyone could want, and despite some technological cantankerousness, about as faithful a car as ever had been built. It got you there and got you back, and that was all, in those days, that anyone could ask. Its fenders rattled, and its hard tires bounced, and it could be balky on a hill, but if you knew how to handle it and mother it along, you never had no trouble.

Those were the days, he told himself, when everything had been as simple as a Model T. There were no income taxes (although, come to think of it, for him, personally, income taxes had never been a problem), no social security that took part of your wages, no licensing this and that, no laws that said a beer joint had to close at a certain hour. It had been easy, then, he thought; a man just fumbled along the best way he could, and there was no one telling him what to do or getting in his way.

The sound of the Model T, he realized, had been getting louder all the time, although he had been so busy with his thinking that he'd paid no real attention to it. But now, from the sound of it, it was right behind him, and although he knew it must be his imagination, the sound was so natural and so close that he jumped to one side of the road so it wouldn't hit him.

It came up beside him and stopped, and there it was, as big as life, and nothing wrong with it. The front-right-hand door (the only door in front, for there was no door on the left-hand side) flapped open—just flapped open by itself, for there was no one in the car to open it. The door flapping open didn't surprise him any, for to his recollection, no one who owned a Model T ever had been able to keep that front door closed. It was held only by a simple latch, and every time the car bounced (and there was seldom a time it wasn't bouncing, considering the condition of the roads in those days, the hardness of the tires, and the construction of the springs)—every time the car bounced, that damn front door came open.

This time, however—after all these years—there seemed to be something special about how the door came open. It seemed to be a sort of invitation, the car coming to a stop and the door not just sagging open, but coming open with a flourish, as if it were inviting him to step inside the car.

So he stepped inside of it and sat down on the right-front seat, and as soon as he was inside, the door closed and the car began rolling down the road. He started moving over to get behind the wheel, for there was no one driving it, and a curve was coming up, and the car needed someone to steer it around the curve. But before he could move over and get his hands upon the wheel, the car began to take the curve as neatly as it would have with someone driving it. He sat astonished and did not touch the wheel, and it went around the curve without even hesitating, and beyond the curve was a long, steep hill, and the engine labored mightily to achieve the speed to attack the hill.

The funny thing about it, he told himself, still half-crouched to take the wheel and still not touching it, was that he knew this road by heart, and there was no curve or hill on it. The road ran straight for almost three miles before it joined the River Road, and there was not a curve or kink in it, and certainly no hill. But there had been a curve, and there was a hill, for the car laboring up it quickly lost its speed and had to shift to low.

Slowly he straightened up and slid over to the right-hand side of the seat, for it was quite apparent that this Model T, for whatever reason, did not need a driver—perhaps did better with no driver. It seemed to know where it was going, and he told himself, this was more than he knew, for the country, while vaguely familiar, was not the country that lay about the little town of Willow Bend. It was rough and hilly country, and Willow Bend lay on a flat, wide flood plain of the river, and there were no hills and no rough ground until you reached the distant bluffs that stood above the valley.

He took off his cap and let the wind blow through his hair, and there was nothing to stop the wind, for the top of the car was down. The car gained the top of the hill and started going down, wheeling carefully back and forth down the switchbacks that followed the contour of the hill. Once it started down, it shut off the ignition somehow, just the way he used to do, he remembered, when he drove his Model T. The cylinders slapped and slobbered prettily, and the engine cooled.

As the car went around a looping bend that curved above a deep, black hollow that ran between the hills, he caught the fresh, sweet scent of fog, and that scent woke old memories in him, and if he'd not known differently, he would have thought he was back in the country of his young manhood. For in the wooded hills where he'd grown up, fog came creeping up a valley of a summer evening, carrying with it the smells of cornfields and of clover pastures and many other intermingled scents abstracted from a fat and fertile land. But it could not be, he knew, the country of his early years, for that country lay far off and was not to be reached in less than an hour of travel. Although he was somewhat puzzled by exactly where he could be, for it did not seem the kind of country that could be found within striking distance of the town of Willow Bend.

The car came down off the hill and ran blithely up a valley road. It passed a farmhouse huddled up against the hill, with two lighted windows gleaming, and off to one side the shadowy shapes of barn and henhouse. A dog came out and barked at them. There had been no other houses, although, far off, on the opposite hills, he had seen a pinpoint of light here and there and was sure that they were farms. Nor had they met any other cars, although, come to think of it, that was not so strange, for out here in the farming country there were late chores to do, and bedtime came early for people who were out at the crack of dawn. Except on weekends, there'd not be much traffic on a country road.

The Model T swung around a curve, and there, up ahead, was a garish splash of light, and as they came closer, music could be heard. There was about it all an old familiarity that nagged at him, but as yet he could not tell why it seemed familiar. The Model T slowed and turned in at the splash of light, and now it was clear that the light came from a dance pavilion. Strings of bulbs ran across its front, and other lights were mounted on tall poles in the parking area. Through the lighted windows he could see the dancers; and the music, he realized, was the kind of music he'd not heard for more than half a century. The Model T ran smoothly into a parking spot beside a Maxwell touring car. A Maxwell touring car, he thought with some surprise. There hadn't been a Maxwell on the road for years. Old Virg once had owned a Maxwell, at the same time he had owned his Model T. Old Virg, he thought. So many years ago. He tried to recall Old Virg's last name, but it wouldn't come to him. Of late, it seemed, names were often hard to come by. His name had been Virgil, but his friends always called him Virg. They'd been together quite a lot, the two of them, he remembered, running off to dances, drinking moonshine whiskey, playing pool, chasing girls—all the things that young sprouts did when they had the time and money.

He opened the door and got out of the car, the crushed gravel of the parking lot crunching underneath his feet; and the crunching of the gravel triggered the recognition of the place, supplied the reason for the familiarity that had first eluded him. He stood stock-still, half-frozen at the knowledge, looking at the ghostly leafiness of the towering elm trees that grew to either side of the dark bulk of the pavilion. His eyes took in the contour of the looming hills, and he recognized the contour, and standing there, straining for the sound, he heard the gurgle of the rushing water that came out of the hill, flowing through a wooden channel into a wayside watering trough that was now falling apart with neglect, no longer needed since the automobile had taken over from the horse-drawn vehicles of some years before.

He turned and sat down weakly on the running board of the Model T. His eyes could not deceive him or his ears betray him. He'd heard the distinctive sound of that running water too often in years long past to mistake it now; and the loom of the elm trees, the contour of the hills, the graveled parking lot, the string of bulbs on the pavilion's front, taken all together, could only mean that somehow he had returned or been returned, to Big Spring Pavilion. But that, he told himself, was fifty years or more ago, when I was lithe and young, when Old Virg had his Maxwell and I my Model T.

He found within himself a growing excitement that surged above the wonder and the sense of absurd impossibility—an excitement that was as puzzling as the place itself and his being there again. He rose and walked across the parking lot, with the coarse gravel rolling and sliding and crunching underneath his feet, and there was a strange lightness in his body, the kind of youthful lightness he had not known for years, and as the music came welling out at him, he found that he was gliding and turning to the music. Not the kind of music the kids played nowadays, with all the racket amplified by electronic contraptions, not the grating, no-rhythm junk that set one's teeth on edge and turned the morons glassy-eyed, but music with a beat to it, music you could dance to with a certain haunting quality that was no longer heard. The saxophone sounded clear, full-throated; and a sax, he told himself, was an instrument all but forgotten now. But it was here, and the music to go with it, and the bulbs above the door swaying in the little breeze that came drifting up the valley.

He was halfway through the door when he suddenly remembered that the pavilion was not free, and he was about to get some change out of his pocket (what little there was left after all those beers he'd had at Brad's) when he noticed the inky marking of the stamp on the back of his right hand. That had been the way, he remembered, that they'd marked you as having paid your way into the pavilion, a stamp placed on your hand. He showed his hand with its inky marking to the man who stood beside the door and went on in. The pavilion was bigger than he'd remembered it. The band sat on a raised platform to one side, and the floor was filled with dancers.

The years fell away, and it all was as he remembered it. The girls wore pretty dresses; there was not a single one who was dressed in jeans. The boys wore ties and jackets, and there was a decorum and a jauntiness that he had forgotten. The man who played the saxophone stood up, and the sax wailed in lonely melody, and there was a magic in the place that he had thought no longer could exist.

He moved out into the magic. Without knowing that he was about to do it, surprised when he found himself doing it, he was out on the floor, dancing by himself, dancing with all the other dancers, sharing in the magic—after all the lonely years, a part of it again. The beat of the music filled the world, and all the world drew in to center on the dance floor, and although there was no girl and he danced all by himself, he remembered all the girls he had ever danced with.

Someone laid a heavy hand on his arm, and someone else was saying, "Oh, for Christ's sake, leave the old guy be; he's just having fun like all the rest of us." The heavy hand was jerked from his arm, and the owner of the heavy hand went staggering out across the floor, and there was a sudden flurry of activity that could not be described as dancing. A girl grabbed him by the hand. "Come on, Pop," she said, "let's get out of here." Someone else was pushing at his back to force him in the direction that the girl was pulling, and then he was out-of-doors. "You better get on your way, Pop," said a young man. "They'll be calling the police. Say, what is your name? Who are you?"

"I am Hank," he said. "My name is Hank, and I used to come here. Me and Old Virg. We came here a lot. I got a Model T out in the lot if you want a lift."

"Sure, why not," said the girl. "We are coming with you."

He led the way, and they came behind him, and all piled in the car, and there were more of them than he had thought there were. They had to sit on one another's laps to make room in the car. He sat behind the wheel, but he never touched it, for he knew the Model T would know what was expected of it, and of course it did. It started up and wheeled out of the lot and headed for the road.

"Here, Pop," said the boy who sat beside him, "have a snort. It ain't the best there is, but it's got a wallop. It won't poison you; it ain't poisoned any of the rest of us."

Hank took the bottle and put it to his lips. He tilted up his head and let the bottle gurgle. And if there'd been any doubt before of where he was, the liquor settled all the doubt. For the taste of it was a taste that could never be forgotten. Although it could not be remembered, either. A man had to taste it once again to remember it.

He took down the bottle and handed it to the one who had given it to him. "Good stuff," he said.

"Not good," said the young man, "but the best that we could get. These bootleggers don't give a damn what they sell you. Way to do it is to make them take a drink before you buy it, then watch them for a while. If they don't fall down dead or get blind staggers, then it's safe to drink."

Reaching from the back seat of the car, one of them handed him a saxophone. "Pop, you look like a man who could play this thing," said one of the girls, "so give us some music."

"Where'd you get this thing?" asked Hank.

"We got it off the band," said a voice from the back. "That joker who was playing it had no right to have it. He was just abusing it."

Hank put it to his lips and fumbled at the keys, and all at once the instrument was making music. And it was funny, he thought, for until right now he'd never held any kind of horn. He had no music in him. He'd tried a mouth organ once, thinking it might help to pass away the time, but the sounds that had come out of it had set Old Bounce to howling. So he'd put it up on a shelf and had forgotten it till now.

The Model T went tooling down the road, and in a little time the pavilion was left behind. Hank tootled on the saxophone, astonishing himself at how well he played, while the others sang and passed around the bottle. There were no other cars on the road, and soon the Model T climbed a hill out of the valley and ran along a ridgetop, with all the countryside below a silver dream flooded by the moonlight.

Later on, Hank wondered how long this might have lasted, with the car running through the moonlight on the ridgetop, with him playing the saxophone, interrupting the music only when he laid aside the instrument to have another drink of moon. But when he tried to think of it, it seemed it had gone on forever, with the car eternally running in the moonlight, trailing behind it the wailing and the honking of the saxophone.

He woke to night again. The same full moon was shining, although the Model T had pulled off the road and was parked beneath a tree, so that the full strength of the moonlight did not fall upon him. He worried rather feebly if this might be the same night or a different night, and there was no way for him to tell, although, he told himself, it didn't make much difference. So long as the moon was shining and he had the Model T and a road for it to run on, there was nothing more to ask, and which night it was had no consequence.

The young people who had been with him were no longer there, but the saxophone was laid upon the floorboards, and when he pulled himself erect, he heard a gurgle in his pocket, and upon investigation, pulled out the moonshine bottle. It still was better than half-full, and from the amount of drinking there had been done, that seemed rather strange.

He sat quietly behind the wheel, looking at the bottle in his hand, trying to decide if he should have a drink. He decided that he shouldn't, and put the bottle back into his pocket, then reached down and got the saxophone and laid it on the seat beside him.

The Model T stirred to life, coughing and stuttering. It inched forward, somewhat reluctantly, moving from beneath the tree, heading in a broad sweep for the road. It reached the road and went bumping down it. Behind it a thin cloud of dust, kicked up by its wheels, hung silver in the moonlight.

Hank sat proudly behind the wheel, being careful not to touch it. He folded his hands in his lap and leaned back. He felt good—the best he'd ever felt. Well, maybe not the best, he told himself, for back in the time of youth, when he was spry and limber and filled with the juice of hope, there might have been some times when he felt as good as he felt now. His mind went back, searching for the times when he'd felt as good, and out of olden memory came another time, when he'd drunk just enough to give himself an edge, not as yet verging into drunkenness, not really wanting any more to drink, and he'd stood on the gravel of the Big Spring parking lot, listening to the music before going in, with the bottle tucked inside his shirt, cold against his belly. The day had been a scorcher, and he'd been working in the hayfield, but now the night was cool, with fog creeping up the valley, carrying that indefinable scent of the fat and fertile land; and inside, the music playing, and a waiting girl who would have an eye out for the door, waiting for the moment he came in.

It had been good, he thought, that moment snatched out of the maw of time, but no better than this moment, with the car running on the ridgetop road and all the world laid out in moonlight. Different, maybe, in some ways, but no better than this moment.

The road left the ridgetop and went snaking down the bluff face, heading for the valley floor. A rabbit hopped across the road, caught for a second in the feeble headlights. High in the nighttime sky, invisible, a bird cried out, but that was the only sound there was, other than the thumping and the clanking of the Model T.

The car went skittering down the valley, and here the moonlight often was shut out by the woods that came down close against the road.

Then it was turning off the road, and beneath its tires he heard the crunch of gravel, and ahead of him loomed a dark and crouching shape. The car came to a halt, and sitting rigid in the seat, Hank knew where he was.

The Model T had returned to the dance pavilion, but the magic was all gone. There were no lights, and it was deserted. The parking lot was empty. In the silence, as the Model T shut off its engine, he heard the gushing of the water from the hillside spring running into the watering trough.

Suddenly he felt cold and apprehensive. It was lonely here, lonely as only an old remembered place can be when all its life is gone. He stirred reluctantly and climbed out of the car, standing beside it, with one hand resting on it, wondering why the Model T had come here and why he'd gotten out.

A dark figure moved out from the front of the pavilion, an undistinguishable figure slouching in the darkness.

"That you, Hank?" a voice asked.

"Yes, it's me," said Hank.

"Christ," the voice asked, "where is everybody?"

"I don't know," said Hank. "I was here just the other night. There were a lot of people then."

The figure came closer. "You wouldn't have a drink, would you?" it asked.

"Sure, Virg," he said, for now he recognized the voice. "Sure, I have a drink."

He reached into his pocket and pulled out the bottle. He handed it to Virg. Virg took it and sat down on the running board. He didn't drink right away, but sat there cuddling the bottle.

"How you been, Hank?" he asked. "Christ, it's a long time since I seen you."

"I'm all right," said Hank. "I drifted up to Willow Bend and just sort of stayed there. You know Willow Bend?"

"I was through it once. Just passing through. Never stopped or nothing. Would have if I'd known you were there. I lost all track of you."

There was something that Hank had heard about Old Virg, and felt that maybe he should mention it, but for the life of him he couldn't remember what it was, so he couldn't mention it.

"Things didn't go so good for me," said Virg. "Not what I had expected. Janet up and left me, and I took to drinking after that and lost the filling station. Then I just knocked around from one thing to another. Never could get settled. Never could latch onto anything worthwhile."

He uncorked the bottle and had himself a drink.

"Good stuff," he said, handing the bottle back to Hank.

Hank had a drink, then sat down on the running board alongside Virg and set the bottle down between them.

"I had a Maxwell for a while," said Virg, "but I seem to have lost it. Forgot where I left it, and I've looked everywhere."

"You don't need your Maxwell, Virg," said Hank. "I have got this Model T."

"Christ, it's lonesome here," said Virg. "Don't you think it's lonesome?"

"Yes, it's lonesome. Here, have another drink. We'll figure what to do."

"It ain't good sitting here," said Virg. "We should get out among them."

"We'd better see how much gas we have," said Hank. "I don't know what's in the tank."

He got up and opened the front door and put his hand under the front seat, searching for the measuring stick. He found it and unscrewed the gas-tank cap. He began looking through his pockets for matches so he could make a light.

"Here," said Virg, "don't go lighting any matches near that tank. You'll blow us all to hell. I got a flashlight here in my back pocket. If the damn thing's working."

The batteries were weak, but it made a feeble light. Hank plunged the stick into the tank, pulled it out when it hit bottom, holding his thumb on the point that marked the topside of the tank. The stick was wet up almost to his thumb.

"Almost full," said Virg. "When did you fill it last?"

"I ain't never filled it."

Old Virg was impressed. "That old tin lizard," he said, "sure goes easy on the gas."

Hank screwed the cap back on the tank, and they sat down on the running board again, and each had another drink.

"It seems to me it's been lonesome for a long time now," said Virg. "Awful dark and lonesome. How about you, Hank?"

"I been lonesome," said Hank, "ever since Old Bounce up and died on me. I never did get married. Never got around to it. Bounce and me, we went everywhere together. He'd go up to Brad's bar with me and camp out underneath a table; then, when Brad threw us out, he'd walk home with me."

"We ain't doing ourselves no good," said Virg, "just sitting here and moaning. So let's have another drink, then I'll crank the car for you, and we'll be on our way."

"You don't need to crank the car," said Hank. "You just get into it, and it starts up by itself."

"Well, I be damned," said Virg. "You sure have got it trained."

They had another drink and got into the Model T, which started up and swung out of the parking lot, heading for the road.

"Where do you think we should go?" asked Virg. "You know of any place to go?"

"No, I don't," said Hank. "Let the car take us where it wants to. It will know the way."

Virg lifted the sax off the seat and asked, "Where'd this thing come from? I don't remember you could blow a sax."

"I never could before," said Hank. He took the sax from Virg and put it to his lips, and it wailed in anguish, gurgled with light-heartedness.

"I be damned," said Virg. "You do it pretty good."

The Model T bounced merrily down the road, with its fenders flapping and the windshield jiggling, while the magneto coils mounted on the dashboard clicked and clacked and chattered. All the while, Hank kept blowing on the sax and the music came out loud and true, with startled night birds squawking and swooping down to fly across the narrow swath of light.

The Model T went clanking up the valley road and climbed the hill to come out on a ridge, running through the moonlight on a narrow, dusty road between close pasture fences, with sleepy cows watching them pass by.

"I be damned," cried Virg, "if it isn't just like it used to be. The two of us together, running in the moonlight. Whatever happened to us, Hank? Where did we miss out? It's like this now, and it was like this a long, long time ago. Whatever happened to the years between? Why did there have to be any years between?"

Hank said nothing. He just kept blowing on the sax.

"We never asked for nothing much," said Virg. "We were happy as it was. We didn't ask for change. But the old crowd grew away from us. They got married and got steady jobs, and some of them got important. And that was the worst of all, when they got important. We were left alone. Just the two of us, just you and I, the ones who didn't want to change. It wasn't just being young that we were hanging on to. It was something else. It was a time that went with being young and crazy. I think we knew it somehow. And we were right, of course. It was never quite as good again."

The Model T left the ridge and plunged down a long, steep hill, and below them they could see a massive highway, broad and many-laned, with many car lights moving on it.

"We're coming to a freeway, Hank," said Virg. "Maybe we should sort of veer away from it. This old Model T of yours is a good car, sure, the best there ever was, but that's fast company down there."

"I ain't doing nothing to it," said Hank. "I ain't steering it. It is on its own. It knows what it wants to do."

"Well, all right, what the hell," said Virg, "we'll ride along with it. That's all right with me. I feel safe with it. Comfortable with it. I never felt so comfortable in all my goddamn life. Christ, I don't know what I'd done if you hadn't come along. Why don't you lay down that silly sax and have a drink before I drink it all."

So Hank laid down the sax and had a couple of drinks to make up for lost time, and by the time he handed the bottle back to Virg, the Model T had gone charging up a ramp, and they were on the freeway. It went running gaily down its lane, and it passed some cars that were far from standing still. Its fenders rattled at a more rapid rate, and the chattering of the magneto coils was like machine-gun fire.

"Boy," said Virg admiringly, "see the old girl go. She's got life left in her yet. Do you have any idea, Hank, where we might be going?"

"Not the least," said Hank, picking up the sax again.

"Well, hell," said Virg, "it don't really matter, just so we're on our way. There was a sign back there a ways that said Chicago. Do you think we could be headed for Chicago?"

Hank took the sax out of his mouth. "Could be," he said. "I ain't worried over it."

"I ain't worried neither," said Old Virg. "Chicago, here we come! Just so the booze holds out. It seems to be holding out. We've been sucking at it regular, and it's still better than half-full."

"You hungry, Virg?" asked Hank.

"Hell, no," said Virg. "Not hungry, and not sleepy, either. I never felt so good in all my life. Just so the booze holds out and this heap hangs together."

The Model T banged and clattered, running with a pack of smooth, sleek cars that did not bang and clatter, with Hank playing on the saxophone and Old Virg waving the bottle high and yelling whenever the rattling old machine outdistanced a Lincoln or a Cadillac. The moon hung in the sky and did not seem to move. The freeway became a throughway, and the first toll booth loomed ahead.

"I hope you got change," said Virg. "Myself, I am cleaned out."

But no change was needed, for when the Model T came near, the toll-gate arm moved up and let it go thumping through without payment.

"We got it made," yelled Virg. "The road is free for us, and that's the way it should be. After all you and I been through, we got something coming to us."

Chicago loomed ahead, off to their left, with night lights gleaming in the towers that rose along the lakeshore, and they went around it in a long, wide sweep, and New York was just beyond the fishhook bend as they swept around Chicago and the lower curve of the lake.

"I never saw New York," said Virg, "but seen pictures of Manhattan, and that can't be nothing but Manhattan. I never did know, Hank, that Chicago and Manhattan were so close together."

"Neither did I," said Hank, pausing from his tootling on the sax. "The geography's all screwed up for sure, but what the hell do we care? With this rambling wreck, the whole damn world is ours."

He went back to the sax, and the Model T kept rambling on. They went thundering through the canyons of Manhattan and circumnavigated Boston and went on down to Washington, where the Washington Monument stood up high and Old Abe sat brooding on Potomac's shore.

They went on down to Richmond and skated past Atlanta and skimmed along the moon-drenched sands of Florida. They ran along old roads where trees dripped Spanish moss and saw the lights of Old N'Orleans way off to their left. Now they were heading north again, and the car was galumphing along a ridgetop with neat farming country all spread out below them. The moon still stood where it had been before, hanging at the selfsame spot. They were moving through a world where it was always three A.M.

"You know," said Virg, "I wouldn't mind if this kept on forever. I wouldn't mind if we never got to wherever we are going. It's too much fun getting there to worry where we're headed. Why don't you lay down that horn and have another drink? You must be getting powerful dry."

Hank put down the sax and reached out for the bottle. "You know, Virg," he said, "I feel the same way you do. It just don't seem there's any need for fretting about where we're going or what's about to happen. It don't seem that nothing could be better than right now."

Back there at the dark pavilion he'd remembered that there had been something he'd heard about Old Virg and had thought he should speak to him about, but couldn't, for the life of him, remember what it was. But now he'd remembered it, and it was of such slight importance that it seemed scarcely worth the mention.

The thing that he'd remembered was that good Old Virg was dead.

He put the bottle to his lips and had a drink, and it seemed to him he'd never had a drink that tasted half so good. He handed back the bottle and picked up the sax and tootled on it with high spirit while the ghost of the Model T went on rambling down the moonlit road.

Clifford D. Simak writes:

This story is pure nostalgia. It is a harking back to the early 1920's, when the Model T was a young man's car, if for no other reason than that he could afford nothing better. In a way, it was a symbol of an age, along with the saxophone, that bleating, blatting, wailing instrument that characterized the popular music of the day.

The Model T, as a matter of fact, was a marvelous mechanism. It marked the watershed between the life style and philosophy of the horse-and-buggy society and the technological complexity that today threatens to utterly overwhelm us. It was a simple and honest machine now embedded in what seems, in retrospect, a blissfully simple age.

It seems to me that the concept of the Roaring Twenties is a modern misinterpretation. To me (who lived through them), the twenties were a time when we had not entirely lost our innocence, when cynicism had not as yet become a national hallmark—a time when we still clung, however feebly, to some belief in not only our country's destiny, but in our own as well.

PLANET STORY

by Kate Wilhelm

There is nothing to fear on this planet.

The planet is represented in our records by a series of numbers and letters, each conveying information: distance from its sun, mass, period of rotation, presence or absence of moons. The seedling colony that will arrive one day will name the planet.

We are twenty-seven men and women planetside—with three more members who remain on the orbiting ship—minimum age twenty-five, maximum age fifty. This is our fourth Earth year of a seven-year contract. There were twenty-eight of us planetside, but Ito went mad and committed suicide twenty days ago, on the seventh day planetside.

There is abundant life here, a full spectrum from viruses to high-order mammals. The animals do not fear us. We walk among them freely. Each is conditioned to fear its predator and to seek its prey. Nowhere in that scheme does man fit in.

The sun is a bright-yellow glow in the clouds; it moves like a searchlight in fog to complete its trip in thirty-four hours. The planet's month is thirty-seven days. On the thirty-eighth day we shall leave. We shall take nothing with us except data: a paragraph in the catalog of worlds. With our lives we are buying insurance for the family of Earthmen.

Olga watches me with brooding eyes, for twice I have spurned her, while I in turn watch Haarlem, a distant figure at the moment, operating his core drill with precision and concentration; it is as if he has become an extension of the mechanism he uses. I wonder at the affinity that sometimes exists between man and his machinery, an affinity that seems reciprocal in that now the will of the human rules, and again he is ruled by the demands of his tool. I concentrate on Olga and Haarlem and on my abstract thoughts, because here, within reach of the ship, in sight of my friends and co-workers, I am afraid.

My buzzer sounds the end of my duty break, and I turn it off and go back to the ship. Since Ito's death we have taken turns at the computer, coding data, transmitting everything to our orbiting ship. Should Haarlem die, another would operate his core drill, complete his geological survey; should I die, another would don doctor's garb and check temperatures, administer to the ill and injured. I wait for my signal to activate the steps and the airlock door to the decontamination chamber, and as I wait, I watch Haarlem, a distant figure. I am eager to be inside, my suit off, breathing the air of the ship, not that from my oxypack. I have become rigid, resisting the impulse to whirl around, to discover finally what it is that makes my heart beat too fast, turns my palms clammy.

I don't turn around. On this gentle continent, on this benign planet, where there is no menace to mankind in the air, on the ground, beneath the ground, no menace of any kind, to yield to baseless fear is to act irrationally. I know what I would see: a broad plain of low vegetation; animals grazing within reach of our people; a hazy sky; a flock of small, furry, flying animals that appear soft and pettable; an iridescent gauzy wing of an insect that hovers, darts away, insectlike.

There are no ruins. No artifacts. No intelligent life has ever walked here until now. There is only the plain that stretches to the horizon to the east, and the hills that are rounded with age and covered with trees, spaced as if planned, gardenlike. Elvil assures us there is no plan; this is how trees grow naturally. There are flowers that grow at the junction of forest and plain: bushes with blue flowers, carpeting plants with yellow masses of blooms, vines that curl and twist their way up the trees on the edge of the forest. Red flowers hang downward, with long slender stamens that sway with the wind, like dancers in yellow tights against a scarlet velvet backdrop. The flowers are the buffer zone, a living flag of truce, promising no encroachment on the part of forest or plain.

The steps descend, and I climb upward and turn momentarily, to see Olga's face lifted, as she watches me with her great brooding eyes. I enter the chamber, and a spray cleanses my suit; lights dry it and finish the process. I discard the garment and step naked into the shower and remain under the warm water for the allotted time, wishing it were longer, and, still naked, go into the dressing room, where Elvil and Derek are checking Derek's planetside suit.

A light signals that the flyer has been decontaminated. "Where are you going?" I ask.

Derek is finished now. "To the ocean group. Jeanne is missing."

My stomach lurches. Jeanne? She is tall and has hair the color of sun on pale sand, blindingly bright, with dark streaks. Her skin is baby-smooth, and there is a joy in her that makes her a favorite of everyone.

"They need the third flyer for the search," Derek says, and enters the decontamination chamber.

"They'll find her," Elvil says, his hand heavy and cold on my bare shoulder. I nod and clasp his hand briefly.

The ship lies on its side while it is on the ground; the seats for thirty become narrow beds, each with a screen that can be closed. When I am relieved at the computer I find Olga waiting for me in my tiny area of privacy.

"Please," she says, "don't make me leave. I only want to talk, I don't even want to touch you."

It is not dark outside yet; my mind is on the search that is continuing along the ocean's edge. But I am very tired. I sit by Olga and draw her close to me and hold her. She is trembling.

"I am so afraid," she whispers. "I keep looking to see what's behind me, and there's nothing. That makes it worse." Her trembling increases, and I lie down with her and stroke her and think of the search.

Olga is beautiful in a broad-hipped, large-breasted way that is pure sensuality. Her response to any touch is always a sexual response. She apologizes for it often, but everyone understands her needs, and few deny her the caresses she craves, the release she must have. Her trembling now, however, is not caused by sexual tension, but fear, and I don't know how to allay it.

We should have a meeting, an open session with everyone present, and air our fears, I decide. After the search is completed, I'll call a meeting, another with the shore party. Derek can preside there. He will know how to conduct it, what to look for, how to force it along certain lines.

Olga moans, and I turn my attention once more to her. She has forgotten her fear, at least for the moment. When I leave her, she is sleeping peacefully.

The captain's office is next to my infirmary. He is a slender man, with delicate hands, and he, like Haarlem, has an affinity for his machines; sometimes it seems that he and the ship are one. His face is deeply carved, and often he is careless with his depilatory cream and misses a fissure, in which dark hairs grow luxuriantly. Those lines make his face look like a caricature. He is studying a monitor on his desk when I enter. He grips the edges of it as if to make it yield up what he requires of it. I read the moving lights as readily as he, but I ask anyway, "Any news yet?"

"Nothing."

We continue to watch together for a few moments, and then I sit down opposite him and say, "She has done it deliberately, then."

He nods. There are constant signals from the suits unless the wearer turns them off. Two buttons are involved, requiring both hands to deactivate the system; it is impossible for it to happen accidentally.

"Like Ito," I say. Not like, but he knows what I mean. Ito hanged himself.

"I'm afraid so," he says. He looks at me, but doesn't turn off his monitor. "Have you any suggestions?"

"None. I would like an open session as soon as possible."

There is no immediate response. He must weigh the possible results: an increase of fear if it becomes acknowledged; a decrease; a cause identified; someone else being driven to suicide. There are ten days remaining to us on this planet. He says suddenly, "Today I found myself stopping to hear if there were footsteps behind me. I have been uneasy before, but not like today. I looked around before I could control myself."

I nod. It is getting worse. Everyone has experienced it, I am certain, and no one has really talked about it. The kindest among us have become withdrawn, short-tempered; the indifferent ones have become quarrelsome; the ones tending toward meanness in the best of times have become vicious. Always before, the ubiquitous dangers of unknown worlds have drawn us closer, but here, in the total absence of any threat, we are struggling to free ourselves from the mutual dependency that is as necessary to our success as the individual skills each brings to the service.

"I look around, too," I say. "There is nothing."

He glances once more at the monitor. "When do you want your session?"

"When we get up, before sunrise." It is a good time, when everyone will welcome a change from the records-keeping chores that occupy us all during the dark hours of the long night.

I rise to leave, and pause before stepping over the portal. "I'm sorry about Jeanne, Wes." I know she was a favorite of his. For a moment his grief is written in the crevices of his face; then he turns away.

High above the atmosphere of this planet the orbiting ship is studying the sun. Closer, spy satellites weave an invisible web as they spin in their separate orbits, mapping the world, sensing mineral deposits, ocean depths, volcanic regions. On the surface, our group, split into halves, makes a minute examination of the soil, the air, the rivers and shores, the animal life. This planet can withhold no secrets from our assault. To date our reports, codified in the computer, rate it as the best possible world for colonizing. There have been no negative reports. But two of our people have died here.

The group that gathers for the open session knows this. We meet in the main room of the ship, where each of us has his own seatbed, with a screen to close or not. The seats are upright now, the screens open.

We know we can trust one another; we know each has proven his bravery and intelligence frequently enough not to have them questioned. We are close enough emotionally to be able to forgo pretense, or preliminaries, intimate enough to recognize any signs of hesitation or evasion. There is doubt and fear, and shock, on the faces that I see before me now.

"I would like to try to get a profile of whatever it is causing our fear," I say. "Since there is nothing anyone can see or detect with instruments, we might approach with the possibility that it is a projection. This is not a conclusion, merely a place to start."

There are nods, and only Haarlem seems disapproving of this beginning. I call on him first. "Have you ever felt a comparable uneasiness that you couldn't rationalize?"

He shakes his head silently, and I feel a flush of annoyance with him.

"Is there anyone who has felt a similar, baseless fear?"

"Once," Louenvelt says, "when I was a child, no more than four. I wakened with a feeling of great fear, afraid to move, unable to say why. Not the usual nightmare awakening, but similar to it. There had been an earthquake, quieted by the time I was thoroughly awake, but I didn't know that at the time." Louenvelt is our botanist, a quiet man who seldom participates in any group activity. I am grateful that he has started the session.

Sharkey is next to speak, and I know I will have to bear this, too.

Sharkey is querulous; conversation with him is always one-sided and endless.

"On my first Contract," he says, with an air of settling in, "we were faced with these bearlike beings. Big! Big as grizzlies, that's why we called them bears, even though they—"

"But you knew what frightened you," I say firmly. "That isn't what we're after right now."

"Well, we knew those bears would tear us limb from limb, and they were smart, even if the computer did rate them nonintelligent. The dominant species! That always is a clue about . . ."

I depress the button of my recorder to underline what he has just said. He has given me something to think about, after all. There is no dominant species on this planet.

Olga has stood up, and there is excitement on her face. "You said it might be a projection," she says. "But what if it isn't? What if there are things that we can't detect simply because we've never had to detect them before?" Sharkey gives way to her amiably. He is used to being interrupted.

"What do you mean?" I ask. Olga is a zoologist, specializing in holographic scanning of animals. She can make replications of animals with her equipment, down to the nerve endings. With her holograms and a blood sample, nail, hoof, or hair clipping, she can tell you what the animal customarily eats, its rate of growth, its lifespan.

"I mean that no matter how much information we have, we always have to add more with new facts. The computer can't be more intelligent than its programmers. We all know that. And if we are faced with something that no one has ever seen before, of course we haven't got that information in the computer. The sensors can't report what they haven't been programmed to sense, any more than a metal detector will indicate plastic." She sits down again with a smug air.

Haarlem says, "And the evidence of our eyes? And our ears? Are we to believe that we cannot hear or see because we have never experienced this before?" Haarlem is very dark; he keeps his head shaved, almost as if he wants to conceal nothing on the outside because he realizes that there are so many hidden places within. Olga has never repressed anything in her life. She is fair, open, quick to be wounded, quicker to heal. Haarlem bleeds internally for a long time.

"Yes, our eyes can deceive us," Olga says with some heat. "If a ghost walked in here, we would every one of us deny our eyes!"

Haarlem laughs and settles back to become a spectator once more.

I study him briefly, wondering at his withdrawal, his almost sullen attitude that has kept me at a distance. I yearn for him in my loins, but in his present mood we only fight when we are together, and it is well that he rebuffs me, I decide. He is wiser in some matters than I am.

Julie tells of a time that she was overcome by fear in a deep woods in the Canadian Rockies, and someone else relates a similar feeling while at sea, standing alone in the stern of the ship. It goes on. Nearly everyone can remember such an incident, and when it is over, I wonder what we have accomplished, if we have accomplished anything. Perhaps we will all speak of it now when it occurs. Mel Souder, our meteorologist, will chart the times and check them against weather changes, wind shifts. I expect little to come of it.

My suit is lightweight and impermeable, my oxypack heavy on my back, an accustomed heaviness accepted, as one accepts a gain in weight or a swollen foot or hand. Awkward, but necessary. We do not breathe the air of the planets we discover. It is for the seedling colonists to take such risks, to adapt to the local conditions if necessary. We adapt to nothing but change.

This is how Jeanne walked away, I think, her footsteps clear in the sand, her tracing clear on the recorder, until suddenly there was no tracing any longer, although the footprints continued up the beach another twenty or thirty meters, and then turned inland and were lost in the undergrowth of the tangled marsh trees and bushes.

There is a pale coloring in the sky now; first comes the lightening with no particular color, and then the clouds glow, as if a fire is raging somewhere, obscured by smoke and fog that lets a crimson band appear first, then a golden flare, then pale pink rolling clouds, and finally the yellow spot that is too bright to look at directly, but is not defined as a sun.

I walk along the edge of the flowers that divide the plain from the forest. The vegetation is grasslike, but not grass. It is broader-leaved, pliable. It springs up behind me and shows no evidence of my passing. A swarm of jade insects rises and forms a column of life that hovers a moment, disperses, and settles once more, hidden again by the plants. There are birds here, songbirds, birds of prey, shore birds. Every niche is filled, from bacteria to mammals, but intelligence did not arise. Nor is there a dominant species.

I could go into the forest, walk for hours, and never become lost. My belt has homing instruments that would guide me back to the ship. My oxypack has a signal to warn me when half of my supply of air is gone. And aboard ship, telltale tracings would reveal my position at a glance to rescuers, should I fall and be unable to continue.

I suppose I am mourning Jeanne, but more than that, I am inviting the fear to come to me now. Always before I have been where I could busy myself instantly, or return to the ship, or seek out another and start a conversation designed to mask the fear. It always comes to one who is alone, in a contemplative mood possibly. Can the fear be courted? I don't know, but I will know before I return to the ship.

The resilient blades under my feet make a faint sighing sound as they straighten up. It is almost musical, a counterpoint to the rhythm of my steps, so faint that only if I concentrate on it does it become audible. I am becoming aware of other sounds. Something in the woods is padding along in the same direction that I walk. I stop and search for it, but see nothing. When I move again I listen for it, and presently it is there. A small animal, curious about me probably, not frightening. If a carnivore should become confused and attack me, I could stop it long before it could reach me. We are armed, and on many planets the arms have been necessary, but not here. I wish to see the small animal, because like it, I am curious.

From the giraffe to the platypus, from the elephant to the shrew, from the crocodile to the gibbon—such is the spread of life that we have accepted on Earth, and wherever we have gone since then, the range has been comparable. There are things that are like, but not the same, and others that are unlike anything any of us has seen before. The universal catalog of animals would need an entire planet to house its volumes. Perhaps Olga is right, perhaps there are things we cannot perceive, because we are too inexperienced.

The small animal has become tired of its game, and walks out from the brush to nibble yellow flowers. It is a pale-gray quadruped, with short coarse hair and padded feet, tailless, and now it evinces no interest in me at all. It is catlike, but no one would ever mistake it for a cat. A herbivorous cat.

The animals have struck a balance on this planet. Checks and balances work here. A steady population, enough food for all, no need for the genocidal competition of other worlds. This, I feel, is the key to the planet. I have stopped to observe the catlike animal, and now I start to walk once more, and suddenly there it is.

There has been no change in anything, as far as I can tell. No sound of parallel steps, no rustling in the grass. The wind hasn't changed. Nothing is changed, but I feel the first tendrils of fear raising the hairs of my arms, playing over my scalp. I study the woods while the fear grows. Then the plain. A small furry animal flies overhead, oblivious of me, intent on his own flight into the woods. Now I can feel my heart race, and I begin to speak into my recorder, trying to put into words that which is only visceral and exists without symbols or signs that can truly define it. My physiological symptoms are not what my fear is. I describe them anyway. Now my hands are perspiring heavily, and I begin to feel nausea rise and spread, weakening my legs, cramping my stomach. I am searching faster, looking for something, anything. Something to fight or run away from. And there is nothing. My heart is pounding hard, and the urge to scream and run is very strong. The urge to run into the woods and hide myself among the trees is strong also, as is the urge to drop to the ground and draw myself up into as tight and hard a ball as possible and become invisible. Nothing in the overcast sky, nothing in the woods, nothing on the plain, nothing . . . From the ground, then. Something coming up from the ground. I am running and sobbing into my recorder, running from the spot where it has to be, and it runs with me.

I am in the woods and can't remember entering them; I remember telling myself I would not enter them. Now I can no longer see the ship in the distance, and the fear is growing and pressing in on me, crushing me down into the ground. I think: If I vomit, I might drown in it. The suits were not made for that contingency. I would have to take off the helmet and expose myself to it even more.

If I turn off all my devices, then it won't be able to find me. I can hide in the woods, then. Even as the thought occurs to me, I start to scream. I fall to the ground and claw and scrabble at it, and I am screaming and screaming.

I begged them not to give me a sedative, but Wes countermanded me and administered it personally, and I slept. Now it is late afternoon and much of the morning is dreamlike, but I know this will pass as the sedative wears off. They think I am mad, like Ito, like Jeanne probably was at the end. I am very sore. I believe I fought them when they found me in the woods clawing a hole in the ground, screaming.

I am in a restraining sheet, and there is nothing I can do but wait until someone comes to see about me. Not Sharkey, I hope. But Wes is too considerate and wise to permit Sharkey access to someone who cannot walk away.

It is Wes who looks in on me, and behind him I can see Haarlem.

"I'm all right," I say. "Pulse normal, no fever, calm. You can release me, you know."

"How did you take your pulse?" Haarlem asks, not disbelieving, but interested.

"In the groin. I have to talk to you, and this sheet makes it damned difficult."

Wes releases the restraint, and I sit up. Before I can start, he says, "If you have found out anything at all, let's have it straight. Now. The clouds have lifted, and for the first time we have the opportunity for aerial reconnaissance, and I want to go along."

The cloud cover of this planet is not thick, not like Venus', but since our arrival there has been a haze; there have been no sharp features that were visible from the aircraft. Probably a spring feature, the meteorologist said, that would not be a factor throughout the rest of the year. With the lifting of the clouds there would be sharp shadows, and clearly defined trees and streams, and peaceful animals that would look with wonder on the things in the sky.

Inside the Chinese-puzzle box are other boxes, each smaller than the last, and our innermost box is the one-man aircraft. "You mustn't go," I say. "Don't let anyone go anywhere alone again."

The captain clears his throat and even opens his mouth, but it is Haarlem who speaks first. "What happened to you?"

I tell them quickly, leaving out nothing. "I recorded all of it," I say. "Until I started to scream. I turned that off."

"You knew you were going to scream?" Wes asks with some surprise, or possibly disbelief.

"I had to. The adrenaline prepares one to fight, or to run. If he can do neither, and sometimes even if he can, the excess adrenaline can change the chemistry of the brain, and the person may go mad. Like Ito. Or lose consciousness. I chose to do neither. Screaming is another outlet, and I had to do something with my hands, or they would have clawed at the buttons of my controls. So I dug and screamed."

"And what have you proved?" Haarlem asks. He sounds angry now.

I continue to look at Wes. "It gets overwhelming if the person is alone, beyond the reach of others or the ship. And there is no living thing present to account for it. Unlike other fear situations, in which the fear peaks and then subsides, this doesn't diminish, but continues to grow."

"You were still feeling it when we found you?"

"I was. It was getting worse by the second." I glance quickly at Haarlem and then away again. "Screaming helped keep me sane, but it didn't do a thing for the terror."

Wes stands up decisively. "I'll cancel the overflights," he says, but he gives me a bitter look, and I know he is resentful because I have denied him this pleasure: flying over a land where no man has walked, seeing what no man has seen, knowing that no man will ever see it this way in the future, for virginity cannot be restored.

"I think the other party at the shore should be recalled," I say, but now I have gone too far. He shakes his head, and presently leaves me with Haarlem.

"You did a crazy thing for someone not crazy," Haarlem says, but he is undressing as he speaks, and contentedly I move over and watch him.

The sun is out, and the perfection of this planet, this day, is such that I feel I could expand to the sky, fill the spaces between the ground and the heavens with my being, and my being is joyful. The air is pristine and indefinably fragrant. The desire to pull off our impermeable suits is voiced by nearly everyone. To run naked in the fields, to love and be loved under the golden sun, to gather flowers and strew them about for our beds, to follow the meandering stream to the river and plunge into the cool, invisible water, where the rocks and plants on the bottom are as sharp and clear as those on the bank —these are our thoughts on this most glorious day.

An urgent message from the shore party shatters our serenity. Tony has gone mad and has broken Francine's neck in his frenzy. He eluded the others and ran into the woods, leaving a trail of instruments behind him.

Wes has ordered the shore party to return to the ship. He has ordered me to the infirmary to wait for Francine, who is dying.

No one suggested we bury Francine. We have her body ready for space burial, and now we orbit the planet and monitor our instruments from a distance. The spy satellites will be finished in three days, and then we shall leave. We voted unanimously that the planet is uninhabitable, and that too will be a note in the paragraph in the catalog of worlds. No one will come here again. There is no need for further exploration; no future seedling colonists will christen this world. The planet will forever remain a number.

* * *

Wes and I are awake, taking the first watch. Although we trust our instruments, our machines completely, we choose to have two humans awake at all times. Always before when I stood watch, it was with Haarlem, but this time I volunteered when Wes said he would be first. Haarlem didn't even look at me when I made the choice.

The Deep Sleep will erase the immediacy of the planet, melt it into the body of other planets, so that only by concentration will any of us be able to feel our experience here again. And there is something I must decide before I permit this to happen. Haarlem said mockingly, "No one believes in heaven, but there is a system of responses to archetypes built into each of us, and this planet has triggered those responses."

I refuse to believe him. Our instruments failed to detect a presence, a menace, a being that made what appeared to be perfection in fact a death trap. I think of the other worlds to which we have condemned our colonists, worlds too hot, or too cold, with hostile animal life, or turbulent weather, and mutely I cry out that this planet that will remain forever a number in the catalog of worlds is worse than any of them. None of the other worlds claimed a life, and this planet has taken four. But my dreams are troubled, and I think of the joy and serenity that we all felt, only to be overcome again by terror.

We all shared the fear. The thought races through my mind over and over. We all shared the fear. The best of us and the worst. Even I.

Even I.

Kate Wilhelm writes:

When I was about twelve, I had the responsibility every afternoon of looking after my two younger brothers until my mother came home from work. One of the things I did to keep them indoors was tell them stories. I told short stories, and novels in serial form, leaving off each day with a cliff-hanger, in the best pulp tradition. I never had seen a pulp and had no idea that that was what I was doing, but it seemed an ideal way to handle this particular situation. I found I could make up incidents as fast as I could talk, and each one led to another, even more exciting. Most of the stories involved other worlds—fairy-tale lands, or alternate universes where wonderful things could and did happen. To reach one of these worlds, my young protagonists had to swim underwater in a pool on an abandoned estate whose grounds were full of statues in disrepair. Near the bottom of the pool was a metal door that never rusted, that opened to a passage where the water turned to sweet air, and led upward into a forest of strange trees. Another story had a trapdoor in a disreputable shanty on the river front, where our heroes fell through to a tunnel into somewhere else.

My brothers and I remember those stories in snatches now, but with great pleasure. Instinctively I had used what must be a universal symbol—the strange world, in which we don't understand the laws or our own ability to deal with them. I am still intrigued by other worlds. Whether they are real, or, more likely, psychic, they have a compelling power to send some of us out again and again to find them, to explore through them another part of ourselves. This story must be a continuation of the search I started when I was twelve, and haven't completed yet.

GRADUATION DAY

by W. Macfarlane

Isserman Stevens stood behind the eucalyptus and trembled violently. He had slipped out of the dormitory ahead of a fat kid who fired and missed. He dodged into the pyrocanthus, foamy with blossom this spring, camouflaging his white school uniform. While other boys and the girls cleared the dorm for sanctuary in the brush and shrubbery, he had scuttled to the service area, his bright-orange tote bag masked by his body.

He stopped shaking and tugged the abstract sculpture from the bag. His sad-faced art professor had said, "Isserman, you've made a worm nest in eight rigid fins. The fifty-centimeter length, the overheft of the vertical members, the unbalance of the wedge crowning your spaghetti farm . . . well, as some have a tin ear for music, you have a glass eye for proportion."

Isserman tried to snap the wedge from its slender base. It would not break. He smashed it onto the concrete platform of the disposal bin. There was a hairline crack, and he pounded until the wedge came free. He checked his gun. He checked his stolen clip. He checked his watch. Four minutes gone of the twenty allotted for the kilometer run to the classroom. A boy sobbed not far away.

He trembled again. He knelt and looked around the eucalyptus. The kid had given up for today. He was walking in the open, polka-dotted with shots. He was covered with twenty or thirty three-centimeter splats of all colors, pink on the back of one hand and an epic blue splash on his right temple. Isserman stopped shaking. The RAD was in sight, lumbering over the turf.

"Recycling Automatic Dispenser, Wayco Manufacturing, Model 22-K," was the title of the operations manual he had studied. The compensators were not precisely in sync. That was why it undulated over the ground. Not enough to bother maintenance yet. It took a phase harmonizer to adjust. You could set it by trial and error with a dash-dot driver. As he watched, he thought he would remember this instant forever.

This was the moment of either-or. This was balancing on the antigravity stick with land instead of the lake below. This was do or flat-out die. He shuddered. The arms of the RAD reached out. The bin door slid down.

Isserman stepped smoothly to the arm. The disposal container was raised and tipped into the RAD. Old uniforms, paper, plastic bottles, shoes, the detritus of dormitory living tilted into the bin. The moment the container was emptied, Isserman rolled through the wide slot. He fumbled for the sculpture. Its edges caught on the bag. With committed calm, he worked it loose. He stood on the uncertain footing and set the base against the very center of the wall. With the other hand he held the wedge end-o against the closure of the door. The door slid up and locked onto it, leaving a twenty-centimeter gap. The RAD moved off.

The hydraulic-ram wall moved toward him. In vertical terms, he figured, an elephant stood on a card table, 1.75 tons per square meter. The ram engaged the sculpture. It held.

The RAD was double-ended for efficiency, so Isserman was looking out the back as it headed for the last school station at the rear of the classroom. He pulled his gun and began squeezing shots as targets offered. His yellow blotch with the personal isotope appeared twenty times on white uniforms. The gun was empty. He groped in the narrow space for the stolen clip in the tote bag.

He snapped eight shots when unsophisticated students tried to run with the RAD for shelter. He had to bend farther over as the trash rose under his feet. His elbow was forced to the line of his shoulders. He ignored the evidence. He made seven more scores before he looked down. The sculpture was failing, plastic turned plastic under the inexorable pressure. The spaghetti lines kept the thick fins in relationship, but he now had only thirty-to-thirty-five centimeters of space. He twisted and wrenched himself split-legged, straddling the sculpture, his narrowest dimension parallel to the ram face.

He held the gun in his teeth and pulled down with all his strength on the horizontal door. It was hard against the wedge and did not give a millimeter with his weight on it. He snorted between amusement and terror. Two hundred meters to the classroom. The RAD had been slowed by the students dodging around it. He looked at his watch. Three minutes to the bell. He squeezed off the last five shots with his hips pressed against the outer wall.

He was bitterly amused by his lack of information after all the research. Pragmatic Ethics said no one ever had enough overt data for a final decision—forget evaluation of the decision—but if he was going to be crushed like a dummy at fifteen and one-half years old, he should have thought to find out if his hips or chest would go first. The ram squeezed tighter. The empirical method! He bared his teeth. Never too late to learn. He would find out.

The RAD stopped, the arms went out, the door lowered, the ram retracted. He swarmed through the opening. He hit the ground between the arms at a dead run. His tote bag swung wide as he turned the corner of the building. The bell began to ring. He was through the door and stuffed his keycard into the counter before it stopped. He walked down the corridor and stepped into the classroom.

His name stood out from all the others in blue fire on the wall. His score 40-0. While his classmates stood and snarled, booed and hissed and cheered, he looked at the 293 names, a few in red; 20-5 was the best score. No one had scored over twenty in his three years of school. There had been only fifty-some graduates from a student body fluctuating at three hundred and under. This was achievement. He stood wire-taut. The names faded.

The wall printed, "Isserman Stevens report to Personnel."

He waved an imperial farewell to his peers and grinned. They cheered him through the door. He staggered down the hall in a fit of reaction, almost losing control of his bladder, trembling, shaking, his mouth working . . . until a student appeared from a room. He walked with swaggering nonchalance.

He tapped his keycard into the slot of the Personnel door. It slid open, and he stepped into the closet. The door shut when he retrieved the keycard. The field built to congruency with the characteristic soft whine, up and beyond the audible range. Coinciding at all points when superimposition occurred, the click came like teeth snapping down a tunnel. The door opened.

"Isserman Stevens," said a woman behind a desk. She nodded to a chair. "I'm Margaret Sandler." The window behind her looked down on a night city—Los Angeles, Mexico City, Buenos Aires? What did it matter—Davenport, Rock Island, Moline—was she personnel chief for the stars or the secretarial pool? Her black hair was sleek, her intelligent brown eyes intimidating. "How did you get hold of that extra clip?"

"I assumed computer identification and called out Lock Theory and Practice, ma'am. The armory alarm is not very sophisticated."

"Did you share access?"

"No, ma'am."

"And how did you get to class all clear?"

His answer matched her brevity. When she asked why he had risked death by crushing, he said he had not figured to die any more than the girl who panicked on the aggie stick and drove into the side of the boat. She looked doubtful. "How did you get out, ma'am?"

"I suborned my peers. When did you realize what school was all about?"

"Weapons or Prag Logic or Exotic Anthro?" he hedged. "Who you shoot or who you don't?" She waited patiently, her eyes probing. "I'm not sure I know now." He said slowly, "The right to make mistakes, maybe, and graduation by ordeal. Oh, I figured this out, but I had a feeling I'd better learn something first. Maybe I was scared. I nearly scheduled Art last year. With no possessions allowed, it's not easy—it's hard to know the right time to go." He stopped speaking.

"How many levels is school about?" she said softly, and answered herself: "Well, you can't feed enough data to a computer, because relative values change. Because the human computer is associational on a value-shifting time-release program, the only meterstick is eating the model." She ignored her confused metaphor. "Go to the next room. When Rawling is done with you, come back here."

Rawling was impersonal, deft, and quick. "Strip down, sir. Step into the fitting booth. Let me snug the collar under your chin. Hold out your arms with the fingers separated. First the lubricant spray and then the moldform. Arms to the side, touch your hands to your shoulders. Squat down, sir, full knee bend. The quadriflex will accommodate with no discomfort. Stand still for the catalyst. Very well, sir. Step out. Slit here and here. Let me help you peel it off."

Left alone at last in the programmed shower, Isserman shook and shook mindlessly while the scrubber and oil and water and foam worked on him.

Spidersilk-soft mesh underwear was waiting. The bronze-rust uniform fit like a second skin. It was engineered to support two guns at his thighs from his shoulders. The boots were red-bronze, and the fingertip-length coat was dull dazzle-striped. "Your complete outfit will be waiting for you, sir," said Rawling. "Will you check your guns now, military jolt load." He watched the holster release when the guns were drawn. He made and set a slight adjustment to the downpull and said Margaret Sandler was waiting.

She looked him over. "Very nice. There's a glass of berryea by your chair." He sat and sipped it. "Do you have a clean handkerchief?" She smiled ruefully. "That's my mother syndrome—it's hard to let you children go. That's why I must follow the book as well as you. My condolences. White uniform plus full score equals graduation. And my congratulations."

"Th-thank you, ma'am."

"You are the new Factor for Laramie."

"F-factor?"

"An early-period planet—Timeless West—out in Boötes somewhere." She watched a tremor shake him. "Muscles and windmills and water power working up to steam. No internal combustion. Despite all the ridiculous conditions, historical-fix planets flourish. You'll go to Laramie because the last Factor was shot two weeks ago."

He stopped trembling at this news, and she continued, "Not from your school. She carried a clean uniform in her tote bag to graduate. That was when we stopped putting out uniforms with the assistance of young men. She extrapolated her talent on Laramie. A wife used a period pistol on her. And before this, a woman filled the post for twenty-six years. She retired to spend more time with her grandchildren. So it always comes down to the individual. But it seemed more politic to send a man this time."

She sat at her desk and punched coordinates at a terminal. She checked her work and tapped Execute and Hold. She stood and said, "Isserman, my only advice is the third law: The exercise of power has an opposite and equal action."

"Somebody must be r-responsible, ma'am."

"Yes. It's a demanding and a weary burden." She led the way to another room. "But it's always been the only game in town. Now you get your choice, Isserman, graduate to your home town with no bias, or go factoring in the Timeless West."

One door in the far wall read "Chicopee Falls, Massachusetts," the other, "Laramie, Laramie." A locker on wheels with his name on it, presumably full of clothing and personal gear, stood between the doors. Without hesitation, he pushed it to "Laramie."

She made a gesture he had never seen before, thumb and forefinger together in a circle. It obviously meant good luck, God bless, goodbye. The door closed. Congruency elided the light-years, the eerie whine, the snap, and the door opened. He pulled out his locker and stood beside it.

The post was a horizontal cylinder, thirty meters interior diameter, corrugated outside, one hundred and twenty meters long. The bottom half contained the support systems. At ground level, Receiving and the Factor's quarters were twenty meters deep, with enclosed passages on either side running the length of the post, giving interior access to the buildings under local control at either end. The rest of the space was open. The far half was elevated seats, with the staging area underneath, the arena, the eleven booths, the First Clerk's desk and files to the left, the locked command console to the right, directly in front of Isserman Stevens.

It was familiar enough from the mock-up at school, but on Laramie it smelled of dust and summer in spite of the standard twenty-one-degree temperature. Fewer than a hundred men and women were in the stands, and a few clerks and handlers idled in the arena in front of the booths. They wore funny hats and peculiar clothing. Silence spread as Isserman Stevens walked to the console. He said he was the new Factor and would open transportation in one hour.

"Where you been, you little son-of-a-bitch?" shouted a virulent drunk on the steps to the arena. "You been dogging it while I dangled here at your pleasure!" He pulled his gun.

Stevens fired first. He aimed for the shoulder, and the man spun like a rag doll, arms flapping, and knocked over a boy carrying a wooden bucket of ice and beer bottles. The military load had a velocity of just under a kilometer per second, and the stun charge left a man numb to stimuli for ten hours. He would recover in two or three days. "Take him to local authority," said Stevens.

He dropped the gun into the holster. The weight was familiar and comforting. He was almost grateful to the drunk, who had triggered this opportunity to establish his persona now.

"Post regulations prohibit firearms and booze," he said firmly. "Either will interrupt orderly progression of our business. Keep in mind that this post exists at your option. Somebody has got to run interstellar transportation, and Earth alone has the radiation belts that make congruency possible. If you don't like our established obligations, your recourse is to terminate the agreement, work for modification from your authority and my own, or develop another method of transport." Three years of school with the quickest kind of pragmatic opportunists made him immune to sneers, smiles, frowns, or applause. "A Factor has discretionary powers, but I'll operate by the book until discretion indicates otherwise."

"Snot-nosed kid!" shouted a woman.

"One month disbarment," said Stevens. He waited while handlers hustled her through the passage under the seats. "Other comment?" He waited. He walked backstage, put his keycard in the door to the Factor's quarters, and shoved in his locker. He closed the door.

He sat in the middle of the floor and howled.

As Factor, he was at the focus of the love-hate that men felt for the Mother of the Stars, the Octopus of Space, cosmocentric Earth. Isserman mourned his own condition, alone, alone.

After the first dozen planets were settled, it became obvious that the paraphernalia of advanced society was too expensive to drop into the stellar void. The emphasis was drastically shifted to any group of a quarter-million people or more who wanted a world. Two hundred and fifty thousand made a reasonable minimum gene pool. The basic agricultural equipment was comparatively inexpensive. Each planet was decreed self-sufficient, to wither or flourish by its own efforts. The trickle of trade that could be handled by one Factor kept a commodity flow open and covered handling costs. Exchange of information by mail was unrestricted.

And he was the man responsible for a planet's exterior communication. He was the link to Earth and some four thousand planets. He was the appointed arbiter, the bottleneck, the master of the post, the focus of resentment. He dumped this overwhelming burden on the carpet and howled.

"You got a problem, Buddy?"

A girl leaned against the doorjamb. She was dressed in the local costume, dark-blue tapered pants and a bandana-print shirt with pearl buttons, but she carried Earth pistols at her hips. Her shoes were pointed-toe boots with high heels. "Got a thorn in your paw? Let Mama—"

He jumped to his feet. "Who're you?"

"Cathy Suddon. I'm the new housekeeper."

"What's 'housekeeper'?"

"I been out shopping. My feet hurt." She hopped on one foot and then the other, pulling off her boots. With the six-centimeter heels her eyes came to his chin. Now he could see that she was a small girl with long legs and a short, trim waist. Her mouth was wide and her lips smooth. She carried her head at a jaunty angle.

"Somebody has to buy food and fix it, Shorty, see the clothes are washed, and scrub bad ideas. Somebody has to keep the post and the planet going. Somebody's got to be responsible for the whole thing, to check and balance and make it work. That's me." She walked to him on stockinged feet and infringed his personal space. "Who's going to take care of you when you get sick of yourself? Who's going to tinker inside your head when you're out of sync and untrack your tangled feet? Me. I'm one of the one-to-one. I'm here to keep this operation in a condition of fine tune. What do you want to eat?"

"Th-thistles!"

"No local artichokes—I'll fix a snack. Where you going?"

"I'm going to inspect Ruh-ruh-ruh . . ." He fled. He stumbled down the hall and out the back door as she called after him that lunch would be ready in ten minutes.

He stood on the loading dock at the far end of the post, with receiving stalls on either side. The native construction was built to join. It was hot and dusty in the pillared log warehouse. A team of horses stood half-asleep, harnessed to a wagon backed to the dock. Men's voices came from one of the storage rooms lining the sides of the barn. Dust motes idled in thin shafts of sunlight through the shingled roof. He leaned against the wall. What color were her eyes? He had no idea. Responsibility and obligation. He groaned.

"Any problem has solutions," he argued silently with the near horse. "Most are unacceptable. I could lock her outside. I could go native. I could always kill myself." The horses sighed and shifted weight. "I could go along. And what's so great about solutions?" he said wearily. "Add apples and oranges to make fruit salad . . ."

A door opened. A man with bowed legs and a leather face walked to the dock and introduced himself as Receiving Chief. He said things were slow, with no exports at the other end. The mail came in, and that was the most of it. He allowed that this was a helluva way to run a railroad. Stevens cheered up at his impersonal pique and said take all the considerations and figure a better way.

He returned to his quarters and picked at the lunch Cathy Suddon had prepared. She said, "You don't like my cooking." He said it was delicious. Her face was woebegone. He snatched his hand away from her shoulder before he patted it. He washed his face and went into the post. Her hair was thick and soft, brown and shining and short. Her eyes? Whatever color, and woebegone, forget it.

The seats were filled with people. The buzz diminished as the First Clerk greeted him. He was a scoop-nosed man with a broom moustache and drooping eyelids. "I'm Moberley Driggs. What happened was, the Mayor let anybody in promiscuous out of the heat. So me and the boys cleared the post and started over. Got numbers drawn, ready to go. Mail's on the line. How long you figure to run?"

Stevens said, "Mail first, and then let's see how it goes. I'm eight personal hours ahead of Laramie time. Tomorrow we'll go on schedule."

"Don't you think maybe. . . ?" began Driggs. Stevens looked at him with level eyes. All interior personnel was appointed and paid by the Factor in local funds. "Um . . . yessir," said Driggs.

Stevens keycarded the console and studied the board. A red eye showed in the BITE panel. "What's with B dock?" Driggs said a new handler had run a skid out of the post, and a gang was carrying it back right now. Stevens looked at him thoughtfully. The Built-In-Testing Equipment panel went green. "I want an efficient, clean, no-foolishness operation," he mused aloud. "I didn't figure on any personnel changes for a week at least." He did not wait for an answer. He turned to the board, checked the mail in the eleventh stall, and pushed the set key for Earth. The mail vanished. The booth gate unlocked.

"Lot one!" announced Driggs in loud relief. "Ten sacks of gold. Shipper, Bye Tompkins. Come *on,* Bye, let's have the destination slip, just don't stand there."

Tompkins sidled up to the console. He had unblinking owl eyes. "Lookee, Factor," he said, "it's not fair. You people take your tenth off the top, and I got caught in the floods last spring in the Poconos, and it washed so bad that the gopher holes stood two meters in the air. . . ."

Stevens walked along the ten booths and said, "Number seven." A clerk with pink armbands took the bag to the eleventh booth. Stevens sat at the console and turned to Bye Tompkins. The pickup carried his voice clearly to the spectators. "Ten percent for transportation is more than fair, and you know it, Mr. Tompkins. And you know the odds are in your favor—nine chances out of ten, if you want to gamble. The post bag might be full of rocks. Give me your consignee slip." He set the coordinates for a planet he'd never heard of. He pushed the Execute button when the board went green. The sacks vanished when congruency occurred. The doors swung open.

Lot two was a shipment of wheat in the standard two-meter-cube containers. Stevens directed the ninth to the post booth. The antigrav skid handlers were clumsy, and one man barely escaped being smashed against the wall. Stevens told Driggs to run the bloody momentum training tape for all handlers, and since this would be a short day, get them some practice time later.

Lot three was bundles of furs, and he chose the ninth again.

Lot four was a mixed consignment of ornamental wrought iron. He chose the ninth for the third time.

Lot five was dried beef in containers, and he picked a random number from the console. Six was bulk corn. He took the opportunity to make the standard warning about concealed transmission of humans. No exceptions, the death rate was 100 percent.

Seven was hides, eight was high-grade chrome ore, and nine a single kunsite crystal sixty-eight centimeters long. Stevens took the speculator's bids, but the shipper waited and paid the post 10 percent of the top figure. The man also had the tenth lot, a thirty-four-centimeter crystal, and let it go to the high bidder with a wolfish grin.

A man of rectitude objected to lot eleven, which he said was immoral: leather images for a degenerate religion. Stevens told him that redress lay with the government of Laramie, which controlled both exports and imports. The Factor's business was not censorship. The man grew offensive and was banned for a month.

Lot twelve was leather; thirteen, bundles of herbs; lot fourteen, three boxes of beauty mud consigned by a woman who never should have sold it; lot fifteen, eight wheels of cheese that went to the high bidder.

Sixteen was a doctor of medicine who wanted drugs from Earth to halt an epidemic. He made a powerful plea. Little children were dying. Driggs watched the Factor with speculative eyes. Stevens quite properly offered his personal sympathy. He asked what the doctor or the government or the people involved proposed to trade. He would do everything he could do to expedite the matter. Next lot.

Seventeen was delicately braided stock whips with snappers to snatch a gout of flesh. Eighteen was announced as boxed silver ingots owned by a man with many friends who haw-hawed and hooted when Stevens picked the ninth for the post. The shipper tried to withdraw the remaining boxes, and the Factor cited transportation terms. The man left with his friends, who loudly demanded drinks and wondered what they were going to do on Aldie Eight with that bunch of drek.

Nineteen was another petitioner, who said his spiritual leader was dying on Themie. He wept, and Stevens said that personal transportation was impossible. The man said it wasn't impossible and that all he had to do was step into the Factor's booth. Stevens said that every man was planet-locked by necessity. There were no study commissions, no diplomatic VIP's, no privileged visitors, no tourists.

Each planet made its own destiny, as each planet made its own bureaucracy.

He was very tired, but he gave a short lecture on the history of Earth and the flight from reality by bureaucrats who wanted to do good to other people, and the near-disaster averted—as it turned out—by the discovery of congruity. Despotism, however benevolent, would destroy the development of any people. The uniculture of Earth would stay shattered. This petition was denied, and further petitions of this nature would not be considered.

He locked the console. He said it was one o'clock in the morning for him, and he'd been up since five.

There was no escape when the Mayor of Laramie invited him to the other planetary end of the building to present him with honorary citizenship. The Mayor also gave him a local-time watch with a tooled leather band and said they halfway figured on a banquet to meet prominent citizens. Stevens said he could not do justice to it, and how about tomorrow night? The Mayor agreed. Driggs had his entire crew cleaning and polishing. Isserman went to his quarters.

He sat on the floor.

Cathy Suddon sat cross-legged in front of him. She said she'd watched the monitor while she made a graduation cake. "Sonny, how come you were so mean to the petitioners? Why can't Earth transport people and send drugs and help out?"

His head was on his wrists, hands locked around his knees. He looked at her, unseeing, fading in and out of his eyes.

She said, "I've been in the Jo'burg warehouse and seen those enormous rooms full of things. Thousands of people receiving and classifying and distributing. And Jo'burg is only one of a hundred and twenty-something, so why not give a little to Earth's children, Buster?"

"Cathy. Knock it off."

" 'Buster'? Well, 'Issy' sounds sissy—"

"I hope you're trying to help," he said with plodding exasperation, "because counterirritation is dumb. You've got more shells than a bag of pine nuts, but don't pour 'em on my head when it's a meter off my shoulders. I feel thick as a shadow, scooped like a muskmelon, hollow as a bell. Don't ring on me. When and how did you graduate?"

"Today. I made a plastic bag to cover me. But how can it be right to let children die—?"

"Shut up!" His wavering attention turned hard as fire in a diamond. "The toughest thing for men to learn is not to mess around with other people. That's what school's about, what all the planets are about, what the conscience of man's about: leave other people alone. Inside society, give them the right to be wrong!"

"Oh, Duke." She snuffled and said, "How come you're not shaking anymore?"

He stretched full-length on the floor. "Who said it was easy?" He closed his eyes. "I think it's inside now, not outside so much." His voice turned dim. "We live between sun and sun. Between black and white on a wavery scale . . . in magnificent gray . . ."

"Duke," she said softly, "is it better or worse?"

"All the wise . . . men say this . . . I dunno . . ."

She said, "We'll have our graduation party when you wake up," but he was asleep. She put a pillow under his head and covered him with a blanket and ran a hesitant finger down his cheek and went to frost the cake.

W. Macfarlane writes:

What's to tell about a story?

I'll tell you. It's got to stand on its own feet.

Rudyard Kipling wrote of a limboland where characters live after "The End," and the damned writers forevermore are haunted by their own failures and misconceptions. Surely there's a special level of limbo for people who write science fiction, where worlds bulge like eggs and imaginary societies hang their writers every day at noon, time without end.

Still and all, it's worth the hazard. Even a gimpy world, imperfectly seen, may be as instructive as a funhouse mirror.

In what other kind of writing are we free to consider answers to all the once and future questions? The gimmickry of space elision is an old idea, and fun enough, but granted multitudinous planets, how do you avoid imperial Earth? How to finance colonies? How do you guard against the peril of self-righteousness? Granted the programming of human beings.

When you look around for exemplars of truth and justice, you find that youngsters know the most about these slippery things. Those of

us grown older are less certain and more susceptible to bent principles. If you agree that men must have laws to live together, then
maybe a smart fifteen-year-old is the only one strong enough to carry
the burden. The able are always exploited, and that could be a good
way to program a thinking animal, too.

I am a hot exponent of fiction, and look slaunchwise at people
chained by current fact. How else in a lifetime can you meet so many
people, and in science fiction so many speculations? In a very real
way, we all make our own world, and if the central core of truth is
unapproachable, we'll know more about it the closer we can come to
a spherical survey.

"Escape," the mentally retarded sneer. "Impossibilities!"

What's more unlikely than our meeting in the pages of a book,
both of us in quest of the entertainment that is the first business of
man: quasars and flatworms and human beings are the entertainment of a cosmos programmed for no easy answers.

What a magnificent way to run things, and it's the only game in
town, the funhouse mirror, well worth the peril of Kipling's
limboland—and the story has got to stand on its own feet.

TIMETIPPING

by *Jack Dann*

Since timetipping, everything moved differently. Nothing was for certain, anything could change (depending on your point of view), and almost anything could happen, especially to forgetful old men who often found themselves in the wrong century rather than on the wrong street.

Take Moishe Hodel, who was too old and fat to be climbing ladders; yet he insisted on climbing to the roof of his suburban house so that he could sit on the top of a stone-tuff church in Goreme six hundred years in the past. Instead of praying, he would sit and watch monks. He claimed that since time and space were *meshuggeneh* (what's crazy in any other language?), he would search for a quick and Godly way to travel to synagogue. Let the goyim take the trains.

Of course, Paley Litwak, who was old enough to know something, knew from nothing when the world changed and everything went blip. His wife disappeared, and a new one returned in her place. A new Golde, one with fewer lines and dimples, one with starchy white hair and missing teeth.

Upon arrival all she said was, "This is almost right. You're almost the same, Paley. Still, you always go to shul?"

"Shul?" Litwak asked, resolving not to jump and scream and ask God for help. With all the changing, Litwak would stand straight and wait for God. "What's a shul?"

"You mean you don't know from shul, and yet you wear such a yarmulke on your head?" She pulled her babushka through her fingers. "A shul. A synagogue, a temple. Do you pray?"

Litwak was not a holy man, but he could hold up his head and not be afraid to wink at God. Certainly he prayed. And in the following weeks Litwak found himself in shul more often than not—so she had an effect on him; after all, she was his wife. Where else was there to be? With God he had a one-way conversation—from Litwak's mouth to God's ears—but at home it was turned around. There, Litwak had no mouth, only ears. How can you talk with a woman who thinks fornicating with other men is holy?

But Litwak was a survivor; with the rest of the world turned over and doing flip-flops, he remained the same. Not once did he trip into a different time, not even an hour did he lose or gain; and the only places he went were those he could walk to. He was the exception to the rule. The rest of the world was adrift; everyone was swimming by, blipping out of the past or future and into the present here or who-knows-where.

It was a new world. Every street was filled with commerce, every night was carnival. Days were built out of strange faces, and nights went by so fast that Litwak remained in the synagogue just to smooth out time. But there was no time for Litwak, just services, and prayers, and holy smells.

Yet the world went on. Business almost as usual. There were still rabbis and chasids and grocers and cabalists; fat Hoffa, a congregant with a beard that would make a storybook Baal Shem jealous, even claimed that he knew a cabalist that had invented a new gemetria for foretelling everything concerning money.

"So who needs gemetria?" Litwak asked. "Go trip tomorrow and find out what's doing."

"Wrong," said Hoffa as he draped his prayer shawl over his arm, waiting for a lull in the conversation to say the holy words before putting on the tallis. "It does no good to go there if you can't get back. And when you come back, everything is changed, anyway. Who do you know that's really returned? Look at you, you didn't have gray hair and earlocks yesterday."

"Then that wasn't *me* you saw. Anyway, if everybody but me is tripping and tipping back and forth, in and out of the devil's mouth, so to speak, then what time do you have to use this new gemetria?"

Hoffa paused and said, "So the world must go on. You think it stops because heaven shakes it . . ."

"You're so sure it's heaven?"

". . . but *you* can go see the cabalist; you're stuck in the present, you sit on one line. Go talk to him; he speaks a passable Yiddish, and his wife walks around with a bare behind."

"So how do you know he's there now?" asked Litwak. "They come and go. Perhaps a Neanderthal or a *klezmer* from the future will take his place."

"So? If he isn't there, what matter? At least you know he's somewhere else. No? Everything goes on. Nothing gets lost. Everything fits, somehow. That's what's important."

It took Litwak quite some time to learn the new logic of the times, but once learned, it became an advantage—especially when his pension checks didn't arrive. Litwak became a fair second-story man, but he robbed only according to society's logic and his own ethical system: one-half for the shul and the rest for Litwak.

Litwak found himself spending more time on the streets than in the synagogue, but by standing still on one line he could not help but learn. He was putting the world together, seeing where it was, would be, might be, might not be. When he became confused, he used logic.

And the days passed faster, even with praying and sleeping nights in the shul for more time. Everything whirled around him. The city was a moving kaleidoscope of colors from every period of history, all melting into different costumes as the thieves and diplomats and princes and merchants strolled down the cobbled streets of Brooklyn.

With prisms for eyes, Litwak would make his way home through the crowds of slaves and serfs and commuters. Staking out fiefdoms in Brooklyn was difficult, so the slaves momentarily ran free, only to trip somewhere else where they would be again grabbed and raped and worked until they could trip again, and again and again until old logic fell apart. King's Highway was a bad part of town. The Boys' Club had been turned into a slave market and gallows room.

Litwak's tiny apartment was the familiar knot at the end of the rope. Golde had changed again, but it was only a slight change. Golde kept changing as her different time lines met in Litwak's kitchen, and bedroom. A few Goldes he liked, but change was gradual, and Goldes tended to run down. So for every sizzling Golde with blond-dyed hair, he suffered fifty or a thousand Goldes with missing teeth and croaking voices.

The latest Golde had somehow managed to buy a parrakeet, which turned into a bluejay, a parrot with red feathers, and an ostrich, which provided supper. Litwak had discovered that smaller animals usually timetipped at a faster rate than men and larger animals; perhaps, he thought, it was a question of metabolism. Golde killed the ostrich before something else could take its place. Using logic and compassion, Litwak blessed it to make it kosher—the rabbi was not to be found, and he was a new chasid (imagine) who didn't know Talmud from soap opera; worse yet, he read Hebrew with a Brooklyn twang, not unheard of with such new rabbis. Better that Litwak bless his own meat; let the rabbi bless goyish food.

Another meal with another Golde, this one dark-skinned and pimply, overweight and sagging, but her eyes were the color of the ocean seen from an airplane on a sunny day. Litwak could not concentrate on food. There was a pitched battle going on two streets away, and he was worried about getting to shul.

"More soup?" Golde asked.

She had pretty hands, too, Litwak thought. "No, thank you," he said before she disappeared.

In her place stood a squat peasant woman, hands and ragged dress still stained with rich, black soil. She didn't scream or dash around or attack Litwak; she just wrung her hands and scratched her crotch. She spoke the same language, in the same low tones, that Litwak had listened to for several nights in shul. An Egyptian named Rhampsinitus had found his way into the synagogue, thinking it was a barbarian temple for Baiti, the clown god.

"Baiti?" she asked, her voice rising. "Baiti," she answered, convinced.

So here it ends, thought Litwak, just beginning to recognize the rancid odor in the room as sweat.

Litwak ran out of the apartment before she turned into something more terrible. Changes, he had expected. Things change and shift—that's logic. But not so fast. He had slowed down natural processes in the past (he thought), but now he was slipping, sinking like the rest of them. A bald Samson adrift on a raft.

Time isn't a river, Litwak thought as he pushed his way through larger crowds, all adrift, shouting, laughing, blipping in and out, as old men were replaced by ancient monsters and fears; but dinosaurs occupied too much space, always slipped, and could enter the present world only in torn pieces—a great ornithischian wing, a stegosaurian tail with two pairs of bony spikes, or, perhaps, a four-foot-long tyrannosaurus' head.

Time is a hole, Litwak thought. He could feel its pull.

Whenever Litwak touched a stranger—someone who had come too many miles and minutes to recognize where he was—there was a pop and a skip, and the person disappeared. Litwak had disposed of three gilded ladies, an archdeacon, a birdman, a knight with Norman casque, and several Sumerian serfs in this manner. He almost tripped over a young boy who was doggedly trying to extract a tooth from the neatly severed head of a tyrannosaurus.

The boy grabbed Litwak's leg, racing a few steps on his knees to do so, and bit him. Screaming in pain, Litwak pulled his leg away, felt an unfamiliar pop, and found the synagogue closer than he had remembered. But this wasn't his shul; it was a cathedral, a caricature of his beloved synagogue.

"Catch him," shouted the boy with an accent so thick that Litwak could barely make out what he said. "He's the thief who steals from the shul."

"*Gevalt,* this is the wrong place," Litwak said, running toward the cathedral.

A few hands reached for him, but then he was inside. There, in God's salon, everything was, would be, and had to be the same: large clerestory windows; double aisles for Thursday processions; radiating chapels modeled after Amiens 1247; and nave, choir, and towers, all styled to fit the stringent requirements of halakic law.

Over the altar, just above the holy ark, hung a bronze plate representing the egg of Khumu, who created the substance of the world on a potter's wheel. And standing on the plush pulpit, his square face buried in a prayer book, was Rabbi Rhampsinitus.

"Holy, holy, holy," he intoned. Twenty-five old men sang and wailed and prayed on cue. They all had beards and earlocks and wore conical caps and prayer garments.

"That's him," shouted the boy.

Litwak ran to the pulpit and kissed the holy book.

"Thief, robber, purloiner, depredator."

"Enough," Rhampsinitus said. "The service is concluded. God has not winked his eye. Make it good," he told the boy.

"Well, look who it is."

Rhampsinitus recognized Litwak at once. "So it is the thief. Stealer from God's coffers, you have been excommunicated as a second-story man."

"But I haven't stolen from the shul. This is not even my time or place."

"He speaks a barbarian tongue," said Rhampsinitus. "What's shul?"

"This Paley Litwak is twice, or thrice, removed," interrupted Moishe Hodel, who could timetip at will to any synagogue God chose to place around him. "He's new. Look and listen. *This* Paley Litwak probably does not steal from the synagogue. Can you blame him for what someone else does?"

"Moishe Hodel?" asked Litwak. "Are you the same one I knew from Beth David on King's Highway?"

"Who knows?" said Hodel. "I know a Beth David, but not on

King's Highway, and I know a Paley Litwak who was stuck in time and had a wife named Golde who raised hamsters."

"That's close, but—"

"So don't worry. I'll speak for you. It takes a few hours to pick up the slang, but it's like Yinglish, only drawled out and spiced with too many Egyptisms."

"Stop blaspheming," said Rhampsinitus. "Philosophy and logic are very fine indeed," he said to Hodel. "But this is a society of law, not philosophers, and law demands reparations."

"But I have money," said Litwak.

"There's your logic," said Rhampsinitus. "Money, especially such barbarian tender as yours, cannot replace the deed. Private immorality and public indecency are one and the same."

"He's right," said Hodel with a slight drawl.

"Jail the tergiversator," said the boy.

"Done," answered Rhampsinitus. He made a holy sign and gave Litwak a quick blessing. Then the boy's sheriffs dragged him away.

"Don't worry, Paley," shouted Moishe Hodel. "Things change."

Litwak tried to escape from the sheriffs, but he could not change times. It's only a question of will, he told himself. With God's help, he could initiate a change and walk, or slip, into another century, a friendlier time.

But not yet. Nothing shifted; they walked a straight line to the jail, a large pyramid still showing traces of its original limestone casing.

"Here we are," said one of the sheriffs. "This is a humble town. We don't need ragabrash and riffraff—it's enough we have foreigners. So timetip or slip or flit somewhere else. There's no other way out of this depository."

They deposited him in a narrow passageway and dropped the entrance stone behind him.

It was hard to breathe, and the damp air stank. It was completely dark. Litwak could not see his hands before his eyes.

Gottenyu, he thought, as he huddled on the cold stone floor. For a penny they plan to incarcerate me. He recited the *Shma Yisroel* and kept repeating it to himself, ticking off the long seconds with each syllable.

For two days he prayed; at least it seemed like two days. Perhaps it was four hours. When he was tired of praying, he cursed Moishe Hodel, wishing him hell and broken fingers. Litwak sneezed, developed a nervous cough, and his eyes became rheumy. "It's God's will," he said aloud.

Almost in reply, a thin faraway voice sang, "Oh, my goddess, oh, my goddess, oh, my goddess, Clem-en-tine!"

It was a familiar folk tune, sung in an odd Spanish dialect. But Litwak could understand it, for his mother's side of the family spoke in Ladino, the vernacular of Spanioli Jews.

So there, he thought. He felt the change. Once he had gained God's patience, he could slip, tip, and stumble away.

Litwak followed the voice. The floor began to slope upward as he walked through torchlit corridors and courtyards and rooms. In some places, not yet hewn into living quarters, stalactite and stalagmite remained. Some of the rooms were decorated with wall paintings of clouds, lightning, the sun, and masked dancers. In one room was a frieze of a great plumed serpent; in another were life-size mountain lions carved from lava. But none of the rooms were occupied.

He soon found the mouth of the cave. The bright sunlight blinded him for an instant.

"I've been waiting for you," said Castillo Moldanado in a variation of Castilian Spanish. "You're the third. A girl arrived yesterday, but she likes to keep to herself."

"Who are you?" asked Litwak.

"A visitor, like you." Moldanado picked at a black mole under his eye and smoothed his dark, thinning hair.

Litwak's eyes became accustomed to the sunlight. Before him was desert. Hills of cedar and piñon were mirages in the sunshine. In the far distance, mesa and butte overlooked red creeks and dry washes. This was a thirsty land of dust and sand and dirt and sun, broken only by a few brown fields, a ranch, or an occasional trading post and mission. But to his right and left, and hidden behind him, pueblos thrived on the faces of sheer cliffs. Cliff dwellings and cities made of smooth-hewn stone commanded valley and desert.

"It looks dead," Moldanado said. "But all around you is life. The Indians are all over the cliffs and desert. Their home is the rock itself. Behind you is Cliff Palace, which contains one hundred and fifty rooms. And they have rock cities in Cañon del Muerto and, farther south, in Walnut Canyon."

"I see no one here but us," Litwak said.

"They're hiding," said Moldanado. "They see the change and think we're gods. They're afraid of another black kachina, an evil spirit."

"Ah," Litwak said. "A dybbuk."

"You'll see natives soon enough. Ayoyewe will be here shortly to rekindle the torches, and for the occasion, he'll dress in his finest furs and turkey feathers. They call this cave Keet Seel, mouth of the gods. It was given to me. And I give it to you."

"Soon there will be more natives about, and more visitors. We'll change the face of their rocks and force them out. With greed."

"And logic," said Litwak.

Moldanado was right. More visitors came every day and settled in the desert and caves and pueblos. Romans, Serbs, Egyptians, Americans, Skymen, Mormons, Baalists, and Trackers brought culture and religion and weapons. They built better buildings, farmed, bartered, stole, prayed, invented, and fought until they were finally visited by governors and diplomats. But that changed, too, when everyone else began to timetip.

Jews also came to the pueblos and caves. They came from different places and times, bringing their conventions, babel, tragedies, and hopes. Litwak hoped for a Maimonides, a Moses ben Nachman, a Luria, even a Schwartz, but there were no great sages to be found, only Jews. And Litwak was the first. He directed, instigated, ordered, soothed, and founded a minion for prayer. When they grew into a full-time congregation, built a shul and elected a rabbi, they gave Litwak the honor of sitting on the pulpit in a plush-velvet chair.

Litwak was happy. He had prayer, friends, and authority.

Nighttime was no longer dark. It was a circus of laughter and trade. Everything sparkled with electric light and prayer. The Indians joined the others, merged, blended, were wiped out. Even a few Jews disappeared. It became faddish to wear Indian clothes and feathers.

Moldanado was always about now, teaching and leading, for he knew the land and native customs. He was a natural politico; when Litwak's shul was finished, he even attended a mairev service. It was then that he told Litwak about "Forty-nine" and Clementine.

"What about that song?" Litwak had asked.

"You know the tune."

"But not the words."

"Clementine was the goddess of Los Alamos," Moldanado said. "She was the first nuclear reactor in the world to utilize fissionable material. It blew up, of course. 'Forty-nine' was the code name for the project that exploded the first atom bomb. But I haven't felt right about incorporating 'Forty-nine' into the song."

"I don't think this is a proper subject to discuss in God's house," Litwak said. "This is a place of prayer, not bombs."

"But this is also Los Alamos."

"Then we must pray harder," Litwak said.

"Have you ever heard of the atom bomb?" asked Moldanado.

"No," said Litwak, turning the pages in his prayer book.

Moldanado found time to introduce Litwak to Baptista Founce, the second visitor to arrive in Los Alamos. She was dark and fragile and reminded Litwak of his first Golde. But she was also a shikseh who wore a gold cross around her neck. She teased, chased, and taunted Litwak until he had her behind the shul in daylight.

Thereafter, he did nothing but pray. He starved himself, beat his chest, tore his clothes, and waited on God's patience. The shul was being rebuilt, so Litwak took to praying in the desert. When he returned to town for food and rest, he could not even find the shul. Everything was changing.

Litwak spent most of his time in the desert, praying. He prayed for a sign and tripped over a trachodon's head that was stuck in the sand.

So it changes, he thought, as he stared at the rockscape before him. He found himself atop a ridge, looking down on an endless field of rocks, a stone tableau of waves in a gray sea. To his right was a field of cones. Each cone cast a flat black shadow. But behind him, cliffs of soft tuff rose out of the stone sea. A closer look at the rock revealed hermitages and monasteries cut into the living stone.

Litwak sighed as he watched a group of monks waiting their turn to climb a rope ladder into a monastic compound. They spoke in a strange tongue and crossed themselves before they took to the ladder.

There'll be no shul here, he said to himself. This is my punishment. A dry goyish place. But there was no thick, rich patina of sophisticated culture here. This was a simple place, a rough, real hinterland, not yet invaded by dybbuks and kachinas.

Litwak made peace with the monks and spent his time sitting on the top of a stone-tuff church in Goreme six hundred years in the past. He prayed, and sat, and watched the monks. Slowly he regained his will, and the scenery changed.

There was a monk that looked like Rhampsinitus.

Another looked like Moldanado.

At least, Litwak thought, there could be no Baptista Founce here. With that (and by an act of unconscious will), he found himself in his shul on King's Highway.

"Welcome back, Moishe," said Hoffa. "You should visit this synagogue more often."

"Moishe?" asked Litwak.

"Well, aren't you Moishe Hodel, who timetips to synagogue?"

"I'm Paley Litwak. No one else." Litwak looked at his hands. They were his own.

But he was in another synagogue. "Holy, holy, holy," Rabbi Rhampsinitus intoned. Twenty-five old men sang and wailed and prayed on cue. They all had beards and earlocks and wore conical caps and prayer garments.

"So, Moishe," said Rhampsinitus, "you still return. You really have mastered God's chariot."

Litwak stood still, decided, and then nodded his head and smiled. He thought of the shul he had built and found himself sitting in his plush chair. But Baptista Founce was sitting in the first row praying.

Before she could say, "Paley," he was sitting on a stone-tuff church six hundred years in the past.

Perhaps tomorrow he'd go to shul. Today he'd sit and watch monks.

Jack Dann writes:

I was born in 1945 in Johnson City, New York. I attended the Manlius Military Academy, studied drama at Hofstra University, and received a B.A. in political science from the State University of New York at Binghamton (Harpur College). I studied law at St. John's University in New York and did graduate work in comparative literature at SUNY, Binghamton. I dropped out of law school to become a "full-time writer" and sold short fiction to Damon Knight's Orbit, *Robert Silverberg's* New Dimensions, *Harlan Ellison's* Last Dangerous Visions, New Worlds, *and many other anthologies. My first anthology,* Wandering Stars, *a collection of Jewish fantasy and science fiction, was published in 1974 by Harper & Row. Forthcoming are* Faster Than Light *(with co-editor George Zebrowski) from Harper & Row,* Future Power *(with co-editor Gardner Dozois) from Random House, and* The Speculative Fiction Yearbook *(with co-editor David Harris from Vintage Books). A book of poetry,* Christs and Other Poems, *is forthcoming this year from Bellevue Press.*

I am currently working on a novel for Gold Medal Books based on my novella "Junction," which was a Nebula Awards finalist in 1973.

Another novel, Starhiker, *will be published by Bobbs-Merrill. I am also editing an anthology of novellas on the theme of immortality for Harper & Row; was the managing editor of the Science Fiction Writers of America* Bulletin *from 1970 to 1974; and am a member of the Science Fiction Writers Speakers Bureau, the World Future Society, and the Mark Twain Society (honorary). I have taught science fiction at Cornell University and Broome Community College and also writing at BCC.*

I have appeared on radio and educational television and on panels at UCLA and the Center for Integrative Studies (SUNY, Binghamton), directed by John McHale. I have at one time or another worked as a law investigator, motel clerk, soup distributor, ghost writer, rug layer, window washer, beerhall piano player, café barker, promo man for a recording artist, and in public relations.

ENCOUNTER WITH A
CARNIVORE

by Joseph Green

The two scout ships slipped below the interference of the thunderstorm almost simultaneously, detected each other, and instantly went to battle mode. The alien wreck was somewhere between them, hidden in the thick jungle below.

The logic of the situation was inevitable, the reaction foreordained. The battle program in each computer took charge, performing an immediate all-sensor scan followed by a probability analysis. Each then devised its first tactical maneuver. The recommendations appeared on the emergency screens of the two pilot consoles. Ten seconds was allowed for the slower biological computers in the heads of the pilots to override, or the plan was automatically confirmed. At the end of the waiting period the two scouts shot toward each other, at the max accel the pilots could safely endure.

As the small ships flashed past one another, each turned off its shield for a few milliseconds at the time in a random program. During these off intervals each computer fired a series of discharges from its ship's discrete magnetic-field generator. When almost through the two programs, each scout finally caught the other with its shield down.

All electronic controls on both ships were fused into instant immobility, except those in the separately protected pilot-escape modules. Each pilot then made the only decision possible, and pressed the two red eject buttons in the proper sequence. And several seconds later two large parachutes opened automatically, and two living pilots descended to the ground, to be swallowed by the waiting green jungle.

Neil Jones hung by his hands from the bottom rim of the escape module, kicking vigorously to start himself oscillating. After several gradually widening swings he was able to lock his legs over a thick limb. He released the escape module and let it fall back, to hang suspended by the ripped and tattered parachute. He was almost thirty meters above the ground.

Keeping a tight grip with his legs, Jones worked his way slowly down the limb to the trunk, then stood up. His uniform boots and spacesuit were not designed for tree climbing. The bole was too thick to grip with arms and legs. To reach the ground, he had to trust his eighty kilos to the vines that wrapped around it in tangled profusion.

The vines proved unexpectedly strong. When his feet touched soil, Jones breathed a big sigh of relief. The Il-Strath, with their feline ancestry and still usable claws, could climb with ease. He had watched Y-Sith's slim form scamper up several trees during the past year. For him it was more difficult.

The jungle was quiet. The animals who had been surprised by his noisy crashing in the treetops were still hidden. And thinking of Y-Sith reminded Jones that he had to get moving. The first one to the wreck could claim it for the home government.

But first he slipped the escape-module emergency pack off his back and opened it. The laser pistol with its separate belt went around his waist. Acting on a program he had memorized a dozen times, but never used except in practice checks, he looked for the spare charge; it was in the pack. Next he slipped the insect-repellent vibrator in his pocket, and swallowed the red capsule that contained a live virus. The strain was one virulent enough to kill any germs he breathed in, but harmless to humans. The concentrates, emergency handtools, protectosuit, and medkit were all there. His wrist sensor indicated that the automatic distress-and-locator signal in the module overhead was steadily sending the bad news back to headquarters.

Jones did a final mental run-through of the emergency planetary-landing procedure. Except for the option of putting on the protectosuit, he had completed all suggested precautions. Now he had to try to reach the wreck before that Il-Strath pilot got there first.

Which aroused an immediate and haunting question. Could the other pilot have been Y-Sith? The timing that had made him the only one available to check out this discovery—just starting leave after a year of shared patrol—might also have applied to his Il-Strath shipmate. If the cats were as shorthanded of pilots as the humans, it quite likely was.

Theoretically, whoever reached the wreck first could claim it, this being a neutral primitive planet. In fact, it belonged to anyone who had the strength to seize and hold it. The agreement under which human and Il-Strath made joint patrols of uncivilized planets did not apply to such discoveries.

Jones lifted the pack to his back and slipped both arms through the straps. There was almost surely going to be a fight, one of the thousands of such encounters never officially acknowledged by the quarreling species. He set off, walking as fast as the tangled ground growth permitted, glancing occasionally at his locator and keeping one hand near the laser. He hoped, oh gods how he hoped, the other pilot had not been Y-Sith!

Y-Sith moved easily through the undergrowth, breathing deeply of the fresh air, admiring the colors of the bright tropical flowers. The gentle breeze carried a hundred different scents, most of them pleasing to the nose. The day was warm, but not uncomfortably so. It was a pleasure to be out of the confining boots, to feel the resilience of growing plants beneath bare feet. This was like being free to roam through a hunting park for an unlimited time, with no worry about making your kill in the allotted span.

Y-Sith stepped soundlessly past a thick growth of weeds. Ahead was an open glade, its grass dappled by sunlight slipping past a high roof of locking branches. A small herbivore was feeding at its far edge. The creature was a long-legged rodent, one of the billions who served no purpose except to become meat for the hunters of the galaxy. A puff of breeze brought its scent across the grass, the smell similar to uncounted lifeforms on a thousand worlds—yet each always subtly different and unique.

Saliva suddenly filled Y-Sith's mouth. To drop the emergency pack; to stretch lean muscles in the joy of chase; to follow the twisting, dodging animal; to inevitably close, talons grasping, the teeth in the furry throat, a quick clean kill, and the taste of blood and fresh meat . . . No, too dangerous to eat the flesh of untested animals. No matter how tired One grew of cooked meat, how alike it all seemed when heated until flavor and texture were lost, still it was safest. Most wild animals carried unknown germs.

Y-Sith stepped forward. The rodent glanced up, saw the tall and unrecognizable figure, and hesitated. And then some ancient instinct identified "hunter," no matter that the stranger was alien to this world. The herbivore turned and loped hurriedly away, glancing back over one shoulder.

Y-Sith suppressed the almost automatic desire to pursue, sighed, and resumed walking. One had to give up a great deal to become civilized. Often the thought came that perhaps the joint human-Il-Strath contact missions took away from primitive peoples as much as they gave.

But that was a disloyal thought. The group share-mother would never approve it in communion. Human and Il-Strath had been locked in this grim posture of cooperation-competition for some forty years now, with little hope of a change in the near future. The contest must go on, until a true peace developed or the humans were driven back from the stars.

At least One could hope the person struggling toward the wreck from the opposite direction was not N-Jones. But if the humans had as few trained pilots as the Il-Strath, then it most likely was. And that would be a shame. To have to fight with N-Jones if he reached the wreck first, to perhaps kill—it was a dreadful thought. The idea that One could learn affection for a hairless human had seemed preposterous before the joint patrol began, but over the months of shared adventure and danger that liking had slowly appeared, until in the end it was perhaps even more. No, killing Jones would be a difficult task. But if duty compelled . . .

Y-Sith stepped up the pace. Best try to reach the wreck, claim it, and then worry over whether the opposing human was indeed N-Jones.

Jones worked his way through an unusually thick tangle, and into trouble. A rumbling growl of warning sounded just to his left. Jones froze, but he was too close, and that was the wrong reaction. The growl changed to a fighting snarl, and seconds later the carnivore who had been sleeping by last night's kill came charging through the brush. It was a wide-bodied, massively muscled creature built like a tank armed with teeth, running low to the ground.

Jones had drawn his pistol after the first growl. He took careful aim, waiting to be certain of a clear shot—a miss could be fatal. The heavy form crashed over the last bush, three meters away, and he burned a hole through one eye to the savage brain.

The four crooked legs kept the dying killer moving. Jones sprang to one side and let it pass. A few meters farther on it stopped, shivered violently for a few seconds, then collapsed in a heap.

Reaction set in, and Jones shivered himself. When his heart slowed to only racing speed, he started walking again.

He thought of Y-Sith, and felt a small stir of envy. This was just the environment she loved, a wild and savage place where she would feel immediately at home. Their year together had taken them to many such uncivilized planets. And she was usually better at dealing with primitive peoples than he, regardless of their physical build. It seemed to be a quality of the mind, a more direct contact with the basic drives of animal life.

Yet the Il-Strath were as capable of abstract thought as Man. Their theories of math were subtly different, and yet beautifully symmetrical and complex. The two species had contributed equally to the design of these jointly operated small scout ships. Their civilization was fully comparable to Man's in technology, though some of their personal habits seemed savage and revolting. Y-Sith had told him that their favorite sport was chasing down animals left wild in parks, killing them with short but still sharp fangs, eating the meat raw and bloody . . . . Jones shivered again.

When Y-Sith had learned how the controlled hunting affected Jones, she asked how anyone could make a habit of using baited hooks to tempt creatures as stupid and harmless as fish. And fishing was still the most popular sport on Earth.

Besides, Il-Strath fangs barely extended past the other teeth, and did not show in a normal smile. Only when the pink, down-turned full lips drew far back in anger—or passion!—had he noticed Y-Sith's carnivorous dentition. In repose her hairless face seemed almost human, the feline ancestry obvious only in the slanted purple eyes and pointed, flexible ears. She wore her hair long, rising in a high crest of rich, brownish red shot through with white, sweeping back from the high forehead and cascading down the back and sides . . . hair that rippled and moved like a living animal when she tossed her head . . . the very white skin of her face never tanned . . . the short, fine hair that covered her body felt like mole fur to the touch, smoother and sleeker than human skin.

Funny, how impossible and alien such a creature could be on first meeting, and how easily he had learned to accept the differences between them—even developing a heightened appreciation of the strangeness. Il-Strath wore a body harness, but no clothes. Y-Sith was almost two meters in height, taller than himself, and very slim. She looked fragile, easily broken, a person that one hard fist could sweep away in collapse. In fact, the streaked-brown-and-red roan fur hid a body of spring steel and powerful muscles. He could lift a greater weight, but Y-Sith could jump her own height in 1G, bound twice that distance forward, and run like a charging lion.

And she was the loveliest woman he had ever seen, on any world.

The two breasts were small, hardly bulging her chest, but the nipples were large and protruded past the fur. To Jones they seemed sexy. If his mind was not occupied, he could become aroused just looking at them. To Y-Sith, and all other Il-Strath, there was nothing erotic about nipples. Nor was there any importance in the fur-covered genitals, though they were prominent on the males. To an Il-Strath, sexual excitement was a matter of intention. They seldom grew amorous through accidental stimuli.

The Il-Strath had evolved on their planet along the same evolutionary path followed by the hominids of Earth. Physically the two species were far more alike than different, so much so that a strong attraction was possible. But culturally they were far apart, and these joint crews used to contact emerging intelligent species were the best cooperation to date. So far, genuine military conflict had been avoided, but a hundred unreported and unacknowledged battles had occurred in the hidden corners of explored space.

There had been many times when Jones thought he and Y-Sith were at the height of a peaceful joint endeavor, only to discover violence lurking close beneath her surface. He rubbed the claw marks on both buttocks, and felt a sympathetic twitch in the scarred skin across the backs of his calves. *She liked to grasp a lover on each buttock, pulling hard, while the long slim legs rose high above their heaving bodies, bent at the knees, the thin feet resting on his calves. And at the height of passion the extensible claws came curving out, gripping and digging into his flesh!*

Though they were not as long and sharp as the killing weapons of their distant ancestors, the Il-Strath claws could still hurt. Yet he had never seen Y-Sith use teeth or claws in a fight. The weapons provided by science were far more potent, and the Il-Strath used them with great skill. Their teeth were employed only for recreational kills, and the claws as the final involuntary caress in a *kil'a'cu* session.

Jones had barely noticed the scarring at the times it happened. But over their last five months on patrol he had been heavily marked by Y-Sith.

Y-Sith glanced at her wrist locator, estimating the distance covered. The other scout had gone down considerably closer to the wreck. In open country One could easily outpace a human, but in this thick jungle she was probably no more than twenty percent faster. Which meant the other pilot was going to reach the wreck first.

That could be an advantage. The first arrival had to occupy the structure, then defend it. His location would be known. The opponent could choose the time and place for an attack.

The Il-Strath had a prior claim; it had been their ship that found the wreckage. But the coldly efficient humans had intercepted the message reporting the giant find, including the fact that the solar observatory making the discovery was not equipped to land. Since the hard-won agreement on alien artifacts specifically required actual possession, the grasping apes had promptly dispatched a scout ship. The scouts were not only jointly designed but identically equipped, leading to highly predictable outcomes when they battled each other.

But on the ground it was a different matter. The humans admittedly functioned well in their vast concrete cities, where the environment they had created was as alien to nature as themselves. Here in the jungles of the galaxy, only the Il-Strath still felt at home.

The humans were cunning, though. Earthmen made a habit of attempting to enforce an agreement even if the circumstances that produced it had changed. They tried to insist that new facts did not justify unilateral amendments to an existing understanding, that both parties had to agree to the changes before they became effective. This was a matter hard for an Il-Strath to grasp. Eventually they had simply accepted the peculiarity, as an alien's way of thinking.

Y-Sith glanced at the chronometer dial on the wrist locator; an estimated two more hours to the wreck. One wondered what could have survived the original crash, and the probable million revolutions the hulk had lain rotting in this jungle. Only a very stable planetary surface had kept it from being buried long ago. But it was a full-sized ship, the first ever found that belonged to the tantalizingly elusive people who had left the marks of their exploration over known galactic space. If they were substantially ahead of Il-Strath and Man in scientific knowledge, the wreck could yield a treasure trove of data. They might even find some powerful weapon or new physical principle that would at last place the Il-Strath in a superior position to the hairless apes.

The human pilot would barely have time to occupy the structure before One would arrive. If One waited until after dark . . . But no, that would give the opponent two hours to prepare a defense. And the tricky devil could rig traps or prepare alerting systems that would more than compensate for an Il-Strath's better night vision. Best to start the attack immediately. The human had to be removed, and all signs of his prior physical presence eliminated. The riches to be gained here belonged to the Il-Strath, by right of discovery. Only the humans would insist the freak of chance that made the observatory ship unable to land did not change the specific terms of the agreement. But their dogged insistence on adhering to their own inflexible cultural patterns had been well demonstrated in the past. One had no choice but to kill the other pilot and hide the body.

And that made One hope again that logic was wrong, and the coming opponent not N-Jones. One had developed too much affection for Jones during that year of forced intimacy. He was a poor partner in *kil'a'cu,* short-winded, quick through to the end, not aggressive enough to give One more than minor thrills—but he was also more considerate of One than an Il-Strath male. Over the second half of the tour, when they had gotten well into the *kil'a'cuing* stage, she had learned to appreciate the unaccustomed gentleness and patience. He was . . . quite different from One's own kind, but oddly satisfying, in a pleasant and less fast-blooded way.

One hoped the humans had sent some pilot other than N-Jones.

Jones did not realize at first that he had found the ship. It loomed ahead like a high rock ridge, covered with trees and brush on the slopes. And then something of the size it must have been dawned, and he frowned. The overly large and the sophisticated seldom went well together. The normal growth of technological expertise was toward precision and smallness.

It had been a relatively easy trip here, even though slowed by the thick growth. He calculated that the Il-Strath pilot had landed at least five kilometers farther away. Perhaps he had an hour before his faster opponent would arrive.

He needed to get inside the wreck, but its size made it obvious several days would be required to run even a preliminary inventory. For now he should mark it "claimed" and then try to gain an advantage over the other pilot. Would it be best to wait inside, or . . . ?

No, that was the obvious move. Jones set off again, paralleling the kilo-long mound. About a third of the way down he saw what he was seeking, an area of bare metal near the top. That was the most logical place to attempt an entrance; otherwise, digging was required. He climbed the sharp slope at that point, sweating heavily from the effort, being careful to leave a noticeable trail. If his opponent was as smart as Y-Sith, she would know he had arrived first, make a circle of the mound, and try to pinpoint his chosen entrance. And if the Il-Strath did the obvious thing, and silently followed his trail . . .

When Jones finally stood on the alien metal, he took a hasty look around the jungle below. He was above most of the trees; only a few growing on the slopes still spread branches several meters over his head. He saw nothing in the wilderness below, of course. But he made a fine target, if there was anyone below to see him. Hastily he crossed to the other slope, where he stayed in the thick brush and headed for the tallest tree—then recovered just in time from what could have been a serious mistake.

Jones changed his course to one of several trees about equal in height. All of them overlooked the area of bare metal he had crossed. If the coming battle was with Y-Sith (*Let it not be! He remembered the peculiar musky smell of her, and how it changed when she was ready for him in* kil'a'cu. *He remembered the long, long talks during the runs between planets, the way her wide mouth opened when she laughed, the feel of the full soft lips against his . . . the funny manner in which she arched and curved her body when he touched her, the way she urged him to be more aggressive, hold tighter. . . . Let it not be!*), she was quite capable of following his thinking. He would have to be extra-clever, unusually subtle. She might ignore the wreck completely, and simply make a silent approach to the tallest tree that looked back over his obvious trail.

Was she capable of shooting him from ambush? It would be her safest bet; he was a better marksman with the laser. Would she be capable of sending a searing beam of coherent light through the body that had held hers so often in *kil'a'cu?* (That marvelous form of Il-Strath lovemaking, where actual sex was only the final caress?) And could he shoot at her, even to save his own life?

Y-Sith was fanatically loyal to her own people, as were all Il-Strath. Did he think equally well of his own? He could leave, return to his escape module, claim he had been unable to find the wreck because of an inadequate fix before the scout was shot down. Did the potential of this old ship matter that much to him?

Jones answered himself that it did. And besides, he could not know for certain it was Y-Sith now making her way through the woods toward him. It might be some other pilot, perhaps even one of the arrogant males, none of whom could get along with a human pilot well enough for a year's tour. Earth sent both sexes on joint patrols, but all Il-Strath were females.

Jones hoped it was a male. Then it could not be Y-Sith.

* * *

Y-Sith stared at the signs of recent passage, thinking hard. If the human wanted One to follow . . . She looked up the steeply rising slope to the single area of bare metal. The obvious first place to try for an entrance, establish a claim. But when One's opponent was a devious, subtle human—like N-Jones, whose mind seemed constantly to explore ramifications whose importance became apparent only later—he might choose to *guard* the entrance area, and from the outside. No other ship would arrive for several rotations. The claim could be established *after* there was no one left to dispute it.

Trying to think like an Earthman was difficult. They so seldom went directly to the point or concentrated on the immediate present. But if One assumed it *was* N-Jones, then One had a background on which to draw. He *would* think of staying outside.

In which case he would find a hiding place overlooking the bare spot and attempt to gain a major advantage over his opponent . . . and if he succeeded, instead of instantly and painlessly burning down the other pilot, probably do something sentimental and foolish when he knew for certain it was Oneself. He might attempt to get One to surrender, or disable without actually killing. There was a certain point with humans at which logic and deepness of thought gave way to self-indulgent emotionalism.

Y-Sith moved several steps through the brush to the right, then slowly worked her way up the slope, paralleling the human trail without following it. In a case like this, One longed for the delicate nostrils of One's ancestors. She knew Jones's odor intimately, especially when he sweated heavily in *kil'a'cu*. A human climbing this slope would be sweating also; but only if he was reasonably close could a modern Il-Strath smell him.

At the edge of the brush, not far from the first shining metal, Y-Sith paused. It was less than an hour before dark. If there was a human watching this area, he almost had to be in one of the nearby trees. . . . Yes, there was the best vantage point, a close one with heavy foliage that stood slightly taller than its companions.

For several minutes Y-Sith remained motionless, watching the highest tree. There was no sign of life. But there wouldn't be, if the man hiding there was N-Jones. He had the patience of a *rabgrul*, waiting all day with just one nostril out of the water, until the herbivores came to drink at dusk.

But if One approached the tree while keeping behind cover . . . Not hard to do in this thick brush. Y-Sith crouched low and moved away, back from the open area and in a wide circle that would bring her toward the tree from the rear. There should be just time enough to reach it before dark. And if One could get close enough, perhaps her nose would tell her if the man waiting in ambush was N-Jones.

Jones stared at the rapidly lowering sun, worry tugging at his mind. Unless the other pilot appeared soon, he would be trapped in this tree for the night. He would not dare descend to the ground after sundown. Even if he could climb down quietly, which was doubtful, he was no match for an Il-Strath in the dark. Not only did they have the hunter's night-vision, they could actually *smell* humans!

There was a brief flicker of movement in the bushes to his left, a lingering afterimage of reddish-brown. Jones's heart seemed to rise and lodge in his throat, choking him.

He knew. Logic, common sense, the inevitable logistics of interstellar transport—all said it had been Y-Sith in that other scout. He had not actually made out the form of the approaching enemy, much less seen the face, but that flash of vivid color was enough.

Careful not to disturb a single leaf, Jones slowly shifted his position and scanned the area ahead of the traveler. The brush was almost impenetrable to the eye on the ground, but from above there were dips and shallow places. Almost directly below his own perch was a small open space, with a line of high bushes at the side facing the tall tree. To someone walking, the spot would seem shielded from view—assuming the enemy was in the obvious place.

And then the brush yielded Jones two more brief glimpses of brown, and finally a partial view of long reddish hair, swinging freely back from a narrow forehead. These civilized Il-Strath did not have quite the stalking capability of the two-legged cats who were their ancestors.

With a hand shaking so badly he could hardly hold the grip, Jones drew his laser. He felt a sense of dark, oppressive foreboding, as though it was himself instead of Y-Sith walking into an ambush. And perhaps, on a level of conscience and morality that would be meaningless to her, he was, and would be trapped forever after a few more steps.

But why was it necessary to think in terms of either-or, as he had learned was Y-Sith's normal pattern? Why not think in *ifs*? *If* he could shoot to wound or to destroy her weapon, *if* he had capture instead of killing as his aim . . .

Jones slowly shifted the barrel of the laser toward the open space below, and waited.

It was less than five minutes before Y-Sith ghosted into the clearing. She stopped, studying the barrier of tall brush at the inner edge. This was the best vantage point she would find to observe his supposed hiding place. Y-Sith drew her laser, seemed to pause a moment, as though gathering resolution for a final effort, then dropped flat and started carefully worming her way through the bushes.

Jones took careful aim, hesitated, and then fired as he simultaneously yelled, *"Y-Sith!"*

Y-Sith involuntarily jerked her hand back as a blue beam smoked into the leaf mold just ahead of her pistol. The voice and the action were enough. Both belonged to N-Jones. He had outthought and outmaneuvered her, but then lacked the strength to kill.

For a frozen second Y-Sith hesitated, still clutching the laser, body outstretched and vulnerable. If One surrendered, and admitted being beaten by a more cunning mind . . . But then the high, hot pride of a thousand ancestors who had died well in the enemy's teeth came to her rescue. She whirled and threw herself to the side, rolling toward the nearest shelter as she brought up the pistol. If One could frighten or jar Jones with a close beam . . . He would be aiming to disable her, probably at the laser again. She kept the gun in motion, weaving the arm separately from her body, sending beam after beam burning upward through the leaves.

And in one flashing glimpse when her face was up, Y-Sith saw the darker shadow that was Jones. She managed to aim, with that instinct that does not require the use of sight. A killing beam lanced upward, one she knew would touch that shadow. And then the fallen trunk toward which Y-Sith had been rolling was close at hand, and after one more turn she was safe. Then the exposed one would be Jones.

Jones fired a final time at the brown-furred hand holding the laser, knowing he would miss again . . . and did. Her last shot had burned a smoking hole through the sole and into the side of his right boot. If he lived through this, he would know pain. But at the moment not even the shock had reached him, and his hand was steady.

With no conscious intent on his part, the laser shifted toward the far larger body, which he could hit even in motion. And in that split-second before Y-Sith would be hidden and himself become vulnerable, a torrent of memories poured through Jones's mind in a confused and tormented stream.

He remembered waking in the night to hear her teeth clicking as she dreamed, the slim body stretching and turning restlessly where it lay against his. . . . The way she tossed her head when she disagreed with him, flinging the long hair back over her right shoulder. . . . The time they had spoken of love, and discovered they had no mutual terms with which to communicate. . . . Above all, her eager mouth and caressing hands in the long, long sessions of kil'a'cu, the many times he had approached total exhaustion, the unbelievable ecstasy when she drew still one more climax from him, and his backbone seemed to melt and flow like heavy oil out of his drained and collapsing body. . . . The day he had realized he could never again be completely happy with a woman of his own species, and what this would mean to his life in later years. . . . And finally, the total numbness of mind and heart he had felt since coming off joint patrol.

And then he pressed the stud.

Jones saw the hit, the instant change of color from brown to black directly below the neck, and knew Y-Sith was dying when she fell out of sight behind the log.

Jones holstered the laser and hurriedly climbed down, feeling the physical pain of his burn now, and an inner pain no medicine could relieve, or time fade from memory.

But death had been almost instantaneous, and he did not reach Y-Sith in time to use the words she had never really understood, and say once more that he loved her.

There was no entrance in the bare area visible above the soil and undergrowth, and the ancient metal proved impenetrable to any cutting tool aboard the survey ship. Finally they admitted defeat, took some seismic profiles by setting off small charges against the stubborn hull, and located a discontinuity on one side. A few well-placed explosives cleared the way, and when the dirt and roots settled, they had found a door—of sorts.

It took another day, but there was an alien psychologist in the crew who could twist his mind into new channels. He solved the apparent secret, and the true simplicity of the mechanism became obvious.

The ship captain was the first man inside, but Jones limped in just behind him. The two men realized almost at once that the imperishable hull and its ingeniously simple door were likely to be all they would find here of value.

The bottom third of the ship was covered with a compost heap of ancient slag, most of it not even metal anymore. Over the eons that the great vessel had lain there, defying the outer elements, the inner machinery had rusted into dust. There was no shape or structure left, no function, not even a hint of purpose. The hull was of one metal, the interior works of many others. There was no conceivable way these ancient grains of metallic dust could be made to tell their story.

As Jones could not tell his.

Joseph Green writes:

One of my abiding interests in life is that hard-to-define human peculiarity we call "prejudice." As a child raised in a small country town in the Deep South, I was exposed to racial prejudice at an early age—in fact, indoctrinated, and quite successfully so. One of my more vivid memories is of fighting two black youths my own age, one after the other, while the older boys of both races gathered in two half-circles and yelled us on. I was about thirteen or fourteen before my omnivorous reading habits brought me into contact with some material that adequately debunked the racial myths.

Like many another American before the Feds tried to integrate the schools of Boston, I thought racial prejudice was confined to the South. It was a terrible disillusionment to move to Long Island in my twenties and discover that supposedly modern New York had just as much prejudice as Florida—it had been removed only from the statute books. I've now traveled or lived in most of the country, and am convinced of one fact: racial prejudice is an abiding and consistent pattern of thought with many millions of people. And I strongly suspect that it has been that way since the dawn of man.

But if we find ourselves reacting unfavorably to the minor physiological differences between black and yellow and brown and white, what will happen when we meet a genuinely alien species?

In most science-fiction stories the "aliens" are humans with oddly shaped bodies and unusual speech patterns. I doubt that it will be this way. I've written a story postulating that it will be impossible for human and alien to have truly meaningful communications, due to totally different cultural backgrounds ("A Custom of the Children of Life," Fantasy & Science Fiction, December 1972). I consider this more likely than that handy and ubiquitous gadget, the "universal translator."

And good ol' sex . . . Yes, what would happen if a human and an alien between whom sex is physiologically possible were placed in circumstances in which each was the other's only possible choice? Would the different smell-feel-response attract or repel? And if the alien is more alien in thought patterns than in body, if the cultures but not the sexual organs are basically incompatible, how will the two react to each other when the cultures clash? It's an interesting line of thought.

LADY SUNSHINE AND THE
MAGOON OF BEATUS

by Alexei and Cory Panshin

1

This is a true story. Some stories are lies, or half-truths. This is a true story of those desperate days when men still confined themselves to the ninety planets of the Dispersion, in the nodding afternoon hours before Nashua summoned the nerve to declare herself an Empire.

This is the story of young Jen, who was as beautiful as you may dream and who was known as Lady Sunshine, and of how she became the partner of the Magoon of Beatus. Lady Sunshine was her own chosen name, but at the time of her meeting with the Magoon it was a true description only of her exterior. She did not radiate. She did not illuminate. She was not fit to be the partner of anyone.

The times were bad for mankind, as bad as any the race has ever known, and Lady Sunshine was a product of the times. Mankind lived on the Ninety Worlds of the Dispersion and did as they thought all the generations of men before them had done. They ruined each other in the name of business, politics, fashion, and fame.

But mankind was sick and horizonless. There was not a man alive who did not know that Earth, the source, the wellspring of man, was dead, ruined by man. Mankind lacked all commonality and purpose. Men whirled in the closed circle of the Ninety Worlds, seeking advantage wherever they could, grasping and seizing.

The universe was limited and life was short.

Lady Sunshine was taught this last lesson by her grandmother, who was Madame O'Severe. Yes, her. Lady Sunshine was the heir of Madame O'Severe and was taught by her to be cynical and treacherous, to deliver more blows than she took, to use power for advantage, and to stand alone.

Madame O'Severe taught Lady Sunshine so well that the day came when Lady Sunshine realized the limitations of their alliance. Whatever Madame O'Severe might say, Madame O'Severe stood alone—a unity sufficient unto herself. And what was Lady Sunshine's place in that unity? She was being ripened to be eaten alive.

Lady Sunshine must flee from that to preserve her own unity. She laid a long plot of escape. She trained and prepared herself. She made herself a spaceship pilot. She used Madame O'Severe's absorption in the busyness of real life to make her own secret plans.

As delicate and precious as she appeared, Lady Sunshine was strong and determined in pursuit of her own purposes. She fought Madame O'Severe, and never admitted that she fought her. She merely said that she was unfond of the planet of her birth, that O'Severe had bent her, and that she wished to travel to some one of the other worlds of men in her spaceship. And she fought so long and well that at last, in order to save her other interests, Madame O'Severe was forced to loose her grip.

Madame O'Severe said, "You disguise your rebellions against me as criticism of this planet."

"But I am the very type of O'Severe," said Lady Sunshine. "It has made me thin and fragile. I wish to see what I would be like elsewhere."

"It is I who made you," said Madame O'Severe, "not this planet. If I had raised you elsewhere than here, you would still be the same."

"I wish to discover this for myself."

"You will shortly enough. Your proper place is here with me, doing as I train you to do. It is only by following my direction that you will ever be a fit instrument to inherit my powers and position. But I am far too occupied at the moment to coerce you properly. So I will indulge you in your whim. You may go. I grant you permission to find out just where it is that your best interests lie. I guarantee that you will learn that they are with me and with O'Severe. Now thank me and go."

"Thank you, good Madame O'Severe," said Lady Sunshine.

"One last thing before you go," said Madame O'Severe, halting her escape. "Remember well all the lessons I have taught you. You will find that you have need of them."

Lady Sunshine ran in her trim white spacecraft to Amabile, which was one of the playground worlds of men. She had in mind to leave her planet and Madame O'Severe far behind her.

There was freedom and gaiety on Amabile, which there never was on O'Severe, and Lady Sunshine tumbled headlong into it. It looked like fun, sporting with rich and handsome men and lovely, carefree women. She threw herself into the whirl and let it do with her as it would.

She was stripped clean by Amabile. She was demeaned and debased by it. She played at pleasure, ever harder and harder, trying to find an end and never finding it. Instead she found that she had good use for every lesson she had ever learned from Madame O'Severe. She did many pointless and destructive things that you would not enjoy hearing about.

She discovered that the people of Amabile and the people who came to Amabile were as bent as the people of O'Severe. Was Madame O'Severe right? Was this life? Was this the entirety of life?

Lady Sunshine woke one day on Amabile. She was alone and she hated herself and what she had become. In desperation, she fled.

She ran again in her spaceship, desperately lunging from world to world in search of a planet that was not as monstrous as Amabile or O'Severe. She was strong in pursuit of her purposes, and it became her purpose to find somewhere among the Ninety Worlds of the Dispersion one world where she would not be bent.

But she did not find it.

She came to Beatus from the planet of Cromartie, which was her sixty-first planet. She was tired and hopeless. She had had small hope of Cromartie. It was for her not a place of search, but a place of retirement.

She had stayed at the home of Lord Brain, who was her grandmother's Vassal on Cromartie. It was unnecessary for Lady Sunshine to encounter anything more of Cromartie than Lord and Lady Brain for her to know that this was not the planet she sought. It was more of the same.

Lord Brain had persisted in trying to amuse her with his minute knowledge of fashion that was new to him but that was irrelevant, not to mention old, to her. Ilis manner was unctuous subservience, which made his matter all the more difficult to endure.

For her part, Lady Brain preferred to meditate aloud on her few well-savored moments of interaction with people of importance. ("My people.") She spent much time in calculation of various stratagems by which the miracle might be repeated, and presented these to Lady Sunshine in hope of approval of the arithmetic.

They inflicted a house party upon her, when all she sought was a moment of peace in which to reorder her own priorities. And they pressed at her a ninny who styled himself the Count de Pagan. He was a pale shadow of the men of Amabile, but by the testimony of

Lord and Lady Brain he was the best that Cromartie had to offer. He pursued her everywhere, urging her to allow him the privilege of harvesting her grapes ere winter's deadly finger touched her vines with frost.

He did not know what she was. He did not know what she had been. He did not know how much his proposals sickened her, and he did not know what she truly sought. None of them knew.

They said to her:

"You are such an inspiration, my lady. It is enough to know there is one like you, a lovely butterfly, flitting from world to world, to give us hope."

Or, "*I* have never traveled through space, and I have no intention of ever doing so. Cromartie is quite good enough. Whatever you may think of me, I do not care. *I* am quite satisfied with myself. So there."

Or, "Forget your fantasies of escape, my sweet Jen. You have no need of other worlds. Reality is *here*. Find the world here in my arms."

She said, "Jen is not a name for your use, Count. To you, I am Lady Sunshine." And turned away.

At last, in desperation, she allowed herself to shock and bewilder them with a brief and partial glimpse of what she really was. In her ship she raced a pilot hired in a pool organized by the Count de Pagan. The pilot's reputation was considerable on Cromartie. She scandalized the party by carelessly distributing the whole sum of the wagers she had won, and had insisted on collecting, to their various servants and mechanicals.

And even so, they did not understand that there had been no risk to her in the race. Even less did they understand that her demonstration of power was no pleasure to her, since it furthered her purposes in no regard. At best, it furthered the purposes of Madame O'Severe, who was pleased to see the power and repute of O'Severe spread farther abroad. To Lady Sunshine, it was a surrender to her own weakness.

She announced her intent to leave immediately for the planet of Beatus. That was a convenient name for her escape, snatched out of fleeting house party conversation.

Beatus, someone had said, was a place where for morale the people wore buttons that said "Beatus is not as bad as Beatans say it is."

Everyone nearby but Lady Sunshine laughed familiarly. The man added, "Only it is. Who ever heard a Beatan speak ill of Beatus?" And everyone laughed again.

Lady Sunshine had heard of Beatus. It was one of the Ninety Worlds of the Dispersion, and it was not far from Cromartie. But she had never heard anything of Beatus to make her think it was the planet she sought where she would not be bent, and she had had no plans to visit the place. For Cromartie, however, Beatus was more than a miserable place. It was the local wellspring of humor.

"What is the difference between Old Earth and Beatus?"

That caught her attention. Lady Sunshine had an interest in Old Earth, the source of the varieties of man.

Several unacceptable answers were tried, to general amusement, before the proper answer was given:

"Nothing. Both are unfit for human habitation."

She asked about Beatus.

Beatans, the jokesters said, were squat and unhealthy men who lived in a deadly blue murk and made machines that did not perform properly. They were guaranteed to operate only on Beatus or in the hands of Beatans, but Beatans did not travel well through the transitions of hyperspace and no one else would willingly live on Beatus.

"What is the difference between a fool and an idiot?"

"A fool is a man with a machine from Beatus. An idiot is a man who travels there."

"Oh. You've heard it before."

Lady Sunshine said: "But the men of Beatus are professional machinists?"

"Of necessity. It is only by virtue of their machines that men live on Beatus at all."

It was small wonder that Lord and Lady Brain were frank enough to ask how they might have offended her, and the means by which they might repair their error. For Lady Sunshine proposed to ruin their house party entirely. Her distribution of the money she had won had shocked Lord Brain, but he had accepted it. He had placed his own wagers on her because that was where he thought his advantage lay whether she won or not, and he had been amazed and pleased by the result. But now this—desertion in mid-party for Beatus, of all places.

Lady Sunshine was politic. She did not inform Lord and Lady Brain that she preferred the blue fog of Beatus to the pleasures of their hospitality. No, she chose instead to tell them that she traveled to Beatus on the chance that it might supply her with a machine, a remote planetary analyzer, that she needed for her purpose.

"You travel to Beatus in search of a machine?"

"Yes, Lord Brain."

"For a machine."

"Yes, Lord Brain." Lady Sunshine had nothing left to her but her purpose. She had no better place left than Beatus to search for a planetary analyzer.

"But what shall we tell your grandmother when she inquires?"

"If my grandmother should inquire after me," said Lady Sunshine, "tell her that I have gone to Beatus."

But she did not think that her grandmother would inquire. Madame O'Severe had given Lady Sunshine permission to find out where her best interests lay, and she did not interfere with her now. She was too busy otherwise to do that.

It was in discouragement that Lady Sunshine came to Beatus. Her purposes were come to nothing, and she feared that O'Severe and Madame O'Severe, waiting patiently for her, were the sum of greatest possibility that yet existed. She hated the thought. Even the transitions of hyperspace, usually a tonic bath, a stimulation of every nerve, were no answer for her discouragement and her lack of hope. The fight against hyperspace left her drained and weary.

When she was given leave to land on Beatus, and was brought down through the murk to a safe landing on a planetary grid, she discovered that the worst that Cromartie had to say of the place was understatement. The men of Beatus seemed hardly human. They were lumpish and hairy creatures, and they did wear buttons that said "Hang on, Beatans!" and "If you think it is bad here, you should see where the Munglies live."

But Lady Sunshine had seen where the Munglies live, and Beatus was worse. It was the most unfortunate and minimal home of man that Lady Sunshine had ever visited.

The machines of Beatus pounded away eternally to keep the men of Beatus alive in their holes and warrens. The cold blue fog of Beatus penetrated even through the protective equipment that she wore. It was corrosive. It made her eyes sore and watery, her throat raw, her lungs painful. It confused her mind and upset her balances. Every moment she spent here demanded double the time elsewhere for recuperation.

But yet, she had come here for the sake of her search. The men of Beatus, whatever else might be said of them and their planet, were technicians and machinists. So down she went into their warrens, doing her best to ignore the seeping blue fog and the pulsing throb of the great machines. She made her usual inquiries and offered her usual inducements:

"I seek a machine by which I may inspect a planet such as Beatus from orbit without the necessity of landing on a grid. A remote planetary analyzer. I am prepared to bear whatever expense is involved."

But all that she received was the usual response:

"My lady, why inspect Beatus remotely? We have a landing grid firmly in place. And, after all, here you are."

"I mean to inspect planets that have no landing grids."

"Pardon my laughter, my lady, but what reason could there be to inspect a planet that lacks a landing grid? If it was worth landing on at all, it would already have a grid so that ships might land there."

And other familiar responses:

"How about another novelty just as good, my lady, but different?"

And, "It is not possible. Begging your pardon, but even to contain such a machine would require a naval vessel of unprecedented size. It is beyond your resources, whatever your willingness or ability to pay."

And, slyly, "How much money might be advanced for preliminary researches into the matter?"

One answer was not usual. It came from a belligerent, lumpish little man who wore not one, but three buttons boosting Beatus:

"What do you suggest? As all Beatus knows, at the Dispersion men were settled on the best existing planets. If a better world than Beatus existed, we would be living within it today. Since we are not, it is hardly in my best interests to build a planetary analyzer, now is it? I am not the fool you take me for!"

But then one day, a man who was lumpish and hairy like other Beatans, but who had more seeming confidence than most Beatans since he wore no buttons, came to her and said, "Please follow me. The Envied One wishes to see you in his hole."

"Who is the Envied One?"

The man was taken aback. "Why, Himself. The Magoon. The mirror in which Beatus sees its hopes reflected."

Ah, the Magoon of Beatus. Lady Sunshine recalled him now by this title. The Magoon was not the mirror for all Beatans, but there were many on Beatus who surrendered the care of their hopes to him. He was a very mysterious figure, reputed to live in deeply dug seclusion.

"Why does he wish to see me?" she asked.

"I don't know," said the man. "I am but a messenger."

There was no hope left in Beatus for Lady Sunshine, but no greater hope elsewhere, so she followed the messenger. She was passed from one pair of confident hands to another, deeper and deeper, until at last she was ushered into a room where the cold blue fog penetrated only in faint nauseating wisps, and there she met the Magoon himself.

The Magoon of Beatus was not beautiful. He was almost as queer and humorous as his title. Like less important men of Beatus, he had been bent by his planet and made squat, lumpish and hairy. He was short and brown. His hands and feet and nose were large. His eyes were sad. He was as ugly as a man may be and still be reckoned human. Lady Sunshine pitied and feared him in his awfulness.

Above the penetrating humble-mumble of great engines, the Magoon said to Lady Sunshine: "I understand that you seek a machine that would sense the nature of a planet at a distance."

"That is true, Magoon," she said, casually mangling his title to demonstrate their true relativity.

"Why do you have need of such a machine, Lady Sunshine? Why don't you use a landing grid like everyone else? If a planet is inhabited, it does not need your analysis. If a planet is not inhabited, it hardly merits analysis. Do you mean to be some sort of spy whirling about our heads and peering down at us?"

"No," she said.

"Then state your purposes."

After a moment she said, "I mean to go to unsettled planets, planets unknown to men, and analyze their fitness for human habitation."

"To what point?" he asked. "Are ninety planets not enough?"

"No," she said. "Some planets are more desirable than others. I seek to find new planets and to distinguish between the more and the less desirable among them. I feel that somewhere there must be a planet more desirable than . . . say, this one."

"But common sense says that if there were some planet beyond the worlds of the Dispersion that was preferable to any world among the Ninety, we would be living there now. Ergo, this planet is more desirable than the next best alternative."

Lady Sunshine stared directly at the Magoon, even though it was impolite to gaze fixedly at what was so deformed.

"Will you not agree that in the haste of the Dispersion, somewhere a planet might have been overlooked that was preferable to Beatus?"

"I cannot believe so," he said. "It would be disloyal."

"Then contemplate this possibility. An error was made five hundred years ago. An agonizing, foolish error. Earth was about to breathe its last, and desperate men—poor clerks—overlooked some better place and condemned their fellows to endure the hell of the Mungly Planet forever."

The Magoon contemplated the possibility. At last he said, "And for this search you need a planetary analyzer so that you may evaluate worlds without landing on them?"

"Yes," she said. "It is essential, if I am to find a world better than the Mungly Planet."

"But isn't this properly the job of some planetary navy? A major vessel on an extended expedition of exploration and survey?"

"Properly, it is," she said, "but no navy cares. Not even the great Navy of Nashua. The interests of Nashua are commerce and power, not search for a hypothetical planet better than that of the Munglies. It is, however, my chosen work. My computer spends all its available time mulling the probabilities of various candidates for my inspection."

"I have asked my advisers," the Magoon said, "and one and all they seriously doubt whether a ship smaller than a major naval vessel could adequately contain a planetary analyzer that meets your specifications."

"Is this idle speculation, or could you build such a machine?"

"It is not idle speculation. I command the best resources of Beatus —the best advisers and the best technicians—and they give me good reason to believe that your desires are impossible. Unless you have a major naval vessel at your command?"

"No," said Lady Sunshine. "Only a modified Podbjelski Model Seven."

And she sighed.

The Magoon said, "However, other possibilities have occurred to me. If you will come—"

Lady Sunshine inhaled in wonder at the phrase "other possibilities," but then coughed and choked on a wisp of blue. Still, she followed the Magoon as he led the way through the intricacies of his warren. As they passed great pulsing machines, Lady Sunshine held her ears against the noise. But the Magoon had been so bent by his planet that he did not even seem to notice the hulking black monsters.

At last they came to a deep interior room at the very heart of the warren, a child's room with many toys and lathes, workbenches and small machines. It was equipped with an airlock. It was a strong room against the blue fog of Beatus, and none penetrated here. Lady Sunshine liked the room on that account.

The Magoon said, "When I was young, I lived my life here. My health did not permit me to leave this room, not even to play in the corridors of the warren. The machines you see about us were my only given playthings. This was my particular favorite. In fact, I have continued to use it until this day."

He patted a metal bowl, polished and featureless, that hung suspended in the air. There was a seat beneath it. The Magoon sat, pulled the bowl over his head like a bucket, placed his hands in gloves, and positioned his feet in stirrups.

"I fail to understand," Lady Sunshine said.

But the sad hillock of a man was wandering in his toy. He did not seem to hear her.

"I do not understand what you mean by this," Lady Sunshine repeated.

There was a sudden rap at the door. Lady Sunshine looked again to the Magoon, but he was lost to the sound.

She answered the door herself. It slid back to reveal a subtle spidery little mechanical about one and a half feet high, crouching there in the airlock on its universal motivator.

It spoke.

"Lady Sunshine," it said thinly, "it is I, the Magoon."

"No," she said. "Is it possible?"

"Indeed," the queer little thing said. "I present you with an alternative to your planetary analyzer."

"This?" she said, looking down at it.

The mechanical hoisted an eye on an extensor until it was on an equal height with her own eyes, and stared directly back. The lens of the extended eye flickered and altered.

"There is green in your eyes, as well as brown," the small mechanical said. "How very strange."

Lady Sunshine looked from the small mechanical to the Magoon, lost in the parent machine, and back again. The mechanical rolled into the room on its motivator and demonstrated its agilities before her.

It said, "I am suggesting that you send a small drone down to the worlds you propose to examine. On board the drone will be a mechanical such as this one. Then, just as I have experienced the surface of my planet of Beatus through my mechanicals, so may you experience the surfaces of these unsettled planets."

"But what is it like?" Lady Sunshine asked of the mechanical circling about her. "What is it like? Permit me to test your system for myself."

The Magoon withdrew his hands from the gloves and raised the large featureless helmet. Consciousness had fled from the mechanical, and it balanced lifelessly on its motivator, a mass of inert metals and plastics.

The Magoon said, "I constructed large parts of the original system myself, and made all of the later modifications, of which there have been many."

"Very clever, Magoon," she said, and was glad somehow that she was taller than he, and that he lacked the extensors of his little mechanical to make himself equal to her.

With his assistance, she put on the cumbersome helmet over her head and put her hands in the gloves. In spite of the fact that both were large enough to fit the Magoon comfortably, it seemed to her that her head was held in a vise and her hands in pinions. She felt loomed about. And she thought that it smelled bad there in the helmet.

But at the same time, she could hear with the little robot's ears. She could see with its eyes.

She looked across the room and saw the Magoon standing over Lady Sunshine in the probe machine, placing her feet in proper position. And yes, she could feel her legs being moved. It was very strange and dissociating to be in two places at once.

But then, suddenly, she could feel the floor move beneath her motivator. She pressed with her right foot and swung right. She pressed with her left foot and wheeled.

"Ha, ha!" she cried, and heard her thin voice with her robot ears. "Wow!"

She tapped at a wall with an experimental extensor as she spun crazily by on her motivator. She felt the shock. She heard the sound, almost as though it were immediate.

"Magoon," she said. "This is very shrewd. What is the price of your machine?"

Its possibilities were incalculable. It was everything the Magoon had said. It was a viable alternative. With this machine she might circle a planet in her trim white spacecraft and see and hear and feel and manipulate it at a distance. That was more than she asked.

The Magoon stepped in front of the progress of the mechanical. Lady Sunshine pulled up short.

"Do you propose to buy me?" he asked. "The wealth of O'Severe means nothing to me. I have wealth enough of my own."

"Do you make me a gift of the machine?" she asked.

"No."

Lady Sunshine moved backward on her motivator. Then she stopped again. She pulled her hands abruptly from the gloves with their fingertip controls. She freed her head and looked at the Magoon, his back to her, standing before the little mechanical.

"So there is a price," she said. "What must I do to earn the use of your machine?"

He turned to face her. Lady Sunshine was amazed to see tears in his eyes.

He said, "I share your ends. I have the hope that there are other worlds where men may live in harmony, rather than in disharmony as here on Beatus. I do not believe that these worlds exist, but I dream that they might. Since I am the mirror of the hopes of Beatus, there are many who share this secret dream of mine. I have never been allowed to chance travel to other worlds. I do not know whether my dream is true.

"You may use my machine, Lady Sunshine, if you will find with it a world to exchange for Beatus. Not the Mungly Planet. Beatus first. The agony of my people must end."

"I will," she said. "You have my word, Magoon. You may have your choice of the worlds I find."

But then she said, "There is one small problem that still concerns me. Your machines have a poor reputation on other worlds. How may I be certain that nothing will go awry at a crucial moment?"

The Magoon waved the criticism aside without rancor.

"There will be no problem," he said. "I guarantee it. I will see the system installed in duplicate, and you have my word that it will work for you in crucial moments."

"We will see," she said. "We will test it on Beatus."

"Agreed," he answered. "Now satisfy my curiosity. You must have given considerable thought to the problem of search. What is your method?"

"I follow the best advice of my ship's computer," Lady Sunshine said.

"I understand," he said. "But on what basis are your computer's choices predicated?"

"Statistical inference," she said.

"Ah, yes. There are interesting possibilities in statistical inference. But what about intuitional methods? Have they no part in your search?"

"No. Intuition plays no part in my search."

"How did you come to land on Beatus?" the Magoon asked. "Was that recommended by your computer?"

"No," she said. "It was an accident."

But it was not an accident. In this universe, those things that are alike find each other out. Affinities gather, and computers be damned. What do computers know of true affinity? Only what they are told.

Computers are also weak in intuition. They cannot jump to wild conclusions and be justified.

2

It took time to install the double system of planetary probe machines in Lady Sunshine's white spaceship, and more time to make the necessary mechanicals and drone landing crafts. All the Magoon's great resources were turned to the problem and he himself oversaw the installation of the probe machines in her ship.

Lady Sunshine meanwhile practiced operation of the mechanical until she was adept at manipulating it on its motivator and directing its various extensors. It was subtle to operate and she wished to be in control when the time came to actually explore another world.

She also asked her computer to devote its spare time to selection of a choice short list of near places of search for the new world she hoped to find. She was interrupted in this by the need of the Magoon to coordinate the probes with the computer. Computer rectification of imperfect data from the distant mechanicals was absolutely necessary.

No matter how directly and immediately one seemed to be in habitation of the mechanical now, the ship's computer was an essential bridging link in exploration from space. Otherwise, what gaps in reality might appear? What blurring?

But there proved to be continuing problems of coordination.

"I don't understand it," said the Magoon.

He found it necessary to adjust the probes again and again, until at last they were in agreement with the computer. It was a long, slow and tedious process. But finally it became time to test the probe machine on Beatus from the spacecraft in orbit.

The Magoon participated in the test. It was only his second opportunity to see his sickly fog-enshrouded world from space. He had never been allowed to travel when he was young, and his sense of responsibility and best advice had kept him confined to Beatus now that he was older and Himself. He was excited. Lady Sunshine beheld him calmly and did not comment on his antics. He was a queer and ugly hairy brown creature, Magoon was.

From orbit they sent a drone vehicle down to the surface of Beatus. All went well, to the Magoon's great delight. When the safe landing of the drone was indicated, Lady Sunshine nodded to the Magoon and donned the probe helmet.

But all was not as it should be. It was not as it had been in all her occasions of practice.

The helmet did not work. The fingertip controls did not respond.

Lady Sunshine became overwhelmed by panic. She smothered. She drowned. She could not breathe in the close confines of the helmet. She could not escape from its grip. At last, she fought free of the probe machine.

She breathed deeply. She had found it frightening. It was all that she feared that was inert and dead.

Then she said, "This machine does not operate properly, Magoon. Will your duplicate machine serve any better, or have I wasted all this great time on Beatus, where the machines are untrustworthy?"

"Perhaps it is a matter of some small adjustment," the Magoon said.

He assumed her place. He put his head in the helmet, his lumpish paws in the gloves, his feet in the stirrups. He was gone for a moment while Lady Sunshine waited, peering at his engulfed body.

But then he raised the helmet and said, "It operates quite satisfactorily for me. Try entering the other probe machine, Lady Sunshine."

She took the other seat and after another deep breath donned the helmet. She found herself in the drone vehicle on the surface of Beatus. She rolled forward on her motivator out of the drone.

It was Beatus beyond question. It was horrid where she found herself. The ground beneath her motivators was spongy and uncertain. It was dotted with viscous purple pools that were vile and of unknown depth. They seethed.

Virulent deep blue roils of fog billowed about her. Lady Sunshine rolled forward tentatively on her motivator and found herself almost immediately surrounded by the pools of oily putrid purpleness, unable to proceed. She paused in the poisoned air and poisoned earth, unable to see, uncertain of her direction. She heard nothing but howling. For the first time in her experience of Beatus, there were no great throbbing machines to show where men made their truces with this awful place. Where to go? She poked a cautious extensor out to test the nearest pool, but paused again in fear that the vileness would dissolve her appendage.

Suddenly a great animal of a Beatan, a large misery, came running out of the fog at her. His protective devices were old and inadequate. He was eaten by sores and his hairiness was untended. He splashed through the purple pools and loomed large before her. She saw that he wore a great plate button.

It said, "I do not understand Beatus, but I accept it."

He cast himself down in the putrid purple slosh. He abased himself before her, coughing and choking and retching in the thick corrosive liquid. He rose and fell in it, thrashing and gasping, but always returning to it.

He cried, "Your pardon, O great Magoon! I have not been among your followers. Forgive me! I never thought to see you here in this solitary corner of mine. You are my one hope! Alter my life! Favor me with your blessing and I will be your faithful follower forever. I have never had a hope before!"

This pathetic creature attempted to paw at her. She rolled backward on her motivator to avoid the contact. With one eye she watched him; with the other she looked to her safe footing so that she would not join him by accident in the vile slop in which he wallowed.

"I am not the Magoon," she said.

To her great relief, she saw the second mechanical then.

"I am the Magoon," it said. It passed her by and rolled up to the Beatan, even into the slop, where it rode gently on the surface of the seething pool. "That is Lady Sunshine. It was a natural error. Now allow me to bless you."

The mechanical soothed and comforted the man, who rose dripping from the rottenness into the poison roils of fog. The Beatan reached vainly toward her.

"Bless me, too, Lady Sunshine! Please bless me! My condition must alter!"

The Magoon looked to her. At last she rolled forward a little distance, reached an extensor out to the man, and touched him with it, as a rock might be prodded with a thin stick.

"Bless you," she said.

The man stood and shook himself with happiness, like a wet dog.

"Oh, grace! Grace unforeseen! I do not deserve, but I will be worthy!"

He ripped off the poor remains of his protective devices and cast them away. He hurled his button into a purple puddle and ran into the fog, shouting and crying his joy.

Lady Sunshine said to the other spidery little mechanical: "Does this happen to you often?"

"Yes," said the other mechanical that was the Magoon. "Often. Their hopes are my chief burden. Their condition must surely alter."

When they faced each other again in Lady Sunshine's orbiting spaceship, Lady Sunshine said, "After that initial difficulty, your machine did all that I could ask. I'm more than satisfied, but I must know—what went wrong?"

The Magoon shook his head. "All that went wrong was that you operated the machine alone. That is all. The machines of Beatus need Beatans to direct them. Otherwise they are uncertain."

Lady Sunshine said, "Then you cannot guarantee the success of the probe when I put it to my own purpose?"

"I guaranteed that the probe would work for you," the Magoon said. "And it will work if I am present. Therefore I propose to accompany you in your search."

"Did you have this in mind from the beginning? Is that why you installed two probe machines?"

"Yes," said the Magoon.

"You were not frank with me."

"No."

"Do you dare to make this journey of exploration?" she asked. "The best advice you have been given has been not to travel."

"Do you dare to travel?" asked the Magoon of her in return. "Who has advised you to make these explorations?"

"No one," Lady Sunshine said. "All have advised against it, but it is my chosen work. And I do not stand the dangers from hyperspace that you Beatans do."

"Who knows what dangers I stand?" the Magoon asked. "I have never traveled through hyperspace. For that matter, who knows what strange and terrible things you may encounter in the course of your explorations? The unknown may be more frightening and dangerous than you can imagine. And yet you persist."

"I have my reasons for persistence," Lady Sunshine said, smiling.

"And I have mine," said the Magoon.

She shook her head. "You may die," she said.

It seemed to her that the Magoon was a frail being for all his gross bulk, and that any great shock might disinhabit this heapish ugly man as firmly and finally as the inert mechanicals they had just abandoned to the various poisons of Beatus.

"I may die tomorrow here at home, and what purpose will my death have served then? Better death in search, even fruitless search, than death in stagnation. I must alter the lives of my people, even though I die in the attempt. For good or for ill, I must cast the hopes of Beatus into the wind of the unknown. And no one may do this thing for me. No one may do this but me.

"So I ask: may I go with you on your journey of exploration?"

Lady Sunshine could not say no. She, too, would rather die in the search for an alternative to all that she had ever known than return to O'Severe to die and become her grandmother.

Moreover, if she were to persist at all, it was quite clear that she needed the Magoon to operate the probe machine.

"Yes," she said, because she could not say no. But she did not like saying yes. It took away from her something that had been hers alone.

The Magoon smiled in great relief, and then he said, "Before we leave, I must alter your computer. It is your ship's computer that has been at fault through all these days of adjustment and readjustment, and not my probe machines. Beatus as we just experienced it is no Beatus that I have ever known before. I have never seen it that blue and vile."

Lady Sunshine asked, "Do you remember that you were not frank with me?"

"Yes."

"I have not been frank with you."

"What do you mean?"

"I have not told you my true purpose. I have not told you all."

"Do you mean to say that your purpose is not to find somewhere a planet more hospitable to man than . . . the Mungly Planet?"

"No," she said. "Though I am sure that I will find such a place in the course of my search."

"Then what is your true purpose?"

Lady Sunshine had confessed her full intent to no one. Who understood her progression from one planet of the Dispersion to another in her own spacecraft? Few. Very few. They called her a butterfly, admired and dismissed her. Who understood her desire to find new worlds outside the tight bounds of the Ninety Worlds? Only the Magoon, this singular foreign creature.

Who would understand her true intent?

She said, "My purpose is to find True Earth, and that is why you may not change the computer. It holds singular precious data."

"I do not understand you, Lady Sunshine," the Magoon said. "Earth was destroyed long ago. There is no Earth anymore. There are only the planets of the Dispersion. Or do you speak of New Earth? That is a fine world, I am told."

"I have been there," Lady Sunshine said. "And it is not the place for which I search. It is not True Earth. Let me tell you my heart. I believe that in the Dispersion men were not taken to the best planets that exist, but were scattered carelessly on first-found worlds. I have been on sixty-two planets, and I know what worlds are like. I have never found a straight one. They have bent us, everyone, every one. They have made us strange and separate. They have made us scrambled and aimless. They have made us hateful. I know. I have been everywhere, and it has been like that everywhere that I have been."

"If New Earth is not True Earth, then for what do you search?" asked the Magoon.

"I search for the one planet where mankind will not be bent, but will grow straight and true. It will not be Beatus. It will not be O'Severe. It will not be New Earth, which is but a pale shadow with a name it does not deserve to bear. Until we find True Earth, we will never know what mankind really is. And I know what True Earth will be like. It will have the mountains of Aurora. It will have the forests of New Dalmatia. It will be made of Amabile, and O'Severe, and New Earth, and even Beatus. It will be all the best and more of sixty-two worlds. That is the standard by which my computer reckons.

"If Beatus was bluer and viler to your eyes than ever before, that is because for the first time in your life you saw Beatus truly, and not as it has bent you to see it."

The Magoon said: "Truer eyes do not improve Beatus."

"No, I suppose they would not," said Lady Sunshine. "But you must realize that by the standard of True Earth, every place looks the less. As the men of True Earth will outmatch the bent men of Nashua, or of anywhere else."

"Your model of True Earth is composed of all the planets that you have visited?" the Magoon asked.

"Yes."

"What of Beatus was added to the standard by which True Earth is to be known?"

"All that which is not blue and vile and lumpish, Magoon," Lady Sunshine said. "Now, if you promise not to alter my computer but accept the truth, then you may still accompany me. You may still venture your adventure and by the way we will discover many worlds that are better than Beatus."

"Your dream of True Earth seems a fancy to me," said the Magoon. "I do not dare to dream your dream. I hardly dare to dream my own dream. But I agree. Let us travel together in search of our dreams, and discover what we may."

The Magoon's departure was opposed by his advisers and his dependents, but he would not be gainsaid. He dared to risk all for his dream, and he prevailed over men who did not. He addressed his people as a whole and named to them the purpose for which he meant to travel. And, as his hope was their hope, they responded as one, and his advisers must then change their advice.

So is it always, when all is risked for a dream.

And so the two set off together in search of a better world than Beatus.

But though they traveled together, Lady Sunshine and the Magoon of Beatus were not yet partners. Lady Sunshine traveled in search of her own purpose, not the Magoon's. She searched for True Earth, the world where her unity would not be bent as it was bent and twisted on other planets.

The presence of the Magoon aboard her ship was no more than a means to this end.

3

Lady Sunshine and the Magoon traveled through hyperspace to the nearest place of those selected for search by the computer. Hyperspace was a stimulation and a joy to Lady Sunshine, a welcome antidote to the debilitations of Beatus. For the Magoon, hyperspace was a shock that left his sad eyes even sadder. But that was an expected reaction. He seemed to survive it ably enough. Lady Sunshine asked if he were all right, and he said that he was.

They emerged from hyperspace near a sun that was living green fire. Lady Sunshine pursued the directions indicated by her ship's computer, and found a planet! An unknown world! A candidate for True Earth.

She settled the ship into orbit around the planet and with the advice of the computer launched a drone. The Magoon looked down at the mystery that waited below them.

"This is more than I ever expected," he said. "And so soon. At this moment, I can almost believe in your True Earth. But I will be more than satisfied if this world is the superior of the Mungly Planet."

But what they discovered was not equal to the Mungly Planet. Not as a place of human habitation. It was not even to be preferred to Beatus.

The two mechanicals rolled forth from the drone. There was nothing to be seen in the somber green light of the distant sun that was not rock or shadow. The shadows were ripe violet in color and strangely cast. There were no clouds in the sky. No wind breathed. All was silence.

Lady Sunshine wheeled slowly on her motivator, looking all about them. The Magoon stood still, but slowly rotated an eye.

The rock that surrounded them was brown, and green, and red-black and gray. In some places these colors were separate. In others they were streaked and intermixed.

The texture of the rock also varied, independently of color. In some places it was delicately roughened, like the hide of a beast. In other places it was as smooth as though it had been finished. And yet, as they looked about them, each in his own separate way, they saw that in still other places it was slick and polished, like a natural glass in which they might see themselves reflected.

There were no straight lines anywhere. All was curves and undulations. The rock was rippled in places like the surface of a pond, and otherwhere it was waved like the surface of an ocean. It was molded in many ways.

In the absence of other life, rock had grown here after its own ways, unmodified. It had slowly fashioned itself. It had made itself into fairy spires, into private abstractions and unknown plastic shapes. Or it brooded through time, considering what it would become.

It was many, but it was all one, for there was nothing in this world but rock, and the shadow of rock. It was natural, but its nature was strange to them. As they were strange to this place.

As they looked about them, they saw that the drone had landed on top of a great singular rock formation, so that they looked at the world about them from a height among heights. They were very near the brink of a smooth and graceful swoop to destruction.

They did not speak to each other, these two mechanicals. How much time passed as they looked about them they did not know, for they did not reckon time.

If this world was strange, it was all the stranger for being judged by the standard of True Earth. That standard was not applicable here. No computer could rectify what the mechanicals perceived, but only make their perceptions more singular and unique. Nothing here could be judged by any human standard. It had its own reasons for being.

At last, Lady Sunshine said, "This is not the world I seek."

She struck at the rock with an edged extensor. The rock gave forth a light hollow sound as though it were brittle. Then it chipped. Now there was a great visible mar in the perfect surface of the planet.

"Nor is it the world I seek, either," said the Magoon. His voice rang thinly, overwhelmed by the towering rock about them.

"And yet," he said, "to think that we stand here where no other sentient observers have ever stood before. Could there be a lonelier place than this? What we see now has never been seen before. When we leave, it will remain unchanged through the eons, never to be seen again."

But the planet gave counterevidence. Where it had been chipped, the rock healed itself. Where it was marred, it slowly grew smooth again. Where fragments lay, they were absorbed by the mother rock.

And then something most strange and awesome happened. The rock face shrugged beneath them. A great blind ripple passed through the surface of the rock as the hide of an elephant might involuntarily shudder to dislodge a fly.

Lady Sunshine was nearer the edge of the formation, close to the long shattering swoop to the lower rock. The surface beneath her motivator was slick and she could not gain traction. The rock undulated again, and she was skidded against her will toward the great hurtling slope. She was helpless to stop her progress. She spun her motivator futilely.

The Magoon did not move to aid her. He watched her silently.

And then as another wave passed, he fell over. She wondered why he made no effort to rise.

He was far away. She was helplessly sliding, falling, and destruction had her. It was like a slow and silent dream.

Then the helmet of the probe was lifted and she was free and safe. The Magoon, that brown and hairy creature with great large nose and deep sad eyes, looked down at Lady Sunshine. She was disoriented.

"I think the mechanicals were best abandoned," he said. "That world is no place for us."

"Yes," she said, still falling. "Yes."

And they did not discuss the world of rock further then. It was too strange a place to be lightly spoken of and their experiences were too much with them.

They put that world far behind them. They went immediately from there to the second place of search indicated by the computer. This was the solar system of a flawless and brilliant white sun.

But search as they might, they found no planet there in the place predicted by the computer. They paused while the computer reintegrated its data. And during that pause, they took silent thought. It was only when they were to leave that they finally were able to speak to each other about Eterna, the rock world.

In the meantime, it occurred to Lady Sunshine that her ship's computer had failed in its first two attempts to find True Earth, or even a world preferable to Beatus. These failures were of course discountable. She had asked the computer for its nearest and best choices, and these had merely been nearest.

Nevertheless, the Magoon might have criticized the computer for its double failure, and had not. She liked him for that. And she liked him for not making an unnecessary fuss over the pains of hyperspace, which she suspected that he suffered and hid. She found that she thought of him as specifically ugly less often now than before.

At last the computer suggested rather abruptly that they had spent altogether too much time in this wasteland solar system where no hospitable planet was likely to be found. So they prepared to leave this sterile emptiness around the white sun.

"We have our release now," Lady Sunshine said. "Let us strike out to see what better place we may find waiting for us at our third rendezvous."

"There is no need to feel disappointment," the Magoon said. "We have had a good beginning. One planet in two attempts is a good beginning. It is more than I expected."

"And that planet was worthy of a visit," said Lady Sunshine. "It was like a cathedral of some forgotten religion. It was awesome and majestic, but also incomprehensible and inhuman."

"Did you think so?" asked the Magoon. "I felt the same, but I thought it must have been a disappointment to you, since it was so clearly not True Earth."

"No," said Lady Sunshine. "That visit was not one I would repeat, but I would not surrender it. The slow power of that place overwhelmed me. I think it has followed another road than ours, one far slower and less headlong, one less improvised, one more well-considered. Even before life arose on Old Earth, I believe that planet was making itself. It has never considered an alternative to being rock. If impetuous man and that which impetuous man becomes are not the true way of the universe, then the rock of that world may slowly demonstrate its own truth. It is an alternative to us. We may not criticize it, but only leave it abide."

"I am sobered by such patience," said the Magoon. "I wonder on what day we will communicate with that world?"

"And on what terms?" said Lady Sunshine.

"And to what ends?"

The third hyperspace transition was longer and more oblique than the first two they had made. Lady Sunshine had always accepted oblique and acute hyperspace transitions as much the same. Now, for the first time, she realized that there were qualitative differences between the two.

The sun of this new place was pink.

Lady Sunshine called the Magoon to view it. And he rose from his bunk once again when they were settled in orbit and she announced another new world in place beneath them.

"A new world! A new enigma!" exclaimed the Magoon. "It looks promising. I wonder what it will reveal to us."

"It is an enigma better resolved with your probe than with the planetary analyzer I never found, Magoon," Lady Sunshine said. "I would not like a remote and bloodless examination half so well as this direct engagement. With a mere analyzer, we would have known no more of the rock world than its unsuitability for human habitation.

"But are you certain you wish to explore so soon after travel? We may rest if you like. I feel a responsibility to your people for you."

"You have no responsibility for me," said the Magoon. "My fate is not in your hands, except now-and-then, and by-the-way. You are not one of my advisers, Lady Sunshine, but there are times when you sound like them."

"I apologize," said Lady Sunshine.

"And rightly so," he said.

"Let us explore now, then."

But as soon as Lady Sunshine saw the planet, she knew it was not True Earth, whatever else it might be. True Earth would have no room for a place as dull as this.

The drone had landed on a featureless gray plain. The sky above was a lighter shade of gray. Plain and sky met at a distant seamless horizon. A tired wind lifted a handful of dust and then let it settle in dribbles. As they silently looked about them at the new world they had found, a great furry-winged flying creature came flying ponderously near, and then was eventually gone, lost to sight in the grayness.

In great excitement, the Magoon said: "Why, this is fantastic! Look at the gauges! Perceive how habitable this world is! Why, it is my dream!"

Was this place better than Beatus? Lady Sunshine inspected her meters and then double-checked them against the Magoon's readings. All readings were startlingly normal, as though this grayness were somehow a boring and temperate average, a mediocre mean. Indeed, seemingly this dusty flat would make a suitable location on which to place row on row of long houses.

Lady Sunshine said, "I wonder if your people of Beatus would be happy here. It seems monotonous after the varieties of your planet."

The Magoon raised an eye on an extensor a great distance in the air and looked all about them. He fixed finally on the direction that the flying creature had flown.

"I see a grove of green in the distance," said the Magoon. "Since you seek variety, let us go investigate it. As we travel, let us propose names for this world we have found."

"Perhaps later, when we know it better," said Lady Sunshine.

They rolled on their universal motivators over the dusty plain in the direction that the Magoon had indicated. The ground was so hard that they left no visible marks of their passage.

Lady Sunshine said: "Does this place delight your heart, Magoon?"

"Indeed it does," he said. "It is living proof of my dreams! I can hardly believe in a world as habitable as this. If I were not within this mechanical and unable, I would hug myself."

A strange reaction! Unless, of course, one had never known any world but Beatus.

"Do you not wonder why I have been so discouraging?"

"Have you been discouraging?" asked the Magoon. "I have not noticed that you have been."

"Perhaps it is a failure in the perceptions of your mechanical," said Lady Sunshine. "For I have been being discouraging. This planet may be better than Beatus, but it is not much of a planet. You would stop here, and rest content."

"You would not?"

"Of course not! I have traveled more than you, Magoon, and I have never seen a planet more lacking in grace! It may be habitable, but it would bend you worse than Beatus has bent you. You would be very strange then, your bentness compounded. We have been here only briefly and distantly, and I feel oppressively bent already."

The Magoon said anxiously, "But perhaps we have already been more than fortunate in finding two planets. How many more than this will we find?"

"Many. In the course of my search for True Earth, many. Worlds so almost perfect they will make you weep and your teeth ache. Take your people of Beatus there.

"Or take them here, if you still prefer. We will remember where this nameless temperate flat was. I will not forget, at any rate."

"But what of this world's groves of green?" asked the Magoon.

Lady Sunshine raised her own eye on its extensor. This gave her the peculiar experience of seeing both near and far simultaneously. With her lower eye, she looked at the Magoon. With her extended eye, she looked in their direction of travel across the gray plain.

She asked, "If there are other groves of green on this planet, are they also giant cabbages?"

"Giant cabbages, Lady Sunshine?" asked the Magoon. "I cannot believe that my grove is giant cabbages!"

"It is not," Lady Sunshine said. "It is one single solitary giant cabbage. That is your grove entire. Do you wish to look for yourself?"

Slowly, in his piping voice, the mechanical that was the Magoon said, "I think you are testing my devotion to this world. I have always found cabbages peculiar."

He rolled forward.

"Pull your eye in," he said. "Let us continue. We will discover soon enough if you are testing me."

Lady Sunshine looked at him with her extended eye, changing the magnification until she saw him whole and clear. He looked quite strange from this angle.

"Very well," she said. "But I, for one, propose that we name this place Cabbage Flat."

The ground under their motivators was now less hard. It was damper and darker. When the green grove was clearly visible to them, even at their proper minor height, the ground had turned to black mud, which tried to enmire them. But their universal motivators were more than equal to mud. Instead of rolling, they now slid smoothly over the top of the bog.

When they came closer, it became apparent that Lady Sunshine had not been testing the Magoon. The grove of green was indeed a single huge plant bearing a distant but distinct similarity to a gigantic cabbage.

It was the center of the local dampness. Indeed, close about it the mud was thick liquid, a sloppy black muck.

Though the great enfolding leaves of the massive vegetable were apparent to them at a distance, the Magoon did not admit its nature until they were close upon the enormous green-and-purple bulk. He stopped in the muck and studied his grove.

"You are right," he said at last. "It is very like a giant cabbage."

"Do you wish to examine it more closely?" asked Lady Sunshine.

"Or does it wish to examine us more closely?" asked the Magoon. "Does it seek to eat us?"

The black muck around the cabbage had begun to swirl slowly. As they rested on the slop, they were being pulled around in a spiral toward the cabbage. Around and around, and closer and closer they were brought to the plant. It looked much the same on all sides—a few leaves spread high and wide, the rest folded together in a central bolus.

They were closer than Lady Sunshine liked when the Magoon finally said: "I have seen as much of this peculiar vegetable as I care to see. Let us retreat a distance."

The swirl on which they were carried seemed so inexorable that Lady Sunshine wondered if they could retreat, or whether they must again abandon their exploratory vehicles. But, in fact, their motivators propelled them easily across the spiraling tide of muck. They settled at a more comfortable distance.

The pull of the swirling current increased, but they resisted it, floating easily in place. It increased yet again, but never becoming more than a frantically stolid movement. They held their place against it lightly.

"Again you see the advantage of your probe to my analyzer," said Lady Sunshine. "An analyzer would have given us a very different picture of this world. It would have reported that this place was temperate, but not that it was Cabbage Flat."

The Magoon said, "If the planetary analyzer were properly made—and if you had a battleship to contain it—it would take such things as cabbages and flatness into consideration."

Suddenly the mud around them ceased its churning. In moments, the face of the bog was still again, the last ripples fading away.

"Observe your meters," said Lady Sunshine. "This planet is less habitable now than formerly. Its disharmony now exceeds that of Beatus."

And, indeed, their gauges did show that the atmosphere around them had become radically altered. There was now an overconcentration of several potent chemicals.

"I suspect the source is the cabbage," said the Magoon.

"Does it seek to attract us, to overcome us, or to repel us?" asked Lady Sunshine.

"How can one tell with a cabbage? Perhaps it is attempting to communicate with us."

The bog began to swirl again, but this time in the opposite direction. Instead of the cabbage drawing them in, it was now doing its best to push them away from itself.

They resisted the movement of sludge and continued to hold their places to see what would happen next.

Then, without warning, the great central bolus of the cabbage fell apart. The overlapping leaves flapped back with the sound of ship's canvas filling. They spread wide, opening the plant but still hiding its interior from their view.

A large furry-winged flying creature, perhaps the same that they had seen earlier, leaped into the air with a raw-voiced cry. It flew to them and seized the little mechanical that was the Magoon of Beatus. It carried him up into the air away from the cabbage with great effortful wing beats, and flew away into the grayness.

Lady Sunshine looked at the unfolded vegetable. She was too small to see over the great spread leaves into the mystery of its interior.

She looked with her other eye at the moving thing in the sky, now only a single undefined spot. She magnified the spot until she saw it clearly again as flying-creature-carrying-mechanical.

She did not know what to do.

Lady Sunshine abruptly pulled her hands from the gloves and raised the featureless metal helmet. It was quiet there in the ship in orbit. She might as well have been all alone.

She looked at the Magoon. She rose and went to him.

Should she rescue him from the machine, as he had rescued her? He was more experienced in its use than she. He might not be as lost as she had been. Would he not abandon the mechanical if he were dropped from a height?

She observed him until she was certain that the Magoon was still in voluntary control of his mechanical's faculties. She saw his feet work his motivator with smooth and knowing precision, and she knew that he was well.

Lady Sunshine left him then and ran back to her probe machine. She had left her curiosity unsatisfied. She hurriedly resumed her place. She pulled the helmet back over her head.

The cabbage had managed to push the mechanical she inhabited to the very edge of the muck while she was gone. But she wished to penetrate its towering bulk. She wished to see from where the flying creature had come.

But the resources of her mechanical exploratory vehicle were insufficient. Lady Sunshine raised her extensible eye to its limit, but the green-and-purple plant would not let her see its unknown interior. It denied her. It lifted its leaves in a tremendous effort that cracked the air loudly, and folded itself together again.

Lady Sunshine looked all around her again. In the distant sky she saw the flying creature returning. She magnified her vision and saw that it was empty-handed. It was returning for her, but she would not let it have her.

She withdrew from the probe machine to save herself. She saw the Magoon rising and standing free of the other machine.

"Are you all right, Lady Sunshine?" he asked.

"Yes," she said. "What happened to you, Magoon?"

"It was quite strange. The flying creature carried me back to the drone and set me down with another raucous cry. Then it flew off without looking back, returning again to the vegetable. What happened to you?"

"Nothing," she said, as though she did not realize the limitations of the mechanical that had just been demonstrated to her. As though she had not been afraid.

Then she said, "While you were being carried, did you think of a better name for this planet than Cabbage Flat?"

"No," said the Magoon. "Cabbage Flat it will be. This is not the planet to replace Beatus. I see now that your dream is a better dream than mine. Mine will produce nothing but Cabbage Flats. But in looking for your dream, perhaps we will find that world better than Beatus for which I and my people hope.

"Let us look on. What is the next place on your computer's list?"

4

The sun that Lady Sunshine saw before her when they emerged from hyperspace was radiant gold of a lustrous richness more orange than yellow. It glowed like her hair, or like a treasure house.

But the Magoon did not rise from his bunk to witness it, though it was lovely. He was not yet recovered from the hyperspace transition.

"Seek our new world, True Earth," he said. "Don't fix your attention on these pains of mine, which will pass."

"You are a dear creature, Magoon," said Lady Sunshine, and turned again to her piloting.

She followed the statistical inferences of her computer and found a planet not too very far from where one was predicted to be. She settled into orbit around it and allowed the computer to calculate the most probably optimal destination for the drone.

But when all was ready, the Magoon was still in pain.

He said, with great effort: "I have not been candid with you, Lady Sunshine. I have been more affected by hyperspace than I have allowed you to know."

"You should have told me so that I might have returned you to Beatus," she said.

"No. What is important is your dream of True Earth, and the fruits of that dream."

"But are you sure that you can survive another transition?"

"No. But that does not matter. You need me, and now I have failed you."

The Magoon ceased to speak then. He did not respond to Lady Sunshine. He was very sick, and she did not know what to do.

She found that he had armed himself with medicine, and that he had used it all. She spoke to him, but he did not answer. She touched him. She washed his face. She felt ashamed.

The Magoon's motives and behavior had been so much nobler than her own. She had selfishly insisted on pursuit of her private goal at all costs. But what had been her true goal? To demonstrate to Madame O'Severe all that Madame O'Severe denied. To show her that there was a world somewhere in which Lady Sunshine could be someone else and not the creature that Madame O'Severe had made.

For this petty end, she had used the Magoon willfully, taking no notice of his pain. Discounting it. Ignoring it. She had not cared what he needed or suffered because she had required his services.

What were her choices in this moment of the Magoon's collapse? She could take him to Beatus. She could take him by the easiest acute hyperspace transition to one of the Ninety Worlds.

But any hyperspace transition might kill him.

Then there was this new enigma, this unknown planet below them that might be more living rock, or more cabbages and flying creatures. This planet might be anything.

If, with all her great skill, she brought her trim white spacecraft down to the planet in the absence of a landing grid, then in spite of her great skill, they would never be able to leave this world again. They would be bound to it forever.

Lady Sunshine was lost in the twists of a great paradoxical knot. She had brought the Magoon to this place to operate the probe machine. Because she could not. Now, however, the Magoon could not operate the probe machine. Because she had brought him here through hyperspace to operate the probe machine. It was for the Magoon's sake that the probe machine was necessary now, to explore the world below them. But without his ability to operate it, the probe machine was useless. Because Lady Sunshine had brought the Magoon through hyperspace to operate the machine. Because she could not.

It was a horrible knot. It made no sense.

She could not land on this planet. Neither could she fly elsewhere through hyperspace. Neither could she do nothing.

She cried in agony. She was alone, more alone than ever before in her life. She was a unity, a singularity, and it was not enough to be that.

She had but one temporization available to her. If she sent the drone down to the planet, the Magoon might recover sufficiently to activate the probe so that they might determine whether or not to land themselves on the secret world below, the unknown planet of the golden star.

She pressed the button to launch the drone. But when it had landed safely, the Magoon had not recovered.

The squat brown creature, ugly and dear, continued to lie unconscious in his bunk. While she looked, he suddenly cried and thrashed behind the glass. Then he became still.

Terror-stricken, she pulled the ship's emergency unit from its private closet. The Magoon was still alive, but he was much worse. She strapped him in and attached the emergency unit. The computer monitored his functions. She could keep him alive in this fashion, but for how long?

For the first time her self-sufficiency failed her. Even in her worst moments on Amabile or in her most discouraging moments of search, she had not been this helpless. She had never needed aid before.

Aid? That was not the way of Madame O'Severe. That was not the way of mankind.

Each for himself. Above all, each for himself, until one stood alone atop the pyramid, master of all. Above all. One.

It suddenly occurred to Lady Sunshine that she had operated the mechanical on Cabbage Flat after the Magoon had quitted the system. He had been standing apart from the machine when she had raised her helmet. Was it possible for her to operate the probe without him?

"Poor Magoon," she said, and touched him. He did not respond, but lay inert in the grip of the emergency unit.

She closed the glass. She checked the automatic functions of the ship.

"Mind your business well," she said to the computer.

Then she went to the probe. She sat down, placed her feet in the stirrups, pulled the helmet over her head and put her hands into the gloves. And immediately it seemed to her like the first time she had tried to operate the machine around Beatus. She was aware of rigidity. Her head was gripped closely. Her hands were imprisoned. Her legs were dead.

But what did that matter? The machine operated!

She could see. She could hear. It was as though she were on the unknown world and not lost in a computer-rectified machine somewhere in orbit above it.

Lady Sunshine looked at the other mechanical beside her, still and silent. She looked out of the drone into the world that awaited her beyond.

It was amazing. It was seeming Arcadia. It was Eden.

It was trees and grass and brilliant golden sunshine. It was a jolly little brook and an alternation of perfect hills stretching to the horizon.

"Can this be True Earth?" she asked, but the other mechanical gave her no answer.

She would have to discover for herself. Amabile had been attractive at first appearance, and also other planets, before they revealed their bentness.

She labored her mechanical body out of the drone. It was an annoyance to labor, but somehow she was unable to work the mechanical smoothly. Her fingers had forgotten themselves. Her feet were asleep.

Was the difference the missing Magoon? Or was it somehow this planet?

Then suddenly she careened forth, ran in a desperate curve, spun helplessly on her motivator, and fell over. A wise little bluebird twittered mockingly at her. It watched her flail to rise and jeered again.

She watched it take to flight as she lay. It disappeared in midair, leaving nothing but a swimming mote of emptiness in her vision. She could not believe what she saw. Had she imagined that she saw the bird? Had she imagined that she saw it disappear?

She finally managed to lever herself upright. Her mechanical body seemed heavy and out-of-balance. Her control was uncertain. At any moment she feared that the mechanical would have a lurching fit, or suddenly refuse to answer her intended direction. She could only move at angles, not in direct forward progression, so she tacked one way and then another in order to proceed.

Was this True Earth? Lady Sunshine wondered why she did not love its golden perfection better.

But then she looked more closely. This was difficult because her mechanical eyes would not focus. But she saw that the world had a plasticene quality. It was overripe. It melted into itself in a way she did not like. Trees intertwined themselves blindly, groping at each other with long tendrils. There were strange distant animals in this pastoral land, moving together. As she watched, a doggish creature—not a dog, more than a dog—rubbed itself intimately against a tree and then urinated on it.

Not knowing why, she was again reminded of Amabile. But why?

She watched a creature that was like a golden-furred rabbit hopping idly on the hillside. It disappeared like the bird, and then appeared again.

There were strange spots of blankness in her vision. The colors of this world drooped and threatened to run together, to spill and mix and whirl. There were flickers at the edges of her eyes. She spun her eye around to catch them, but though she rotated it madly, they always managed to elude her.

She did not like this place. It made her uneasy. And yet to appearance it was perfect and golden like some California or Huy Brasil. Was the fault in the machine? Or was it this place?

She moved forward, tripped over something she didn't see, skated wildly, fell, bounced fortuitously, and came to rest upright. It was so strange. She could not move properly. She could not see clearly.

Lady Sunshine felt the need of the Magoon. There were spaces in her expectations, and she was deeply disturbed.

She began to watch one particular area of blankness in her vision, a swimmingness that moved this way and then that, and could not be pinned down. She was determined to see through it.

She raised an eye on an extensor to see it from a height. She did this with all due carefulness lest she fall over, which she felt that she might do. She watched the mote with separate eyes and it did not go away.

She became certain then that it was not the computer that was at fault. It was not the mechanical. It was not herself. The source of strangeness lay in the planet.

She heard a piercing squeal which unnerved her. Then suddenly the blankness—that blankness—was no longer there.

Instead, she saw a black rabbit-creature mounted on the golden rabbit she had seen before. It turned its face to her as it thrust and pumped, and she saw that it had long sharp unrabbitlike teeth. Then it fell off and lay panting, its little pink penis extended from its furry sheath.

The golden doe tried vainly to hop away, but the black buck leaped up again. It seized the golden doe by the neck and bit down savagely. The doe squealed again and then its neck was broken.

It thrashed helplessly, exposing its underbelly. And then Lady Sunshine saw that it was not a doe at all, but another buck, and that it had an erection of its own in the throes of death. Even before it stopped moving, the black rabbit-creature fell to feeding on its warm body.

Lady Sunshine retracted her extended eye. She feared she could not move without falling with her vision radically split.

She moved forward carefully. She was successful except for one inadvertent reckless lurch.

The rabbit-thing continued to feed greedily on its fellow until she was close. Then it lifted its head, gave her a knowing look, hastily licked the blood from its black-furred mouth with a delicate pink tongue, and hopped away into an anomaly. It was gone into a swimming blur, disappeared again.

The look it gave Lady Sunshine remained with her. It had included her somehow in its crimes with that look, and the knowledge frightened her. She wanted to separate herself, but the golden corpse remained, bloody and mangled, lying on the hillside, as though it were hers. Her property.

Abruptly, a loud moan began, starting low, rising, breaking into howls. What was that? It was painful and intimidating. It unnerved her to hear. It came from nowhere and from everywhere. It surrounded her and filled her ears, filled her world. It was as though the whole uncertain planet were shrieking its pain at her.

Lady Sunshine wished that it would stop. When it became too much, she cried for it to stop.

It stopped.

Then two people suddenly appeared. They seemed to walk out of a bush with brown and crumbling leaves. One was a woman with long black hair and sharp foxy features. She led a man who was covered with overlapping triangular scales. Both were naked. Her muff hair was as golden as the dead rabbit-creature. His penis was slippery and wet, and dripped mucilaginous strings of gleet.

Lady Sunshine was amazed to see people here. This planet was not one of the Ninety Worlds of the Dispersion from Old Earth.

Naked people.

The woman saw Lady Sunshine first. She put one hand to her muff and the other to her mouth, sucking her fingers in a parody of concern. She prodded the man with an elbow and made a suggestive twaddle to Lady Sunshine with the fingers from her crotch.

Then the woman and the man walked through each other and were a place of emptiness. They were not visible. Gone, impossibly gone.

Lady Sunshine tried to calm her distress by placing the worlds of origin of the two naked people. They seemed definite types, as definite as the Magoon from Beatus. As definite as a lace-veil butterfly from O'Severe. These people were formed, malformed, bent into special shapes.

But Lady Sunshine could not remember any place where the people looked so vulpine. Or any place where men had evolved scales like a pineapple. And that was even more distressing.

In the emptiness about her head, there were suddenly tears, screams and silence. Silence. Then more screams.

She looked wildly about her. Nothing, nothing, nothing but golden sunshine and a sky as blue as the benighting fog of Beatus.

The planet uttered a final explosive raw-voiced agony, which turned to laughter and trailed away.

"There are those who need time to get used to it here," someone said in an exquisite throaty voice.

The voice came out of nowhere.

"And then there are those who take to it right away."

The voice seemed to come from above, out of a tree. A mass of creepers, tendrils and black writhing vines lowered itself. There was a flickering within the web, at times flashes of paleness, at other moments only writhing blackness. The squirming nest reached the ground and broke open. But there was nothing within the tentacles but unfocused shimmer, an anomaly.

Then a dryad stepped forth, out of the nothingness. She was fat, middle-aged, coy and horrid. She was naked and flabby and white as rice. She looked like an evil pig. A great festering wound, a gumma, had eaten away most of her nose and turned it into an open snout. A few of the black creepers broke away from the main mass and remained with her, winding and twining intimately about her body like snakes. Where they touched her they left welts on the whiteness like intense broken red veinlets.

The creature of the tree, this dryad, reached out to Lady Sunshine, who started back from her, nearly toppling.

"May I touch you?" the dryad asked pleasantly. "I want very much to touch you. May I? I like to be the first to touch new people. It is almost my only vice."

The gumma seemed to shift on her face. Her nose was now there, where it had not been before. It was a red blobby thing. But now part of her forehead was eaten to the bone, which showed whitely through the open wound. And a lip was lifted high to reveal skeleton teeth smiling at Lady Sunshine.

"No!" said Lady Sunshine. She did not want to be touched. Above all, she did not want to be touched.

The dryad said, "I just thought that I would ask while it occurred to me. You mustn't think I was insisting, just because it occurred to me."

She walked in a circle around Lady Sunshine, while Lady Sunshine watched her with a wary rotating eye, ready to lurch if the dryad attempted to move in her direction. Then, suddenly, the dryad sat down beside her. She stroked and petted her various creeping companions, and moved a favored thick black tendril into her crotch where it curled itself around her leg and snuggled intimately.

The dryad licked her lips obscenely, tongue running over white teeth where she had no lip, and leaned toward Lady Sunshine. Lady Sunshine inched away.

"From what planet do you come, my dear?" she inquired.

"O'Severe," Lady Sunshine said. "Originally."

"O'Severe. That's nice! That is such a distance to have come. Your need for us must have been very great. Why, that means that sooner or later I will see more of you, doesn't it? But it would be so nice to be first. You are so sweet and fragile. I do like that in a girl."

The dryad, that fat fountain of unknown delight, suddenly stood again.

"You must excuse me, really," she said. "I have tarried too long with you. For here is someone new that has been sent to me. And I must not be selfish, must I?"

She turned and galloped off to intercept one of the distant animals that Lady Sunshine had seen, which now approached them. Or was it a man? Or a boy? Or was it a creature part human and part something other than human?

Lady Sunshine could not say. His genitals made him male. But he had the narrow-hipped, smooth-muscled body of an adolescent boy. His skin was mottled green and yellow, and seemed of different textures, smooth where it was yellow, pebbled like a turtle or lizard where it was green, everywhere hairless. His tiny head was bald and chinless and bobbed atop a neck fully two feet long as though it had a life of its own separate from its body.

This strange and improbable creature took no notice of the maiden of the tree come tripping to intercept him. He detached a bit of yellow from his green leathery body, tossed the gobbet into the air, and snapped it down with a lunge of his long neck.

Lady Sunshine realized then that the yellow patches on his skin were fleshy moving things like creeping leeches. He plopped another with great relish into his lipless mouth, and bulged his eyes hugely.

"Match for unity," the dryad challenged him. She seized him by his limp dangling member, and her black-creeper familiars bound him to her otherwise.

He nodded and picked a yellow blob off his body. He squeezed it until it popped and ran like dripping custard. He smeared it on her face, and she gagged and sputtered.

"One for me," he said, laughing. "Unity."

They began to contend, to wrestle, to twine like the trees of this planet. The doggish creature that Lady Sunshine had seen earlier came trotting over as they swayed for advantage. It sniffed them closely, snapped at their genitals, and was slapped smartly by the thick tendril that the dryad wore as guardian of her privacy. The doggish one whined, and then deliberately urinated on them.

"Unity," it said audibly, and trotted briskly away. Lady Sunshine was amazed to hear it speak.

The gross dryad never let go of the green boy's penis. She ripped at it with her nails. She gnawed at it with her skeleton teeth. She rubbed and snorted it in her decayed nose. Lady Sunshine could hardly bear to watch.

The turtle boy whimpered and chittered at her attack, but in spite of all her painful work, he did not yield to her. He had weapons of his own. He bashed, nudged and butted her blindly with his small bald head on its long neck. He struck her again and again with great blows. With soft, nailless fingers he strove to pry away the thick black tentacle that protected her.

He suddenly broke away with a triumphant cry, holding the tendril. His neck grew stiff. His tiny head grew dark and engorged. He struck the dryad with her tendril and she screamed and loosed her grip on his penis.

The green boy-creature made the dryad bend and present her rear to him. He whipped her with the tendril and she screamed with each blow. Her body was a mass of red welts. He cried, "Louder! Louder!" and whipped her ever harder.

Then he penetrated her with his bald head on its long neck. He plunged into the dryad again and again, and she filled the world with the sound of her pleasure and agony. The tendrils that clung to her stood out from her body and writhed blindly.

And then, at the climactic moment when the green leather-skinned creature was about to expend himself within her, somehow the black tendril he used as a whip wrapped itself tightly around his neck. He was blocked, prevented. The tendril squeezed tighter and tighter, and the rising tide within him had no outlet.

He withdrew his lipless, chinless head. He was under stress. He was in dire straits. He pointed to his neck desperately. With his other hand he pried vainly at the thick tentacle. His green skin was almost black.

The dryad snapped his neck with sharp impertinent fingers. She slapped his cheeks. She prodded him in the gut. At last, she recovered her black companion and stood aside.

The boy rang the world with his howl. Then he vomited gouts of delayed yellow matter that had been blocked from ejaculation.

"One for me," the dryad said. "Unity."

"Unity," everyone cried, and applauded her. They knew a winner when they saw one.

The poor sick boy looked at the great crowd that had gathered. He retched and cried. He flickered madly, and then disappeared.

The dryad showed her teeth in her most hideous smile, and then yawned elaborately. She passed her black familiar between her legs. It wrapped itself around her right leg and nestled into its home again.

Lady Sunshine looked at the many beings gathered around her. It was impossible to say how many there were because they became and they unbecame.

All of this awful world threatened to come unpinned about her now. There was more flicker than stability.

All the strange and naked people she saw standing around her in the dark rainbow drip and swirl were diseased. Or they were deformed. Or they were inhuman.

There was one being that looked like a baboon with immensely swollen genitals. It had the face of a lovely woman. It sat on the ground and played with crawling spiders.

A woman with skin like rough tree bark fondled a balloon-headed dwarf. A creature with the body of a man and the head of an elephant groped them both with its trunk. The woman seemed to be unaware of where she was, of what she did, and of what was done to her. The dwarf smirked.

Another woman with twin lines of dugs that stretched from chest to groin lay on her side on the ground while an assorted brood of squirming things fought each other for her tits. Two fought to the death. Their wet nurse picked up the parts of their bodies and tossed them to the sharp-toothed rabbit-thing, which savaged them.

Lady Sunshine whirled on her motivator, but everywhere she looked, it was the same. She felt dizzy. This place was not an accident. It was intentional. It was directed at her. It was a trap for her.

She had a vision of this planet: plants, animals, humans, and creatures in between, all intertwined in one great rapacious, battling, steaming, creaming, moaning, sucking, fucking, slavering, groping, dying, crying, pyramidal unity.

The creatures whirled in a sickening flux around her and sang to her:

"Earth is dead."

"Nothing matters."

"Sufferance."

"Desolation."

"Pleasure."

"Unity."

"Forever and ever, amen."

Lady Sunshine was bewildered and beset.

"Who shall initiate her into the mysteries?" the creatures asked.

The dryad stepped forward. She wriggled her wet and gaping snout.

"I saw her first," she said. "I should have first turn."

"You've had your first turns, darling," said a filthy grandmother with a neck that hung in wattles like a turkey, and empty withered breasts. She gnawed on the leg bone of a child. "But I have experience, and experience counts."

"Match experience," said the dryad. "Match your unity against mine."

"Very well," said the grandmother. "Have a nibble," she said, and handed her bone to the dryad.

"And you," said the dryad, handing her black companion to the ancient.

The fat dryad munched at the leg bone. The filthy old woman tried to bite the wriggling creeper she held, but it evaded her and struck at her wrinkled neck.

The old woman snapped like a mongoose and the tendril was caught and bitten in two. It fell limp. The dryad shuddered and ululated. Then she flickered and was gone.

"One for me," said the old one. "Unity."

The crowd shuddered and cried, "One for you."

"As you see, it is experience that counts. Oh, what I will teach this sweet child."

But then a man stepped forward, naked except for black socks. In this company he was unusual, because he looked fully human. He did not flicker at all unless you watched him very closely, and his dark hair was neatly combed.

He said, "You forget me."

"I did forget you, Dr. Wrongsong," said the grandmother, "but only for the merest moment. Let us step aside and match ourselves one against one."

Dr. Wrongsong smiled sincerely. "One against one," he said.

"Unity," said everyone. "Unity above all."

They all disappeared, the man, the grandmother, and all the various creatures. The world around Lady Sunshine shattered, sharded, pinwheeled, blurred, spilled, swirled and ran. There was only one stability in all the chaos. That was the doggish creature.

It came sniffing up to Lady Sunshine. She tried to back away from it, but could not move.

"Try to leave," said the doggish creature. "Just try to leave us. You will find that you cannot. We are yours, and you are ours. I will be last. I'm always last. But in the end there will be one for me."

To her horror, it lifted its leg and urinated all over her, and she could not prevent being marked.

"Unity," it said. Then it disappeared, too.

Lady Sunshine was helpless and alone, lost in lovelessness. She tried vainly to move, but her head was vise-gripped. Her hands were cuffed. Her fingers were paralyzed. She could not move her motivator. She could not extend her extensible eye. She could not rotate her rotatable eye.

She could not leave the mechanical. She could not retire from this place. She could not take her ship through hyperspace and escape as she wanted. She could not move at all.

She knew now why this place reminded her of Amabile. But it was far more terrible than Amabile had ever been.

She realized that Madame O'Severe was right.

She had hoped to remain aloof from corruption. She had longed to remain untouched. But now she was lost, eternally damned.

This was the entire universe, forever and ever. And it was the same everywhere:

Disease . . .

Decay . . .

Death . . .

Devolution . . .

$$O'Severe = Amabile = Beatus$$

As counterpoint to her thoughts, this planet played for her its single eternal song of ecstatic revulsion, of solitary abandonment and humiliation. It filled Lady Sunshine's head and heart as the one real thing.

But no! There was a realer thing. There was one hope.

There was True Earth. Somewhere there was True Earth.

No matter what else, there was True Earth.

The awful keening stopped as abruptly as it had begun. There was silence. Long, empty silence.

Then the sincere man stepped into being through the swirling colorful dissolve. He was alone.

Dr. Wrongsong's hair was still perfectly in place, but he was now missing a sock. Lady Sunshine saw that his bare foot was not human, but was other.

"Here I am at last," he said, licking his lips and teeth clean of blood. "Have I kept you long?"

Lady Sunshine looked blindly at him and tried to hold onto her dream of True Earth.

"You think you understand now," Dr. Wrongsong said, "but of course you don't. You must be dominated. Experience is the only true teacher."

She protested. "I don't understand! I won't understand!"

"No false innocence. You say you don't understand, but of course you do. Deep in your heart, you do. You did not come here by accident. You sought us out. This is the place for which you have longed."

"What do you mean?" she cried.

"This is True Earth."

No! If this was True Earth, then there was no hope.

"And now you must be touched," Dr. Wrongsong said.

He reached out, and she could not prevent him. She could not resist. She could not help herself. There was no escape.

Escape? To what? To where?

He touched her. He spun her ruthlessly on her motivator, and around and around she went. She spun in her mind. Helplessly.

Hopelessly she cried cried cried to be saved.

And then, all around Lady Sunshine the dissolving spinning world split apart and there was light. The helmet of the probe machine was lifted from her head and she lay open to the radiance of a new universe.

"Magoon," she said. "It's you."

5

He had come somehow. Out of his coma. Out of the grip of the emergency unit. From behind his closed doors.

The Magoon was naked and hairy. He dripped tubes, wires, and broken needles, but he took no notice of them. His eyes were for her, otherwise unseeing.

He said, "I heard you call for me, and I came."

She hugged and kissed him desperately.

"Bless you, Magoon," she said. "This is an awful place and we must get away from it."

The Magoon looked at Lady Sunshine.

"This is the place," he said. "I know it. There is no other."

And he collapsed.

She cried, and laughed, and gasped because he was hurt and he was her love. She plucked the thorns and darts from him. With impossible strength, she carried him in her arms to her bed.

She had not yet thought of him when she said they must leave, but now she did think of him. She thought of him above herself.

The Magoon could not go elsewhere than this planet. And she must take him there, for his sake.

If this was True Earth, it did not matter. One place was like another. The one thing she was sure of was the Magoon, and if they were together, it did not matter where they traveled. The Magoon transformed the universe.

She kissed him and tenderly stroked his hairiness.

Then she turned to her piloting. With the aid of the computer and her own skill, she brought her white spaceship safely to land not far from the drone on this planet without landing grids, this awful world she had just quitted. And felt relief.

Not far distant, Lady Sunshine could see her former mechanical body. It stood alone. Abandoned. Inert.

But something was strange. She felt as she had never felt before in all her life, and she did not know what it meant. She glowed within herself. Her heart was lifted.

What did it mean?

This was not the way it had been when she inhabited the mechanical. That was remote and queer. And this might almost be a different world. Or was the difference in her?

This world was changed. It was not the same. She saw it differently.

She threw open the doors of the spaceship and stared about her in wonderment. The planet was lit from within itself. Colors were everywhere pure and luminescent. They glowed and streamed with inner life like the slowly pulsing breath of a stained glass dove.

The planet was filled with notes that hummed and fluttered and chimed. Occasional notes that came and went, or stayed, or changed. Rare harmonies. And the colors interplayed and shifted with the notes of the song the planet sang. All in goldenness and sunshine.

The Magoon joined her, risen from her bed, and she turned to him. He was well. He was healed. His eyes were no longer sad. He was beautiful.

He was beautiful, but at the same time no less the Magoon that had been. He was not altered. He was transfigured. And he smiled at her.

Lady Sunshine looked at him, and in him she saw enhanced all that was good in herself and all that was glorious in this strange planet. She loved him, not as ultimate truth, but for the ultimate truth that she saw within him.

And if he was made well, so was she. She, who had not even realized that she was sick.

A great oppression that had been with her always was now lifted. And it was only with its passing that she realized its existence.

She, who had been bent, was no longer bent.

"I love you, my dear Magoon," she said. "In you, I see more than I can ever say."

"And I love you," he said.

It was then that they became partners. They were no longer solitary selfish unities, but were joined together in a Oneness that was more than either of them, that was more than their sum.

They exchanged names. Hers was Jennet. His was Lester, which means "lustrous."

She had never told her true name to anyone before.

They turned to the planet again and went out into the world together, hand in hand. Lady Sunshine cast her white clothing from her and let herself be touched by the winds of color. They played on her body and she laughed in surprise. She was lifted into the air on a chiming note and became part of the dance of color and the song of songs. She was ecstatic. Her bare body sailed in the iridescent streaming rainbow swirl.

It was all so strange and wonderful. It was the same world that she had encountered before, but it was seen with transformed eyes.

As they played, knowledge came to them. It surrounded them. Knowledge was this world, and in their play they became knowledge. They knew truth.

There was no more bentness.

They saw the computer's standard of "True Earth" as the poor, partial composite that it was. This planet could not be recognized by any sum of addition. It was of another order.

They saw the probe mechanicals in all their inadequacy. How could truth be perceived as truth by means of this fractional version of human perception? It could not.

And they saw themselves for what they had been: distorted, half-human creatures.

And they knew other things. Together Lady Sunshine and the Magoon laughed and shouted, rolling through the singing shafts of luminous color. They were together with each other and with this world. They were locked together in Oneness.

Love was experienced. Love was known to them.

This world was love, and love was knowledge. Knowledge, love, and knowledge this world.

And then suddenly the sounds and colors around them were altered to new orders of complexity, far beyond their range. They looked and found themselves in the presence of three people—a boy, a mature woman, and an old man, all clothed in reclarified light.

"Welcome," they said. "Welcome. The celebration of your homecoming is in progress, and we have been sent to bring you. Array yourselves and come."

Homecoming!

Lady Sunshine said, "Is this True Earth?"

They laughed.

The woman said, "No. True Earth is every human world."

And Lady Sunshine suddenly perceived

O'Severe = True Earth = Beatus

The Magoon—Lester, the Lustrous One—said, "Yes! Yes! And now I know how to make the Ninety Worlds True Earth."

"Of course," the boy said. "That is what you came to learn."

Lady Sunshine said, "But if this is not True Earth, what place is it?"

"This is Livermore," the old man said. "This is the world where everything is possible to those who can perceive."

6

When it was fully time for Lady Sunshine and the Magoon to leave Livermore, there was another celebration. Then the others made a grid in their minds to hurl the white spaceship into space.

They went first to O'Severe by long passage. Hyperspace was no trial now to the Magoon, for he knew better.

Madame O'Severe said, "So you are returned at last. You took long enough about it."

"You gave me permission to find out where my best interests lie," Lady Sunshine said.

"And here you are. I should not have thought it would take you this long. Who is this grotesque that accompanies you?"

Lady Sunshine said, "This is the Magoon of Beatus. He is my love and partner."

"You have never had good judgment," said Madame O'Severe. "You have never known what was important and what was not. My patience with you is nearly at an end. You must rid yourself of this monster if you would be my instrument."

"I will not be your instrument," said Lady Sunshine. "I know now where it is that my best interests lie, and they do not lie with you."

"I disown you," said Madame O'Severe. "You are not a serious person."

Lady Sunshine and her partner, the Magoon, traveled to Beatus. There they turned the mighty machines of the planet to new purpose. They changed the blue fog into dissipating mist, and performed other wonders.

Lady Magoon and the Sunshine of Beatus.

And that was not the last of what they did. They healed many worlds, among them O'Severe.

Alexei and Cory Panshin write:

We were married in June 1969, just before the bright and hopeful days of the sixties that produced Sgt. Pepper *and* Lord of Light *were*

*declared officially dead by Richard Nixon, Spiro Agnew, and John
Mitchell. Six months before Altamont.*

*Darkness and confusion hadn't yet seized control. Woodstock, the
last muddy flower of the counterculture, was still two months away.
But signs were already in the air. In the week before we were married, Alexei finished his third Anthony Villiers story,* Masque World,
*a book with a darkness of tone that wasn't there in the two that came
before it.*

*Both our apartment leases ran out that summer, Alexei's in New
York, Cory's in Cambridge. We looked for a new place to live, but
we could find no place for ourselves in the city. Then, in August,
through a chain of circumstances totally strange, we found ourselves
living in isolation on a farm in Elephant, Pennsylvania.*

*Do you know the story of the elephant in the dark? If you passed
through Elephant, Pennsylvania, in the dark, you wouldn't even
know it was there.*

*The farm is on a hilltop. At night, the stars are bright overhead.
People and society are only rumors, glows at the horizon.*

But what is the center of things? And where is the periphery?

*Elephant has been a place to think, a stillness in the midst of
storms, a calmness in the midst of confusion. We have done a lot of
thinking here, about who we really are and what we are doing. Our
three-year series of columns in* Fantastic, *probing into the mysterious
nature of science fiction, was a product of Elephant.*

*Elephant has also been a place in which to change. The greatest
part of* Farewell to Yesterday's Tomorrow, *a book of short stories
about the possibility and necessity of change, was written in Elephant. So was our novel,* The Son of Black Morca, *which is about
giving up one self-definition in favor of another.*

So was "Lady Sunshine and the Magoon of Beatus."

If the darkness and night of Masque World *were an unconscious anticipation of the decadence and repression of the early seventies, then
what have we unconsciously anticipated in "Lady Sunshine"?*

A lifting of clouds? New brightness?

". . . FOR A SINGLE YESTERDAY"

by George R. R. Martin

Keith was our culture, what little we had left. He was our poet and our troubadour, and his voice and his guitar were our bridges to the past. He was a timetripper too, but no one minded that much until Winters came along.

Keith was our memory. But he was also my friend.

He played for us every evening after supper. Just beyond sight of the common house, there was a small clearing and a rock he liked to sit on. He'd wander there at dusk, with his guitar, and sit down facing west. Always west; the cities had been east of us. Far east, true, but Keith didn't like to look that way. Neither did the rest of us, to tell the truth.

Not everybody came to the evening concerts, but there was always a good crowd, say three-fourths of the people in the commune. We'd gather around in a rough circle, sitting on the ground or lying in the grass by ones and twos. And Keith, our living hi-fi in denim and leather, would stroke his beard in vague amusement and begin to play.

He was good, too. Back in the old days, before the Blast, he'd been well on his way to making a name for himself. He'd come to the commune four years ago for a rest, to check up on old friends and get away from the musical rat race for a summer. But he'd figured on returning.

Then came the Blast. And Keith had stayed. There was nothing left to go back to. His cities were graveyards full of dead and dying, their towers melted tombstones that glowed at night. And the rats—human and animal—were everywhere else.

In Keith, those cities still lived. His songs were all of the old days, bittersweet things full of lost dreams and loneliness. And he sang them with love and longing. Keith would play requests, but mostly he stuck to his kind of music. A lot of folk, a lot of folk-rock, and a few straight rock things and show tunes. Lightfoot and Kristofferson and Woody Guthrie were particular favorites. And once in a while he'd play his own compositions, written in the days before the Blast. But not often.

Two songs, though, he played every night. He always started with "They Call the Wind Maria" and ended with "Me and Bobby McGee." A few of us got tired of the ritual, but no one ever objected. Keith seemed to think the songs fit us, somehow, and nobody wanted to argue with him.

Until Winters came along, that is. Which was in a late-fall evening in the fourth year after the Blast.

His first name was Robert, but no one ever used it, although the rest of us were all on a first-name basis. He'd introduced himself as Lieutenant Robert Winters the evening he arrived, driving up in a jeep with two other men. But his Army didn't exist anymore, and he was looking for refuge and help.

That first meeting was tense. I remember feeling very scared when I heard the jeep coming, and wiping my palms on my jeans as I waited. We'd had visitors before. None of them very nice.

I waited for them alone. I was as much a leader as we had in those days. And that wasn't much. We voted on everything important, and nobody gave orders. So I wasn't really a boss, but I was a greeting committee. The rest scattered, which was good sense. Our last visitors had gone in big for slugging people and raping the girls. They'd worn black-and-gold uniforms and called themselves the Sons of the Blast. A fancy name for a rat pack. We called them SOB's too, but for other reasons.

Winters was different, though. His uniform was the good ol' U. S. of A. Which didn't prove a thing, since some Army detachments are as bad as the rat packs. It was our own friendly Army that went through the area in the first year after the Blast, scorching the towns and killing everyone they could lay their hands on.

I don't think Winters was part of that, although I never had the courage to flat-out ask him. He was too decent. He was big and blond and straight, and about the same age as the rest of us. And his two "men" were scared kids, younger than most of us in the commune. They'd been through a lot, and they wanted to join us. Winters kept saying that he wanted to help us rebuild.

We voted them in, of course. We haven't turned anyone away yet, except for a few rats. In the first year, we even took in a half-dozen citymen and nursed them while they died of radiation burns.

Winters changed us, though, in ways we never anticipated. Maybe for the better. Who knows? He brought books and supplies. And guns, too, and two men who knew how to use them. A lot of the guys on the commune had come there to get away from guns and uniforms, in the days before the Blast. So Pete and Crazy Harry took over the hunting, and defended us against the rats that drifted by from time to time. They became our police force and our army.

And Winters became our leader.

I'm still not sure how that happened. But it did. He started out making suggestions, moved on to leading discussions, and wound up giving orders. Nobody objected much. We'd been drifting ever since the Blast, and Winters gave us a direction. He had big ideas, too. When I was spokesman, all I worried about was getting us through until tomorrow. But Winters wanted to rebuild. He wanted to build a generator, and hunt for more survivors, and gather them together into a sort of village. Planning was his bag. He had big dreams for the day after tomorrow, and his hope was catching.

I shouldn't give the wrong impression, though. He wasn't any sort of a tin tyrant. He led us, yeah, but he was one of us, too. He was a little different from us, but not *that* different, and he became a friend in time. And he did his part to fit in. He even let his hair get long and grew a beard.

Only Keith never liked him much.

Winters didn't come out to concert rock until he'd been with us over a week. And when he did come, he stood outside the circle at first, his hands shoved into his pockets. The rest of us were lying around as usual, some singing, some just listening. It was a bit chilly that night, and we had a small fire going.

Winters stood in the shadows for about three songs. Then, during a pause, he walked closer to the fire. "Do you take requests?" he asked, smiling uncertainly.

I didn't know Winters very well back then. But I knew Keith. And I tensed a little as I waited for his answer.

But he just strummed the guitar idly and stared at Winters' uniform and his short hair. "That depends," he said at last. "I'm not going to play 'Ballad of the Green Berets,' if that's what you want."

An unreadable expression flickered over Winters' face. "I've killed people, yes," he said. "But that doesn't mean I'm proud of it. I wasn't going to ask for that."

Keith considered that, and looked down at his guitar. Then, seemingly satisfied, he nodded and raised his head and smiled. "Okay," he said. "What do you want to hear?"

"You know 'Leavin' on a Jet Plane'?" Winters asked.

The smile grew. "Yeah. John Denver. I'll play it for you. Sad song, though. There aren't any jet planes anymore, Lieutenant. Know that? 'S true. You should stop and think why."

He smiled again, and began to play. Keith always had the last word when he wanted it. Nobody could argue with his guitar.

A little over a mile from the common house, beyond the fields to the west, a little creek ran through the hills and the trees. It was usually dry in the summer and the fall, but it was still a nice spot. Dark and quiet at night, away from the noise and the people. When the weather was right, Keith would drag his sleeping bag out there and bunk down under a tree. Alone.

That's also where he did his timetripping.

I found him there that night, after the singing was over and everyone else had gone to bed. He was leaning against his favorite tree, swatting mosquitoes and studying the creekbed.

I sat down next to him. "Hi, Gary," he said, without looking at me.

"Bad times, Keith?" I asked.

"Bad times, Gary," he said, staring at the ground and idly twirling a fallen leaf. I watched his face. His mouth was taut and expressionless, his eyes hooded.

I'd known Keith for a long time. I knew enough not to say anything. I just sat next to him in silence, making myself comfortable in a pile of fresh-fallen leaves. And after a while he began to talk, as he always did.

"There ought to be water," he said suddenly, nodding at the creek. "When I was a kid, I lived by a river. Right across the street. Oh, it was a dirty little river in a dirty little town, and the water was as polluted as all hell. But it was still water. Sometimes, at night, I'd go over to the park across the street, and sit on a bench, and watch it. For hours, sometimes. My mother used to get mad at me."

He laughed softly. "It was pretty, you know. Even the oil slicks were pretty. And it helped me think. I miss that, you know. The water. I always think better when I'm watching water. Strange, right?"

"Not so strange," I said.

He still hadn't looked at me. He was still staring at the dry creek, where only darkness flowed now. And his hands were tearing the leaf into pieces. Slow and methodical, they were.

"Gone now," he said after a silence. "The place was too close to New York. The water probably glows now, if there is any water. Prettier than ever, but I can't go back. So much is like that. Every time I remember something, I have to remember that it's gone now. And I can't go back, ever. To anything. Except . . . except with that . . . ." He nodded toward the ground between us. Then he finished with the leaf, and started another.

I reached down by his leg. The cigar box was where I expected it. I held it in both hands, and flipped the lid with my thumbs. Inside, there was the needle, and maybe a dozen small bags of powder. The powder looked white in the starlight. But seen by day, it was pale, sparkling blue.

I looked at it and sighed. "Not much left," I said.

Keith nodded, never looking. "I'll be out in a month, I figure." His voice sounded very tired. "Then I'll just have my songs, and my memories."

"That's all you've got now," I said. I closed the box with a snap and handed it to him. "Chronine isn't a time machine, Keith. Just a hallucinogen that happens to work on memory."

He laughed. "They used to debate that, way back when. The experts all said chronine was a memory drug. But they never *took* chronine. Neither have you, Gary. But I know. I've timetripped. It's not memory. It's more. You go back, Gary, you really do. You live it again, whatever it was. You can't change anything, but you know it's real, all the same."

He threw away what was left of his leaf, and gathered his knees together with his arms. Then he put his head atop them and looked at me. "You ought to timetrip someday, Gary. You really ought to. Get the dosage right, and you can pick your yesterday. It's not a bad deal at all."

I shook my head. "If I wanted to timetrip, would you let me?"

"No," he said, smiling but not moving his head. "I found the chronine. It's mine. And there's too little left to share. Sorry, Gary. Nothing personal, though. You know how it is."

"Yeah," I said. "I know how it is. I didn't want it anyway."

"I knew that," he said.

Ten minutes of thick silence. I broke it with a question. "Winters bother you?"

"Not really," he said. "He seems okay. It was just the uniforms,

Gary. If it wasn't for those damn bastards in uniform and what they did, I *could* go back. To my river, and my singing."

"And Sandi," I said.

His mouth twisted into a reluctant smile. "And Sandi," he admitted. "And I wouldn't even need chronine to keep my dates."

I didn't know what to say to that. So I didn't say anything. Finally, wearying, Keith slid forward a little, and lay back under the tree. It was a clear night. You could see the stars through the branches.

"Sometimes, out here at night, I forget," he said softly, more to himself than to me. "The sky still looks the same as it did before the Blast. And the stars don't know the difference. If I don't look east, I can almost pretend it never happened."

I shook my head. "Keith, that's a game. It *did* happen. You can't forget that. You know you can't. And you can't go back. You know that, too."

"You don't listen, do you, Gary? I *do* go back. I really do."

"You go back to a dream world, Keith. And it's dead, that world. You can't keep it up. Sooner or later you're going to have to start living in reality."

Keith was still looking up at the sky, but he smiled gently as I argued. "No, Gary. You don't see. The past is as real as the present, you know. And when the present is bleak and empty, and the future more so, then the only sanity is living in the past."

I started to say something, but he pretended not to hear. "Back in the city, when I was a kid, I never saw this many stars," he said, his voice distant. "The first time I got into the country, I remember how shocked I was at all the extra stars they'd gone and stuck in my sky." He laughed softly. "Know when that was? Six years ago, when I was just out of school. Also last night. Take your pick. Sandi was with me, both times."

He fell silent. I watched him for a few moments, then stood up and brushed myself off. It was never any use. I couldn't convince him. And the saddest part of it was, I couldn't even convince myself. Maybe he was right. Maybe, for him, that was the answer.

"You ever been in the mountains?" he asked suddenly. He looked up at me quickly, but didn't wait for an answer. "There was this night, Gary—in Pennsylvania, in the mountains. I had this old beat-up camper, and we were driving through, bumming it around the country.

"Then, all of a sudden, this fog hit us. Thick stuff, gray and rolling, all kind of mysterious and spooky. Sandi loved stuff like that, and I did too, kind of. But it was hell to drive through. So I pulled off the road, and we took out a couple of blankets and went off a few feet.

"It was still early, though. So we just lay on the blankets together, and held each other, and talked. About us, and my songs, and that great fog, and our trip, and her acting, and all sorts of things. We kept laughing and kissing, too, although I don't remember what we said that was so funny. Finally, after an hour or so, we undressed each other and made love on the blankets, slow and easy, in the middle of that dumb fog."

Keith propped himself up on an elbow and looked at me. His voice was bruised, lost, hurt, eager. And lonely. "She was beautiful, Gary. She really was. She never liked me to say that, though. I don't think she believed it. She liked me to tell her she was pretty. But she was more than pretty. She *was* beautiful. All warm and soft and golden, with red-blond hair and these dumb eyes that were either green or gray, depending on her mood. That night they were gray, I think. To match the fog." He smiled, and sank back, and looked up at the stars again.

"The funniest thing was the fog," he said. Very slowly. "When we'd finished making love, and we lay back together, the fog was gone. And the stars were out, as bright as tonight. The stars came out for us. The silly goddamn voyeuristic stars came out to watch us make it. And I told her that, and we laughed, and I held her warm against me. And she went to sleep in my arms, while I lay there and looked at stars and tried to write a song for her."

"Keith . . ." I started.

"Gary," he said. "I'm going back there tonight. To the fog and the stars and my Sandi."

"Damnit, Keith," I said. "Stop it. You're getting yourself hooked."

Keith sat up again and began unbuttoning his sleeve. "Did you ever think," he said, "that maybe it's not the drug that I'm addicted to?" And he smiled very broadly, like a cocky, eager kid.

Then he reached for his box, and his timetrip. "Leave me alone," he said.

That must have been a good trip. Keith was all smiles and affability the next day, and his glow infected the rest of us. The mood lasted all week. Work seemed to go faster and easier than usual, and the nightly song sessions were as boisterous as I can remember them.

There was a lot of laughter, and maybe more honest hope than we'd had for quite a while.

I shouldn't give Keith all the credit, though. Winters was already well into his suggestion-making period, and things were happening around the commune. To begin with, he and Pete were already hard at work building another house—a cabin off to the side of the common house. Pete had hooked up with one of the girls, and I guess he wanted a little more privacy. But Winters saw it as the first step toward the village he envisioned.

That wasn't his only project, either. He had a whole sheaf of maps in his jeep, and every night he'd drag someone off to the side and pore over them by candlelight, asking all sorts of questions. He wanted to know which areas we'd searched for survivors, and which towns might be worth looting for supplies, and where the rat packs liked to run, and that sort of thing. Why? Well, he had some "search expeditions" in mind, he said.

There was a handful of kids on the commune, and Winters thought we ought to organize a school for them, to replace the informal tutoring they'd been getting. Then he thought we ought to build a generator and get the electricity going again. Our medical resources were limited to a good supply of drugs and medicines; Winters thought that one of us should quit the fields permanently and train himself as a village doctor. Yeah, Winters had a lot of ideas, all right. And a good portion of 'em were pretty good, although it was clear that the details were going to require some working out.

Meanwhile, Winters had also become a regular at the evening singing. With Keith in a good mood, that didn't pose any real problems. In fact, it livened things up a little.

The second night that Winters came, Keith looked at him very pointedly and swung into "Vietnam Rag," with the rest of us joining in. Then he followed it up with "Universal Soldier." In between lyrics, he kept flashing Winters this taunting grin.

Winters took it pretty well, however. He squirmed and looked uncomfortable at first, but finally entered into the spirit of the thing and began to smile. Then, when Keith finished, he stood up. "If you're so determined to cast me as the commune's very own friendly reactionary, well I guess I'll have to oblige," he said. He reached out a hand. "Give me that guitar."

Keith looked curious but willing. He obliged. Winters grabbed the instrument, strummed it a few times uncertainly, and launched into a robust version of "Okie from Muskogee." He played like his fingers were made of stone, and sang worse. But that wasn't the point.

Keith began laughing before Winters was three bars into the song. The rest of us followed suit. Winters, looking very grim and determined, plowed on through to the bitter end, even though he didn't know all the words and had to fake it in spots. Then he did the Marine hymn for an encore, ignoring all the hissing and moaning.

When he was finished, Pete clapped loudly. Winters bowed, smiled, and handed the guitar back to Keith with an exaggerated flourish.

Keith, of course, was not one to be topped easily. He nodded at Winters, took the guitar, and promptly did "Eve of Destruction."

Winters retaliated with "Welfare Cadillac." Or tried to. Turned out he knew hardly any of the words, so he finally gave that up and settled for "Anchors Aweigh."

That sort of thing went on all night, as they jousted back and forth, and everybody else sat around laughing. Well, actually we did more than laugh. Generally we had to help Winters with his songs, since he didn't really know any of them all the way through. Keith held his own without us, of course.

It was one of the more memorable sessions. The only thing it really had in common with Keith's usual concerts was that it began with "They Call the Wind Maria," and ended with "Me and Bobby McGee."

But the next day, Keith was more subdued. Still some kidding around between him and Winters, but mostly the singing slipped back into the older pattern. And the day after, the songs were nearly all Keith's kind of stuff, except for a few requests from Winters, which Keith did weakly and halfheartedly.

I doubt that Winters realized what was happening. But I did, and so did most of the others. We'd seen it before. Keith was getting down again. The afterglow from his latest timetrip was fading. He was getting lonely and hungry and restless. He was itching; yet again, for his Sandi.

Sometimes, when he got that way, you could almost see the hurt. And if you couldn't see it, you could hear it when he sang. Loud and throbbing in every note.

Winters heard it too. He'd have had to be deaf to miss it. Only I don't think he understood what he heard, and I know he didn't understand Keith. All he knew was the anguish he heard. And it troubled him.

So, being Winters, he decided to do something about it. He came to Keith.

I was there at the time. It was midmorning, and Keith and I had come in from the field for a break. I was sitting on the well with a cup of water in my hand, and Keith was standing next to me talking. You could tell that he was getting ready to timetrip again, soon. He was very down, very distant, and I was having trouble reaching him.

In the middle of all this, Winters comes striding up, smiling, in his Army jacket. His house was rising quickly, and he was cheerful about it, and he and Crazy Harry had already mapped out the first of their "search expeditions."

"Hello, men," he said when he joined us at the well. He reached for the water, and I passed my cup.

He took a deep drink and passed it back. Then he looked at Keith. "I enjoy your singing," he said. "I think everybody else does, too. You're very good, really." He grinned. "Even if you are an anarchistic bastard."

Keith nodded. "Yeah, thanks," he said. He was in no mood for fooling around.

"One thing, though, has been bothering me," Winters said. "I figured maybe I could discuss it with you, maybe make a few suggestions. Okay?"

Keith stroked his beard and paid a little more attention. "Okay. Shoot, Colonel."

"It's your songs. I've noticed that most of them are pretty . . . down, let's say. Good songs, sure. But sort of depressing, if you know what I mean. Especially in view of the Blast. You sing too much about the old days, and things we've lost. I don't think that's good for morale. We've got to stop dwelling so much on the past if we're ever going to rebuild."

Keith stared at him, and slumped against the well. "You gotta be kidding," he said.

"No," said Winters. "No, I mean it. A few cheerful songs would do a lot for us. Life can still be good and worthwhile if we work at it. You should tell us that in your music. Concentrate on the things we still have. We need hope and courage. Give them to us."

But Keith wasn't buying it. He stroked his beard, and smiled, and finally shook his head. "No, Lieutenant, no way. It doesn't work like that. I don't sing propaganda, even if it's well-meant. I sing what I feel."

His voice was baffled. "Cheerful songs, well . . . no. I can't. They don't work, not for me. I'd like to believe it, but I can't, you see. And I can't make other people believe if I don't. Life is pretty empty around here, the way I see it. And not too likely to improve. And . . . well, as long as I see it that way, I've got to sing it that way. You see?"

Winters frowned. "Things aren't *that* hopeless," he said. "And even if they were, we can't admit it, or we're finished."

Keith looked at Winters, at me, then down into the well. He shook his head again, and straightened. "No," he said simply, gently, sadly. And he left us at the well to stalk silently into the fields.

Winters watched him go, then turned to me. I offered him more water, but he shook his head. "What do you think, Gary?" he said. "Did I have a point? Or did I?"

I considered the question, and the asker. Winters sounded very troubled and very sincere. And the blond stubble on his chin made it clear that he was trying his best to fit in. I decided to trust him, a little.

"Yes," I said. "I know what you were driving at. But it's not that easy. Keith's songs aren't just songs. They mean things to him."

I hesitated, then continued. "Look, the Blast was hell for everybody, I don't have to tell you that. But most of us out here, we chose this kind of life, 'cause we wanted to get away from the cities and what they stood for. We miss the old days, sure. We've lost people, and things we valued, and a lot that made life joyful. And we don't much care for the constant struggle, or for having to live in fear of the rat packs. Still, a lot of what we valued is right here on the commune, and it hasn't changed that much. We've got the land, and the trees, and each other. And freedom of a sort. No pollution, no competition, no hatred. We like to remember the old days, and the *good* things in the cities—that's why we like Keith's singing—but now has its satisfactions too.

"Only, Keith is different. He didn't choose this way, he was only visiting. His dreams were all tied up with the cities, with poetry and music and people and noise. And he's lost his world; everything he did and wanted to do is gone. And . . . and well, there was this girl. Sandra, but he called her Sandi. She and Keith lived together for two years, traveled together, did everything together. They only split for a summer, so she could go back to college. Then they were going to join up again. You understand?"

Winters understood. "And then the Blast?"

"And then the Blast. Keith was here, in the middle of nowhere.

Sandi was in New York City. So he lost her, too. I think sometimes that if Sandi had been with him, he'd have gotten over the rest. She was the most important part of the world he lost, the world they shared together. With her here, they could have shared a new world and found new beauties and new songs to sing. But she wasn't here, and . . ."

I shrugged.

"Yeah," said Winters solemnly. "But it's been four years, Gary. I lost a lot too, including my wife. But I got over it. Sooner or later, mourning has to stop."

"Yes," I said. "For you, and for me. But I haven't lost that much, and you . . . you think that things will be good again. Keith doesn't. Maybe things were *too* good for him in the old days. Or maybe he's just too romantic for his own good. Or maybe he loved harder than we did. All I know is that *his* dream tomorrow is like his yesterday, and mine isn't. I've never found anything I could be that happy with. Keith did, or thinks he did. Same difference. He wants it back."

I drank some more water, and rose. "I've got to get back to work," I said quickly, before Winters could continue the conversation. But I was thoughtful as I walked back to the fields.

There was, of course, one thing I hadn't told Winters, one important thing. The timetripping. Maybe if Keith was forced to settle for the life he had, he'd come out of it. Like the rest of us had done.

But Keith had an option; Keith could go back. Keith still had his Sandi, so he didn't *have* to start over again.

That, I thought, explained a lot. Maybe I should have mentioned it to Winters. Maybe.

Winters skipped the singing that night. He and Crazy Harry were set to leave the next morning, to go searching to the west. They were off somewhere stocking their jeep and making plans.

Keith didn't miss them any. He sat on his rock, warmed by a pile of burning autumn leaves, and outsung the bitter wind that had started to blow. He played hard and loud, and sang sad. And after the fire went out, and the audience drifted off, he took his guitar and his cigar box and went off toward the creek.

I followed him. This time the night was black and cloudy, with the smell of rain in the air. And the wind was strong and cold. No, it didn't sound like people dying. But it moved through the trees and shook the branches and whipped away the leaves. And it sounded . . . restless.

When I reached the creek, Keith was already rolling up his sleeve.

I stopped him before he took his needle out. "Hey, Keith," I said, laying a hand on his arm. "Easy. Talk first, okay?"

He looked at my hand and his needle, and returned a reluctant nod. "Okay, Gary," he said. "But short. I'm in a rush. I haven't seen Sandi for a week."

I let go his arm and sat down. "I know."

"I was trying to make it last, Gar. I only had a month's worth, but I figured I could make it last longer if I only timetripped once a week." He smiled. "But that's hard."

"I know," I repeated. "But it would be easier if you didn't think about her so much."

He nodded, put down the box, and pulled his denim jacket a little tighter to shut out the wind. "I think too much," he agreed. Then, smiling, he added, "Such men are dangerous."

"Ummm, yeah. To themselves, mostly." I looked at him, cold and huddled in the darkness. "Keith, what will you do when you run out?"

"I wish I knew."

"I know," I said. "Then you'll forget. Your time machine will be broken, and you'll have to live today. Find somebody else and start again. Only it might be easier if you'd start now. Put away the chronine for a while. Fight it."

"Sing cheerful songs?" he asked sarcastically.

"Maybe not. I don't ask you to wipe out the past, or pretend it didn't happen. But try to find something in the present. You know it can't be as empty as you pretend. Things aren't black and white like that. Winters was part right, you know—there *are* still good things. You forget that."

"Do I? What do I forget?"

I hesitated. He was making it hard for me. "Well . . . you still enjoy your singing. You know that. And there could be other things. You used to enjoy writing your own stuff. Why don't you work on some new songs? You haven't written anything to speak of since the Blast."

Keith had picked up a handful of leaves and was offering them to the wind, one by one. "I've thought of that. You don't know how much I've thought of that, Gary. And I've *tried*. But nothing comes." His voice went soft right then. "In the old days, it was different. And you know why. Sandi would sit out in the audience every time I sang. And when I did something new, something of mine, I could see her brighten. If it was good, I'd know it, just from the way she smiled. She was proud of me, and my songs."

He shook his head. "Doesn't work now, Gary. I write a song now, and sing it, and . . . so what? Who cares? You? Yeah, maybe you and a few of the others come up after and say, 'Hey, Keith, I liked that.' But that's not the same. My songs were *important* to Sandi, the same way her acting was important to me. And now my songs aren't important to anyone. I tell myself that shouldn't matter. I should get my own satisfaction from composing, even if no one else does. I tell myself that a lot. But saying it doesn't make it so."

Sometimes I think, right then, I should have told Keith that his songs were the most important thing in the world to me. But hell, they weren't. And Keith was a friend, and I couldn't feed him lies, even if he needed them.

Besides, he wouldn't have believed me. Keith had a way of recognizing truth.

Instead, I floundered. "Keith, you could find someone like that again, if you tried. There are girls in the commune, girls as good as Sandi, if you'd open yourself up to them. You could find someone else."

Keith gave me a calm stare, more chilling than the wind. "I don't need someone else, Gary," he said. He picked up the cigar box, opened it, and showed me the needle. "I've got Sandi."

Twice more that week Keith timetripped. And both times he rushed off with a feverish urgency. Usually he'd wait an hour or so after the singing, and discreetly drift off to his creek. But now he brought the cigar box with him, and left even before the last notes of "Me and Bobby McGee" had faded from the air.

Nobody mentioned anything, of course. We all knew Keith was timetripping, and we all knew he was running out. So we forgave him, and understood. Everybody understood, that is, except Pete, Winters' former corporal. He, like Winters and Crazy Harry, hadn't been filled in yet. But one evening at the singing, I noticed him looking curiously at the cigar box that lay by Keith's feet. He said something to Jan, the girl he'd been sleeping with. And she said something back. So I figured he'd been briefed.

I was too right.

Winters and Crazy Harry returned a week, to the day, after their departure. They were not alone. They brought three young teen-agers, a guy and two girls, whom they'd found down west, in company with a group of rats. "In company," is a euphemism, of course. The kids had been slaves. Winters and Crazy had freed them.

I didn't ask what had happened to the rats. I could guess.

There was a lot of excitement that night and the night after. The kids were a little frightened of us, and it took a lot of attention to convince them that things would be different here. Winters decided that they should have their own place, and he and Pete began planning a second new cabin. The first one was nearing its crude completion.

As it turned out, Winters and Pete were talking about more than a cabin. I should have realized that, since I caught Winters looking at Keith very curiously and thoughtfully on at least two occasions.

But I didn't realize it. Like everyone else, I was busy getting to know the newcomers and trying to make them feel at ease. It wasn't simple, that.

So I didn't know what was going on until the fourth evening after Winters' return. I was outside, listening to Keith sing. He'd just barely finished "They Call the Wind Maria," and was about to swing into a second song, when a group of people suddenly walked into the circle. Winters led them, and Crazy Harry was just behind him with the three kids. And Pete was there, with his arm around Jan. Plus a few others who hadn't been at the concert when it started but had followed Winters from the common house.

Keith figured they wanted to listen, I guess. He began to play. But Winters stopped him.

"No, Keith," he said. "Not right now. We've got business to take care of now, while everybody's together. We're going to talk tonight."

Keith's fingers stopped, and the music faded. The only sounds were the wind and the crackle of the nearby burning leaves. Everyone was looking at Winters.

"I want to talk about timetripping," Winters said.

Keith put down his guitar and glanced at the cigar box at the base of concert rock. "Talk," he said.

Winters looked around the circle, studying the impassive faces, as if he was weighing them before speaking. I looked too.

"I've been told that the commune has a supply of chronine," Winters began. "And that you use it for timetripping. Is that true, Keith?"

Keith stroked his beard, as he did when he was nervous or thoughtful. "Yeah," he said.

"And that's the *only* use that's ever been made of this chronine?"

Winters said. His supporters had gathered behind him in what seemed like a phalanx.

I stood up. I didn't feel comfortable arguing from the ground. "Keith was the first one to find the chronine," I said. "We were going through the town hospital after the Army had gotten through with it. A few drugs were all that were left. Most of them are in the commune stores, in case we need them. But Keith wanted the chronine. So we gave it to him, all of us. Nobody else cared much."

Winters nodded. "I understand that," he said very reasonably. "I'm not criticizing that decision. Perhaps you didn't realize, however, that there are other uses for chronine besides timetripping."

He paused. "Listen, and try to judge me fairly, that's all I ask," he said, looking at each of us in turn. "Chronine is a powerful drug; it's an important resource, and we need all our resources right now. And timetripping—anyone's timetripping—is an *abuse* of the drug. Not what it was intended for."

That was a mistake on Winters' part. Lectures on drug abuse weren't likely to go over big in the commune. I could feel the people around me getting uptight.

Rick, a tall, thin guy with a goatee who came to the concerts every night, took a poke at Winters from the ground. "Bullshit," he said. "Chronine's time travel, Colonel. Meant to be used for tripping."

"Right," someone else said. "And we gave it to Keith. I don't want to timetrip, but he does. So what's wrong with it?"

Winters defused the hostility quickly. "Nothing," he said. "*If* we had an unlimited supply of chronine. But we don't. Do we, Keith?"

"No," Keith said quietly. "Just a little left."

The fire was reflected in Winters' eyes when he looked at Keith. It made it difficult to read his expression. But his voice sounded heavy. "Keith, I know what those time trips mean to you. And I don't want to hurt you, really I don't. But we need that chronine, all of us."

"How?" That was me. I wanted Keith to give up chronine, but I'd be damned before I'd let it be taken from him. "How do we *need* the chronine?"

"Chronine is not a time machine," Winters said. "It is a memory drug. And there are things we *must* remember." He glanced around the circle. "Is there anyone here who ever worked in a hospital? An orderly? A candy-striper? Never mind. There might be, in a group this size. And they'd have seen things. Somewhere in the back of their skulls they'd *know* things we need to know. I'll bet some of you took shop in high school. I'll bet you learned all sorts of useful things. But how much do you remember? With chronine, you could remember it all. We might have someone here who once learned to make arrows. We might have a tanner. We might have someone who knows how to build a generator. We might have a *doctor!*"

Winters paused and let that sink in. Around the circle, people shifted uneasily and began to mutter.

Finally Winters continued. "If we found a library, we wouldn't burn the books for heat, no matter how cold it got. But we're doing the same thing when we let Keith timetrip. We're a library—all of us here, we have books in our heads. And the only way to read those books is with chronine. We should use it to help us remember the things we must know. We should hoard it like a treasure, calculate every recall session carefully, and make sure—make *absolutely* sure—that we don't waste a grain of it."

Then he stopped. A long, long silence followed; for Keith, an endless one. Finally Rick spoke again. "I never thought of that," he said reluctantly. "Maybe you have something. My father was a doctor, if that means anything."

Then another voice, and another; then a chorus of people speaking at once, throwing up half-remembered experiences that might be valuable, might be useful. Winters had struck paydirt.

He wasn't smiling, though. He was looking at me. I wouldn't meet his eyes. I couldn't. He had a point—an awful, awful point. But I couldn't admit that, I couldn't look at him and nod my surrender. Keith was my friend, and I had to stand by him.

And of all of us in the circle, I was the only one standing. But I couldn't think of anything to say.

Finally Winters' eyes moved. He looked at concert rock. Keith sat there, looking at the cigar box.

The hubbub went on for at least five minutes, but at last it died of its own weight. One by one the speakers glanced at Keith, and remembered, and dropped off into awkward silence. When the hush was complete, Keith rose and looked around, like a man coming out of a bad dream.

"No," he said. His voice was hurt and disbelieving; his eyes moved from person to person. "You can't. I don't . . . don't *waste* chronine. You know that, all of you. I visit Sandi, and that's not wasting. I need Sandi, and she's gone. I have to go back. It's my only way, my time machine." He shook his head.

My turn. "Yes," I said, as forcefully as I could manage. "Keith's right. Waste is a matter of definition. If you ask me, the biggest waste would be sending people back to sleep through college lectures a second time."

Laughter. Then other voices backed me. "I'm with Gary," somebody said. "Keith needs Sandi, and we need Keith. It's simple. I say he keeps the chronine."

"No way," someone else objected. "I'm as compassionate as anyone, but *hell*—how many of our people have died over the last few years 'cause we've bungled it when they needed doctoring? You remember Doug, two years ago? You shouldn't need chronine for that. A bad appendix, and he dies. We butchered him when we tried to cut it out. If there's a chance to prevent that from happening again—even a long shot—I say we gotta take it."

"No guarantee it won't happen anyway," the earlier voice came back. "You have to hit the right memories to accomplish anything, and even *they* may not be as useful as you'd like."

"Shit. We have to *try*. . . ."

"I think we have an obligation to Keith. . . ."

"I think Keith's got an obligation to *us*. . . ."

And suddenly everybody was arguing again, hassling back and forth, while Winters and Keith and I stood and listened. It went on and on, back and forth over the same points. Until Pete spoke.

He stepped around Winters, holding Jan. "I've heard enough of this," he said. "I don't even think we got no argument. Jan here is gonna have my kid, she tells me. Well, damnit, I'm not going to take any chances on her or the kid dying. If there's a way we can learn something that'll make it safer, we take it. Especially I'm not gonna take no chances for a goddamn weakling who can't face up to life. Hell, Keithie here wasn't the only one hurt, so how does *he* rate? I lost a chick in the Blast too, but I'm not begging for chronine to dream her up again. I got a new chick instead. And that's what you better do, Keith."

Keith stood very still, but his fists were balled at his sides. "There are differences, Pete," he said slowly. "Big ones. My Sandi was no chick, for one thing. And I loved her, maybe more than you can ever understand. I know you don't understand pain, Pete. You've hardened yourself to it, like a lot of people, by pretending that it doesn't exist. So you convinced everybody you're a tough guy, a strong man, real independent. And you gave up some of your humanity, too." He smiled, very much in control of himself now, his voice sure and steady. "Well, I won't play that game. I'll cling to my humanity, and fight for it if I must. I loved once, really loved. And now I hurt. And

I won't deny either of those things, or pretend that they mean any less to me than they do."

He looked to Winters. "Lieutenant, I want my Sandi, and I won't let you take her away from me. Let's have a vote."

Winters nodded.

It was close, very close. The margin was only three votes. Keith had a lot of friends.

But Winters won.

Keith took it calmly. He picked up the cigar box, walked over, and handed it to Winters. Pete was grinning happily, but Winters didn't even crack a smile.

"I'm sorry, Keith," he said.

"Yeah," said Keith. "So am I." There were tears on his face. Keith was never ashamed to cry.

There was no singing that night.

Winters didn't timetrip. He sent men on "search expeditions" into the past, all very carefully planned for minimum risk and maximum reward.

We didn't get any doctor out of it. Rick made three trips back without coming up with any useful memories. But one of the guys remembered some valuable stuff about medicinal herbs after a trip back to a bio lab, and another jaunt recalled some marginally good memories about electricity.

Winters was still optimistic, though. He'd turned to interviewing by then, to decide who should get to use the chronine next. He was very careful, very thorough, and he always asked the right questions. No one went back without his okay. Pending that approval, the chronine was stored in the new cabin, where Pete kept an eye on it.

And Keith? Keith sang. I was afraid, the night of the argument, that he might give up singing, but I was wrong. He couldn't give up song, any more than he could give up Sandi. He returned to concert rock the very next evening, and sang longer and harder than ever before. The night after that he was even better.

During the day, meanwhile, he went about his work with a strained cheerfulness. He smiled a lot, and talked a lot, but he never *said* anything much. And he never mentioned chronine, or timetripping, or the argument.

Or Sandi.

He still spent his nights out by the creek, though. The weather was getting progressively colder, but Keith didn't seem to mind. He just brought out a few blankets and his sleeping bag, and ignored the wind, and the chill, and the increasingly frequent rains.

I went out with him once or twice to sit and talk. Keith was cordial enough. But he never brought up the subjects that really mattered, and I couldn't bring myself to force the conversations to places he obviously didn't want to go. We wound up discussing the weather and like subjects.

These days, instead of his cigar box, Keith brought his guitar out to the creek. He never played it when I was there, but I heard him once or twice from a distance, when I was halfway back to the common house after one of our fruitless talks. No singing, just music. Two songs, over and over again. You know which two.

And after a while, just one. "Me and Bobby McGee." Night after night, alone and obsessed, Keith played that song, sitting by a dry creek in a barren forest. I'd always liked the song, but now I began to fear it, and a shiver would go through me whenever I heard those notes on the frosty autumn wind.

Finally, one night, I spoke to him about it. It was a short conversation, but I think it was the only time, after the argument, that Keith and I ever really reached each other.

I'd come with him to the creek, and wrapped myself in a heavy woolen blanket to ward off the cold, wet drizzle that was dripping from the skies. Keith lay against his tree, half into his sleeping bag, with his guitar on his lap. He didn't even bother to shield it against the damp, which bothered me.

We talked about nothing, until at last I mentioned his lonely creek concerts. He smiled. "You know why I play that song," he said.

"Yeah," I said. "But I wish you'd stop."

He looked away. "I will. After tonight. But tonight I play it, Gary. Don't argue, please. Just listen. The song is all I have left now, to help me think. And I've needed it, 'cause I been thinking a lot."

"I warned you about thinking," I said jokingly.

But he didn't laugh. "Yeah. You were right, too. Or I was, or Shakespeare . . . whoever you want to credit the warning to. Still, sometimes you can't help thinking. It's part of being human. Right?"

"I guess."

"I know. So I think with my music. No water left to think by, and the stars are all covered. And Sandi's gone. Really gone now. You know, Gary . . . if I kept on, day to day, and didn't think so much, I might forget her. I might even forget what she looked like. Do you think Pete remembers his chick?"

"Yes," I said. "And you'll remember Sandi. I'm sure of that. But maybe not quite so much . . . and maybe that's for the best. Sometimes it's good to forget."

Then he looked at me. Into my eyes. "But I don't *want* to forget, Gary. And I won't. I won't."

And then he began to play. The same song. Once. Twice. Three times. I tried to talk, but he wasn't listening. His fingers moved on, fiercely, relentlessly. And the music and the wind washed away my words.

Finally I gave up and left. It was a long walk back to the common house, and Keith's guitar stalked me through the drizzle.

Winters woke me in the common house, shaking me from my bunk to face a grim, gray dawn. His face was even grayer. He said nothing; he didn't want to wake the others, I guess. He just beckoned me outside.

I yawned and stretched and followed him. Just outside the door, Winters bent and handed me a broken guitar.

I looked at it blankly, then up at him. My face must have asked the question.

"He used it on Pete's head," Winters said. "And took the chronine. I think Pete has a mild concussion, but he'll probably be all right. Lucky. He could be dead, real easy."

I held the guitar in my hands. It was shattered, the wood cracked and splintered, several strings snapped. It must have been a hell of a blow. I couldn't believe it. "No," I said. "Keith . . . no, he couldn't . . ."

"It's his guitar," Winters pointed out. "And who else would take the chronine?" Then his face softened. "I'm sorry, Gary. I really am. I think I understand why he did it. Still, I want him. Any idea where he could be?"

I knew, of course. But I was scared. "What . . . what will you do?"

"No punishment," he said. "Don't worry. I just want the chronine back. We'll be more careful next time."

I nodded. "Okay," I said. "But nothing happens to Keith. I'll fight you if you go back on your word, and the others will too."

He just looked at me, very sadly, like he was disappointed that I'd mistrust him. He didn't say a thing. We walked the mile to the creek in silence, me still holding the guitar.

Keith was there, of course. Wrapped in his sleeping bag, the cigar box next to him. There were a few bags left. He'd used only one.

I bent to wake him. But when I touched him and rolled him over, two things hit me. He'd shaved off his beard. And he was very, very cold.

Then I noticed the empty bottle.

We'd found other drugs with the chronine, way back when. They weren't even guarded. Keith had used sleeping pills.

I stood up, not saying a word. I didn't need to explain. Winters had taken it all in very quickly. He studied the body and shook his head.

"I wonder why he shaved?" he said finally.

"I know," I said. "He never wore a beard in the old days, when he was with Sandi."

"Yes," said Winters. "Well, it figures."

"What?"

"The suicide. He always seemed unstable."

"No, Lieutenant," I said. "You've got it all wrong. Keith didn't commit suicide."

Winters frowned. I smiled.

"Look," I said. "If you did it, it would be suicide. You think chronine is only a drug for dreaming. But Keith figured it for a time machine. He didn't kill himself. That wasn't his style. He just went back to his Sandi. And this time, he made sure he stayed there."

Winters looked back at the body. "Yes," he said. "Maybe so." He paused. "For his sake, I hope that he was right."

The years since then have been good ones, I guess. Winters is a better leader than I was. The timetrips never turned up any knowledge worth a damn, but the search expeditions proved fruitful. There are more than two hundred people in town now, most of them people that Winters brought in.

It's a real town, too. We have electricity, and a library, and plenty of food. And a doctor—a real doctor that Winters found a hundred miles from here. We got so prosperous that the Sons of the Blast heard about us and came back for a little fun. Winters had his militia beat them off and hunt down the ones who tried to escape.

Nobody but the old commune people remember Keith. But we still have singing and music. Winters found a kid named Ronnie on one of his trips, and Ronnie has a guitar of his own. He's not in Keith's league, of course, but he tries hard, and everybody has fun. And he's taught some of the youngsters how to play.

Only thing is, Ronnie likes to write his own stuff, so we don't hear many of the old songs. Instead we get postwar music. The most popular tune, right now, is a long ballad about how our army wiped out the Sons of the Blast.

Winters says that's a healthy thing; he talks about new music for a new civilization. And maybe he has something. In time, I'm sure, there will be a new culture to replace the one that died. Ronnie, like Winters, is giving us tomorrow.

But there's a price.

The other night, when Ronnie sang, I asked him to do "Me and Bobby McGee." But nobody knew the words.

George R. R. Martin writes:

The facts go like this:

I was born in September 1948. Home was Bayonne, New Jersey, a big oil-refining town just across the bay from New York City. I grew up there, mostly in a federal housing project that sat by the deep-water channel connecting New York and Newark bays. So I spent a lot of time watching big ships come and go, fascinated by their flags. I went to grade school (Mary J. Donohoe) and high school (Marist High), read a lot (mostly comics and SF), and wrote. Since the dawn of time, it often seems. At least since the dawn of my time.

I made my first sale when I was in grade school; it was a short monster story, the first of a series. I printed it in pencil on notebook paper and sold it to another kid in the project for a penny. The price included a dramatic reading by yours truly. (In those days I did great werewolf sounds, but I have since forgotten how. Tsk.)

I wrote and sold four other stories in the same series (for fees up to a nickel, which even in those days wasn't much, but I liked making werewolf sounds), and my literary career was going great until one of my reader-listeners started having nightmares. With werewolves in them, I guess. His mother complained, and suddenly I was back to writing stories for my trunk. My trunk has a lot of old stories in it, since I never throw away anything.

Then there was high school, during which time I decided I wanted to be a writer because everybody kept laughing when I told them I wanted to be an astronaut. In high school I read a lot more SF, started a chess team, got thrown off the school newspaper in a censorship dispute, and began to devour comic books and write stories for comic fanzines (y'know—amateur magazines put out by fans). That was when I discovered my stories looked a lot more impressive in print than in pencil, even though they didn't pay me anything and I didn't get to make werewolf sounds (not even one).

In 1966 I finally left Bayonne; off to Evanston, Illinois, to attend Northwestern University. I came out five years later, with an M.S. in journalism, but sometime in there I started writing SF and submitting to professional magazines. One day in the summer of 1970, a hairy orange first reader at Galaxy found one of my stories in his slush pile, and his boss bought it, and that was my first sale since grade school. They paid me ninety-four dollars, which is only a little bit better than a nickel.

Since then I've sold nearly thirty stories, and I've been nominated for a Hugo and a Nebula and a John W. Campbell Award. Lost all three. Sigh. At the moment I live in Chicago, fly around and run chess tournaments on weekends, write on weekdays. I no longer do monster stories, but my ex-roommate says that I make great flying-saucer sounds.

BLOODSTREAM

by Lou Fisher

On Wednesday morning, in response to the postcard, Craig Stafford brought his eleven-year-old son to the New York State Medical Center, which in Kingston was located in a quadrant of the license bureau. Randy's examination started right on time; and in less than an hour the computer in Albany had read the sensors and scanned the blood, urine, and skin analyses and turned the holorays into digital bits of physiological data. From then on it was only a matter of waiting for the transmission lines to free up for the report.

The doctor was smiling as the printout spewed from his deskside terminal.

"Good news, Mr. Stafford," he said, tearing the paper from the console with a professional flourish. "Randy's in excellent condition. In fact, I'd go so far as to say that this is the best report I've seen this week."

Stafford frowned. "That means you'll be taking him."

"Well, I wouldn't put it that way."

"What way, doctor—how *would* you put it?"

The doctor glanced again at the bottom line of the report, the sum of the digits. "Randy's a lucky boy," he said. "Actually, there's less than half a chance of making it on the first examination; and many children, unfortunately, are never considered healthy enough, despite our chemotherapy programs. But your son is ready now. No problem. He can go to the hospital this week."

For an instant Stafford thought it sounded almost convincing, but then, as he got out of his chair, the tight marks deepened in his long face and his compatibly long fingers curled into fists of defiance. It occurred to him that Randy was still out in the waiting room, anxious to hear the happy verdict; but to Stafford it was the worst possible result. He had hoped for a negative report. He had hoped at least for a postponement.

He said, "I don't want him to go."

"But it's the hospital . . ."

"Forget it, I just don't want him there. Leave him alone."

"I can't permit . . ." The doctor paused. He folded the computer listing, creasing each seam, and put it into a preprinted envelope. "That's a bad attitude, Mr. Stafford," he began again in a bedside manner inherited from past medical generations. "First of all, the law is absolute and uncontestable, as you well know, for the good of the general public. It's obviously not a matter for voluntary choice. How can a child decide? How can you decide for him? No, no, it's simple enough. If he qualifies for the hospital, he goes there. . . . And if you understand the purpose of the hospital, you must want Randy—"

"I know all about it," Stafford countered, "even if I didn't get to go there myself. You put a strong, healthy kid in the hospital for almost a year. You have him contract every known disease, one by one; then you cure him, one by one, so he's loaded with permanent antibodies and immune to everything and spends the rest of his life in perfect health."

"Well, that in itself—"

"Is bullshit!" Stafford went on, striding closer to the desk and leaning over it. "Sure, the good old AMA has it all worked out. Give the kid cancer, diabetes, all the heart disorders, a couple hundred viruses, and everything else that God knows. Build up his immunities so he can live to a hundred and eighty . . . live with a body full of scars and plastic parts, and memories of a year in hell."

If the doctor was the least bit disturbed, he didn't let on. Going about his business, he put the envelope in a stiff folder and removed a small blue card that was attached to the front of the folder.

"You have the wrong impression," he said flatly. "Without the hospital, your son would be lucky to reach ninety."

Stafford shook his head. "It's not worth it."

"Of course it is. You know that Randy would get many of the illnesses naturally, as his life went on. By taking them all at once, under supervision, and at an early age, when he can fight them off, he can gain quick cures and double his life expectancy."

"What about all the suffering?"

"Well, there's some price to be paid," the doctor said. "Frankly, Mr. Stafford, the only easy way to build up antibodies is through the use of vaccines. But vaccines are effective for only a limited number of diseases; they are not permanent—especially after the age of one hundred; and humans have become somewhat resistant to them. Vaccines, after all, are a much weaker dose than the real thing."

Stafford's shoulders sagged.

The doctor nodded. "It'll be all right," he said, as he double-checked the blue plastic card.

Apparently satisfied, he handed the card to Stafford. There was nothing to see but a few punched holes and a serial number. Stafford looked up questioningly.

The doctor explained, "Randy must check into the hospital on Friday afternoon. The processing will go quite rapidly if you have this card with you. Will you be able to bring him yourself?"

"Yes," Stafford told him. "It's not my workyear."

He turned the plastic card over and over in his fingers, leaving faint damp marks on both sides. He knew he couldn't stop what was happening. Once Randy passed the health review, the hospital was the compulsory next step. Actually, he should be a proud father like everyone else in his situation. *But that terrible year.*

"Some of them die," he said.

The doctor stood up and came around the desk as if to cue an end to the pointless discussion.

"That's true," he admitted. "Some die. In many cases, though, they are children in borderline physical condition who never should have been admitted. Their parents probably used official influence to get them in. Myself, I think we should make the requirements stricter. At any rate, don't worry—we have a ninety-four-percent survival record. Very good odds, you know."

"Worse than I thought," was Stafford's bitter reply. Pocketing the admission card, he started toward the outer office to get his son, knowing that he would have to meet Randy's cheers with at least a faint smile of enthusiasm.

Like a laugh in the dark.

At home, Myra was waiting for them outside the front door, up on her toes, her pretty face full of hope, her delicate hands clasped between her small breasts, all of her lit up in anticipation. Stafford waved artificially from the car in the driveway, but it was Randy who ran up to give her the word.

"Mom, I'm going," he said excitedly. He was also up on his toes, reaching for her. Short for his age, and slim, and somewhat soft. Much like Myra's side of the family, Stafford thought. Still, strong and healthy in his own right, as the doctor had proven this morning, Randy would probably survive the immunizations.

But in what condition? Through what agony? At what cost?

Stafford trembled briefly, and moved away from the car.

"Friday, Mom," Randy was saying. "I'm going to the hospital on Friday. It's all set."

Myra hugged him.

"That's so wonderful, Randy. Oh, I prayed and prayed . . . and I'm happy for you." Her bright eyes were not aware of her husband's leaden steps as he came up to join the celebration, and even the metallic edge on Stafford's words didn't break through her glow of wishes-come-true.

Once more he asked his son, "Do you really want to go?"

"Sure, Dad," Randy answered, acting victorious. "Only the best people go. Mom says so. Everybody wants to go to the hospital."

"But everybody can't go."

"Yeah. . . . Especially Joey," Randy said, a little more quietly. "If Joey was going with me—"

"Never mind," Myra put in. "You'll make new friends at the hospital. Now, go upstairs and change clothes, and then you can go over to tell Joey the news." With her arm resting on Randy's shoulder, she guided him to the accessway; and when she came back to Stafford, it was with a further explanation. "Joey took the exam last week, and he was underweight. They turned him down. His mother was frantic, she was so sure."

Stafford made a vague gesture that indicated nothing but that temporarily covered his end of the conversation. A moment later, when he was sure that his son was out of earshot, he gave in to the feelings that were knotted in his stomach.

"The whole thing stinks," he said, but Myra had heard his opinion many times before.

"Please don't start that now. It's all settled, and there's nothing more you can do about it."

"But damnit, Myra, you've seen the hospital. You know what it's like in there."

"It's not that bad."

"Not that bad? How can you—"

"Stop it, Craig!" This time there was a snap to her usually mild voice, and he could see the start of angry tears. "You're being ridiculous, and you know it. It's a great chance for Randy." She wheeled and stalked out of the room, leaving Stafford cut off from further debate.

He was tired of arguing about it, anyway. The doctor, his wife, his son, the world.

The whole goddamned world.

No one ever listened.

He sank into the cushions of his telereading chair, but he drew no comfort from it. Neither did a deep breath do anything to extinguish his nerves. Shuddering, he wondered why he always saw a completely different hospital. Maybe he was wrong, or unreasonable, or just stubbornly old-fashioned. After all, the hospitals were created by medical geniuses as an answer to mankind's plea for a longer life, and every father dreamed of having his children admitted, of giving his children something more than he had, a shot at two hundred years.

Almost every father.

Somehow he couldn't stand the image of Randy in the hospital. He could see him there writhing near death, in masses of agony, rattles of pain. Suffering, screaming. Sleeping only with drugs. And one after another: asthma, leukemia, tumors, cataracts, pneumonia . . . No relief, no end, not for a year. . . .

At that point he heard Randy calling from upstairs.

He found the boy stretched out across the bed, face-down. He touched Randy's shoulder, and the muffled voice blurted, "I don't want to go."

Stafford sat next to him.

"But you said you did."

"That was before, Dad. Now I'm scared. I don't know what's going to happen to me. There's going to be a bunch of people I never saw before, and they never saw me before. And I don't like hospitals, anyway. . . . I want to stay here."

"Take it easy," Stafford told him. Then he bit his tongue and said, "I wouldn't send you there if it wasn't all right."

He took his son's arm affectionately, helping him to turn over and up, trying to discover the real look on his face. If Randy was afraid now, he thought, what would happen when he was really in the midst of that ghoulish infirmary . . . when he was plugged into electronic nurses and tubes of plasma . . . when they came at him with hypodermic needles and surgical knives . . . when the errant strains of earthwide bacteria swarmed through his eleven-year-old body?

Or when he found out that it hurt all the time?

Sitting up on the bed, Randy swallowed hard and put a little bravery back in his chin, as if realizing that the meeting was man-to-man as well as father-to-son.

He said, "I'd probably be okay if Joey was going, too. If he was there, you bet I wouldn't be scared at all. Can't you tell them to let Joey go with me?"

"Maybe he'll make it next time," Stafford replied. He rustled Randy's dark hair. Then his hand slipped down to Randy's neck, pulling him just a little closer. "Tell you what, though. I'm going to ride out and take a look at the hospital tomorrow, to make sure they've got things in good shape for you."

Being in the second of his three offyears, Craig Stafford had acquired the habit of sleeping until ten o'clock in the morning—mainly because Myra, who tired easily, managed to sleep that late every day of every year. But on Thursday morning Stafford had his breakfast coffee at the throughway Savarin as the day was just beginning, and he pulled his car into the hospital grounds at the very start of visiting hours.

The fence was a miles-long plastic ribbon that formed a semicircle down to the Hudson River. Within it, Stafford followed the wide road that led up to the hospital; once there, he tried to read, but couldn't concentrate on, the huge plaque of dedication that had been signed by President Cooper in 1996. The building itself loomed up in front of him; like its many duplicates across the country, it was forty-five stories high, windowless, and immaculately white.

And assuredly soundproof.

The few other visitors in the south wing of the fifth floor were women and they moved silently with Stafford around the railing that circled above the ward. Below him, the huge room of beds was encased in a clear plastic dome that made it open and public, offering an unhampered view of the entire arena. The outside walls were a checkerboard of servogear and electronicaides. The beds were the latest in four-by-six-floaters. The lighting was indirect-nonreflective, which meant that it could be left on all day and all night with only minor automatic adjustments to its intensity. And in the main aisles that crisscrossed between the beds, a moving center strip—it seemed like a treadmill—allowed the skittering men and women in white uniforms to review their hundreds of patients.

To Stafford it was a pitiful zoo. He stopped walking, folded his arms on the railing, peering in.

He wasn't sure why he'd come or what he was looking for. Reassurance, no doubt. But it wasn't there. Instead, there was visible evidence of torture and murder. In the beds, every one of them filled, he saw the empty faces of unknown children—sad and hopeless strangers trapped in nothing they had asked for. From where he stood, he couldn't hear their screams, but he felt every one that echoed inside the enormous cage.

A red-haired girl ripped the stuffing from her pillow.

Another girl pounded her stomach with angry fists.

A boy coughed and choked and went on crying.

Another boy tore a gash in his face.

One boy slept.

"Which one is yours?" a woman's voice asked, and Stafford turned to give her half of his attention. She was close to Myra's age, but a little bigger all around.

"Not here yet," Stafford replied without emotion.

"Oh, that's certainly too bad," she lamented. "But don't give up, he might make it. Or is it a girl? Tell me, have you tried vitamins?"

"It's a boy—my son."

"Oh, then you must try exercise, too. Exercise and vitamins."

"He's really all right. In fact, he's scheduled here for this Friday—tomorrow."

She brightened sincerely. "I'm certainly glad for you. . . . That's mine over there, at the head of the third row. See him? That's Mike, our oldest child."

The boy Stafford saw was a quivering wreck. The cheeks were sunken. The hair was awry. And the eyes were clamped shut, as if to avoid the cold stares of the dials and gauges and cathode-ray tubes that were arranged in a forest around him. Stafford was about to offer his sympathy, but the woman wasn't in tune.

"He's almost finished with cirrhosis of the liver," she boasted. "Next week he'll probably start on arthritis. That's an easy one—takes only a few days."

Stafford nodded skeptically, unable to find the right answer or the right tone of voice. Like Myra, he thought, the woman had been brainwashed with the benefits of advanced medicine and was completely oblivious to the cruelty that completed the process. He stood by for a moment before he walked away from her; then, as he moved on, his eyes searched the ward from child to child—seeing Randy in every bed, sick and hurt, begging for relief. Finally, he turned his back to it all and started slowly towards the elevator.

Down.

As the doors slid open on the main floor, Stafford caught sight of the arrow sign that pointed to the office of the director; and the same impulse that had brought him to hell, or to the hospital, struck another hot link in his nerve chain and sent him striding down the corridor in the indicated direction.

Luriwist, the director of the hospital, was fat. Most of the excess flesh was around his waistline, indented by his belt. Some of it also lay around in his cheeks, which, together with flashing teeth, made him seem always happy. All in all, he looked like a man who appreciated second helpings, morning chats, and the huge executive offices.

He, of course, did not see any cause for Stafford's complaints.

"Your son is in very good health," Luriwist said, reading the record from the green glow of a display tube. "You've got nothing to worry about."

"I just don't want him here," Stafford repeated. He was standing at the far end of a banquet-size desk and had begun the conversation by pounding on it.

Luriwist clicked off the tube. "Best thing that could happen to him. Wish to God I could take it myself. Why, when the boy gets to be *twice* your age, he'll look and feel better than you do now."

"Maybe."

"Do you doubt it?"

"Sure I doubt it. It hasn't been done long enough to know one way or another. Show me a generation of two-hundred-year-olds."

"That's academic," Luriwist argued with smiling complacency. "It's all based on sound medical knowledge, and there were countless treatments on experimental subjects—animal and human. We were able to *triple* the lifespan of some of the smaller animals. Anyway, it was proven in all cases that the level of antibodies produced in the bloodstream was more than enough—"

"I don't care about that!" Stafford shouted. He was beginning to feel battered and worn. "Did those medical geniuses ever measure the emotional scars that come from a year in this place? Did they ever try it themselves? What do you think—did they care about anything but antibodies?"

Luriwist flopped back in his chair. Only his eyes reflected a change in the stoic outlook, and those eyes were fixed on Stafford's face.

"What the hell is the matter with you, Stafford?"

Stafford gave it some thought. "The pain, the suffering, the whole year—I can't have Randy go through it."

The director raised a brow.

"Oh, one of those guys, huh?" He tapped his fingers on the edge of the desk, and his voice became less superficial. "Well, we run into your kind now and then, and sometimes we work out a deal. But it'll cost you, say, a thousand superdollars."

"For what?" asked Stafford. "To keep Randy out?"

Luriwist shook his head. "No way to do that. But what we *can* do . . . Is Randy your real son? Not adopted or anything?"

"Of course he's mine. Would I be—?"

"Then I suppose we can do business," the director said. He leaned forward and used one hand to underline his words. "But the deal is off the record. Strictly off the record. *Understand?* Anyway, we can fix it so that your son will feel no pain at all."

"Safely?" Stafford wondered, then had his doubts. "I don't see how you can do that."

"Why not? Pain is only a message that's sent through the nervous system to the brain. The secret is to divert the message." Luriwist put some of the secret into his smile. "So we divert the message," he continued. "We block the nervous system in just the right places. We take the pain away from the patient and transfer it to another person of his immediate family."

"You mean that I'd feel the pain instead of Randy?" Stafford said, half-breathing, half-speculating.

"It could be arranged," was the reply, "if you've got the thousand."

Stafford's mind was a tape of quick thoughts. It was easy enough to get the money. The pain was another matter. *Could he himself take a year of it?* He'd seen enough to know its awful touch; but the strength of a large man was a lot tougher target than the inexperience of a small boy, and somehow, just knowing that Randy was escaping it . . . So it would hurt, Stafford told himself firmly and finally. The physical pain would be no worse than the mental anguish it saved.

But he still wasn't convinced.

He said, "It doesn't seem possible."

"It's very possible," Luriwist assured him. "Look, we don't publicize it, because people would claim that it's like black magic. And maybe it is. There you are, Stafford—call it black magic."

"I don't like black magic."

"All right, then I'll tell you the truth. It's based on a medical practice that was thoroughly discredited at the end of the century. But a couple of experts on our staff kept playing around with it, and the best thing they found was *pain transfer*. We've used it successfully a number of times."

"That's not much of an explanation—"

"Cut it out, Stafford!" Luriwist seemed to be growing weary and ill-tempered. "I'm not going to give you a classroom lecture. Either you want to do it, or you don't. Make up your mind."

Stafford moved his legs apart to a ready stance.

"I'll bring the money with me tomorrow."

"Cash, please," said Luriwist.

The guard at the gate checked with registration, then signaled them on with a flick of his hand. Randy was wedged in the front seat of the car with his head leaning on his mother's shoulder. Stafford glanced down. For some reason the boy seemed younger than ever, almost a baby again.

"How do you feel?" Stafford said.

"Okay, I guess," his son answered quietly.

Myra tightened her arm around him. "Do you remember everything I told you? Remember that the doctors and nurses are there to help you. And don't forget to look for us on weekends." She paused, recounting.

"Mom?"

"What is it, dear?"

"Joey didn't even come over to say good-bye this morning."

"Never mind that. There are plenty of boys just your age right here in the hospital."

Randy wiped his eyes. "Dad?"

"You'll be all right," Stafford said, and he saw a parking space far down the line.

Once they reached the check-in area, the blue plastic card lived up to its promised expediency and brought on a single piece of paper to be signed and two male escorts in white uniforms who greeted Randy with brave, cheery words and much-used smiles, both before and after they hooked onto him.

And quickly, Stafford saw him go.

He turned Myra around and led her to the elevator, which they took up to the seventeenth floor. It was quite crowded; Friday afternoons were used for general admissions, and 17H was the ward of the day. They edged to a place on the rail close to the plastic window; they got there in time to see Randy ushered to a bed, his mouth open, the clean, crisp hospital gown dragging slightly below his feet.

Myra stood on her toes and waved. Stafford bit hard. "I'll be back in a few minutes," he told her.

On the lower level, once again in the lavish office, Stafford put the money on the desk and waited while the director counted it. He still felt that it might be some sort of con game, some weird scheme without fulfillment or redress. At best it was a gamble.

He said, "Are you sure it'll work?"

Luriwist shoved the money into a drawer.

"I don't see why not. It always has," he explained. "A top man on the staff will be giving the treatments. Each treatment will divert the pain from your son for months at a time; and as that happens, the nerve sensations will automatically find you, his own flesh and blood. I hope you're strong enough to take it."

"I'm ready," Stafford said.

"Then I'll send up the word, and you'd better start for home immediately." For the first time, a note of sympathy could be heard in Luriwist's voice. "Good luck, Stafford."

Myra felt his touch and turned her head to him.

"Oh, you're back. I'm glad," she said anxiously. "There's something strange going on with Randy. Do you see that man in the dark suit?"

Stafford looked down into the ward. A dark-suited man with a small black case was standing at Randy's bedside.

"What about him?"

"Well, he just came along and stopped the doctors from giving Randy his first injection. I can't imagine who he is."

"Probably a specialist," Stafford said, knowing it was the truth. "The hospital always makes sure that everything gets off to the right start. Let's watch for a minute and see what he does."

What he did was open the black case and take out a handful of stainless-steel needles. The shafts were of various lengths and seemed to be knurled down to within an inch of the points.

What he did was twirl the needles rapidly as he inserted them—two in each of Randy's ears, four more at selected points around Randy's spine.

What he did was attach an electronicaide to the the end of each needle. Immediately a redline graph began pulsing on a wall display, and Randy's hands began to shake.

Stafford watched it all, astounded.

"Acupuncture," he mumbled, mostly to himself, but Myra picked it up.

"Why, I thought nobody used that anymore."

Stafford calmed himself. He considered his words carefully. "Evidently they use it here, Myra. I'm sure it's nothing to worry about. This is one of the best hospitals."

Inwardly, he was still amazed. Acupuncture! What had Luriwist said? *A medical practice that was thoroughly discredited at the end of the century.* The ancient art of acupuncture. Chinese medicine. Needles in the skin.

Well, why not? was Stafford's second thought. What else but acupuncture could produce the miracle of diverting Randy's pain? . . . And suddenly it occurred to him that he should have left the hospital right after he made the arrangements.

"Really, Craig," Myra was saying, "I think we ought to ask about it. I've never heard of anyone—"

"Let's just leave it to the experts," Stafford replied firmly, checking his watch.

It took a while to get Myra away from the ward and out to the car; but then Stafford drove rapidly, recklessly, anxious to get home before anything started on him. He wondered how soon it would be. Of course, Myra would have to know, he told himself. He'd need all her help to get him through it. *Would she understand?* He glanced over, finding her outwardly happy and proud, but also seeing a deeper strain of worry and loneliness. Well, she'd feel better when she found out. . . .

At that instant she grabbed his sleeve. She clutched her stomach. She doubled over and bit into his arm. Then she twisted her head to stare up at him, her eyes wide and pleading as she let out the first scream.

Lou Fisher writes:

First of all I must confess to all the readers of this anthology that I am not a prolific writer. This note, by itself, is a considerable addition to my total output, and one that I will probably include in future tallies to make them seem like more. It's not that I don't want to write in continuous streams, that I don't want meaningful fictions to pour out of me like they pour out of Barry Malzberg or Evan Hunter or any of the prolific *writers I admire. I dream of writing like that. But the magic eludes me; whatever it is.*

In my case, there are a number of good-sounding excuses. There is a full-time job as writer-editor of programming manuals for a computer company. And a house that needs handling and three cars that need oil. Of course, there is an energetic wife who needs to share her experiences, and two teen-age daughters who need to be guided (ha!) through their tumultuous years. Not to mention hours of all-out devotion to tennis, softball, volleyball, golf, bowling, bridge, cribbage, and reading. Anyone can see that I go to extremes to use up my time so I won't feel guilty about not writing. It doesn't work. There is plenty of time left over, and it has never been the problem. The problem, obviously, is in the mind, in the spirit.

Now that I have started to confess, I might as well go all the way. For the first time I will lean over my records and see what I have done in the way of published works. It will turn out to be much less than what I had hoped for when I first started to call myself a writer. Okay, here it is, starting in 1958: eighteen stories in a number of splashy men's magazines, four paper-back novels, also in the men's field; and five (only) science-fiction stories. That doesn't include reprints. God, all of my men's stories and novels were reprinted and reprinted in later years under new and dramatic titles; it's no wonder I never knew until now how many I actually had written.

There was something else. For about a year I wrote a monthly column of gambling advice for one of the men's magazines. (The far-seeing editor decided that I was a gambling expert because the hero of my four novels was a bookie named Chet McCoy.)

Naturally, I am happiest writing science fiction, and lately I have been trying to stay with it. My stories so far have appeared in F&SF, Fantastic, *and* Galaxy; *a story called "Triggerman" reappeared in* The Best from Galaxy, Volume II.

But about this *story. Well, every once in a while my writing urge overcomes my writing block, and an idea that's been stewing for months in my middle consciousness expands into all sorts of weird images, and I try to put it together the best I can.*

EXISTENCE

by *Joanna Russ*

IMITATIO QUASI IMAGO IN HONOREM JACOBI BLISH MULTA CUM ADMIRATIONE FELICITATIS SUI IN ARTIBUS RECONDITIORIBUS*

It is impossible to call up the Devil when women are present, I mean real women, that is to say hermaphrodites, for men (real men, who exist) are the people who look at the women, and the women are therefore the people who are looked at by the men. So that women (when they are alone) must be either men or nothing. There are a great many women who were supposed to have called up the Devil, all those witches and so on, but the question remains: what did they really call up? Or better still: did they exist? Maybe they called up something else. Or if it was true, and women really can *call up* the Devil, what does that make the Devil? Or are women really male? I have no answers to these questions.

With men, there's no problem. See the men? There are four of them. They have good, straight, legal, logical, one-track masculine minds. Wicklow, the fat one, wants to blow up the world; Ludlow, the *magister magici,* is going to do it for him; Albano, the third one, will try to stop it (they have to have him there for legal reasons); and the fourth man—oops, it's a woman—is Mr. Wicklow's private secretary. One could be forgiven the mistake. He employs this woman because she has an eidetic memory and no mind of her own; she's been in love with him for years. Her name is Estrellita Baines. Estrellita means "little star."

The men have no first names. Why should men need first names?

Wicklow, the bully, fat and merry, who bullies his secretary.

Ludlow, indescribably commonplace, lean, smells bad somehow

---

* "Representation in the form of a picture in honor of James Blish, with much admiration for his felicity in the more recondite arts."

(through no fault of his own, you can't place it), and takes no pleasure in the mauling that interests Mr. Wicklow. Has awful eyes.

Albano, the monk, who's been taking a lot of spiritual mauling lately, the solid, stolid peasant with big feet. Nurses impossible dreams of personal glory and is violently ashamed of them. He's not speaking to anyone.

Wicklow: thick cream, *lots* of money.

I

All around the marble chamber (which resembles a Greek columbarium at Forest Lawn) in various positions on the tessellated floor, posing against the walls like figurines, like lamiae, like snakes, are the bad doctor's demon assistants, girls with big eyes, girls with silky thighs, lovely girls with undulant bodies, golden hair, arms like waves, moist pits, impossible bones. They smile or scowl.

Beat me.

Tease me.

Love me.

Rape me.

II

All around poor Estrellita Baines in her gray suit and her rimless spectacles. She wears a skirt and carries a pocketbook so you can tell who she is. Her hair is pulled back in a tiny bun. It just won't grow, no matter what she does.

It matters what women look like.

III

Then they got tired of waiting. After discussing what the catastrophe is to be—Plague or the Bomb—they disperse to their separate circles. Demons are not allergic to electric light, and so the lights go on. Circles, pentacles, alb, stole, cope (you can read all this in books). Insofar as she thinks at all, Estrellita Baines thinks that whatever Mr. Wicklow wants must be right. The world is lucky to be done in by him when it's going in any case. Mr. Wicklow is feeding the fire on the lamia's magical body. Ludlow's fat cat lies very regardant and strange by the altar at Ludlow's feet, from time to time turning his huge eyes on his own ginger fur and giving himself a self-regarding lick. He weeps like a human.

"*. . . mulier hominis est confusio . . .*"

Estrellita Baines wonders why she feels so sleepy. The room is filling with smoke.

"*. . . felix conjunctio . . .*"

Frater Albano wonders at the words. Ludlow sounds like a bandsaw; it's impossible to make anything out.

"*. . . quicquid, te, cara, delectat. Quid iuvat deferre, electa?*"

Wicklow feeds the fire.

"*. . . ave, formosissima . . . iam, dulcis amica, venito . . . Vestiunt silve tenera merorem virgulta, suis onerata pomis . . .*"

What *is* the man saying? The cat lies on its back and bats at the air. Something cold seems to glide in across the floor under the smoke. Wicklow, shaking himself awake, drops more resin into the fire: resin and honey, sparks snap from the dead body of the lamia. Ludlow has explained everything very carefully; magic is an art, like science, *I mean* (thinks Wicklow) *like mathematics. Or perhaps an exact art, that's better.* Anyway, there are rules. Inflexible rules. It's all to do with the nature of the Personages that lie behind the appearance of things—or in connection with the appearance of things? Wicklow shakes his head to clear it, earning a sharp look from the magician. *And Albano is here because of some pact the Devil has made with God, or God with the Devil, who can tell? But he must only observe, not interfere. That's clear. Why? The limits on Good. Evil breaks the rules, Good must obey the rules. Very simple. And to our advantage.*

"*. . . imperatrix mundi . . .*"

"*. . . Dione . . .*"

"*. . . mundi luminar . . .*"

And the cold, rising, somehow does not clear the smoke, but makes it blacker. Frater Albano is almost entirely lost in the dark. The empty pentacle in front of the altar begins to glow, not light but rather darkness visible, and into this column whirl the magician's girl-demons, sucked around and around, distorted souls flattened and glowing, somehow dimmed as if caught in a waterspout. A mutter comes from Frater Albano's direction, absolutely contrary to the rules.

"*Aliquid mihi faciendum est!*" cries Ludlow. The altar flames. Stifled words come from Albano, and much coughing.

"*. . . vini, vidi . . .*"

"Quid nunc, O vir doctissime, tibi adest?" exclaims Ludlow.

"... *vici* ..." finishes Albano in his corner, barely able to speak.

"Veni, audivi, exii!" Ludlow shouts, and as these last words sink into the cold (sink into it but do not penetrate it, do not neutralize it, refuse to mingle with it, but only trail wisps of human heat after them), the light in the pentacle condenses to a tiny star, a mote of light that seems to drift farther and farther away. It does not become less, but somehow draws back as if in obedience to the laws of some other perspective, until it is very far away (but still within the room); and then—at the point of becoming too small to see—it expands soundlessly until it fills everyone's sight, a magnesium flare, intense and colorless, in which one looks at one's neighbor and sees bleakly and without emotion that he has not even greed or wrath, but that he is hollow.

"I don't like this," says Estrellita Baines. Ludlow raises his wand, black eyes blazing like balls of pitch. A head seems to be forming in the room (they are all inside it). The head grins, mottled, quicksilver-mouthed, simultaneously behind the doctor and before him, at the ceiling and around their ankles; Estrellita Baines says more positively, "I don't like this *at all.*

"And why," she continues crossly, "do you always have to grin like a wolf? It's so dull. Why can't you grin like a chihuahua?" At the sound of her voice, the ceiling and floor exchange places, causing an almost unbearable nausea. They settle, and Ludlow raises his wand. *If she moves* ...! And simultaneously, Frater Albano, disabled by coughing, manages to croak *"reprobare, reprobos!"* which is the end of a verse that can be used only once; and somehow in the world, now shaking and gliding like a crack-the-whip, up and down, back and forth, racked with alternate light and darkness, the *magister magici* sees dependable Estrellita Baines preparing to step out of her circle. The lenses of her spectacles reflect the fragmented images of a dissolving world. He raises his wand to blast her.

Broad daylight. Silence. Sunlight streams over the raised gallery at the end of the room. The Sabbath Goat sits on the edge of the gallery, swinging His animal's hooves. He is as solid a horror as anything can be, emblematic from the crown of lit candles on His human head to His erection to the Star of David on His forehead to His oozing breasts to His slit-pupiled eyes. Goats and cats belong to Him. Estrellita steps out of her circle, foolish and confused. She says, "You look silly." He lifts His head and opens His mouth; the magician's cat backs carefully onto Ludlow's feet and settles there with a groan. Estrellita has taken off her glasses, as if trying an experiment (can she see without them?), but this is one of those ladies who look even worse that way; nobody says, "You're beautiful without your glasses." So she puts them back on. She wanders out between the chalked figures on the floor, studying them with interest. Her voice, one knows, will be strong but not sweet:

I don't fancy giving you my world to play with.

Give up, magician. I don't exist apart from the particulars, so you can't touch me.

"I thought," says Frater Albano, finding the words, or the words finding him, "that you would be more beautiful."

Why? I'm not a picture. And I'm not the Virgin, either. She hikes up her stockings and begins to climb the stair at the side of the gallery. Albano covers his face with his hands. Holding her drab skirt above her knees with one hand, she trudges up the steps—dogged, plain, and slow. She kicks off her shoes.

I could be beautiful if I wanted to. I could be anything if I wanted to. But there's nothing emblematic about me; I must use what's to hand. So if your aesthetic sense isn't too violently offended, gentlemen, I'll stay as I am.

The Sabbath Animal yawns. Little Star climbs the steps. Either the steps are higher than they look or she isn't really walking, for it seems to take her forever to get there. And as she toils away from the three on the floor, she grows larger—though still climbing one step at a time—until, miles away, large as a monument at the head of a stair, huge as a pyramid, she can pick up the Goat in one hand, which she does. Her spectacles flash like the Lunar Apennines. He wriggles furiously in her fingers, and she brings him close to her face, to look at him. Sitting on the gallery, feet reaching the floor and head bent to avoid the ceiling, she presses her knees carefully together, ladylike. The gallery sags and creaks. She puts her free hand behind her back, and when she brings it out again, there is in it another furiously wriggling little man. A golden squiggle to match the red-and-black squiggle. She holds them almost at her nose.

Neither of these is the genuine article. Of course, there is no genuine article.

Ludlow breaks his wand in two and points the raw ends at Little Star. She does not look up.

No use, magician. What a funny little man you are, with your hot temper and your subtlety and all your logic! You have played for years with your pacts and laws and compulsions without the slightest suspicion that anyone was trying to cheat you. And you spoke for years with what you believed to be Infernal Personages without ever once thinking that the real mark of a Personage—as distinct from a Thing—was Its ability to change Its mind. Someone has been making fun of you.

Ludlow continues his incantation.

If the characteristic of a Thing, says Little Star, is its invariability, then surely the characteristic of a Person is passion, volition, and reason. And where is that to come from if not from you? Ah, We had grand times in the early days when there were only vegetable and animal souls to draw our being from, grand times but bland times, I must admit; then you came along and We have developed amazingly since. We have developed into beauts, doctor, if I may so express myself, into real lollapaloozers, the human coloration of which never ceases to amaze me.

"Who are you?" says Albano in a croak.

I (says Estrellita Baines) *am The One Who Puts Things Back Where They Belong. I am She Who Confines Fancies to the Space Between the Ears, The Lady Who Makes Things Concrete, The Woman Who Insists on Facts, I am The I-Am, I Am The What-Is. Something of a paradox, you will admit, for a supernatural being. But I am one of the two real Personages.*

"Why are you here?" cries Wicklow. "Why are you interfering? And why are you my secretary?"

Because (says the woman-mountain) *I am The Decider Who Decides That To Make A Real Bang You Must Use A Real Bomb. Anything else offends Me.*

"That is not logical," says Ludlow, the master magician, in a hard, tight, furious voice.

It is not, says Little Star, *but it is both reasonable and real,* and thrusting both arms under her skirt, she appears to release Good and Evil into the space between her legs, then doing the same with the magician and the monk, whose arms and legs twinkle a violent protest as they are shoved back into the womb. She seems to get no pleasure from it. Her lips are thin and priggish. The huge hand lowers above Wicklow, who throws himself flat on his face.

"I don't believe it!" Boss Wicklow shouts. "It's not possible!"

Why not? I am the effluvium of billions of souls, a billion and a half women who turn uneasily in their sleep, a billion and a half men who resent the uneasiness of the women. My brother is What-Is-Not

*and he is also my father, my lover, and my son: The One Who
Broadcasts Dreams, The Man Who Believes, The Inside Turned Outside, The Yes-It-Is, The All-Is-All, The Great Somebody Else. And
to complicate matters still further, we are really each other, but since
that's impossible, we take turns. It's the women's turn today; it'll be
the men's tomorrow, when the men become women, when the women
become men, when they both become zebras. I'll still be here.*

"Go away!" He shuts his eyes.

*The trouble with men is that they have limited minds. That's the
trouble with women, too. But I know everything.*

"GO AWAY!"

All right.

He opens his eyes, to find Estrellita Baines—his own size now—
kneeling over him. There is a very disapproving look on her face.

"Mis-ter Wick-low!" she says.

"I'm all right," says merry Wicklow.

"I think," says Miss Baines, "that we had better go home, Mr.
Wicklow, and that after this, Mr. Wicklow, you had better consult me
about anything you plan to undertake. You have wasted both your
money and our time."

"All right," says rich Wicklow.

"And I think," continues Miss Baines, "that, while I'm at it, I
might as well tell you the plans I have for this palazzo, which is to be
turned into a karate school for high-school girls. Your life will not be
worth living, Mr. Wicklow."

"I know it," Wicklow groans.

"You will not like it, Mr. Wicklow."

"Yes, yes," he says.

"Considering what I know about the firm, you may even have to
make me a partner, Mr. Wicklow."

His head snaps up. "Miss Baines!" She is standing just inside the
door to the great marble room. She's sizing him up. She's wondering
mildly where that idiot Albano and that idiot Ludlow and the cat and
all those silly girls have got to. She seems remarkably graceful. She
pirouettes on one heel; it's wonderful how good a woman can look
when she knows there's no competition around. He hates her.

"Mis-ter Wick-low!"

He follows her.

Appendix: The Latin

It's no wonder they call up the Great Mother, considering the invocations they use. If you are interested:

mulier hominis est confusio—Chaunteclere to Pertelote: woman is man's damnation

felix conjunctio—happy conjunction (of a boy and girl)

quicquid, te, cara, delectat, etc.—everything, dear, to delight you. Why put it off, sweetheart?

ave, formosissima, etc.—oops, can't find it; more medieval love poetry

imperatrix mundi—empress of the world

Dione—another name for Aphrodite

mundi luminar—light of the world

Aliquid mihi, etc.—There exists something which must be done by me. (Bad Latin)

Quid nunc, etc.—a facetious cry for which I am indebted to T. H. White's *Mistress Masham's Repose:* "What is biting you, O learned man?"

veni, vidi—I came, I saw

vici—I conquered

Veni, audivi, exii!—I came, I heard, I left!

magister magici—nasty neologism

reprobare, reprobos—to reprobate reprobates (written by one)

Joanna Russ writes:

Assuming this to be free advertising space, I will now put in a plug for writers, who—with a very few exceptions—are day laborers paid piecework in an industry that is shaky, badly advertised, and poor, largely due not to its choice of books or its editing of them, but to an impossible distribution system for paperbacks (in which the distributors and the retail outlets do not share in the risk and in which books are merchandised like Kleenex) and a vehement confusion between old-style paperback selling (impulse buying) and the emerging reality that soon there ain't gonna be hardbacks except for specialized books and library sales. Nobody has adjusted to this yet. Nobody knows who buys books where and why. It is a mess.

It is rude and crude to rend the lovely veils of spidery illusion which blow so gently over our work, but for a field that prides itself on being down-to-earth there is an extraordinary reluctance to look at the economic facts. Many Americans seem to be like this—maybe art is supposed to be Above All That.

My own, quixotic dream for the paperback-book industry is a giant Sears-Roebuck-ish, centralized store which will carry remaindered books at lowered (or raised) prices (depending on their bibliographic value and the rise due to inflation) and have wee beautiful catalogs in every hamlet, village, and town where people (now that the movies are too expensive) can go when TV palls and find old Phyllis Whitney gothics (Look! I found a copy of Fear in the Old Castle!*) or HPL (Look!* Horrible Monsters from Old New England!*) or controversial books (How can anybody bear to talk about such filthy things in public? I'll buy it.), order them (see? no problems with shelf space), pay for them, and get them (quickly). The books would move only when paid for, copies would not be shredded (as they are now when they're not sold within about ten days). But how would prices on old paperbacks be changed? With a goddamn supermarket stamp, nudnick!*

College bookstores (as three of them have told me) always sell SF if it remains on the shelves long enough. *The real problems are distribution and information (really identical).*

Of course, such an operation would require a vast capital outlay. Or would it? Specialized bookstores do this kind of thing already. At any rate, it points in the proper direction, I think. The first step is for some brilliant sociologist or computer programmer out there (hello, hello?) to get a grant to study just who buys books and why, something about which there are a lot of publishers' theories and no facts.
A big grant. *And then . . . ?*

Say, why don't one of you readers . . . ?

INTERFACE

by A. A. Attanasio

Morning sunlight running invisibly through the long, slender glass windows gives the laboratory a surreal attitude. The walls are white, circular, and indifferent. And the remote ceiling is a luminescent circle with an eleven-meter diameter. The cylindrical room itself is a menagerie of electrical equipment describing the circumference of an amphitheater recessed in the center of the room. In the amphitheater is a mechanized chair of graying leather before a television screen. The floor is well waxed.

Dr. Michel Ibu advances several paces into the laboratory and looks across the amphitheater at a small bank of data collaters, mute in the sunlight. Their metallic faces, catching the sun, wear several small rainbows.

Dr. Ibu walks around a crowd of oxygen tanks and stands at the edge of the amphitheater. He is lanky and has a slight stoop. His face would be virtually flat except for high, prominent cheekbones laced with fine wrinkles in the black skin. His temples are gray.

"Dr. Reed?" he calls tentatively.

"Be with you in a minute," a distracted female voice answers.

Dr. Ibu folds his arms and grins.

So this is how we meet, he thinks.

A slender, dark-haired woman in a light-blue lab smock emerges from behind a portable canvas partition that has a large, assertive red ! printed on it. She is tall, and her hair is loose, falling about her shoulders.

"Yes?" she asks.

"Dr. Reed, I'm Michel Ibu from the marine labs."

She raises her eyebrows in a gesture of surprise. "So you're the neurophysiologist-biophysicist I've been warned about," she says without a smile.

"I've been tracking you down for two weeks." Ibu grins. "It seems you're kept quite busy here."

"Frankly, Dr. Ibu, I've just been trying to avoid you."

He cracks a disconcerted smile. "Why?"

"I'm not interested in working with terminal patients."

"How do you know I'm going to ask you to?"

"Are you going to be coy?"

"Who told you about the project?"

"I received your first invitation to work on the project, and then I went to Comptrol, and I looked into it myself. I'm just not interested in working on it."

"But do you understand what it's about?"

"I don't understand why you have to use a terminal patient."

"Look, Dr. Reed, have you had breakfast yet?"

"Yes."

"Well, I'd like to talk with you—to familiarize you with the project."

"I'm listening."

"Well, why don't you let me take you down to the marine labs so I can show you what we're doing?"

"I haven't got the time, Dr. Ibu."

"Okay," he says, exasperated, running one hand over his face. "In a nutshell, I'm on the verge of interspecies communication. I'm working with Lenny, a dolphin, and Heath Underhill, an eighteen-year-old terminal."

"Underhill? Do you mean he's from Underhill Clone?"

"Yes. But it would be more accurate to say that he's a reject from Underhill Clone. He's a 'cdd'—the defect is on an independent geriatric allele. In a short while, two or three years, he'll start decomposing. But right now he's in perfect health and with an IQ that easily categorizes him as a genius. He was purchased for just those reasons.

"Underhill Clone sent me Heath when he was six months old. As a 'cdd' he would have been euthed immediately. But we kept him here, and when he turned seven, we introduced him to Lenny. They've grown up together; their psyches have been interacting for most of their lives. They have a good, healthy relationship."

"You talk as if they're equals."

"If anything, Lenny is Heath's superior. The dolphin has a cerebral cortex the size of a human's. But the parietal area, the silent zone linked to abstract thinking, is almost twice as large. When I began to study dolphin sounds, I found they had an immensely more complex communication system than we do. This is what led me to question whether we might establish interspecies communication. Our biggest problem right now is structural. The dolphin language is sonic, but it's waterborne and is therefore ten times faster than ours. We just think too slowly to talk with a dolphin. But that's where you come in."

"And how's that?"

"Your field is psychobiology. Your specialty is neurology. And your research project for the past six years, since you first came to the clinic, has been autonomous visceral control. I know that you've taught subjects how to control their heartbeat, blood pressure, even certain glandular excretions. What I'd like is for you to teach Heath much of the same, only more intensively."

"But what has that to do with talking dolphins?"

"Dr. Madoc, the psychophysicist here, has synthesized a hallucinogen that, in some way I'm not familiar with, mobilizes awareness. It distorts temporal perception so radically that, for any practical purposes, time for the user no longer exists. Most remarkably, it's possible when using this drug to shift consciousness to any part of the body. There's one drawback: even the smallest trace quantities of this drug are enough to dislocate consciousness for hours. And he's found, working with rats, and in the six volunteer cases he's had, that it's impossible to survive without extensive conscious visceral control. Many of the primitive parts of the brain are shut down by the drug, and normally independent functions simply stop. Only one of the six volunteers survived."

"I still don't see where the talking dolphins come in."

"It's the mutual belief of Dr. Madoc and myself that within the expanded state of awareness of this drug, it will be possible to 'race up the mind,' so to speak, to the faster rate of communication that the dolphin employs. With the proper precontact training, most of which in Heath's case is unnecessary, considering the *simpático* between him and Lenny as it is, we may establish the first interspecies communication; we may be exposed to a culture whose structure is totally alien to us."

Dr. Reed deliberates for a brief moment. Presently she says, "There are two others in this department who have been working on visceral control—Kapowitz and Jennings."

"Yes, but only you have had extensive experience with humans. Heath may be synthetic, but he's still human, and you're the most qualified to deal with him."

"All right," she says, shrugging. "I have to admit you've interested me. When do we begin?"

"You may begin whenever you're ready," she says, securing the headrest. "Take it from sixty-four to one hundred and ten."

Dr. Reed walks to the front of the amphitheater and steps behind a console, from where she can monitor the heartbeat of the young man in the mechanized chair and still observe him. The subject's face is calm, and his eyes are fixed on the TV screen in front and slightly above him.

Several minutes of inactivity pass, and then a small red light on the face of the screen blimps once, indicating an alteration in the heartbeat of the young man.

Focus on that, Dr. Reed thinks.

Another red light blimps. A moment passes, and then there is another flash. And then another. The TV screen registers an acceleration of heartbeat by displaying a cardiograph with more frequent spikes. With deliberation, the rate climbs to one hundred and ten beats per minute.

"Okay, now bring it down to fifty," Dr. Reed orders.

Immediately another red light flashes on the screen. This occurs once more before the spikes on the cardiograph become more separated, spacing out to fifty beats per minute.

"Fine," she says. "Now maintain that rate, and increase your blood pressure. Take it to one-twenty over ninety."

Another graph flicks onto the TV screen, showing his relative blood pressure. Thirty seconds pass before the graph indicates an increase in the pressure. It increases steadily, leveling off at the assigned pressure.

"Very good," Dr. Reed says, recording the time intervals on a clipboard.

"He's progressing well, I take it," a gravel voice says at her side. It's Dr. Ibu.

"Hold it there for another minute," she directs, and then turns her attention to Ibu. "Yes, his will is remarkably well integrated. He's a good subject to work with."

"I'm glad to hear that you're satisfied," Ibu says. "Would you say, then, that he's ready?"

"Ready for what? Short-term suspension of visceral control—yes. Prolonged suspension—no."

"You've been working with him for six weeks. How much longer before he can master his visceral responses?"

"Master them for what period of time?"

"Indefinitely."

Dr. Reed turns back to the experiment. "That's it for now, Heath." She looks at Ibu. "I'll need another two weeks, at least."

Ibu's mouth slips open. "Two weeks! My dear, do you realize how impatient I am?"

"I'm doing as thorough a job as I can, as quickly as I can, doctor," she says, studying her console and recording some final data. "You yourself pointed out that if he doesn't master this, his life may be forsaken. Besides, if you didn't hog all of his time, this process would have been over long ago."

"I'm not hogging his time. It's Lenny. But that's necessary, too. Their relationship is important."

She shrugs.

"I just think you're jealous of Lenny," Ibu says mock seriously.

Dr. Reed puts down her clipboard and regards him with a solemn stare. She looks vexed.

"Hello, Michel," Heath says, approaching them. He is of average height, perhaps a trifle smaller. His complexion is light and smoothly clear, enhancing his pleasing features—prominent jaw and soft gray eyes. His physique is ideal.

"Hello, Heath," Ibu responds with a smile. "Elisabeth tells me that she's very satisfied with you."

Heath grins and makes a sarcastic gesture.

"Listen, you," Elisabeth says with feigned anger, "keep that up, and tomorrow you'll get a real workout in the chair. As for you"—she glares at Ibu—"why don't you go tell it to your fish . . . or . . . or mammal, or whatever it is."

Ibu laughs his staccato laugh, indicating his own satisfaction. "I'm going to do that right now," he says, putting his arm around Heath's shoulders. "It's just about time for Lenny's session."

Heath faces Elisabeth. "Why don't you come with us?" he asks.

"I don't think I can afford the time now," she says. "I've got all of today's data to correlate, still."

"You can do that tonight," Heath says. "Besides, I'm tired of showing off in front of Michel and his cronies. It'd be more satisfying for me if you were there."

Ibu chuckles. "What can you say to that?"

"I'm coming," she says. The young man's abruptness makes her nervous.

It is a long, cool walk through the air-conditioned halls of the clinic from the neurology labs to the marine labs. Occasional artistic blurbs of multicolored geometric designs printed on walls and doors relieve some of the monotony of the otherwise bland white corridors.

The marine labs take up the entire west face of the complex of buildings that make up the clinic. It faces the sea.

The particular lab that they enter is more like an enormous gymnasium. The ceiling is several stories high, and many naked steel beams cross each other up there. On the tile floor of the lab, besides a series of bleachers and several large water-purifying units, there is a red stripe that outlines a hundred-meter pool. Ibu leads up to the demarkation and finds a metal ring that opens a door in the tile floor. Ibu and Elisabeth descend into an observation room that is a chamber whose one wall is a glass side to the pool.

The pool is connected to a large underwater tunnel that leads directly to the sea. It is rarely closed off, and all manner of sea life find their way. Dr. Ibu learned long ago that to confine a dolphin against his will was futile. They just won't cooperate. He found that the creatures responded better to his experimentation when they were treated warmly and consistently and were allowed to come and go as they pleased.

Elisabeth touches her fingertips to the glass. The water is pellucid enough to see the surface clearly. Up there Heath is stripping.

"It'll be a few moments before Lenny gets here," Ibu says, looking at his watch.

"Does he always come on time?"

"Always."

The sound of someone singing in a falsetto seeps through the walls from unseen corridors. It is a happy tune.

"Tell me, Michel," Elisabeth says, studying her reflection in the glass (she considers herself good-looking; most men would agree), "is there any possibility of . . ."

There is a blurred, elusive movement in front of her. Focusing her eyes, she sees a dolphin, slightly larger than a man, its gray form sleek. It darts longitudinally across her field of vision.

"Punctual, indeed," Ibu says, his flat, black face bright with pride. He returns his attention to Elisabeth. "Excuse me. What was it you were going to ask?"

She had meant to ask about Heath, and if there were any chance of his life being prolonged. She knows it is hopeless and thinks it better not to give Ibu any more reason to suspect that she is infatuated with Heath.

"My answer is out there," she says, gesturing toward the water. "I was going to ask if Lenny was really coming or not."

A silvery-blue congeries of bubbles thrusts itself soundlessly before the glass wall, resolving itself into a human form that gracefully arcs back up toward the surface, completing a perfect parabolic sweep.

Heath returns immediately, but this time he is clinging to Lenny's back, trailing his legs behind him. The duo complete several spirals and then surface for air.

"They'll play for a couple of hours," Ibu says.

In the pool, Heath is completing the transition between two worlds. He lets the above world slip away, shrugging off its gravity. The below world, the world of muted colors and buoyant substance, adopts him—not a foster world, though, nor less genuine, but more congenial than above, more real.

He skims along the surface of the pool, Lenny keeping time beside him, his bottle nose and permanent smile above water. Then, with a stretch of stroke, Heath picks up the pace, and with dazed and jumping eyeballs he looks once more above, then dives below. He reaches the bottom, touches it with hands and knees, and then unforms and sprawls shapeless as a dead man, hanging limply in suspension.

Lenny slips under him and pushes him.

They latch together and streak up. The green edges of the pool whirl, dizzy with the eruption of their surfacing, and the pumping heart shakes the brilliance from the electric lights.

Heath loops his arms around Lenny again, and they somersault below, easing into a slow sweep of the bottom.

Heath feels his body become exhilarated with the smooth effort. His brain is hurled from platitude, the forced lungs cry for meager air, organs of sense are strained beyond their common catch, and the world and tortured body pulse into chaos. Together they unmake old realms.

Having to halt, they drift to the surface. Heath gasps for breath and hears the blood grow soft and usual. Seeing the green pool's edge and his pile of clothing, he feels stale threats come up abreast and reassert their normalcy, before whose arrogance he straightens, fills his lungs, begins to dive.

"Yes, they'll play for hours together," Ibu says, his eyes glazed over.

*   *   *

Dr. Corin Madoc, sitting in his cramped office with the glass panel that looks out into his cramped lab, sees Elisabeth Reed as soon as she enters the lab. She walks toward his office with a straight-backed, slow step that he is very fond of in her. He doesn't know her very well—only by word of mouth and his own sexual curiosity—but he has admired her for a long time, since his wife died (that long? really?).

Having seen him staring at her, she does not bother to knock. He likes that, too.

"Dr. Madoc, I'm Dr. Reed," she announces congenially.

"Come in and sit down, if you wish," Dr. Madoc offers in a voice with a trace of Australian accent. "I'd ask you to make yourself comfortable, but the room's too small for that."

"Yes, you're really tight—even your lab."

"It's unfortunate, all right. Comptrol thinks that because all of my work is molecular, I can do with correspondingly diminutive working space."

Dr. Reed smiles and sits down in a worn green overstuffed chair flanked by stacks of equally worn journals. "I've come to talk about your drug—the psychotrope that'll be used in Dr. Ibu's experiments."

"US-Twelve," Dr. Madoc confirms.

"I wasn't aware of its name."

"It doesn't have a name yet. That's just a temporary label. It stands for Unspecified Structure. I determined the structure, despite the current label, long ago—I just never got around to registering an official IUPAC name with Comptrol."

She nods. "Well, if I can be direct, I'm contributing to Dr. Ibu's project, too, and I'm curious to know exactly what the nature of US-Twelve is. It seems no one really knows."

Dr. Madoc smiles. Though he is forty-one, his sullen eyes, behind tinted, silver-framed glasses, look much older, dark and netted with wrinkles. Dr. Reed recalls having seen him at the computer center occasionally and remembers him as what some of the female techs there described as "dark, tall, and lonely." Though he still wears a wedding band, she also remembers having heard from someone that his wife had died a few years ago. She pities him, almost. She believes he is the kind of introverted scientist-type who'll probably never again go out of his way to meet another woman.

"US-Twelve, admittedly, is strange," Dr. Madoc says. "Only five or six molecules of it are required to precipitate a psychotomimetic experience in an average male. It works directly on the reticular activating system, initiating a seretonin-based chemical reaction within the RAS that very quickly affects the cerebral cortex and, in the only way I can describe it, dislocates consciousness."

"That, specifically," Dr. Reed says, "is what I'm curious about. What do you mean? You're not talking about 'out-of-body experiences'?"

Dr. Madoc shakes his head. "No—if anything, the opposite. By a remarkable biochemical rearrangement, the scope of awareness is infinitely enhanced by the drug. The sensory level of our consciousness is limited to the few sense organs by means of which we make our fumbling contact with the external world. This somatic level of consciousness is limited to the organs and tissue centers of the body.

"A large enough dosage of US-Twelve, four to five milligammas, which I suppose most of us would call 'trace quantities,' activates the cellular level of consciousness. There are as many distinct levels of consciousness as there are anatomical, cellular, subcellular, and neural structures within the body. And this drug can activate any of them."

"But that's not related to Dr. Ibu's work?"

"No, it isn't. He merely wants to increase the somatic consciousness of his subject to enable quicker neural responses. We'll use eight molecules for that."

"Have you experimented with that quantity before?"

"Six times."

"What were your results?"

"Five of those subjects died as a result of being unable to cope with the effects of the drug—specifically, loss of autonomic visceral control."

"What about the other one?"

"He survived, but he had been trained to. Indirectly, though. He was a Yogin. That's how we stumbled onto the necessity for conscious control of visceral responses. But if I'm not mistaken, that's your role in the project. Isn't it?"

"Yes, it is."

"Well, then, we may be working together quite soon."

Dr. Reed frowns quizzically.

"I'll be supervising the administration of the drug during the preliminary experiments. There are some exercises the subject should master before he's introduced to the drug; other than that, though, he'll be chiefly your charge. By the way, what's his name?"

* * *

"Heath!" she shouts, her hands funneling her mouth. She feels a moment of desperation.

The young man has drawn far ahead of her and is running along the wet, flat sand, following the slow curve of the shrunken sea. Three hundred yards to his left, the small waves are breaking, running in shallow streams along the smooth beach. Huge black rocks, crusted with gray barnacles below the high-water line, rip out of the sand at random intervals, upsetting the perfect flatness of the landscape in a peculiar way. They remind Heath of bent witches, draped by heavy, dark shrouds.

He splashes through a knee-deep pool and runs up to a narrow, natural jetty made up of a collection of small black boulders. He stands with his back to the low sun and the broad expanse of the sea reach.

After a few minutes, Elisabeth, her hair falling long past her shoulders and stringy with salt, jogs up to the jetty and sits down at Heath's feet. She is breathing hard from her run, and there are small droplets of sweat at her temples.

She is wearing denims, cut very short, and the top of a white bathing suit.

"I can't run any farther," she breathes.

"Okay, let's stay here and watch the sun set," Heath says, squatting beside her.

The slanting beams of sunset ripple off the distant thin line of ocean and touch the many pools of water around them with a fiery glow. The repeated call of some bird, sharp and discordant, is all that disturbs the silence of the world.

Heath sits with his chin resting in one hand, his profile catching a vague line of light that follows the outline of his features: soft lines, but with sharp touches—maturity emerging from childhood. His fair hair curls around the small ears and along the sleek tendons of his neck, not quite hiding a blue vein.

Elisabeth shifts so that they are touching, pleased by the warmth and firmness of his flesh. For the first time, she is caught up in the thought that he might accept her physically.

"*Istigkeit*," Heath says, without removing his eyes from the horizon. "That's the word Meister Eckhart liked to use."

"Is-ness?" she translates.

He turns, focusing his steady gaze on her. "That's a funny thing to say, isn't it? But that's what this reminds me of. Being. The chant of the sea rolling in, with the sea breeze, and those colors. Three different things that produce one feeling. They are simply one."

Elisabeth turns to look away, and he watches how her hair slips back from her rounded shoulder. She's confused, he realizes, but she doesn't want to pursue.

"Ignorance is a bliss we can never afford," he murmurs. "We have to understand the self as thoroughly as we can."

She glances at him, catching the odd tone, but her mind is still on their touching, thinking about how it might be extended, thinking how to narrow their proximity.

"You're sounding pedantic," she says curtly. She stretches her legs out; they are long and slender, and she is proud of them.

Heath pretends not to notice. He studies her face, seeing the up-angled cheeks, the lime-toned eyes, the olive complexion, and the expressive mouth.

"Don't blame me for that," he says flatly. "I learned to talk in a laboratory, not a classroom."

"So?" she asks with uninterest.

"So I may not talk like normal people."

"We shouldn't have wandered this far from the city," she says, facing to look down the strand they had walked up.

He sees that she hasn't been listening to him, focuses on her words, wondering why she sounds frustrated. He looks down at her legs, sees the white flesh of her thighs spilling from the tight denims.

"How have you been getting along with Corin?" she asks suddenly.

"Let's not talk about that now."

"No. Let's," she presses. "Tomorrow's the first preliminary experiment. I want to know if you and Corin have had any more scraps. His training is important. I'm concerned."

"As a scientist?" he asks with a grin that his boyish features make mischievous.

She trains her eyes on the remote undulation of the falling waves. "How else would I be interested?"

He speaks quickly because here is a fact and a change of subject. "I may not be human, but I do have real feelings. And I know that you're attracted to me."

She stares hard at him, a defiant ripple along her jaw.

"When are you going to stop harping on your identity? I hate that!"

He feels a pang of foolishness surge through him. "I can only be what I am," he says in a strained voice. "I can't delude myself."

"But you don't have to be so hard all the time. You're strong, you're intelligent, and you're beautiful."

"And I'm a carrier of defective DNA," he adds in a sardonic tone. "A 'cdd.' What does that do for my strength and my intelligence and beauty? They're all synthetic—and more temporary than a third of your life."

"Listen, Heath, I've heard it all before," she says, sharply. "Why don't you cut it?"

In the silence that comes between them, a breeze fingers their hair.

"You're acting like a child," she says, breaking the pause with a bitterness that is final. She stands up and walks toward the water. He watches her slow, deliberate stride, observing how the sleek muscles tighten and loosen, flowing under the tan skin. She is physically perfect, thanks to modifications of her own alleles. He pushes that thought out of his mind and entertains the idea of going after her.

He unbends, stretching in the suddenly cooler air. He begins to walk after her slowly, swinging his legs loosely, stooping several times to pick up and examine seashells, and then snapping them toward the sea. In his head, an extravagant fantasy begins to jell into an idea. He feels suddenly bold.

He saunters up beside her and runs a damp hand along the curve of her back.

"*Are* you attracted to me?" he asks, stopping and holding her by both of her elbows.

"Why do you think I can't stand to watch you tear yourself apart?"

"Just say yes."

"Yes." She feels her back and her thighs harden.

"I've felt that way about you for a long time."

She hears the nervousness in his voice.

He moves his hands up her arms, past her shoulders, glancing her neck; and pressing his palms to her cheeks, he moves his lips over hers. This, it seems to her now, is a bandit pleasure.

They walk, holding each other tightly, to a large, overhanging black rock. They sit down at its base, and Heath pulls her close to him. She is warm and soft. Her eyes are large and clear and make her willingness apparent. His hands are gentle, and he caresses her in such a way that she feels he is confident. That pleases her.

His hand undoes her denims and her white top and then retreats to his canvas shorts.

Her dusky body reclines, the neck and the swelling breasts, the curve of the hips, the belly with its beginning traces of dark down, the full thighs, the legs stretched out, wide apart, and the black fleece, provocative, proffered, henceforth available.

He smiles and bends over her in the failing light.

Noverim me, noverim Te, he thinks wryly.

There is a long and pleasing physical interlude that ends reluctantly in the twilight.

When he has collapsed, Elisabeth pushes his weight off. In the ensuing stillness, the cool darkness licking the sweat from their bodies, she experiences a moment of clarity. She realizes that there is no longer any feeling. She had failed or refused to see that her passion was produced by the restraints that were opposed to her sexual impulse. Now lying limp, she sees the object of her desire as a frustrated adolescent gripped by the absolute fear of an imminent and unavoidable future. To think that she had craved his total acceptance so adamantly makes her smile without mirth. She knows he feels some degree of pride, and this irks her.

The return walk to the clinic is long and tedious.

In front of the canvas partition with the large red ! printed on it, Dr. Ibu and Dr. Reed stand. They are looking into the pit of the amphitheater where Dr. Madoc, sitting on a stool, is addressing a white-smocked Heath.

Heath shifts his weight in the leather chair, his eyes closed, hearing the dull voice of Dr. Madoc resonate in his right ear.

"I'm going to place a breathing mask over your nose and mouth," Madoc is saying. "Take one deep breath and hold it for as long as you can. There will be no immediate effect, except for a slight dizziness."

Heath has read all of Madoc's papers on the psychotrope: he knows its structure, the paths of its synthesis, and its physiological effects perfectly well; and he is annoyed that Madoc still treats him as if he knew absolutely nothing.

The mask is clear plastic and fits snugly. Heath drags the thick air in slowly, recognizing the mixture of oxygen and helium by its sweet odor. But undetectable within it are a handful of large, clumsy adrenochrome molecules.

The mask is removed, and tightening his lips, Heath lets the muscles in his arms and legs relax, waiting for the first effect, which will be an outstanding intensification of visual stimuli.

"If you open your eyes," Madoc says, "in a few moments you'll become aware of an alteration in your color perception."

Heath's lids slip open. The expectant dizziness has not come. As yet, he is feeling unaffected.

Dr. Reed has moved into his line of vision. She walks to a console where she can monitor his metabolism. She is wearing a skirt and no stockings, and he admires her legs, toast-colored.

Looking up, he sees that she is watching him, and he gives her a sly, mischievous grin that makes her look away.

Just in front of her, the metallic face of the console catches the sunlight that is streaming into the laboratory. To Heath, the light is shattering off the metal in complicated broken lines and spirals, webbing bright stars, and fainter ones that are reflecting with it.

He snaps his attention out of its focus, realizing that the first effect of the drug has manifested itself.

Elisabeth's hair, tumbling about her shoulders, seems to glow with a living light; the natural wave of the hair presses against the space around it, bending the air almost as if with heat waves. Her green eyes are like crystals, faceted, casting off color in all directions, and her face, impassive, caught in an instant of remote or vacuous emotion, is like a detail from a Vermeer—perfectly still and radiant.

Heath lets his gaze scan the room, becoming more and more aware of the relationships between patterns. Two silver oxygen tanks with blue waistbands stand at attention in the twilight of a shadow cast by an overbearing piece of computer machinery; all of this comes together like some modern interpretation by Braque or Juan Gris. It's a still life, but without realism, lacking depth.

He again pulls his attention away, realizing that he must stop his mind from wandering independent of his volition. Down that path, when the full effect of the drug comes over him, lies madness. Instead, he must strive to maintain a constant and unstrained alertness.

"Within the next sixty seconds," Madoc's voice begins again, "you will experience your first temporal lapse. Remember to keep your attention fixed on your metabolic responses programmed on the screen and not to allow them to trespass beyond the indicated tolerance points. When the lapse is over, indicate so to me with a raised hand."

Heath looks up at the screen before him, where four graphs are registering his heart rate, blood pressure, respiration, and brain waves. On each of the graphs, two red lines indicate the safety limit of that graph. For any of the four graphs to range into those regions means almost certain death.

Closing his eyes, he concentrates on his mental disciplines. They are all now that is between him and oblivion.

Sitting there, with the sterile light of the laboratory filtering pink through his lids, he recalls Spinoza's statement that "blessedness is not the reward of virtue, but is virtue itself"; and whereas, before, this had been to him a vaguely pregnant piece of intuition, now it is clear, and he cannot understand why he could not fully grasp it before. But to someone who has trained himself in goodness, training his desires, his will, as he has trained his own responses, diligently, relentlessly, virtue really is blessedness.

Heath opens his eyes. There is an absolute quiescence about the laboratory. Movements—Elisabeth moving her hand, Ibu walking behind her—are slowing down. They continue to brake, until Ibu, in the midst of negotiating a turn, is casting an unchanging shadow.

Sunlight itself appears different, darker in hue, like a thin plasma stretched to web thickness over the entire room.

He attempts to speak, but opening his mouth demands intense concentration, and the heart and blood-pressure graphs both nosedive toward toleration limits.

He reasserts his mental discipline, focusing his attention over the entire neural extent of his being. He endures by his own will.

Now, with his metabolism regulated semiconsciously, a vast expanse of time lies before him. The temporal lapse, he recalls, will last only two minutes, but that, in this almost timeless state, will be experienced as indefinite duration.

Heath shifts his attention to Ibu. His skin is dark black, almost blue-black. The flat face, caught in midstride, is slightly drawn, but the features are plain: the practically nonexistent nose, merely two flaring nostrils; the thin lips, tight against the face; and the texture of the skin itself, very smooth, like polished stone. The whole face emits energy, and Heath realizes that he is seeing more of Ibu's face than he had ever been aware of. It is now more than just spatial relationships—it is visionary beauty.

He shuts his eyes again. The rosy darkness unmasks inner sensations that he had never faced before. He can feel his eyes, still tense from their exposure to light, retaining a ghost image of the laboratory. He is aware of the entire eye, warm from the light, the entire multilayered swamp of rods and cones, hungry for light.

He holds his eyes open to mere slits. Streams of light energy flood into him, so that his head becomes dizzy with sensation. He shuts his lids.

It's true what Bergson said—that the sense organs are *eliminative*. But now this drug has unfettered him.

Within his darkness he can feel his whole body: other than his open awareness to messages from the autonomic nervous system, he is conscious of a linkage to every cell within his body, so that he knows he can map any somatic sensation.

But there is more.

He feels himself sinking down into the soft tissue marsh of his own body, drifting slowly down dark capillary canals, propelled through endless cellular factories, ancient fibrous clockworks.

Presently, after an indeterminable time, Heath gathers his attention and opens his eyes to see if the temporal lapse has completed itself.

There is a brief flash of seeing the laboratory—white, brilliant, with Madoc's face, motionless and very near—and then it passes, dissolving into a shimmering filigree of pulsating white waves.

For an instant Heath panics and the light intensifies; but then he realizes what he is seeing: the subcellular worlds of neural energy shuttling everywhere within him. It is an endless sea of dancing particles, and even though he knows what it is, he feels cold and apprehensive. His violent longing to return to normalcy makes a fiercer chill run through him, and he fights a strange, oncoming ice age of the will.

He tries to remember seeing. He holds a winter landscape in his mind. Known tracks, habitual roads are covered now by a blank sameness. There are many trees bunching up to the horizon, hazy skeletons in the cold.

"Try the respirator again," Madoc orders softly.

"But he's breathing perfectly well," Reed retorts.

"The oxygen may loosen him from the coma," Madoc explains, looking at his watch. "He's been catatonic for twelve hours now."

"But why, Madoc?" Ibu asks in a raspy voice.

"I don't know."

"How long before the drug runs itself out?" Ibu asks.

"It ran itself out nine hours ago," Madoc replies calmly.

"Well, why is my boy like that?"

"I don't know."

"Why don't you know? Haven't you done this before?"

"Yes, of course. You know that . . . but only one has survived."

"This project is my life, Madoc. He better survive."

"I'm sorry, Michel. This is beyond my control."

Ibu's face is taut. "Keep me posted." He turns sharply and leaves the lab.

"This *is* everything to him," Elisabeth apologizes.

"I told him about the risks," Madoc says quietly, readjusting a sensor on the boy's temple. He holds the respirator to Heath's nose and mouth.

Elisabeth watches him, noting the detached efficiency with which he toils over the reclining boy. Not once during the past tense hours has he raised his voice or displayed anything but complete self-control. She is impressed by this.

"Let's get a glucose unit in here," he says. "We're just going to have to sit back and wait."

Ibu returns four times in the next six hours, the last time merely standing over the boy and clenching his fists.

"Madoc," he says, not facing the doctor, "if my boy dies, I'm going to file a report with Comptrol against you."

Madoc says nothing. He sips his coffee and thumbs through a journal.

Ibu, his eyes red, walks slowly out of the lab.

Elisabeth, who is sitting behind the console, looks across at Madoc. "Why didn't you say something?"

"What was there to say?"

"He can't file a report. You did nothing wrong."

"I know. And he knows, too."

"Then you shouldn't have let him threaten you like that."

Madoc says nothing. He riffles through several pages.

"You're due for some sleep," Elisabeth says after a brief silence.

"Yes . . . I guess so," he says, standing up. He checks over the console and walks toward the door. "I'm sorry," he says, looking back.

Twenty-four hours after the experiment had begun, Ibu leaves the laboratory and Dr. Reed comes on. It is raining outside, and the large room has a lazy, nocturnal feeling to it.

Madoc is sitting at the console, flipping the pages of another journal. He is not wearing a tie, as he usually does; his dark, heavy hair is uncombed; and his sullen eyes are listless.

He watches Elisabeth's straight-backed, slow step as she walks around to examine Heath. The physician has just left, but Madoc feels there is no harm in her looking.

She is more beautiful than his wife was, he realizes, but she does not have the same quiet ways of doing things that he loved his wife for. She has too much emotional remove, too. She is demanding and cold, Madoc sees.

She comes around the console and moves a chair so that she is sitting beside him. The fragrance of her body lotion, vague and feminine, reaches him and he remembers the warm odor of his wife.

A week ago, with the strength of surprise, he had seen a rumpled advertisement photograph of a woman who reminded him of his wife. It had shocked him. It lay on the third step down of a subway entrance. He took it up; the nose and chin did not really match, after all, but the harm was done.

"Why don't you get more sleep?" Elisabeth asks him.

"No. I'll stay here for a while."

"What are you thinking about?"

"My wife."

Ibu, who has just returned, stops in the doorway, unnoticed.

"Forgive me for asking, but how did she die?"

Madoc remains quiet. He recalls vividly the wild night, walking in the dark and the wind over broken earth, half-made foundations and unfinished drainage trenches and the spaced-out circles of glaring lights marking streets that were to be, walking with her, but so far from her, his arms full of linen—that daring venture to the laundry, going downriver four blocks away, to the train somewhere underground that was to bring them to their living place. As if by design, from out of the dark air and the cold wind, four figures emerged. Cruel decision: enjoy . . . . A boy with a pimply face pulled the magenta ribbons from her hair; the short, bearded one gripped a fold of her skirt; the pale, severe one pushed him from his wife and approached her with icy and painful motives and gestures half-familiar from worlds of shadow violence. There was a brief struggle by the hidden river, and when it was over, he turned from them and fled.

"I'm sorry, Corin . . . I didn't . . ."

"Well, why don't you tell her, Madoc?" Ibu says, stepping several paces into the laboratory.

"Stay out of this," Madoc says, his voice breaking. "I don't want to discuss it."

"She was raped one night while Madoc watched," Ibu says. "She died that night in a hospital . . . and he was nowhere to be found. It took a witness and two good lawyers to get him off the hook."

Madoc stands up and walks quietly out of the room.

Elisabeth glares at Ibu and walks out after Madoc.

He is standing at the end of an adjacent corridor, staring out one of the glass walls at a courtyard six stories below. The rain has streaked the window, making the wide, desolate concrete court look even more dismal.

He had met his wife one hot evening in Amman. She was not beautiful then, nor was she ever, but she was attentive to what he said, and he liked her voice and quiet mannerisms. She was American, and so they hit it off together right away, because he was an Australian working for his American citizenship papers at the American-sponsored clinic at Tel Aviv. They spent two weeks together in Amman.

The day before he was due back in Jerusalem, fighting erupted again, and the roads were blocked off. Ann, later his wife, went to work at one of the field hospitals, and though Corin was classified as "valuable personnel," he had grown very fond of Ann and followed her to the field. He applied what little medical training he had to fulfilling his role as a medic, and at night he spent all of his time with her. They had been sleeping together for two months when an envoy, in passing, brought orders to return Madoc to Tel Aviv. They had wanted to get married then and there, but most of their papers were missing.

She wrote to him often; he wrote back less often. She wrote about the wounded and about how much she loved him and needed him and wanted to have his babies; he wrote about his research, about the kind of home he wanted them to have, about how much money he could save for them.

After a time, he was discharged and given his citizenship papers. He wanted to go straight to America, and had his research material shipped immediately. But Ann was reluctant to leave at once, because her parents were in America, and all the friends she didn't want to see. They quarreled about it, and he left, feeling bitter, but with her promise that she would follow in a few months.

He rented a flat outside of San Diego, near the clinic. He wrote more often to Ann, but her letters were shorter and arrived less frequently. It frustrated him to have so much to say and not be able to get an immediate response.

It was lonely and hot in Amman, and Ann made friends with the son of an Arab colonel. He was, himself, only a corporal, but he was very impressive; and besides, it was lonely and hot that time of year. She wrote to Corin that she had met the son of an Arab colonel, and that he was friendly, and she was sure that he wouldn't mind the soldier taking her to lunch now and then, because it was awfully hot and lonely. They finally made love at his apartment, and she soon moved in with him, writing to Corin that she was more involved now with the soldier and that it was only a childish, quick affair and that she would come to the States when it was over, and they would get married, for she said she really loved him and said she felt nothing whatever for the soldier.

Madoc did not write back. At first, he thought he would never see her again. But he was very fond of her, and he thought he loved her. Two months later he made arrangements with her to come to him. They spent over a year making him understand it was only a quick, childish affair, and then they married.

"The pressure's really getting you down, isn't it?"

Her contralto is jolting, and Madoc turns from the window.

"Don't let Ibu pressure you," she says. "I don't care what he says. Nor do I care about your wife or your past. I'm sorry I started that."

Madoc says nothing.

"I like you," she says to him. "I thought you should know."

She turns and walks back to the lab.

Thirty-seven hours, forty-three minutes, and eight seconds after the beginning of his initial exposure to US-Twelve, Heath awakens.

"It's night," he mumbles sitting up. "How long have I been out?"

"Thirty-eight hours," Elisabeth says, as if in greeting. She undoes the sensors and rubs both of his cheeks. "You really had us scared."

Heath grins slyly, his face beginning to flush. "You especially?" he asks.

"Michel, if anyone," she says, brushing a loose piece of tape from his face. After having seen him impassive for all those hours, Elisabeth feels an uncertain excitement just to watch him move and hear him talk.

Madoc and Ibu appear almost simultaneously in the door. Michel runs up to Heath, his face lighting up.

"Heath! My God, are you all right?" he blurts.

"I'll go get the physician," Elisabeth says, leaving the room.

"I didn't realize how much time had passed," Heath explains.

"What happened?" Madoc asks.

"Apparently I internalized my awareness," he says. "I knew exactly where I was all the time, but I had no concept of duration."

"Then you just willed yourself out?" Madoc asks.

"Yes. The same way I willed myself in."

"Why the hell did you will yourself out in the first place?" Ibu asks.

Elisabeth and a physician enter, and the doctor immediately begins his examination.

"I was bored," Heath answers, sitting up straighter.

"You were bored?" Ibu repeats.

"After the time lag began, I had nothing to do."

"What did you experience?" Elisabeth asks.

"It's difficult to explain."

"Don't move your eyes, please," the physician says, fixing Heath's lids open.

"I actually saw cellular activity in my body—visually, clearly," Heath says. "And then I went deeper, and I saw neural activity—an incredible array of brilliant light energy. I was a little frightened of it all."

"That's pure nonsense," Ibu says sternly.

"Don't be so quick," Madoc warns. "We know that the brain receives information about every process in the body; all of the 'biologically useless' information is screened out by the reticular activating system . . . and it is the RAS that is affected first by the drug. It's very possible that Heath had shifted his awareness to that center of the brain."

"It's also very possible that Heath merely hallucinated the entire experience," Ibu says. "I feel that's something we should leave for the psych people."

Madoc shrugs his shoulders. "You didn't remember our lessons," he says to Heath, who is now flat on his stomach. "Remember, I told you to fix your attention on a single object or idea, otherwise you'd lose your awareness during the temporal lapse."

"Yes, I know," Heath says, "but I didn't expect the experience to be that total. It was more than just my eyes—it was everything that I am."

"He's going to need some sleep," the physician says. "I'd like him moved to an observation room, too. Just as a safety precaution."

"Fine," Ibu says. "Do whatever you feel is best." He faces Madoc. "I'd like to speak with you, outside."

In the corridor, Ibu assumes a paternal air. "Corin, I've known you for seven years, and I was instrumental in getting your research qualified here. I'm not saying this to make you feel indebted, but I do want you to have a sense of how important this project is for me. I'm not holding you responsible for what happened. I flew off the handle, but you know that's my character. You also know that I'm a scientist, as you are. We are not like the psych people. We work in areas where we can apply the laws of nature. So, because we are scientists and because I head this project, I don't want you using my subject to test any of your theories. I don't want to hear about internalization—I want him to externalize, to reach out and communicate with that dolphin. And remember, I own Heath. He's my lab property, and I have the last say about what he does and doesn't do. Clear?"

"Of course," Madoc says indifferently, and turns to leave.

"Corin."

"Yes."

"Keep in mind that despite his IQ, he's still just a teen-ager."

"Sure."

Heath's room is narrow and not very long. The ceiling is one fluorescent light. The two longer white walls are broken up by large prints by Ernst Fuchs. At the far end of the room, opposite the door, is an oval window that looks out onto the bay. Two large, flat speakers emerge from the face of one wall over his desk. When Madoc enters, Heath is lying on his low bed, listening to Gesualdo's *Moro lasso,* which is playing rather loudly.

Heath rises and turns down the music.

"Hello, Corin! What brings you to this quarter of the known world?" he asks with a chuckle.

Madoc sits on the edge of Heath's desk. "I want to talk about to-morrow's preliminary."

"Look, I've got it straight about the time lag."

Madoc holds up his hand. "Not that. I want to ask you to give up the project entirely."

Heath raises his eyebrows inquisitively.

"I'd like you to work for me," Madoc says.

"No. I can't do that."

"Why?"

"I'm personally committed to this project."

"You mean Lenny?"

"Aye, that's it, mate," Heath says, miming Madoc's accent.

"Won't you consider it?"

"There's no reason to. That dolphin and I are too close as it is for me to stop now. Sometimes, in the pool, I feel that I *can* communicate with him. I'm not about to lose an opportunity like this."

Madoc nods his head and stands up. Above Heath's bed is a Chinese ceramic square of exceptional subtlety and beauty. It depicts a cuckoo about to alight on a thin branch. He stares at it for a moment and then leaves.

Heath takes a long drag from the face mask. He looks down at Madoc's hand, focusing on his wedding ring. He stares at the ring until the golden glow diffuses and then collects itself in a single sharp star of reflected light. He moves his eyes across the extent of his field of vision. Madoc's glasses, tinted by the sunlight in the room, look opaque. Ibu is standing just on the edge of the amphitheater, his long white lab coat draped about him like a cloak. He is standing still, and Heath moves his eyes away from him until he finds Elisabeth, who is sitting by her console, clipboard propped in her lap. She is wearing a white skirt and has her long tanned legs crossed. Her suspended foot is wagging anxiously, and Heath pays it special attention.

The lighting of the room seems to dull, as if a cloud is passing the sun. Gradually, Elisabeth's foot rocks to a stop. The time lag has commenced.

Heath notices the small bones in the ankle, which create soft shadings. He examines the region where her foot enters the white shoe. A small callus is there, barely visible from his perspective, which he picks out because he knows it is there. He tracks his eyes over the shoe, noting each scuff mark carefully, scrutinizing the seams. Finally he rests his eyes on the heel, and then begins all over again at the ankle. He does this thirty-one times before the foot begins to wag again.

The foot is moving slower than it had been, and Heath notices that if he focuses his eyes, the foot moves more quickly. He is on the interface of different rates of time.

He raises his hand to indicate that he is out of the time lag.

Madoc places a set of black headphones over his head, covering his ears.

"Are you comfortable?" Madoc asks, adjusting a tiny microphone that snakes around his cheek.

Heath hears the question normally, but his visual perception of Madoc's lips is not synchronized with his audio perception. He nods.

"Fine," Madoc says. He looks over his shoulder at the pudgy physician who is standing there. The physician catches the glance and approaches Heath. He examines Heath's reflexes. When he is done, he nods at Madoc approvingly.

"Okay, let's play," Madoc says, swinging around on his stool so that he is facing a desk machine with a typing face. He punches out a pattern, and five digits flash on the screen before Heath for an instant. Heath moves his hand over a similar machine resting just above his thighs. He taps out the same figure.

Madoc repeats the procedure, this time with six digits, flashing more briefly on the screen. Finally, he lets the computer take over, moving at a rate his fingers cannot.

For over an hour they play, with more numerals and geometric patterns, more and more quickly. By the end of the session, Heath's fingers are a blur, the screen blinking nonsensically.

Madoc shuts down the computer.

Heath settles into the white leather.

"How'd I do?" he asks with a grin.

"You're remarkable," she says, her voice muffled in his shoulder.

Elisabeth and Heath are lying naked on his bed. The *Sanctus* in Beethoven's Mass in D is seething through the room. She is lying on her stomach, her dark hair spreading its tendrils over his chest.

When the music is over, Elisabeth gets up from the bed and scans the row of tapes just above Heath's desk. She selects the *Vespers* by Claudio Monteverdi. After injecting the cartridge into the player, she moves to the window. The sea is still breaking violently, and night has steamed into the bay. Two white lights are moving along the horizon. They are lusterless in the thin fog and remind her of cabin windows on a stranded hulk heavy with sand.

Heath watches her from the bed.

"Where were you born?" he asks.

"In Madaket."

"Where's that?"

"Massachusetts, on Nantucket Island. Why do you ask?"

"Just curious."

He turns his head to look into the darkness by the door, and then he asks, "Why did you change your mind?"

"About what?"

"About sleeping with me."

"You don't snore."

Heath laughs, a very natural laugh. "Is it because Madoc disappoints you?"

Elisabeth says nothing, but walks up to the bed and sits down.

"He's still strongly affected by his wife," he says. "He would never go for you. For him, you have *noli me tangere* written all over your yummy body."

"How can you say that?"

"I've listened to him talk. And I know how you operate."

"I don't like him. He's a coward."

"He only believes he's a coward."

"Same difference."

"What do you see in him?"

"Are you jealous?"

"Maybe. Am I being crude?"

"How hard are you trying?"

"Not very. Again, I'm just curious. I like Corin."

"Why?"

"He's brilliant. For me, he's the easiest person to communicate with—besides you, of course."

"Of course."

"He's not the stereotyped psychophysicist with chemical formulae for love and hate. He's truly interested in the human psyche. Do you know, he actually asked me to continue internalizing so that he might study the time-dilation effect of his drug? If it wasn't for Lenny, I know I'd do it."

"Michel would kill you."

"True, but I don't like Michel. He strong-arms everybody."

"He's highly regarded by Comptrol, and he's in well with the security force. He can get anything he wants."

"He's a bully. His personality is twisted."

"Value judgment."

Heath grunts and rolls over so that he is facing her.

"Again?" she asks.

"Sure."

"Do you love me?"

"No."

In the pool, Lenny is circling. Madoc, in a green polo shirt that reveals a physique with no signs of middle age, is briefing Heath, who is sitting forward in a large mechanized chair at the edge of the pool. Several heavy computer components on casters outflank the chair.

Ibu is standing on the other side of the pool with Elisabeth and a short bald man who is a Comptrol representative.

"Off the record, Michel," the bald man is saying, "how does this computer tie-up work, and where'd you get the idea?"

"The dolphin world is almost strictly acoustic," Ibu explains, "just as ours is visual. The total amount of information received by dolphins and humans from their environment is roughly the same. But the types differ.

"Before the war, research on dolphin sounds was not uncommon. Here in the States, in fact, dolphins were taught to mimic our speech. Well, in this experiment something very similar is being done. Our subject has had his world 'speeded up,' so to speak, to permit him to work comfortably with a sound system that will feed acoustic patterns into the pool at about the rate of dolphin communication.

"Quite simply, we're going to start establishing rudimentary communication today. We don't really expect any profound intercourse for some time."

"Why must you use the boy at all? What's wrong with computers?"

Ibu smiles. "A typical question from a Comptrol man," he says. "That type of communication has been attempted time and again by myself and others, with minimal success. We don't know why, yet, but dolphins have a predilection for man. I'm betting my professional career and a lot of your money that I can exploit that predilection. Heath, our subject, has grown up with that dolphin. By broadcasting his voice to the dolphin, we're making it clear that he, the dolphin's companion, wants to communicate. We've had excellent results with preliminary experiments along this line."

Heath, sitting back in the chair, looks at the frozen world around him. Ibu, Elisabeth, and the Comptrol man at the far end of the pool look like mannequins posed realistically. The banks of computer components that an instant before were faces of winking lights have tilted, the lights freezing. He shifts his gaze to the water, where he can see the gray, submerged form of Lenny.

After studying the still surface of the water several times, Heath realizes that the temporal lag is lasting too long. It should have ended long ago.

He tries to look at Madoc, but he is out of his visual scope. He looks across the pool; the mannequins there have changed their positions slightly. Now he knows that the time lag is excessively long.

Returning his gaze to the pool, he detects a faint odor. He smells the esters of some sweet substance, like aloe.

It's the drug. There is a leak in a tube just alongside of his neck.

The odor becomes more acrid, pinching his nostrils. He tries to hold his breath, but the light vapors rise up his nose.

He fights to maintain his calmness. *Too much of this can kill me,* he realizes. Such a stupid accident, absurd . . . . Or is it an accident?

The water of the pool has become completely transparent, so that it no longer exists. Suspended in the pool is Lenny, looking up at him. The dimensionality of the vision startles Heath, and he attempts to avert his eyes, but he cannot. He is totally paralyzed.

Did Madoc do this? he wonders. *Is Madoc forcing me to internalize?*

He tastes the vapors in his nostrils, in the roof of his mouth, in his eyes—a biting sweetness.

Dizzy.

He feels that he can no longer keep his eyes open without becoming nauseated, yet he cannot close them.

The air around him becomes hot and close, and he has trouble breathing. His stomach is nervous, sending spasms of sour pain down into his bowels.

Lenny, hanging before and below him, has become Heath's entire visual universe. Every detail, every gradation of shading on the dolphin's body, is revealed to him.

Suddenly he is very close to Lenny, so close that he can feel the smooth skin on the dolphin's nose and can see every close detail of the dolphin's left eye. The tactile-visual image grates on his mind with an undreamlike quality that arrogates his fright.

This is real, he thinks with a calmness that surprises him. *I've externalized myself.*

He draws closer to the eye, aware that he is commanding some kind of psychokinesthetic extension of himself. He sees a silhouette in the black iris, ghosts of motion, but with no proximity.

He floats up even closer, free of the contiguities he has always known . . . and then he is within the cloudy mirror, and like some wide-eyed Alice, turns to look back at the world he has left. But there is nothing there in the gray light.

A cry catches in his absent throat, while the thin walls of the alien cornea thicken like distance, and he is most alone.

* * *

Ibu scrambles along the side of the pool, stopping short of Madoc. "What's wrong?" he asks, suppressing his anger.

"I don't know," Madoc replies.

"Has he internalized?"

"It looks that way."

A physician who has been standing by a computer component runs up and bends over Heath. He looks up at Ibu. "Get this apparatus off him, and have him moved to an observation room."

Ibu and Madoc quickly respond. After Heath has been removed from the lab, Ibu faces Madoc, says, "You're going to have to explain this."

Elisabeth, who has been standing behind Ibu, asks, "Why? You've known about the risks all along."

Madoc shakes his head. "Elisabeth."

Ibu steps back, relaxed, studying Elisabeth silently.

"You can't hold Corin responsible," she says.

"Dr. Reed," Ibu says in a quiet tone, "your job on this project is over. Please don't concern yourself with my job."

The short bald man from Comptrol steps up behind Ibu. "What's happened, Michel?"

"It seems that Dr. Madoc has made an extravagant error. Our subject has ODed."

Elisabeth faces Madoc. He avoids her eyes, and it takes her a moment to put down the upsurge of rage that threatens to overcome her. She speaks in a faltering voice, "Dr. Madoc was not responsible for what happened. The risk of the subject inter—"

"Dr. Reed!" Ibu barks. "That's enough from you."

"The risk of what has just occurred," she continues, "has always been understood by all concerned."

Ibu slashes the back of his hand across her face, so that she stumbles back with the impact. "I said that's enough!"

Madoc steps forward, eyes flashing.

Ibu fixes his stare on him. "Yes, Madoc?"

Madoc drops his gaze to the floor.

The Comptrol man glares at Ibu, asks Madoc, "Just what has happened to the boy?"

"I don't know."

"Don't you understand the effects of your drug?"

"Not fully."

"Then why is it being employed?"

"Dr. Ibu and I . . ."

Ibu fires an intent look at Madoc. "Don't try to transfer the responsibility, Madoc."

"Apparently," the Comptrol man intervenes, "the drug being employed is not backed with the proper research to qualify its use. I think we should shut down this project until more data regarding the drug can be acquired."

He walks toward the exit. Ibu flashes Madoc one threatening glance and then follows after.

Elisabeth touches Madoc's arm. "This time, I'm sorry."

He walks to the exit.

She watches him until he is out of sight.

"Coward," she breathes.

The sun is striking over the void observation room as Dr. Ibu walks in. Six vacant beds occupy the long room, each one under a slender window. Audible from an adjacent room is a lutanist plucking away at "Rocky Raccoon." Ibu walks toward the music.

He enters the adjacent room, and against the glare of a window, he recognizes the curly-headed physician who is playing the song. Seeing Ibu, he puts aside his instrument and stands up.

"Your boy was discharged earlier this morning," the doctor says.

"I know that. I was told that the final reports would be ready for me by now."

"Let me see." The physician walks to a cluttered desk and fumbles among the papers. He comes away with a blue folder, the contents of which he examines at length.

"Well, what's the story?" Ibu asks.

"It seems he's in excellent physical shape. Suffered no damage whatsoever from the experiment. However . . ." He remains silent while he studies the folder again.

"Well?"

"There's a marked difference in his personality profile. The psych who examined him indicates here that your boy is less aggressive, displays signs of potentiating away from the death fixation all of his previous examinations have turned up, and, to put it bluntly, he's lost his sexual identity."

"What does that mean?"

"He's lost his sexual potential. You might even say he's very close to being asexual."

* * *

"I always thought that you and Liz were having an affair," Madoc says. He is sitting on a park bench of twisted metal.

"Was it that apparent?" Heath asks.

Madoc nods, grinning softly.

"Maybe for you it would have been," Heath says.

They are in a sunburned park on Sunday, in the wide waste beyond the city. Two teams in gray deploy through the sunlight.

"What was that supposed to smack of?" Madoc asks.

"I just think that you admire Liz and would have noticed something like that."

Coming in stubby and fast, the baseman gathers a grounder in fat green grass, picks it stinging and clipped as wit into the leather; a swinging step wings it dead-eye down to first. Smack.

"Attaboy," Heath says.

"Well done," Madoc agrees. He wipes the sweat from his brow, removing his glasses to do so. "Tell me about what happened with Lenny again."

The catcher reverses his cap and squats in the dust. The pitcher rubs the ball on his pants, chewing, spits behind him. He nods past the batter, taking his time.

"I extended myself—there was that gas leak."

"I wasn't responsible for that, Heath."

"I believe you," he says, though he is not sure. "Anyway, I extended beyond my body. I actually . . . merged consciousness with Lenny."

"That's what I want you to expound on."

The batter settles, tugs at his cap. A spinning ball comes at him, and he steps and swings to it, catching it with hickory before it ducks.

"Socko, baby!" Heath yells.

Cleats dig into the dust. The outfielder, on his way, looking over his shoulder, makes it a triple.

"Tell me again about the dolphin consciousness," Madoc says.

"Why do you persist?" Heath asks. "No one would believe you if you told them."

"I want to know."

"All right. But let's get away from this game. It's too compelling."

They walk toward a remote colony of trees, the afternoon sun pacing their shadows before them.

"Everything I'm going to tell you now," Heath says, "I've acquired by the mind meld I experienced with Lenny. I don't know if I can make you understand it." He says nothing more for several seconds, as he gathers his thoughts.

"The difference between dolphins and humans is not a matter of intelligence or spirituality—it's a difference in direction. Man is constantly striving outward. All of his serious sciences attempt to explain and cope with what is around him. The dolphins, on the other hand, have done just the opposite. They've moved inward, researching the inner universe that each individual dolphin possesses. While we've banded together into social units to probe everything around us, the dolphins have remained essentially individuals, but they have progressed inwardly at a collective rate."

"But how is that possible?" Madoc asks.

"You're suffering from a problem that most of us are stymied by. As far as physical science is concerned, we have long since gone beyond the eighteenth-century notion of dead hunks of matter moving in the black void of space. Yet our psychological sciences are still restricted to eighteenth-century mechanistic notions: minds are simply located hunks of gray matter moving in the black void of time. The dolphins, however, realize that the mind of their species, just like the mind of mankind, is a collective and interpenetrating field.

"The unconscious is not personal, but in order not to be swamped by infinite information, the brain functions as what Aldous Huxley called a 'reducing valve.' It shuts out the universe so that the individual can do what is in front of him. The million signals a second must be reduced to a few. But the intuition and the imagination maintain an opening to the unconscious, which contains all the information that could not register in immediate consciousness. Where we ignore intuition and imagination in favor of deduction and the logical sequence, the dolphins have exploited those faculties to penetrate into their collective unconscious, and to advance inwardly, as we have advanced outwardly. And that's why they have no 'culture' as we recognize it—no cities, museums, no artwork or history books. All of that and much more is available to them in their unconscious."

"But how do they mark their progress?"

"In a more unified way than we do. We have history, they have their whole collective memory, right back to the beginnings of their species. They're not hindered by time because they've almost eliminated their immediate consciousness. Since the immediate consciousness must work in a step-by-step incremental sequence of events, its perception of time is linear. Certainly all the information cannot be restricted to that line, and so the time of the unconscious is out of time; the line must be widened and lengthened until it becomes a sphere if you want to achieve the consciousness of the dolphin.

"And while I was one with Lenny, I experienced that."

"You were aware of the future?"

"There was no future. Time was not linear."

They enter shadows shattered by sunlight and sit beneath the trees.

"You know, Heath, since you first told me about them, I've wanted to join you."

"Why don't you?"

"I can't take US-Twelve."

"If you had the training you could."

There is a long pause; then: "I'll have to think about it."

Heath frowns. "One thing you learn when you minimize immediate consciousness, and that is not to think too much. You have to be able to act gracefully, and thinking makes you heavy and clumsy. Any decision in life can be decided any number of ways. I've learned to think like a strategist and act like a savage."

A quick length moves as a slip of silver light, not disturbing the slick surface of the pool. Lenny circles the pool twice and then breaks the water in a jumping invitation to Heath, who is standing on toes at the edge. He strips off his cotton shirt and knifes into the water.

Lenny is cruising the bottom of the pool and rises to meet him. Together they dance in the filmy world, bobbing slowly to the surface for air.

Skimming the surface, Heath shakes the water from his face and sees the stark figure of Dr. Ibu at the poolside, staring down at him. He strokes toward him, lifting himself into the heavy gravity.

"I've been looking for you," Ibu says, sitting on his heels.

"I heard Comptrol shut down the project temporarily," Heath says, wiping water from his eyes. "I thought I'd be the last person you'd want to see for a while."

"Where've you been?"

"With Madoc."

"I don't like you seeing him."

"Why?"

"He's subversive."

"In what way?"

"Isn't it apparent? He's no scientist. He's a mystic. He doesn't want to understand. He wants to be enlightened."

"How can you say that?"

"I know very well that Madoc asked you to work for him, so he could study the internalizing effect of his drug."

"How'd you find out?"

"He approached me and told me. He wanted to buy you, of course."

"I don't like to be discussed financially. You told me that I can do what I want, when I want. You told me you're never going to exercise your ownership rights."

"Oh, let's be realistic, Heath. I *do* own you. I *can* do whatever I want with you."

Heath looks down at his knees and says nothing.

"I don't want you working for Madoc," Ibu says.

"What makes you think I will?"

"Nothing. But I know that he's applied here and at two other clinics to continue his research with US-Twelve. I'm going to do everything I can to thwart him, the way he thwarted me."

"He didn't thwart you."

"It was his failure that shut down my project—that has meant your whole life has been lived in vain."

"My life has been fulfilling. I am satisfied . . . just disappointed that you didn't get your money's worth. And your blaming Madoc for a technical flaw is nonsense."

"Nonsense or not, you're not to cooperate with him. I forbid it."

Heath looks at him passively, as if studying his features.

"And don't get smart with me," Ibu says. "My signature can have you euthed at any time."

He makes his last remark as he is standing; then he turns and walks away with clipped steps.

Heath stares out over the water until Lenny slices the surface, beckoning him with sharp, happy cries. Holding his nose, he slips into the pool.

I feel dead, he thinks. *I feel as if I were the residue of a stranger's life, that I should pursue you.*

He sinks toward the bottom, and Lenny passes over him.

I feel imperfect, unable to tell you that I understand you but cannot follow, and that it was a mistake that placed you in that world, and me in this; or that misfortune placed these worlds in us.

After the first lesson in Dr. Reed's laboratory, Madoc rises from the white-leather chair, stifling a yawn. "How'd I do?"

Elisabeth steps out from behind her exclamatory partition, regarding her clipboard, and with a pencil-in-mouth accent replies, "Lousy."

"That bad?"

"Probably worse, but I've an uncontrollably optimistic attitude."

"Well, how long will it be?"

She raises her eyebrows and widens her eyes in feigned surprise. "Didn't they teach you that a scientist's chief virtue is his patience?"

"They never mentioned that at Austral—but then, that's purely a technical school, and you can't expect such refined ethical training."

She laughs warmly.

"Where'd you study?" he asks.

"Harvard, ten years."

He moves around her and puts on his buckskin vest. It fits him well, but Elisabeth thinks it is somewhat incongruous with his white shirt, and white slacks and shoes.

"It's lunchtime," he announces. "May I join you?"

"If you'd like."

The elevator dip and the four turns to the cafeteria are accompanied by a strained silence. Madoc puts his hands in his pockets and tries to walk as casually as he can.

He selects the meatloaf with mashed potatoes and string beans, she the swordfish and baked potato. Both have tea.

Sitting under the parabolic steel arc of a main support, they are silhouetted by a china-blue sky that hovers over the thousands of green acres that separate the clinic from San Diego.

"You've quite a physique," she says, spreading her potato.

"Your physique isn't so bad, either."

"Oh, come on, Corin. That line died before the war."

His face flushes hot and red. He stuffs his mouth with mashed potato.

"Do you work out a lot?" she asks.

"Occasionally. But I haven't that much time. I'm involved with Nayaka's karate forum."

Genuine surprise crosses her face. "Sincerely?"

"Don't be too impressed. I've been at it for seven years now, and I'm still his worst student."

They eat for a moment in silence.

"I've been meaning to ask you about Heath," she says. "He's changed quite a bit hasn't he?"

Madoc feels some disappointment at the bend of the conversation. "Why ask me?"

"You and he do spend a considerable amount of time together, don't you?"

"I thought that you knew him better than I do."

"Not lately," she answers honestly. "He hasn't avoided me, but he hasn't been around to pursue me, either."

"You miss that, I assume."

"He's decidedly attractive."

"I wouldn't know."

She regards him with a contemplative expression.

He sees that and is afraid of what she's about to say, so he speaks first. "The incident at the pool was almost mystical for him; at least, that's what he told me. All of his interests have changed."

"For the better or worse?"

"You'll have to decide that for yourself."

She walks down the boulevard alone. It is late afternoon, the sunlight is thick yellow, and she feels like she is about to cry again. She remembers that she hasn't felt this way in almost eight years. It makes her tired to think it's been that long.

She stops at a corner and tries to get her bearings. She has to return to the clinic before nightfall. There is no place for her to stay in the city. She has no money.

She turns down an intersecting road that leads to the highway that leads to the expressway. She wipes the tears from her eyes, but they return immediately.

She thinks about being alone in Cape Cod that summer eight years ago. She had had many technical lovers by that time, and she had lost count. But she loved him as she had loved only one person before him.

She recalls how it hurts your eyes to watch the sunrise coming off the bay. They had quarreled that night before she had gone out. He had whored the whole time they were together, and then, when that was over, he had wanted one of his whores to move in with them.

She despised him then and ran off, as she has run off now. No money, just hurt. She had walked for hours, but that had failed to kill her despair. It was night when she had made it into Boston. She had no place to stay, so she stayed with a nicotine-perfumed journalist who had picked her up on a park bench. His apartment was cramped, his breath was stale, and his only compliments were that he liked dark-haired women and was enthusiastic about needing no pillow under her buttocks.

She hitched to Cambridge the next morning, and as soon as she got to her flat, she got sick.

She stands on the macadam, her thumb out. Two cars hum by before a dirt-caked, formerly red, old-fashioned gas-piston jerks to a stop. She hops in, and the car has lurched off before she regards the driver.

He is bulky, strong-looking, and with close-cropped hair and bright, lidless eyes. He's wearing only an undershirt without sleeves, and there is a green-and-blue stain on his bicep that she strains to recognize as a tattoo. He is close to fifty and unshaven.

"Hi. Name's Bill," he says. His voice is expectantly deep and gruff.

"I'm Elisabeth."

"Where you goin', Liz?"

"The expressway."

"Fine. So'm I. Where down that?"

"The Diego Clinic."

"What you want with that?" he asks, giving her a narrow-eyed glance. He smiles broadly. His teeth are yellow-brown. "What you want with them scientist types?"

"I work there."

He opens his window and spits out. "You mean *you're* a scientist?" he says with a chuckle.

"Yes."

He stops laughing. "Sorry, ma'am," he says, his face serious. "You look much too fine to be a scientist."

"But I am."

"You're fine, all right."

The car turns onto the expressway and accelerates. They drive for fifteen minutes in silence; then he pulls off the expressway and careens down a winding dirt road.

She looks at him. "What are you doing?"

He says nothing, merely smiles his dirty smile.

"Stop the car," she orders.

"Will do, love. Will do," he says, laughing. The car rocks to a stop, and Elisabeth jumps out before he can grab her. She starts running toward the expressway, hears the car door slam behind her and the quick scratch of his pursuit.

"Now, hold on, love," he calls.

When he is directly behind her, she spins about, feeling inside the pocket of her jacket. He grabs her left arm and pulls her toward him. In one smooth, unified motion, she withdraws the knife from her pocket, hisses it open under his chin, and slashes his neck. Blood drools over his chest, and he jumps back with a startled gasp.

She turns about and runs to the expressway. The fourth car that passes picks her up. The driver, a bony businessman, sees the blood on her hand and cuff but says nothing. He is going past the clinic, and leaves her off at the ramp entrance.

It is time for the ocean to move on. Somehow, sheathed in the warm current of the pool, he'd lost his desire for the sea. He usually left with the tide, but today he feels comfortable staying. He falls shuddering among the detritus of kelp that has washed into the pool from the ocean. His belly touches the smooth bottom as he runs aground on his own shadow. In the world above, two legs dangle, thrashing for the fun of it, thirty feet above the weary shadow.

Lenny noses up for air. He rises slowly, a long gray feather slendering up through the dense air of the sea. His eyes of bolted glass are fixed on a roundness as of sun and white flesh, glittering like stars above his brain; the dolphin rises gradually. He is very tired. As he rises, his shadow pales and enters the colorless bottom, dissolved in the whirling liquid that his thrusting tail spawns.

A sense half of anguish overcomes him. A desire to sleep in the currents fights against the strong enchaining links of hungry lungs.

He knows the path up is direct, but the dolphin is tired. He dawdles awhile, swerves, pauses, turns on his side, and cocks a round eye up at the dense thrashing. In the calm water, ten feet down, twisting, he thinks himself around and around in a slow circling of doubt, powerless to be a dolphin. He rises slowly.

Heath climbs out of the pool, kneels facing Madoc, and pulls his canvas trunks up.

"He's sick," Heath says.

"Can we do anything?"

"Very little." He stands up, dripping. "I've fed him. I'm going to just let him be until tomorrow. He may get over it."

He walks to a pile of clothing and extracts a thick pink towel and begins drying himself.

"Have you seen Elisabeth today?" he asks Madoc.

"Yes, I had my lesson."

"How are you progressing?"

"It's been only four weeks."

"How's Liz?"

"She seemed to be upset, but she wouldn't talk about it."

"Yeah," Heath sighs, stripping off his trunks.

"Do you know what's happened?"

"We went into the city yesterday. I really didn't want to—that was my mistake. You should *never* surrender yourself to anything. Always battle to the end."

"What?"

"I should have told her here, and not gone into the city with her, but I didn't think she'd take it that hard."

"You mean, she loves you?"

"Don't be silly. Love is respect and admiration. It has nothing whatsoever to do with sex, despite anything and everything those marriage manuals say. Sex is a biological drive."

"But you told her that you're not interested in her anymore?"

"Yes. She started arguing about it—got quite vicious, too. Then she just ran away."

Heath finishes toweling himself and then crawls into his clothes.

"Always treat *everything* with respect," he says. "That was my heroic flaw." He grins broadly. "I gave myself up to Elisabeth for a time. You can't do that. You can't surrender yourself to anything—not even your death. That's how dolphins think."

"Do they put much emphasis on death?"

"More than anything else. You must often think of your death, wonder about it, explore it. Do that so your life will be more defined."

"That sounds rather grim."

"Naw. It's just the paradox of our reality. Only the tragic sense of life is capable of sustaining an enduring strength and joy."

"Once you told me that we must act more and think less. Do I smell the dregs of a paradox?"

"You're smelling the stink of your confusion. Act your life out, don't think it out. You can't think your death out—that, you'll act when the times comes whether you want to or not. But the constant knowledge of it provides the clarity we need to act without looking back."

"It's too pat for me."

Heath smiles. "What else is life but a journey to death?"

It is late night or early morning. The large laboratory housing the pool is not shaken by the rising wind, but a plate-glass window rattles. Heath stands alone at the pool's edge, where the dripping of the filter machine, at any silence of the wind, can be heard tapping like a blind man through the lab.

Lenny floats in the pool, most gray, turning up his grinning head. He is without life.

Heath covers his face with his hands and prepares to sob, but he does not. There is no reason to. Everything he has been taught, everything he has learned from the dolphin, does not permit tears. Instead, he wonders why. He is convinced that Lenny was poisoned. There can be no other explanation. But who? And how to proceed to find the murderer without misleading sophism? Or is that possible?

Elisabeth? She was at the clinic yesterday, and certainly she is angry enough, and that makes up for cruelty.

Ibu? That makes no sense. Lenny was a vital part of his beloved experiment.

Madoc? Incredible jealousy? Hardly likely. But was he responsible for that gas leak that was almost fatal? Using that as a pawn to strike Ibu? And now using Lenny, too? Possible. There is enough suppressed emotion. It is possible. But only that, possible.

Who, really?

A stocky, towering man with a football-shaped head and a nose almost flat against his big-boned face enters the dim-lit room with the grace of a ballet dancer. Like a large cat, he squats obscenely in the center of the room. Another door opens, and Dr. Ibu steps out on a carpet of light. He is wearing only a cotton robe. His face is haggard with want of sleep. He had not truly wanted the dolphin killed. He had changed his mind even as he was administering the poison. But that is irrevocable. It was a means of venting his torment. As irrational and prodigal as anything that is man's.

"I want Madoc dead," he whispers.

The big man sits quite still, staring forward as if he has heard nothing.

"I will invite him here tomorrow night," Ibu continues. "He will have to pass through the marine lab to get here. I have made arrangements with the security patrol that night so that they will avoid the area. Four dangerous adolescent delinquents, drugged and looking for adventure, will break into the lab just as Madoc is passing through. He will be assaulted and most unfortunately drowned in the pool. We will supervise the affair but not interfere."

The hulking man rises and leaves.

It is nine-thirty. Dr. Madoc is standing in his laboratory examining a distilling apparatus. There is nothing about him but glassware mating with glassware. A single row of fluorescent lights is on overhead, and most of the small lab is crowded with shadows. The fragrance of volatile esters is strong.

He looks up at the wall clock, which has just clicked 9:33, and reminds himself that he is due at Ibu's apartment at ten. He turns to lower the heating unit under the boiling flask. It is an abrupt turn, too precipitous, and his cuff catches the end of a stand. There is a crack, the sound of splintering glass, followed by a moment of uncertain panic as Madoc faces about to see the damage. A sweet aloe odor catches him full in the face, and he collapses to the floor with the realization of what it is.

He falls on his back, and the row of fluorescent lights retreats further and further. Madoc senses memories rolling in his mind—the few weeks of training with Elisabeth. The room, his workbench, the air above him, bent waves from a Bunsen burner—all compress themselves in his field of vision. He tries to recall everything Elisabeth has told him.

He pulls himself to his feet. It will be a minute, maybe longer, before the time lag hits him. It all depends on how much of the drug caught him. He cups his hands over his mouth and staggers from the lab. Behind him, he hears the distant crash of glassware.

The corridor he stumbles down, he sees in a broken symmetry. His legs are beginning to feel rubbery, and he knows he won't make it to Heath's room.

Time becomes a sequence of layers, so that each step seems to propel him durationally and not spatially. If he stops moving, he has the terrible feeling that all time will stop.

Do I know enough to survive?

He falls to his knees with a groan and slides along the wall of the corridor. His arm, which is falling before him, suspends itself in the air. He watches it, aware that at the same instant a tight fist has clenched itself in his chest.

I can't breathe!

There is a stark pain that shoots along his left shoulder and down his back. He feels the blood in his veins slowing.

No!

The tightening increases.

No! No!

The cramp and the pain ease and then subside.

Silence.

His mind is now a bin without a bottom, filling with visual sensations. His suspended arm appears to be a magnificent work of art, positioned just for his observation. The white sleeve, like a closed Chinese fan, appears very delicate. But he knows it is a mountain that not even faith can move.

It is a long time later when the arm collapses in his lap. He moves his head, but everything is wrong. The colors are not right. These walls were white once. Now they're anything but that.

He struggles to his feet and falls again. He crawls along the corridor several feet and then attempts to rise. With much difficulty he gets his leg under him, and he forces himself to his feet. He staggers for a moment, and then he vomits, collapsing again. He retches for several minutes, holding the pain in his sides with both white-knuckled hands. When the spasms have stopped, he braces himself against the wall and stands. Lacking all coordination, he limps down the hall, holding his eyes to mere slits to reduce the nauseous shifting of his vision.

He reaches an elevator and takes it down to the floor he wants. Riding, he vomits again and collapses. After getting to his feet, he edges his way toward the marine lab.

Entering, he recognizes only the saltwater odor. The room is dense with shadows, and he is afraid to advance farther, remembering how Lenny was found yesterday, like a fetus dead in the womb.

There is a movement, he thinks. He looks for it again and sees it. He tries to call out, but he cannot vocalize.

The movement disappears. There is a dull thud, and then the heavy sigh of generators being turned on, and the electric lights flood the room.

Madoc staggers back and falls, stumbling over his feet. Shoes clamber toward him, and a figure blots out the light.

It is Heath.

"Corin! What's happened?"

They are words heard through a cotton blanket.

Heath opens Madoc's mouth and smells his face. The aloe odor is faint.

"Did you do the drug?"

Madoc rolls his eyes, gasps, "Yes."

"Okay," he says, picking him up by the armpits. "Let's get to my room."

They struggle together into the lab toward the exit on the other side. "It's a good thing I was coming to see you," Heath says. "How'd you survive the time lag?"

There is a metallic scream. A door is being kicked open. At the far end of the pool, four young men dressed in stained overalls and carrying nightsticks climb over each other into the room. Screaming war cries, they charge toward Heath and Madoc.

Heath pushes Madoc against the generator. "If you can move, get out of here," he says.

Heath runs to meet the assailants and then slumps forward. He spins to his left as he sees the foremost attacker raise his arm to bring his nightstick down on Heath's new position. He leaps up and catches his opponent's arm with both of his hands, pulling it back and down, simultaneously driving his knee into the man's groin. There is a crackle as the shoulder joint snaps.

Before the man crumbles, Heath lifts the club from him and blocks the attack of the next man. He buries his free open hand under the man's sternum and falls behind him, using his body as a temporary shield.

The two other men have drawn knives and are approaching slowly, trying to outflank him. He charges one of them, screaming wildly, and then, in midstep, turns his body about and hurls his nightstick with a yelp at the unapproached assailant. The club catches the man between the eyes and splits his skull.

The final attacker is upon Heath, his knife catching Heath's arm. They struggle together briefly and then tumble into the pool. In his element, Heath disarms his opponent by applying pressure to his wrist and then drags him to the bottom of the pool, where he strikes the man's windpipe and drowns him.

He surfaces slowly, his arm oozing blood. Leaning at the edge of the pool, he looks for Madoc, who is gone. He remains clinging to the side, breathing hard. Then, from behind a computer component, Dr. Ibu and a powerfully built man emerge. They approach Heath, and the large man offers his hand. He helps the boy out of the water.

"Thanks," Heath says, holding back a sneeze.

Ibu looks at the giant and nods. The man grabs Heath and bends him backward over his knee, forcing his forehead back with the palm of his hand until the neckbone snaps. Then he casts the rag-doll body into the pool.

Madoc stumbles back into the lab. Three reluctant security men are with him. He runs along the pool, but stops short when he sees Heath's body floating.

"We just arrived, officers," Ibu explains. "It appears that four thugs had broken in. Two of them are dead . . . and so is my subject. They murdered him."

* * *

From Heath's window Elisabeth watches the ebb slip from the rocks, the sunken rocks lifting streaming shoulders out of the slack. The slow west is sombering its torch. A ship's light shows faintly, far out, over the weight of the ocean, on the low clouds.

A footfall makes her turn slowly. It is Madoc.

"Hello," he says.

She returns her gaze to the sea.

"I've looked for you so I might say good-bye," he says.

"You're leaving?"

"Cumberland has reviewed my work and is giving me a grant to continue research."

"When do you leave?"

"Tomorrow. My material's being shipped after me."

She continues to look out of the window for a long time, and then faces Madoc.

"I shouldn't mourn him, should I?"

Madoc shakes his head. "He wouldn't approve."

He turns to leave.

"Corin?"

He looks over his shoulder.

She smiles.

He smiles back and is gone.

She looks out of the window again to the sea, where great waves awake and are drawn like smoking mountains bright from the west.

It is quite late when Ibu enters Madoc's lab. He is dressed as usual in his lengthy white lab coat and dark-blue tie.

Madoc, dressed entirely in white, is easily spotted in the dark lab, sitting on one of his lab tables, accompanied by rows of glassware.

"Come in, Michel."

Ibu walks up to Madoc and stands before him. "I hope you'll excuse my intrusion, Corin," he says.

"I wasn't doing anything, not even thinking."

"A remarkable feat."

"It comes with practice."

"You're leaving tomorrow?"

"Yes."

"You've gotten a grant to continue your work?"

"Yes."

"How fortunate. My own project has been reviewed here again

and considered too impractical. It's been shut down permanently."

"How unfortunate."

"Yes, you can joke. You've lost nothing."

"I squandered nothing."

"Do you imply that I have?"

"I am merely suggesting that you might have."

"Well, it so happens that you are very right, Corin. I have squandered all of my resources. All of them."

"What are you going to do now?"

"Do I detect a hint of apprehension?" Ibu smiles. "I'm jealous of you, Corin. But more importantly, more intensely, I am angry with you. In fact, it is you that I see as the cause of my misfortune." He slips his hand into his pocket, and Madoc tenses.

"Don't be afraid. I'm not going to kill you." He withdraws something white. "It's only a handkerchief." He unwraps it and moves to hold it to his face, but with a turn of his wrist he faces it toward Madoc and reveals a thin aerosol can. Ibu sprays a fine mist. The odor, sweet, like aloe, envelops Madoc's face. He throws his arms out wildly, kicking and falling backward. The sound of glassware shattering is very far away.

Iron hands on his collar jerk him into a standing position.

"How ironic, letting your own drug do you in." Ibu laughs loud and long.

Madoc is breathing hard through his mouth, his hands at his throat.

Ibu spins him about so that they are facing. Madoc feels that in the darkness of the room everything is dominated by degrees of smallness: Ibu appears to be at the far end of a long tunnel, like some small trinket of an African god.

"My God, Madoc!" Ibu mockingly shouts. "You've just accidentally inhaled a gas mixture of your own drug!" He pushes Madoc, so that he skips backward, falling against the bench. More glassware collapses in the distance.

"And now, scared for your life . . . Oh, you do get so scared for your life, don't you, Corin?" Ibu laughs again, gripping Madoc's collar and dragging him out of his lab. "Scared for your life, you run madly out of your lab. You run and run," Ibu screams, "you run and run until everything slows. EVERYTHING STOPS!"

Ibu heaves him down the corridor, and Madoc sprawls to the floor and slides.

Inside his head, the confusion rages for a moment. Only a moment. His chest is tightening uncontrollably, and a burning pain sears his whole back and left side.

No!

"Yes, moan, you bastard!"

No! No!

Ibu's laughter is uncontrollable, echoing in the corridor and in Madoc's ears until the physical universe comes to a halt.

He tries to focus on a mark on the floor, but his vision is blurring. His glasses are half off, and he cannot focus his eyes. His head feels as if it has been disconnected from his body, but the pain is gone. He has mastered his responses again.

The time lag ends with a burst of spaced-out, distant laughter.

Madoc feels quite calm, despite it, quite serene.

Ibu pulls Madoc to his feet. "So you survive the initial tests of your own creation. But you are still dazed, and you stagger blindly down the hall, groping."

Ibu pushes Madoc forward, holding him by his hair and arm.

The corridor seems to stream past him. But he can control his vision now. His glasses are intact, and he has some grip on his senses.

"You come to the elevator, and you wait for it, uncertain where you are headed, only running scared."

Footsteps, quick footsteps, crash down the hall. A young orderly rounds the bend.

"Hey! What's going on?" he calls.

Ibu releases Madoc. The orderly draws closer, and Ibu whips his aerosol can out, spraying the man in the face. The boy gags once and slams himself against the wall, a surprised look on his face.

"You fool, Madoc! In your mindless flight you kill an innocent man whose only intent was to help you."

The elevator arrives, and Ibu kicks Madoc in. When it stops, Ibu drags him out and down the corridor. The smell of the sea is strong.

"Driven mad by your drug, you walk aimlessly into the Marine Lab. Here you will unwittingly drown yourself."

You must not surrender yourself. For Madoc, suddenly, everything begins to clarify itself. He stands in the doorway to the lab. The pool is still, a soft blue light is reflecting off it. There is absolute silence in there. The smell of brine is cool and relaxing. The combined effect reminds him of a temple. *Can violence be permitted here?*

Ibu pounds him in the back of the neck, and Madoc lunges into the room, more from his own power than from the force of the blow.

In his mind, his years of defensive training flash almost visibly through his awareness. But he knows that it does not matter whether he understands it or not. He must feel it. It must be automatic. Action, not thought.

A hulking figure appears to his left, approaching him.

Madoc rises to his feet and crouches. The drug has enhanced all of his perceptive powers. Simultaneously, he can watch the giant and Ibu, study their movements, know their thoughts.

He begins sidling to the right, toward the pool.

"What do you think you're doing, Madoc?" Ibu calls, hilarity breaking his voice. "You're not seriously going to fight?" He erupts into peals of laughter.

Madoc stares through the shadows at the giant. The man's body looks like knotted whipcord and layers of solid muscle.

He feels no fear, only serenity—his mind and body one. One will.

He circles warily, opposite the huge man, his muscles poised and ready.

Madoc sees the motion from behind him. It is Ibu, and he delays responding for a fraction of an instant, waiting until he can skip to the side.

He maneuvers, and Ibu hops past him clumsily. Madoc shifts his weight and kicks out and up, catching Ibu on the side of his head. The black man falls down heavily.

Now Madoc circles the giant. With unexpected speed, the man pounces, catching Madoc's right arm. Madoc screams loudly and drives his fingers to the man's throat.

The giant howls and pulls away, the realization sweeping over him that this is no untrained fighter.

Madoc presses the fight now, circling but not attacking.

The giant leaps high, feinting so that Madoc draws back to the pool's edge.

Trapped!

The giant, crouched low, large hands ready, closes in. He sweeps out with his arms in a blurred movement. Madoc shifts his weight, using the drug to follow the giant's movements, and ducks below the arms. Then he springs up, screaming, driving his right foot forward and high. It catches the giant in the face, full force, and topples him. Madoc moves swiftly and delivers a death blow to his temple.

He looks up. Ibu is standing, blood glistening on his cheek. He is breathing hard, frightened. The dim light catches on a knife he is holding, and he charges.

Madoc crouches, accepts the charge. Over Ibu's shoulder, he sees approaching shadows. He catches the knife arm in one hand, drives his foot into Ibu's groin, and pushes him away.

Four security officers scramble behind Ibu, pistols withdrawn.

"Shoot him!" Ibu yells, his voice frantic.

Madoc remains crouched, hands at shoulder height, eyes intent. Death is acted, he thinks.

They level their guns, hesitant.

"He's mad! Shoot him! You know me! Shoot him!"

There is a barrage of fire. The impact lifts Madoc off his feet and kicks him into the pool.

When the echoes stop and the smoke has cleared, his body resurfaces, the blue light reflecting on it.

A. A. Attanasio writes:

"Interface" is the first science fiction I ever wrote. I began it in the seventh grade, in Mr. Nunez's algebra class. It stewed in my unconscious caldron five years before I found it in a bedraggled notebook and rewrote it. I never thought anything creative would come out of Nunez's class, but such is the synchronous symphony of being oneself. Since completing "Interface" I have been hemorrhaging ink, writing poetry and fiction. My work habits, however, have expansive phases. When I begin writing, something leads the days through me the way the wind herds light through the bones of the unburied. During the months that I don't write, I walk the flat of the blade, seeking the edge where the dark is sliced from the light. I am constantly stumbling over my tall. Aside from the tarot, the calender of shadows, which shows me its small eyes, I have no close relations. But like the magician who rolls over in his sleep and wakes the fool, the world sustains me on unknown paths, and I am not lonely. We have invented ourselves. Have you forgotten already?

BLOODED ON ARACHNE

by *Michael Bishop*

Ethan Dedicos stood at the turnstile in the sapphirine depot with the other disembarked passengers of the *Dawn Rite*. Outside, the wind blew and the world fell away. Among the dronings of people sounds, it was his turn.

"I've come to be blooded," he told the man at the stile. Because of the noise, he had to repeat himself, shouting.

"Go the H'Sej," the stile-tender said out of a skinned-looking face.

Ethan looked around: bodies, polarized glass, a series of plastic domes, red sandstone beyond, a pinprick sun. "I don't—"

"There, by the footslide. That one, boy. The hag-sage with the spider crown. Move on, Ethan Dedicos, you make us lag."

He went through. Bodies pressed behind him, angry of elbow, flashing-loud of teeth. Hands shoved at him, hands pushed him this way and that. By the footslide the H'Sej was staring at him, a man maybe old, with skin the color of burgundy wine and brown satchel clothes that swallowed him. The spider crown was made of blue metal, and the tips of its eight legs seemed to grow into the hag-sage's narrow skull.

"I'm Ethan Dedicos," the boy said. "I've come to be blooded."

"Who sends you, Ethan?"

"The Martial Arm. I'm to be a star-bearer, an officer of the Arm. Isn't that why you're here, H'Sej? Didn't you come to meet me?"

"I know you, Ethan Dedicos. But I have to know if you know what you want. Now you can come with me."

The hag-sage turned, ignoring the crowd in Scarlet Sky Depot, and maneuvered agilely onto the footslide. How old, the boy wondered how old the H'Sej assigned me? He followed the burgundy man.

"Can you tell me your name?" he shouted.

"Integrity Swain, Child of Learned Artifice," the maybe-old man said, grabbing Ethan's arm and pulling him alongside. The name was a genealogy, not solely a descriptive designation. Learned Artifice had been this hag-sage's father, and their people lived in the salt gardens on the margin of Arachne's desolate sea bottoms. That was where you went when you were blooded, and that was all you knew until the H'Sej made you aware of more. "Sej, only Sej, is what the outli people call me, boy."

Then they were out of Scarlet Sky Depot, on the precipice-stair that fell into the basin where Port Eggerton lay: white larvae nestled plastically against the red sandstone. Other people went quickly into air tunnels that led down to the administrative complex.

The wind blew. The pinprick sun hurled glitterings across the sky, and even here the noise of a world continuously eroding and reshaping itself made real talk impossible. Dizzied, Ethan put an arm over his eyes to block the blowing sand, the scathing light, the fear of falling.

"Sej!" he shouted. "The tubes! Can't we take the tubes down?"

"We aren't going into Port Eggerton, lamb's eyes."

"I must report to the Martial Arm!"

"You report afterward!"

And the maybe-old blooder of boys led him away from the drop-tube terminals, away from the precipice-stair, across an expanse of plateau. They fought the wind to a chimney of rocks beyond Scarlet Sky Depot, now a shimmering bubble-within-a-bubble-within-a-bubble at their backs, and plunged down the wide abrasive chimney into silence.

On a ledge they halted, and Ethan Dedicos could see nothing but the dark-red rocks surrounding them. Above, maybe the sky. Below, faceted cliffs without bottom. In the wide stone chimney he trembled with a calmness as eerie as drugsleep.

"What do we—?"

"We wait, Ethan Dedicos."

"Why do we wait here, Sej?"

"For transport and because you aren't to see a friend-face until the blooding's done. You aren't to think of Earth or probeship voyagings. We provide now, my people of the salt gardens."

"And the blooding—what must I do?"

"Survive, of course." The hag-sage chuckled. "We play old games on Arachne."

And the maybe-old blooder of boys squatted on the ledge so that his brown vestments billowed around him and his burgundy hands hung over his knees like the bodies of skinned rabbits. He stopped talking, and darkness began climbing up the faceted cliffs below. Ethan leaned on the cold rocks, studied Sej's spider crown, and waited.

And stiffened with his aloneness.

On the other side of the plateau, down in the red basin, there were people just like him. Not just wind-burned hag-sages; not just the promise of cranky spidherds, arrogant in their gardens of salt and sandstone.

Impatience burned in Ethan Dedicos like a secret fuse.

Then from deep in the chimney of rock a golden spheroid rose toward them, a ring of luminous orange coursing about its circumference. The coursing ring emitted a hum more musical than a siren's song. The entire canyon glowed with the spheroid's ascent.

"Sej!"

"The nucleoscaphe from Garden Home. Our transportation."

"Such a vehicle! I didn't think—"

"The spidherds of Garden Home aren't barbarians, unblooded one."

Humming, the nucleoscaphe hovered beside them. The brilliant-orange ring swept upward and became a halo over the spheroid rather than a belt at its middle. A door appeared, and a ramp reached out to them like a silver tongue. The H'Sej, ignoring the chasm that fell away beneath the ramp, entered the nucleoscaphe. Reluctantly Ethan Dedicos followed, his eyes fixed on the darkness inside the humming spheroid.

Then he was inside, and the howling ruggedness of Arachne seemed light-years away. Beside the maybe-old blooder of boys he found himself in a deep leather chair the color of Mediterranean grapes. The chair swiveled, but the curved walls of the nucleoscaphe bore nothing upon them but silken draperies. Directly overhead, there was a stylized insignia depicting a spider as drawn from the top.

When the nucleoscaphe's ramp retracted and its door sealed shut, man and boy could not see out. Alone, in a gargantuan atom.

Soon they began to move. Unearthly music droned in their ears.

"Sej, this is a wonderful thing, this vehicle. Couldn't you have had it come to Scarlet Sky Depot? Did you have to make me climb down a hundred rocks to hitch a ride to Garden Home?"

"The nucleoscaphe belongs to the spidherds, boy, not to your outli folk in Port Eggerton. A long-ago gift of Glaktik Komm and the Martial Arm. You don't like climbing, heh?"

Ethan said, "Will it take us to Garden Home?"

"Close, close. We'll have to walk a few last kilometers, down from the perimeter cliffs." The H'Sej laughed. "But only because I like to climb, to walk, to hike. And your feet, lamb's eyes, how will they fare?"

Ethan was silent.

In only a few minutes, it seemed, the nucleoscaphe had stopped. It hovered, hummed insanely and ran out its ramp for the maybe-old man and the boy to disembark upon. They went out into the night and the chill, onto a brutal ledge. The nucleoscaphe closed up behind them and dropped goldenly into the abyss, disappearing like a coin sinking through water. Overhead, the stars mocked.

"Come with me, Ethan Dedicos."

Along the ledges, down the uneven sandstone steps, the H'Sej and the boy struggled. At last they came upon a salt plain and left the escarpments behind. In the starlight, monstrously alone again, they walked across an empty whiteness. They walked all night. When dawn began reddening the yardangs that had at last begun to appear in the desert (grotesque, plastically shaped rocks suggesting the work of a demented sculptor), they finally sighted Garden Home.

"There," Sej said. "Punish your feet some more, darling Ethan."

In the morning's attenuated light Ethan Dedicos saw the salt towers surrounding the central butte of Garden Home: Garden Home, an assemblage of yellow syntheskin tents huddled in a cove beneath the encircling pillars of white. Forty or fifty such tents, all of them large. The encircling pillars, larger yet, pitted with arabesque holes by Arachne's winds. It was a dream city, but as cruel and as real as eroded rock.

"How can you live out here?" Ethan asked.

"Nowhere else is so dear. For three hundred years there have been spidherds in Garden Home, supported at first by Glaktik Komm but living here now like even our own arachnids. And each year the Martial Arm sends us its stringclinging neostarbs to be blooded. Such as you, lamb's eyes."

"Why was Glaktik Komm a patron, Sej? In the beginning?"

"Someone must care for the spiders, they said. Must keep them away from the new depot. In their saliva is a terrible virus that can affect almost any kind of living cell, a virus to which the arachnids themselves are evolutionarily immune. We must study the Stalking Widows, they said, we must have people who will watch them and destroy their poisons. The first scientists who watched them invented the symbodies you carry in your veins, Ethan Dedicos, to keep your blood lucid starwhen and starwhere. The spidherds of Garden Home are the children of the makers of the symbody, the children of the outli folk who killed disease, for always."

They were close enough to see people among the yellow tents.

"Why must you stay here now?" Ethan asked. "Why must anyone remain in this angry desert of salt?"

"To call the spiderlings home, boy, to sing them back to Garden Home when they have gone ballooning."

Ethan remembered something vague. "Isn't that but once a year?"

"Aye. But we love our leggy beasts. They are as thought-bright as you or any stringclinging manbud in the Martial Arm. We stay because we belong to them, because we talk the spidherd–Stalking-Widow talk."

"You talk to them? And understand their talk?"

"Talk to them, croon to them, pipe to our spiderlings the homing call of Garden Home. The Stalking Widows are a people, too, unblooded Dedicos."

Ethan said nothing. They strode into a crowd of burgundy people who moved among the plastic buildings. A few of these people hailed the H'Sej wordlessly by dancing their fingers like spider legs. The sun was now full up. Its strange light glittered on people, tents, and stones alike. Ethan felt lost, alone in the long shadows that rippled from the fanciful salt pillars: lovely, sensuous, weird.

They were in front of a tent. A piece of plastic facing unzipped, and a woman darker than the red wines of Jerez stepped from behind the yellow flap into their paths.

The boy saw that she was not a maybe-old woman, she was antiquity given flesh. Her hair was stringy magenta. Her albino eyes stared out of the crimson-brown stain of a face riveted with time webs. She wore brown sacks. A witch for really real, the boy thought. And the witch twisted her head upward in order to see him from her stoop.

"Allo, N'tee Swain," she said to the H'Sej. (A voice like the high notes played on Musikman Belzer's aeolectic flute.) "Is this the boy you bring us to put out for blooding?"

"Ethan Dedicos he is," Integrity Swain said. And then the blooder of boys added, "This is the Widows' Dreadwife, Ethan. Embrace her well."

The neophyte star-bearer embraced her. Surprisingly, she had no smell, even though her face flesh was against him close. Then she drew back. Albino eyes stooped to see him and crinkled in their mask.

"Come inside, unblooded one. Breakfast for you. Then to the top of Garden Home to see the Stalking Widows and their chirren."

They entered the large tent and ate sand locust from earthen bowls. Ethan noticed a vacuum well in the center of the tent—a sparkling chrome mechanism that could tap water from deep within any planet's crust. Odd to see it in the hands of this semiprimi people, so backwardly backward. The Widows' Dreadwife fetched him a bowl of water, and her fluty voice echoed in the big syntheskin canopy.

"It never rains on Garden Home, nor on the sea bottoms beyond. We spidherds'd die if Glaktik Komm took back our well."

"True it is," Sej said. "The Stalking Widows and the sand locust have their own ways to water, but the vacuum well is ours. Blood our boys and keep our well, they say."

"And you eat only the sand locust?"

"No, no," the Dreadwife said. "Dull eatings, if so. Also eaten are murdered husbands of the spider people, egg sacs, sea-bottom merkumoles, and our own dead when such dyings come." The Dreadwife laughed, a falsetto piping. "I am soon to be eaten, I think."

Unblooded Dedicos asked no more about the spidherds' diet.

They went out into the hot bright morning—Dreadwife, hag-sage, and boy. Through the paths among the yellow tents they ambled, to a natural stairway leading through salt glens to the roof of Garden Home. This wide, uneven roof overlooked the sea bottoms, which were hidden from the city in the cove by the enclosing pillars themselves.

Before they reached the high place, they stopped beside several valleys in the rock where spidherds tended their charges and sang to the Stalking Widows out of dutiful throats.

"Look upon them with your lamb's eyes, boy." Sej pointed. "Down there you'll see the people who go eight-legged and wraithly in our hearts."

And so he looked down into a bleached, grassless glen and saw a burgundy boy of his own age singing in the lovely patois of Garden Home to a horde of ghostly, stilt-standing mistresses. Fifty or sixty Stalking Widows—tall white ladies whose bodies were almost transparent—moved jauntily about in the glen, and the spider-boy moved among them. Ethan could not believe it. They were as tall as elephants.

The burgundy boy stooped now and again to stroke the colorless hairs on his ladies' bellies, sometimes even blowing voluptuously on the wind-sensitive trichobothria furring their legs. When he did this, his ladies reared up, waved their foremost limbs, and opened their jaws—but more from pleasurable excitation than from fear or anger. The boy's song, the boy's breath, worked on them almost sexually, but without the end result by which they divorce themselves forever from their spider husbands. The boy was not eaten.

"Can they hear his singing?" Ethan asked. "I didn't think some spiders could hear."

"On Arachne," the Dreadwife said, "they hear, they hear."

The spectacle hypnotized Ethan Dedicos. The wind in his own hair prompted pointless stirrings in his loins. Then the burgundy boy in the glen saw the three of them looking down and waved his loose fingers at them in the characteristic greeting of the spidherds.

"Threnody Hold," the Dreadwife said. "A masterful touchsinger."

They went on. They looked down into other valleys, saw other spidherds touchsinging, watched the stilt-legged giantesses dance. And Ethan Dedicos felt the planet's heat in him like unrequited desire.

They reached the roof of Garden Home and stood looking across the sea bottoms stretching endlessly away to the horizon. And beyond, Ethan thought. The wind blew blastingly here, but not as hard as it had on the plateau outside Scarlet Sky Depot. They did not have to shout to make themselves heard.

"We drop you in the bottoms on the morry," the Dreadwife said.

"What?" Ethan looked down at her sharp profile.

"That's where your blooding begins, as you know," Sej said. "But we begin tomorrow."

"What do I do out there?"

"Come back to us, sweetling," the Widows' Dreadwife piped. "Come back to us with blood on your hands—all bedighted in a grown-up's skin."

"Allo, Baby Tranchlu!" Sej suddenly shouted. He hailed a girl of seven or eight who had just appeared at the top of the path on the other side of the butte and who was walking across its wind-pitted surface toward them.

The girl had a wide Oriental face stained a tentative mauve. She drove before her a group of spiderlings so colorless they seemed to be made of glass. They were a third of the size of the prancing ladies they had seen in the salt glens, but still as tall as Baby Tranchlu herself. Mere babies, they moved on splinter-thin legs, as clumsy as new-born colts. Only the scopulae on the pads of their feet kept Arachne's winds from blowing them away.

Ethan stepped back as the little girl and her spiderlings approached. He wanted to fall into the planet's sky. And drown.

"Come here, Tranchlu. Say allo to this summer's neostarb, here to be blooded."

"Allo," Tranchlu said.

Her spiderlings, nine or ten in all, tottered about the four human beings and ruminantly waggled their mouth parts. Pedipalpi. A combination of hands and soft teeth, these mouth parts; a strange melding. Baby Tranchlu stared at Ethan.

The Dreadwife asked her, "Have you brought these chirren for the wind, small girl?"

"These be firsties," Tranchlu said. "More on the morry. Goose summer we have. They go fly."

"It's gossamer time," Sej translated. "The spiderlings disperse. These that Tranchlu has attempt the wind today, but tomorrow thousands will go ballooning. Many will die. Every year a thousand spidikins fly, and one boy is blooded."

"Go on," the Dreadwife said. "Put them about it, pert smirl."

Baby Tranchlu did a gangly little dance and sang to her babies in the lilting patois that Ethan couldn't understand. She turned, and pirouetted, and danced along the butte to a place where several salt spires thrust up into the sky. The spiderlings followed, stilt-legging in her wake and flashing glassily in the sun.

"Watch how it is," Sej told Ethan.

The spiderlings, as if on the pert smirl's commands, climbed the pitted rocks and fought both wind and gravity with sticky feet. Ethan lifted his head to watch. Clinging precariously to the spires as they moved, the spiderlings turned in slow circles and ejected strands of silk, which floated on the wind. Their underslung spinnerets paid out more and more glistening thread, more and more. And more and more.

The sky was a pale crimson suspended in a crystalline net, a color captured in webs.

"There they go, Tranchlu!" Sej shouted.

And the leggy babies, still clinging to their skyey umbilicals, lifted from the rocks. Upward they were dragged like parachutists jumping backward for the door of an invisible aircraft. Ethan felt as if he were watching a film being run the wrong way. Up, up, up, the spiderlings floated.

"But where are they going?" Ethan asked. "Out there are the sea bottoms—nothing else."

"Out there is all of Arachne," the maybe-old man said.

"What happens to them?"

"Some of them die, some of them come back. None of the people of the Stalking Widows live anywhere but here at Garden Home."

"Then why should these little ones go out at all? Why disperse, if only to die or come back?"

"Goose summer it is, lamb's eyes," the H'Sej said. "They go out."

And when Baby Tranchlu's babies were lost in the webby welkin, the hag-sage, the Dreadwife, and Ethan Dedicos descended the paths of the salt-garden butte to the yellow tents in the cove.

The winds died, the afternoon trekked by, and night came out like a dark maiden wearing candles. There was food, and talk. Then Ethan laid himself down among the bodies of murmuring spidherds, closed his eyes, and slept his first sleep on Arachne. While he slept, the maybe-old man touched his face and whispered, "I love the boys I blood. Remember that, lamb's eyes." Ethan heard an orange humming. Groggy, he rolled over.

And woke up on the sea bottoms.

He got to his feet. The sun was already up. He turned around. In every direction, whiteness whiteness whiteness whiteness.

"Sej!"

There was not even an echo. Only a dead word falling from his mouth, and a hint of wind. The desert air smothered the word, and he wondered if he had shouted anything at all. The sun glowered.

"SEJ!"

Again and again he turned around. It was impossible to be this alone. How could they have done this to him? With the nucleoscaphe only. He remembered its humming. *Be sure, be sure.* Kneeling, he looked at the floor of the sea bottom and saw no tracks, no footprints, no telltale striations on its hard white surface. He stood up. He turned around again. There were no landmarks anywhere. Where was his hag-sage?

"SEJ, YOU BURGUNDY BASTARD!"

This was his blooding. Drugsleep they had hyped him with in Garden Home and put him out to cope. The Widows' Dreadwife had told him how it would be. Sej had said, "Survive. We play old games on Arachne."

Ethan Dedicos was a neostarb of the Martial Arm, and neostarbs were blooded. So be it. He would play. He would think, and grapple, and run. Very well. What had they given him to play with? What survival pieces had he at hand?

Ethan Dedicos looked at himself and enumerated:

—The silver-blue, seemingly seamless uniform in which he had come to Arachne: light, indestructible, proof against weathers.

—A curved knife: heavy, elaborate of haft, hurtful.

—Two narrow cylinders of water fitted like cartridges into the belt on which he had found the knife: a maybe-supply for two days.

—Nothing else but his wits.

"Sej!" he shouted. "Sej, how are you blooder of boys when you leave your charge to blood himself?"

Irony of name-making. Cruelty of trust. Ethan Dedicos, doubting his neostarb's soul, turned around and around on the salt sea bottom and cursed the probeship fathers, every one. In his head his blood beat loud. And Arachne ached around him like a whitened world wound.

Knowing no directions, Ethan struck out toward the midmorning sun. He walked and walked. The horizons remained ever distant, ever smooth, annoyingly undisturbed. He looked behind him to see his own footprints, and saw none. He walked some more.

In the midday heat he uncapped a cylinder and drank his first drink: one, two, three drops on the tongue. And walked toward the place where the sun no longer was. And took his second drink: four, five, six drops moistening a cobwebbed mouth.

Then knelt in the middle of nowhere and shut his mind off, *click*. His gut, rumbling, would not so obligingly click off.

Thoughtless, he squatted.

His eyes saw a little hole on the sea bottom, a crumbly place in the whiteness. Ethan Dedicos told his mind to come on. *Click*, it did. Then he dug at the hole and pulled away salt shards and stabbed down with his knife. Scrabbling with his hands, he caught a stunned merkumole and pulled it free of its burrow: an ugly beastie with a hair-horn nose and spatulate feet. In the hot sun Ethan slew it and ate it, sucking the sinewy flesh as if it were candy, crunching the mush-marrowed bones. He drank off his first cylinder of water. The skin and hair horn of the merkumole he thrust back into the caved-in hole contemptuously.

Then shut down his mind, *click*. And walked on the feet of his

own shadow, offmindedly trying to step on the shadow's elusive gray
head—a bobbing, shadowboxing shadow's head.

His mind would not stay off. What he saw was too strange to look
at out of dreamily dead eyes. He halted and gawked at the horizon,
the horizon before him. Pale light pinked its curving edge, but higher
up, the sky was streaming with movement.

It was raining there.

"No," Ethan said aloud. "It doesn't rain on the sea bottoms."

But what he saw *resembled* rain—even though the only clouds in
sight were three or four miles up, and as feathery as goose down.
Didn't the distant sky glitter with columns of down-pouring moisture?
Didn't the density and height of those columns verify a desert squall?
An advancing shower?

"It's not supposed to rain out here!" He shook his fist at the translucent columns for trying to deceive him. He wanted a rain, but
dared not hope. Looking at the lofty cirrus he thought: As feathery
as goose down.

Analogy into equation:

Goose down: goose summer: gossamer.

And suddenly he knew that he was looking at neither a mirage nor
an on-sweeping squall. "Spiderlings coming to see me!" he shouted.
"Tranchlu's ballooning babies and all their thousand cousins!"

The wind in his mouth, he sprinted toward the arachnid aviators
on their glistening silken tethers—a shower of blowing cobwebs. If
they were coming toward him, then Garden Home must lie behind
their filamentous squall line. All he need do was walk in that direction and he would survive his blooding. His time in the wilderness
would be successfully won through. Thinking that, Ethan Dedicos let
out a joyous yelp. He was sixteen.

But not stupid. He halted again and reconsidered. He had only one
remaining cylinder of water. What were his chances of stumbling on
the burrow of another merkumole? The spidherds of Garden Home
had said farewell to their tottering glass babies early that morning,
had watched them fly off, most likely, right after sunrise. How far
might the spiderlings have ballooned in twelve hours' time? Maybe,
Ethan decided, as much as two hundred kilometers, conservative estimate.

"Sej, you burgundy bastard," he hissed. "Glaktik Komm, child
murderers, and sadists. Venerable starbs of the Arm, go to Vile Sty."

He hoped these maledictions covered everyone. He would not be able to walk two hundred kilometers, or more, before his water ran out and he fell over from the heat. Doornail Dedicos.

Standing there with the sun at his back and before him curtains of proteid thread catching the sun's last light, he peeled a strip of dead flesh from his nose, crisped it between his fingers, and thought. Glaktik Komm, the Martial Arm, and Integrity Swain were indeed child murderers; they murdered the child so that a man might move in and reanimate the vacated corpse. Absolutely. There had to be a way out of the sea bottoms. The Martial Arm did have probeship officers, after all, and every one of them had been blooded.

About a kilometer away Ethan caught sight of a single drifting spiderling. Sunlight ricocheted off its body and twinkled from the five or six incredibly lengthy threads streaming from its spinnerets. Cephalothorax down, the spider floated toward him. In less than five minutes, as best as Ethan could judge, it would sweep right by him. Then the others, the hundreds of others who were still together, would come ballooning past, too.

"You're my way out," Ethan said. "I'll board you."

But the first balloonist drifted by overhead, out of reach.

Ethan Dedicos waited. In another ten minutes six more of the advance guard had floated by, all of them either too high or too far to his left or right to permit a hijacking. He left off waiting and once again sprinted forward.

On Arachne the afternoon was deepening inexorably into twilight. The air seemed to be laden with melancholy music played upon countless strings.

Ethan, still running, was surrounded by showers of gauze. At last he caught the forelegs of one of the airborne spiderlings and attempted to hoist himself over its outraged eyes into the saddle between its abdomen and cephalothorax. For a moment his feet were off the ground, pedaling air. Then several of the spider's leg joints broke off in his hands, and he crashed back down on the sea bottom, still holding severed leg pieces. He got up and cast them aside. Rocking back and forth, the maimed spiderling floated on.

Half panicked, Ethan turned in rapid circles in the eye of the silk storm. His hands felt sticky. He stopped turning and looked at them. A viscous goo—the colorless blood of the spider people—adhered to his palms.

As he watched, this goo began taking on a faint pinkish cast; in another moment it had turned the brilliant burgundy that was the hallmark of the Garden Home spidherds. Contact with air. A chemi-

cal reaction. Ethan realized suddenly that he had been blooded.
Symbolically blooded. Now all he had to do was survive the very real
ordeal of getting back to Garden Home—the part of the blooding that
counted.

He wiped his hands on his uniform. "I'll board one of you!" he
shouted. "I'll outlive all of you!" He was sixteen.

But he was crying. He wept for himself and the spider whose legs
he had pulled away. Sej had as much as told Ethan that the Stalking
Widows were intelligent creatures, sentient in the manner of man—or
in a manner totally their own, at least. And he, Ethan Dedicos, had
cruelly hurt one of their people.

It was not to weep about. He had to try again. Most of the
ballooning arachnids were too high to reach, much too high to reach,
and the sun had already set; soon they would be flown into starlit
darkness. He pulled his belt tight and ran forward, his eyes half
misted shut and the immense desertscape glinting with buoyant silk.

Ethan leaped. He caught a spiderling about its thin middle and
desperately hung on.

For a moment he feared that the strands supporting it would crum-
ble beneath his additional weight and come cascading down around
both of them. He lifted his knees beneath him. The floating spider
dipped, then dipped again. Ethan's toes dragged the hard sea bottom,
slowing their progress. He lifted his knees again and curled his toes
away from the earth. Come on, he thought, come on.

They were up, the spiderling and he—up in the pearly evening sky
among hundreds of other airborne travelers, an assault force with
no one to make war against. Ethan shut his eyes completely and
stretched his legs out. They hung free now, just as he hung free. And
the wind washed around his dangling body as if he had been submerged in a beautiful, giddy-making tonic.

Finally Ethan opened his eyes and found himself in a jungle of
writhing legs. His head was pressed against the spider's belly. He
pulled himself up, squeezing his way between two of the creature's
hind legs to its chitinous back. He straddled the spiderling, facing
rearward, and grasped two of the threads that emerged from its spinnerets. He leaned forward and hung on. After a while his unwilling
mount ceased to struggle.

Over one shoulder, Ethan could see the white sea bottoms receding
beneath them. The planet's horizons broadened, and broadened, and
broadened even more. But only the sea bottoms filled this broadening
expanse. Where were they flying off to?

Ethan locked his legs together, tested his grip on the silken cords, and was soon rocked to sleep—deep adolescent sleep, womb-warm slumber. He dreamed that he was piloting the *Dawn Rite* through the surreal glooms of id-space, lost in a comforting nightmare of power.

He woke once, remembering where he was almost immediately. Since it was too dark to see the ground, he closed his dreaming eyes again. The air seemed refreshingly cool, not at all cold. He let the wind sail him back to sleep.

When Ethan Dedicos next woke up, he did so because his spiderling was twisting about in a determined way, as if hoping to dislodge him. He hung on with locked legs and aching hands. It was light. Sort of. He could see neither ground nor sky. The two of them were drifting in a luminous fog, insulated from the outside world. Tatters of insubstantial silver-gray floated past Ethan's face, but the spider's persistent twisting kept him from enjoying the scenery. A cloud bank they were in—a fog of turbulent, wispy batting. Where were the other balloonists?

"Stop it!" Ethan shouted. "Damn you, you . . ." He promptly christened the spiderling Bucephalus. "Damn you, Bucephalus!" His voice was muffled by the fog, smothered in moisture.

Bucephalus continued to writhe and sway. The boy wondered how far he would fall if the creature did dislodge him. Several times he felt himself slipping, but gathered his strength and clung like a cat on a bedspread. Shortly he was hanging head-down, while Bucephalus faced skyward and used its forelegs to hoist itself up the silken threads creasing its belly and disappearing into the moving clouds high above.

"What are you doing?" Ethan shouted. "You can't climb up your own balloon wires, you leggy spidikin!"

Then the beast ceased climbing; it left off torquing about. Their frail airship achieved a kind of rocky equilibrium. Looking over his shoulder, upward, Ethan saw Bucephalus joggle several drops of condensed moisture down the flowing silk into its pedipalpi: a drink in flight. Better than Ethan himself could manage.

They floated on for a time, through the silver-gray fog, and then the spider abruptly released its grip on its balloon wires and dropped until joltingly caught up at its own spinnerets. Ethan screamed but held on. When the beast at last stopped bucking, the boy was head-up again.

"You damn near did me that time, Bucie. You damn near did."

They rose through the mist, at last breaking through into painful sunshine. Beneath them their cloud bank undulated like a wide living fleece; above them the sky was the thin Arachnean scarlet that Ethan had almost forgotten. At unhailable distances Ethan saw several other ballooning spiders. He counted nearly forty, whereas before there had been hundreds. The dispersal, he supposed, was progressing as a dispersal ought.

"But to no point," Ethan said aloud. "You either die or return to Garden Home. I hope you're a returnee, Bucephalus. I don't like cloud-walking, it's not first on my list of career priorities."

Through a break in the cloud bank the boy saw that they were over water, water of multicolored blue. The waves sparkled, but it was impossible to judge how high he and his spiderling were. When the clouds at last thinned to mere ghostly wisps, nothing but ocean lay beneath them.

For two or three hours they sailed casually over water. Twice Ethan Dedicos looked on in amazement as companion balloonists reeled in a bit of thread and slowly tailspun into the sea, suiciding. After collapsing upon them, the downed flyers' webs bobbed in random patterns on the bright surface. It was not until these odd self-drownings that Ethan realized his own spiderling might have some control over where they were going.

"Say, Bucie Belle, are you my pilot?"

Ethan looked up at the wind-weaving threads bearing them aloft and tried to discover where the threads ended. He could not. The sun made him squint. Was Bucephalus manufacturing more proteid secretion and silently paying it out? Was it reeling some in, his pilot? Had this been going on all along?

"I wish I knew your talk, Bucie. What kind of blooder of boys fails to teach his neostarb the spidikin lingo?"

Sej, he thought, Sej, you treacherous spidherd.

Far away he saw red cliffs rimming the sea. Their airship drifted in that direction. Eighteen or twenty balloonists still accompanied them, that Ethan could actually see and count. The remainder were gone now, having either plunged into the water or shrunk to invisibility with distance.

Ethan was hungry. Maybe Bucephalus could survive on a drop or two of water every morning, but Ethan wanted food. The taste of yesterday's merkumole was still acrid in his mouth; nevertheless, his stomach made noises as if he had not eaten for a week. But for the moment the boy satisfied himself with a careful sip from the cylinder that Sej and the Dreadwife had provided him.

He looked down and saw earth instead of water, intricate topography instead of the sea's smoothness. Infertile and brownish-red, all of it. Fit country only for predatory arachnids. Why had Glaktik Komm come here? Was it solely to blood probeship captains for the Martial Arm?

No, not solely.

Once, many many years ago, scientists had ogled through microscopes the virulent, shape-changing virus in the saliva of the Stalking Widows. They had done so in order to devise a plastic, semiliving symbody, an adaptable counter to almost any antigen that might enter the bloodstream. Ethan carried these artificial counters in his own blood, while the spidherds of Garden Home had long since developed natural immunity to the arachnid virus.

"How about that, Bucie? You got a mouth full of hungry germs?"

Later Arachne had become an administrative and commercial center, a seedy port. A number of those who came to Arachne were touri-tramps, rugged crazies who sometimes ventured out to Garden Home or even into the dead sea bottoms.

"Not much to see in them, though," Ethan Dedicos told his pilot. "Except the silk storms—and they happen only once a year. Right?"

Bucephalus, the spiderling, kept its own counsel.

They passed over cliff after cliff of creviced sandstone. The entire planet now seemed to be made of lusterless copper. First, white desert. Then, ocean. Now, sandstone.

Shortly it was night again. As myriad stars commenced to burn, the earth blanked out.

Weakened by a night and day aloft, Ethan Dedicos hung on to Bucephalus lethargically. Now another night lay ahead. He uncapped his second cylinder and emptied it in a single breathless gulp. Then the cylinder fell from his fingers and tumbled into darkness. He had eaten nothing all day. His stomach lurched painfully with each new gust of wind. His lips were chapped, his cheeks and forehead blast-burned. And if he went to sleep again, how could he be sure that Bucie would not suicide during the night, plummeting them both to destruction?

He could not. That was the answer: he could not. Knowing the answer too well, he slumped across the spiderling's upturned rear, gripped the threads emerging from its spinnerets, and went to sleep.

When he awoke, only ten other arachnid aviators remained in sight, all a good ways in front of them and conspicuously higher. In the dawn glow over the land Ethan saw a vista depressingly similar to yesterday's endless sandstone. Except that now there were canyons in the rock—monstrous canyons, labyrinthine and cruel. The canyons were new.

Ethan remembered climbing with the H'Sej from Scarlet Sky Depot into a crevice like the mighty ones below. He remembered the nucleoscaphe. Might not these canyons be tributaries to the one he and Sej had traveled in? Did Port Eggerton lie near? Did Garden Home lie near? Probably not, Ethan thought. We have crossed an ocean.

His speculations ceased when Bucephalus began writhing its legs and threatening to topple him into skyey space. Time for a morning drink. Midnight moisture on the balloon wires. Symbolically blooded Dedicos prepared for the spider's topsy-turvy toast to dawn. Inebriate of dew, he silently cursed. Drunken whoreson!

And he was suddenly upside down, admiring red rock.

Then, moments later, he was traumatically upright again, wind whirling blue in his mouth, sun stitching his eyes into a squint.

That day was a dull one. Several times he thought about trying to control the direction of their travel himself—either by cutting a silk strand free or attempting to pull more thread from one or two of the spinnerets. But he was afraid to experiment. And if he could control their climb and descent, where would he take them? Enigmatic Arachne gave few topographical clues, all of them dreary-dull. Dull. As this marvelous floating was finally dull.

Ethan's hunger grew. His weakness, he realized, would soon be an obstacle to his survival. Faint, fatigued, feverish, he would be bucked into free-falling anonymous death by bronco Bucephalus' next dipsomaniacal quest for water. And he would die. It was as simple as that. He—Ethan Dedicos, neostarb of the elitist Martial Arm—would die, his body burst upon abrasive rock or abusive sea, his grave a canyon or a watery grotto. Just another abortive blooding.

Die.

And so, as the afternoon wore on, Ethan made up his mind to kill the spiderling. He didn't want to. He had to. To be successfully blooded, one had to survive. That meant that Bucephalus would have to die.

"I'm sorry," Ethan Dedicos said, meaning it. "I'm sorry to have to do this."

He removed the knife from his belt, locked his legs farther down the creature's cephalothorax than usual, and reached his arms around the abdomen in order to find the soft membrane where its legs joined its body. Only here could his knife penetrate the horny skeleton. Bucephalus, exasperated, languorously waved its legs, but Ethan found the spot anyway.

And stabbed. And jerked the blade sideways. And stabbed again.

The spiderling spasmed. Its body hiccuped violently. Lame, its legs thrashed. Overhead, silken streamers buckled in the wind, buckled and fluttered. But, forearmed and resolute, the boy survived these gimpy, aerial throes. He hung on for drear death—the spiderling's, not his own.

Its spasming done, they floated on almost as before.

When Ethan next looked at his hands, they were covered with clear, viscous fluid. He watched as the discharge turned bright burgundy. This new stain overlapped the old—from his palms and knuckles, all the way up his wrists. He felt a murderer, a Jacobean villain, a deranged hero. Oh, blood, blood, blood, he thought.

And put the thought out of his mind, *click*. So that he could ensure his own survival. Pilotless now, he had to hurry. An hour or so ought to suffice, time in which to eat and plan a second hijacking. If he remained too long aboard Bucephalus' dead husk, the winds might eventually send him flailing into nowhere. Only living spiders made it back to Garden Home. He needed a pilot.

Ethan Dedicos, hanging on with one hand, used his knife to crack open the chitinous back of the spiderling. Imagine it's lobster, he told himself. Same phylum, after all. Arthropoda. This knowledge proved uncheering.

Deliberately, Ethan ate of the clear tubular heart, squeezing it section by section through the hole he had punched in Bucephalus' back. He ate until he could eat no more. The taste was vile. His uniform was blotched with wine-colored stains on his chest, and on his thighs, where he had wiped his hands. Again and again he willed himself not to vomit. When he could force no more down, he pulled out still more of the heart and cut loose a large section to hang from his belt. For tomorrow, he told himself. Imagine it's lobster.

By this time, the spiderling's translucent body, open to the air, was shot through with marblings of deepest ruby. To lighten the load that the balloon threads had to bear, Ethan methodically cut away each one of the corpse's legs. He dragged out reddening entrails and heaved them into the wind. They dwindled slimily in the late-afternoon sunlight, spiraling downward in dreamy slow motion.

And as he had hoped, his pilotless airship began to rise.

Four balloonists floated above him now. No more. He had not

seen any of the other six spiders plunge into the knife-edged canyons that day; they had simply sailed off. These four remaining ones were his last hope. He had to board one of them before the twilight deepened into night, before night scattered his last hope beyond the prospect of capture. He had to maneuver his fragile craft by body shifts and tuggings of line—expertly, as if he had flown on streaming silk his entire life.

Clumsily, Ethan Dedicos managed. Seldom looking down, he leaned and yanked his way alongside the slowest of the four spiderlings—the slowest and the heaviest. Even so, it bobbed several meters out of reach, to his left and above him. A chasm of air intervened, a frightening chasm of air.

Ethan hacked away portions of Bucephalus' body until he had almost nothing to cling to. Using the toe of one foot against the heel of the other, he pulled his boots free and kicked them into the dropping sun, where they seemed to catch fire and disintegrate. Very little time remained. It was like his last evening on the sea bottoms all over again—but more urgent, more insanely desperate.

Ethan leaned and yanked on the tethers, shifted his weight, and muttered incoherently into the wind. He looked up and saw that Bucephalus' threads were weaving themselves among those of the spider that he hoped to board. Indifferently, the beast watched him approach. He could almost touch its dangling forelegs, almost look into its mouth. But he wasn't rising anymore. An unbridgeable gap existed, a chasm.

Not knowing what else to do, Ethan unfastened the belt the spidherds had given him and let it drop. Food supply and all: Bucephalus' tubular heart.

Like a buccaneer, he held his knife between clenched teeth. Come on, he thought. Come on. Maybe coincidentally, maybe because of his action, his craft bobbed higher. Then higher again.

And instantly Ethan Dedicos jumped.

He was conscious of his knife slicing his mouth, spinning silverly away. He was conscious of rocking impact and blurred, out-of-kilter horizons. Then he felt his newly filled stomach plummeting canyonward, and his body irresistibly following.

A tailspin. Silk tearing on the sky. This is it, Ethan said to himself. This is it.

At which point he was yanked up by the gossamer canopy pouting from the spiderling's tail, and the world snapped back into place with a *pop*. Miraculously, he was still astride his hijacked arachnid, but now he could see their elongated twilight shadow on a wall of rock below. How far they had fallen! His entire body trembled, his blotched, clinging hands most of all.

Far, far above them the mutilated corpse of Bucephalus rode the gusts ever upward. Ethan felt empty, alone.

"I'm not going to name you," he told his new pilot. "I promise you that: I won't give you a name."

By the time it was completely dark, his heart had stopped its riotous beating, and they had gained a bit of altitude again. Both relieved and exhausted, Ethan pressed his body against his host's, tightened his grip on the silks, and, for the third time in as many nights, went to sleep as if in a treetop cradle. He slept the big drugsleep, he bobbed on the lullaby winds. And dreamed of solid ground grown over with lovely grass.

In the middle of the cool night he opened his eyes and thought he heard the distant sloshing of waves. He did not look down. Soon he was asleep again, dreaming of clip-on epaulets and probeship glory. A venerable starber was he in his sleep rhythms.

The following morning he survived the spiderling's flipover for water, and, head-down, got a good view of the sea. The same sea as before, or a new one? Multicolored and sparkly, it looked just like the other, but there was no way for Ethan to be sure. White froth and indigo; cream combers and lilac—but not a seacoast or sailing vessel in sight.

Not even in the air was there a sailing vessel. Rightside-up again, he quickly determined that they were alone. The last three balloonists had skyed away during the night, or maybe crumpled down in the dark, to drown. Not again would he be able to switch courses in mid-scream (a thought not hateful, so breathstopping had his jump been). Nor could he kill off his current mount for food—but for desperation, but for sheer desperation.

"You're my ticket, trick, and trump," the boy whispered. "You're it, beastie."

Then Ethan himself shook water down the silks, and drank. He was not desperate. Not yet. And all that day they floated where the wind and the spiderling willed—over bright ocean. Until the late afternoon brought land into view once more, a whiteness punctuated with bizarre yardangs; then the red rocks again. A maybe-new continent. He couldn't tell for certain.

Then, at eventide, he suddenly saw Port Eggerton!

And the sapphirine bubble-within-a-bubble-within-a-bubble of Scarlet Sky Depot, high on a cliff above the nestling city!

"We've circled around!" Ethan shouted. "You've brought us back!"

He thought about trying to wrench the airship to earth, about crash-landing on the plateau by the depot. Maybe these bubbles and domes signaled his last chance to look upon the work of man. It would be dark soon, his fourth night aloft. But the Widows' Dreadwife had said, "Come back to us sweetling. Come back to us with blood on your hands." He had to trust in his spidikin pilot, he had to go cruising craftily back to Garden Home. Otherwise the blooding would be blotted, an all-for-naught mistake. What, what should he do?

With poignant regret Ethan Dedicos watched Port Eggerton slip away beneath them. An opportunity lost. After which, remorseless night fell.

But this night Ethan could not sleep. He made no attempt to sleep. To sleep would be madness. This night, he felt sure, they would balloon their way to the salt escarpments above the spidherds' cove of yellow tents. His journey would be over, his blooding complete. The petty demands of the body—hunger, thirst, weariness—could not eclipse the importance of such a fulfillment.

Adrenaline flowed in the boy, a tiny glandwind raging where Arachne's winds could never roar.

The passing hours, the turning stars, mocked his excitement. He and the spiderling drifted in darkness. Nothing happened. Nothing at all. Had the winds changed again? Would morning again find them over water?

"Weave a spell for us, hag-sage. Burnish your spider crown, Sej, and lift lovely Garden Home out of the desert. Put it anywhere you like, but put it close. Put it goddamn close."

To no avail, this plea. They dipped, and rose, and stuttered in nearly utter blackness, only the stars gleaming. Ethan began to despair. He thought of another day aloft, of his wind-scorched lips and his knotted sinews and the idea of dying at sixteen.

Why not simply slide backward off the arachnid's stupid snout and let whatever lay beneath snuff out his life? In that thought was some sweetness, a temptation like young girls' bodies. It seduced him, almost.

A thin singing saved him, a fluty piping on the wind.

Through the tall darkness, Ethan Dedicos heard this music, and the child of the Stalking Widows heard it too. Instantly they dropped several meters. Ethan's stomach told them that they had dropped. He gripped the silks and pulled himself up a little, so that in a moment he saw far in front of them two tiny flames, like matches burning, and the slowly emerging silhouette of a jagged landform.

It was the roof of Garden Home!

Or was it a dream, a cruel deception?

"No, no." Ethan said. "It's the spidherds' fortress, the Stalking Widows' roost. Home in on that singing, Widows' babe. Home in on it, I tell you!"

They homed. The silver singing, as unearthly as everything else he had encountered on Arachne, led them in.

As they approached the great butte of the Stalking Widows, he could see that the match flames were torches. The dark, milling forms of many people crowded the opening between two salt spires, an opening toward which his pilot was apparently navigating.

And around them, around them in the dark, he somehow knew there were other balloonists sailing in. A very few at a time. Homing in on the eerie song that they had all heard from afar, picking it up long before he himself had heard it. The survivors of goose-summer madness, riding their gossamer tides back home.

And he, Ethan Dedicos, among them. Decorously blooded.

They swept toward the gap in the rock. Torchlight illuminated the strange upturned faces of a hundred burgundy spidherds. He heard cheering, cheering that overrode the ghostly song of the Widows' Dreadwife, for it was she who had sung them in. As they gusted in, he thought he saw her albino eyes flashing out of a fire-tattered face. She was apart from the others, standing on a high ledge. Singing.

The spiderling and boy swept through the gap. Hands caught at him, friendly hands—the hands of spidherds. The cheering swelled until he thought it would rupture the very darkness and spill daylight over all Arachne. Hands clutched at him. Hands held him upright. The press of celebrating bodies bore him staggering, grinning, away from his glassy beast, along a narrow path. Faces among the hands, Baby Tranchlu's and Threnody Hold's. Torches bobbingly accompanied them.

Solid ground, Ethan thought. I'm on solid ground.

And then their procession of faces and hands abruptly halted. And numbly turning up his eyes, Ethan saw a burgundy-dark, maybe-old man in the path in front of them. A hag-sage wearing loose brown sacks and a glinty-blue spider crown. The H'Sej, flickering brightly there.

"Oh, what a man you are now," Sej said. "You're stained and smeared and shredded, just like a spidherd. Just like a spidherd, lovely one."

For a moment Ethan Dedicos stared uncomprehendingly. Then grinned. Then felt a cold, violent ache in his heart. Then crumpled in the hands of the gentle rowdies who had led him to his blooder.

Just like a spidherd Ethan looked, just like a spidherd. Now the Martial Arm would let him drop probeships into id-space. Why did his gut hurt so? His heart, too?

Lurching forward on his knees against the many friendly hands, he heaved up undigested bits of something saddening. Spittle dripped from his lips and chin. Then he heaved up air, only air. Then he threw back his sweaty face and looked at the imperceptibly lightening sky, where winked a thousand scornful stars.

Just before he passed out, Ethan whispered the word "Bucephalus." No one heard him. No one knew his hurt.

Michael Bishop writes:

What to say about "Blooded on Arachne"? Not a great deal, really. I set myself the goal, before beginning, of writing a sort of Technicolor entertainment with no slowdowns and a suitably imageful and cadenced style. The title—a deliberately garish one, redolent, I hope, of one of SF's "Golden Ages" and the old pulps—preexisted the story and provided me with its impetus. Then I studied up on spiders a little bit and began. During the writing, when I reached an impasse of some kind, I simply resolved to hurtle it, and either introduced a new character or took steps to advance the purely physical action. The story, as it now stands, is no sort of landmark at all, either in the field or, more modestly, in my own development as a writer; but I think it succeeds in precisely those areas I wanted it to succeed in. The word from here, then, is simply this: Enjoy.

LEVITICUS: IN THE ARK

by Barry N. Malzberg

I

Conditions are difficult and services are delayed. Conditions have been difficult for some time, services have been delayed more often than being prompt, but never has it weighed upon Leviticus as it does now. Part of this has to do with his own situation: cramped in the ark, Torahs jammed into his left ear and right kneecap, heavy talmudic bindings wedged uncomfortably under his buttocks, he is past the moments of quiet meditation that for so long have sustained him. Now he is in great pain, his body is shrieking for release; he has a vivid image of himself bursting from the ark, the doors sliding open, his arms outstretched, his beard flapping in the strange breezes of the synagogue as he cries denunciation. *I can no longer bear this position.* There must be some Yiddish equivalent for this. Very well, he will cry it in Yiddish.

No, he will do nothing of the sort. He will remain within the ark, six by four, jammed amidst the holy writings. At times he is sure that he has spent several weeks within, at others, all sense of time eludes him; perhaps it has been only a matter of hours . . . well, make it a few days since he has been in here. It does not matter. A minute is as a century in the Eye of God, he remembers—or did it go the other way?—and vague murmurs that he can hear through the not fully soundproofed walls of his chamber inform him that the service is about to begin. In due course, just before the adoration begins, they will fling open the doors of the ark and he will be able to gaze upon them for a few moments, breathe the somewhat less dense air of the synagogue, endure past many moments of this sort because of his sudden, shuddering renewal of contact with the congregation, but, ah God! . . . it is difficult. Too much has been demanded of him; he is suffering deeply.

Leviticus turns within the limited confines of his position, tries to find a more comfortable point of accommodation. Soon the service will begin. After the ritual chants and prayers, after the sermon and the hymn, will come the adoration. At the adoration the opening of the ark. He will stretch. He will stand. He will stretch out a hand and greet them. He will cast light upon their eyes and upon the mountains: that they shall remember and do all his commandments and be holy unto him.

He wonders if his situation has made him megalomaniac.

II

Two weeks before, just at the point when Leviticus' point of commitment to the ark loomed before him, he had appeared in the rabbi's cubicle and made a plea for dispensation. "I am a sick man," he had said, "I do not think that I will be able to stand the confinement. Also, and I must be quite honest with you, rabbi, I doubt my religious faith and commitment. I am not sure that I can function as that embodiment of ritual which placement in the ark symbolizes." This was not quite true; at least, the issue of religious faith had not occurred to Leviticus in either way; he was not committed to the religion, not quite against it either, it did not matter enough . . . but he had gathered from particularly reliable reports going through the congregation that one of the best ways of getting out of the ark was to plead a lack of faith. Perhaps he had gotten it wrong. The rabbi looked at him for a long time, and finally, drawing his robes tightly around him, retreating to the wall, looked at Leviticus as if he were a repulsed object. "Then perhaps your stay in the ark will do you some good," he had said; "it will enable you to find time for meditation and prayer. Also, religious belief has nothing to do with the role of the tenant. Does the wine in the goblet conceive of the nature of the sacrament it represents? In the same way, the tenant is merely the symbol."

"I haven't been feeling well," Leviticus mumbled. "I've been having chest pains. I've been having seizures of doubt. Cramps in the lower back; I don't think that I can—"

"Yes you can," the rabbi said with a dreadful expression, *"and yes you will,"* and had sent Leviticus out into the cold and casting light of the settlement, beginning to come to terms with the realization that he could not, could not under any circumstances, escape the obligation thrust upon him. Perhaps he had been foolish to have thought that he could. Perhaps he should not have paid credence to the rumors. He returned to his cubicle in a foul temper, set the traps to *privacy* and sullenly put through the tape of the *Union Prayer Book, Revised Edition: For the High Holy Days.* If you really were going to have to do something like this, he guessed that a little bit of hard background wouldn't hurt. But it made no sense. The writings simply made no sense. He shut off the tapes and for a long time gave no further thought to any of this, until the morning, when, in absolute disbelief, he found the elders in his unit, implacable in their costume, come to take him to the ark. *Tallis* and *tefillim.*

III

In the ark, Leviticus ponders his condition while the services go on outside. He has taken to self-pity during his confinement; he has a tendency to snivel a little. It is really not fair for him, a disbelieving man but one who has never made his disbelief a point of contention, to be thrown into such a position, kept there for such an extended period of time. Ritual is important, and he for one is not to say that the enactment of certain rote practices does not lend reassurance, may indeed be a metaphor for some kind of reality which he cannot apprehend . . . but is it right that all of this should be at his expense? He has never entered into disputation with the elders on their standards of belief; why should they force theirs upon him?

A huge volume of the Talmud jabs his buttocks, its cover a painful little concentrated point of pain, and cursing, Leviticus bolts from it, rams his head against the beam forming half of the ceiling of the ark, bends, reaches, seizes the volume, and with all his force hurls it three feet into the flat wall opposite. He has hoped for a really satisfying concussion, some mark of his contempt that will be heard outside of the ark, will impress and disconcert the congregation, but there simply has not been room enough to generate impact; the volume falls softly, turgidly across a knee, and he slaps at it in fury, little puffs of dust coming from the cover, inflaming his sinuses. He curses again, wondering if this apostasy, committed within the very place in which, according to what he understands, the spirit of God dwells, will be sufficient to end his period of torture, release him from this one kind of bondage into at least another, but nothing whatsoever happens.

He could have expected that, he thinks. If the tenant of the ark is indeed symbol rather than substance, then it would not matter what he did here or what he thought; only his presence would matter. And fling volumes of the Talmud, scrape at the Torahs, snivel away as he will, he is nevertheless in residence. Nothing that he can do will make any difference at all; his presence here is the only testament that they will need.

Step by tormenting step Leviticus has been down this path of reasoning-after-apostasy a hundred times during his confinement. Fortunately for him, these are emotional outbursts which he forgets almost upon completion, so that he has no memory of them when he starts upon the next; and this sense of discovery—the renewal of his rage, so to speak, every time afresh—has thus sustained him in the absence of more real benefits and will sustain him yet. Also, during the long night hours when only he is in the temple, he is able to have long, imagined dialogues with God, which to no little degree also sustain him, even if his visualization of God is a narrow and parochial one.

IV

The first time that the doors had been flung open during the adoration and all of the congregation had looked in upon him, Leviticus had become filled with shame, but that quickly passed when he realized that no one really thought anything of it and that the attention of the elders and the congregation was not upon him but upon the sacred scripts that one by one the elders withdrew, brought to the podium, and read with wavering voice and fingers while Leviticus, hunched over naked in an uncomfortable fetal position, could not have been there at all, for all the difference it made. He could have bolted from the ark, flung open his arms, shrieked to the congregation, "Look at me, look at me, don't you see what you're doing!" but he had not; he had been held back in part by fear, another part by constraint, still a third part from the realization that no one in the ark had ever done it. He had never seen it happen; back through all the generations that he was able to seek through accrued knowledge, the gesture was without precedent. The tenant of the ark had huddled quietly throughout the term of his confinement, had kept himself in perfect restraint when exposed; why should this not continue? Tradition and the awesome power of the elders had held him in check. He could not interrupt the flow of the services. He could deal with the predictable, which was a term of confinement and then release, just like everyone who had preceded him, but what he could not control was any conception of the unknown. If he made a spectacle of himself during the adoration, there was no saying what might happen then.

The elders might take vengeance upon him. They might turn away from the thought of vengeance and simply declare that his confinement be extended for an indefinite period for apostasy. It was very hard to tell exactly *what* they would do. This fear of the unknown, Leviticus had decided through his nights of pondering and imaginary dialogue, was probably what had enabled the situation to go on as long as it had.

It was hard to say exactly when he had reached the decision that he could no longer accept his position, his condition, his fate, wait out the time of his confinement, entertain the mercy of the elders, and return to the congregation. It was hard to tell at exactly what point he had realized that he could not do this; there was no clear point of epiphany, no moment at which—unlike a religious conversion—he could see himself as having gone outside the diagram of possibility, unutterably changed. All that he knew was that the decision had slowly crept into him, perhaps when he was sleeping, and without a clear point of definition, had reached absolute firmness: he would confront them at the adoration now. He would force them to look at him. He would show them what he, and by implication they, had become: so trapped within a misunderstood tradition, so wedged within the suffocating confines of the ark that they had lost any overriding sense of purpose, the ability to perceive wholly the madness that they and the elders had perpetuated. He would force them to understand this as the sum point of their lives, and when it was over, he would bolt from the synagogue naked, screaming, back to his cubicle, where he would reassemble his clothing and make final escape from the complex . . . and leave *them,* not him, to decide what they would now make of the shattered ruins of their lives.

The long period of confinement, self-examination, withdrawal, and physical privation had, perhaps, made Leviticus somewhat unstable.

V

Just before the time when the elders had appeared and had taken him away, Leviticus had made his last appeal, not to them, certainly not to the rabbi, but to Stala, who had shared to a certain point his anguish and fear of entrapment. "I don't see why I have to go there," he said to her, lying tight in the instant after fornication. "It's stupid. It's sheer mysticism. And besides that, it hasn't any relevance."

"But you must go," she said, putting a hand on his cheek. "You have been asked, and you *must.*" She was not stupid, he thought, merely someone who had never had to question assumptions, as he was now being forced to. "It is ordained. It won't be that bad; you're supposed to learn a lot."

"*You* go."

She gave a little gasping intake of breath and rolled from him. "You know that's impossible," she said. "Women can't go."

"In the reform tradition they can."

"But we're not in the reform tradition," she said; "this is the high Orthodox."

"I tend to think of it more in the line of being progressive."

"You know, Leviticus," she said, sitting, breathing unevenly—he could see her breasts hanging from her in the darkness like little scrolls, *like little scrolls,* oh, his confinement was very much on his mind, he could see—"it's just ridiculous that you should say something like that to me, that you should even *suggest* it. We're talking about our tradition now, and our tradition is very clear on this point, and it's impossible for a woman to go. Even if she wanted, she just couldn't—"

"All right," he said, "all right."

"No," Stala said, "no I won't stop discussing this, *you* were the one to raise it, Leviticus, not me, and I just won't have any of it. I didn't think you were that kind of person. I thought that you accepted the traditions, that you believed in them; in fact, it was an encouragement to me to think, to really think, that I had found someone who believed in a pure, solid, unshaken way, and I was really *proud* of you, even prouder when I found that you had been selected, but now you've changed everything. I'm beginning to be afraid that the only reason you believed in the traditions was because they weren't causing you any trouble and you didn't have to sacrifice yourself personally, but as soon as you became involved, you moved away from them." She was standing now, moving toward her robe, which had been tossed in the fluorescence at the far end of his cubicle; looking toward it during intercourse, he had thought that the sight of it was the most tender and affecting thing he had ever known, that she had cast her garments aside for him, that she had committed herself trustfully in nakedness against him for the night, and all of this despite the fact that he was undergoing what he took to be the positive humiliation of the confinement; now, as she flung it angrily on herself, he wondered if he had been wrong, if that casting aside had been a gesture less tender than fierce, whether or not she might have been —and he could hardly bear this thought, but one must, after all, press on—perversely excited by images of how he would look naked and drawn in upon himself in the ark, his genitals clamped between his thighs, talmudic statements by the rabbis Hill and Ben Bag Bag his only companions in the many long nights to come. He did not want to think of it, did not want to see her in this new perspective, and so leaped to his feet, fleet as a hart, and said, "But it's not fair. I tell you, it isn't fair."

"Of course it isn't fair. That's why it's so beautiful."

"Well, how would *you* like it? How would *you* like to be confined in—"

"Leviticus," she said, "I don't want to talk to you about this any more. Leviticus," she added, "I think I was wrong about you, you've hurt me very much. Leviticus," she concluded, "if you don't leave me right now, this moment, I'll go to the elders and tell them exactly what you're saying and thinking, and you know what will happen to you *then*," and he had let her go, nothing else to do, the shutter of his cubicle coming open, the passage of her body halving the light from the hall, then the light exposed again, and she was gone; he closed the shutter, he was alone in his cubicle again.

"It *isn't* fair," he said aloud, "she wouldn't like it so much if this was Reform and *she* were faced with the possibility of going in there someday," but this gave him little comfort; in fact, it gave him no comfort at all. It seemed to lead him right back to where he had started—futile, amazed protest at the injustice and folly of what was being done for him—and he had gone into an unhappy sleep thinking that something, something would have to be done about this; perhaps he could take the case out of the congregation. If the ordinators were led to understand what kind of rites were being committed in the name of high Orthodoxy, they would take a strong position against this, seal up the complex, probably scatter the congregation throughout a hundred other complexes . . . and it was this which had given him ease, tossed him into a long, murmuring sleep replete with satisfaction that he had finally found a way to deal with this (because he knew instinctively that the ordinators would *not* like this), but the next morning, cunningly, almost as if they had been informed by Stala (perhaps they had), the elders had come to take him to the ark, and that had been the end of that line of thought. He supposed that he could still do it, complain to the ordinators—that was, after his confinement was over—but at that point it hardly seemed worth it. It hardly seemed worth it at all. For one thing, he would be out of the ark by then and would not have to face it for a very, very long time, if ever. So why bother with the ordinators? He would have to take a more direct position, take it up with the congregation itself. Surely once they understood his agony, they could not permit it to continue. Could they?

VI

In the third of his imaginary dialogues with God (whom he pictured as an imposing man, somewhat the dimensions of one of the elders but much more neatly trimmed and not loaded down with the paraphernalia with which they conducted themselves) Leviticus said, "I don't believe any of it. Not any part of it at all. It's ridiculous."

"Doubt is another part of faith," God said. "Doubt and belief intertwine; both can be conditions of reverence. There is more divinity in the doubt of a wise man than in the acceptance of fools."

"That's just rhetoric," Leviticus said; "it explains nothing."

"The devices of belief must move within the confines of rhetoric," God said. "Rhetoric is the poor machinery of the profound and incontrovertible. Actually, it's not a matter of doubt. You're just very uncomfortable."

"That's right. I'm uncomfortable. I don't see why Judaism imposes this kind of suffering."

"Religion is suffering," God said with a modest little laugh, "and if you think Judaism is difficult upon its participants, you should get a look at some of the others sometime. Animal sacrifice, immolation, the ceremony of tongues. Oh, most terrible! Not that everyone doesn't have a right to their point of view," God added hastily. "Each must reach me, each in his way and through his tradition. Believe me, Leviticus, you haven't got the worst of it."

"I protest. I protest this humiliation."

"It isn't easy for me, either," God pointed out. "I've gone through cycles of repudiation for billions of years. Still, one must go on."

"I've got to get out of here. It's destroying my health; my physical condition is ruined. When am I going to leave?"

"I'm sorry," God said, "that decision is not in my hands."

"But you're omnipotent."

"My omnipotence is only my will working through the diversity of twenty billion other wills. Each is determined, and yet each is free."

"That sounds to me like a lousy excuse," Leviticus said sullenly. "I don't think that makes any sense at all."

"I do the best I can," God said, and after a long, thin pause added sorrowfully, "you don't think that any of this is easy for me either, do you?"

VII

Leviticus has the dim recollection from the historical tapes, none of them well attended to, that before the time of the complexes, before the time of great changes, there had been another kind of existence, one during which none of the great churches, Judaism included, had been doing particularly well in terms of absolute number of participants, relative proportion of the population. Cults had done all right, but cults had had only the most marginal connection to the great churches, and in most cases had repudiated them, leading, in the analyses of certain of the historical tapes, to the holocaust that had followed, and the absolute determination on the part of the Risen, that they would not permit this to happen again, that they would not allow the cults to appropriate all of the energy, the empirical demonstrations, for themselves, but instead would make sure that the religions were reconverted to hard ritual, that the ritual demonstrations following would be strong and convincing enough to keep the cults out of business and through true worship and true belief (although with enough ritual now to satisfy the mass of people that religion could be made visible) stave off yet another holocaust. At least, this was what Leviticus had *gathered* from the tapes, but then, you could never be sure about this, and the tapes were all distributed under the jurisdiction of the elders anyway, and what the elders would do with material to manipulate it to their own purposes was well known.

Look, for one thing, at what they had done to Leviticus.

VIII

"I'll starve in here," he had said to the elders desperately, as they were conveying him down the aisle toward the ark. "I'll deteriorate. I'll go insane from the confinement. If I get ill, no one will be there to help me."

"Food will be given you each day. You will have the Torah and the Talmud, the Feast of Life itself to comfort you and to grant you peace. You will allow the spirit of God to move within you."

"That's ridiculous," Leviticus said. "I told you, I have very little belief in any of this. How can the spirit—?"

"Belief means nothing," the elders said. They seemed to speak in unison, which was impossible, of course (how could they have such a level of shared anticipation of the others' remarks; rather, it was that they spoke one by one, with similar voice quality—*that* would be a more likely explanation of the phenomenon, mysticism having, so far as Leviticus knew, very little relation to rational Judaism). "You are its object, not its subject."

"Aha!" Leviticus said then, frantically raising one finger to fore-stall them as they began to lead him painfully into the ark, pushing him, tugging, buckling his limbs. "If belief does not matter, if I am merely object rather than subject, *then how can I be tenanted by the spirit?*"

"That," the elders said, finishing the job, patting him into place, one of them extracting a rag to whip the wood of the ark speedily to high gloss, cautiously licking a finger, applying it to the surface to take out an imagined particle of dust, "that is very much your prob-lem and not ours, you see," and closed the doors upon him, leaving him alone with scrolls and Talmud, cloth, and the sound of scrambling birds. In a moment he heard a grinding noise as key was inserted into lock, then a snap as tumblers inverted. They were lock-ing him in.

Well, he had known that. That, at least, was not surprising. Tradi-tion had its roots; the commitment to the ark was supposed to be voluntary—a joyous expression of commitment, that was; the time spent in the ark was supposed to be a time of repentance and great interior satisfaction. . . . But all of that to one side, the elders, bal-ancing off the one against the other, as was their wont, arriving at a careful and highly modulated view of the situation, had ruled in their wisdom that it was best to keep the ark locked at all times, excepting, of course, the adoration. That was the elders for you. They took ev-erything into account, and having done *that,* made the confinement, as they said, his problem.

IX

Now the ritual of the Sabbath evening service is over, and the rabbi is delivering his sermon. Something about the many rivers of Judaism, each of them individual, flowing into that great sea of tradi-tion and belief. The usual material. Leviticus knows that this is the Sabbath service; he can identify it by certain of the prayers and chants, although he has lost all extrinsic sense of time, of course, in the ark. For that matter, he suspects, the elders have lost all extrinsic sense of time as well; it is no more Friday now than Thursday or Saturday, but at a certain arbitrary time after the holocaust, he is given to understand, the days, the months, the years themselves were recreated and assigned, and therefore, if the elders say it is Friday, it is Friday, just as if they say it is the year thirty-seven, it is the year thirty-seven, and not fifty seven hundred something or other, or whatever it was when the holocaust occurred. (In his mind, as a kind of shorthand, he has taken to referring to the holocaust as the H; the H did this; certain things happened to cause the H, but he is not sure that this would make sense to other people, and as a matter of fact wonders whether or not this might not be the sign of a deranged consciousness.) Whatever the elders say it is, it is, although God in the imaginary dialogues has assured him that the elders, in their own fashion, are merely struggling with the poor tools at their command and are no less fallible than he, Leviticus.

He shall take upon himself, in any event, these commandments, and shall bind them for frontlets between his eyes. After the sermon, when the ark is opened for the adoration, he will lunge from it and confront them with what they have become, with what they have made of him, with what together they have made of God. He will do that, and for signposts upon his house as well, that they shall remember and do those commandments and be holy. Holy, holy. Oh, their savior and their hope, they have been worshiping him as their fathers did in ancient days, but enough of this, quite enough; the earth being his dominion and all the beasts and fish thereof, it is high time that some sort of reckoning of the changes be made.

Highly unfair, Leviticus thinks, crouching, awaiting the opening of the ark, but then again, he must (as always) force himself to see all sides of the question: very possibly, if Stala had approved of his position, had granted him sympathy, had agreed with him that what the elders were doing was unjust and unfair . . . well, then, he might have been far more cheerfully disposed to put up with his fate. If only she, if only someone, had seen him as a martyr rather than as a usual part of a very usual process. Everything might have changed, but then again, it might have been the same.

X

The book of Daniel, he recollects, had been very careful and very precise in giving, with numerology and symbol, the exact time when the H would begin. Daniel had been specific; he had alluded to precisely that course of events at which period of time that would signal the coming (or the second coming, depending upon your pursuit); the only trouble with it was that there had been so many conflicting interpretations over thousands of years that for all intents and purposes the predictive value of Daniel for the H had been lost; various interpreters saw too many signs of rising in the East, too many beasts of heaven, stormings of the tabernacle, too many uprisings among the cattle or the chieftains to enable them to get the H down right, once and for all. A lot of them, hence, had been embarrassed; many cults, hinged solely upon their interpretation of Daniel and looking for an apocalyptic date, had gotten themselves overcommitted, and going up on the mountaintops to await the end, had lost most of their membership.

Of course, the H had come, and with it the floods, the falling, the rising and the tumult in the lands, and it was possible that Daniel had gotten it precisely right, after all, if only you could look back on it in retrospect and get it right, but as far as Leviticus was concerned, there was only one overriding message that you might want to take from the tapes if you were interested in this kind of thing: you did not want to pin it down too closely. Better, as the elders did, to kind of leave the issue indeterminate and in flux. Better, as God himself had (imaginarily) pointed out, to say that doubt is merely the reverse coin of belief, both of them motes in the bowels of the Hound of Heaven.

XI

The rabbi, adoring the ever-living God and rendering praise unto him, inserts the key into the ark, the tumblers fall open, the doors creak and gape, and Leviticus finds himself once again staring into the old man's face, his eyes congested with pain as he reaches in trembling toward one of the scrolls, his cheeks dancing in the light, the elders grouped behind him attending carefully; and instantly Leviticus strikes: he reaches out a hand, yanks the rabbi out of the way, and then tumbles from the ark. He had meant to leap but did not realize how shriveled his muscles would be from disuse; what he had intended to be a vault is instead a collapse to the stones under the ark, but yet he is able to move. He is able to move. He pulls himself falteringly to hands and knees, gasping, the rabbi mumbling in the background, the elders looking at him with shocked expressions, too astonished for the instant to move. The instant now is all that he needs. He has not precipitated what he has done in the hope of having a great deal of time.

"Look at me!" Leviticus shrieks, struggling erect, hands hanging, head shaking. "Look at me, look at what I've become, look at what dwells in the heart of the ark!" And indeed, they are looking, all of them, the entire congregation, Stala in the women's section, hand to face, palm open, extended, all of them stunned in the light of his gaze. "Look at me!" he shouts again. "You can't do this to people, do you understand that? You cannot do it!" And the elders come upon him, recovered from their astonishment, to seize him with hands like metal, the rabbi rolling and rolling on the floor, deep into some chant that Leviticus cannot interpret, the congregation gathered now to rush upon him; but too late, it has (as he must at some level have known) been too late, from the beginning, and as the rabbi chants, the elders strain, the congregation rushes . . . time inverts, and the real, the long-expected, the true H with its true Host begins.

Barry N. Malzberg writes:

I was born in 1939, married in 1964, had a daughter in 1966 and another in 1970, presently live in the pastoral serenity of Bergen County two miles from the Ridgefield Park Oil Dump & Refinery. I have written more than seventy novels, some of them science fiction, and more than a hundred and fifty short stories, almost all of which have been (or at least have been published as) science fiction. My favorite of all novels is Underlay *(Avon Books, 1974), which is invisible. I am a full-time writer; have been for about seven years.*

CAMBRIDGE, 1:58 A.M.

by Gregory Benford

Gregory Markham returned to the Cavendish Laboratory at 9:13 P.M. Instead of going to his cluttered office, he descended into the basement. The corridors were poorly lit, and many laboratories yawned empty, stripped of equipment.

When he entered the large room reserved for the nuclear-resonance group, he nearly bumped into a tall, thin man standing just inside the door.

The man turned and smiled slightly. "You must be Markham," he said, holding out his hand.

"Right. How did you know?"

"You're the only one here who looks as though he might be an American."

"Ah. I've been here six months, but apparently there's something British that doesn't rub off on visitors."

"You're better dressed than we are, for one thing."

"You mean for a scientist I'm better dressed. Those tweeds of yours are quite fashionable."

"We do a bit better in the government. It's about all we seem to be doing well, these days," the man said wryly.

"Oh, you must be Ian Peterson, then."

"Didn't I say that? Stupid of me. Yes, I rang you up two days ago. Sorry, I'm wandering around in a daze, I guess."

"Crisis?"

"Of course, there's always one these days. The Emergency Council has been in executive session since this morning. I was barely able to get the train down here in time."

"Worried about North Africa?"

"That, yes. Looks as though it's a full-scale dieback this time."

"Damn. Is it all due to the drought?"

"Plus not having any food reserves. Disease is killing most of them now, though."

Markham gestured into the laboratory. "Say, there's Renfrew. Have you met?"

"No, I've only just arrived. He's the heavyset one?" The two men stood on a raised platform overlooking a sprawl of scientific equipment. There were eight technicians working among the aisles. Roughing pumps chugged laboriously, and there were muffled conversations, but otherwise the laboratory was quiet.

"I'd like a word before I meet Renfrew," Peterson said. "I didn't have much chance to sound you out on the telephone the other day."

"I don't have much of an opinion so far," Markham said precisely.

"Nonetheless, you're the fellow the Americans elected to send. You must know how they feel about this."

"Strictly speaking, they didn't 'send' anyone. I'm here with the Cavendish theory group, sabbatical leave. The National Science Foundation wired me last week to act as liaison."

"Yes, you're from the University of California at Irvine, right? A plasma physicist."

"Most of my work has been in plasmas until the last few years. I wrote a paper on tachyons long ago, before they became fashionable. I suppose that's why the NSF asked me to be here."

Peterson lowered his voice. "There's the rub, you see. I haven't any technical background in this sort of thing. No one on the council has. We've got ecologists and systems people and that sort of thing, but . . . well, look, tell me, do you think this experiment might be of any real help?"

"Without being melodramatic," Markham said slowly, "I believe it could save millions of lives."

"If it works."

"We know the technique works. It's whether we can actually communicate with the past that we don't know."

"And this setup here—" Peterson swept his arm out across the laboratory bay—"can do that?"

"If we're damned lucky. We know there were similar nuclear-resonance experiments in the Cavendish and a few other places in the States and the Soviet Union functioning as far back as the 1950's. In principle they could pick up coherent signals induced by tachyons."

"So we can send them telegrams?"

"Yes, but that's all. It's a highly restricted form of time travel, if you want to put it that way. This is the only way anyone's figured how to send messages into the past. We can't transmit objects or people."

Peterson shook his head. "I did a degree in math, computers. But even I know there's a paradox involved here somewhere. The old thing about shooting your grandfather, isn't it? Someone on the council brought that up yesterday. We almost booted the whole idea out because of that, you know."

"A good point. I made the same error in a paper back in 1970. It turns out there are paradoxes, and then, if you look at things the right way, paradoxes go away. Maybe I can explain—"

"Sorry, but I haven't time for that now. The whole point, as I understand it, is to send these telegrams and tell somebody back in 1955 about our situation here."

"Well, something like that. Warn them against chlorinated hydrocarbons, sketch in the effects on phytoplankton. Describe—"

"Hello, Greg! Glad to see you here." Unnoticed, John Renfrew had mounted the catwalk from the bay below. He was a large, swarthy man with his white shirt partially untucked in his trousers. Lines of fatigue made his face seem ashen. Despite the chilly English spring, there were crescents of sweat in the cloth around his armpits. "And you're Mr. Peterson, I expect," Renfrew said with considerably less enthusiasm. "Come to see if I've been spending the council's special appropriation wisely?"

"Something of the sort," Peterson said distantly.

"I'm grateful for it, mind you that, and we'll be showing you some results later on. But Professor Markham is here because I think the only way to really accomplish anything is to get the Americans to come in."

"Since I'm not so essential," Peterson said, "you might have scheduled this experiment at some more reasonable hour."

"Couldn't. Noise level in the day is too high, and anyway, the electric-power chaps won't let us run in the peak usage times. We use a lot of high-tension devices to put out short bursts of tachyons, and they—"

"I'm sure," Peterson said. "Could I please see the experiment?"

"Ah, yes, certainly." Renfrew turned and led the way down the catwalk to the floor of the laboratory. The room was of bare stonework, outfitted with old-fashioned electrical connections and rather newer cables strewn through the aisles of apparatus. Some old, gray cabinets were of English manufacture, but most of the newer equipment was housed in brightly colored compartments from Maxwell

Laboratories, Physics International, and other American firms. Peterson gathered these garish red-and-yellow units came from the council appropriation.

Renfrew led them to a complex array housed between the poles of a large magnet. "Superconducting setup, of course. We need the high field strength to get a nice sharp line during transmission."

Peterson studied the maze of wires and meters. Cabinets housing rank upon rank of electronics towered over the men; he found the mass of it oppressive. He waited for Renfrew to begin, but when the man said nothing, Peterson pointed out a particular object and asked as to its function.

"Oh, I didn't think you'd be wanting to know the technical side," Renfrew said.

"Try me."

"We've got a large nuclear source in there, see . . ." Renfrew pointed at the encased volume between the magnet poles. "We modulate the electric fields around the source—it's cesium—in such a way that the nuclei give off tachyons. Particles that travel faster than light, you know. On the other side"—he pointed around the magnets, leading Peterson to a long cylindrical tank that protruded ten meters away from the magnets—"we draw out the tachyons and focus them into a beam. They're a particular type of tachyon, ones that resonate only with cesium nuclei. Ordinary matter is transparent to tachyons, do you see?"

"Until they run into something," Peterson said.

"No, no, that's the point," Renfrew said sharply. "Tachyons just don't interact with most ordinary matter. They pass right through."

"That's why we can shoot them halfway across the galaxy without having them stopped," Markham interjected.

"Except for cesium," Renfrew said. "When one of our tachyons hits a cesium atom in a strong magnetic field—a situation that doesn't occur naturally very often—it will be absorbed. The struck nucleus recoils then, with a very high momentum. It sends out shock waves in the lattice of the cesium sample."

"That's some other fellow's cesium, I suppose?" Peterson said.

"One operating in 1955," Renfrew said.

Markham added, "We hope."

"We're hoping the fellows doing the experiments back then will notice some large signals—they'll perceive them as sound waves—carrying a message," Renfrew said. "The whole point is that there must be enough tachyons striking that 1955 block of cesium metal to show up clearly. For that we have to concentrate a burst of tachyons and aim it just so—"

"Hold on," Peterson said, putting up a hand. "Aim for *what?* Where is 1955?"

"Quite far away, as it works out," Markham conceded. "Since 1955 the Earth has been going around the Sun, while our star itself is revolving about the hub of the galaxy. Add on to that the motion of our galaxy relative to the fixed rest frame of the center of mass of the universe—"

"You mean 1955 is in a different place, then?"

"Certainly. So we send out a broad beam that sweeps the volume we believe was occupied by the Earth at that particular time in the past," Markham said.

"Sounds impossible."

Markham shrugged. "It may be. The trick is that Renfrew here is creating tachyons with essentially infinite speed, so if we can hit the right spot in space, we can send a message back quite a long way. How far back we can go is related to the distance."

"We're aiming for a particular space-time point along the Earth's geodesic," Renfrew began.

"You're traveling a bit too fast for me," Peterson put in. "What were these results you were talking about?"

"We've been working with noise problems the last few months, that's the main thing. The signal has to appear above the thermal background, so it's accessible to the fellows back in the 1950's, with their relatively crude equipment."

Peterson shook his head. "I'm amazed you got the money for this."

Renfrew's face tightened. "Well, we did get it. Though it's bloody well not enough."

"You think you won't be able to get through?" Markham said.

Renfrew turned to the American. "It'll be a near thing. We need a lot more power to be sure. That's where the Americans come in, if they will."

"But you'll try?" Peterson said.

"Right. The rig is set; we've been working on it all day."

"When can we run?" Markham said.

"Now."

It was 9:34 P.M.

* * *

José Basquan waited for the first threads of dawn to lighten the sky. Slowly he put his loose fishing gear in a mesh sack. He squatted at the threshold of a dark stone house, listening to the slowly gathering sounds of people arising through the village. He tried to ignore the gnawing, rumbling hunger in his belly.

He debated with himself for a moment and then decided a mouthful of wine would give him energy to begin. The cork came out with a dry pop, and he carefully trickled a pool of it into his mouth. It was sharp and rough; the fumes seemed to burn his nostrils. RODAS CABERNET. He read each letter to himself, moving his lips. José could still remember letters, but the words made no sense to him. Downslope from his house was a long, low wooden building with a sign atop it. To pass the time he slowly spelled the letters out to himself, as he had many times before. MITSUBISHI PACKING CORP.

There was no movement around the building, no lights were burning. There had been little work for months there, José knew, and some of the men who had learned that trade had moved away to another village in search of another job.

José heaved to his feet. If there was to be work for anyone, he had better get down to his boat. The bleak village of scattered one-story houses depended utterly upon the fishing fleet. There had been precious few hauls of fish in the last few weeks. The familiar casting areas yielded nothing. José and a few other men had found some shallow spots farther up the coast that occasionally gave a modest catch, but everyone knew those places were not dependable.

He walked slowly down the damp cobblestoned street. A drizzle began. He heard the high notes of excitement from the direction of the plank pier. There was also a low bass sound, like angry men yelling. José walked faster. A small hill hid the view of the ocean from him. He took a shortcut through a clump of stunted brown trees. A dead bird lay in his path, but he did not notice it. He rounded the brow of the hill.

The shouting grew louder. He squinted through the drizzle, and suddenly his eyes widened. Normally at dawn the Atlantic was dark and oily. Today it was a mottled red. A stench of rotting sea life rose from the narrow beach.

José did not have to go out in his skiff today to know he would find no fish. Something had happened. The ocean was dying.

November 16, 1991

Dear Alex:

I'm not going to make it down for Thanksgiving; there's just too much to do here at Cal Tech. The last few weeks have been extremely exciting. I'm working with a couple of other people, and we really don't want to break off our calculations, even for a holiday in Baja. I shall miss the prickly cactus and that delicious dry heat. Sorry, and maybe we can make it next time.

After breaking a promise like this, I really suppose I ought to tell you what's stirred me up so. Probably a marine biologist like you won't think all this is of such great concern—cosmology doesn't count for much in the world of enzymes and titrated solutions and all that, I suppose—but to those of us working in the gravitational-theory group it looks as though there's a genuine revolution around the corner. Or maybe it's already arrived.

You must remember Malcolm Walmesley, the fellow who was best man at Jim and Hilary's wedding? He's tied into this, though somewhat indirectly. He and two others were the first to notice that quasars are clustered into two groups in our sky. This was way back in 1966, and you will get some idea of how difficult the observations are when I tell you that it has taken this long to follow up those first measurements in depth. It turns out the quasars are clumped together, representing a really large-scale clustering of matter in the universe.

This is related to a problem that's been hanging around astrophysics for a long time. If there is a certain quantity of matter in the universe, then it is a closed geometry—like the surface of a sphere, you can move around on it, but you can't escape. So people in our line of work have been wondering for some time if there is enough matter in our universe to close off the geometry. It would be nice to see if the geometry is closed by a direct experiment—say, by sending out a beam of light and seeing if it curves around and comes back eventually—but that experiment takes about twenty billion years to finish.

Just counting the luminous stars in the universe gives a small quantity of matter, not enough to close off space-time. But there's undoubtedly a lot of unseen mass such as dust, dead stars, and black holes.

We're now pretty sure that most galaxies have large black holes at their centers. That accounts for enough missing matter to close off our universe. What's new is that the recent data on quasar distribution mean there are large fluctuations in matter density throughout our universe. If galaxies clump together somewhere in our universe, and their density gets high enough, *their* local space-time geometry could wrap around on itself, in the same way that our universe is closed.

We now have enough evidence to believe Tommy Gold's old idea —that there *are* parts of our universe which have enough clustered galaxies to form their own closed geometry. They won't look like much to us—just small areas with weak red light coming out of them. The shocker here is that these local density fluctuations qualify as *independent* universes. The time for forming a separate universe is independent of the size (it goes like square root of Gn, where G is the gravitational constant and n the density of the contracting region). Thus it's independent of the size of the miniuniverse! A small universe will close itself off just as fast as a large one. This means all the various-sized universes have been around for the same amount of "time." (Defining just what time is in this problem will drive you to drink, if you're not a mathematician.)

The point here is that there may be closed-off universes *inside* our own. In fact, it would be a remarkable coincidence if our universe was the largest of all. We may be a local lump inside somebody else's universe! Remember the old cartoon of a little fish being swallowed by a slightly larger one, in turn about to be swallowed by another bigger one, and so on ad infinitum? Well, we may be one of these fishes.

The last few weeks, I've been working on the problem of getting information about—or out of—these universes inside our own. Clearly, light can't get out of one universe into the next. Neither can matter. The only possibility might be some type of particle that doesn't fit into the constraints set by Einstein's theory. There are several candidates like this, but Thorne (the grand old man around here) doesn't want to get into that morass. Too messy, he says.

Some of us here think otherwise, which is why I'm working so hard on the problem. There's a chance of a first-class discovery in this. We've had the devil of a time pursuing things, with the food strike and the big fire in L.A. And I scarcely think anyone will give much of a damn, with the world in its present state. But that's what the academic life is for.

I'm going to try to get through to La Jolla sometime soon, and maybe we can see each other then. Sorry about Baja.

Sincerely,
Charles

At 10:22 P.M. John Renfrew began tapping slowly on a signal key. Markham and Peterson stood behind him. Technicians monitored other output from the experiment and made adjustments.

"It's this easy to send a message?" Peterson said.

"Simple Morse," Markham said.

"I see, to maximize the chances of it's being decoded."

"Damn!" Renfrew suddenly stood up. "Noise level has increased again."

Markham leaned over and looked at the oscilloscope face. The trace danced and juggled, a scattered random field. "How can there be that much noise in a chilled cesium sample?" Markham asked.

"Christ, I don't know. We had trouble like this all along lately."

"It can't be thermal."

"Transmission is impossible with this going on?" Peterson put in.

"Of course," Renfrew said irritably. "Broadens the tachyon resonance line and muddles up the signal."

"Then the experiment can't work?" Peterson said.

"Bloody hell, I didn't say that. There's just something wrong now. I'm sure I can find the problem."

A technician called down from the platform above. "Mr. Peterson? Telephone call, says it's urgent."

"Oh, right." Peterson hastened up the metal stairway and was gone. Renfrew conferred with some technicians, checked readings himself, and fretted away several minutes. Markham stood looking at the oscilloscope trace.

"Any idea what it could be?" he called to Renfrew.

"Heat leak, possibly. Maybe the sample isn't well insulated from shocks, either."

"You mean people walking around the room, that sort of thing?"

Renfrew shrugged and went on with his work. Markham rubbed a thumbnail against his lower lip and studied the yellow noise spectrum on the green oscilloscope screen. After a moment he said, "Have you got a correlator you could use on this rig?"

Renfrew stopped for a moment and thought. "No, none here. We have no use for one."

"I'd like to see if there is any structure we could bring out of that noise."

"Well, I suppose we could do that. Take a while to scrounge up something suitable."

Peterson appeared overhead. "Sorry, I'm going to have to go to a secured telephone. Something's come up." Renfrew turned away without saying anything. Markham climbed the stairway and said, "I think there will be a delay in the experiment, anyway."

"Ah, good. I don't want to return to London just yet, without seeing it through. But I'll have to talk to some people on a confidential telephone line. It will probably take an hour or so."

"That bad?"

"Seems so. There's a large diatom bloom off the South American coast, Atlantic side."

"Bloom?"

"Biologist's word. It means the thyloplankton are coming to terms with the chlorinated hydrocarbons we've been using in fertilizer. Apparently marine animals can't get along with this new diatom. They're dying off, and the whole food chain might be threatened."

"I see. Can we do anything about it?"

"I don't know. We've been trying some methods in the Indian Ocean, anticipating something like this might happen. I don't know if we can shift resources to the lower Atlantic that fast."

"Well, I won't keep you from the telephone. I've got something to work on, an idea about Renfrew's experiment. Say, do you know the Whim?"

"Yes, it's a pub in Jesus Green."

"I'll probably need a drink and some food in an hour or so. Why don't we meet there?"

"It's, let's see, ten-forty-five. Yes, that's a good idea. See you near midnight."

The Physical Review D, Vol. 2, No. 2, 263-265, 15 July 1970
"The Tachyonic Antitelephone"
G. A. Markham, D. L. Book, and W. A. Newcomb
Lawrence Radiation Laboratory, University of California,
Livermore, California
(Received 23 June 1969)

The problem of detecting faster-than-light particles is reconsidered in relation to Tolman's paradox. It is shown that some of the experiments already under way or contemplated must either yield negative results or give rise to causal contradictions.

Hypothetical faster-than-light particles (tachyons) have recently received considerable attention, both theoretically[1-3] and experimentally.[4-6] Still, there are difficult questions of causality associated with faster-than-light signals. We hope to show that these have not been adequately resolved. In particular, it appears that at least some current attempts to produce and detect tachyons are foredoomed to failure on fundamental grounds.

In 1917 Tolman [7] presented an argument (Tolman's paradox) showing that if faster-than-light signals can be propagated, then communication with the past is possible. That is, they would comprise an "antitelephone."

Recently Bilaniuk, Deshpande, and Sudarshan [1] have attempted to answer this argument with a "reinterpretation principle." They note that a tachyon of negative energy $-E$ leaving point 1 at time t_1 and arriving at point $_2$ at an earlier time t_2 may be reinterpreted as a tachyon of energy $+E$ traveling from 2 to 1. Thus the earlier of the two events can always be viewed as an emission and the later as an absorption. They point out that the end of the tachyon's world line that appears "earlier" depends on the reference frame of the observer. That is, emission of a tachyon may be viewed as absorption by another observer. As we shall see, this statement is not sufficient of itself to refute Tolman's paradox.

Note that Tolman's paradox deals only with faster-than-light *communication*. It does not rule out tachyons, which for some reason may not be used as a signaling system. There is no paradox associated with an unmodulated tachyon beam. Current theories deal mainly with noninteracting tachyons. The moment interactions are introduced, Tolman's paradox must be faced. . . .

James Whyteborn was late for work. He hastily shook out his jacket and hung it in the dark narrow cloakroom. He put on his white smock and fumbled with the buttons. His head was blurred and it ached, either from the cheap Algerian red of the night before or simple fatigue. He hated this job; maybe that had something to do with it.

He pushed open the heavy door into the preparation room. The chill air made Whyteborn shiver, and the foreman gave him a significant look. He hurried to his post. Well, hell. He wouldn't have been late if he hadn't had to take the damned bus from Croydon through Caterham, and then run into that jam at the railway crossing. Nothing ever seemed to work right these days.

He took out his working case, the chemical analyzers and needles and the rest. He was reasonably sure that he understood most of the checks he was to make, but the government seemed to add a new test every time he turned around. Whyteborn got his kit in order and went to the first line of carcasses. He looked aside as he approached, wanting to delay the moment until the last. It didn't seem to matter whether it was pork or beef or lamb, the sight of a carcass hanging from a hook, partially chopped to pieces and still bleeding, made him ill. If he wasn't a vegetarian, maybe it would be easier.

He did the first row all right, drawing out the samples and making the color-coded checks required. He ignored the gobs of yellow fat that dangled in the air, the stringy meat interlaced with blue and brown streaks.

By the second row he had begun to feel the dull buzzing pain behind his eyes again, and his attention wavered. Whyteborn checked his watch; still quite a long time till tea break.

He came to a line of pigs neatly strutted and cleaned. There was a special set of tests for these, recently started by the government inspectors. Something to do with the protein supplements given the hogs, ground-up cod and whitefish marrow, something like that.

He inserted a needle, took a sample, and tested it in the analyzer. The color indicator came out neutral. Whyteborn felt his headache getting worse. He shuffled on to the next body and repeated the process. This result was somewhat worse, but Whyteborn knew he probably wasn't doing the test right. It seemed likely this meat would come out all right if he was careful about his procedures. He looked down the long row of silently hanging hog carcasses and felt the room spin around him. God, it was really bad this morning. He shouldn't have drunk the wine. He should have called in sick.

He put away his kit. That was enough for this line. The tests came out neutral or maybe a little better, and anyway, what did it matter, the tests weren't that good in any case, and Whyteborn wasn't about to eat any of this rubbish. Christ, only the rich could buy this stuff now.

He coughed and his head felt worse. He decided to take his tea break early. What a piss-up of a day this was.

*   *   *

The Whim was gloomy, even considering the energy shortage. Ian Peterson pushed his way through a crowd near the front door and stood for a moment trying to get his bearings. A yellowed poster announced that some menu items were discontinued—temporarily, of course. The Whim was surprisingly crowded; then Peterson remembered that most experimental work at Cambridge was done at night, due to its low priority. The university crowd had apparently adapted well; some of them even seemed to be in good spirits.

He made his way across the crowded eating section, through blue curls of pipe smoke layered in the air. Someone called his name, and he peered around until he saw Markham in a side booth.

"It's chancy finding anyone here, isn't it?" Peterson said as he sat down.

"I was just ordering. Thought I might have the tongue, though it's incredibly expensive."

Peterson studied the menu. "Lot of salads, aren't there? There doesn't seem to be anything worth eating these days."

"Anything with meat in it is just impossible."

"Yes, except the cheaper cuts. I don't see how you can eat tongue, knowing it came out of some animal's mouth."

"Have an egg instead, then?"

Peterson laughed. "I suppose there's no way to turn. But I think I'll splurge and have the sausages. That should do up my budget pretty nicely."

When the waitress had brought Peterson's ale and Markham's Mackeson stout, Peterson suddenly noticed an odd sour tang in the air. "Is that what I think? They allow that in here?"

Markham looked around and sniffed the air. "Marihuana, sure. All the mild euphorics are legal here, aren't they?"

"They have been for a year or two. But I thought by social convention, if there's any of that left, one didn't smoke it in public places."

"If the government wants to distract people from the news, there's no point in requiring them to do it only at home," Markham said mildly.

"Score to you. Despite all the rhetoric, I'm sure that's why it was legalized. I'll bet the rate of use goes up pretty soon, too."

"The news that bad?"

"Worse, if anything."

"How much does the bloom cover?"

"Apparently almost all the south Atlantic. The large fishing areas are gone. As far as patrols can tell, there is nothing left alive inside. And the perimeter is growing."

"We'd better get Renfrew's experiment on the air, then."

"That's what I don't understand. I may be a nonspecialist, but how in hell do you get around that grandfather paradox bit? How can we possibly change the past?"

"Quite honestly, no one knows for certain. Renfrew's is the first experiment done with tachyons that deliberately tries to reach the past. All the ideas he's working under depend on new advances in cosmology and relativity and particle physics. No one has been able to put all these ideas together in a coherent philosophical package."

"Then how the hell can you say this might work?"

"There are good theoretical reasons to think it might. The trick is that you can change the past so long as the physical circumstances of the experiment aren't also altered in the process."

Peterson shook his head. "Don't follow."

"Look, we want to get word that use of fertilizer-sensitive grains won't work in the long run, that the oceans are so damned vulnerable, more so than anything else. That whole countries will begin to go down the drain by the 1980's. We can send that information—the laws of physics and causality will let us—as long as we don't solve the problem so well that the Renfrew experiment never gets performed. That is, unless we do something that cuts off the message itself. So we *can* make things better. At least, there isn't any reason in the theory why we can't."

"That's what you're asking the government to support?"

"The council did, didn't it?"

"Only on advice. Do you think the National Science Foundation will come in with some money for Renfrew?"

Markham shrugged. The waitress arrived with their food, and both men began to eat quickly. "If Renfrew's personality has anything to do with it, I think we can write off the whole affair."

"Yes, I'm rather amazed that he's so hostile," Peterson said. "Any idea why?"

"Sure. He's had to scrounge and fight like billy-hell to get this thing together. I think he's getting paranoid about it. Yet he's doing just what should be done. He's checking important implications of a new cosmological theory that uses tachyons as an essential part. It took half a century for Weber to test for Einstein's gravitational waves, you remember. Well, Renfrew is speeding up the process a bit for tachyons."

"He's already found them, hasn't he?"

"Yes, but to *use* them—there's the rub."

"That settles it, then. The council secretary wanted me to return to London immediately, but I won't. I'll stay a few more hours to see if this thing comes out. Shouldn't we be getting back over to the laboratory?"

Markham took a long pull at his stout. "I suppose so," he sighed. "What time is it?"

"Morning already. One-oh-eight."

The stars were out as Markham and Peterson made their way back to the Cavendish. Their walk took them through the Euclidean perfection of Kings College, through an ivy arch, and down a small, cobbled lane. They went along the backs, Markham rather relishing the experience as only Americans do at Cambridge, and then passed through the Great Court of Trinity. The air was heavy and damp, giving their footsteps an odd hollow ring.

As they entered the nuclear-resonance laboratory, Renfrew looked up and waved energetically. "Where've you been? We've got everything set up."

"Sorry, I was delayed," Peterson said.

Renfrew nodded to two technicians and beckoned them down the

(From *The Geography of Calamity: Geopolitics of Human Dieback,* by J. Holdren)

		Attributable Deaths (estimated)
1984-1986	Java	8,750,000
1986	Malawi	2,300,000
1987	Philippines	1,600,000
1987-Present	Congo	3,700,000
1989-Present	India	68,000,000
1990-Present	Colombia	
	Ecuador	
	Honduras	1,600,000
1991-Present	Dominican Republic	750,000
1991-Present	Egypt	
	Pakistan	3,800,000
1993-Present	General Southeast Asia	113,500,000

stairs. "I have a Scott correlator rigged in, as you asked," he said to Markham. "But our noise problem is just as bad."

"I expected so," Markham said. When Renfrew seemed surprised, he went on, "I've been doing some calculations and a bit of reading since I left. I think there may be an explanation for the anomalous noise level. It's not thermally generated at all, if I'm right. Instead, the noise comes from tachyons. Your cesium sample isn't transmitting tachyons, it's receiving them. There's a tachyon background we've neglected."

"A background?" Renfrew said. "From what?"

"Let's see. Try the correlator."

Renfrew made a few adjustments and stepped back from the oscilloscope. "That should do it."

"Do what?" Peterson put in.

"This is a lock-in coherence analyzer," Markham said. "Which means it can cull out the genuine noise in the cesium sample—sound-wave noise, that is—and bring any signals up out of the random background."

"Which is just what it's doing," Renfrew said quietly. He stared intently at the oscilloscope face. A complex wave form wavered across the scale.

"It seems to be a series of pulses strung out at regular intervals," Renfrew said. "But the signal decays in time." He pointed at the fluid line that faded into the noise level as it neared the right hand of the screen.

"Quite regular, yes," Markham said. "Here's one peak, then a pause, then two peaks together, then nothing again, then four nearly on top of each other, then nothing. . . . Strange."

"What do you think it is?" Peterson asked.

"Not ordinary background, that's clear," Renfrew answered.

"It's coherent, can't be natural," Markham said.

Renfrew: "No. More like . . ."

"A code," Markham finished.

It was 1:56 A.M.

"Let's take some of this down," Markham said. He began writing on a clipboard. "Is this a real-time display?"

"No, I just rigged it to take a sample of the noise for a hundred-microsecond interval." Renfrew reached for the oscilloscope dials. "Would you like another interval?"

"Wait until I copy this."

Peterson said, "Why don't you just photograph it?"

Renfrew looked at him significantly. "We have no film. There's a shortage, and priority doesn't go to laboratories these days, you know."

"Anyone here know Morse?" Markham interrupted.

Renfrew shook his head. Peterson said, "I probably still remember some."

Markham handed him the clipboard. "Try that. Meanwhile, let's have another interval analyzed."

Renfrew made an adjustment, and another pattern appeared on the scope, this time covering only half the time period before it was submerged in the noise level. Markham began copying its features.

"Odd," Peterson said. "It decodes to 'Nd Meat I'—that's all."

"At least it's English," Markham said. "Try this."

Renfrew wrinkled his brow. "What's happening?"

"Someone is sending us time telegrams, I'd say," Markham said. "Telegrams to one-fifty-eight A.M., Cambridge. They're having trouble getting through the noise level."

"Word from the future," Renfrew said slowly. "They must know we set up this attempt to signal back to the 1950's. So they're trying to reach us, too. Makes sense, doesn't it?"

"Trouble is," Markham said, "can *you* transmit through that noise?"

Renfrew thought a moment. "I don't believe so. This is the best equipment I could muster. I might be able to pick up a factor of two in sensitivity with a few modifications, but I doubt it. And there's no point in going to lower temperatures, if the noise level is this high."

Peterson held up the clipboard. "'AMSNU QUEALSEUD POH3E4C.' Gibberish."

"I was afraid of that, too," Markham said.

"What are you talking about?" Renfrew said sharply.

"All that background noise doesn't arise naturally, or at least, that's my guess. It's formed by overlaying a lot of different coherent signals, from many different sources. Every once in a while this particular space-time point we're at gets a burst of a coherent signal somewhat larger than the rest. That's what we've been decoding. But the noise level is so high, not much can get through before it's swallowed up again. Apparently focusing is difficult. If our technology is strained right now, I doubt we'll get very much more."

Renfrew began pacing back and forth with sudden energy. He waved at the laboratory technicians who had left their posts and gathered around the three men. "Keep an eye on," he called, and motioned them away. When he turned back, Peterson could see clearly the lines of fatigue in the man's face. "Look, if you're right, why are there so many signals coming in?"

"And why does this second message come out nonsense?" Peterson added.

Markham gestured at the oscilloscope screen. "Try another one, John. I'll bet you find that quite a few of the signals that get above noise level are incomprehensible."

Renfrew moved to the oscilloscope, and when he had a new trace, Peterson began copying it. Markham went on, "There's going to be gibberish simply because either the senders don't use Morse or the senders don't speak our language."

"You mean from the far future, then?" Peterson said.

"No, not necessarily. Though that's possible." Markham made a tent of his fingers and smiled into it in what was clearly his favorite academic gesture. "John, I know you've been busy with this experiment and haven't had time to keep up with theoretical developments. But the very existence of tachyons and the rest of the so-called 'new relativity' leads to far-reaching, almost incredible conclusions."

"I don't have time for much reading," Renfrew said with a note of dismissal.

"Leisure of the theory class," Markham said laconically. "Not that there are that many technical journals left—I've gotten most of this from Thorne's group at Cal Tech. The astrophysical data pretty well show now that there are quite a few 'nested universes' inside our own. They look like infrared emission readings to us. The light we are getting is from the era before the space-time geometry closed off in those areas."

"This one says 'DI4KLT O RYE3'—it appears you are right," Peterson said.

"Um. Well, perhaps. We should do quite a few more before we conclude anything," Renfrew conceded. "But what's this about astrophysics? I've not paid much attention to that. Those fellows seem to speculate in ideas like stockbrokers."

Markham smiled and nodded. "Granted, they often take a grain of truth and blow it up into a kind of intellectual puffed rice . . . but this time they may have a point. Charles Wickham sent me some calculations that look convincing. The reason it ties in with your work, John, is that tachyons are the only thing that can even theoretically escape from a closed space-time geometry."

"Why's that?" Peterson said.

"Well, they violate the tenets of the old relativity theory, Einstein's. That's a clue in itself. But let's not go into that. The only point I want to make is that we are getting tachyon noise. It's unlikely that natural effects will give much tachyon noise—Christ, we're measuring a hundred times the expected value. I think we're getting the signals emitted by other civilizations, signals that have escaped from the nested universes inside our own."

"Well, I suppose that makes sense," Peterson said. "Other societies might try to use tachyons too. After all—and I still don't understand why faster-than-light particles can let you communicate back in time—"

"It's simple," Renfrew interjected, "comes right out of special relativity. The—"

"We'll skip it," Peterson said firmly. "Aliens sending tachyon signals makes sense, though I can't see that it's any use to us."

"Here's another," Renfrew said, handing a sheet to Peterson. "Decode it."

Peterson wrote for a moment and then read out, "'CE RN 4 KJ QOEC.'"

"At first I thought it might be something about CERN, the European nuclear agency," Markham said, "but the rest is just random."

Renfrew compressed his lips. There was a long silence. Between the magnet coils, the liquid nitrogen bath that immersed the nuclear sample gave off a pale fog. There came an occasional snap as ice formed on its jacket.

Abruptly Renfrew stood up. "Not much bloody chance of CERN being in the picture, is there?" He turned to Peterson. "Our brilliant crisis managers shut it down three years ago."

Peterson studied him coldly. "The fact remains, Dr. Renfrew, that you have failed to live up to your promises. You cannot contact the past."

Markham: "But look, all we have is an idea about why it doesn't work. We have to see if this is galactic-scale background. We can check again, see if there is some angular dependence to the incoming noise. It might be avoidable someway."

Peterson pointed at Renfrew. "You yourself said you couldn't improve sensitivity much more."

"I can't, but—"

"The Emergency Council hasn't got funds or time for pursuing your hobbies. There's no point in studying theoretical questions like this tachyon business if we're all heading slam-bang for the rapids ahead," Peterson said.

Renfrew had begun pacing again, but he suddenly turned on Peterson and said savagely, "Yes, no use at all, is it? Research is nothing to you buggering power-mad bastards. Climbing all over each other to direct the latest disaster."

Markham raised his hand and began, "Now, John—"

"Sure enough, we're headed for the rapids, but if so, what's the point of everybody trying to pilot the boat, eh? That doesn't stop you council sons-of-bitches from—"

Peterson sprang to his feet. "From trying to stop runaway technology, yes!"

"That's all your type thinks about, isn't it? Bad technology got you into this, so you're going to get out using solely your wits, is it? Only the Americans can get us out of this bloody mare's nest now. Only they've kept up any kind of respectable science and engineering. . . ."

The cold seeps into his bones. José Basquan sits on the doorstep of his house and watches the cobblestoned streets. He has been waiting for two days. They have all been waiting, the entire village, for the promised truckload of food from the government regional storehouse. The truck is late. Some say it will not come.

The children in the streets do not play anymore. They stare dully ahead, unable to focus properly. Few people pass by his house. José watches a woman shuffle by, her belly distended. She is carrying a basket, but there is nothing in it. He has heard the tales of dysentery, the word of the radio about cholera. His fingers toy with the cut on his wrist. It has not closed completely, though it is three days old. José knows it will not heal unless he gets food. He should get up and search for something, but the villagers have already scavenged the countryside around. There is no place left to go. He sits and watches the street and waits for the truck.

(AP) United Airlines Flight 347, London to Washington, D.C., encountered turbulence on its approach to Dulles Airport and crashed in the early hours of the morning. The plane went down in a wooded area and burned upon impact. Witnesses said the plane appeared to explode as it struck the trees. Early reports mention no survivors. This latest in a series of airline disasters has . . .

Peterson awakes slowly. There is a murmur of movement around him, but he is lethargic, his limbs slack. He studies the latticework of glass and metal standing beside his bed for a long moment and then decides he must sit up and continue writing the telegram. He struggles up and finds his pen. He begins to write, but the noise in the ward is distracting. Patients lie on temporary pallets, some of them moaning and others staring unmoving at the ceiling. Peterson concludes that the food poisoning must be more widespread than he thought. The nurses move quickly through the ward, stepping primly over the patients in the aisles, and ignore the chorus of pleadings that come from all sides.

Peterson shuts the scene out of his mind. He continues writing.

. . . though I sent my report several days ago, I expected at that time that it would be considerably reinforced at the National Science Foundation by the in-person appearance of Dr. Markham. Only yesterday did I learn that he died when his return flight to Washington went down. Dr. Markham told me before he left that he thought the rash of airline crashes was not pure accident, that defective manufacturing in the airplanes themselves was responsible, and I fear that had I not urged him to go in person, he would not have flown at all. It was only because of Dr. Markham that I realized the potential significance of the Cavendish tachyon experiments. I have some personal difficulties with Dr. Renfrew, but I was persuaded by Dr. Markham to overlook these in the light of the gathering crisis.

I will not describe to you the chaos and near starvation that prevail all around me today. I imagine similar scenes must be going on in many other of the Western nations. I hesitate to think what the rest of the world is like.

I have telephoned my office to send you the copies of Dr. Markham's notes that I retained. As you study them, you will undoubtedly conclude that the entire matter of communicating with the 1950's or 1960's, which gives us enough lead time to measurably affect the present day, is technically very difficult. But if only a small bit of information can get through, we must make the effort.

The technical argument speaks for itself. I am unqualified to add anything further about that. But there is something about the Renfrew experiment that has only today occurred to me, and I feel I should bring it up.

We received a few scattered bits of signals that momentarily peaked above the tachyon noise level. It seems to me that the existence of these signals is in itself of momentous importance. They are evidence that someone in the future still speaks English and can send tachyon signals. We have no way of knowing how far in the future that time might be. A pessimist might say that the fact that people in the future want to communicate with us is in itself a bad sign. What disasters lie ahead, that others would reach back into the past and try to alter events?

I take the other view. That men can still send tachyon signals from the future is a sign that there are solutions to these crises. Our ecosystems may not be fatally unstable. Perhaps something can be done.

I urge immediate action on my report of . . .

Rain spattering in his face awakens him. The cold numbs his legs, but he is too weak to stand. There is no one in the street now, only a huddled form lying in a doorway down the hill. The form has not moved for a day now. José rests his head in his hands, rocking from side to side. He knows the truck is going to come. If he can sit here in the cold stone doorway long enough, the truck will come.

A brown organic bloom begins to spread off the coast of Spain. Fishermen report it, but at first their descriptions are not understood by local officials, and word does not reach the oceanographic community until the bloom is several hundred kilometers in diameter. A stench begins to rise from the sea. Fish are dying in unparalleled numbers; the bloom becomes redder as it spreads. Similarities to the South American bloom multiply. Biologists soon agree that the phenomena are related: Manodrin, a chlorinated hydrocarbon used in insecticides, has opened a new life niche among the microscopic algae. A new variety of diatom has evolved; it uses an enzyme that breaks down Manodrin. The diatom silica also excretes a breakdown product that interrupts transmission of nerve impulses in animals. Dendritic connections fail. In Lisbon birds fall from the sky and die within minutes. The beaches are dark with rotting sea life. The bloom spreads.

John Renfrew works late, alone, though he is weak from dysentery. Most of his technicians have not appeared for work since the breakdown of the food-supply network. It is rumored that many people are fleeing to the countryside. Every sound Renfrew makes echoes hollowly in the Cavendish. He is the only man left in the building. The heat was long ago turned off. Electrical power is low but still functioning. The campus itself seems nearly entirely abandoned; for the last few days he has seen only a few figures in the distance. The trains have stopped. He has not heard the distant rumble of an airplane for many days.

The tachyon noise level remains constant. Occasionally he can resolve a few brief snatches of coded signals, but never as much as a complete sentence. Most of the messages are clearly not Morse. Some are complex wave forms, others almost pure sine waves.

Nothing Renfrew can do reduces the noise level. He cannibalizes electronics gear from other untended experiments in the Cavendish, but there is little improvement. The dysentery becomes worse. He feels his brow and realizes he has a fever. He hears strange, distant sounds like voices, but when he goes to investigate, there is no one else in the building. There is only the gritty scraping of his own shoes on the stone floor.

He drinks great quantities of water, but nothing stops the dysentery. His throat burns. As he works, the laboratory shifts in and out of focus, as though under water.

He tries to think calmly and cleanly about what Markham said in the train station, about Kerr black holes and the riddle of cosmology. Even Einstein's theory carried acausal loops in it, Markham said, matter swallowed into the net of space-time and spitting out elsewhere in the differential geometry, elsewhen. Elsewhen. And now tachyons and worlds sliding into other worlds, G times n, tensor geometries folding inward, blindly, following the squiggles and jots of Riemann and Littenberg.

There is an ache behind his eyes. Renfrew shivers as the cold seeps into him. He reads the latest fragment. "ENZYME INHIBITED B." That is all.

He scans the other bits of signal, hoping for something that makes sense. They all mean something to someone, but who? Where? When? His apparatus opens up communication with all the rest of the universe, instantly. Men could talk to great cultures that span the stars. A telegram from Andromeda would take no longer than one from London. Even other, enclosed universes are accessible. There may be macrouniverses, larger than our own, all sending tachyon messages that leak out of the space-time curvature and sleet through this laboratory, through Renfrew, through everything.

He shakes his head. Incredible. Unless there is some unsuspected natural source of tachyons, the random yellow jitter on his oscilloscope is a wealth of information. But all the form and structure is eroded into noise by overlapping too many messages. Because everyone is talking at once, no one can hear.

But no, Renfrew thinks to himself, rocking back and forth to keep warm. No, they aren't all talking at once. All times are represented, all places, each split nanosecond, all things smeared together in a vast ocean of noise.

The universes are all connected, he sees, as behind him the pumps cough, the electronics gear gives an occasional *ping*. Tachyons of 10^{-13} centimeters size flash across whole universes, 10^{28} centimeters of cooling matter, in less time than Renfrew's eye takes to absorb a photon of the pale, watery light. The tachyons zip by, carrying word of alien thoughts. All size scales, all distances, are wound in upon each other. Singularities suck up the stuff of creation, event horizons ripple, worlds coil into worlds.

Renfrew shakes himself. Christ, the fever. It claws at him, runs glowing smoke fingers through his mind.

Again he tries his equipment. The oscilloscope gives a complex wave, but the decoding makes no sense. Perhaps there is no message, never was. Causality weighs its leadened hand on events. But where were cause and effect in such an infinite matrix of worlds? Where the past, which the future? No beginning or end, only an endless series of nested universes.

He smiles to himself with flinty irony. Attempting to sidestep causality, he is caught again in its snare. The grandfather paradox remains; an infinite series of grandfathers will live out their lives safe from Renfrew. The noise wins, the noise prevents his tinkering.

The only thing left was to forget the past, let it lie in musty pages, on gravestones. Renfrew sees he must turn to the future. There is someone up there, in the times ahead, still sending.

ENZYME INHIBITED B. Someone is calling.

Hello, 7:11 A.M., 1995. Hello. ENZYME INHIBITED B.

Whispers flit across the tachyon spectrum, embedding soft words of tomorrow in the cesium. Someone is there. Someone brings hope. The infinite goddamn universe has not beaten him yet.

The room is cold; Renfrew huddles by his instruments. He is trying a modification of the signal correlator when suddenly the lights flicker and wink out. All power is gone. Utter blackness rushes in.

Renfrew takes a long time to feel his way out of the basement laboratory and into sunlight. It is a bleak, gray morning, but he does not notice this; it is enough to see light at all. As he stands outside the Cavendish, he can hear no sound whatever from the entire town of Cambridge. The breeze carries a sour tang.

He feels a curious heady lightness. He does not know what lies ahead. Perhaps Peterson has gotten through to the Americans. If there is no causality, then nothing is known, the past and future are equal riddles. Renfrew takes a few hesitant steps across a geometrically flattened green and feels a surge of something he cannot name. He moves more firmly. With resolution, puffing slightly, he sets out to walk into the countryside.

Nested universes collapse inward on nested universes, onionskin within onionskin. They hum in the infrared. Tachyons sputter from their cores.

The galaxy is a swarm of colored dots, turning with majestic slowness in the great night.

The bloom laps at the Dover coast. Surf foams pink on the beaches.

Ian Peterson's cable reaches Washington.

Gregory Benford writes:

Theorem: Time travel is impossible.

Proof: If a time machine exists, it can be used to make paradoxes. Cause and effect will be reversed. This means logical contradictions can exist in the operating of the universe. This is unacceptable.

So goes the logic, and quite neat it is. I am a theoretical physicist, and the argument looks compelling to me. In fact, I wrote a paper on the subject in 1970, with David Book and William Newcomb.

In the late 1960's, much dust was being raised about a hypothetical particle, the tachyon, which could travel faster than light. Now, faster-than-light travel (FTL) is a mainstay of science fiction. One might think that a scientist who was also a writer of fiction would leap at the possibility of FTL. After all, tachyons seemed to promise a reasonable explanation for those galaxy-spanning ships so beloved in SF. But I didn't cheer the advent of tachyons; instead, I attacked it.

The reason lies in the theorem announced above. Einstein's Special Theory of Relativity can be used to show that if FTL particles exist, they can be employed in a transmitter; and the signals emitted by this tachyonic telephone could be sent back in time. So FTL implies time travel, paradoxes, and all the elaborate games that SF writers have played with the idea since H. G. Wells.

David Book, William Newcomb, and I worked out a simple proof based on Einstein's theory, especially designed to overcome an argument that certain particle theorists had constructed. These theorists wanted to avoid the time-paradox problem, and thought they had. Book, Newcomb, and I showed that if tachyons could be detected in an experiment at all, they implied communication through time. And if somehow tachyons couldn't be detected, but existed anyway . . . what was the use of doing experiments to find them?

Since those days, tachyons have fared rather badly. The experiments designed to detect them failed to find anything, and despite a spate of tachyon theories, no one has gotten around the time-paradox problem.

But still . . . sometimes I wonder. Suppose time paradoxes are not totally disallowed in our universe, but are merely highly unusual? In a certain sense, paradoxical events can occur within the boundaries of the General Theory of Relativity. In the last few years we've gotten quite accustomed to black holes and white holes, places where matter may "tunnel through" space itself, to reappear in distant galaxies.

I don't think the tachyon ferment is totally resolved, and indeed it may never be. It's very difficult to show that something doesn't exist.

All these thoughts led me to think about the time-travel stories so beloved in SF, and whether they seemed probable. Even if time travel was possible, would it really come about that way? So I tried to deal with the problem in a fashion that felt right to me—that seemed dramatically interesting and had some reasonable scientific underpinning. (Not correct, just reasonable!) All time-travel stories are dreams, really, and this one is no different. If the real thing comes along someday, it will undoubtedly be unlike anything I've guessed . . . I hope.

RUN FROM THE FIRE

by Harry Harrison

1

"You can't go in there!" Heidi shrieked as the office door was suddenly thrown wide.

Mark Greenberg, deep in the tangled convolutions of a legal brief, looked up, startled at the interruption. His secretary came through the doorway, propelled by the two men who held her arms. Mark dropped the thick sheaf of papers, picked up the phone, and dialed the police.

"I want three minutes of your time," one of the men said, stepping forward. "Your girl would not let us in. It is important. I will pay. One hundred dollars a minute. Here is the money."

The bank notes were placed on the blotter, and the man stepped back. Mark finished dialing. The money was real enough. They released Heidi, who pushed their hands away. Beyond her was the empty outer office; there were no witnesses to the sudden intruders. The phone rang in his ears; then a deep voice spoke.

"Police Department, Sergeant Vega."

Mark hung up the phone.

"Things have been very quiet around here. You have three minutes. There will also be a hundred-dollar fee for molesting my secretary."

If he had meant it as a joke, it was not taken that way. The man who had paid the money took another bill from the pocket of his dark suit and handed it to a startled Heidi, then waited in silence until she took it and left. They were a strange pair, Mark realized. The paymaster was draped in a rusty black suit, had a black patch over his right eye, and wore black gloves as well. A victim of some accident or other, for his face and neck were scarred, and one ear was missing. When he turned back, Mark realized that his hair was really a badly fitting wig. The remaining eye, lashless and browless, glared at him redly from its deepset socket. Mark glanced away from the burning stare to look at the other man, who seemed commonplace in every way. His skin had a shiny, waxy look; other than that and his unusual rigidity, he seemed normal enough.

"My name is Arinix, your name is Mark Greenberg." The scarred man bent over the card in his hand, reading quickly in a hoarse, emotionless voice. "You served in the United States Army as a captain in the adjutant general's office and as a military police officer. Is that correct?"

"Yes, but—"

The voice ground on, ignoring his interruption. "You were born in the state of Alabama and grew up in the city of Oneida, New York. You speak the language of the Iroquois, but you are not an Indian. Is that true?"

"It's pretty obvious. Is there any point to this questioning?"

"Yes. I paid for it. How is it that you speak this language?" He peered closely at the card as though looking for an answer that was not there.

"Simple enough. My father's store was right next to the Oneida reservation. Most of his customers were Indians, and I went to school with them. We were the only Jewish family in town, and they didn't seem to mind this, the way our Polish Catholic neighbors did. So we were friends; in minorities, there is strength, you might say—"

"That is enough."

Arinix drew some crumpled bills from his side pocket, looked at them, and shoved them back. "Money," he said, turning to his silent companion. This man had a curious lizardlike quality for only his arm moved; the rest of his body was still, and his face fixed and expressionless, as he took a thick bundle of bills from his side pocket and handed it over.

Arinix looked at it, top and bottom, then dropped it onto the desk.

"There is ten thousand dollars here. This is a fee for three days' work. I wish you to aid me. You will have to speak the Iroquois language. I can tell you no more."

"I'm afraid you will have to, Mr. Arinix. Or don't bother, it is the same to me. I am involved in a number of cases at the moment, and it would be difficult to take off the time. The offer is interesting, but I might lose that much in missed fees. Since your three minutes are up, I suggest you leave."

"Money," Arinix said again, receiving more and more bundles

from his assistant, dropping them on Mark's desk. "Fifty thousand dollars. Good pay for three days. Now, come with us."

It was the man's calm arrogance that angered Mark, the complete lack of emotion, or even interest, in the large sums he was passing over.

"That's enough. Do you think money can buy everything?"

"Yes."

The answer was so sudden and humorless that Mark had to smile. "Well, you probably are right. If you keep raising the ante long enough, I suppose you will eventually reach a point where you can get anyone to listen. Would you pay me more than this?"

"Yes. How much?"

"You have enough here. Maybe I'm afraid to find out how high you will go. For a figure like this, I can take off three days. But you will have to tell me what is going to happen." Mark was intrigued, as much by the strange pair as by the money they offered.

"That is impossible. But I can tell you that within two hours you will know what you are to do. At that time you may refuse, and you will still keep the money. Is it agreed?"

A lawyer who is a bachelor tends to take on more cases than do his married associates—who like to see their families once in a while. Mark had a lot of work and a lot of money, far more than he had time to spend. It was the novelty of this encounter, not the unusual fee, that attracted him. And the memory of a solid two years of work without a single vacation. The combination proved irresistible.

"Agreed. . . . Heidi," he called out, then handed her the money when she came into the office. "Deposit this in the number-two special account and then go home. A paid holiday. I'll see you on Monday."

She looked down at the thick bundle of bills, then up at the strangers as they waited while Mark took his overcoat from the closet. The three of them left together, and the door closed. That was the last time that she or anyone else ever saw Mark Greenberg.

2

It was a sunny January day, but an arctic wind that cut to the bone was blowing up from the direction of the Battery. As they walked west, it caught them at every cross street, wailing around the building corners. Although they wore only suit jackets, neither of the strange men seemed to notice it. Nor were they much on conversation. In cold and silent discomfort they walked west, a few blocks short of the river, where they entered an old warehouse building. The street door was unlocked, but Arinix now secured it behind them with a heavy bolt, then turned to the inner door at the end of the hall. It appeared to be made of thick steel plates riveted together like a ship's hull, and had a lock in each corner. Arinix took an unusual key from his pocket. It was made of dull, ridged metal, as thick as his finger and as long as a pencil. He inserted this in each of the four locks, giving it a sharp twist each time before removing it. When he was done, he stepped away, and his companion put his shoulder against the door and pushed hard. After a moment it slowly gave way and reluctantly swung open. Arinix waved Mark on, and he followed them into the room beyond.

It was completely commonplace. Walls, ceilings, and floor were painted the same drab tone of brown. Lighting came from a translucent strip in the ceiling; a metal bench was fixed to the far wall next to another door.

"Wait here," Arinix said, then went out through the door.

The other man was a silent, unmoving presence. Mark looked at the bench, wondering if he should sit down, wondering too if he had been wise to get involved in this, when the door opened and Arinix returned.

"Here is what you must do," he said. "You will go out of here and will note this address, and then walk about the city. Return here at the end of an hour."

"No special place to go, nothing to do? Just walk around?"

"That is correct."

He pulled the heavy outer door open as he spoke, then led the way through it, down the three steps, and back along the hall. Mark followed him, then wheeled about and pointed back.

"Those steps! They weren't there when we came in—no steps, I'll swear to it."

"One hour, no more. I will hold your topcoat here until you return."

Warm air rushed in, bright sunlight burned on the stained sidewalk outside. The wind still blew, though not as strongly, but now it was as hot as from an oven door. Mark hesitated on the doorstep, sweat already on his face, taking off the heavy coat.

"I don't understand. You must tell me what—"

Arinix took the coat, then pushed him suddenly in the back. He stumbled forward, gained his balance instantly, and turned just as the door slammed shut and the bolt ground into place. He pushed, but it did not move. He knew that calling out would be a waste of time. Instead, he turned, eyes slitted against the glare, and stared out at the suddenly changed world.

The street was empty, no cars passed, no pedestrians were on the sidewalk. When he stepped out of the shadowed doorway, the sun smote him like a golden fist. He took his jacket off and hung it over his arm, and then his necktie, but he still ran with sweat. The office buildings stared blank-eyed from their tiered windows; the gray factories were silent. Mark looked about numbly, trying to understand what had happened, trying to make sense of the unbelievable situation. Five minutes ago it had been midwinter, with the icy streets filled with hurrying people. Now it was . . . what?

In the distance the humming, rising drone of an engine could be heard, getting louder, going along a nearby street. He hurried to the corner and reached it just in time to see the car roar across the intersection a block away. It was just that, a car, and it had been going too fast for him to see who was in it. He jumped back at a sudden shrill scream, almost at his feet, and a large seagull hurled itself into the air and flapped away. It had been tearing at a man's body that lay crumpled in the gutter. Mark had seen enough corpses in Korea to recognize another one, to remember the never-forgotten smell of corrupted flesh. How was it possible for the corpse to remain here so long, days at least? What had happened to the city?

There was a growing knot of unreasoned panic rising within him, urging him to run, scream, escape. He fought it down and turned deliberately and started back toward the room where Arinix was waiting. He would spend the rest of the hour waiting for that door to open, hoping he would have the control to prevent himself from beating upon it. Something had happened, to him or the world, he did not know which, but he did know that the only hope of salvation from the incredible events of the morning lay beyond that door. Screaming unreason wanted him to run; he walked slowly, noticing for the first time that the street he was walking down ended in the water. The buildings on each side sank into it as well, and there, at the foot of the street, was the roof of a drowned wharf. All this seemed no more incredible than anything that had happened before, and he tried to ignore it. He fought so hard to close his mind and his thoughts that he did not hear the rumble of the truck motor or the squeal of brakes behind him.

"That man! What are you doing here?"

Mark spun about. A dusty, open-bodied truck had stopped at the curb, and a thin blond soldier was swinging down from the cab. He wore a khaki uniform without identifying marks and kept his hand near the large pistol in a polished leather holster that swung from his belt. The driver was watching him, as were three more uniformed men in the back of the truck, who were pointing heavy rifles in his direction. The driver and the soldiers were all black. The blond officer had drawn his pistol and was pointing it at Mark as well.

"Are you with the westenders? You know what happens to them, don't you?"

Sudden loud firing boomed in the street, and thinking he was being shot at, Mark dropped back against the wall. But no shots were aimed in his direction. Even as they were turning, the soldiers in the truck dropped, felled by the bullets. Then the truck itself leaped and burst into flames as a grenade exploded. The officer had wheeled about and dropped to one knee and was firing his pistol at Arinix who was sheltered in a doorway across the street, changing clips on the submachine gun he carried.

Running footsteps sounded, and the officer wheeled to face Arinix's companion, who was running rapidly toward him, empty-handed and cold-faced.

"Watch out!" Mark called as the officer fired.

The bullet caught the running man in the chest, spinning him about. He tottered but did not fall, then came on again. The second shot was to his head, but before the officer could fire again, Mark had jumped forward and chopped him across the wrist with the edge of his hand, so that the gun jumped from his fingers.

"*Varken hond!*" the man cried, and swung his good fist toward Mark.

Before it could connect, the runner was upon him, hurling him to the ground, kicking him in the head, again and again, with a heavy boot. Mark pulled at the attacker's arm, so that he lost balance and had to stagger back, turning about. The bullet had caught him full in the forehead, leaving a neat, dark hole. There was no blood. He looked stolidly at Mark, his features expressionless, his skin smooth and shiny.

"We must return quickly," Arinix said as he came up. He lowered the muzzle of the machine gun and would have shot the unconscious officer if Mark hadn't pushed the barrel aside.

"You can't kill him, not like that."

"I can. He is dead already."

"Explain that." He held firmly to the barrel. "That and a lot more."

They struggled in silence for a second, until they were aware of an engine in the distance getting louder and closer. Arinix turned away from the man on the sidewalk and started back down the street. "He called for help on the radio. We must be gone before they arrive."

Gratefully Mark hurried after the other two, happy to run now, run to the door to escape this madness.

3

"A drink of water," Arinix said. Mark dropped onto the metal bench in the brown room and nodded, too exhausted to talk. Arinix had a tray with glasses of water, and he passed one to Mark, who drained it and took a second one. The air was cool here, feeling frigid after the street outside, and with the water, he was soon feeling better. More relaxed, at ease, almost ready to fall asleep. As his chin touched his chest, he jerked awake and jumped to his feet.

"You drugged the water," he said.

"Not a strong drug. Just something to relax you, to remove the tension. You will be better in a moment. You have been through an ordeal."

"I have . . . and you are going to explain it!"

"In a moment."

"No, now!"

Mark wanted to jump to his feet, to take this strange man by the throat, to shake the truth from him. But he did nothing. The desire was there, but only in an abstract way. It did not seem important enough to pursue such an energetic chain of events. For the first time he noticed that Arinix had lost his hairpiece during the recent engagement. He was as hairless as an egg, and the same scars that crisscrossed his face also extended over his bare skull. Even this did not seem important enough to comment upon. Awareness struck through.

"Your drug seems to be working."

"The effect is almost instantaneous."

"Where are we?"

"In New York City."

"Yes, I know, but so changed. The water in the streets, those soldiers, and the heat. It can't be January—have we traveled in time?"

"No, it is still January, the same day, month, year it has always been. That cannot be changed, that is immutable."

"But something *isn't;* something has changed. What is it?"

"You have a very quick mind, you make correct conclusions. You must therefore free this quick mind of all theories of the nature of reality and of existence. There is no heaven, there is no hell, the past is gone forever, the unstoppable future sweeps toward us endlessly. We are fixed forever in the now, the inescapable present of our world line. . . ."

"What is a world line?"

"See . . . the drug relaxes, but your brain is still lawyer-sharp. You live in a particular present because of what happened in the past. Columbus discovered America, the armies of the North won the Civil War, Einstein stated that $E=MC^2$."

He stopped abruptly, and Mark waited for him to go on, but he did not. Why? Because he was waiting for Mark to finish for him. Mark nodded.

"What you are waiting for is for me to ask if there is a world line where Columbus died in infancy, where the South won, and so forth. Is that what you mean?"

"I do. Now, carry the analogy forward."

"If two or three world lines exist, why, more, any number, an infinity of world lines can exist. Infinitely different, eternally separate." Then he was on his feet, shaking despite the drug. "But they are not separate. We are in a different one right now. There is a different world line beyond that door, down those steps—because the ground here is at a different height. Is that true?"

"Yes."

"But why, how . . . I mean, what is going on out there, what terrible thing is happening?"

"The sun is in the early stages of a change. It is getting warmer, giving out more radiation, and the polar ice caps are beginning to melt. The sea level has risen, drowning the lowest parts of the city. This is midwinter, and you saw how warm it is out there. You can imagine what the tropics are like. There has been a breakdown in government as people fled the drowning shorelines. Others have taken advantage of it. The Union of South Africa has capitalized on the deteriorating conditions, and using mercenary troops, has invaded the North American continent. They met little resistance."

"I don't understand—or rather, I do understand what is happening out there, and I believe you, because I saw it for myself. But what can I do about it? Why did you bring me here?"

"You can do nothing about it. I brought you here because we have discovered by experience that the quickest way that someone can be convinced of the multiplicity of worldliness is by bringing them physically to a different world line."

"It is also the best—and quickest—way to discover if they can accept this fact and not break down before this new awareness."

"You have divined the truth. We are, unfortunately, short of time, so wish to determine as soon as possible if recruits will be able to work with us."

"Who is *we?*"

"In a moment I will tell you. First, do you accept the idea of the multiplicity of world lines?"

"I'm afraid I must. Outside is an inescapable fact. That is not a stage constructed to confuse me. Those dead men are dead forever. How many world lines are there?"

"An infinite number; it is impossible to know. Some differ greatly, some so slightly that it is impossible to mark the difference. Imagine them, if you will, as close together as cards in a pack. If two-dimensional creatures, clubs and hearts, lived on each card, they would be unaware of the other cards and just as unable to reach them. Continue the analogy, drive a nail through all of the cards. Now the other cards can be reached. My people, the 'we' you asked about, are the ones who can do that. We have reached many world lines. Some we cannot reach—some we dare not reach."

"Why?"

"You ask why—after what you saw out there?" For the first time since they had met, Arinix lost his cold detachment. His single eye blazed with fury, and his fists were clenched as he paced the floor. "You saw the filthy things that happen, the death that comes before the absolute death. You see me, and I am typical of my people, maimed, killed, and scarred by a swollen sun that produces more and more hard radiation every year. We escaped our world line, seeking salvation in other world lines, only to discover the awful and ultimate secret. The rot is beginning, going faster and faster all the time. You saw what the world is like beyond that door. Do you understand what I am saying, do the words make any sense to you?

"The sun is going nova. It is the end."

4

"Water," Arinix called out hoarsely, slumping onto the metal bench, his single eye closed now. The inner door opened, and his companion appeared with a pitcher and refilled the glasses. He moved as smoothly as before and seemed ignorant of the black hole in his forehead.

"He is a Sixim," Arinix said, seeing the direction of Mark's gaze. He drank the water so greedily that it ran down his chin. "They are our helpers; we could not do without them. Not our invention. We borrow what we need. They are machines, fabrications of plastic and metal, though there is artificial flesh of some kind involved in their construction. I do not know the details. Their controlling apparatus is somewhere in the armored chest cavity; they are quite invulnerable."

Mark had to ask the question.

"The sun is going nova, you said. Everywhere, in every time line— in *my* time line?"

Arinix shook his head a weary no. "Not in every line; that is our only salvation. But in too many of them—and the pace is accelerating steadily. Your line—no, not as far as we know. The solar spectrum does not show the characteristic changes. Your line has enough problems as it is, and is one we use for much-needed supplies. There are few of us, always too few, and so much to be done. We must save whom we can and what we can, do it without telling why or how we operate. It is a great work that does not end, and is a most tiring one. But my people are driven, driven insane with hatred, at times, of that bloated, evil thing in the sky. We have survived for centuries in spite of it, maimed and mutated by the radiation it pours out. It was due to a successful mutation that we escaped even as we have, a man of genius who discovered the door between the world lines. But the unsuccessful outnumber a million to one the successful in mutations, and I will not attempt to describe the suffering in my world. You may think me maimed, but I am one of the lucky ones. We have escaped our world line but found the enemy waiting everywhere. We have tried to fight back. We started less than two hundred years ago, and our enemy started millions of years before us. From it we have learned to be ruthless in the war, and we will go on fighting it until we have done everything possible."

"You want me to do something in that world outside the door?"

"No, not there; they are dead. The destruction is too advanced.

We can only watch. Closer to the end, we will save what art we can. Things have been noted. We know a culture by its art, don't we? We know a world that way as well. So many gone without record, so much to do."

He drank greedily at the water, slobbering. Perhaps he was mad, Mark thought, partly mad, at least. Hating the sun, trying to fight it, fighting an endlessly losing battle. But . . . wasn't it worth it? If lives, people, could be saved, wasn't that worth any price, any sacrifice? In his world line, men worked to save endangered species. Arinix and his people worked to save another species—their own.

"What can I do to help?" Mark asked.

"You must find out what happened to our field agent in one of our biggest operations. He is from your world line, the one we call Einstein because it is one of the very few where atomic energy has been released. He is now on Iroquois, which will begin going nova within the century. It is a strange line, with little technology and retarded by monolithic religions. Europe still lives in the dark ages. The Indians rule in North America, and the Six Nations are the most powerful of all. They are a brave and resourceful people, and we had hoped to use them to settle a desert world—we know of many of those. Imagine, if you can, the Earth where life never began, where the seas are empty, the land a desert of sand and rock. We have seeded many of them, and that is wonder to behold, with animal and plant life. Simple enough to introduce seeds of all kinds, and later, when they have been established, to transfer animals there. Mankind is not as easy to transfer. We had great hopes with the Iroquois, but our agent has been reported missing. I have taken time from my own projects to correct the matter. We used War Department records to find you."

"Who was your agent?"

"A man named Joseph Wing, a Mohawk, a steel worker here in the city in your own line."

"There has always been bad feeling between the Mohawk and other tribes of the nations."

"We know nothing about that. I will try to find his reports, if any, if that will be of any assistance. The important thing is—will you help us? If you wish more money, you can have all you need. We have an endless supply. There is little geologic difference between many worlds. So we simply record where important minerals are on one world, things such as diamonds and gold, and see that that is mined on another. It is very easy."

Mark was beginning to have some idea of the immensity of the operation these people were engaged in. "Yes, I'll help, I'll do what I can."

"Good. We leave at once. Stay where you are. We go now to a world line that is called Home by some, Hatred by others."

"Your own?"

"Yes. You will perhaps understand a bit more what drives us. All of our geographical transportation is done on Hatred, for all of the original transit stations were set up there. Also, that is all it is really good for." He spat the words from his mouth as though they tasted bad.

Again there was no sensation, no awareness of change. Arinix left the room, returned a few seconds later.

"You wouldn't like to show me how you did that?" Mark asked.

"I would not. It is forbidden, unthinkable. It would be death for you to go through that door. The means of transit between the world lines is one we must keep secret from all other than ourselves. We may be partially or completely insane, but our hatred is of that thing that hangs in the sky above us. We favor no group, no race, no people, no species above the others. But think what would happen if one of your nationalistic or religious groups gained control of the means to move between world lines, think of the destruction that might follow."

"I grasp your meaning but do not agree completely."

"I do not ask you to. All else is open to you; we have no secrets. Only that room is forbidden. Come."

He opened the outer door, and Mark followed him through.

5

They were inside a cavernous building of some kind. Harsh lights high above sent long shadows from great stacks of containers and boxes. They stepped aside as a rolling platform approached laden with shining cylinders. It was driven by a Sixim, who was identical, other than the hole in the forehead, to the one with them. The door they had just closed behind them opened, and two more Sixim came out and began to carry the cylinders back into the room.

"This way," Arinix said, and led the way through the high stacks to a room where bales of clothing lay heaped on tables. "Go on to repair," he ordered the damaged Sixim that still followed them, then pointed at the gray clothing.

"These are radiation-resistant. We will change."

As bereft of shame as of any other emotion, Arinix stripped off his clothing and pulled on one of the coverall-type outfits. Mark did the same. It was soft but thick and sealed up high on the neck with what appeared to be a magnetic closure. There were heavy boots in an assortment of sizes, and he soon found a pair that fitted. While he did this, Arinix was making a call on a very ordinary-looking phone that was prominently stamped "Western Electric"—they would be surprised if they knew where their apparatus was being used—speaking a language rich in guttural sounds. They left the room by a different exit, into a wide corridor, where transportation was waiting for them. It was a vehicle the size of a large truck, a teardrop shape riding on six large, heavily tired wheels. It was made of metal the same color as their clothing, and appeared to have no windows. However, when they went inside, Mark saw that the solid nose was either transparent or composed of a large viewscreen of some kind. A single driver's seat faced the controls, and a curved, padded bench was fixed to the other three walls. They sat down, Arinix at the controls, and the machine started. There was no vibration or sound of any exhaust; it just surged forward silently at his touch.

"Electric power?" Mark asked.

"I have no idea. The cars run when needed."

Mark admired his singleness of purpose but did not envy him. There was only one thing in the man's life—to run from the solar fire and save what possibly could be saved from the flame. Were all of his people like this?

Strong headlights glared on as they left the corridor and entered what appeared to be a tunnel mouth. The walls were rough and unfinished; only the roadway beneath was smooth, dropping away at a steep angle.

"Where are we going?" Mark asked.

"Under the river, so we can drive on the surface. The island above us—what is the name Einstein—?"

"Manhattan."

"Yes, Manhattan. It is covered by the sea now, which rises almost to the top of the cliffs across the river from it. The polar caps melted many years ago here. Life is very harsh, you will see."

The tunnel ahead curved to the right and began to rise sharply. Arinix slowed the vehicle and stopped when a brilliant disk of light became visible ahead. He worked a control, and the scene darkened as though a filter had been slipped into place. Then, with the headlights switched off, he moved forward until the light could be seen as the glaring tunnel mouth, growing larger and brighter, until they were through it and back on the surface once more.

Mark could not look at the sun, or even in its direction, despite the protective filter. It burned like the open mouth of a celestial furnace, spewing out light and heat and radiation onto the world below. Here the plants grew, the only living creatures that could bear the torrent of fire from the sky, that welcomed it. Green on all sides, a jungle of growing, thriving, rising, reaching plants and trees, burgeoning under the caress of the exploding star. The road was the only visible man-made artifact, cutting a wide, straight slash through the wilderness of plant life, straining life that leaned over, grew to its very edge, and sent tendrils and runners across its barren surface. Arinix threw more switches, then rose from the driver's seat.

"It is on automatic control now. We may rest."

He grabbed for support as the car slowed suddenly; ahead, a great tree had crashed across the road, almost blocking it completely. There was a rattle of machinery from the front of the car, and a glow sprang out that rivaled the glare of the sun above. Then they moved again, slowly, and greasy smoke billowed up and was blown away.

"The machine will follow the road and clear it when it must," Arinix said. "A device, a heat generator of some sort, will burn away obstructions. I am told it is a variant of the machine that melted the soil and rock to form this road, a principle discovered while observing the repulsive sun that has caused this all, making heat in the same manner the sun makes heat. We will turn its own strengths back upon it."

He went to the seat in the rear, stretched out on it with his face to the cushions, and appeared to fall instantly asleep. Mark sat in the driver's chair, careful to touch nothing, both fascinated and repelled by the world outside. The car continued unerringly down the center of the road at a high speed, slowing only when it had to burn away obstructions. It must have utilized radar or other sensing devices, for a sudden heavy rainstorm did not reduce its speed in the slightest. Visibility was only a few feet in the intense tropical downpour, yet the car moved on, speed unabated. It did slow, but only to burn away obstructions, and smoke and steam obscured all vision. Then the storm stopped, as quickly as it began. Mark watched until he began to yawn, so then, like Arinix, he tried to rest. At first he thought he could not possibly sleep, then realized he had. Darkness had fallen outside, and the car still hurried silently through the night.

It was just before dawn when they reached their destination.

The building was as big as a fortress, which it resembled in more ways than one. Its walls were high and dark, featureless, streaked with rain. Harsh lights on all sides lit the ground, which was nothing more than sodden ash. Apparently all plant life was burned before it could reach the building and undermine it. The road led directly to a high door that slid open automatically as they approached. Arinix stopped the vehicle a few hundred yards short of the entrance and rose from the controls.

"Come with me. This machine will enter by itself, but we shall walk. There is no solar radiation now, so you may see my world and know what is in store for all the others."

They stepped out into the damp airlessness of the night. The car pulled away from them, and they were alone. Rivulets of wet ash streaked the road, disappearing in runnels at either side where the waiting plant life leaned close. The air was hot, muggy, hard to breathe, seemingly giving no substance to the lungs. Mark gasped and breathed deeply over and over again.

"Remember," Arinix said, turning away and starting for the entrance, "this is night, midwinter, before dawn, the coolest it will ever be here. Do not come in the summer."

Mark went after him, aware that he was already soaked with sweat, feeling the strength of the enemy in the sky above, which was already touching fire to the eastern horizon. Though he panted with the effort, he ran and staggered into the building and watched as the door ground shut behind him.

"Your work now begins," Arinix said, leading the way into a now familiar brown room. Mark got his breath back and wiped his streaming face while they made their swift journey to the world line named Iroquois.

"I will leave you here and will return in twenty-four hours for your report on the situation. We will then decide what must be done." Arinix opened the outer door and pointed.

"Just a minute—I don't know anything that is happening here. You will have to brief me."

"I know nothing of this operation, other than what I have told you. The Sixim there should have complete records and will tell you what you need to know. Now, leave. I have my own work to do."

There was no point in arguing. Arinix gestured again impatiently, and Mark went through the door, which closed with a ponderous thud behind him. He was in darkness, cold darkness, and he shivered uncontrollably after the heat of the world he had just left.

"Sixim, are you there? Can you turn on some lights?"

There was the sudden flare of a match in answer, and in its light he could see an Indian lighting an ordinary kerosene lamp. He wore thong-wrapped fur leggings and a fringed deerskin jacket. Though his skin was dark, his features were Indo-European; once the lamp was lit, he stood by it, unmoving.

"You are the Sixim," Mark said.

"I am."

"What are you doing here?"

"Awaiting instructions."

These creatures were as literal-minded as computers—which is probably what their brains were. Mark realized he had to be more specific with his questions, but his teeth were chattering with cold, and he was shivering hard, which made it difficult to think.

"How long have you been waiting?"

"Twelve days, fourteen hours, and—"

"That's precise enough. You have just been sitting here in the dark without heat all that time! Do you have a way of heating this place?"

"Yes."

"Then do it, and quickly . . . and let me have something to wrap around me before I freeze."

The buffalo-skin robe made a big difference, and while the Sixim lit a fire in a large stone fireplace, Mark looked around at the large room. The walls were of logs, with the bark still on, and the floor bare wide boards. Crates were piled at one end of the room, and a small mound of skins was at the other. Around the fire, it was more domestic, with a table and chairs, cooking pots, and cabinets. Mark pulled a wooden chair close and raised his hands to the crackling blaze. Once the fire was started, the Sixim waited stolidly again for more orders.

By patient questioning Mark extracted all that the machine man seemed to know about the situation. The agent, Joseph Wing, had been staying here and going out to talk to the Oneida. The work he did was unknown to the Sixim. Wing had gone out and not returned. At the end of forty-eight hours, as instructed, the Sixim had reported him missing. How he had reported, he would not say; obviously there were questions it would not answer.

"You've been a help—but not very much," Mark said. "I'll just have to find out for myself what is going on out there. Did Joseph Wing leave any kind of papers, a diary, notes?"

"No."

"Thanks. Are there any weapons here?"

"In that box. Do you wish me to unlock it?"

"I do."

The weapons consisted of about twenty well-worn, obviously surplus M-1 rifles, along with some boxes of ammunition. Mark tried the bolt on one—it worked smoothly—then put the rifle back in the box.

"Lock it up. I'm not looking for trouble, and if I find it, a single gun won't make that much difference. But a peace offering might be in order, particularly food in the middle of winter."

He carried the lantern over to the boxes and quickly found exactly what he needed. A case of large smoked hams. Picking one out, he held the label to the light. "Smithfield Ham," it read, "packed in New Chicago, weight 6.78 kilos." Not from his world line, obviously, but that didn't matter in the slightest.

And he would need warmer clothes, clothes that would be more acceptable here than gray coveralls. There were leggings and jackets —obviously used, from their smell—that would do nicely. He changed quickly in front of the fire, then, knowing it would be harder the longer he waited, tucked the ham under his arm and went to the door and pulled back on the large wooden bolt.

"Lock this behind me, and unlock it only for me."

"Yes."

The door opened onto an unmarked field of snow with a stand of green pines and taller bare-limbed oak trees beyond. Above, in the blue arch of the sky, a small and reasonable winter sun shed more light than heat. There was a path through the trees, and beyond them a thin trickle of smoke was dark against the sky. Mark went in that direction. When he reached the edge of the grove, a tall Indian stepped silently from behind a tree and blocked the path before him. He made no threatening moves, but the stone-headed club hung easily and ready from his hand. Mark stopped and looked at him, saying nothing, hoping he could remember Iroquois after all these years. It was the Indian who broke the silence and spoke first.

"I am called Great Hawk."

"I am called . . . Little-one-talks." He hadn't spoken that name in years; it was what the old men on the reservation called him when he first spoke their own language. Great Hawk seemed to be easier when he heard the words, for his club sank lower.

"I come in peace," Mark said, and held out the ham.

"Welcome in peace," Great Hawk said, tucking the club into his waist and taking the ham. He sniffed at it appreciatively.

"Have you seen the one named Joseph Wing?" Mark asked.

The ham dropped, half-burying itself silently in the snow; the club was clutched at the ready.

"Are you a friend of his?" Great Hawk asked.

"I have never met him. But I was told I would see him here."

Great Hawk considered this in silence for a long time, looked up as a blue jay flapped by overhead, calling out hoarsely, then examined with apparent great attention the tracks of a rabbit in the snow—through all of this not taking his eyes from Mark for more than a second. Finally he spoke.

"Joseph Wing came here during the hunter's moon, before the first snow fell. Many said he had much orenda, for there were strange lights and sounds here during a night, and no one would leave the long house, and in the morning his long house stands as you see it now. There is great orenda here. Then he came and spoke to us and told us many things. He said he would show the warriors a place where there was good hunting. Hunting is bad here, for the people of the Six Nations are many, and some go hungry. He said all these things, and what he showed us made us believe him. Some of us said we would go with him, even though some thought they would never return. Some said that he was Tehoronhiawakhon, and he did not say it was not the truth. He said to my sister, Deer-runs, that he was indeed Tehoronhiawakhon. He told her to come with him to his long house. She did not want to go with him. By force he took her to his long house."

Great Hawk stopped talking abruptly and looked attentively at Mark through half-closed eyes. He did not finish, but the meaning was clear enough. The Oneida would have thought Joseph Wing possessed of much orenda after his sudden appearance, the principle of magic power that was inherent in every body or thing. Some had it more than others. A man who could build a building in a night must have great orenda. So much so that some would consider him to be Tehoronhiawakhon, the hero who watched over them, born of the gods, who lived as a man and who might return as a man. But no hero would take a maiden by force; the Indians were very practical on this point. Anyone who would do that would be killed by the girl's family; that was obvious. Her brother waited for Mark's answer.

"One who does that must die," Mark said. Defending the undoubtedly dead Joseph Wing would accomplish nothing; Mark was learning pragmatism from Arinix.

"He died. Come to the long house."

Great Hawk picked up the ham, turned his back, and led the way through the deep snow.

6

The Oneida warriors sat cross-legged around the fire while the women served them the thin gruel. Hunting must have been bad if this was all they had, for it was more water than anything else, with some pounded acorns and a few scraps of venison. After eating, they smoked, a rank leaf of some kind that was certainly not tobacco. Not until the ceremony was out of the way did they finally touch the topic that concerned them all.

"We have eaten elk," Great Hawk said, puffing at the pipe until his eyes grew red. "This is an elkskin robe I am wearing. They are large, and there is much meat upon them." He passed the pipe to Mark, then reached behind him under a tumbled hide and drew forth a bone. "This is the bone of the leg of an elk, brought to us by someone. We would eat well in winter with elk such as this to hunt."

Mark took it and looked at it as closely as he could in the dim light. It was a bone like any other, as far as he could tell, distinguished only by its great length—at least five feet from end to end. Comparing it with the length of his own femur, he could see that it came from a massive beast. Surely an elk or a cow would be smaller than this. What had this to do with the dead Joseph Wing? He must have brought it. But why, and where did he get it? If only there were some record of what he was supposed to be doing. Hunting, of course —that had to be it; food for these people who appeared too many for the limited hunting grounds. He held up the bone and spoke.

"Was it told to you that you would be able to hunt elk like this?"

There were nods and grunts in answer.

"What was told you?" After a silence, Great Hawk answered.

"Someone said that a hunting party could go to this land that was close by but far away. If hunting was good, a long house would be built for the others to follow. That was what was said."

It was simple enough. A hunting party taken to one of the seeded desert worlds, now stocked with game. If the trip was successful, the rest of the tribe would follow.

"I can also take you hunting in that land," Mark said.

"When will this be?"

"Come to me in the morning, and I will tell you."

He left before they could ask any more questions. The sun was low on the horizon, sending long purple shadows across the white snow. Backtracking was easy, and the solid log walls of the building a welcome sight. When he was identified, the Sixim let him in. The fire was built even higher now, and the large room was almost warmed up. Mark sat by the fire and stretched his hands to it gratefully; the Sixim was statuesque in the shadows.

"Joseph Wing was to take the Indians to another world line. Did you know that?"

"Yes."

"Why didn't you tell me?"

"You did not ask."

"I would appreciate it if you would volunteer more information in the future."

"Which information do you wish me to volunteer?"

The Sixim took a lot of getting used to. Mark took the lantern and rummaged through the variety of goods in the boxes and on the loaded shelves. There were ranked bottles of unfamiliar shape and labeling that contained some thing called *Kunbula Atashan* from someplace that appeared to be named Carthagio—it was hard to read the letters, so he could not be sure, but when he opened one of them, it had a definite odor of strong alcoholic beverage. The flavor was unusual but fortifying, and he poured a mugful before he returned to the fire.

"Do you know whom I must contact to make arrangements for the transfer to the other world line?"

"Yes."

"Who?"

"Me."

It was just that simple. The Sixim would give no details of the operation, but he would operate the mechanism to take them to the correct world and return.

"In the morning, first thing, we'll go have a look."

They left soon after dawn. Mark took one of the rifles and some extra clips of ammunition; that had been a big elk, and he might be lucky enough to bag another. Once more the sensationless transfer was made and the heavy outer door pushed open. For the first time there was no other room or hallway beyond it, just a field of yellowed grass. Mark was astonished.

"But . . . is it winter? Where is the snow?" Because it was phrased as a question, the Sixim answered him.

"It is winter. But here in Sandstone the climate is warmer, due to ocean-current differences."

Holding the rifle ready, Mark stepped through the door, which the Sixim closed behind him. Without being ordered, the Sixim locked the door with the long key. For the first time Mark saw the means of world-line transportation not concealed by an outer building. It was a large box, nothing more, constructed of riveted and rusty steel plates. Whatever apparatus powered it was inside, for it was completely featureless. He turned from it to look at the world named Sandstone.

The tall grass was everywhere; it must have been seeded first to stabilize the soil. It had done this, but it would take centuries to soften the bare rock contours of what had once been a worldwide desert. Harsh-edged crags pushed up in the distance where there should have been rounded hills; mounds of tumbled morain rose above the grass. Groves and patches of woods lay scattered about, while on one side a thick forest began and stretched away to the horizon. All of this had a very constructed air to it—and it obviously was. Mark recognized some of the trees; others were strange to him. This planet had been seeded in a hurry, and undoubtedly with a great variety of vegetation. As unusual as it looked now, this made ecological good sense, since complex ecological relationships increased the chance the ecosystem had of surviving. There would certainly be a variety of animal life as well—the large elk the Oneida knew about, and surely others as well. When he moved around the rusty building, he saw just what some of that life might be—and stopped still on the spot. No more than a few hundred yards away, there was a herd of elephants tearing at the leaves on the low trees. Large elephants with elegant swept-back tusks, thickly covered with hair.

"Hairy mammoth!" he said aloud, just as the nearest bull saw him appear and raised his trunk and screamed warning.

"That is correct," the Sixim said.

"Get your key, and let's get out of here," Mark said, backing quickly around the corner. "I don't think a thirty-caliber will make a dent in that thing."

With unhurried, steady motions the Sixim unlocked the door, one lock after another, while the thunder of pounding feet grew louder and closer. Then they were through the door and pushing it shut.

"I think the Oneida will enjoy the hunting," Mark said, grinning wryly, leaning against the thick wall with relief. "Let's go back and get them."

When he opened the outer wooden door in Iroquois, he saw Great

Hawk and five other warriors standing patiently in the snow outside. They were dressed warmly, had what must be provision bags slung at their waists, and were armed with long bows and arrows as well as stone clubs and stone skinning knives. They were prepared for a hunting expedition, they knew not where, but they were prepared. When Mark waved them forward, they came at once. The only sign of the tension they must be feeling was in their manner of walking, more like stalking a chase than entering a building. They showed little interest in the outer room—they must have been here before—but were eyeing the heavy metal door with more than casual interest. The deceased Joseph Wing must have told them something about it, but Mark had already decided to ignore this and tell the truth as clearly as they could understand it.

"Through that door is a long house that will bear us to the place where we will hunt. How it will take us there I do not know, for it is beyond my comprehension. But it will take us there as safely as a mother carries a papoose on her back, as safely as a bark canoe carries us over the waters. Are you ready to go?"

"Will you take the noise stick that kills?" Great Hawk asked, pointing with his thumb at the rifle Mark still carried.

"Yes."

"It was one time said that the Oneida would be given noise sticks and taught the manner of their use."

Why not, Mark thought, there were no rules to all this, anything went that would save these people. "Yes, you may have them now if you wish, but I think until you can use them well, your bows will be better weapons."

"That is true. We will have them when we return."

The Sixim pulled the heavy door open, and without being urged, the Indians filed into the brightly lit room beyond. They remained silent but held their weapons ready as the door was closed and the Sixim went through the door to the operating room, only to emerge a moment later.

"The journey is over," Mark said. "Now we hunt."

Only when the outer door was opened onto the grassy sunlit plain did they believe him. They grunted with surprise as they left, calling out in wonder at the strange sights and the warm temperature. Mark looked around nervously, but the herd of mammoth was gone. There were more than enough other things to capture the Indians' attention. They saw animals where he saw only grass and trees and called attention to them with pleased shouts. Yet they were silent instantly when Great Hawk raised his hand for silence, then pointed.

"There, under those trees. It looks like a large pig."

Mark could see nothing in the shadows, but the other Indians were apparently in agreement, for they were nocking arrows to their bows. When the dark, snuffling shape emerged into the sunlight, they were ready for it. A European boar, far larger than they had ever seen. The boar had never seen men before either; it was not afraid. The arrows whistled; more than one struck home, the boar wheeled about, squealing with pain, and crashed back into the undergrowth. Whooping with pleasure, the Oneida were instantly on its trail.

"Stay inside until we get back," Mark told the Sixim. "I want to be sure *we* can get back."

He ran swiftly after the others, who had already vanished under the trees. The trail was obvious, marked with the blood of the fleeing animal, well trampled by its pursuers. From ahead there came even louder squealing and shouts that ended in sudden silence. When Mark came up, it was all over; the boar was on its side, dead, its skull crushed in, while the victorious Indians prodded its flanks and hams happily.

The explosion shook the ground at that moment, a long, deep rumbling sound that hammered at their ears. It staggered them, it was so close and loud, frightening them because they did not know what it was. Mark did. He had heard this kind of noise before. He wheeled about and watched the large cloud of greasy black smoke roiling and spreading as it climbed up the sky. It rose from behind the trees in the direction of the building. Then he was running, slamming a cartridge in the chamber of the rifle at the same time, thumbing off the safety.

The scene was a disaster. He stumbled and almost fell as he emerged from beneath the trees.

Where the squat steel building had stood was now only a smoking, flame-licked ruin of torn and twisting plates. On the grass nearby, one leg ripped away and as torn himself, lay the Sixim.

The doorway between the worlds was closed.

7

Mark just stood there, motionless, even after the Indians came up and ranked themselves beside him, calling out in wonder at the devastation. They did not realize yet that they were exiled from their tribe and their own world. The Sixim raised its head and called out hoarsely; Mark ran to it. Much of its imitation flesh was gone, and metal shone through the gaps. Its face had suffered badly as well, but it could still talk.

"What happened?" Mark asked.

"There were strangers in the room, men with guns. This is not allowed. There are orders. I actuated the destruct mechanism and attempted to use the escape device."

Mark looked at the ruin and flames. "There is no way this room can be used again?"

"No."

"Are there other rooms on this world?"

"One that I know of, perhaps more. . . ."

"One is enough! Where is it?"

"What is the name of your world line?"

"What difference does that make? . . . All right, it's called Einstein."

"The room is located on an island that is named Manhattan."

"Of course! The original one I came through. But that must be at least two hundred miles away from here as the crow flies."

But what was two hundred miles as compared to the gap between the worlds? His boots were sound, he was a couple of pounds overweight, but otherwise in good condition. He had companions who were at home in the wilds and knew how to live off the land. If they would come with him . . . They had little other choice. If he could explain to them what had happened and what they must do . . .

It was not easy, but the existence of this world led them to believe anything he told them—if not believe it, at least not to doubt it too strongly. In the end they were almost eager to see what this new land had to offer, what other strange animals there were to hunt. While the others butchered and smoked the fresh-killed meat, Mark labored to explain to Great Hawk that they were physically at the same place in the world as the one they had left. The Indian worked hard to understand this but could not, since this was obviously a different place. Mark finally forced him to accept the fact on faith, to operate as if it were true even though he knew it wasn't.

When it came to finding the island of Manhattan, Great Hawk called a conference of all the Indians. They strolled over slowly, grease-smeared and happy, stomachs bulging with fresh meat. Mark could only listen as they explored the geography of New York State, as they knew it and as they had heard of it from others. In the end they agreed on the location of the island, at the mouth of the great river at the ocean nearby the long island. But they knew they could not get there from this place, then went back to their butchery. They fell asleep in the middle of this; it was late afternoon, so he gave up any hope of starting this day. He resigned himself to the delay and was eating some of the roasted meat himself when the Sixim appeared out of the forest. It had shaped a rough crutch from a branch, which it held under its arm as it walked. Arinix had said the creatures were almost indestructible, and it appeared he was right.

Mark questioned the Sixim, but it did not know how to get to Manhattan, nor did it have any knowledge of the geography of this world. When the sun set, Mark stretched out by the fire with the others and slept just as soundly as they did. He was up at first light, and as the sun rose in the east, he squinted at it and realized what he had to do. He would have to lead them out of here. He shook Great Hawk awake.

"We walk east toward the sun," he said. "When we reach the great river, we turn and follow it downstream to the south. Can we do that?" If there were a Hudson River on this world . . . and if the Indians would follow him . . . Great Hawk looked at him solemnly for a long moment, then sat up.

"We leave now." He whistled shrilly, and the others stirred.

The Indians enjoyed the outing very much, chattering about the sights along the way and looking with amazement at what was obviously a happy hunting ground. Game was everywhere—creatures they knew and others that were completely strange. There was a herd of great oxlike creatures that resembled the beasts of the cave paintings in Altamira, aurochs perhaps, and they had a glimpse of a great cat stalking them that appeared to have immensely long tusks. A sabertooth tiger? All things were possible on this newly ripening desert world. They walked for five days through this strange landscape before they reached what could only be the Hudson River.

Except that, like the Colorado River, this river had cut an immense gorge through what had formerly been a barren landscape. They crept close to the high cliffs and peered over. There was no possible way to descend.

"South," Mark said, and turned along the edge, and the others followed him.

A day later they reached a spot where a tributary joined the Hudson and where the banks were lower and more graded. In addition, many seeds had been sown or carried here, and strands of trees lined the shore. It took the Indians less than a day to assemble branches, trunks, and driftwood to make a sizable raft. Using strips of rawhide, they bound this firmly together, loaded their food aboard, then climbed aboard themselves. As the Indians poled and paddled, the clumsy craft left shore, was carried quickly out into the main current, and hurried south. Manhattan would be at the river's mouth.

This part of the trip was the easiest, and far swifter than Mark had realized. The landscape was so different from what he knew of the valley, with alternate patches of vegetation and desert, that he found it hard to tell where they were. A number of fair-sized streams entered the river from the east, and there was no guarantee that the East River, which cut Manhattan off from the mainland, existed on this world. If it were there, he thought it another tributary, for he never saw it. There were other high cliffs, so the Palisades were not that noticeable.

"This water is no good," Great Hawk said. He had scooped up a handful from the river, and he now spat it out. Mark dipped some himself. It was brackish, salty.

"The ocean, tidewater—we're near the mouth of the river! Pull to shore, quickly."

What he had thought was a promontory ahead showed nothing but wide water beyond it, the expanse of New York Harbor. They landed on what would be the site of Battery Park on the southernmost tip of the island. The Indians worked in silence, unloading the raft, and when Mark started to speak, Great Hawk held his finger to his lips for silence, then leaned close to whisper in his ear.

"Men over this hill, very close. Smell them, smell the fire, they are cooking meat."

"Show me," Mark whispered in return.

He could not move as silently as the Oneida did; they vanished like smoke among the trees. Mark followed as quietly as he could, and a minute later Great Hawk was back to lead him. They crawled the last few yards on their stomachs under the bushes, hearing the sound of mumbled voices. The Indian moved a branch slowly aside, and Mark looked into the clearing.

Three khaki-clad soldiers were gathered around a fire over which a smoking carcass roasted. They had heavy rifles slung across their shoulders. A fourth, a sergeant with upside-down stripes, was stretched out asleep with his wide-brimmed hat over his face.

They spoke quietly in order not to waken him, a strangely familiar language deep in their throats.

It was Dutch—not Dutch, Afrikaans. But what were they doing here?

Mark crawled back to the others, and by the time he had reached them, the answer was clear—too clear, and frightening. But it was the only possibility. He must tell them.

"Those men are soldiers. I know them. Warriors with noise sticks. I think they are the ones who took over the room and destroyed it. They are here, which must mean they have taken over the room here. Without it we cannot return."

"What must we do?" Great Hawk asked. The answer was obvious, but Mark hesitated to say it. He was a lawyer, or had been a lawyer—a man of the law. But what was the law here?

"If we are to return, we will have to kill them, without any noise, then kill or capture the others at the room. If we don't do that, we will be trapped here, cut off from the tribe forever."

The Indians, who lived by hunting, and were no strangers to tribal warfare, were far less worried about the killing than was Mark. They conferred briefly, and Great Hawk and three others vanished silently back among the trees. Mark sat, staring sightlessly at the ground, trying to equate this with his civilized conscience. For a moment he envied the battered Sixim, who stood by his side, unbothered by emotions or worries. An owl called and the remaining Indians stood and called Mark after them.

The clearing was the same, the meat still smoked on the spit, the sergeant's hat was still over his eyes. But an arrow stood out starkly from his side below his arm. The huddled forms of the other soldiers revealed the instant, silent death that had spoken from the forest. With no show of emotion, the Indians cut the valuable arrows free of the corpses, commenting only on the pallid skin of the men, then looted their weapons and supplies. The guns might be useful; the arrows certainly were. Great Hawk was scouting the clearing and found a—to him—clearly marked trail. The sun was behind the trees when they started down it.

The building was not far away. They looked at it from hiding, the now familiar rusted and riveted plates of its walls, the heavy sealed door. Only, this door was gaping open, and the building itself was surrounded by a palisade of thin trees and shrubs. A guard stood at the only gate, and the enclosure was filled with troops. Mark could see heavy weapons and mortars there.

"It will be hard to kill all of these without being killed ourselves," Great Hawk said. "So we shall not try."

8

The Indians could not be convinced even to consider action. They lay about in the gathering darkness, chewing on the tough slabs of meat, ignoring all of Mark's arguments. They were as realistic as any animal, and not interested in suicide. A mountain lion attacks a deer, a deer runs from a lion—it never happens the other way around. They would wait here until morning and watch the camp, then decide what to do. But it was obvious that the options did not include an attack. Would it end this way, defeat without battle . . . and a barren life-time on a savage planet stretching ahead of them? More barren to Mark, who had a civilized man's imagination and despair. The Indians had no such complications in their lives. They chewed the meat, the matter dismissed and forgotten, and in low whispers discussed the hunting and the animals while darkness fell. Mark sat, silent with despair; the Sixim loomed silent as a tree beside him. The Sixim would follow orders, but the two of them were not going to capture this armed camp. Something might happen—he must make the Indians stay and watch and help him. He doubted if they would.

Something did happen, and far sooner than he had thought. Great Hawk, who had slipped away to watch the building, came back suddenly and waved the others to follow him. They went to the fringe of the trees once more and looked at the activity in the camp with astonishment.

The gate was standing open, and there was no guard upon it.

All of the soldiers had drawn up in a semicircle facing the open door of the building. Fires had been lit near it. All of the heavy weapons had been trained on the opening.

"Don't you see what has happened!" Mark said excitedly. "They may control this building and others like it in other lines, but they cannot possibly control them all. They must be expecting a counterattack. They can do nothing until the attackers appear except wait and be ready. Do you understand—this is our chance! They are not expecting trouble from this flank. Get close in the darkness. Wait. Wait until the attack. Then we take out the machine guns—they are the real danger—sow confusion. Taken from the front and rear at the same time, they cannot win. Sixim, can you fire a rifle? One of these we captured?"

"I can. I have examined their mechanism."

"How is your aim?" It was a foolish question to ask.

"I hit what I aim at, every time."

"Then let us get close and get into positions. This may be our only chance. If we don't do it this time, there will probably be no second chance. Once they know we are out here, the guns will face both ways. Come, we have to get close now."

He moved out toward the enclosure, the Sixim, rifle slung, limping at his side. The Indians stayed where they were. He turned back to them, but they were as solid and unmoving as rock in their silence. Nothing more could be done. This left only the two of them, man and machine man, to do their best.

They were almost too late. While they were still twenty yards from the palisade, sudden fire erupted from inside the building; the South African guns roared in return. Mark ran, drawing ahead of the Sixim, running through the open gate, to fall prone in the darkness near the wall and to control his breathing. To squeeze off his shots carefully.

One gunner fell, then another. The Sixim was beside him, firing at target after target with machine regularity. Someone had seen the muzzle blast of their guns, because weapons were turned on them, bullets tearing into the earth beside them, soldiers running toward them. Mark's gun clicked out of battery, empty of cartridges. He tore the empty clip away, struggled to jam in a full one; the soldier was above him.

Falling to one side with an arrow in his chest. Darker shadows moved, just as a solid wave of Sixim erupted through the open doorway.

That was the beginning of the end. As soon as they were among the soldiers, the slaughter began, no mercy, no quarter. Mark called the Indians to him, to the protection of their own battered Sixim, before they were also cut down. The carnage was brief and complete, and when it was over, a familiar one-eyed figure emerged from the building.

"Arinix," Mark called out, and the man turned and came over. "How did all this happen?"

"They were suspicious; they had been watching us for a long time. That officer we did not kill led them to this building." He said it without malice or regret, a statement of fact. Mark had no answer.

"Is this the last of them? Is the way open now?"

"There are more, but they will be eliminated. You see what happens when others attempt to control the way between the worlds?" He started away, then turned back. "Have you solved the problem with the Indians? Will they settle this world?"

"I think so. I would like to stay with them longer, give them what help I can."

"You do not wish to return to Einstein?"

That was a hard one to answer. Back to New York and the pollution and the life as a lawyer. It suddenly seemed a good deal emptier than it had. "I don't know. Perhaps, perhaps not. Let me finish here first."

Arinix turned away instantly and was gone. Mark went to Great Hawk, who sat cross-legged on the ground and watched the operation with a great deal of interest.

"Why did you and the others come to help?" Mark asked.

"It seemed too good a fight to miss. Besides, you said you would show us how to use the noise sticks. You could not do that if you were dead."

The smoke from the dying fires rose up in thin veils against the bright stars in the sky above. In his nostrils the air was cold and clean, its purity emphasized by the smell of wood smoke. Somewhere, not too far away, a wolf howled long and mournfully. This world, so recently empty of life, now had it in abundance, and would soon have human settlers as well, Indians of the Six Nations who would be escaping the fire that would destroy their own world. What sort of world would they make of it?

He had the sudden desire to see what would happen here, even to help in the shaping of it. The cramped life of a lawyer in a crowded world was without appeal. He had friends that he would miss, but he knew that new friends waited for him in the multiplicity of worlds he would soon visit. Really, there was no choice.

Arinix was by the open door issuing orders to the attentive Sixim. Mark called out to him.

The decision had really been an easy one.

Harry Harrison writes:

The parallel-world story uses what is perhaps the only SF theme that was not invented by H. G. Wells. Time machines follow "The Time Machine," countless hordes of mutants shuffle after "The Island of Dr. Moreau," while his short story "The Land Ironclads" started all the engines of scientific warfare. But you will find no parallel worlds in the pages of Wells. In fact, this is one of the neglected themes in all of science fiction. Very few novels, almost as few short stories, and that is that.

I wonder why? I personally find it a most rewarding area of speculation—in the short-story form, as represented here, or as in my novel A Transatlantic Tunnel, Hurrah! *(Retitled, despite muttered grumbles of the author, as* Tunnel Through the Deeps.*) I can understand why authors avoid the book length, since a great deal of thought and research must go into the construction of a world much like our own, though changed greatly by events in the past. Ward Moore's admirable* Bring the Jubilee *is a perfect example of this, the change here caused by the South winning the Civil War. Moore makes wonderfully logical conclusions about the world today if the past had been altered in this manner. I know that Kingsley Amis is working on a novel in which Protestantism never occurred and Mother Church rules supreme; I look forward to reading that!*

Perhaps it is the extra labor that keeps so many writers away from this general theme: you must do your homework well. I feel that far too much of modern SF is written in a rush of emotion and is empty of any content as a result. A bad trend, since content is what put SF on the map in the first place. Many SF writers today can plead lack of technical or scientific knowledge, which is a plausible reason for not writing solid-fuel SF. But there are a lot more rooms in our ramshackle mansion than the early fathers of SF ever dreamed of. Scientific knowledge is not always needed. Writing the parallel-world story requires a lot of thought and some recourse to the history books. Both of these seem within the realm of possibility for practicing writers. Therefore I encourage my brethren in this field to consider not only the future but also the manifold possibilities for a changed present.

THE APERTURE MOMENT

by Brian W. Aldiss

WAITING FOR THE UNIVERSE TO BEGIN

Chin Ping Neverson went through the indignities of Customs and emerged into a bustling street. Color fountains flared. There were no views of Outside. He was in the heart of the urbstak.

He caught a petulent and moved according to the map he had been given. At Indigo Intersection, a man in a frilled blouse bumped into him.

"You in a hurry, sunshine?" Chin Ping asked.

"It's the whole going human concern." It was the correct password.

They turned off together into an afrohale parlor. The man ordered two double nostrils of polkadot aframosta, and they sniffed. Floating, they moved into the gents' room. Nobody else was there, except a guy flat out in the drying chamber, being massaged by a molycomp.

"Hand it over, Earthie."

"Let's see my inducement."

The man in the frilled blouse wore a flesh mask, a tissue of sentient, symbiotic skin that clung to the outlines of his face, making him unidentifiable. Chin Ping scanned the eyes, but they gave nothing away. They did not even have a color. Unblinkingly, they watched Chin Ping as their owner extended a jewel to him.

Chin Ping whipped a pen from his pocket, snapped it open, and peered through it at the jewel.

"Spectral signature says it's a doppler," he agreed.

"Now the goods."

Going over to a splash basin, Chin Ping ran warm water around his skull and brow. He brought a damp tissue from a cachet and rubbed it on the same area. Then he peeled off his toupee.

Stuck to the underside of the toupee was a thin envelope. He flung the toupee into a trash basket and handed the envelope to the man in the frilled blouse. The man took it, passed over the doppler, and was gone.

And Chin Ping was free to visit his father.

Two men were working amid an organized clutter of machines. So intent were they on what they were doing that speech was rare between them. The main noises were electronic hums and sighs, the flicker of figures through various synthesizers, and the occasional clatter as data readouts moved up on a monitor screen. They were near the end of one stage of their work; a certain intensity in their attitudes revealed the fact.

The room was a mixture of workshop and luxurious rest room. The machines were grouped at one end, with coaxial cable and flow charts littering the floor. The other end of the room contained thick plummy floor sofas, a bar, still and movie projectors, and a screen. There was a tall window with striking views of the great outer sweep of the urbstak of Magnanimity IX, on which the sun always shone.

On one wall hung a large oil painting. It represented a historical scene. A Roman soldier clad in armor and gripping a spear stood on guard at the entrance to a narrow alley; or perhaps it was part of a gateway. Over his shoulder, in the street behind the gateway, a scene of terror and chaos was observable. Molten lava and cinder rained from darkened skies, overwhelming people who tried to escape from what was apparently a doomed city. A man and a woman struggled down the littered way in panic. Only the sentry stood fast. Orders to leave his post had not reached him, and he remained on duty, eyes turned apprehensively to the sky.

Copies, charts, dissections, and abstractions of this picture lay about the room, often in stacks. Magnetic lettering on a whiteboard announced APERTURE MOMENT FOR FAITHFUL UNTO DEATH, with color charts and diagrams appended.

"We're ready, Archie," Hazelgard Neverson said. "Switch on the processor."

Archie depressed a key. A new humming note. The two men went and stood together, looking down at a delivery chute in the side of the fax-prod machine. Neverson lit a mescahale. Ten seconds passed.

Neverson was a tall man with an air of battered calm about him. Although solidly built, he could look flimsy at will. Friends who knew him, women who loved him, claimed they loved but never knew him.

Color slides clicked neatly down the chute, stacking themselves for

presentation. When there were twelve of them, Archie switched off
the instrument and picked out the slides. He took them over to the
other end of the room and inserted them in the projector. Neverson
dimmed the lights.

On the screen, volcanic ash leaned steeply up against the walls of a
town, while a volcano distantly jetted fire. An inconsequential view of
a gate, lit by fire, part veiled by smoke. A view of two Roman soldiers, one about to leave. A street, an old man with his robes aflame.
A building toppling, partly covering the corpse of a young girl. The
sentry at his gate, looking up apprehensively, horror in the background. Dark shot of a tavern interior, with an aged woman huddled
in a corner, trying to quiet a frightened dog. The sentry again, at the
other end of the passageway, stones and ash falling about him. A
knot of people, hurrying, led by a man with a gray beard. The
graybeard trying to pull the sentry from his post. The street again, its
houses burning, more fire raining from the clouds, with a flaming
cart. The sentry, overcome by fumes, sprawled unconscious in the
darkening passageway.

The pictures were crude, constructed by a pointillistic technique
that proved, on close inspection, to consist of myriads of tiny squares.

The two men stared at each other. Finally Archie rose and held
out his hand.

"Congratulations, Hazelgard. It is going to work."

"We've a long way to go yet," Neverson said. "Let's have a
drink."

He stood gazing out at the curve of Magnanimity IX.

"The frozen present," he said.

"An illusion of the Zodiacal Planets, just because they have no
diurnal revolution."

"More than that. They have no diurnal revolution because we built
them in our image. They are the expression of our inward state."

"You know, I don't feel that at all."

"Nevertheless, even for you the present is frozen, Archie!"

"And when your paintings move, will that free you from the ice?"

"A start has to be made somewhere. We have made that start."

They spoke passionlessly, sipping their drinks at the same time.
They had had this conversation many times before in the course of
the present project. In the same indifferent tone, Neverson said,
"Let's have the rest of the day free. You can go and join the junket-
ing in the streets. I have to go to my life adviser."

"Don't forget, your son is supposedly arriving on Magnanimity today."

"I'm so busy . . ."

The two men looked each other in the eyes.

"Archie, you have reservations about the tremendous developments we are cooking up here, haven't you? Don't you see we are opening new dimensions of art? Why won't you understand?"

The younger man cast his eyes down and said, "Our sets of values may be very different, sir."

Neverson encountered his son in the hall, and did not bother to conceal his annoyance.

"I'm off to the life adviser, and I'm late already."

"Your usual loving welcome, Father! I'll come along with you, if I may."

"Please yourself." As he and Chin Ping climbed into the feeder, he said, "Why are you wearing that absurd uniform?"

"It happens to be all the fashion on Earth, Father. Why are you living on Magnanimity IX under an assumed name?"

"When one registers as one-year resident or inhabitant, it is customary on a Zodiacal Planet to change one's terrestrial name. It is the courteous thing, let's say. As to why I'm here, I believe that Aldo Wattis Karmon is one of the best life advisers anywhere, and so I settled near him."

"Does he make you feel any happier, Father?"

Neverson stared into the distance. "He is helping me to live with myself."

His look was so weary that silence fell between them. The feeder had been programmed, and was traveling now in fast tube along the outer surface of the man-made planetoid. Below them, they could see festivity, which Chin Ping watched through binoculars. A long procession was wending its way through a public place, bearing effigies of a beaked creature, either animal or bird.

The vehicle branched into a slower tube and entered a pile-apt, slowing as it went.

"How did you get here from Earth?" Neverson said. "The fare's expensive. You haven't been . . . ?"

"No more theft offenses, Father," Chin Ping said bitterly. "I'm on bigger things now."

"I don't know what's to become of you. I've done my best."

"You . . ." Chin Ping checked whatever he was about to say. The feeder had arrived at the heart of the building, had signaled, and had been admitted into an apartment.

Father and son climbed out, and Neverson announced them at an elevator door. As they were cleared, the door opened; they entered, and were carried down one floor.

"If you've never been in a life adviser's before, you may find this one interesting."

"I've never had need of one, thank God."

"Just keep thanking him."

The receptionist who greeted them was a standard polyclone female.

"Herr Karmon won't be long," she said, showing them into a dim room with crimson draperies. Electronic music played faintly. They sank into lounges.

"Are you writing any more fiction?" Chin Ping asked.

"No."

"I'm sorry."

"You needn't be. I'm involved in something much more important. Do you understand how petrified we all are in time? The popular understanding of time is that it flows, that present moments always turn into past moments, that days and weeks slide by. That idea is erroneous. We age, our brains store and lose information, but that is change, not time, and is internal, not external. Time, I believe, is frozen. We are inside an iceberg. We do not know it, but we are waiting for the universe to begin. The Big Bang has yet to occur and set cosmic time in process. Till then, we retain in our heads merely the broken dreams of a past universe."

"How, then, do we live, converse, have children?"

"We do not. We merely dream that we do. Our belief that we eat, talk, procreate, is false, a belief shaped by distorted legends of greater and more meaningful acts that we as instruments will be able to accomplish when time does finally begin. We cannot fully understand yet."

Chin Ping was silent. Then he said, "Father, I did not mean to speak sharply to you. Please forgive me. I never seem to give you the correct password. I was upset by the journey here."

"It is absurd to believe that one generation follows another. They all coexist, like cards in a new pack. As yet, time is congealed, unidimensional. Do you understand me?"

"You've been overworking."

The polyclone reappeared. "Herr Karmon will see you now, Mr. Neverson."

"Will you wait here for me, Chin Ping?" Neverson asked, rising.

"Of course, if you want me to."

"I shall be a long while. You'll be gone when I come out."

"No, I won't."

"Well, we'll see."

Aldo Wattis Karmon was a slight man who managed to combine a cold, reserved manner with outgoing facial expressions. It was difficult to tell whether it was the cold, reserved manner or the outgoing facial expressions that had been acquired, or both. He wore a long silvery alchemical gown, trimmed with fur, under which were black trousers and a white shirt. A whimsical figure, but still a considerable one.

One end of his long consulting room was given over to his finches, fifty of them, which fluttered about in bursts of color.

"How's the animation going?" he asked.

"We've had the first crude results in this morning. They do suggest that eventually I shall be able to achieve complete sequential high-probability animation for any painting I wish."

"Or any photograph?"

"My interests at present lie entirely in Victorian paintings of what I call the Aperture Moment variety."

"All the same, your company will have to develop. And you will need funds and investments at all stages."

Neverson made no answer. After a silence he said, "Let us talk about my soul rather than my work."

"By all means. Though they are not readily separable."

Karmon crossed to a screen, and it lit at a wave of his hand. He pointed to a line of figures on it.

"As you will observe, we have now analyzed your schizophrenia group. You are a Schizo AM 26a, which is rather a rare group. We have examined the enzyme content of platelets in your blood samples, and determined the percentages of monoamine oxidase, or MAO—"

"Just a minute. What has monoamine oxidase to do with the state of my soul? I told you, since my wife died, I just need a madwoman, or a succession of madwomen. Something a little violent."

"Your obsession with copulation with the insane is directly related to MAO. Deficiency of MAO is directly related to a number of schizoid states. The MAO deficiency index in your brain has affected your response to temporal stimuli to such an extent that—"

Neverson held up his hand. "I admit I'm sick. I admit I'm in need of help. That's why I came to you. I'm in pain and misery and depression. All the same, you'd better not forget that I'm a dedicated artist, and my work—my genius, if you like—means more to me ultimately than my happiness. I'm in a state of rapture. I'm not having you tamper with my enzymes, even if it 'cures' me, so—"

"The treatment would be quite painless and entirely trouble-free. You must have been subject to a genetic weakness, and in the grief of your wife's death, your secretion of MAO fell below normal. A monthly booster shot—"

"Normal? My dear Herr Karmon, don't make me teach you the facts of life! Normality is a statistical fiction. I'm proud to belong to my schizoid group if it means I can see farther than other people in some directions. My art relies upon what you call my response to temporal stimuli. I'm glad of your diagnosis, but you can keep your cure."

The physician nodded in mandarin fashion. He went to sit on a dais close to the finches and rested his hands on his knees.

"Such was what I anticipated your answer would be. It is entirely characteristic of your schizoid group. We grow to love our chains. Freedom is for suckers. So I have prepared to help you in another way, which I hope you will find more acceptable."

"I'll listen, of course." He lit a mescahale.

"The finch-alternative method is for you. By rejecting a cure, you have, in effect, chosen a certain mode of living, of engaging with future events, the course that will conform to your group, bearing in mind a number of other factors. Had you accepted the offer of cure, then you would have chosen an alternative course. You understand?"

"Continue."

"The course you will take through life will not be random. We could chart it absolutely, given all the other life factors you will encounter. Naturally, we are not given those factors, but we have enough data on you—your age, weight, disposition, predilections, financial circumstances, history, ancestry, etc.—to give us a very good idea of what the future may hold for you. You understand?"

"The process you outline sounds not dissimilar to certain techniques I am investigating myself. You are going to synthesize all these factors through a computer and give me, in effect, later timephase versions of my present self?"

Smiling, Karmon said, "I do not use a computer. My birds are my computer. These homeopathic finches, as you know, have a life cycle of two days. I have four of them already prepared, their systems loaded with toxics that will influence their actions in such a way that, when released, they will perform flight paths to correspond with the possible paraments of your later career."

"Ah. Now you've lost me!"

"We shall find you, Mr. Neverson, a number of years from now."

He walked over to the desk and fanned the bell contact. In came the polyclone, bearing a plasite box containing four inert finches. Karmon, meanwhile, pulled back a curtain to reveal a large glass-fronted cage, three sides of which were covered with small square shutters lined in rank after rank. The shutters were painted in various colors, apparently at random.

Taking the plasite box over to the cage, Karmon pressed a plunger on its upper surface, releasing a crimson gas into the box, where it immediately disappeared. He placed the box on the bottom of the cage before the finches could revive.

As the birds came to life, they struggled to their feet. The lid of the box sprang open. Out flew the birds.

In strange, erratic flight, they darted this way and that with a great flutter of wings. Whenever their plunging bodies touched a shutter, it fell open, revealing a number underneath.

"This is where the calculator comes in," Karmon said. "It is noting the numbers in the order that they are revealed, and keying them to a behavioral code. Watch—the birds are almost exhausted now."

The finches were flying more slowly, making more frequent attempts to settle on the bottom of the cage. They fluttered up, releasing more shutters. Then they fell dead to the floor in four untidy little mouthfuls of feather.

The polyclone tore a printout from the compterminal on Karmon's desk and gave it to him. He read it, striking out a line here and there, nodding as he did so, frowning, pushing his bottom lip far out over his top lip.

"And what has this mumbo-jumbo *proved?*" Neverson asked sarcastically, after a moment's silence.

"Oh, perhaps I let you think that the method was totally reliable. Of course, it cannot be. We do have errors. . . . I'm sure this time we have an error."

"Why?"

Karmon cleared his throat and stroked his chin. He also looked at his watch and nodded dismissively toward the polyclone. "The homeopathic finches appear to forecast so many disasters for you. People's lives are not full of disaster—only in films and cinecasts—however much they may want them to be. I think we must have a few more sessions, and then we will try again. I reject these projections."

In a stride, Neverson was at the other's side and had grasped him by the wrist. Immediately, a stinging shock ran up his arm, and he staggered back.

Nursing his hand, he said, "Since I have no intention of believing this mumbo-jumbo, you'd better tell me what it says."

"Just keep your hands off me. You will be worse injured next time. My body electricity is marshaled to repel foreign bodies. The finch-alternative method, if you insist on knowing, predicts that you will very shortly meet the sort of woman you are hoping to meet, and she will fulfill—and more—all your wishes. Your friend and helper will turn against you, eventually to reveal himself as one of your unassuageable enemies. You will manage to turn your present theories into reality through the strength of your obsessions. But those obsessions will cause the emotional ruin and perhaps worse of those who depend on you. Moreover, your success will prove a disaster for the very art you vociferously claim to love. I have also to tell you that I see here your death—blood and a flight of shallow steps are involved, somewhere in the open air—at the hands of the woman who you think loves you dearly."

"Give me that rubbish!" Neverson jumped forward and snatched the strip of paper from Karmon's grasp, sustaining another shock as he did so. "You damned quack, you're just trying to scare more money out of me!"

He screwed up the scroll and flung it at the finch cage.

"You'd better come back next week and hear the rest!" Karmon exclaimed, but his patient was already bursting out of the door.

The feeder took them back to Neverson's pile-apt. Traffic-flow control directed the vehicle down to lower levels, so that they slid evenly among gigantic structures.

"I gather the guy in the cloak upset you," Chin Ping said, interpreting his father's silence. "That was a real nuthouse in there— you shouldn't take stick from anyone in a shower like that."

"Why don't you talk correct English? That slobby talk is only an affectation, and you know it. How did you manage to get here to Magnanimity, in any case?"

"If I told you I was smuggling go-go, you'd believe me, wouldn't you?"

"I wouldn't put it past you. You know it's criminal."

There was silence between them. They threaded their way through a square where dancing and festivity were going on to the sound of a band. Some of the onlookers carried effigies of a white, beaked animal.

"What are they all feeling so good about?" Chin Ping asked.

"This is a great day on several Zodiacal Planets. They are sporting their domesticity emblem, Donald the Duck. This is his day."

"Never heard of him."

"A matter of mythology—not your strong point."

"Uh . . . like you, Father, I'm waiting for the universe to begin. . . . Do we have to be at each other's throats like this? Let's take that white bird for a symbol of peace. I came here because I genuinely wanted to see you. I understood you were ill."

"You understood correctly. Did you also understand you could cure me?"

Chin Ping waved his arms a bit. "Look, defreeze, will you? See me real, will you? Like, I didn't kill Mother, I am not responsible for her death, and you can't make me be! I grieve for her more than you do. *You* killed her with your lack of concern—did your phony life adviser ever happen to tell you that?"

"Ah, here we are now at my home," Neverson said pleasantly, as the feeder slowed. "I'm sure you won't want to come in?"

They climbed out into the hall and stood looking at each other, both locked in the hopeless complexity of their relationship.

"You're caught in yesterday's cobwebs, Father. Step out of them, step right out of them and go on living again! Before it's too late for both of us."

"What does that mean, exactly?"

The boy hung his head. "Life isn't easy for me either."

"You always made things difficult for yourself."

Archie appeared, putting on the flowery outer coat that he affected. He looked surprised.

"Are you back already? It's later than I thought. I've been running the Faithful slides through again. Are you going to stay with your father, Chin Ping?"

"No, he is returning to Earth immediately," Neverson said. "I'm sorry, Chin Ping, but I've just had a disturbing diagnosis, and your presence upsets me too much. You must go."

"If you want it that way. Don't forget, I've warned you."

Archie put a hand on Neverson's arm, which was immediately withdrawn. "Hazelgard, he is your son—"

But the outer door slammed. Chin Ping had left. Neverson turned away.

"You know the boy loves you. . . ."

"Don't reproach me, Archie—I can't bear to be reproached. Perhaps I was too standoffish, but I have just been informed that I'm liable to be murdered by a woman. Why isn't there just work? Why all this other side of life, this messy side? I love him, too, but there's time enough to sort all that out when our work here is done."

"There may not be time enough for your son. Not all of us live in your frozen time, Hazelgard."

Neverson stood stiffly, his face grim. "For all your money, you're my assistant, not my life adviser. Why don't you see if Karmon has a job open for you?"

He hastened toward his workshop and the safety of his art. Outside, the beaked creatures went by unnoticed, people thronged the streets, solar energy beamed down almost inexhaustibly.

BUT WITHOUT ORIFICES

Keith Road said to Miss Brangwyn and her daughters, "I've traveled a long, long way. . . ."

The words hung for a while in Miss Brangwyn's living room, and were finally removed by a molycomp.

"A curious reaction to the only genuine Tiepolo-Neff inside or outside an art gallery!" said Miss Brangwyn. Her manners were always formal.

"Oh, I do like it . . . I admire it immensely," Keith said. "It's all that Tiepolo is, and oh, how much besides!"

She switched it off; the screen went blank, and hanging on the wall was merely a bulkily framed Tiepolo etching, *Castle Scene with Penitents*. She stood silently by. Her daughters, Polly and Polkadot, stood silently by her, half-looking at Keith Road, as if aware that all four of them were merely a study for some ideal group of four, arranged with careful regard for the long-unused light of evening coming horizontally through the glass wall behind them.

"Why I said what I said was that . . . the Tiepolo-Neff seemed to sum up for me the distances of my life. That's why I said I'd come a long way. It was purely in admiration of your Neff, Miss Brangwyn."

"I understand," said Miss Brangwyn. "Neff gave this work to my grandmother, Faith Brangwyn. That is how it came into my possession."

The room was full of precious porcelain.

"Mr. Road has traveled a long way, Mother," Polkadot said. She was the one Keith liked.

"Yes, and by *road,* too," said Polly. She was the one Keith did not like.

Both girls wore blue.

"I'll walk with him back to his car," Polkadot said. "You'll probably be glad to get out of the Experimental Experience area, won't you, Mr. Road?"

"Oh, I like it . . . I mean, yes, it is my first time in an EE area, yes, Miss Brangwyn. I've been among the Zodiacal Planets."

"What were you doing there?" inquired Miss Brangwyn.

"I was on a rerethinking course, Miss Brangwyn." He tried to copy their correctness.

He walked through the grounds with Polkadot. "It was great of your mother to let me see her treasure, Polkadot, I mean, Miss Brangwyn. I do much appreciate the privilege."

"Shit, we pretend to keep up conventional behavior—it's all the rage—but you go too shit-holing far, Mr. Road. Don't you want to seduce me or something, or not even so much as get a finger up?" Sunlight made her dress blink.

"Yuh, uh, well, you're a pretty girl, Miss Brangwyn, I mean Polkadot, but I mean, why, we only just been reprod . . . uh, introduced."

"Fuck that, do you want to lay me, or do you want to lay me not?"

The grounds were beautiful. There were stately pink flamingos walking by the lakeside, not a dozen paces away.

"'Course I bastarding well want to lay you!" he shouted. He clutched her. Their lips met. Her mother's and sister's applause came faintly to their ears. Her arms went around his neck, her hair curled against his cheek. His hands ripped away the blue dress. He groaned with pleasure and got her down on the lawn. The grass was thick with flamingo shit.

*   *   *

There ends, unfortunately, the last story ever to fall from the computer of Hazelgard Neff. The fragment has a title: "But Without Orifices." It leaves us with a mute surmise, as does Charles Dickens' *Mystery of Edwin Drood,* also uncompleted at death. Was Polkadot to prove without orifices? Would she prove to be a simulacrum (artifice-fiction—the so-called "artifiction"—of the third decade of the twenty-first century is full of simulacra)? Or does Neff's title refer to some event as yet unrevealed, as seems more likely?

Neff's son, Chin Ping Neff, reminds us that Neff's earliest work was *The Golden Orifice,* and here the word was used in a metaphorical sense. Neff refers more than once to "the fudged vents of the soul," a phrase later plagiarized by other writers.

Chin Ping says, "Miss Brangwyn was probably an amalgam of women that Father knew, right? One of them was almost certainly Catherine Cleeve, known in certain circles as Capodistria Kate. They were lovers at one period, despite the somewhat cagey tone of their first meeting, see."

Neff: "I like your dress."

Cleeve: "Do you? This is the first time I've worn it."

Neff: "It's beautiful."

Cleeve: "The boutique where I bought it called it 'très cad, presque snob.'"

Neff: "There's a split in the seam by your left shoulder."

Cleeve: "It's designed for looks, not durability, darling."

Neff: "That goes for a lot of us."

Cleeve: "I have to be going myself now."

The conversation has come down to us because both Neff and Catherine Cleeve were wired for sound. Both had a mania for recording the transient; indeed, Neff's whole life was directed toward imposing order on the fleeting moment and banishing impermanence; it was the fulcrum of his art. This obsession it was that brought him and Catherine together. Her two daughters were already grown up and living in EE cities, Vienna, Austria, and Trieste, Italy.

NeffPanimation was the brain child of Neff and Catherine and their computers. The mating of their computers, charged as they were with life data, was fully as traumatic as the mating of the two human beings.

And NeffPanimation exploited to the full that Neffian obsession with the transient.

"This all happened before I was locked away for antiexperimental behavior," Chin Ping says, inserting the thumb of his right hand in his left ear. "Father had this thing about Victorian paintings, which were very fashionable again in the 2020's. He saw in them what he called the Aperture Moment, a frozen moment of time typically defined by artists from John Martin's day to Sickert's. Their whole range of pictures just doesn't make sense unless and until you ask yourself the sort of extra-artistic question 'What happens next?' right?

"I mean, like take one of the most famous paintings of the period, Holman Hunt's *The Awakening Conscience,* well, it's not just a composition featuring some Victorian skirt rising from a piano—at least, it's only that from the narrow old academic art tradition. It's an Aperture Moment, my father said, where Hunt makes you expand a whole new section of your mind—new in Victorian times, I mean—and say to yourself, 'What happened before now? How did this skirt get in this predicament at the piano with her boyfriend? How long did they know each other? Why doesn't she like his tune, right?' And the Aperture Moment also makes you think about the future, right? So you say to yourself, 'What happened after this? Did she give the guy the brush? Who got the house? What's that cat doing eating the pigeon? Was the artist there looking on all the time, like God?' What you'd call metaphysical questions, right?

"And Father said that it was by inventing—or at least perfecting, we'd better say, and accelerating, if you follow me—this Aperture Moment that the Victorian artists reflected the new dimensions of the age in which they lived, as exemplified by Darwin's theories, which widened the stage of human affairs, back far into the past and forward into the future. So painters like Hunt helped ordinary slobs to appreciate the new expansion of the mind of which we are capable."

Chin Ping Neff was shot on Tuesday, May 1, 2051, two centuries to the day after the opening of the Great Exhibition. The execution was carried out in 577 Buki Tinghi Street, Singapore, before a member of the World Judiciary.

"Sure, I remember the dress," Catherine Cleeve said. She was still beautiful in a Socratic fashion. She spoke without gesture, sitting absolutely composedly. A chill radiated from her. "It was a nice dress. There was a split in the seam by the left shoulder the very first time I wore it. No, the right shoulder. It came from a boutique in Singapore. The girl who sold it to me said it was 'très cad, presque manic,' or something."

"You worked with Neff on his first Animation, I believe."

"Maybe it was the left shoulder. I know Hazelgard commented on it. Sure, I worked with him. Panimating Hunt's *Awakening Conscience* was my idea. Or my computer's, at least. He had done a Poynter before that, which he destroyed. I had a turquoise Tanzyme 5505 All-Digit. It never gave me any trouble. What we did, we fed into Hazelgard's big computer all the data we could get concerning Hunt's painting. Centrally, the data about the picture itself, of course, so that the comp could match color values and everything—the proportions, relationships of figures to background, light readings, dynamism with frame—together with details about objects in picture, structure, type, make, material used, style, period, and so on. Great fun to do. A lot of research needed. We were lovers at the time. My daughters still took up much of my life."

Remaining immobile, she changed only the focus of her eyes, so as to gaze into some inaccessible distance.

"Hazelgard had always longed for an affair with a madwoman. And I was certified mad at the time. It is perfectly true that I had killed my brother to terminate our long and rather intense incestuous relationship. Oh, I can face the facts now. Hazelgard was marvelous. I owe my life to him. I can only say he treated me like a brother, in every way. . . .

"We both had a mania for the transient. He was waiting for the universe to begin. That was what brought us together. No, it was the seam on the right shoulder that went. Mind you, the side seam split the second time I wore it. I know I told Hazelgard that it was designed for appearance rather than permanence, and he said, 'Aren't we all!' Very funny, I thought it was. His whole life was directed toward a study of the fleeting moment, with all its chaos and mystery. That was all he wanted from life."

"That was why you animated Holman Hunt?"

"Basically, yes. We also fed the computer all the possible parameters of Hunt's life. First, his painterly techniques, complete data on palette, brushes, mode of work, analysis of lengths of brushstroke, all that kind of thing. Then his other pictures. Facts about his personal life, why he was blackmailed, how he ate the original scapegoat that died, his Christianity and his involvement with the slums through his mistress, Annie Miller—a very Victorian story! It all went in, together with a stack of information on the other Pre-Raphaelites and the society of the time."

She sat stock-still, not speaking, not thinking. Her hands were long and narrow.

"That business about the flamingo shit. A complete fabrication. I believe there was a goose turd somewhere, but nowhere near Bobbie and me."

"And when you had fed all the data into the computer?"

"It was programmed on strict probability transference to produce a sequence of 4,320 reproductions of *The Awakening Conscience,* using Hunt's original as central Aperture Moment, and using time as a factor of variance. These were to be projected in the form of film. At sixteen frames per second, we had a four-and-a-half-minute film that was in all respects a genuine Hunt original."

"I believe there has been some argument on that score, Miss Cleeve."

"Believe what you will. It was a genuine Hunt, its subject matter enduring in time linearly as well as instantaneously. The brushwork was Hunt's, and everything. Oh, I know what Sir Archibald McTensing said, but other critics were entirely on our side. Archie was a dirty little man, for all that he was the Big Panjandrum on Art. He buggered Eskimo boys, it was well known."

"At least the film was a great success."

"Success? Success! My dear girl, it was a revolution! It was . . . it was a new art form, and we had invented it. It's the schizos who explore and extend the world. Yes, Archie actually buggered them in the snow, if you can believe it. In the end, he caught frostbite where he least wanted it."

"What did your Hunt film show?"

"It showed *The Awakening Conscience* as it really would have been if Hunt had had access to our manipulative techniques. It was Hunt's film, not ours. The lady rises from the piano stool, where she has been playing 'Home, Sweet Home' with the man she loves. No, 'Come into the Garden, Maude.' She goes to the door, opens it, walks into the hall, and . . ."

For a moment her immobility is broken, she bends double in the chair to utter a coarse laugh.

". . . and she nips into the lavatory for a pee! Ha ha ha. . . ."

The interviewer reaches out and slaps the aging lady on the face, hard, three times, left cheek, right cheek, left cheek.

"Think what you are saying, Kate, you old bitch! You aren't in Capodistria now, or Koper either! This is Vienna, Austria, nor are we out of it, so you'd better answer my questions properly. Who am *I*, for a start?"

Catherine looked blearily up at her questioner. The woman was possibly in her late thirties, attractive, well-built, a splendid head of tawny hair. Something hard about her mouth.

"I know we've met before."

"Of course we've met before. I'm Polkadot, your daughter. Remember me now?"

The older woman in the wheelchair began to cry.

"You're trying to make me unhappy. I don't have any daughters. I had two, but they died when they were small. I remember burying them in their party dresses, I remember how pretty they looked and how I cried—"

"You remember, you remember! Jesus Christ, is that all the human race ever does? Why not forget for a change? What about the future, what about what's going to happen? Doesn't that excite your intellectual curiosity just one little titsy bit?"

"Not half as much as the past does, darling." Catherine had pulled herself up in the wheelchair and was affecting a deep masculine drawl. "Besides, you forget I'm mad, baby, and madness is all to do with the past, isn't it? You must have read your Freud and your Stekel and your Stockmeyer and your Rhukaiser if you're any sort of a daughter of mine! The little webs in the grass, functional long after the spider's dead, the old fridge on the waste lot, still trapping kids. . . . Come on, will you? Why isn't there any air in here? You breathing it all?"

"In your presence I never breathed. You were always a suffocating presence, even when Polly and I were small. I remember running out into the fresh air and panting, clinging to the big old Spanish chestnut and just trying to get the whole atmosphere of you out of my lungs."

"Didn't do your asthma any good, did it?"

"You see, you do remember me! You aren't mad, you've never been mad! You're just sick, aren't you?"

"Why do I have to remember you, just because you're my mother?"

Polkadot screamed and made a filthy face.

"I'm not your stinking mother, I'm your daughter! Oh, Jesus, why do you make me live, why is there all this mess blowing around all the time, like I can never get free of it? I was mad to come here at this of all times, just when . . ."

She walked about the room, big and bleak, behind the wheelchair, gesturing as she went.

". . . just when I'm in this dreadful emotional state, and my whole psyche seems to be breaking up. Do you know what I dreamed last night? I dreamed my little girl came all the way from Sacramento in a pink frock, and she just went to the Rowlandsons' house next door to get her dolly, and she wouldn't come to me at all, and I thought she was coming, but when she got as near as the gate, she hitched a lift from a car and was gone, and I ran out to stop her, screaming 'Dorothy, Dorothy!' and there was her little dolly lying in the gutter, all bleeding and broken." She broke into convulsive sobs.

Catherine started to laugh.

"Hazelgard had bad dreams too. He'd tell me about them at breakfast, and we'd laugh at them over the grapefruit."

Choking back her tears, Polkadot came around to confront her mother and said, "You killed Hazelgard, didn't you? You shot him!"

"What gives you that idea? I liked him as well as any man I've ever known. He loved me, and he was faithful to me. Faithful unto me, *Faithful Unto Death*—that's the title of Poynter's dreadful Pompeii canvas, the first thing Hazelgard ever worked on. . . ."

"His Panimation exhibition was so badly received that you shot him, didn't you? There are several nasty streaks in you, Mother, but the worst is that while you're a failure yourself, you can't bear failure in others, can you? You think I'm a failure, don't you?"

The older woman lit a mescahale. "Go back to your husband, if he'll have you. I shouldn't think you're much of a lay. I *know* you're a failure. What's even more boring is that you keep on coming around every so often, begging me to tell you so. As for Hazelgard, he wasn't like you, he was a real man, he had a strong will to success, something every artist should have. When it seemed as if everyone turned against his invention, he couldn't bear that. He shot himself more in anger than sorrow. I was there, my dear child, I saw him run out on the terrace and do it. I went to him, but he'd blown half his head off. Before I had strength enough to call for help, I went back into the living room, and I remember his coffee still stood there, the cup half full. It wasn't cold yet."

"If he shot himself, then why are you in this criminal institution?"

She was looking into the distance again. "You know what Hazelgard always said? That reality was designed for looks, not durability! I really liked that remark. It was one of the things that won me to him. 'Kate,' he'd say 'reality is designed for looks, not durability.'

And the reality that killed him wasn't at all enduring. If only he'd sweated it out a bit. . . . The tide of opinion soon turned. People were soon on his side. They wanted the product. . . . Poor Hazelgard! I loved him like a brother. . . ."

Fidgeting, Polkadot said, "Well, that's my cue to leave, Mother dearest. We all know you killed your brother."

"Do you remember that? I didn't think you were born then. Funny how you get confused about such matters. Well, give my love to little Dotty. . . ."

"I have a job now, Mother, believe it or not. I do women's features for Eurovision. I'm going to write up this interview for them."

"Want a picture of me?"

"I have one. Shows you with your hair as you used to do it when we were at Salzburg."

"Oh, I remember. That big antique tortoiseshell comb I had."

"Was it genuine tortoiseshell?"

"The man said it was. And you and your sister used to wear black-velvet bows in your hair. Fashions were so pretty then."

"I guess that 2035 was about my favorite year."

"That was the year we had those donkeys!"

"Oh, the donkeys! And that holiday in the Amundsen Sea!"

"Wasn't that fun, with the Polynesian music?"

"Lovely! Oh, Mother, let's do it all again sometime! You're not too old."

"Of course I'm not! I'm still wired for sound. Just you wait till they let me out of here—you'll see!"

"I'll wheel you back to your cell now."

AIMEZ-VOUS HOLMAN HUNT?

The private viewing of the NeffPanimation Exhibition was well under way, and some of the reporters and critics were already glancing tipsily toward the exit, when Valery Mallarmaine entered with Polly Neff and Sir Archibald McTensing. Quimpax, Sir Archie's young Eskimo valet, followed close behind the trio. The two celebrated critics were having a loud and sophisticated conversation.

"He was a terribly talented young man, and I dearly loved him," Sir Archie was saying. "You know he was one of the founders of EE, one of the first to realize that whereas a majority of the population cling to Traditional Experience, there is nevertheless a considerable minority who prefer Experimental Experience, and that the two groups would be happier when separated. The New Renaissance dates from that perception."

"A touch of Leonardo and Dirac about him, I agree."

Sir Archie smirked. "And Beardsley. . . ."

"He and his sister Kate did really have it off together?"

"Not a doubt! They were both so proud of it that they set many incidents on film. Careful what you say, though, Val—she'll be here, Kate'll be here, hanging on friend Neff's arm. He always said he yearned for an affair with a madwoman." They tittered.

A gallery assistant brought them both catalogs. The men watched the beaten-silver pages turn themselves over.

"No expense spared," Sir Archie murmured.

"Neff always liked to impress," Val said, catching sight of the artist in the far corner of the room, wearing a silver alchemist's gown. Catherine Cleeve was with him.

"I see he's included Poynter's *Faithful Unto Death*. Temperamental affinity, I always thought," said Sir Archie. "Neff's like Pompeii—all very quiet and Roman and enduring for a long while, then suddenly, *puff*, the volcano erupts and everyone has to run from the boiling lava."

"Of course, you used to work with him—you should know."

"That was donkeys' years ago. I bear no grudges. I doubt if he even remembers me."

"We'd better go over and be nice to him."

"He's okay if you give him the right password." He gestured to the valet to follow.

There were ten Panimations on display in the exhibition, embodying single works by Turner, Egg, Wallis, Burne-Jones, Millais, Waller, Poynter, and Sickert, and two by Holman Hunt.

The private showing was a fashionable one, among those present being Naseem Bata, V. T. P. Naipaul, Anna Kavan, Francis Parkinson Hunt, and two especial friends of Catherine Cleeve's, Freddie Rhukaiser and Frank Krawstadt. Slightly apart from the others stood Heinlette van Ballison, the leading writer of artifiction, his android close behind him.

For once, many of the guests were paying closer attention to the exhibits than to each other. Although the attic in Gray's Inn with Chatterton dying caused some excitement, most of the interest centred on Hazelgard Neff's earliest completed creation, *The Awakening Conscience*.

* * *

Albert is playing the piano.

The soft tinkling notes of Edgar Lear's "Tears, Idle Tears" come from the stuffy little room, over which the eye roves among dull indigoes and reds. All is overfurnished; even the window open onto spring trees discloses only a claustrophobic little garden.

Suddenly there is a break in the music. Annie Miller has pulled the sheet off the stand.

"You *are* in a pet this afternoon," Albert says. "That's what comes of lying in bed so late of a Sunday morning instead of going to church like a respectable girl."

"You know why I was late getting up," she says, half-sulking, half-coquettish.

He sniggers and starts to play "Oft in the Stilly Night." The rosewood piano tinkles a little. She perches on the arm of his chair and sings with him. The tabby cat bursts savagely in through the window, a sparrow in its mouth. Her embroidery is unfinished. The wallpaper pattern of corn and vine is oppressive; thieving birds prey on the fruit. He always had longed to have an affair with a madwoman. Old webs capture prey long after the spider has gone. A slight breeze stirs the net curtain. A copy of Noel Humphrey's *The Origin and Progress of the Art of Writing* lies in elaborate binding on the table. Albert's novel *The Golden Oriole* has stuck on chapter six, at the words ". . . hoped that there would be more alternatives than his life had so far offered. . . ."

Annie's voice falters and stops. She rises, moisture trembling on her eyelashes like dew in grass.

"Come on, Annie! Let's hear you!

> The eyes that shone,
> Now dimmed and gone,
> The cheerful hearts now broken . . ."

But Annie moves away, tall in her sad, silly, complex dress. Her face is a study in pained intensity. In Ruskin's words, her eyes are filled "with the fearful light of futurity and with tears of ancient days."

She strides from the room, closing the door behind her. The hall is dark. She passes a tall hall stand, crammed with coats and brushes; visiting cards lie on a little silver tray. A mirror catches a dim glimpse of her as she passes. She goes to a rear door and unlocks it, bending slightly to do so. There is a frosted panel of glass in the door, set around by lozenges of various colors.

Annie lets herself into the garden. There is an attempt at lawn, but the garden is east-facing, and a high brick wall keeps out sunlight, so that the grass is thin or strangled by moss. Sun catches the boughs of their single plane tree. Two daffodils flower in a far corner. She closes her eyes, squeezing out a tear, and commences to walk back and forth. Once, a word comes from her lips, either a curse or perhaps the word "Mother." An inquisitive small boy peers at her over the wall from the next-door garden. He wears a deerstalker hat. He clutches a hoop. The tinkle of the piano is thin in the Victorian air.

At the window, Albert appears, grinning. He rests his face on one hand and lets his jaw hang down in a mockery of Annie's dejection.

"Come on! Cheer up! I'll give you a drink, old girl!"

She hesitates, then looks toward him. Smiling, she begins her return to the house. All in genuine Holman Hunt brushstrokes.

"It seemed to go quite well," Neff said.

"I wonder how many of them realized that they were attending the birth of a new world of art?" Catherine said.

They were riding together on donkeys, moving steadily through the extensive grounds of the asylum. Huge black or white screens had been erected here and there to set off special trees or clumps of trees. Lights burned underground. A few people walked, many of them alone. It was very early.

The odor of cigars still hung about him from the night before; flat champagne cluttered his kidneys, making him pensive.

"See the schizos taking their exercise! They're our kind, yet not like us. The ability to turn sickness into art is a survival trait."

"The schizos are exploring the real world, the world of artifice. You spoke to Van Ballison last night, I hope?"

He was watching an inmate who had walked up to his donkey and was frowning as they rode by. "Funny thing about reality. There's a split in the seam by the shoulder. It's designed for looks, not durability."

She said dreamily, turning the donkey's head for home, "Reality's for machines. We're coming to realize that now. Humans were never happy there. They just had to live there because we had no alternatives before. Now, with EE and all the rest of it, we have alternatives."

His cloak was gray, her robe saffron. The long gold strikes of the early sun made them both the same color. There was dew underfoot, and little clever webs made of minute pearls, which the hooves of the animals broke. The grass bent and sprang upright again as they passed. Catherine sang wordlessly under her breath.

"Are you happy, Catherine?"

"I'm never happy, Hazelgard. We live so long, and we have to live so many lives, so many broken bits of miscellaneous lives. My daughters' lives . . . Are you going to be able to face what the critics say?"

He gave no answer for a while. They rode back along an avenue of poplars, where sunlight painted the shadows behind their eyes red and green. The android at the stables took charge of their mounts. As they climbed the shallow steps into Neff's living room, he said, "Rapture. That's what I always feel. Used it not to mean 'possession'? In that case, I'm possessed. Sometimes I think I really am a considerable artist, on that score alone. Whether happy or miserable, I am always in a state of rapture. . . ."

"You don't care that these steps were the scene of a foul murder last week?"

He paused, looking into her eyes. Her face, her expression, still and always gave him a shock. There had never been anyone like her. The spider had created its web and left forever.

"No, I recall no murder here."

"Perhaps it's next week," she said. In anyone else, the reply would have rung like a feeble joke; from Catherine, the remark was merely confusing. For a moment Neff saw dirty arterial blood everywhere. It stained the walls and curtains as he entered the living room.

There he turned and confronted her. "You can no more take my rapture from me than I can take your madness from you."

"Isn't that why our relationship is impermanent? You always wanted an affair with a madwoman, but I as a person am meaningless to you. Only my madness awakes a response. Isn't that so?"

He cast his gaze down. "Isn't it enough that . . . ?" The sentence was never completed.

"Let's see what the critics have to say," Catherine said.

She walked over to the fax machine, which had delivered six duplos. Looking through them, she selected one, pushed it into the go slot, and switched on. The words of Sir Archibald McTensing spoke from the morning edition of *The European Times*.

* * *

What the NeffPanimation studio has achieved is little short of a miracle. Yesterday evening, I saw a new Holman Hunt. In many respects, it was a genuine Holman Hunt. It was our old friend *The Awakening Conscience,* that mawkish bit of kitsch of the Pre-Raphaelite school, which shows a woman having a touch of remorse about the things that were. I have never admired the quality of the thought or the handling of this picture. The paint surface is mere-tricious. But yesterday evening we were not invited to dwell on such exacting considerations, or to stretch our minds far toward an aesthetic response to an aesthetic act. What we were invited to do was to admire—and admire we did—the ingenuity of NeffPanimation in endowing the Holman Hunt with life. This was a world of peep shows, not painting.

Accordingly, we saw the woman and her lover at the piano. We heard the piano playing, as the fancy man (wearing his gloves, mark you) gave us "I Stood on the Bridge at Midnight" and the woman sang. Then she broke off, went outside, and walked about the garden until the fancy man called her in again.

All this in the peculiarly beastly palette of Holman Hunt, in suffocating pinks and indigoes. It was a Holman Hunt we were watching, a Holman Hunt given the extra dimension of time.

You may think there was nothing particularly momentous in what we saw, that this was just one more tiresome technical trick. I disagree. I believe I have never seen anything so momentous.

We were witnessing the death of art, nothing less. As photography killed the portrait, so now the computer has killed the whole aesthetic of pictorial composition. I was assured by Mr. Neff that his computer could have been programmed to produce the whole life story of Hunt's wretched woman and her banal involvements. All he needs is backers; and can we doubt that in an age like ours, backers will be forthcoming? When painting is transformed overnight into a tarted-up version of the comic strip, can we doubt that the Philistines will be there in their hordes?

For what we see here may be, in many respects, a genuine Holman Hunt; but it entirely subverts the artist's original intention, which was precisely that his subjects and subject matter should not move, that the piano should make no sound, that the light at the window should be forever frozen. Only thus could he achieve his intention of forcing the viewer to reflect on such profundities and delights as he, Hunt, had to offer. There was room, even in Hunt's limited art, for the connoisseur. Now the connoisseur is banished forever. Thanks to Hazelgard Neff's computer, the connoisseur has been elbowed out of the way by the rubberneck.

It would be vain to claim much majesty for Hunt's original conception, but at least he strove to present us, as honestly as he could, with the dilemma of a fallible woman. All that has been banished now. Instead, we have the privilege of following her into the toilet.

There are nine other pictures in this exhibition, all of which have been subjected to the same perverted ingenuity. One may watch—to name the most saddening victims of Neff's new technique—the horses led off and the old house closed in Samuel Waller's *Day of Reckoning;* Chatterton, the golden boy, quaff down his poison as dawn comes up in those hues uniquely Henry Wallis'; Poynter's Roman sentry overcome by the disaster at Pompeii; and J. M. W. Turner's little steam train cross a viaduct in a storm and its passengers alight at Maidenhead station.

As yet, we may remain, if not entirely calm, at least composed. For, as yet, the Neff studios have desecrated no major artist, with the exception of Turner. But I give warning now. Rembrandt, Giotto, El Greco, Botticelli, Titian, Tiepolo—none can rest easy in their graves. Within five years I predict, we shall have the Mona Lisa smiling and waving at us, and shall be able to follow her as she trips away to sweep down her back porch.

The long struggle between art and science is at last over. Science has won. Given a few more years, it alone will possess the field.

Hazelgard Neff took off his cloak without speaking.
Catherine walked over to him and laid a hand on his shoulder.
"How's the rapture, honey?" she asked.
"There's a split in the seam," he said. He hid his face in his hands. "You try to give . . . you try to give . . . You devote your life to it. And they don't understand."
She clutched at him, but he brushed her away.
"That is the artist's role—to strike out always for something new, to break away, to defy, to . . . to grapple with the unfamiliar . . .".
He staggered out to the terrace, confronted the long shallow steps, stared toward the ever-changing aspect of parkland.
Only the familiar ghosts confronted him, the deserted webs of other lives, other epochs.
She went to make some coffee.

Brian W. Aldiss writes:

My story is about a current preoccupation—the future of the arts in a world where technology increasingly intrudes on the personal. I have written several such stories, but this one embodies the future art machine that pleases me most, though the fulcrum of the story is not so much the machine as possible responses to it.

The format of the story is a tripartite one I have been using increasingly of late. By telling three overlapping stories that the reader is able to read all together, a greater density and complexity can be achieved.

Writers mainly fall into two groups; either they are forest clearers or explorers. Some like to tidy the world and reduce it to a clear and understandable diagram. Others prefer to wander in the wilderness, rejoicing in it for its own sake. I like the wilderness. I have tried to put down a few human ambiguities without attempting to tidy them away.

NIGHTBEAT

by Neal Barrett, Jr.

The wakechimes touched me with the sound of cinnamon. I stretched, turned over, and watched the clockroach play time games against the wall. It marked the spidery minutes in fine script and left crystal dungtracks behind.

It was half-past blue, and a lemon moon spilled color into the room. Its light burnished Bethellen's hair to silver and brushed her flesh with coffee shadow.

She stirred once, and I slid quietly away, padded to the shower cage, and let cool spicewater bring me awake. There were cocoa-cubes where Bethellen had left them, but I passed them by and trotted back to the nightroom. My Copsuit sprang from its hollow with a sunfresh scent, and I slipped into it quickly.

I would have liked to look at myself. A small vanity, but mine own. I take a pride in the uniform. It's a Copsuit in the classical cut—basic whipcord in umber and vermilion, sepia pullover, and fringe-leather vest. The jackboots, gloves, and chainbelt are traditional indigo. The Marshal's Star of David is cadmium-gold, and the Peacemaker by my side is finest quartz and ivory.

Set. Ready to go, and a last look at Bethellen. She had turned in her sleep to catch the moonwaves. Citron limbs bared to an ocher sea. By morning, I'd taste lemon on her lips.

Outside, the prowlbug hummed to electric life. The moon was high now, and a second had joined it—a small saffron tag-along. Lime shadows colored the streetways. The dashglow winked me into service, and I switched the roadlights and moved along.

The street ribboned over soft hills furred with bonebrake, and through dark groves of churnmoss. Raven blossoms hung from high branches nearly to the ground. I swung the prowlbug into Bluewing, whispered through Speaklow, and coasted down the steep circle to Singhill.

There were people all about now. If I listened, I could feel the sound of their sleeping. From Tellbridge I watched lonelights far and away. Not everyone slumbered, then, but all were snug in their homeshells till the day. None would stir before Amberlight polished the world. For that was as it was—the day belongs to us, but not the night.

I have often stopped the prowlbug and dimmed the lights and watched the darklife. In moments, the night fills with chitter-hums and thrashes. A beetlebear stops to sniff the air, pins me with frosty muzzle and razoreyes. For a while there is pink carnage in her heart; then she scutters by clanging husky armor. Jac-Jacs and Grievers wing the dark hollows. A Bloodgroper scatters his kill. There is much to darklife, and few have seen it as it is.

A quarter till yellow. The dashglow hemorrhages, coughs up a number. The prowlbug jerks into motion, whines up the speedscale. Sirens whoopa-whoopa-whoopa through the night, and I switch on the traditional lilac, plum, and scarlet flashers.

There are no strollwalkers to pause and wonder. No other bugs abroad to give me away. Still, there are customs to keep alive, bonds with the past.

The address was nearby. Prowlbug skittered up the snakepath around Henbake. Pressed me tight against the driveseat. Pink lights to port. A homeshell high on Stagperch, minutes away.

Around a corner, and green sparkeyes clustered ahead—nightmates and shadelings hunkered in the streetway. The prowlbug whoopa-ed a warning, and they scattered like windleaves.

They were waiting for me, portal open. A big man with worry lines scribbled on paper features. His handstrobe stitched my path with lightcraters to shoo stray nightlings. The woman was small and pretty. Hands like frightened birds. I moved through them up turnstairs past buffwalls to the boy's room.

I'd been there before, but they didn't remember. No-face in a uniform.

A child in Dreamspasm is not a pretty sight. I punched his record on the bedscreen, scanned it quickly. Twelve and a half. Fifth Dream. Two-year sequence. No complications. I gripped one bony arm and plunged Blue Seven in his veins. The spasms slowed to a quiver. I touched him, wiped foamspittle from his cheeks. His skin was cold, frogdank. Waterblue eyes looked up at nothing. The small mouth sucked air.

"He's all right." The man and woman huddled behind. "Take him in in the morning. Don't think he did internal damage, but it won't hurt to check."

I laid a vial beside the bed. "One if he wakes. I don't think he will."

"Thank you," said the man. "We're grateful." The woman nodded his words.

"No problem." I stopped in the hall and faced them again. "You know he could secondary."

They looked startled, as if they didn't.

"If he does, stay with him."

They frowned questions, and I shook my head. "Punch in if you like, but there's nothing else I can do. He can't have Seven again. And a strong secondary's a good sign." I sent them a Copgrin. "He's old enough. You could be out of the woods."

They gave each other smiles and said things I didn't hear. The prowlbug was turning all my buttons red and shrieking whoopas into the night. I bounded down turnstairs and tore out the portal. No time for strobes and such. If nightlings got underfoot, they'd get a jackboot for their trouble.

The prowlbug scattered gravel, skit-tailed into the streetway. It was wound up and highwhining and I held on and let it have its way. Stagperch faded, and the snakepath dizzied by in black patches. I prayed against sleepy megapedes bunked in on the road ahead. A tin medal for Bethellen. Early insurance.

The dashglow spit data, but I already knew. Bad. Category A and climbing. Name of Lenine Capral and long overdue. First Dream and fifteen.

The Rules say punch before you practice. No way with Lenine Capral. No record, no time, no need. The Dream had her in nighttalons. Down on the dark bottom, and nothing for it. Lost, lost Lenine.

I drew the Peacemaker, pressed the muzzle between her eyes. Her body arched near double, limbs spread-eagled. I pulled back lids and looked. Milkpools. Silverdeath darting about. The little shiverteeth nibbling away.

I tossed my jacket aside. Grabbed a handful of hair and pinned her neck where I wanted it. Put the muzzle low behind the ear and up. This time, shock jerked a small arm and snapped it like crackwood. But nothing snapped Lenine.

I couldn't shoot her again. More would burn her skull bone-dry. And nothing in the little glass tubes. Blue Seven was fine for the boy —about as good as mouse pee for Lenine.

Okay. One deep breath and down to dirty fighting. I ripped the sheet away. Stripped her bare. She was slim and fragile, too close to womantime. I spread her wide, and the motherperson made little noises.

"Out."

The man understood and moved her.

Dreamspasm is a thing of the mind. But that door's closed for helpers. The physical road is the only way. Peacemakers. Blue Seven. Redwing. And after that: physical stimuli to build mental bridges back home. Countershock for young minds. For Lenine Capral, therapeutic rape. Thumb the Peacemaker to lowbuzz and hope this one's led a sheltered life.

Hurt her good.

Whisper uglies in her ear.

Slap and touch and tear. No gentle Peacemaker funsies. Only the bad parts. A child's garden of horrors. Everything Mother said would happen if the bad man gets his hands on you.

Orange.

Red-thirty.

Coming up violet. Cream-colored dawn on the windows.

And finally the sound you want. Lenine the wide-eyed screamer. The violated child awake and fighting. Afraid of real things, now. Scared out of Dreamspasm One.

Quickly out and past the hoverfaces. No gushy gratitude here. Mother doesn't thank the Coprapist.

Outside, dawnbreeze turns the sweat clammy cold. A medbug has braved the nightlings all the way from Fryhope. Lenine will get proper patching.

The prowlbug has a homepath in mind, as well it might. Only I am not ready for Bethellen and breakfast. Both are out of temper with the night's affairs. Instead, I brave the prowlbug's grumblings, move past Slowrush, and wind down to Hollow. The road ends, and prowlbug will duly record that I have violated Safecode and am afoot before the dawn. The nightlings don't concern me. They've fed before

Firstlight and bear no ill. At the stream I hear their thrums and splashings as they cross back over to find hugburrows for the day.

The stream is swift and shallow and no wider than a childstep. It makes pleasant rillsongs and winds beneath green chumtrees. It has no name. It is simply the stream that divides the world. Dark from light. Night from day.

There is still nightshadow on the other side. The groves are thick and heavy. I watch, wait, and listen to the stream music.

Timebug says half-past violet. While I wait, I polish dun-glasses. Put them on. They help to see what is, and temper what isn't at all. Wait.

Watch the waterlights.

A blink and a breath and he's there. As if he'd been there all along.

For a moment my stomach does its tightness. But it's not so bad for me. They make teetiny headchanges in policemen. Little slicecuts that go with the Copsuit. But there is still a childmind to remember. Dreamspasms in dark nightrooms.

Through the dun-glasses I can see bristly no-color. Hear his restless flickersounds. See him move with the shape of frostfur. Hear him breathe hot darkness. Sense his crush-heavy limbs.

Only, I cannot see or hear these things at all.

I wonder if he watches, and what he sees of me. I have to look away. And when I look again, he is gone. Nothing has changed in the thickgroves.

What would I say to him? That wouldn't need the saying?

Back to the prowlbug. Ten till indigo now. Amberlight dares the high ridges. Sucks away darkness.

I imagine him. Thromping and shiffing. Dark fengroves away. Safe against the sunstar. And all the young darklings purged of manfear. Only fright-thoughts, now—fading daydemons named Lenine.

Who can tell such a thing? The stream divides the world. Whatever could be said is what he knows. That there are pinchfew places left. That mostly there is nothing. That we will have to make do with what there is to share.

Neal Barrett, Jr., writes:

It is no news that we're running out of bunks on this small green dormitory of ours—a problem we handle, at best, with cautious pessimism and renewed apathy. You are my polite intruder, and I am yours. We have erected dampers and defenses to keep each other at bay. Courteous walls divide your sins from mine, but nothing works too well. For we live perilously close to one another. The aroma of your Big Mac enhances my coq au vin not at all. Your TV growls ominously at mine. Your lovemaking comes to me in fiberboard fantasies. I know that you are there.

So far, your dreams do not intrude upon mine. But this too may come to pass, with someone/something, on one world or another. Which is what "Nightbeat" is all about.

One could argue the credibility of such a tale. For it is inconceivable, now, that we should ever find ourselves planetary roommates with an alien life form. It's a vast, lonely universe out there; innumerable clusters of ripe green Edens hang on the big galactic bush.

Hopefully, that's the way it is. Certainly the way it ought to be. And if it isn't? Well, we've been wrong before. And we can always take solace in the words of Florida's redoubtable developer, Ponce de León, who said: "Just park the trailer anywhere, baby. There's plenty of room for everyone. . . ."

UNEASY CHRYSALIDS, OUR MEMORIES

by John Shirley

JULY 4, 1993

I have been told by my history tutor that since I am an American, today should have some special significance for me. I should feel patriotic and grateful to my country. Or at least I should feel guilty if I don't feel that way. But none of those emotions are present because I didn't know about the importance of the Fourth of July until today. Or at least, the person who I now am didn't know, though probably the old Jo Ann Culpepper did. Marsha, a cheery and energetic girl who I have been told was my best friend, said that I was once quite patriotic as a little girl, and should have been as a woman, especially after the big revival of nationalism after 1986.

A president and three of his cabinet members were assassinated with a bomb, and that sparked off another sort of uprising shortly after July 1986. I gather that most of the insurgents and guerrillas in the U.S. were purged. At least, that is what Mr. Zelenke, my history tutor, tells me, though some of the things he tells me are so outrageous that I often wonder if he makes them up.

According to Marsha, I knew all those historic things before I lost that portion of my memory two years ago, but when I hear them now, they don't actually ring with familiarity.

Dr. Fosdick said that my memory was fractured in September 1991 because of what he called "a permanent complication from glandular damage causing a chemical imbalance rendering mnemonic banks inaccessible, with pathological implications of dementia praecox." I think that was it. He said that it will be impossible for me to get my old memory back, so they will try to give me a background with tutoring.

This diary is supposed to be an exercise for recall. I'm still terribly absentminded, even in small things. I forgot to turn off the tap, and water flooded the house; I forgot to feed my fish, and they died.

Dr. Fosdick said that I could repair my reflexes but that I'll have to settle for what little I have left of my life.

I remember my mother, some. She was tall, thin, dark-haired, like me. That's where I got most of my looks. Even the black eyes with the blue circles under them. It looked good on my mother, but not on me. She was a speedy, nervous person, I think. Always doing something, easily startled. I'm not like that, really I'm not. I'm rather slow with my reactions, and boring to talk to. People get tired of me easily.

But it's not as if I had nothing to say. I was even thinking of starting an organization to help people with messed-up memories like mine. A lot of people suffer from it, especially politicians, I've noticed.

I don't remember my father much. I doubt if I liked him, somehow.

I wish I could remember more about my mamma. I have to admit I'm lonely. People shouldn't have to *admit* that they're lonely; it's too much like signing a confession. But I feel guilty that I'm lonely, like I've failed socially. Dr. Fosdick says give it time.

They say I was an only child. I once had lots of friends and a boyfriend. I wonder what happened to my boyfriend? No one seems to know. Some of my friends come to see me once in a while. No, that isn't true. Dr. Fosdick said that this journal should be extremely honest. Actually, none of them ever come to see me because of what happened to my parents during the purge by the vigilantes. A lot of people don't like to be associated with me because of my antinationalist background. I wish I could remember my "antinationalist background."

JULY 8, 1993

Dr. Fosdick took me to one of the Independence Day government-sponsored festivals a few days ago. Free beer or pop or hot dogs. I didn't think he'd ask me to go anywhere with him. I thought that his interest in me would be purely clinical. But he has spent an awful lot of time with me.

We were sitting together, leaning our elbows on Minnesota. Each of the fifty tables at the festival was shaped like one of the states, and at the height of the evening they push them all together to symbolize the strengths of nationalism. All the tables together make the shape of the United States, with mustard stains and crumpled paper cups on it. We were drinking Coke, the National Drink (state-owned), out of bottles shaped like Polaris missiles, and eating hot dogs. Those were the only things on the menu. There were a lot of boisterous people making toasts and singing the anthem all around us (see, Dr. Fosdick? I'm using words from my vocabulary exercises when I talk. Like you wanted! Boisterous!), but they had looks of strain, like the celebration was out of character. We were a little island of quiet in the middle of colorful festivity. The festival was on top of the Ford Defense Building, in the open air under the bubble of the smog shield, through which I could barely make out the half-moon. The waiters looked silly dressed in red rags like the Communists wear, and Dr. Fosdick explained that it was supposed to be symbolic of something because they were serving us. I thought that it was symbolic of the silliness of the organizers of the festival, but I couldn't say that.

I sat quietly, wondering if Dr. Fosdick had ever had connections with the vigilantes. I am sure that he didn't, because he took me in after they killed my parents, and no nationalist would shelter the daughter of impurities.

Dr. Fosdick said something strange to me, then: "Sometimes it's a valuable asset to have no memory. You have no regrets that way. I envy you at times, Jo Ann." That was the first time he'd ever called me Jo Ann. Always it was Miss Culpepper. I didn't know what to say, so I smiled.

I was sort of disappointed the first time I met Dr. Fosdick. I had thought that he would be an imposing Germanic figure with thick spectacles and an accent and a white laboratory smock. That was how a scientist was supposed to look, I thought. But when I was introduced to him seven months ago, I met a short little man with coarse black hair greased back like a cowboy's, no glasses over his shiny blue eyes. Dr. Fosdick has a rusty face. He wears jeans and a plaid shirt, even at work, never touches a white smock, and he listens to country music. We had to leave the festival early when some vigs recognized me. So we didn't get to see the sky rockets or the floggings.

JULY 10, 1993

I underwent something ugly today. It is running around in my head like a dog that's chained in one place so long it tracks a circular rut around itself in the dirt.

They made me relive the incident that took away my memory. I didn't want to do it. I wish that the incident itself was washed out, but for some reason, only everything before it is gone. They aren't sure if it was the thing that happened or the blow I got on the head that took it away. Maybe both.

My memory goes back two years. It starts with the incident, and everything before that is gone except for a few fragments: high-school graduation, studying English (Marsha says that I gave up my ambition to be an English teacher after the book burnings), women's-infantry-corps initiation and the recovery in the hospital after the initiation, a trial of some kind (though I can't remember what I was tried for), some childhood pictures of my mother happily working in her garden, my aunt on her deathbed, a dog biting my ankle, a date with a boy who insisted on sodomy instead of the usual . . . and then the incident.

The nurses at the clinic are very sympathetic when I tell what happened. They make tsk noises about the men who killed my parents, but none of them ever say anything directly against the vigs. I'm not bitter.

Before the incident, my memories of education leave off with a little geography, ability to write (I had to relearn how to read), the names of the nations in the UN except for the United States. Some math and grammar, but almost no lit, which was once my specialty.

And the incident. The men who came into our apartment and what they did with knives to my mother and father. The blood, the blades, the screams, the curious neighbors looking in the open door. I can't understand why it wasn't erased. The memories of my parents that might have made me hate their killers are lost.

I had to relive it once today, so I'd rather not go into it more now.

JULY 30, 1993

I haven't written in this journal for so long because so many wonderful things have happened that I just didn't know how to express it.

Well, perhaps that is an exaggeration. To make myself feel better. Because there are some things I've been worried about, too.

I didn't think anyone would ever care about me much, because I'm pretty shallow and I have this habit of running myself down. But Dr. Fosdick says that if people look down on me it's because I look down on myself. And someone *does* care about me. Dr. Fosdick. I guess it's okay to talk about all this here, though I feel funny talking about Dr.

Fosdick, because I know he's going to read this. I'm supposed to be honest, so that he'll know how much I've improved and all.

Dr. Fosdick made love to me yesterday at my apartment. I think he had been considering it for a while, because he had insisted that I take birth-control pills, though I was sure that no one would ever want to sleep with me. He must have cared about me right off, to have prepared for it so long ahead of time.

He came to my apartment unexpectedly, with the usual dope that people bring on social visits; but it wasn't the government-issue green-weed kind, it was the white powdery sort that makes you excited. He really didn't need to give me cocaine for *that,* however. I had waited for a long time. I can't really remember any of my other lovers, so I can't compare Dr. Fosdick to anyone. (It's funny, but he has never asked me to call him by his first name, and I don't even know what it is. I had to call him Dr. Fosdick when he made love to me.) He was nice, and he didn't even mind that I was in my period. He was energetic, like those really fast pistons you see on the Eagle car commercials on the viddy.

But something else has happened. After we made love, he gave me an injection in my right arm (it's still sore) with a syringe from a leather case he had in his coat pocket. He said that it was a serum that might bring back my memory.

I asked him why he couldn't give it to me at the clinic, and he replied that it was still a bit experimental and that he hadn't had it officially approved as yet. The medical board wouldn't let him use it until it was too late. It had to be injected within a certain period of time after the original loss of memory, he told me, or else it wouldn't work. He held my hand and said very earnestly that the medical board didn't care about my recovery like he did.

The only thing that really disturbed me was that he injected it into my arm without asking me first, or even telling me. I turned away from him for a moment, and the next thing I knew, there was a needle stinging my arm.

He explained that he had wanted it to be a surprise.

AUGUST 4, 1993

Two things happened today that should mean something to me, I think, though they seem distant and removed from me.

I was walking with Dr. Fosdick in the lower corridors of the subterranean shopping center looking at the "new" Revolutionary War-style dresses in the shop windows. It was Friday, so the walk was crowded with people going to the free U.S.-history exhibitions in the auditorium down the way. Among that crowd, I saw one of the men who had stabbed my mother and father. He was a big man with his hair shaved into the star and his eyes very red from dope. He was walking with another man I didn't recognize. The first man pointed at me and laughed, taking a step toward me. Dr. Fosdick motioned for me to remain where I was. He walked briskly over to the man with the star on his square head and said something to him I couldn't hear. The man laughed again, but nodded and walked away.

I felt very detached from the whole scene, but there was a certain sense of *déjà vu*.

The other thing that happened was the headline on the front page of *The Daily Loyalty:* UNITED STATES WITHDRAWS FROM UN. Mr. Zelenke says that the withdrawal marks the end of a disappointing era.

We were discussing the event at my lesson, after I came back from the shopping center. He said that the withdrawal was a further step toward the "Purification of Resources" goal the Hearth government had set for itself.

Mr. Zelenke is a spindly, kindly man with a large nose and eyes that slant downward so mournfully I always feel I should agree with whatever he says to keep him from crying. He always seems to be on the point of tears.

But this time something grated in me when he said "purification."

"But couldn't it be," I objected in a coarser tone than I am used to, "that they are pulling out of the UN because they're scared?"

Mr. Zelenke was upset and probably would have started crying if I hadn't taken it all back.

AUGUST 6, 1993

Some cruelly surprising things happened today.

I was sitting with Dr. Fosdick in his office. He had an arm around my shoulders, and he was reading a poem to me from a book called *Flowers of Evil* by Charles Baudelaire.

"This book was my wife's favorite," he said casually as he flipped through the yellowed pages with his rough right hand. I leaned against him, pretending to look at the book. I don't have much to myself, really. Very little memory. I feel like a sort of scarecrow in personality, just a rag on some broomsticks. Because people are made of memories. And leaning against Dr. Fosdick makes me feel like his memories are mine, too, somehow.

"Are you separated from your wife?" I asked. I asked mostly out of obligation, because I really didn't want him to think about her.

"No. She's dead two years. Killed in a . . . landslide. It was one of those stupid, unexpected accidents. We were hiking . . ." His voice got husky.

Strange. My parents have been dead two years. The timing of our tragedies was the same.

"I understand," I said, feeling bad for bringing it up at all. "You don't have to talk about it."

He took a deep breath. "Anyway, this was her favorite poetry." He began to read out loud. I didn't like the poetry much, but maybe I didn't understand it right. And I was distracted by the sore place on my arm where Dr. Fosdick had injected me again that afternoon.

But two stanzas sounded almost familiar, and I can't get them out of my mind. They are from a poem called *The Flask:*

> . . . and hinges creak or in a press
> in some deserted house where the sharp stress
> of odors old and dusty fill the brain
> an ancient flask is brought to light again
>
> And forth the ghosts of long dead odors creep
> there, softly trembly in the shadows, sleep
> a thousand thoughts, funereal chrysalids
> phantoms of the old folding darkness hide . . .

A woman was standing in the office with us! There was no way that she could have gotten in; the door was locked. The woman was lovely and covered with white mist that still revealed the outlines of her nude body, her blond hair streaming over her white shoulders.

I gasped, and Dr. Fosdick asked, almost eagerly, "What's wrong? Did the poem upset you?"

I pointed at the woman. He looked in that direction, right through her, then looked back at me and shrugged.

"Don't you see her?" I whispered.

The woman was coming toward us. And now I could see that she was looking at Dr. Fosdick with hate in her narrow green eyes.

Then she vanished. Just like that.

Dr. Fosdick says that it was a hallucination symptomatic of the return of my memory. He says that she is probably some important figure out of my past whom I didn't recognize yet.

But there was no familiarity about her at all. She looked Scandinavian, about thirty. Where would I have met such a person, and seen her naked?

I was scared the rest of the day, knowing that she was somewhere around.

AUGUST 20, 1993

Dr. Fosdick asked to see this journal last Friday. I told him that I had destroyed it because it contained parts which embarrassed me. He seemed to repress anger, but he insisted that it was very important to my progress for him to know my inner feelings. I apologized and said that I would start another journal.

Of course, I didn't really destroy it, but I hid it. I don't know why exactly. Or perhaps I do know. I hate to think about it, but I don't trust Dr. Fosdick anymore. I wanted to trust him. I wanted to fall in love with him. But I can't. Maybe it's because he says that he is in love with me, and I cannot believe that anyone could love me.

But disquieting things have happened lately.

The woman has come back many times. I would see her in the corners of the room, sitting, looking at me as if I were a mirror. I didn't tell Dr. Fosdick about it.

I have had some strange recollections. I seem to recall being a little girl on a dairy farm owned by my parents. Perhaps my memory of my mother as tall and thin is a distortion of the chemical imbalance I was supposed to have, because the woman I remember as my mother on the dairy farm had red hair and freckles and a tall blond husband.

I remember going to medical school, though Marsha didn't tell me anything about that. The faces around me at the school are indistinct and unidentified. There is an alien sense to these memories that makes me feel like an actress who has memorized her lines, only to find herself in the wrong play.

I have one peculiarly vivid memory of walking alone in a park. It is a spring day tempered by a cool breeze, the heaters under the bushes adding to the faint warmth that comes to us from the sunlight penetrating the smog shield. I'm in a secluded place, though the path is well beaten by lovers. There is lush greenery on all sides, with little firecracker tongues of red and yellow flowers. The background detail of the dream is lucid, but the human events are blurry, like a camera shot that shifts in and out of focus confusingly.

I am looking at a blue jay who is looking back at me from a branch of a pussy willow a few feet from my face. The bird cocks its head as if it's listening to my thoughts and doesn't want to miss anything. Its eyes are shining like the beads of sweat on my forehead. We regard each other for a minute, and then it screams raucously and flurries at my face. I put up my hands to shield my eyes, but the bird flies over my shoulder, and I hear someone cry out behind me. There are two men there, one with his hands to his face. He grunts: "Why did it attack me? Damn thing. Kill it!"

"Too late. It got away," the other man says in a voice that is almost familiar. "You must have come too near its nest. Blue jays are temperamental like that."

The first man drops his hand, and there are three long hyphens reddening his right cheek where the bird clawed him. "Well, the woman's still here, she ain't flown off. Let's take care of her." He takes a step toward me.

But the other man puts a restraining hand on his companion's arm. I cannot see the face of the second man; it is as if he wears a mask of mist.

"No, leave her alone. Our information was wrong. She goes to my school. She's not one of them, she's a nationalist."

I nod hastily, and note the Captain America armbands on the right bicep of each man. Nationalist vigilantes.

I feel like I should know the man who intervened for me, but his face is lost. He puts a rough hand on my arm, smiling. . . .

The memory ends there. It is like the chrysalis of some strange creature struggling to emerge. But I know I was never a nationalist. My father was a dissenting liberal. That's why the vigs killed my parents.

Did the stranger with the lost face lie for me?

Somewhere, there is a very important lie.

SEPTEMBER 1, 1993

I'm frightened. I'm scared of myself because I have developed an unreasoning hatred for Dr. Fosdick. I think of excuses to avoid my therapeutic sessions with him, and I've broken all our dates.

And when I reread my diary, parts of it—especially the last part— sound like they were written by someone else. "The chrysalis of some strange creature . . ." Did I say that? I don't know what I meant by that. And the handwriting in the August 20 section of my diary is smaller than usual, almost crabbed. Maybe I was just in a hurry.

But this morning I went to get my hair done. They asked me if I had an appointment, and I said, "Yes, of course. The same time I've come to this hairdresser's every week for four years." And then I caught myself and wondered why I had said that. I hadn't been to that hairdresser before. I usually do my own hair. And they said they had no appointment for me. The secretary gave me a strange look and took off her reading glasses to watch me as I left.

I had made an appointment; I remember it distinctly. I remember playing with the cat with a pencil while calling the hairdresser's on the phone. But I don't have a cat.

And I've been sleepwalking. I woke up last night in the kitchen. I'm afraid to tell anyone about all this. They'd put me away for sure.

So I just sit in my drab apartment and try not to think about it. I try to read, but I'm too nervous to sit still enough to concentrate.

My apartment has two rooms—bathroom and the combination living room, bedroom, and kitchenette. It's paid for by my parents' insurance. The rooms are undecorated. I took down the pictures Dr. Fosdick gave to me.

I shift uncomfortably in my wooden chair as I write this, because my clothes are tormenting me. They are all too small, though I haven't gained any weight. I no longer like the colors and textures of my clothing. Too drab. Crude. I can't imagine why I chose them.

There is something missing in my room, as if it should have another life in it besides mine. Something small to warm up the corners and add motion. A pet. A small dog? A cat! I've never wanted one before, but I have an empty spot in me, like a little drawer pulled open in my chest where a miniature life should fit in to supplement my own. . . .

When I read, it's always poetry. I disliked poetry before, but lately I've been reading Baudelaire. I'm beginning to see the veins of death that he talks about, veins that run through the walls of any place you have grown accustomed to. The old man living upstairs is part of a conspiracy to convince me that old age is inevitable so that I will make supplications to time.

I no longer see the woman, but I feel her presence. And I can catch glimpses of a small animal that I can't identify running around the floor in the room, poking its nose from behind chairs or hiding under cushions, darting just on the periphery of my vision. I suspect that it is my lost pet. It is like the panther in Rilke's poem who was behind bars so long that its existence is so wholly subjective it might as well be dead.

Rereading this diary, I am growing more and more worried. Because I am certain that Jo Ann Culpepper had never read Rilke. She disliked poetry. And she would never have said anything about "supplications to time" and all that. And the handwriting is almost a scribble.

I find it increasingly easy to refer to Jo Ann Culpepper almost formally, as if I were speaking of a relative who had passed away. . . . Someone whose memory I can regard as I would a caged animal.

SEPTEMBER 1, 1993

Marsha came to see me today, just as I was feeding the two cats I got from the pound.

Marsha is an Irish dumpling, springy and so optimistic that it makes me pessimistic. I don't know why I feel vindictive toward her all of a sudden. I think we were once good friends. It is cruel of me. But I felt antipathy from the moment she came into my room.

"Hello, hello! Ohhh, it's been so *long,* Jo Ann, no *kid*ding. I've been really *worry*ing *about* you. Dr. Fosdick, too. He asked me to—"

I glared the dimples from her round cheeks. "Did Dr. Fosdick tell you to come?"

"What's wrong?" Her saccharine voice faltered, and she put a hand to her doughy face as if to adjust a feature slipped out of place. I just looked at her, trying to remember.

But I felt no friendship for her. She was brown and hamsterlike, a rodent snuck into my room, an invader, a stranger come to sell me something.

"I don't want anything," I said. I had picked up a vase with one hand without noticing having done it. When she looked at the vase, I quelled the urge to brain her with it, and set it back on the table. My trembling fingers left it slightly rocking.

"What? Jo Ann—"

"I don't need you or Dr. Fosdick."

"*Jo Ann.*" She was hurt.

"I'm sorry," I said, seeing the blond woman standing in the corner, her jade-green eyes stony with loathing. I saw her only in my mind's eye this time, but so vividly I thought that she was about to slap

Marsha across the face. But Marsha smiled, reassured, as I said, "Well . . . How have you been?"

We chatted uncomfortably for a while, until the estrangement grew into embarrassment. Then she left, murmuring about coming back soon, calling the clinic, they're worried.

I hope I never see her again. If she gives me that "It's-been-so-long" crap again, I'll feed her to my cats.

SEPTEMBER 5, 1993

I was afraid that he'd come and smash my door down if I didn't, so I went to visit Dr. Fosdick today. I forced myself.

"Thank God," he said, nervous, embarrassed at his unprofessional outburst. "I've been worried sick about you. Why didn't you answer the door when I knocked?" His mouth worked as if he were trying to keep something from escaping from it, and his lips were the parting folds of a chrysalis.

"I . . . must have been asleep, Doctor."

He looked into my eyes and raised a brow. "Really?"

How dare he question *my* honesty! I thought furiously. Fake it. He can have you committed.

I shrugged. "I haven't been well. Sleep too deeply."

"What? Not well? Here, sit down." I sat by him on the con-foam couch in his office and toyed with the leaves of a potted plant, shredding them one by one between my grotesquely thin fingers.

"In some ways I have been improving. I've been more . . . articulate lately. Words come to me more easily than they used to. I've begun to remember some books I must have read before . . ." Then I sensed that I was telling him things he shouldn't know.

"You *do* look more confident. . . . But what is it that you have been remembering?" He put an arm around me. I pushed it off. He frowned but only opened his desk drawer for the little tape recorder for the session. In that swift movement I saw in the open drawer a framed photo of the woman of my apparition. She was sitting on a lawn in an evening gown, surrounded by three large cats. One of the cats was very black and perched itself on one of her soft shoulders, nestling in her lush blond hair. The cat seemed to be looking at me, until Dr. Fosdick closed the drawer on its golden eyes.

The woman in the photo had been Dr. Fosdick's wife. I remembered; she remembered.

"There is a surprise waiting for you back at your flat," Dr. Fosdick was saying. "I had it sent—" But I cut him off with as hard a slap as I could manage, leaving a red imprint on his cowboy jaw. I turned and ran from the office, pushing an astounded secretary to the floor in a flurry of overturned papers as I rushed past. A bus was just loading outside. I hopped aboard and turned to look at Dr. Fosdick as he ran, unheeded, after the bus a block back. His face, getting smaller, was the face of the man of my memory—the vigilantes in the park, the medical student, Dr. Lawrence Fosdick, my husband. Older, but undeniably it was he.

Jo Ann Culpepper didn't know him before the loss of her memory.

But I remember a night in a beach cabin on the coast of Maine. I could map the topography of his hands over my breasts; on breasts fuller than Jo Ann's, between hips wider than hers.

I remember our quiet marriage, our work together at the clinic, the exhaustive private work at the laboratory after our regular hours at the clinic.

And Lawrence's warnings. He said that I should not make fun of the vigs. But I hated the nationalists. They controlled Lawrence, and through him puppeted me. Since Lawrence was vigilante coordinator for our sector, he was expected to live up to a vig model. They made a ridiculous cartoon of our private life.

He warned me again. But I derided the nationalists at our parties, where a quarter of our guests were vigs.

I think I knew they would kill us. But: *Death may rise, a sun of another kind, and bring to blossom the flowers of their minds*. Baudelaire again.

I wanted to kill us both, but only one of us died.

He stood behind me on the mountainside, and I knew what he was going to do.

I didn't try to stop him, because I thought he would pull us both over the edge. But he pushed only me. I fell, saw him receding, getting smaller against the sky, and I felt the giant hand crumple me in granite fingers. The landslide skinned me alive under jagged rocks. A million points of penetration.

I lay in shock, my exposed face shredded into a red sponge soaking up pain. I watched my husband scuttle down the hillside path, jumping over sagebrush and winding around the tormented bristlecone pines, himself an animate root. He stood over me with his face twitching in a thin-sauce parody of my agony. I remember the moment of death shining like the jeweled eyes of a rapacious blue jay.

I remembered all, seeing him get smaller as the bus left him behind, as if I was falling from the cliff again. Smaller. I hurried back to my room, managed to get there before he did.

There was his "surprise." A fat and butter-yellow canary in an ornate cage with a note tied to it with a ribbon. I didn't bother to read the note, but I took the cage inside. The bird fluttered in its confinement like a memory that wants to be forgotten. It reminded me of Marsha. So, while I was packing my bags, I left the cage door open with the cats in front of it.

By the time I had everything I needed—I would travel light, leave most of Jo Ann's clothes behind, and buy new things later—the cats were finished. I brushed stray feathers from their whiskers and took them along in a paper sack, grabbed up the suitcase, and took a cab to a hotel. On the way to the hotel we passed through a neighborhood that Lawrence and I had once lived in. We had lived in this neighborhood, across from the playfield of the elementary school, during the time we unlocked the memory code.

Experimenting on rats, Lawrence and I found that the memory of the sound of an electric bell was chemically recorded into an eight-segment chain of six amino acids. When the chemicals were isolated from the brain and injected into other rats that were not trained to the sound, the untrained animals acted as if they had been conditioned to the bell. My husband simply extrapolated it into humanity. . . . Typical of him to find it easy to compare people with trained animals.

Combinations of twenty amino acids produce peptides that are programmed with certain memories, according to which sequence of amino acids is chosen. Larry found which combinations of amino acids correlated with general memories in rats. It wouldn't be difficult —merely tedious—to carry the process into evaluation of the human memory system.

He never told me what he had intended to do with the results. Perhaps the national Hearth would use it to train soldiers, injecting memories synthesized from a trained fighter pilot into the brain of a trainee. Or maybe extract information from prisoners by withdrawing their memories and reinjecting them into volunteers. If I can help it, they'll never use it for anything. I put up with the vigs for convenience's sake, but they forced the issue. I should have known where Lawrence's loyalties would be, him and his fucking cowboy music.

The day after the final proofs of success, he was called to a vig meeting. They were voting as to whether to purge a Professor Culpepper. The vote was affirmative. Larry, in his capacity as regional coordinator, signed the death order. But he asked that the professor's only child, the girl, be spared and turned over to the clinic. He had use for her. No one objected. It didn't matter if the girl attempted to tell the authorities who'd killed her parents. The vigs are "officially" frowned upon, but actually sanctified by the national Hearth government. They are never brought to court.

The girl was just seventeen, ripe time in the development of her memory coordinations. But it turned out even better than he had hoped. Her memory had blanked from the shock of witnessing her parents' murder. There would be no complications of her prior memory patterns if he were to introduce new combinations of peptides. But first he had to obtain them. A day later he received an ultimatum from the vigs. His wife must be killed because of her impurities, or he . . .

He told me about the ultimatum and said that we would hide in our cabin in the Ozarks until the danger was over.

Then he killed me to save his skin and his position.

No. He killed *her. But he carried her back, to the cabin where he'd hidden the equipment, and extracted the mnemonic peptides. And he injected a large portion of Sandra's mnemonic peptides into me.*

I was lucky. He also saved the memories of my father; he still has them, frozen. He might have tried to put those in me, and I would have killed myself by now if he had. He injected too much of Sandra in me, because I remember more than he wanted.

I am tall, thin, five-foot-eight, weigh a hundred-ten. But someone who weighed one-hundred-thirty and who was five inches shorter than I is trying to fit herself into my body. There isn't enough room. There is an overwhelming nausea, as if I'd overeaten to the point of vomiting. I feel like the whole nation must have felt in 1986. Usurped. Cut open from the inside.

The husband of the string of cold chemical memories ordered the vigs to kill my father, then killed his wife. Then he made her memories mine. Why? Because he wanted her back? He must have been crazy with remorse.

Crazy with remorse? What crap. Jo Ann is an idiot if she believes that. Vigilantes know no remorse. He brought me back because he's an inept incompetent.

But Jo Ann deserves everything she got. It makes me nauseated to read the first part of her diary. It's full of fatuous and naïve comments like "I was even thinking of starting an organization to help people with messed-up memories . . ." and "He was nice, and he didn't even mind that I was in my period." And I'm revolted by the big-eyed innocence in the way she looks at things. She let him dominate her. "Leaning against him . . ." I think he was able to justify killing me to himself because I would never let him dominate me. The gullible little ass trusted him right from the start, let him dominate her until he shot her up with me, erasing bit by bit the last of her vestigial personality.

Lawrence and I used to talk of the possible meanings of our discoveries. Obviously, personality is merely the persistence of memory. Motives are just chemicals. If there are such things as souls, then all souls are alike, distinguished only by their arbitrary trappings of memory.

There is a sickness in my body this evening. Perhaps the air-conditioner isn't working and the carbon monoxide is seeping in.

The night is gathering itself up in dismal layers. First the dusk, then the noises of the car fiends outside, their customized horns braying like donkeys or grunting like bulls; tires squealing, engines grinding piston teeth together. Then a layer of my own exhaustion. My cats escaped their shopping bag when I got out of the cab at the hotel door. I've been out all day prowling around the park, looking for them. No luck. I haven't slept much in the past few days, and there is a decaying night radiation below the strata of my weariness.

If I find the cats I'll kill them for leaving me. I'll feed their remains to an eagle at the zoo when no one's watching.

My mind is formed like the design of a spin painting, dollops of color in a whirlwind.

SEPTEMBER 10, 1993

It makes me feel better to keep this journal. For Jo Ann it was a release. But for me it's a confession.

I went into the clinic when I knew Lawrence would be there alone. I wasn't sure what I was going to do.

He was alone at his desk. He didn't feign felicity as I had expected. He knew that I remembered everything. His eyes were grave and his voice monotonous. "I want you to understand, Sandra—"

"If it were just me, maybe I could go away and forget. I can't stand that naïve little bitch you seduced, but something about the way you killed her parents and then took her for experiments and then killed me, all within a couple of days—"

"No. They would have been killed even if I hadn't signed the death order. The vote was almost unanimous. This is a democratic country, after all." He smiled bitterly.

"And how did you vote?"

He turned his back to me, opened a cabinet, extracted the leather case containing the hypodermic.

I broke a chloroform bottle over his head and jumped back with a handkerchief to my mouth. He fell amid the broken glass, his tense body slowly unraveling, going limp.

When he was unconscious, I dragged him to the nearest table and set to work. The method he had used on Jo Ann was permanent, because it was implemented gradually. In our early experiments we tried injecting memories into an unconscious man whose own memory was undamaged. If done with unerring precision, this technique worked temporarily. And then left the subject a babbling moron for the remainder of his life. We wanted something more permanent and less wasteful. But it would do for my purposes. I went to the freezer and found the mnemonic solution for Professor Culpepper.

Two hours later Professor Albert Culpepper, temporarily housed in Lawrence, awoke and sat up, rubbing his temples. I had my face disguised by a surgical mask on the off-chance that he might recognize his daughter, though she'd changed with age.

Culpepper bridled, looked startled, quickly scanned the room with frantic eyes.

"Where are they? Jo Ann? Sadie?" He croaked.

"Take it easy," I said. He jumped to his feet and whirled into an antagonistic crouch, hands outstretched, face infuriated. Seeing me— not one of the party of vig killers he remembered—he relaxed some but remained wary. "Professor Culpepper. Your wife and your little girl are dead. Murdered. You saw your wife stabbed, remember?"

"Yes." His eyes showed whites all around the pupils. He began to grow agitated, gritting his teeth, fingers clenching and unclenching. "Where are they? The vigs!" From between clenched teeth. Lawrence had extracted a heavy dose of Culpepper's last-moment emotions. Mostly hate.

I handed him the automatic pistol I'd found in Lawrence's desk. "The vigs will be having a meeting in twenty-five minutes at this address. Five blocks from here." I gave him the slip of paper. He put it in his pocket with trembling hands.

I was about to launch into a speech designed to convince him to wreak vengeance on the vigs. No need to bother. He ran from the room growling incoherently.

He had an hour and a half as Culpepper. He would make it. He'd probably get five or six of them before they got him.

As for me . . .

I say *me*, not *we*. There is only one. Oh, when I look into the mirror, I see Jo Ann Culpepper's washed-out, neurotic face. My hands are her ugly claws. I hate Lawrence for sticking me with this body. He had no respect for me. He might have found something with elegance. But this clumsy relic has a foul stink to it I can't quite wash away. I deserve better than this. But I'm trapped, whole, in this ungainly parody of womanhood. I'm tired from pounding the bars of this cage. I'm in my hotel room. No sign of the cats. So tired I can hardly think. Pages are blurring.

Maybe Jo Ann, the plebeian whore Jo Ann, was not taken in by Lawrence. Maybe they were working together. The bitch would have done anything for him. So she trapped me in this unclean cell. Brain cells have bars.

If she gets too near the cage, I can reach out through the bars and grab her by her skinny throat and throttle her. She's a fool. She expects me to believe that this is my body. It's not, and I can prove it. I'm going to kill her. I'm going to get the razor and slash her throat. And get out. She thinks she has me hypnotized to believe I'm stuck in here. I'll have my own purge, in a way.

I'm not sure where I'll go after that. Run and hide, I suppose. Maybe I'll sell "Dr. Fosdick's" notes to the men in the red rags.

I'm going now. To get the razor. But I have a nagging feeling that there is something that I have forgotten.

John Shirley writes:

The fact that there is a red-and-white-striped barber pole with a gold ball on top planted in Antarctica at the exact geographical location of the South Pole keeps me awake at night. I saw it on a TV special; some Coast Guard kid put it there. On hearing about this barber pole at the South Pole, Steven P. Brown was heard to remark, "Walt Disney really is God!"

But I beg to differ. After all, that is not a very pious thing to say.

Because Walt Disney far outranks God, and Steve's statement shows little respect for Disney. As a matter of fact, Disney was an artist, in his repressed way. He made his sick self-image respectably ameliorated by streamlining it down into a cute li'l cartoon character. And that is only the inherent perfidy of any artist, no more. He was an artist. And God, you see, is the whipping boy of art. God is a groveling sycophant unto art.

Mother Mary, or Venus, as she was once called (also Mother Nature, or any female fertility archetype), is the handmaiden (as they say at the massage parlours) of art.

The Devil is the slave of art. But that is certainly more illustrious than God's station: cuckold, scapegoat, lackey—somebody for the boss to kick around when he gets pissed.

Of course, an artist has a choice. He can choose to make God perform, do tricks, juggle, or flail himself like a dwarf Harlequin. Or he can demand that Mary come to bed. Or he can command the Devil to caper and dance or cook barbecued chicken. It is the function of the artist to make arbitrary choices.

Most artists tend to concentrate on rapport with one or the other— Devil, Mary, or God.

Me, I prefer to work with the Devil. He's a regular guy, cooks some fine chicken, and knows when to keep his mouth shut. God, the Devil, Mary, or the impression of self—these are delusions of memory (which is what this story is about), and memory is an illusion of art. And art is the biggest delusion of all.

THE DOGTOWN
TOURIST AGENCY

by Jack Vance

CHAPTER 1

Hetzel composed a letter, writing a crisp and angular hand in black ink, with a short-nibbed pen:

> Dear Madame X:
>
> Complying with those instructions transmitted to me by messenger, I traced the person known as Casimir Wuldfache to Twisselbane on Tamar in the Nova Celeste Sector, where he arrived Ianiaro 23 Gaean, of the current year.
>
> At Twisselbane, Vv. Wuldfache secured employment at the Fabrilankus Café as a waiter, using the name Carmine Daruble. Evenings he worked at the local Mirrograph when not otherwise occupied as a paid escort for ladies in need of such a service.
>
> About three months ago he departed Tamar in company with a young woman whom I have not been able to identify. At the spaceport I circulated Vv. Wuldfache's photograph and received information that his destination was the planet Maz, unlikely as this may seem.
>
> I have exhausted your retainer, and will exert no further effort until further instruction reaches me.
>
> > With sincere best wishes,
> > Hetzel, Vv.

Hetzel addressed the letter to "Subscriber, Box 434, Ferraunce" and dropped it into an expedition slot. The case was now terminated or so he assumed. The turbulence of Madame X's emotions would subside in due course; Casimir Wuldfache, or whatever his name, would no doubt exercise his austere blond beauty upon a succession of other impressionable ladies.

The planet Maz? How could such a place draw a man like Casimir Wuldfache? Hetzel shook his head in perplexity, then gave his attention to other matters.

CHAPTER 2

Sir Ivon Hacaway decided to conduct personally the interview with Hetzel; the matter was too important to be entrusted to the discretion of an underling. Nor were the company offices in Ferraunce suitable for the occasion; a thousand underlings observed his every act, and Hetzel was essentially an unknown quantity, no more than a name and a reputation in a field at the questionable brink of respectability. Rather than risk a compromise of his dignity, Sir Ivon elected to manage the business in privacy at Harth Manor.

Hetzel arrived at the appointed hour, and was conducted out upon the terrace. Sir Ivon, who disliked surprises, frowned to see not the furtive ruffian he had expected but a personable dark-haired man of obvious competence and a certain calm elegance that might have done credit to a gentleman. His clothes, neutral and unobtrusive, by some trick of reversal suggested not a neutral personality but flamboyance held under careful control.

Sir Ivon gave a perfunctory nod and gestured toward a chair. "Please be seated. Perhaps you will take a cup of tea?"

"With pleasure."

Sir Ivon touched a button, and briskly addressed himself to business. "As you must know, I am chairman of the board at Palladian Micronics. We manufacture a variety of highly intricate mechanisms: robot brains, automatic translators, psychoeidetic analogues, and the like. These articles require a vast amount of hand labor; automatic assembly is impossible, and our products are generally quite expensive.

"A most curious situation has arisen. We have our competitors, naturally; Subsikon Corporation, Pedro Gomayr Associates, Gaean Micronics, are the most important. We all market comparable products at competitive prices, and coexist with no more than the usual skulduggery. We are now being afflicted by unusual skulduggery." Sir Ivon glanced at Hetzel to gauge the effect of his exposition, but Hetzel merely nodded politely. "Continue."

Sir Ivon cleared his throat. "About six months ago a company

known as Istagam began to market several high-cost items at prices
we can't hope to match. Naturally, my engineers have examined these
products, looking for areas where economies have been made, without success. The articles are constructed at least to the standard of
our own. Who is Istagam, you ask? Well, we're asking ourselves the
same question."

From the house, pushing a teacart, came a portly woman wearing
a voluminous gown of pink and black silk. Hetzel rose gallantly to his
feet. "The Lady Hacaway, I take it?"

"Oh, no, sir, I'm Reinhold, the housekeeper. Please sit down; I'll
lay out the tea."

Hetzel bowed and resumed his seat. Sir Ivon eyed him sidewise, a
rather grim smile on his lips. He said, "To you this may seem a
footling business: a question of a few million SLU.* Rather more is
at stake. If Istagam expands, then we—and by 'we' I mean the
members of the legitimate micronics industry—are in serious trouble."

"An urgent affair, no doubt," said Hetzel. "However, I must explain that I undertake no industrial espionage, unless the fee were
truly astronomical, and even then—"

Sir Ivon held up his hand. "Hear me out," he said testily. "The situation is extraordinary; otherwise I would simply turn the matter
over to one of the large agencies. And I must remark in passing that
your fee, while adequate, will be something less than astronomical.
Otherwise I would do the work myself."

Hetzel sipped tea. "I'll certainly listen to you without prejudice."

In a measured voice Sir Ivon continued his exposition. "Istagam
distributes its products from at least three or four depots—all out to
the north of Jack Chandler's Gulf. One of these is a warehouse at an
inconsequential little town known as Ultimo, on the planet Glamfyre.
I don't suppose that you're acquainted with the place?"

"Not even superficially."

"Well, Glamfyre is a rather bleak place, just about at the edge of
the Reach. I communicated with our own district factor and asked
him to make a few inquiries." Sir Ivon brought forth a sheet of paper,
which he passed across the table to Hetzel. "This is his report."

The letter had been indited at Estance Uno, Glamfyre, a month
previously by a certain Urvix Lamboros.

---

* SLU, Standard Labor-value Unit, the monetary unit of the Gaean Reach,
defined as the value of an hour of unskilled labor under standard conditions.
The unit supersedes all other monetary bases, in that it derives from the single
invariable commodity of the human universe—toil.

Hetzel read:

Sir Ivon Hacaway
Harth Manor on the Meadows
Harth, Delta Rasalhaque

Esteemed Sir:

In response to your request I journeyed to Ultimo, where I made local inquiry to this effect. Shipments were received at the Istagam warehouse on these dates, Gaean Standard Time: March 19, May 4, July 6. I thereupon made inquiries at the Ultimo spaceport, which is served by the Krugh Line, the Red Griffin Line, and occasionally the Osiris Line. Proximately before the dates mentioned above the following ships discharged cargo at Ultimo:

March 12	*Paesko*	(Red Griffin)
March 17	*Bardixon*	(Krugh)
May 3	*Voulias*	(Krugh)
July 3	*Cansaspara*	(Krugh)

I was unable to determine the previous ports of call of these vessels.

With utmost respect and with hopes for your continued patronage, I am,

Urvix Lamboros, Vv.

Hetzel returned the letter. Sir Ivon said, "I communicated with officials of the Krugh Line and learned that these three ships had taken on cargo at only one port in common." He paused to heighten the drama of his disclosure. "That port was Axistil, on the planet Maz."

Hetzel sat up in his chair. "Maz?"

"You seem startled," said Sir Ivon.

"Hardly startled," said Hetzel. " 'Surprised' or 'perplexed' would be a better word. Who on Maz manufactures micronic components?"

Sir Ivon sat back in his chair. "Exactly. Who indeed? The Gomaz? Absurd. The Liss? The Olefract? Incredible. We have here a mystery of fascinating implications."

Hetzel agreed. "The case certainly exceeds the ordinary."

Out upon the terrace stepped a tall woman of striking appearance wearing a modish afternoon gown of brown, red, and gold pleats, with a panache of black feathers in a forehead band of black velvet. Her manner was rather imperious, and she quite ignored Hetzel, who had again risen to his feet, as, somewhat more slowly, did Sir Ivon.

"Ivon, I implore you to exert yourself," said the woman. "Something must be done! Felicia has not yet returned from Graythorpe, and you will recall that I gave her most explicit instructions."

"Yes, my dear," said Sir Ivon. "I'll deal with the matter in due course, but at this moment I am occupied with business, as you see." He glanced toward Hetzel, hesitated, then performed a rather grudging introduction. "This is Vv.* Miro Hetzel, an effectuator. He will be conducting certain investigations for the consortium. Vv. Hetzel, I present the Lady Bonvenuta Hacaway."

"I am honored to make your acquaintance," said Hetzel.

"It is a pleasure," said Lady Bonvenuta in a frigid voice. To Sir Ivon she said, "I insist that you have a serious talk with Felicia. There are often questionable people at Graythorpe, as you well know."

"I'll certainly deal with the matter," said Sir Ivon. "In the meantime, you might call Graythorpe and make your feelings known to Felicia."

"I shall do so." Lady Bonvenuta favored Hetzel with an inclination of the head and returned into the manor. Sir Ivon and Hetzel resumed their seats. Sir Ivon continued his exposition. "So, then—the Istagam shipments appear to derive from Maz, which seems most remarkable."

"No question as to this. Exactly, then, what do you want me to do?"

Sir Ivon darted Hetzel a puzzled side glance, as if wondering at his naïveté. "Our first objective is information. Are the Liss or the Olefract attempting a commercial penetration of the Gaean Reach? If so, will they allow a counterflow? If not, who or what is Istagam? How does it contrive such remarkable economies?"

"This appears straightforward."

Sir Ivon folded his hands across his belly and looked off across the vista. "I need hardly point out that Istagam represents a nuisance which ultimately must be abated. Naturally, I don't advocate sabo-

---

* Vv., an abbreviation for Visfer, originally Viasvar, an Ordinary of the ancient Legion of Truth; now a low-grade honorific used to address a person lacking aristocratic distinction.

tage or assassination; that goes without saying. Still, your methods are your own, and they have won you an enviable reputation."

Hetzel knit his brows. "You would seem to be saying that I have earned a reputation for murder and destruction, which you envy."

Sir Ivon turned Hetzel a sharp look, and chose to ignore the tactless jocularity. "Another matter, which may or may not be connected with Istagam. At times I keep certain important documents here at Harth for a day or two, or as long as a week, in order to study them at my leisure. About three months ago a portfolio containing valuable marketing information was stolen from the premises. These papers would considerably benefit my competitors; to Istagam they would be invaluable. The theft was accomplished with finesse; no one saw the criminal; he left no traces, and I discovered the loss only when I opened the portfolio. I mention this matter if only to put you on your guard against Istagam. The people involved are evidently unscrupulous."

"I will certainly take your warning to heart," said Hetzel, "assuming that you decide to entrust this dangerous and difficult matter to me."

Sir Ivon raised his eyes toward the sky as if in search of divine proscription against Hetzel's avarice. He reached into his pocket and brought forth a pamphlet, which he handed to Hetzel. "I have here a map of Axistil, published on Maz by the local tourist association. Axistil, as you see, is a very small community. The Plaza and Triskelion are under Triarchic jurisdiction. The Gaean sector is tinted green and includes the Gaean spaceport, the Beyranion Hotel, where you will be staying, and part of the settlement known as Dogtown. Far Dogtown, in Gomaz territory, lies beyond Gaean authority and is a refuge for criminals and riffraff. The Liss sector is indicated by purple shading and includes the Liss spaceport. The Olefract sector is shown in orange stipple." Sir Ivon became earnest and affable. "A fascinating city, so I am told. A place possibly unique in the galaxy: the juncture of three interstellar empires! Fancy that!"

"This well may be," said Hetzel. "Now, as to my fee—"

Sir Ivon held up his hand. "Let me recapitulate. Istagam ships its products through the Gaean spaceport. Where do they originate? There would seem three possibilities. In the Liss Empire, or in the Olefract Empire, or on the planet Maz itself. In the implausible event that the Liss or the Olefract are producing trade goods and attempting to sell them across the Reach, the matter is vastly important. Both Liss and Olefract are xenophobic; they would tolerate no retaliation in kind. So, then—Maz. Implausible again. The Gomaz, for all their remarkable qualities, lack discipline; it is difficult to imagine a group of Gomaz warriors occupied at an assembly line." Sir Ivon spread out his hands. "So there you have it: a fascinating puzzle."

"Quite so. And now, a matter of considerable importance—"

"Your fee." Sir Ivon cleared his throat. "I am authorized to pay what I consider a most generous sum—thirty SLU per diem, plus adequate expenses, and a bonus should your work prove highly satisfactory, that is to say, should our maximum objectives be achieved."

Hetzel sat frozen with wonder. "Surely you are joking!"

"Let us not bore each other with spurious histrionics," said Sir Ivon. "Your circumstances are known to me; you are a clever man, with the soul of a nomad and pretensions beyond your class. You are currently living at a rather disreputable inn, which suggests—"

Hetzel said, "You have not achieved eminence through tact or flattery, so much is clear. But your attitude clears the air, in that I can now freely state my opinion of the commercial mentality—"

"My time is too valuable to be spent on impudence or psychoanalysis," said Sir Ivon. "Now then, let us—"

"A moment," said Hetzel. "I am normally too proud to haggle, but I must meet you on your own ground. You put forward a ridiculous figure. I could counter with another as unreal, but I prefer to state my minimum requirements at the beginning."

"Such as what?"

"You have come to me because you know my reputation for subtlety, resource, and competence; you want to derive the beneficial use of these qualities. They do not come cheap. You may write your contract to the tune of a hundred SLU per standard Gaean day, plus a cash advance of five thousand SLU for necessary expenses and an open draft upon the bank at Axistil, should additional sums be required, plus a bonus of five thousand SLU should the investigation be completed to your satisfaction within the month, with the clear understanding that 'investigation' does not include murder, theft, destruction, or suicide, unless necessary."

Sir Ivon's face became pink. "I never conceived demands so capricious as these! Certain of your remarks have merit, and I might be willing to adjust my preliminary figure . . ."

The conversation continued an hour before a final understanding was reached; Hetzel agreed to depart at once for Maz, at the edge of the Gaean Reach.

Sir Ivon, once more composed, gave Hetzel final instructions. "The

Gaean representative at the Triarchy is Sir Estevan Tristo. I suggest that you immediately introduce yourself and explain your purposes; there is no reason why he should not give you all aid possible."

"In cases such as this," said Hetzel, "the obvious and reasonable courses of action are usually the least productive. However, I must start somewhere; why not with Sir Estevan Tristo?"

CHAPTER 3

Maz, a small world submerged under a heavy atmosphere, swung around the white dwarf sun Khis, in company with a large frigid moon. A nimbus of smoky orange, unique in Hetzel's experience, surrounded Maz, nor had he ever seen a moon so bland, blank, and featureless—a globe of frosted silver.

The passenger packet *Emma Noaker* of the Barbanic Line made the required rendezvous with the Triarchic patrol ships. The Liss and the Olefract vessels drifted above and to the side, and all the passengers craned their necks to study the artifacts of these exotic transgalactic intelligences, who allowed so little to be known of themselves. From the Gaean corvette came a pilot to take the *Emma Noaker* down to Axistil and to ensure against the landing of illicit weapons.

Down dropped the packet. The landscape of Maz was that of an ancient world—a half-dozen shallow seas, a few ranges of low hills separated by swamps or undulating plains, with sluggish rivers meandering here and there like the veins on the back of an old man's hand.

Axistil, headquarters of the Triarchic superintendency, occupied a site on a low plateau somewhat to the north of the equator. Halfway into the morning, local time, the *Emma Noaker* grounded at the Gaean spaceport half a mile east of the Triskelion. Landing formalities were brief; in company with thirty or forty other Gaeans, mostly tourists, Hetzel was passed into the depot. He immediately telephoned the Beyranion Hotel to confirm his reservation, and learned that he had been assigned their choicest accommodations, a suite in the garden annex, at a rate considerably higher than he would have been content to pay had he been settling his own account. A carryall from the Beyranion was on hand; Hetzel entrusted his valise to the driver and set out on foot along the Last Mile, toward the Plaza of the Triarchy.

A world eerily beautiful, thought Hetzel. To look up at the sky was like looking off into sea-green water. Halfway along its morning arc the white star Khis glittered like a sequin. To the left a wasteland mounded with hummocks of moss faded into haze; to the right, a similar landscape sloped down into that nondescript clutter of shacks, huts, and a few substantial buildings of whitewashed marl known as Dogtown. Ahead, the structures of Axistil, blurred by the haze, were perceived only as a set of unlikely silhouettes.

Hetzel met no one along the way; indeed, during his entire stay, the disparity between the monumental structures of Axistil and the near-absence of a population produced a unique, almost hallucinatory quality, as if Axistil were no more than a titanic stage setting bereft of players.

The Last Mile ended at the Plaza. Here a sign read:

> You stand at the edge of the Gaean Reach, and are about to enter Triarchic jurisdiction. Conventional behavior is required and will usually provoke no unforeseen inconveniences. It is most wise, however, to obtain a copy of *Special Regulations* at the Triskelion or at your hotel, and be thereby guided.
>
> *Urgent warning:* never venture into enclaves of the Liss or the Olefract, at the certain risk of profoundly unpleasant consequences.
>
> Attempt no familiarity with the indigenous Gomaz! At Axistil they are normally not aggressive; however, they react unpredictably to attempts at social intercourse. You may observe them as closely as you like, but do not touch them or attempt conversation. The Gomaz are adept telepaths; the extent, however, to which they can comprehend human thought is still a matter of conjecture.
>
> *Most important!* Do not offer, present, display, barter, or sell weapons to the Gomaz! The penalty is confinement for life in the Exhibitory. There are no exceptions; the regulation is strictly enforced by the Triarchs, two of whom are Liss and Olefract. Neither sympathizes with adventurous folly or drunken bravado. If you violate this rule, your visit to Maz will surely terminate in tragedy.

A rather dampening notice, thought Hetzel. The ordinary touristic pleasures all seemed punishable by death, lifetime imprisonment, or unpredictable attack. Still, this very thrill of danger no doubt accented the zest of a visit to Maz.

Hetzel took a step forward and thereby departed the Gaean Reach. He walked out upon the Plaza, an expanse paved with silver-gray schist that seemed to give off a glimmering light of its own. To one side loomed the spires, domes, eccentric columns, and asymmetric blocks of the Triskelion—a structure designed in three segments by the architects of three races, a remarkable and unique edifice. Beyond the Triskelion, to southwest and northwest, lay the Liss and Olefract sectors, each with its cluster of buildings. At the north side of the Plaza, opposite the Triskelion, stood a pair of monuments that the three empires had conjoined to maintain: the Rock of Pain, where the Gomaz chieftains, numb with the weight of disaster, had surrendered to the Triarchy; and the multicelled slab of glass and black copper known as the Exhibitory. Both objects were encompassed within a small park, where a few trees with eggplant-purple foliage grew from a dim green sward. To the northeast rose the facade of the Beyranion Hotel, to which Hetzel now directed his steps.

The Beyranion Hotel and its precincts constituted the smallest independent principality within the Gaean Reach. A garden of three acres surrounded the hotel proper; to one side stood the new garden annex. Hetzel registered at the main desk, and was conducted to his suite.

Hetzel discovered his quarters to be more than satisfactory. The sitting room overlooked the garden, a place of odd colors, bizarre shapes, and nose-twitching scents. Black spindle trees as tall as the hotel shaded tussocks of purple-black moss; from a pond grew clumps of horsetail with pewter stems and orange whisks. There were banks of blue geraniums, twinkling candle blossom, and Maz mint, all of which added pungency to the smoky-sour reek of the moss. Newly arrived tourists now roamed the garden, marveling at the exotic growths and unfamiliar odors. Hetzel inspected the bedroom and discovered a view across Dogtown, which he would visit later in the day. First to business.

He went to the telephone and put a call through to the office of the Gaean Triarch at the Triskelion. The screen brightened to show the face of a delicately pretty receptionist with blond ringlets and a rose-petal complexion. She spoke in a voice cool and tinkling, like far-off wind chimes. "The office of Sir Estevan Tristo; how can we serve you?"

"My name is Miro Hetzel. I would like a few minutes with Sir Estevan at the first convenient opportunity, on a matter of considerable importance. Can I see him this afternoon?"

"What is your business, sir?"

"I require information in regard to certain conditions on Maz—"

"You may apply for information to Vvs. Felius at the Triskelion Information Desk, or at the Dogtown Tourist Agency. Sir Estevan concerns himself exclusively with Triarchic business."

"Nonetheless, this is an important matter, and I must request a few minutes of his time."

"Sir Estevan is not in his office at the moment; I doubt if he'll appear until the next session of the Triarchs."

"And when will that be?"

"Five days from now, at half-morning. After the session, he allows an occasional interview. Are you a journalist?"

"Something of the sort. Perhaps I could see him at his home?"

"No, sir." The girl's features, as clear and delicate as those of a child, showed neither warmth nor sympathy for Hetzel's problems. "He conducts all public business at the Triarchic sessions."

"Ah, but this is private business!"

"Sir Estevan makes no private appointments. After the Triarchic session he works in his office for an hour or two; perhaps he will see you then."

Hetzel tapped the off switch in exasperation.

He searched the directory for Sir Estevan's home residence, without success. He telephoned the clerk at the Beyranion reception desk. "How can I get in touch with Sir Estevan Tristo? His secretary gives me no help at all."

"She's not allowed to help anyone. Sir Estevan has had too many problems with tourists and letters of introduction. The only place to catch him is at his office."

"Five days from now."

"If you're lucky. Sir Estevan has been known to use his private entrance when he wants to avoid talking to someone."

"He appears to be a temperamental man."

"Decidedly so."

The time was noon. Hetzel crossed the garden to the Beyranion's wood-paneled dining room, which had been decorated with picturesque Gomaz artifacts: fetishes; cast-iron war helmets, spiked and crested; a stuffed gargoyle of the Shimkish Mountains. The tables and chairs had been carved from native wood; the tablecloths were soft bast, embroidered with typical emblems. Without haste Hetzel lunched on the best the house afforded, then sauntered out upon the Plaza. At the Exhibitory he paused to inspect the prisoners peering forth from their glass cells—gunrunners and weapons smugglers, who would never leave their cells alive. The pallid faces wore identical expressions of sullen passivity. Occasionally one or another exerted himself sufficiently to make an obscene gesture or display his naked backside. Hetzel recognized none of his acquaintances or former clients. All were Gaean, which Hetzel considered a significant commentary upon the human character. Men, as individuals, seemed more diverse and enterprising than their Liss or Olefract counterparts. The Gomaz, he reflected, lived by extremes peculiar to themselves.

Hetzel turned away from the Exhibitory. The prisoners—pirates, outcasts, mad gallants—awoke him to no pangs of pity. For the sake of gain they had sought to arm the Gomaz, heedless of the fact that the Gomaz, if furnished even a meager weaponry and the means to transport themselves, would go forth to attack the entire galaxy, including the worlds of the Gaean Reach, as forty-six years before they had demonstrated.

Hetzel continued across the Plaza, an expanse of such grand dimensions that the structures around the periphery loomed in the thick air like shadows. He walked in solitude, like a boat in the middle of a lonely ocean. Perhaps a dozen other dark shapes moved here and there across the silver-gray perspectives, too distant to be identified. A curious vista, thought Hetzel, strange as a dream.

The Triskelion solidified as he approached. He altered his direction in order to circle the structure, in effect entering areas in which the Liss and the Olefract exerted at least theoretical control, and certainly a psychological influence. He passed a Liss on its way to the Triskelion—a lithe dark creature in a scarlet robe—and a moment later he saw an Olefract at a somewhat greater distance. Both seemed indifferent to his presence; both affected him with a curious mixture of fascination and repugnance, for reasons he could not quite define. Returning to the Gaean frontage, Hetzel felt the lifting of a subtle oppression.

He climbed three steps, passed through a crystal portal into a lobby centering upon a triangular information desk. The Liss and Olefract sections lacked both personnel and information seekers. At the Gaean segment two clerks were more than occupied with recently arrived tourists. A burly round-faced man in a splendid, if overtight, blue-and-green uniform stood to the side, inspecting all who entered with benign contempt. Silver epaulets and silver filigree on the visor of his high-peaked cap marked him for an official of importance. He fixed Hetzel with an especially stern gaze, by some instinct recognizing a person whose business he might or might not consider legitimate.

Hetzel paid him no heed and went to the information desk. The chief clerk, a portly black-haired woman with a large lumpy nose and a nasal accent, pursued her duties with little grace or patience: "No, sir; the Triarch can't be seen. . . . I don't care what you heard, he definitely does not receive visitors at his home." . . . "No, sir, we are not agents for organized tours; we are the staff of the Gaean administration. In Dogtown you'll find a tourist office. They operate a number of inns in scenic regions, and they offer air cars for rent." . . . "I'm sorry, madam, under no circumstances will you be allowed into the Liss sector. They are absolutely rigid in this regard. . . . What will they do? Who knows what happens to the people they take away —put them in zoos, perhaps." . . . "In Dogtown, sir, you can buy souvenirs." . . . "No, sir, not until the next session, in five days. The public is admitted." . . . "You may photograph the Liss and the Olefract segments of the desk, yes, madam."

The second clerk, a tall young man with a pale, earnest face, was less crisp and perhaps less efficient. ". . . recommend a hotel in Dogtown? Well, I don't know. You'd be far more comfortable at the Beyranion. Don't forget, Far Dogtown is beyond *everybody's* jurisdiction. You could get killed there, and nobody would even bury you. . . . Yes, Dogtown itself is Gaean. But don't wander past the green fence unless you're an adventurer. . . . Actually, Far Dogtown isn't all that bad if you keep your wits about you and carry no more than two or three SLU. Don't drink there, and be sure not to gamble there." . . . "No, sir, I have no knowledge or schedule of the Gomaz wars. They take place, certainly, and if you want to be chopped into two hundred pieces, go try to find one. That's why the tourist agency won't rent you an air car without a qualified guide. . . . That's correct, you can't just hire an air car and go off by yourself. It's only for your own protection. Don't forget, this is the end of the Reach—right here."

The portly chief clerk spoke to Hetzel. "Yes, sir, what do you wish?"

"Are you Vvs. Felius?"

"I am she."

"I have a rather unusual problem. I must discuss an urgent matter with Sir Estevan, but I am told that he cannot be reached."

Vvs. Felius sniffed. "I can't help you. If Sir Estevan doesn't want to see people, I can't force him to do so."

"Certainly not. But can you suggest some dignified way I could get his attention for a few minutes?"

"Sir Estevan is a very busy man; at least, he says he is, with his reports and recommendations and all. We see him only during the sessions. The rest of the time he's off somewhere with his lady friend, or his fiancée, whatever she's called." Vvs. Felius used her prominent nose to produce a disapproving sniff. "I'm sure it's his business, of course, but he simply won't be interfered with when he's not in his office."

"In that case, I suppose I'll have to wait. Do you have at hand any informational material, especially in regard to, say, the opportunities for investment capital?"

"No. Nothing of the sort." Vvs. Felius gave an incredulous titter. "Who would want to invest out here, away from everything?"

"Istagam seems to be doing very well."

"Istagam? I don't know who you're talking about."

Hetzel nodded. "What about the Gomaz? Are they willing workers?"

"Hah! Offer them a gun and they'll pay you all they own, but they wouldn't work a minute for you. That's against their pride."

"Odd! At the hotel I saw chairs carved ostensibly by the Gomaz."

"By the Gomaz bantlings. They put their young to toil, instead of letting them kill themselves in play wars. But full-fledged warriors work for hire? Never."

"Interesting," said Hetzel. "And you believe that I must wait five days to see Sir Estevan?"

"I certainly can't suggest any other way."

"One last question. I arranged to meet a certain Casimir Wuldfache here on Maz. Can you tell me if he has arrived?"

"I have no such information at hand. You might ask Captain Baw; he's the commandant." The woman indicated the burly officer in the green-and-blue uniform.

"Thank you." Hetzel approached Captain Baw and put his question, receiving for a reply first an uninterested grunt, then: "Never heard of such a person. They come and they go. There's a hundred down in Far Dogtown I'd like to get my hands on, I'll tell you for certain."

Hetzel expressed his gratitude and departed.

* * *

North of the Exhibitory a wide road paved with what Hetzel took to be tamped gravel and crushed shell sloped away from the Plaza and down to Dogtown: the so-called Avenue of Lost Souls. A wind from off the downs blew in Hetzel's face, smelling of smoke and peat and exhalations less familiar. Hetzel was alone on the road, and again felt the brush of dream time. . . . He stopped short and bent to study the road. The bits of shell and gravel of the surface were not, as he had first assumed, tamped or rolled; they quite clearly had been fitted piece by piece into cement, to form a mosaic. Hetzel looked back the way he had come, then down to Dogtown. An enormous amount of toil had been expended on this road.

Two tall spindle trees loomed over the road; Hetzel passed below and into Dogtown. The Avenue of Lost Souls broadened to become a plaza, the center of which had been dedicated to a park where grew thickets of cardinal bush, Cyprian torch, and flowering yellow acacia; under the water-green sky and against the somber downs to the north, the scarlets and lemons and golds made a peculiarly gratifying contrast. The structures surrounding lacked uniformity except for a certain easy shabbiness. Timber, marl, stucco, vitrified soil, slag bricks, all figured in the schemes of construction, which were as various as the men who had chosen to build out here at the brink of the Reach. Shops sold imported foods, hardware, and sundries; there were four or five taverns, as many hotels of greater or lesser respectability, a few business offices: exporters of Gomaz artifacts, an insurance agent, a tonsorial salon, a dealer in energetics and power pods. A relatively imposing structure of glistening pink concrete had been divided into a pair of adjoining offices. The first displayed a sign:

MAZ TOURIST ASSOCIATION
Information, Tours, Outback Accommodation

Or more familiarly, thought Hetzel, the Dogtown Tourist Agency. The premises next door showed a more subdued facade, and was identified by an inconspicuous plaque reading:

BYRRHIS ENTERPRISES
Development and Promotion

Hetzel looked into the tourist agency, to find a similar or perhaps the same group of tourists he had encountered at the Triskelion. They crowded the counter, talking to a pretty dark-haired girl with melancholy eyes, who answered their questions with a charming mixture of reserve, good humor, and courtesy.

Hetzel stepped into the office and waited, listening with half an ear to the conversation.

". . . seven inns," said the girl. "They're all in dramatic locations and very comfortable. At least, so I'm told; I've never been out to them myself."

"We'd like to see the *real* Maz," declared one of the women. "The places tourists don't go. And we'd just love to see one of the wars. We're not bloodthirsty or anything like that, but it must be wonderfully exciting!"

The girl smiled. "We couldn't possibly arrange such a spectacle. In the first place, it would be dangerous. The Gomaz are very proud people. If they saw tourists, they'd halt their war and kill the tourists, and then proceed with the war."

"Hmmf. Well, we're not exactly tourists. We like to think of ourselves as travelers."

"Of course."

A man spoke, "What about these inns? If the Gomaz are that sensitive, it might be dangerous leaving Dogtown."

"Not really," said the girl. "The Gomaz are actually oblivious of Gaeans, unless they commit some kind of nuisance, just as you might ignore birds in a tree."

"Can't we visit the Gomaz castles? Like that one on the wall?"

The girl gave the woman a smiling shake of the head. "It can't be done. But some of our inns are built in ancient Gomaz castles, and they're really quite comfortable."

Hetzel inspected the posters: *Warriors March to Battle on Tusz Tan Steppe; The Flyers of Korasman Castle Soar and Veer; Kish Castle at Sunset; Conclave of the Jerd Nobles.* Then he turned his attention back to the girl, who was no less interesting to look at than the pictures. At first glance Hetzel had thought her slight and frail, but on closer inspection he decided that she could bear up very well under a bit of playful rough-and-tumble. He moved a few steps closer to the desk. The girl turned her head and gave him a flicker of a smile. Charming, thought Hetzel.

". . . all seven inns, if you have the time. We naturally arrange transportation."

"But we can't rent our own air car?"

"Not without one of our guides. It really wouldn't be safe, and it's also against Triarchic regulations."

"Well, we'll think it over. Which is the best tavern in Dogtown—the most typical and picturesque?"

"I think they're pretty much alike. You might try the Last Resort, across the square."

"Thank you." The tourists departed. The girl looked at Hetzel. "Yes, sir?"

Hetzel approached the counter. "I don't quite know what I want to ask you."

"There must be something."

"The situation is this. A friend of mine has come into some money, and now he wants to invest it. The question is: where?"

The girl laughed incredulously. "You want *my* advice?"

"Certainly. Unconventional ideas are best, because they haven't occurred to anyone else. Assume that I'm about to place a million SLU in your hands. What would you do with it?"

"I'd buy a ticket out of here," said the girl. "But that isn't what your friend has in mind."

"Let me put the matter this way: how could a person invest here on Maz and hope to make a profit?"

"That's quite a problem. The only people in Dogtown who seem to make money are the tavern keepers."

"I was thinking of enterprises on a larger scale, somewhat on the order of Istagam. In fact, where would I find the director of Istagam? I'd like to ask his advice."

The girl gave him a curious side glance that Hetzel could not interpret. She said, "That's something I know nothing about."

"Surely you're aware of Istagam's existence?"

"That, and not much more. But why don't you talk to Vv. Byrrhis? He's far more expert than I am on such subjects." She looked toward a door that connected to the adjoining office. "But I don't think he's in just now."

"What are Vv. Byrrhis' enterprises? Or is he a broker?"

"Vv. Byrrhis has his fingers in almost everything: tourist agency, back-country inns, air-car rental. He also operates Maz Transport for the Triarchy."

"Maz Transport?"

"Just old air buses that bring Gomaz into Axistil and back to their castles. It's a free service; the Gomaz wouldn't use it if they had to pay."

"The Gomaz haven't adapted to a money economy, then."

"They haven't adapted to anything." The girl reached to a shelf and brought forth a pamphlet, which she presented to Hetzel. He glanced at the title: *The Warriors of Maz*. "Thank you," said Hetzel. "When do you expect Vv. Byrrhis in his office?"

"I'm not sure. He comes and goes. You can always telephone."

A new group of tourists entered the office; Hetzel departed. He sauntered around the square, looking in shop windows, then stepped into the Last Resort for a mug of ale. Here he ruminated over his findings to date, which were few and could be expressed very simply:

1. Sir Estevan Tristo went to extraordinary lengths to avoid casual visitors.
2. If Vv. Byrrhis were not directly involved in Istagam, he almost certainly knew everything there was to know about it.
3. The clerk at the tourist agency was not the sort of person one might expect to find in a settlement at the end of the Reach.

Hetzel brought forth the pamphlet the girl had given him: *The Warriors of Maz*. On the cover appeared a sketch labeled: "A Flyer of Castle Korasmus." The Gomaz stood on a parapet, wings of withe and membrane attached to his back. The caption read: "Under favorable conditions the Gomaz flyer can soar in the dense air of Maz. He is able to flap the wings by thrusting his legs and manipulating the forward ribs with his arms. In general, however, the flyer swoops down from the heights to attack his enemy."

The Gomaz, Hetzel learned, were an ancient race, culturally static across a period of perhaps a million years. They showed a generally anthropomorphic configuration, after which, similarity to the human race dwindled. The Gomaz skeleton, partly internal, partly external, was formed of a tough, flexible siliceous cartilage reinforced with fibers of calcium-magnesium-carbophosphate, which on exposure to air hardened into a tough white chitin; this material sheathed their heads and formed the substance of three parallel crests that each sept carved into distinctive patterns of spikes, denticles, and barbs.

As an individual, the Gomaz was typically unpredictable, captious, mercurial, with personal gratification as his primary motivation. Yet in this aspect of himself he merely reflected the character of his sept, to which he was telepathically linked. He was the sept, the sept was himself. While the sept lived, the warrior could not die, hence his absolute fearlessness, and the Gomaz warrior thereby became in human terms a creature of paradox, reconciling as he did total personal autonomy to total identification with a social institution.

The Gomaz wars were of three varieties: wars of hate, which were in the minority; wars of rivalry, economic necessity, or territorial control; wars that no xenologist or sociologist or journalist could resist calling "wars of love." The Gomaz were monosexual and reproduced by implanting zygotes in the bodies of vanquished enemies, apparently to their mutual exaltation, which the victor augmented by eating a nubbin of a gland at the back of the vanquished warrior's neck. This gland yielded the hormone *chir* which stimulated growth in the bantlings and martial zeal in the adult warrior. The thought of *chir* dominated the lives of the Gomaz. The bantlings in their mock battles ingested the *chir* of those they had bested and killed; in the adult battles the warriors performed the same act and were thereby exalted, strengthened, and endowed with a mysterious *mana; chir* conceivably fertilized the zygotes.

The Gomaz used a few glyphs and symbolic objects, but knew neither a written language nor other than the most primitive mathematics, for which telepathic facility was held to blame.

Geison Weirie, the renegade Gaean, had discovered Maz sixty years before, and had recruited a force of Gomaz warriors for use as shock troops against Sercey, his native planet. The Gomaz, quickly grasping the potentialities of Gaean weaponry, subordinated Weirie and his band of cutthroats to their own purposes; they captured a fleet of space ships and set forth to conquer the universe. Their raids took them into the hitherto unknown empires of the Liss and the Olefract; eventually, forces of the three empires, acting in concert, destroyed the Gomaz fleet, captured Geison Weirie, built the Exhibitory to hold him, and placed a permanent injunctive agency of three parts upon Maz to prevent future irruptions. The Gomaz returned to their previous mode of existence, paying the Triarchy the ultimate insult of indifference.

Hetzel glanced through the rest of the pamphlet, which listed the septs, described their peculiarities, and located their home castles on a map of Maz. The Gomaz language, which they used in conjunction with emotional keys or colorations transmitted by telepathy, consisted of whistles, grindings, and squawks incomprehensible to both the Gaean ear and mind. Communication with the Gomaz was achieved through the use of micronic translators.

Gomaz weapons were few: a three-foot staff attached to a ten-foot bola, to assist in trapping the enemy; tongs worked by motions of the forearm; harpoons of three flexible barbs; a short heavy sword. Elite warriors employed wings to hover and swoop; on the rare occasions when a castle was to be stormed, the Gomaz built siege engines of great ingenuity. For transport they used wagons pulled by domesticated reptiles; their diet consisted of substances gathered or harvested by the bantlings, who performed all the work of the sept.

Hetzel returned the pamphlet to his pocket and called for a second mug of ale. He asked the bartender, "At a guess, how many local people work for Istagam?"

"Istagam? Who's he?"

"The Istagam Manufacturing Company."

"Never heard of it. Ask Byrrhis, across the square; he knows everything."

Hetzel finished the ale and went out into the street. The bartender's advice had much to recommend it, and if Vv. Byrrhis were unavailable, he could always put further inquiries to the dark-haired girl in the tourist office.

Hetzel crossed the square to Byrrhis Enterprises and tried the door, which, somewhat to his surprise, opened. Hetzel stepped inside.

At a desk, speaking into the telephone, sat a stocky man with a square, muscular face and a mane of lank black hair parted in the middle and cut square above the ears, in a style currently fashionable among the planets of the Fayence Stream. Byrrhis' nose was long and straight; his eyes were small and steady; his chin was massive. He wore a loose shirt of embroidered green velvet, breeches of purple-and-yellow-striped whipcord, and a fine scarf of white silk knotted to the side of his neck. The garments were informal, almost festive; the man's expression was agreeable enough; his voice was soft and pleasant as he spoke into the telephone: ". . . very much the same idea. . . . Exactly. I've got a visitor; I'll call you back."

Byrrhis rose to his feet and performed a conventionally polite salute. "What can I do for you?"

Hetzel thought that Byrrhis had terminated his telephone call somewhat abruptly. "Quite honestly, I don't know. I've been asked to inquire as to the possibility of local investment, and it might be that you prefer to keep such information to yourself."

Byrrhis acknowledged the pleasantry with a smile. "Not at all. Quite frankly, there isn't a great deal of scope out here for investment. The tourist business isn't all that big and may not get much bigger. Maz is no longer the novelty it used to be."

"What about import and export? Will the Gomaz buy Gaean goods?"

"What we can sell them, they don't want. What they do want, we're not permitted to bring in. And then, there's the matter of payment. They don't have any means of payment, except a few handicrafts and war helmets. Not much chance for any large-scale operation."

"What of Istagam? It seems to be doing well."

Byrrhis responded with easy facility. "That's an affair I know nothing about. It appears to be some sort of transshipment operation. Maz, of course, levies no taxes, which might mean a great deal to some struggling new business."

"You're probably right. What about minerals?"

"Nothing to speak of. The Gomaz take up some bog iron, but the deposits are pretty well used up. The Gomaz have been working them for a million years, more or less. Maz is essentially a worn-out planet."

"What about business with the Liss? Or the Olefract?"

Byrrhis gave a sour chuckle. "Are you joking?"

"Naturally not. Trade is a normal condition, provided that both parties are able to profit."

"The Liss are xenophobic to the point of obsession. The Olefract are incomprehensible. We can deal with the Gomaz easier—far easier. Did you notice the road up to the Plaza? The Kish and the Dyads sent out five thousand bantlings, and the road was finished in three weeks. We paid them in pneumatic wheels for their wagons. But there's no money to be made selling roads on Maz. If I had money to invest, I'd go to Vaire on Lusbarren and trawl for angelfish. Do you know what they fetch a pound at Banacre?"

"I know they're expensive. At a guess, two SLU a pound."

"That's close. And at Vaire, just off the Dal coast, they swim in shoals."

"It's an idea to bear in mind. I understand that you operate the air-car-rental service."

"That's correct. It's a miserable business, what with maintenance and downtime and Triarch directives. A new one just came through: I can't rent an air car unless I get prior clearance from the Triarch. Some tourists decided to visit the Disik castle and barely escaped with their lives."

Hetzel frowned. "I need a clearance from Sir Estevan Tristo before I can hire an air car?"

"That's correct."

"I'll get one this evening, if you'll direct me to his house."

"Ha ha! You can't put salt on Sir Estevan's tail quite so easily. He performs official tasks only at the Triskelion."

"I'm in no great hurry. One more question: where can I locate Casimir Wuldfache?"

Byrrhis' face became absolutely impassive. "I am not acquainted with the gentleman." He looked at his watch. "Sorry, I've got an appointment."

Hetzel rose to his feet. "Thanks for the information." He went out into the square. The tourist agency was dark; the girl had gone home—wherever home might be. Hetzel returned up the Avenue of Lost Souls. Sunset was close at hand. Khis showed as an orange spark low behind the western murk; the Plaza was dim and eerie. Hetzel found it easy to imagine himself a wraith wandering a dead landscape. . . . He was not wholly satisfied with the events of the day. He had been forced to ask questions, and thereby identify himself as a curious man. If Istagam were illicit, he must have sent tremors through the organization, and he might well encounter a reaction. Personal violence could not be excluded. Out on the Plaza, Hetzel felt isolated and vulnerable; he quickened his pace. The Exhibitory loomed ahead; the prisoners could not be distinguished. Two dark figures stood silently nearby; they watched Hetzel pass but made no attempt to intercept him. Liss? Olefract? Gomaz? Gaeans? Their nature could not be distinguished through the gloom.

With nothing better to do, Hetzel loitered over his dinner. As he was about to leave the dining room, a thin man in a suit of soft gabardine came quietly into the room. Hetzel studied him a moment or two, then went over to his table. "May I join you for a moment?"

"Certainly."

"You are the hotel's security officer?"

The man in gray showed a faint smile. "Is it so obvious? My official title is 'night manager.' My name is Kerch."

"I am Miro Hetzel."

"Miro Hetzel. . . . Somewhere I have heard the name."

"Perhaps you'll answer a few questions for me. Discreet questions, of course."

"You might get discreet answers."

"My business concerns itself with an entity—a society, a business, a group—known as Istagam. Have you heard the name mentioned?"

"No, I believe not. What is the function of this so-called 'entity'?"

"Apparently it uses the Axistil spaceport to export complicated and expensive machinery into the Reach. There's been speculation that Maz might function as a depot or staging area for goods produced outside the Reach."

"I know nothing about such an enterprise. The hotel occupies most of my attention."

"Surprising!" said Hetzel. "The Beyranion appears absolutely placid."

"So it is, at the moment. But consider: a walk of only ten or fifteen minutes separates our clientele from the population of Far Dogtown. Is it unpredictable that the foxes occasionally raid the chickenyard? I recommend that you entrust your valuables to the hotel strongbox —especially if you are out in the annex, our most vulnerable area."

"I will be sure to do so," said Hetzel. "But surely you take precautions?"

"Indeed we do. Our detection devices are carefully maintained, and as often as not, the thief is apprehended."

"And then?"

"There is an investigation. The guilty individual is assigned counsel, who holds a preliminary hearing with the prosecuting official. He is then tried and adjudged. He is allowed to appeal his sentence, and recommendations for leniency are carefully considered, after which an appropriate penalty is imposed."

"This seems a complicated operation for such a small environment."

"Not at all," said Kerch. "I comprise all these functions within myself. I investigate, I prosecute, I judge, I sentence, I execute the sentence and occasionally the criminal. The process often requires no more than five minutes."

"The procedure seems efficient and definite," said Hetzel. "May I order a bottle of wine for our joint consumption?"

"Why not?" said Kerch. "I find myself in congenial company, and there is no better occasion upon which to drink."

CHAPTER 4

In regard to Istagam, Hetzel capitulated the possibilities:

I. Istagam manufactured its products:
    1. Within the Gaean Reach
    2. Outside the Gaean Reach

      3. Upon the planet Maz.
   II. Istagam was an operation:
      1. Illicit
      2. Licit but clandestine
      3. Licit, with the operators indifferent to either se-
         crecy or notoriety.
  III. The operators of Istagam:
      1. Would use any means whatever to discourage in-
         vestigation
      2. Would use misdirection and deceit to discourage
         investigation
      3. Were indifferent to investigation.

Hetzel considered the permutations of the listed concepts, hoping that some course of action applicable to all might suggest itself, and this in fact was the case. He discovered that he had very little choice but to wait for the next session of the Triarchy, at which he could interview Sir Estevan Tristo.

Meanwhile, supposing propositions I-3, II-1, and III-1 to be accurate, he could reasonably expect that a certain degree of uneasiness must be affecting the operators of Istagam, and he must conduct himself accordingly.

Hetzel enjoyed three days of leisure. He breakfasted in his sitting room, lunched in the Beyranion garden, took his evening meal in the hotel dining room. He strolled about the Plaza, looked across the frontier into the Liss and Olefract sectors, explored Dogtown, and at all times he attended to the promptings of his subconscious. Once or twice he was tempted to investigate Far Dogtown, but decided that here, if anywhere, the risk might be real.

At the northwest corner of the Plaza was the Maz Transport depot. According to Kerch, anyone might freely ride the carriers, but he might not debark at any of the castle stations. Additionally, the adventurous passenger must be prepared to tolerate the unpleasant odor of the Gomaz. The carriers were slow, the routes indirect, the seats uncomfortable. The pilots of these carriers, thought Hetzel, might well provide meaningful items of information, and on the afternoon before the Triarchic session, he went to the landing plat and waited while the afternoon carrier landed.

Three Gomaz alighted—tall chieftains magnificent in capes of black leather and ropes of braided green feathers. They wore cast-iron war helmets with three rows of spiked crests accentuating their own crests of white bone. Wonderful, terrible creatures, thought Hetzel as he watched them stalk off across the Plaza. They were certainly more desirable as allies than enemies: a concept upon which the Triarchy was based, each party more fearful of conspiracy than of the Gomaz themselves.

The pilot refused even to listen to Hetzel's questions. "Ask at the tourist agency," he said. "They've got all that information. I'm busy and I'm late; excuse me."

Hetzel shrugged and moved away. For want of any better destination, he strolled down the Avenue of Lost Souls into Dogtown. The girl in the tourist office might be leaving at about this time, and if he met her on the street, who knows what might ensue?

The trifle of shiny tinsel which was the dwarf star Khis had dropped behind a field of herringbone cirrus, gray-green on the green sky; the light was rather poor, and Hetzel did not immediately recognize the man who stepped from Byrrhis' office. Hetzel halted, stared, then ran forward. He called out, "Casimir! Casimir Wuldfache!"

The man—Casimir Wuldfache?—hesitated not a step. He turned into the road leading to Far Dogtown, and when Hetzel reached the corner, he was nowhere to be seen.

Hetzel retraced his steps. The tourist agency was dark; the door into the premises of Byrrhis Enterprises was closed, and no one responded to his knock.

Hetzel returned up the Avenue of Lost Souls, and around the edge of the Plaza to the Beyranion.

On the morrow, the Triarchic session, and the meeting, or interview, or confrontation—whatever it might be—with Sir Estevan Tristo.

Hetzel awoke in the dark. What was the time? Midnight? The green moon Oloë, a great gibbous ellipsoid, almost filled the frame of the window. What had awakened him?

Hetzel searched his recollection: a gnawing sound, a faint scratching, somehow sinister. . . . Hetzel listened. Only silence. Now a quiet sigh, almost inaudible. Hetzel lay still a moment, gathering his wits. The air seemed stale, a trifle acrid. Hetzel swung his legs to the floor, stumbled from his bed and out into the sitting room. Here the air also seemed acrid. He ran to the door; it refused to open. To the back window he tottered on legs that felt numb. He threw open the pane, and the wind from off the downs blew into his face. Hetzel gasped, inhaled, exhaled, clearing his lungs. His senses swam; he leaned on the windowsill.

Hetzel awoke to find himself back in bed. Morning sunlight slanted through the window; on a chair nearby sat a nurse. Hetzel rubbed his head, which throbbed and ached. Dreary recollections drifted into his mind. Death gas? Sleep gas? Murder? Robbery? Revenge?

The nurse leaned over him and held a goblet to his mouth. "Can you drink? You'll feel better."

Hetzel drank the potion and indeed felt somewhat better. He focused his eyes on his watch. Today the Triarchy met in executive session. . . . In consternation he saw the time, and thrust himself up into a sitting position. The nurse expostulated. "Please, Vv. Hetzel, you must rest!"

"It's more important that I get to the Triskelion. Where are my clothes?"

The nurse ran to the telephone while Hetzel coerced his stiff limbs into his garments. Kerch appeared. "You seem to be alive."

"Yes, I'm alive. I've got to get over to the Triskelion."

"Easy, then. Do you feel capable?"

"Not altogether. What happened to me?"

"Gas—I don't know what kind. They came into your rooms and set off alarms, but they escaped out the back window. Are you missing any valuables?"

"My money is in the hotel safe, with most of my papers. My wallet is missing, with about a hundred SLU and a few documents. Nothing important."

"You are lucky."

Hetzel bathed his face in cold water, drank another cup of the nurse's potion, drew a few deep breaths. The throbbing in his head had subsided; he felt weak and limp, but capable of ordinary activity. Perhaps robbery had been the motive for last night's incursion, perhaps someone had not wanted him at the Triarchic session. Too bad for his assailants. They had gained small loot, and he would attend the session. Somewhat late, perhaps, but he would be there. He assured Kerch and the nurse of his viability and set off across the Plaza, trotting, then walking.

The Triskelion loomed above him. Hetzel referred to his watch. If the session began punctually, on the hour, he would be late. He mounted the three wide steps, crossed the forecourt. As he reached to push open the crystal portal, it slid abruptly wide, and Hetzel was thrust aside by the furious passage of a Gomaz warrior. Hetzel received an instant impression of a pinched face of polished bone, black optic balls blazing with an inner star; he sensed the creature's rancid odor; then it was gone in a jangle of chain and medals, striding off across the Plaza. Hetzel looked after it, thinking to recognize one of the Gomaz who had alighted from the carrier on the previous evening. Where were its fellows? Odd, thought Hetzel. Why should the creature act in this fashion?

He continued into the central lobby and immediately sensed stress and excitement. At the Gaean leg of the reception desk, portly Vvs. Felius stood quivering and pale; the young man leaned forward, peering toward a curved flight of stairs.

Hetzel approached. "I came to attend the session," he told the young man. "I hope I'm not too late."

Vvs. Felius emitted a choking, half-hysterical laugh. "Too late, ha ha! Too late indeed! There'll be no session now! No more sessions ever; they've all been killed!"

The young man muttered, "Come now, Vvs. Felius; control yourself."

"No, Vv. Kylo, let me be; it's all so terrible!"

"What's this?" asked Hetzel. "Who's been killed?"

"The Triarchs—all! Poor Sir Estevan, ah, poor man!"

Vv. Kylo spoke in annoyance. "Just a minute; we don't really know what's happened. There's Captain Baw; he'll tell us the facts."

Vvs. Felius called out, "Captain Baw, oh, Captain Baw! Whatever in the world has happened?"

Captain Baw, his round face pink and purposeful, his mouth coiled into a rosebud, paused by the desk. "Assassination, that's what's happened."

"Oh, Captain Baw, how dreadful! And who—?"

"The Liss and Olefract Triarchs—both struck down, and a pair of Gomaz as well."

"Ah! Aliens all. But what of Sir Estevan?"

"I called a warning to him; he dropped behind his desk and escaped by the flicker of an eyelash."

"Great praise!" cawed Vvs. Felius, rolling up her eyes. "I vow a thousand pastilles for the Sacred Arch!"

Vv. Kylo spoke in annoyance, "Just a minute; we don't really seems to have been the hero of the occasion."

"I did no more than my duty," declared Captain Baw. "I'd do as much ten times a day."

"One fact is yet unclear," said Hetzel. "Who was the assassin?"

Captain Baw turned Hetzel a head-to-toe glance under raised eyebrows. He clearly had forgotten their previous meeting. Noting neither opulent garments nor aristocratic insignia, he began to formulate a curt reply; then, meeting the gray clarity of Hetzel's gaze, he cleared his throat and rendered a rather more respectful response. "The assassin was a crazy young Gaean—a vagabond with a grudge, a sectarian, a cultist. In my affable innocence I took him into the chamber, and now you can imagine my remorse!"

"Why, I spoke to that very man!" cried Vvs. Felius. "To think of it! It gives one an utter qualm! He wore no proper tokens, although he was so disheveled that they would never have been seen. Bold as a baron, he asked for Sir Estevan, and I sent him over to Captain Baw; why, he might have killed all of us!"

"And what of this mad cultist? He is in custody?"

Captain Baw spoke tersely. "He escaped. By now he's safe in Far Dogtown."

Vv. Kylo uttered a rather tactless sound of astonishment. "Escaped? With you right beside him?"

Captain Baw puffed out his cheeks and stared across the chamber. He spoke in a measured voice. "I was not at his very side; I had stepped forward to attract Sir Estevan's attention. After the shots, there was confusion, and at first I thought to blame the Gomaz, until I saw that two of his fellows were down. By this time the assassin was halfway to Dogtown, curse his heels. Never fear, we'll winkle him out by one trick or another, or maybe arrange his demise. I assure you, he'll not escape so easily."

"A sad affair," said Hetzel. He spoke to Vvs. Felius. "Inasmuch as my business with Sir Estevan is urgent, I prefer to see him now, rather than wait for another session of the Triarchy."

Vvs. Felius said in a haughty voice, "Sir Estevan is certainly too shaken to conduct business at this moment."

"Why not consult Sir Estevan on this score? I suspect that he has more fortitude than you give him credit for."

With a sniff, Vvs. Felius spoke into a mesh. She listened to the quiet reply, and, vindicated, turned back to Hetzel. "Sir Estevan is seeing no one today. I'm sorry."

Hetzel stood on the great Gaean porch, wondering what to do next, and not particularly anxious to do anything. In the aftermath of last night's adventure, his legs were flaccid, his throat felt raw, his head seemed to expand and contract as he breathed. Had he been dosed with sleep gas? Or death gas? It would be interesting to know. The ramifications and possibilities were too large to grasp. Speculation at the moment was futile.

Hetzel descended the steps to the Plaza and moved off in the general direction of the Beyranion. He passed beside the Exhibitory and on sudden thought halted to reexamine the apathetic faces. None bore the semblance of Casimir Wuldfache. No surprise, of course, especially if that man he had glimpsed the previous evening had for a fact been Wuldfache.

Hetzel turned away. On a bench nearby sat an unkempt young man in ragged garments and scuffed ankle boots. Matted blond hair and a half-grown beard blurred his rather prominent and overlarge features, but failed to disguise an expression of rage and hate. Hetzel halted to look the man over and received a lambent blue glare for his pains.

Hetzel asked, "May I share the bench with you?"

"Do as you like."

Hetzel seated himself. The man smelled of sweat and filth. "My name is Miro Hetzel."

The young man returned only a surly grunt. Hetzel inquired, "And your name is . . . ?"

"None of your affair." A few seconds later he blurted, "Who are you? What do you want with me?"

"As I say, I am Miro Hetzel. What do I want with you? Perhaps only a few minutes of idle conversation."

"I do not care to talk to you."

"As you wish. But you should know that a man approximating your description has just committed a serious crime. Unless the actual criminal is captured, you would be wise to prepare yourself for inconvenience."

For a moment it appeared that the man would make no reply. Then, in a rasping voice he asked, "Are you the police? If so, look elsewhere for your criminal."

"I am not connected with the police. May I ask your name?"

"Gidion Dirby."

"Have you just paid a visit to the Triskelion?"

"You might call it that."

"During this visit, did you expunge two of the Triarchs?"

Gidion Dirby spoke in a wondering voice, "Two Triarchs? Which two?"

"The Liss and the Olefract."

Gidion Dirby laughed softly and leaned back upon the bench.

"The news comes as no great shock," Hetzel observed.

"I was supposed to kill the Gaean," said Gidion Dirby. "The plan went wrong. After all that work, after all that effort . . ."

"The more you explain, the less I understand," said Hetzel. "In simple language: why did you disregard this complicated plan and kill the aliens instead of Sir Estevan?"

"What are you saying? I killed no one whatever. Not that I wouldn't like to."

Hetzel said thoughtfully, "The description of the assassin—a man vehement, dirty, and wild—is not too much different from your own."

Gidion Dirby laughed again, a hoarse, hacking sound. "There can't be two of me. Sometimes I doubt if there's even one."

Hetzel hazarded a shot in the dark. "Istagam has dealt unfairly with you."

Gidion Dirby cut short his mirth. "Istagam? Why Istagam?" He seemed concerned and puzzled.

"You don't know?"

"Of course I don't know. I don't know anything."

Hetzel reached a decision. He rose to his feet. "Come along with me. At the Beyranion, Captain Baw can make no demands upon either of us."

Dirby made no move. He blinked across the Plaza, then looked back at Hetzel. "Why?"

"I want to hear your story as a coherent unit, especially in regard to your dealings with Istagam."

Dirby grunted and rose to his feet. "I've got nothing better to do."

They moved off toward the Beyranion.

CHAPTER 5

Upon entering the suite, Hetzel indicated the bathroom. "Clean yourself. Drop your clothes down the chute."

Gidion Dirby grumbled something without conviction and went into the bathroom. Hetzel telephoned for a barber and fresh garments.

In due course Gidion Dirby stood in the center of the room clean, shorn, shaved, and dressed in clean clothes. Only his surly expression remained. Hetzel surveyed him with qualified approval. "You're a different person. Without risk you could return to the Triskelion and assassinate Vvs. Felius."

Gidion Dirby ignored the rather mordant pleasantry. He inspected himself in a mirror. "I haven't looked at myself like this for . . . I don't know how long. Months, I suppose."

Waiters appeared with a catering cart and laid out a meal. Gidion Dirby ate with an appetite he made no effort to conceal and drank more than half a bottle of green wine.

Hetzel presently asked, "What, in general, are your plans?"

"What good are plans? I have none. The police are looking for me."

"Not too diligently, perhaps."

Gidion Dirby looked up, suddenly alert. "Why do you say that?"

"Isn't it strange that an assassin could kill two Triarchs while Captain Baw looked on, then run away unscathed? I may, of course, be overestimating Captain Baw's competence."

"I'm not an assassin," said Gidion Dirby in a flat voice. "Why did you bring me here?"

"I am interested in Istagam. I want to hear what you can tell me. It's that simple."

"Not all that simple. You are a police official?"

"No."

Dirby's voice became sarcastic. "A philanthropist. An amateur of oddities?"

"I am an effectuator," said Hetzel.

"It makes no difference, in any case. I have no secrets." He took a gulp of wine. "Very well, I'll tell you what happened to me. You can believe me or not; it's all the same. My home is Thrope on the planet Cicely. My father owns an estate on one of the northern islands—Huldice, if you happen to know Cicely. It's a quiet place where nothing ever happens except the turn of the crops and the hussade championships, and even our hussade is stately and we denude no sheirls, more's the pity. . . . To be brief, I grew up to wanderlust, and when I left Dagglesby University I took a job with the Blue Arrow Line as supercargo. At Wolden Port, on Arbello, we picked up cargo for Maz —perhaps some of this very wine we drink now."

"Not this wine. This is Medlin-Esterhazy, from Saint Wilmin."

Dirby made an impatient gesture. "We discharged our cargo at the spaceport yonder and took aboard a new cargo of crated merchandise. The consignee was Istagam at Twisselbane on Tamar."

"Twisselbane? And there you met Casimir Wuldfache? Or Carmine Daruble?"

"I met neither. We discharged cargo, and then I went across town to the Pleasure Gardens, where I met a beautiful girl with dark hair and a wonderful soft voice. Her name was Eljiano. She had just arrived in town from one of the backlands, or so she told me. I fell in love with her, and one thing led to another, and two days later I woke up with no money and no Eljiano. When I managed to get myself to the spaceport, my ship was gone and far away.

"A man came up to me and asked if I wanted to earn some easy money. I asked, 'How much and how easy?' This was my second mistake. My first was at the Pleasure Gardens. The man said his name was Banghart and his game was smuggling. Well, I needed money, and I agreed to the proposition. We loaded an old barrel of a hulk with unmarked crates, and they might have been the same crates we had brought away from Maz, except that they were far heavier. But I knew that Istagam was somehow connected with the affair. Banghart told me nothing.

"We took off on the hulk and presently stood off a planet surrounded by an orange nimbus. Banghart identified the planet as Dys, wherever that is. We discharged our cargo by moonlight, on an island in a swamp."

"Dys has no orange nimbus," said Hetzel.

Gidion Dirby paid him no heed. "Banghart approached the planet with great caution, and I believe he was waiting for a signal, because all of a sudden we dropped like a stone down to the night side. We landed on an island in a swamp and all night long discharged cargo by hand, under a beautiful big full moon, green as a gooseberry."

"Dys has no moon," said Hetzel.

Dirby nodded. "We were here on Maz. When the hold was empty, Banghart told me that I had to stay and guard the cargo, that I was to be sent out on another job. I complained, but in a reasonable voice, because I had nothing to back up my arguments. I said, 'Yes, Mr. Banghart, certainly, Mr. Banghart, I'll really guard this shipment.' The ship left. I was sure I was going to be killed, so I climbed a tree and hid in the branches.

"I began to think. I watched the moon; it was big and round and green and I knew then that I was back on Maz. The crates must certainly contain weapons for the Gomaz. I could see that my chances were poor. If the Gomaz caught me, they'd kill me; if the Triarchy patrol caught me, they'd seal me into the top floor of the Exhibitory.

"The moonlight was too green and dim to see by. I sat in the tree until daylight; then I climbed to the ground. The day was overcast and almost as dim as the night, but I noticed a path leading off across the swamp, with timbers laid across the worst spots.

"Even now I hesitated. Banghart had told me to guard the cargo, and I was deathly afraid of him. I still am. Worse now. But I finally decided to try the path. I walked about two hours. I had a few minor adventures, but no real emergencies, and I finally came to dry land. A stone fence ran along the shore. By this time nothing seemed strange. The path led to a gate, and here a man waited, and this is where the story starts to become insane. I'm not insane, mind you; it's just what happened to me. This man was tall and as handsome as Avatar Gisrod. He wore a white robe, a white turban, a veil of white gauze embroidered with black pearls. He seemed to be expecting me. I said, 'Good morning, sir, can you direct me to civilization?'

"He said, 'Of course. Step over here.' He took me to a tent. 'Just wait inside.'

"I said I'd just as soon wait outside in the open; he just pointed into the tent. I went in, and that's all I remember; Handsome must have had put-out gas waiting for me." Gidion Dirby heaved a sad sigh.

"I came back to life in a large bare room. There were no doors or windows. The floor measured twelve paces in one direction, fourteen and a half in the other. The ceiling was high; I could barely see it. I must have been unconscious for two or three days; my beard had grown; I was weak and thirsty. There was a chair, a table, a couch, all built of rough timber, but I wasn't overly critical." Dirby paused. "What do you think of the story so far?"

"I haven't thought. I'm just listening. Offhand, there doesn't seem any relationship between its various phases."

Dirby could not restrain a grim smile. "Quite right. Where does it start? When I left Dagglesby University? When I first came to Maz? At the Pleasure Gardens? When I took up with Banghart? Or has this always been my destiny? This is a most important question."

Hetzel said, "Perhaps I lack perceptiveness . . ."

Dirby showed no impatience. "The point is this. . . . But, no. I'll just go on with the story. It's quite absurd, don't you think?"

Hetzel refilled the goblets. "There may be a pattern not yet evident to either of us."

Dirby shrugged, to indicate that he cared nothing one way or the other. "I looked around the room. Light came from two high fixtures.

The walls were white plastic. The floor was covered with a gray composition. Across one end of the room was a platform, as high as my waist and four feet wide—a stage, with flush doors at both sides. On the table was a jug. It seemed to hold water, and I drank. The water had an odd flavor, and after a few minutes I was bent over with stomach cramps. I decided that I had been poisoned, and I was ready to die. But I vomited instead, time after time, until I was too weak to vomit anymore. Then I crawled to the couch and went to sleep.

"When I awoke, I felt better. The room looked exactly as before, except that someone had kindly cleaned up the vomit, and on the table beside the jug was a photograph of Handsome. Something nagged at my mind. Was I in the same room? The walls were pale yellow instead of white. I stood up, and I was still hungry and thirsty. On the stage I noticed a tray with bread, cheese, fruit, and a glass mug full of beer. I looked at it a minute. Maybe it was poisoned, like the water. I decided I didn't care; I'd just as soon be poisoned as starve. I picked up the bread and cheese. It was rubber. The beer was some sort of gel. At the bottom of the mug I found a photograph of a man winking at me—Handsome.

"I made up my mind to be stoic. Someone was watching me—a lunatic, or a sadist, or Handsome, or all three. I'd give him no satisfaction. I turned away and went to sit down in the chair. It gave me an electric shock. With great dignity I went to the cot. It was sopping wet. I sat on the table. A few minutes later I looked back at the stage, and the tray had been moved. Somehow it looked different. I sat for a moment or two, then leisurely got up to investigate. This time the food was real. I brought it back to the table and ate. Without thinking, I was sitting in the chair. As soon as I remembered, I began to expect another shock, but nothing happened. This, incidentally, was how I was fed during my entire stay. Sometimes the food was real, more often not. The intervals were irregular. I never knew when I would be fed." Dirby gave a sad laugh. "When the waiters brought in our meal, I half-expected it to be rubber, and I would not have been surprised."

"It seems that you were the victim of a careful and systematic persecution."

"Call it what you like. The food trick was trivial compared to what else went on; after a while, I hardly thought about it. I was never shocked again, incidentally. I always half-expected it. And after that first jug of water, the food never poisoned me again.

"When I finished that first meal, I looked at the back wall, which was blue. I was sure all the walls had been yellow. I began to wonder if I were insane after all. The walls kept changing colors—never when I looked at them: white, yellow, green, blue, occasionally brown or gray. I learned to dislike brown and gray, because they usually—not always—meant that something unpleasant was about to happen."

"A very strange proceeding," mused Hetzel. "Perhaps some sort of experiment?"

"That's what I thought at first. I changed my mind. . . . The first few days, nothing much happened, except the rubber food and the walls changing color. Once, when I lay on the cot it tossed me out; another time, the chair collapsed. Occasionally I'd hear small noises behind my back, noises very near—a footstep, a whisper, a giggle. Then there was Handsome. One day the walls turned gray. When I noticed the stage, I saw that a doorway had opened at the back to show a long hall. At the far end, a man appeared. He wore Old Shalkho costume—tight breeches of white velvet, a pink-and-blue jacket with gold tassels, a ruffled cravat. He was a tall, strong man, very stately in his manner, very handsome. He came to the edge of the stage and looked toward me—not at me, but toward me—with a peculiar expression I can't describe: amused, bored, supercilious. He said, 'You're making yourself quite comfortable. Too comfortable. We'll see to that.'

"I called out, 'Why are you keeping me here? I've done nothing to you!' He paid no attention. He said, 'You must think more intently.' I said, 'I've been thinking about everything there is to think about.'

"Again he paid no attention. 'Perhaps you're lonely, perhaps you'd like some company. Well, why not?' And out on the stage ran a dozen beasts, like weasels, with spiked tails and long fangs and prongs growing from their elbows. They ran at me squealing and hissing. I climbed up on the table and kicked them back when they jumped. Handsome watched from the doorway, with an absolutely quiet expression—not even smiling. Two or three times the weasels almost had me; then they gave up and began to roam the room. When one came close, I jumped on it and crushed it to the floor, and I finally killed them all. Handsome had gone away long ago.

"I piled the dead things in a corner and went to look at the doorway where he had stood. The wall seemed solid, so here was another mystery, although now mysteries were simply ordinary events—a way of life, so to speak. Still, if Handsome wanted me to think, he had his way with me, because I did little else.

"I wondered why they worked such elaborate pranks. Revenge?

Except for my sad little smuggling exploit, I had lived a blameless life. An experiment with my sanity? They could have proceeded much more harshly. Mistaken identity? Possibly. Or perhaps I was in the hands of some mad prankster who enjoyed practical jokes. Nothing seemed reasonable."

"And did you see Handsome again?"

"I did indeed, and the back wall turned gray before every time, although sometimes it turned gray and Handsome never appeared. But other things happened, silly, strange things. One day I heard a fanfare, then music, and a troupe of trained birds ran out on the stage. They danced and ran in circles and jumped over each other and marched back and forth; then they all turned somersaults off the stage. The music became a caterwauling, blatting and clanging and thumping; then it stopped. I heard a girl giggling, and then there was silence. The girl sounded like Eljiano, even though I knew this to be impossible. Then I thought: impossible? Nothing was impossible.

"About an hour later, the lights went out, and the room was pitch dark. A minute or two passed; then a tremendous green flash filled the room, and a clap of noise. I was startled and almost fell out of the cot. I lay in the dark expecting another flash, but after five minutes the usual lights turned on.

"A jailer began to appear in the room—a creature half-man and half-woman. His right side was masculine; his left side was female. He—I'll call it a 'he'—never spoke, and I never spoke. He'd walk around the room, look here and there, wink and grimace, perform some silly caper, and go. He came about five times; then I never saw him again. But one time I awoke and found three naked girls crawling around the room on their hands and knees. When they saw I was awake, they ran out of the room. One of them was Eljiano—I think. I'm not sure. About this time my meals began to appear in articles of the most extraordinary shape and size: a tiny bowl with an enormous lopsided spoon; a ten-gallon kettle twisted into a half-spiral, with a bit of cheese at the bottom; tangles of tubes and bulbs in which I was served my drink; a tray half an inch across and three feet long holding three peas. I found these amusing rather than otherwise, though I never had enough to eat.

"The lights went out a second time, and I lay on the couch waiting for another flash of green light, but this time the ceiling billowed with luminous gas. It dissipated, and there was a view out over my old home at Thrope. It changed to other landscapes of the neighborhood, and then others that I couldn't recognize. All these pictures were dis-

torted; they all shuddered and quivered and crawled. My own face
appeared, then the top of my head. Two hands cut away my scalp
with a saw, and there was my brain. A tiny naked girl appeared—I
think it was Eljiano. She climbed over the rim of the skull and ran
back and forth across the brain. Eljiano ran away; the picture
changed and became a calm stern face—Handsome. Mind you, this
was not a dream. My dreams during this time were havens of normality. . . . The lights went on. I sat up on the couch and yawned and
stretched, as if I were accustomed to such visions. I'd now decided
that Handsome was deliberately trying to drive me insane. I still
think so."

Hetzel made a gesture that might have signified almost anything;
Dirby turned on him a resentful scowl. "Other incidents occurred.
The sounds behind me—whispers and giggles. About every third day
the lights would gradually go dim, and I'd start to wonder why I
couldn't see; was I going blind? Then they'd play music—a simple
tune that would meander through all kinds of meaningless phrases
and never resolve, or go through a hundred repetitions. And of
course, Handsome. He came twice more to the doorway that opened
on the stage, and once I turned around, and there he stood in the
room with me. He wore a different costume—a suit of silver scales, a
silver morion with cusps across his cheeks, a nasal protecting his
nose, and three silver spikes at his forehead. He spoke to me. 'Hello,
Gidion Dirby.'

"I said, 'So you know my name.'

" 'Of course I know your name!'

" 'I thought you might be making a mistake.'

" 'I never make mistakes.'

" 'Then why are you keeping me here?'

" 'Because I choose to do so.' He went to the table. 'This must be
your breakfast. Are you hungry?' He took the lid off the pot, and
there was the contents of my commode—or somebody else's commode. When I looked down, he turned the pot over my head, then
left by the door at the side of the stage.

"I cleaned myself up as well as I could, and went to sit on the
couch. Presently I became drowsy and fell asleep, and when I woke
up, I was in a new and different place—a bench outside a building of
iron and glass, which I saw to be the Maz space depot. I sat for a few
minutes gathering my wits. Could it be that I was free? No one paid
any attention to me. I checked my pockets and my pouch: there was
nothing but a few coins and a zap gun; no papers.

"A guard came up to me and asked what I was up to; I told him I was waiting for a ship. He asked for identification; I said I'd lost my papers. In that case I'd have to get new papers from the Gaean Triarch. Luckily for me, so he said, the session was just starting, and he set me off along the avenue to the Triskelion. I went into the lobby. A big red-faced official asked what I wanted. I said I must see the Gaean Triarch on urgent business. He took me into a chamber with three desks. There were three Gomaz ahead of me. The security officer led me to one of the desks and said, 'This man claims urgent business with you.' To me he said, 'This is Sir Estevan Tristo; state your business.' But I couldn't state anything, because this was Handsome. He looked at me, and I looked at him. Then I just turned and walked away, too confused even to talk. Behind me I heard zaps going off. I looked around. Handsome had dropped behind his desk, and there was a great deal of shouting. I saw that two of the Gomaz were on the floor. The official made a dive for me, but I knocked him down and ran out the side door. I had nowhere to go, so I ran across the Plaza and sat down on the bench, and there you found me. I see now that I was wrong running away; I should have stayed and told the truth. Mind search would have proved me out. . . . Of course, they might have shot me first and asked questions later. Maybe I acted correctly."

"Not really," said Hetzel. "You should have continued down to Dogtown. Far Dogtown, that is. Sitting in the Plaza, you're fair game for Captain Baw. Even a confused pseudo-lunatic should know better than to pose invitingly before the Exhibitory. Why did you stop there?"

Dirby's face became dark and sullen. "I don't know. I saw a bench, and I sat down. Must I explain everything?"

Hetzel ignored the question. "You suffered a perplexing experience. At least, from your point of view. Sir Estevan is definitely Handsome?"

"I'd know his face among ten thousand."

"And he recognized you?"

"He said nothing. His face showed nothing. But he must have recognized me."

CHAPTER 6

Hetzel went to the window and stood looking out over the Plaza. Dirby slumped back in his chair and stared morosely down into the goblet.

Hetzel turned back to Dirby. "You are still carrying the zap gun?"

Dirby brought it forth; Hetzel examined the charge meter, slid out the power cell, examined the meter once more. "It shows a charge, but the cell is dead. The meter has been jammed." He tossed the gun aside. "I assume that you were meant to be captured. Some element of the plan went wrong. You escaped. Or were allowed to escape."

Dirby frowned. "So . . . what do I do now?"

"Send a message to your father. Ask him to send out legal aid and a Gaean marshal as quickly as possible. Then, don't stir from the premises of the Beyranion, or you'll be subject to the jurisdiction of the Triskelion. If you were put on trial now, your chances would be poor."

"Mind search would prove that I'm telling the truth," Dirby muttered.

"Mind search would prove that you subscribe to a maniac's dream in which Sir Estevan Tristo is your persecutor. You would be declared criminally insane and guilty of murder."

Dirby growled. "Either way, I lose."

"You don't have a chance unless you can corroborate your story."

"Very well. You're an effectuator. Effect an investigation."

Hetzel reflected a moment. "I have other commitments. There might be a conflict of interest. Still, on the other hand, I might be able to sell the same work twice, which is all to the good. I presume you intend to pay me?"

Dirby looked up with a rather unpleasant sneer. "With what? I don't have a zink.* If you're worried, I'll make out a draft upon my father's bank, which he will certainly honor."

"We'll discuss this in due course. But first an understanding. I commit myself only to investigation. I undertake neither to assert your innocence nor to defend your guilt. You must secure legal representation elsewhere. Is this agreeable?"

Dirby gave an indifferent shrug. "Whatever you say. I'm in no position to argue."

"By any chance are you acquainted with a certain Casimir Wuldfache? No? What about Carmine Daruble? I'd like you to examine a photograph . . ." Hetzel stopped short. His wallet, with eighty-five SLU and the photograph of Casimir Wuldfache, had been stolen from him. "Well, no matter."

---

* Zink, a coin representative of a man-minute, the hundredth part of an SLU. Gaean time is based upon the standard day of Earth, subdivided into twenty-four hours, after ancient tradition. A minute is the hundredth part of an hour; a second is the hundredth part of a minute.

A chime sounded. Hetzel went to the door and slid it open, to reveal two men—the first a ponderous and immaculate gentleman whom Hetzel recognized for the hotel manager, and Kerch, the hotel security officer.

"I am Aeolus Shult, manager of the Beyranion," said the large man in a dry, precise voice. "This is Nello Kerch, our security officer. May we come in?"

Hetzel stood back; Shult and Kerch entered the room. Hetzel said, "Allow me to introduce my guest, Vv. Gidion Dirby."

Shult refused to acknowledge the introduction. Kerch gave Dirby an uninterested nod. "I am here in connection with Vv. Dirby," said Shult. "Unfortunately, I must ask him to depart the premises at once."

"This is a curious demand," said Hetzel.

"Not at all. I have received notice to the effect that Vv. Dirby has committed a serious crime, namely, the assassination of two dignitaries. The Beyranion cannot function as a sanctuary for criminals."

"Vv. Dirby does not fit this description," said Hetzel. "He tells me that he is innocent of wrongdoing. Furthermore, he is not a casual intruder upon the premises; he is here as my guest."

Shult's face became obdurate. "Captain Baw of the Gaean Security Force has made a specific statement. He identifies Vv. Dirby as the assassin."

"This is more puzzling than ever. Captain Baw told me that he merely heard the shots. Who made the identification?"

"Captain Baw vouchsafed no details."

"But details are the gist of the matter. Several other persons were present when the assassinations occurred, including three Gomaz, two of whom were killed."

"I cannot judge any of this," said Shult. "Captain Baw is waiting in my office; he insists that I expel Vv. Dirby into his custody."

"You would thereby set a very dangerous precedent," said Hetzel. "Do you want Captain Baw appearing every few days to demand one or another of your guests, who for some reason or another has annoyed the Triarchs? Or the Liss authorities? Or the Olefract? They have rights equal and equivalent to Captain Baw."

Kerch said, "Vv. Hetzel is quite right on this score."

Shult pursed his lips. "Naturally, I want nothing of the sort. Still, my responsibility extends only to patrons of the hotel."

"I have already pointed out that Vv. Dirby is my guest."

"He is not registered as such."

"That is irrelevant. I have rented a suite of rooms, not a single occupancy; I have the right to entertain as many guests as I wish. Now, there is another point that you have not considered. The Triskelion is a special entity, and not subject to Gaean law. The Beyranion Hotel is very definitely subject to Gaean law. Vv. Dirby has been proved guilty of nothing. If you irresponsibly turn him over to Captain Baw, and should he thereby suffer harm, you are liable for damages and a punitive fine, perhaps ten or twenty million SLU. You are treading upon exceedingly thin legal ice."

Shult now exhibited signs of nervousness. He glanced at Kerch, who merely shrugged and turned away. "This is all very well, but I still cannot allow myself to harbor an assassin."

"Who says he is an assassin?"

"Well . . . Captain Baw."

"I suggest that you ask Captain Baw to assemble his witnesses and his evidence and bring everything here, and then we can decide upon Vv. Dirby's guilt or innocence. Even then, you are not obliged to respond. We stand on Gaean territory; yonder is a joint jurisdiction of three races, two of whom are alien. Under no circumstances can you allow yourself to be intimidated by Captain Baw."

Aeolus Shult heaved a deep sigh. "There is something in what you say. We must always act with due regard for Gaean justice." He gave Hetzel a doleful salute and departed, followed by Kerch.

After several moments Dirby spoke. "So . . . I'm a prisoner at the Beyranion."

"Until you prove yourself innocent."

Dirby lapsed into mulish silence. Fifteen minutes passed. The telephone chimed. Hetzel touched the audio button. The screen lit up to display the tea-rose delicacy of Sir Estevan's blond receptionist. "Hetzel speaking."

"This is the office of the Gaean Triarch. Sir Estevan Tristo regrets that he was unable to meet with you earlier today; however, he is free now and requests that you call at his office."

"Now?"

"If it is convenient."

Hetzel reflected a moment. "Please connect me with Sir Estevan."

"Just a minute, sir. Will you be good enough to press your video button?"

"When Sir Estevan comes on."

"Very good, sir."

The screen brightened, to show a keen-featured face. Dirby came forward and stared intently at the image. He nodded to Hetzel. "That's Handsome."

Hetzel touched the video button. Sir Estevan said, "You are Vv. Miro Hetzel, who called at the Triskelion earlier today?"

"Quite correct, sir."

"I would be pleased to see you now, if you are at liberty."

"That is kind of you. However, another matter must be taken into consideration."

"You refer to Gidion Dirby?"

Hetzel nodded. "I would like to call on you, but I do not care to be seized as soon as I leave the Beyranion and held on some trumped-up charge. If this is to be the case, I would prefer that you came here to see me."

Sir Estevan smiled a wintry smile. "Let me check with the commandant."

The screen went blank. Hetzel switched off the audio and looked at Dirby. "So that's Handsome."

Dirby nodded. "His hair is different. He wears it more formally."

"What of his voice?"

Dirby hesitated. "It's somewhat different. Considerably different, in fact."

"Has it occurred to you that on the two occasions you saw Handsome at close hand he wore first a veil and then a morion that concealed a good part of his face? On the other occasions, he stood in a doorway in a section of wall where no doorway existed."

"What are you suggesting?"

"That your experience of Handsome for the most part was a projected image, and that the voice might or might not have been his own."

Dirby scowled. "So that Handsome wasn't out there at all."

"It seems that diligent efforts were made to arouse your antagonism against Sir Estevan."

Dirby laughed. "Then they bring me here to the Triskelion, give me a dead zap, and show me Sir Estevan. Why all this?"

"Two Triarchs were killed—an Olefract and a Liss. It would be more difficult to arouse animosity against these two."

Dirby shook his head. "I don't understand it."

"I don't understand it either," said Hetzel. "You call him Handsome. I call him Casimir Wuldfache."

Sir Estevan returned to the screen. Hetzel restored the sound. "I have conferred with Captain Baw," said Sir Estevan. "Understandably, he is anxious for information."

"All of us share this anxiety, including Gidion Dirby. For instance, he would like to know why you turned a pot of ordure over his head."

Sir Estevan Tristo raised his eyebrows. He reached out and made an adjustment on the clarity control. "I don't believe I heard your remarks correctly."

"No matter," said Hetzel. "I want only your assurance that if I leave the hotel I won't be subjected to inconvenience."

"If you transgress our laws, or if you have done so, you will face the ordinary consequences. However, Captain Baw tells me that to the best of his knowledge you have committed no such acts."

"I then have your explicit assurance that I will not be arrested?"

"Not unless you commit a crime."

"Very well," said Hetzel. "I'll risk it."

CHAPTER 7

Hetzel set off across the Plaza toward the murky outline of the Triskelion. He observed no persons in the blue-and-green uniform of the Gaean Security Patrol, and when he arrived at the Triskelion, the officer on duty paid him no extraordinary attention. Captain Baw was not in evidence.

Hetzel approached the Gaean section of the reception desk. The Liss and Olefract sides of the triangle, as usual, were vacant. Vv. Kylo, who was on duty alone, directed Hetzel to a door across the lobby. Hetzel entered an antechamber where Sir Estevan's pretty blond receptionist sat at a desk. The telephone image failed to do justice to the girl. Her coloring, thought Hetzel, was exquisite—pale-blond hair like winter sunlight, flower-petal skin, features delicate, almost overrefined, as if she derived from generations of aesthetes and aristocrats. For Hetzel's taste she was perhaps too sensitive, too fastidious and meticulous, and perhaps humorless as well; nevertheless, she added a great deal of tone to Sir Estevan's office.

"Vv. Hetzel? This way, please."

Sir Estevan arose from his desk to meet Hetzel—a man tall and stern, but undeniably handsome. He was, thought Hetzel, older than Casimir Wuldfache. The resemblance, though strong, dissipated somewhat upon close inspection.

Sir Estevan indicated a chair, and seated himself. "You are an almost obsessively cautious man."

"Captain Baw's zeal compels such an obsession," said Hetzel.

Sir Estevan allowed himself a faint smile. "I think you referred to Gidion Dirby as your client?"

"By no means. His situation interests me, and I am acting informally as his adviser. He is not my client. The distinction is important."

"You were previously acquainted?"

"I met him for the first time today. His predicament attracted my attention, and the story he tells aroused my professional interest."

"I see. May I inquire your profession?"

"I am an effectuator, of a specialized sort—in fact, something of a dilettante. I rescue distressed maidens, I undertake interesting missions, I search for lost fortunes."

"In which of these categories does Gidion Dirby fit?"

"He is hardly a maiden in distress," said Hetzel. "Nonetheless, I am attempting to protect him from his enemies."

Sir Estevan laughed his chilly laugh. "And who protects the enemies against Gidion Dirby?"

"I wish to discuss this matter with you. First, do you believe Gidion Dirby to be the assassin?"

"I see no other possibility, nor does Captain Baw. Consult him; he was much closer to the action."

"You did not observe Dirby shoot his gun?"

"No. Captain Baw obscured my view. I heard the sound of the pellets; I saw two Gomaz killed, and dropped behind my desk. Essentially, I saw nothing of what happened."

"You never saw Vv. Dirby at all?"

"Not clearly."

"Did you recognize him when you saw his face in the view plate?"

"No, he is a stranger to me."

"Why should he—or anyone else, for that matter—attempt to assassinate the Triarchs?"

Sir Estevan leaned back in his chair. "I assume that the murderer was and is insane. There is no other explanation. The deed is absolutely pointless."

"What if the surviving Gomaz were the assassin?"

Sir Estevan shook his head. "It is not the nature of the Gomaz to assassinate. He kills for his own private reasons—'lusts' might be the applicable word; otherwise, he is neither violent nor murderous, unless he is molested."

"You have apparently made a close study of the Gomaz."

"Naturally; why else am I here?"

"The Liss and the Olefract share your interest?"

Sir Estevan shrugged. "We have little communication between us. Certainly no informal contacts. The Liss are suspicious and hostile; the Olefract are contemptuous and hostile. But still no reason to kill their Triarchs."

"And how will they react?"

"Reasonably enough, or so I imagine. If Dirby is deranged, they'll accept the killing as an aberrated act."

"Assuming that Dirby is indeed the killer."

"There's no other possibility."

"Captain Baw was in the chamber."

"Ridiculous. Why should he perform such an act?"

"Why should Gidion Dirby?"

"Insanity."

"Perhaps Baw is insane."

"Rubbish."

Hetzel indicated a door. "This leads into the Triarchic chamber?"

"It does."

"Your receptionist at all times had the door under observation?"

"She certainly would have noticed someone standing here shooting at me."

"Perhaps someone was hidden in the chamber?"

"Impossible. I was fifteen minutes early into the chamber. No one was hidden there."

"Well, then . . . what about yourself?"

Sir Estevan showed his cold smile. "I'd prefer to fix the guilt on Gidion Dirby, or the Gomaz, or even Baw, for that matter."

"And the Gomaz—why were they here?"

"They had no opportunity to explain themselves."

"Won't this assassination cause problems? Raids? Demonstrations?"

"Probably not. The Gomaz are linked telepathically to the unitary consciousness of their sept, and they are not disturbed by death. This is an element of their ferocity." Sir Estevan tossed a pamphlet across his desk. "Read this, if you're interested in the Gomaz."

"Thank you." The pamphlet was entitled *The Gomaz Warriors of SJZ-BEA-1545 (Maz), Prepared by the Hannenborg Institute for*

Xenological Research. He inspected the diagram on the cover. "Two hundred and twenty-nine septs. The Gomaz who visited you this morning—what was their sept?"

"Ubaikh." Sir Estevan gave his fingers an impatient twitch. "Surely you did not come here to discuss the Gomaz?"

Hetzel opened his mouth to mention Istagam, then had second thoughts. It might be wise to secure an air-car-use permit for reasons other than investigating Istagam. "At the moment, I am preoccupied with Gidion Dirby and his extraordinary plight."

"What is so extraordinary about it?"

"I would like you to hear Gidion Dirby's story from his own mouth. Could you step over to the Beyranion for a few minutes?"

"I'd prefer that you give me the gist of it here."

"Gidion Dirby declares that he was held captive and subjected to a number of fantastic tricks; you were the chief trickmaster, and terminated the proceedings by turning a chamber pot over his head."

Sir Estevan grinned. "I deny this."

"You have never seen Gidion Dirby previous to today?"

"Never, to my knowledge."

"Are you familiar with a long corridor with blue-and-white-tile walls and an arched white ceiling?"

"Certainly. Such a corridor connects the loggia of my residence to the morning room. Why do you ask?"

"This hall figures in Gidion Dirby's account, and it tends to authenticate his story."

Sir Estevan considered. "If Dirby is innocent, then either I or Captain Baw must be guilty of murder. Or conceivably my secretary, Zaressa, if your imagination can cope with the image of her standing in that doorway and gunning down a Liss, an Olefract, and two Gomaz."

"If Dirby is innocent, then you, Captain Baw, Zaressa, or the Gomaz must be guilty. I agree to this."

"It would be most tiresome," said Sir Estevan, "especially since the Gomaz must be removed from the list. Far better that an addle-brained zealot be declared the assassin, whether he is guilty, as I believe him to be, or not."

"Dirby might concede this point of view," said Hetzel, "if he were granted safe-conduct away from Maz and recompensed for his inconvenience. At the moment, he is annoyed and unhappy, and he is anxious to bring the facts to light."

"This, of course, is his option. How does he propose to perform the illumination?"

"The Gomaz was present; why not question him?"

Sir Estevan leaned back in his chair and pondered. "Gomaz make poor witnesses. They are unresponsive—contemptuously unresponsive, I should say—to our laws and customs. They will say what they wish to say, and no more. It is impossible to coerce a Gomaz, and it is also impossible to appeal, shall we say, to his better nature."

"Incidentally, what was their business with the Triarchy?"

"Before a statement could be made, the assassinations occurred."

Hetzel thought to detect evasiveness. "Did they not state their business for your agenda?"

"No." Sir Estevan's reply was curt.

"And you yourself do not know what their business might have been?"

"I would not care to speculate."

"From Dirby's point of view, the surviving Gomaz is a prime witness. It would seem that if a Gomaz testified at all, he would speak the truth."

"The truth as he saw it. By no means the truth as we see it."

"Still, in all fairness, we should hear what he has to tell us."

Sir Estevan hesitated a moment, then took up a schedule, which he studied a moment. He punched a button on his telephone. The screen became bright; a face looked forth; a voice spoke. "Maz Transport. Yes, Sir Estevan."

"Has the Route Five carrier left on schedule?"

"Yes, sir, half an hour ago."

"How many passengers were aboard?"

"One moment, sir. . . . Seven passengers: two Kaikash, two Ironbellies, a Ubaikh, an Aqzh, and a Yellow Hellion."

"Look out into the corral. Do you see any Ubaikh?"

"It's empty, sir. Everyone left on the transport."

"Thank you." Sir Estevan switched off the screen. "The Gomaz has returned to his castle, and must be considered inaccessible."

"Not necessarily. I can be on hand when the carrier puts him down, and interview him there."

"Hmmf." Sir Estevan studied Hetzel a long ten seconds. "How will you communicate with him?"

"You must have a suitable translator."

"Naturally. A valuable piece of equipment."

"I'll post bond on it, if you wish."

"That's not necessary. Zaressa will get it for you. You can rent an air car from the tourist agency in Dogtown." He scribbled a note, handed it to Hetzel. "That's your permit. They'll send one of their personnel with you; that's our invariable rule, to keep inexperienced people out of trouble. Maz is a dangerous planet, and naturally you go out at your own risk. The agency man will know how to find the Ubaikh depot. Don't go near the castle; they'll kill you. At the depot you're safe enough." He looked at the schedule. "You've got ample time. The carrier won't arrive at Ubaikh until tomorrow afternoon. I'll want to look over the tape of the interview; is that understood?"

"Certainly. Now, one other matter . . ."

Sir Estevan glanced at his watch. "I'm a bit pressed for time."

"I came here to Maz to inquire about Istagam, as the concern is known. My principals are concerned by Istagam's low prices; they fear that the Liss and the Olefract are using Maz as a port of entry from which to flood the Gaean markets."

Sir Estevan's lip curled. "You can assure them otherwise. Neither Liss nor Olefract want contact with the Gaeans, or with each other."

"Then who or what is Istagam?"

Sir Estevan spoke almost primly. "I have heard the word mentioned, and I believe that there is no illegality involved. You may so inform your principals, and they will have to trim their sails to the wind."

"Can you identify the directors of Istagam, or tell me anything about their mode of operation?"

"I'm sorry, sir; this is a matter that I can't discuss."

"On what grounds?"

"Caprice," said Sir Estevan. "That's as good a reason as any. I'm sorry that I now must terminate our discussion."

Hetzel rose to his feet. "Thank you for your courtesy. It has been a pleasure talking with you."

"Bring me back the translator tape; I'll want to check it over."

"I'll be sure to do so."

Captain Baw stood three inches taller than Hetzel; his shoulders, chest, and abdomen bulged with muscle; his round, flat face was cold and wary. He rose briskly to his feet when Hetzel entered his office, and stood sternly erect during the period of the interview.

"You are Captain Baw, I believe."

"I am he."

"Sir Estevan suggested that I consult you, in order to clarify exactly what happened this morning."

"Very good, then, consult away."

"You were present when the killings occurred?"

"I was indeed."

"What was the precise sequence of events?"

"I brought in a man named Gidion Dirby, who claimed urgent business with Sir Estevan. As I stepped forward to attract Sir Estevan's attention, he produced a gun and opened fire."

"You saw him shoot the gun?"

"He stood behind me, from where the shots originated."

"What of the Gomaz? They stood behind you as well."

"Gomaz are not allowed to carry guns."

"Assume that through some unusual circumstance, one of the Gomaz did in fact carry a gun—what then?"

"First: he would not kill in cold blood. Second: he would not kill his fellows. Third: he would not depart without making a thorough job of it."

"What happened to the weapon?"

"I have no information in this regard. You must put the question to Gidion Dirby."

"As a matter of fact, I have done so. Somewhat to his surprise, he did find a gun in his pocket. The cells were discharged and the contacts were corroded. The gun has not been fired for months. What do you say to that?"

In a voice of long-suffering patience, Captain Baw replied, "Sir, it is not my place to argue with you. Ask your questions of fact; I will respond as well as I can."

"You state that you did not actually see the gun being fired."

Baw lowered his eyelids, and his eyes became such narrow lines of leaden gristle that Hetzel wondered how he could see. "I will merely assert, sir, that the shots came from the vicinity of Gidion Dirby. I glimpsed the action from the corner of my eye; I was somewhat preoccupied with the Gomaz, who had become restless and upset."

"Why did you not immediately rush forth and capture Gidion Dirby?"

"My first duty was to Sir Estevan. I assured myself that he was not seriously hurt, and had a brief discussion with him. Then, when I went to seek Vv. Dirby, he was nowhere to be seen. I assumed that he had taken himself to Far Dogtown, where we lack jurisdiction."

"You might have caught him, had you hurried."

"Perhaps so, sir, but there was no basis on which I might have arrested him, and this was the subject of my discussion with Sir Estevan. Dirby's shots killed a Liss in Liss territory, an Olefract in Olefract territory, and no one has bothered to pass a law against killing Gomaz. The shoe is on the other foot. We have no formal extradition procedures with either Liss or Olefract, nor have they as yet made any representations to us."

"All this seems highly abstract," said Hetzel. "I would expect that when you observe a man killing two Triarchs, you would capture him first and worry about charges later."

Baw condescended a small smile. "This procedure might be feasible within the Reach. You do not understand how carefully we must deal with the Liss and Olefract. We adhere to the exact letter of our contract; they do the same with us. Only in this way can we accommodate each other."

"So, then, what is Dirby's status as of this moment?"

"We have issued a complaint of misdemeanor against Gidion Dirby, asserting that he fired weapons during official proceedings of the Triarchy and disrupted the session."

"This is not the statement you made to Aeolus Shult, at the Beyranion."

"At the Beyranion I have no official status. I can use unofficial language and perform unofficial acts, such as laying hold of Dirby and dragging him out on the Plaza to where I could arrest him."

"On misdemeanor charges?"

"Exactly."

"What is the penalty for such an offense?"

"He must be adjudged."

"By whom?"

"In connection with small crimes, I generally act as magistrate."

"And how do you adjudge Gidion Dirby?"

"Guilty."

"And his penalty?"

Captain Baw's thinking had not proceeded so far. "I must consult the statutes."

"Why not do so now? I will pay the fine."

Captain Baw made a brusque gesture. "If you think to pay some trifling sum in Gidion Dirby's name and win him away free and guiltless, you are mistaken."

"You have done this much yourself."

Captain Baw's mouth became a loose O of indignant astonishment. "How so?"

"You have tried and adjudged him of firing shots in the Triarchy chamber, and found him guilty. Regardless of his guilt or innocence, a man may not be twice held to account for the same charges."

Captain Baw's face began to turn pink. He spoke in a heavy voice. "This interpretation will not carry weight, I assure you."

"I thought not," said Hetzel.

"There may be an additional charge, such as felonious attack upon the life of Sir Estevan Tristo."

"How can this be? Only four shots were fired, and four individuals were killed!" This remark was a casual essay; Hetzel had no notion whatever as to how many shots had been fired.

"The number of shots fired is not germane," said Baw laboriously. "Gidion Dirby must surrender himself at once, or seriously compromise his position."

"I will tell him so," said Hetzel, "and I thank you for your courtesy. But one more matter puzzles me. I identified the Gomaz as Kaikash—"

"Kaikash? Nonsense. They were Ubaikh. Kaikash wear a peaked helmet and black leggings, and they smell different. I can't read the smells so that I know what they mean, but I can tell a Kaikash from a Ubaikh."

"What did they want from the Triarchs?"

"The matter lies beyond my province."

"But you know?"

"Of course I know. It is my business to know everything."

"Sir Estevan declared that you would answer all questions freely."

"In my opinion, Sir Estevan is far too liberal. There is no reason why we should explain official business to every astounded tourist. I will say this much: the Ubaikh consider themselves an elite. They led all the septs in the great war, and now they hold themselves first among the Gomaz, and they are always the first to complain of any and every fancied encroachment."

"I would consider Istagam more than an encroachment," said Hetzel. "No reasonable man could say otherwise."

Captain Baw looked off across the room. "In this regard, there can be no discussion."

"It is foolish to ignore a notorious reality," said Hetzel.

"Not all that notorious," grumbled Captain Baw. "A trivial matter, really."

"Then why should the Ubaikh come here to complain?"

"I don't know, and I don't care!" roared Captain Baw. "I can talk no more today!"

"Thank you, Captain Baw."

CHAPTER 8

Hetzel found Gidion Dirby sitting on a hummock of purple-black moss in that corner of the garden overlooking Dogtown. He seemed morose and preoccupied, and when Hetzel approached, he turned a resentful glance over his shoulder. Gidion Dirby, thought Hetzel, was not a likable man. Still, he must be excused a certain degree of peevishness. After similar treatment, Hetzel might also become misanthropic.

Dirby asked, "Well . . . did you see Sir Estevan?"

"Yes. He told me nothing we don't already know. I also spoke to Captain Baw, who seems somewhat uncertain. He tells me that the deed for which you are held liable is a simple misdemeanor. The Triarchs have never established a mutually binding legal code; no one trusts anyone else, and each party enforces its own laws upon its own subjects. Gaean interest in the missiles that killed the Liss and the Olefract ends as soon as those missiles cross the lines of jurisdiction. Killing Gomaz is not yet illegal. Hence, even had you shot the gun, your offense is a simple disorderly conduct. This is the theory. In effect, Sir Estevan might informally extradite you to the Liss or the Olefract. Though this I somehow doubt. He is a complex man, a puzzling man. He seems very confident."

Dirby gave an inarticulate growl. "They purposely allowed me to escape, because they couldn't risk a public trial, with mind-search evidence."

"I'm sure of nothing," said Hetzel. "Sir Estevan tells me that there is a long blue-and-white-tiled hall in his residence. Someone photographed him walking along this hall and adapted the film to your situation. . . . I neglected to ask who might have so filmed him."

"And when he turned the pot over my head—that was also a photograph?"

"That might not have been Sir Estevan. In fact, almost certainly it was Casimir Wuldfache."

Dirby rose to his feet and stood rubbing his chin. "If my offense is just simple misdemeanor, why not go over to the Triskelion and pay a fee?"

"It's not quite that simple. Captain Baw comprises the whole legal system in himself. He might sentence you to thirty lashes, or eighteen years in the Exhibitory, or expulsion into Liss territory. You had better remain at the Beyranion until you have legal counsel and a Gaean marshal on the job."

"That will be a month, or maybe two months."

"Do as you like," said Hetzel. "Shall I continue the investigation?"

"I suppose you might as well."

"If you turn yourself in, I'm going to stop. I can't collect money from a dead man."

Dirby only grunted.

Hetzel drew a deep breath and went on. "We've only scratched the surface of this case. Right now, at least, several matters seem important. Where is Banghart? Where is Casimir Wuldfache? Where were you confined? Is your case linked with Istagam? If so, how?"

"Don't ask me," said Dirby. "I'm just the turkey."

"Does Banghart have other names or a Gaean index by which he might be traced?"

"Not to my knowledge."

"What does he look like?"

Dirby scratched his chin. "He's older than I; stocky, with a square face and black hair. He doesn't seem particularly impressive until he gives you orders and looks at you. He's cold inside. He likes to dress well; in fact, he's something of a dandy. He spoke once or twice of a place called Fallorne."

"Fallorne is a world on the other side of the Reach. Anything else?"

"He had a strange way of singing. I can't quite describe it—as if singing two tunes at once, a kind of counterpoint. I can't think of much else."

"Very good. Now, you were put down on a swampy island. Do you remember the weather?"

"It was just an ordinary clear night."

"Could you see stars?"

"Not distinctly. The air blurs them out, and the moon was stark full, which concealed even more stars."

"How high did the moon rise above the horizon? In other words, what was its maximum height in degrees?"

Dirby shrugged peevishly. "I hardly noticed. I wasn't concerned with astronomical observations. Let me think. I don't believe it went higher than about forty-five degrees—halfway up the sky. Don't ask me about the sun, because I didn't notice; in fact, I hardly saw it."

"Very well, but you noticed where the sun rose?"

Dirby allowed himself a sour smile. "In the east."

"In the east is correct. Now, then, on the night previously, did the moon climb the northern sky or the southern sky?"

"The southern sky. But what difference does all this make?"

"Any information might be useful. In the room where you were held, did you notice any indication of the passing days? Any difference between night and day?"

"No."

"But you think you were held prisoner two or three months."

"About that. I don't really know."

"You never heard sounds outside your room? Conversation?"

"Nothing. Never."

"If you think of anything," said Hetzel, "make a note of it."

Dirby started to speak, then held his tongue. Hetzel watched him a moment. Perhaps his adventure had, for a fact, distorted his thinking processes. His perceptions must have been honed; he would experience events in terms of contrasts and extremes. All colors would seem saturated; all voices would ring with both truth and duplicity; all acts would seem pregnant with mysterious symbolism. In a certain sense, Dirby must be regarded as irresponsible. Hetzel spoke in an even voice. "Remember, do not leave the grounds of the hotel; in fact, you would be wise to stay indoors."

Dirby's reply confirmed his suspicions. "Wisdom doesn't work as well as you might imagine."

"Everything else works much worse," said Hetzel. "I have some business in Dogtown, and I'll be gone for an hour or two, or perhaps the rest of the afternoon. I suggest, first, that you rayogram your father, then sit quietly somewhere. Talk to the tourists. Relax. Sleep. Above all, don't do anything to get yourself kicked out of the hotel."

From the rear of the Beyranion Hotel a flight of rock-melt steps zigzagged down the face of a sandstone bluff, to join the road connecting the space depot and Far Dogtown. Hetzel had not yet visited this district southeast of Dogtown proper, in Gomaz territory and outside the Gaean Reach. This was the Dogtown of popular imagination, the so-called City of Nameless Men. Every other building appeared to be an inn of greater or lesser pretension, each stridently asserting its vitality with a sign or a standard, painted, sometimes crudely, sometimes artfully, in colors that gave zest to structures built of drab stone from the bluff, or planks of local wormwood, or slabs sawed from burls.

The time was now late afternoon; the folk of Far Dogtown had come forth to take a draft of beer, or a flask of wine, or a dram of spirits, at rude tables before taverns or under the acacias that grew down the center of the street. They sat alone or in small groups of twos and threes, talking in confidential mumbles punctuated with an occasional guffaw or a jocular curse, eyeing each passerby with stony, speculative gazes. Hetzel recognized garments and trinkets from half a hundred worlds. Here sat a man with hair in varnished ringlets after the fashion of Arbonetta; there sat another with the cropped ears of a Destrinary. This man with the slantwise velvet cap and the dangle of black pearls past his ear might be a starmenter from Alastor Cluster; what could bring him so far across the galaxy?

And those two girls, sisters or twins, with pale snub-nose faces and orange hair; they seemed very young to be so far from Marmonfyre. But most of the folk taking their ease at the taverns of Far Dogtown wore garments much like those of Hetzel himself—the unobtrusive dress of the galactic wanderer, who preferred to attract a minimum of attention.

The street took a jog and widened by a few yards; here was a cluster of small shops: food-markets; a pharmacy and dispensary; a haberdasher with racks of ready-to-wear garments and crates of boots, shoes, and sandals; a newsstand with journals from various sections of the Reach. . . . Hetzel felt a sudden uneasy pang. Halting to study an offering of fraudulent identification papers and packets of counterfeit money, he managed to glance back the way he had come, but the man following him, if such there were, had stepped into a public urinal.

Hetzel continued. His instincts were right more often than not, and if he were indeed being trailed, the fact should come as no surprise. Hetzel was nonetheless displeased. To be followed elsewhere in the Reach might indicate simple curiosity; in Far Dogtown, such attention might mean death.

The road passed under a wooden archway; Far Dogtown became Dogtown, where Gaean law prevailed. Hetzel proceeded to the central square, and paused again to look behind him. Nothing, except the street and a few individuals out upon their errands. Hetzel strolled around the square and proceeded past the office of tourist information, to a shop offering Gomaz boneware for sale. He sidled quickly into the dim interior. He could not be certain, but a dark form might have stepped into the acacia grove that occupied the center of the square.

The proprietor approached—a frail old man in a white smock with lens cups over his eyes. "What would you care to examine, sir?"

"These bowls here—what is their worth?"

"Aha! These are adult Zoum skulls, with palladium rims and a palladium foot. Excellent craftsmanship, as you can see. The material is dense as stone, and of course has been carefully cleaned and sterilized. Think what a conversation you'll have when you serve your guests their broth! The price for a dozen is a hundred and fifty SLU."

"A bit more than I care to pay," said Hetzel. "Can't I outrage my guests more cheaply?"

"Well, yes, of course. These ladles are fashioned from the skulls of Voulash bantlings. Their play wars are as deadly as the efforts of the adults, as perhaps you know."

No one had emerged from the acacia grove. Hetzel disliked such uncertainty. The ambience of Far Dogtown no doubt had stimulated him to hypersensitivity.

". . . back scratchers are the shins and toes of very young bantlings, a clever and unusual article."

"Thank you. I will keep your recommendations in mind." Hetzel gave the square a last inspection. He stepped forth and walked to the office of tourist information.

At the counter stood the same young woman to whom he had spoken previously. Today she wore breeches of beige velvet gathered at the ankles, a dark-brown jacket with gold brocade, a gold fillet to confine her dark hair. Hetzel thought that she recognized him, but her voice was institutionally polite. "Yes, sir; can I be of help?"

"Are you able to produce an astronomical almanac?"

"An astronomical almanac, sir?"

"Any information relating to the movement of the sun, the moon, and Maz in their orbits should be sufficient."

"This little calendar shows the phases of the moon. Will that help you?"

"I'm afraid not." Hetzel gave the sketch a cursory glance. "Just a minute; let me reconsider. The plane of the orbit of the moon appears to cut the plane of Maz's orbit at right angles."

"Yes; it's quite unusual, so I'm told."

In such a case, Hetzel reflected, the moon would be at full when it crossed the plane of Maz's orbit directly behind Maz in relation to the sun. Hetzel checked the calendar and noted the date of this occurrence. On this date, Gidion Dirby had sat on a swamp island with the moon approximately halfway up the southern sky. Since the moon at this instant had been very close to the plane of Maz's orbit, the latitude of the swamp island would be approximately 45° North, plus or minus the tilt of the ecliptic plane.

"Perhaps," said Hetzel, "you have a reference book that might provide general information in regard to Maz?"

The girl produced a pamphlet. "If you explained what you wanted to know, I might provide the answer."

"You might," said Hetzel, "but more likely not. Let me see, now. The Maz year is 441 days, each of 21.74 standard hours. The plane of rotation is inclined twelve degrees to the plane of the ecliptic . . ." Hetzel returned to the calendar. "What is considered the middle of summer and the middle of winter?"

"We don't have much of either. It's mostly a wet season in summer and a dry season in winter. It's now fall, and we're well into the dry period, lucky for you. When it rains, it rains a torrent. The calendar uses the standard month names—only here the months are ten days longer than they were at home on Varsilla."

"Varsilla! The world of nine blue oceans and ten thousand sea peaks and eleven million islands."

"And twelve billion sand flies and sixteen billion glass nettles, and twenty billion tourist villas. So you know Varsilla?"

"Not well."

"Have you visited Palestria on Jailand?"

"I never had occasion to leave Meyness."

"That's a pity; Jailand is so beautiful and placid. Too placid, I used to think. But I wish I were there now. I'm bored with Maz. Anyway, Iulian is summer there, and summer here. The months naturally don't come at the same time."

Hetzel studied the calendar. The summer solstice occurred about the first day of Iulian. It appeared, then, that the moon had reached full almost exactly at the autumnal equinox. Hence there would be neither subtraction nor addition of degrees, and the swamp island, if Dirby's estimate were accurate, must be found somewhere near latitude 45° North.

The girl was watching Hetzel curiously. "Have you reached an important decision?" Her mouth showed an impish twitch.

"So!" said Hetzel. "You consider me solemn and foolish!"

"Of course not! I never think thus of tourists!"

Hetzel merely raised his eyebrows. "Can you show me a large-scale map of Maz, preferably a Mercator projection?"

"Of course." She touched a dial and pressed a button; on the hard white surface of the wall appeared a map as tall as Hetzel and twelve feet wide. "Is that satisfactory?"

"Excellent. Where is Dogtown?"

The girl put her finger on the map. "Here." She looked over her shoulder. "Excuse me a moment." She went back to the desk to deal with a pair of tourists in white suits and wide-brimmed white hats with souvenir emblems pinned to the ribbons.

"Where can we see the Gomaz warriors in a real battle?" asked the man. "I'm hoping to get some shots for a travelogue."

The girl smiled politely. "Battles aren't all that easy. The Gomaz refuse to keep us informed. Very churlish of them, of course."

"Oh, dear," said the woman. "We promised everyone we'd bring back films. I understand we're not allowed in the tribal castles?"

"I'm afraid that is so. But we've remodeled a number of ancient castles into very comfortable inns, which I'm told are very typical. I've never visited one myself."

"Can't you arrange to find a battle for us? I very much wanted to film an authentic Gomaz war."

The girl smilingly shook her head. "You'd probably be killed if you ventured that close."

"Where would you say we have the best chance of seeing a good battle?"

"I don't know what a good one would be like," said the girl, "or a bad one either, for that matter. It's probably just a matter of luck—'misfortune' might be a better word, because these affairs are very dangerous."

Hetzel found latitude 45° North. He traced it over oceans, mountains, uplands, and moors. A thousand miles north of Axistil, a river flowing down from the northern moors wandered out upon a flatland and dissipated into a thousand trickles and rills. This was the Great Kykh-Kych Swamp. Hetzel inspected it carefully. Nearby, he noticed a black dot.

The tourists departed. A door from the adjoining office opened, and a burly man looked forth—Byrrhis. Today he wore a modish suit of dark-green twill, with a black-and-scarlet cravat. "Janika, I'm leaving for the day. Transfer any calls to my villa."

"Yes, Vv. Byrrhis."

"Mind you, lock up well. Don't forget the back windows."

"Yes, Vv. Byrrhis, I'll be careful."

Byrrhis gave Hetzel a friendly nod, which might or might not have connoted recognition. He retreated into his office, evidently planning to leave by a different exit.

Hetzel asked, "What did he call you?"

"Janika."

"Is that your name?"

"It's short for my girl-name, which most people consider rather queer—Lljiano. Two L's sounded on your side teeth. It's an old Hiulak name."

"I didn't know the Hiulaks settled on Varsilla."

"They didn't. My father's name is Reyes; he's part Maljin and part White Drasthanyi. He met my mother on Fanuche and brought her back to Varsilla. And she's a quarter Semric, which makes me something of a mongrel."

"A very healthy-looking mongrel."

"Where are you from?"

"I was born on Old Earth. My name is Miro Hetzel. I am told that I come of decadent stock because all the enterprising persons long ago immigrated to the stars."

"You don't seem decadent; you seem quite ordinary."

"I'm sure you intend a compliment."

"Of a sort." Janika laughed. "Did you find what you were looking for?"

"I think so. What are these red stars?"

"They're the sites of the touristic inns—all picturesque and comfortable, so I'm told. I've never visited any of them."

"And what is this black circle?"

"You'll see several of them on the map. They're ruins that are especially quaint, where Vv. Byrrhis wants to establish new inns."

"The others do well?"

"Moderately well. Lots of tourists insist upon a Gomaz war, which we can't produce. Of course, we've never tried, but I doubt if the Gomaz would take kindly to the idea."

"The Gomaz are a humorless lot. I understand that I can rent an air car through this office."

"It's the only agency in Dogtown. You must have a clearance from Sir Estevan Tristo, and you must be accompanied by an official guide, to prevent you from smuggling weapons or selling the air car."

"I have the clearance, and also a good idea. Why don't you come along as the official guide?"

"Me? I couldn't stop you from smuggling weapons."

"That's a restriction I'll agree to right now—no smuggling."

"Well . . . it sounds pleasant. When did you have in mind?"

"Tomorrow."

"I'm supposed to work tomorrow, but that's no real problem. A substitute could take over. Where did you plan to go?"

"Oh, I don't know. Off in this direction, I suppose; we could have lunch at this inn."

"That's Black Cliff Castle, which is supposed to be very dramatic. But it's a long way off." She glanced sidewise at Hetzel. "It's actually more than a one-day trip."

"All the better. Book a couple rooms for us, then we won't need to rush. Are you doubtful? Of your job? Or of me?"

" 'Doubt' is not quite the word." Janika laughed rather nervously.

"Caution? Apprehension?"

"No, none of these. . . . Oh, well, why not? I haven't been out of Dogtown in all the time I've been here. Vv. Byrrhis can fire me if he wants; I don't really care."

"How long have you worked here?"

"Only three months, and just about ready to think 'why not?' again and go back to Varsilla."

"Is Vv. Byrrhis so harsh a taskmaster?"

"He has his crotchets." Janika put on as prim and stern an expression as her features were capable of forming. "I must insist that I pay my own expenses."

"Just as you like," said Hetzel. "The only person to profit will be a certain Sir Ivon Hacaway, who can well bear the expense."

Hetzel returned to the Plaza by way of the Avenue of Lost Souls. The time was early evening; the sky swam with violet and pale-green murk. He crossed the dim Plaza to the Beyranion Hotel, and found Dirby in the lobby, sitting quietly in a lounge chair with a journal. Dirby looked up with mingled suspicion and curiosity. "What have you learned in Dogtown?"

Hetzel evaded the question. "You've never been there?"

"When I was here on the *Tarinthia* I went down for an evening or two. I've seen better places."

Hetzel nodded agreement. "Still, there's a special atmosphere to Dogtown: vain regrets, lost causes—they hang in the air like smoke."

"If I ever get away," muttered Dirby, "I'm going back to Thrope. I'll work my father's loquat orchard and never again look at the sky."

"Perhaps I'll join you there," said Hetzel. "Especially if you find yourself unable to pay my fee."

"I'll pay you off in loquats if necessary." Dirby's eyes gleamed with malicious humor, which Hetzel found at least preferable to sulkiness and self-pity.

"Tomorrow I fly out into the back country," said Hetzel. "I'll be gone a day or two; you'll have to fend for yourself until I get back."

"Be as mysterious as you like," Dirby grumbled, once more his usual self. "I'm in no position to complain."

CHAPTER 9

Hetzel arrived at the transport depot early in the morning, to find that Janika had already arranged the rental of an air car. "It's an old Ray Standard, and it's supposed to be dependable."

"There's nothing a bit faster? We have considerable ground to cover."

"There's a new Hemus Cloudhopper, but it's more expensive."

"Money means nothing," said Hetzel. "Let's take the Hemus."

"They want to be paid in advance in case we kill ourselves: twenty SLU for two days, which includes insurance and energy."

Hetzel paid the account. They climbed into the air car. Hetzel checked out the controls and energy level, then took the vehicle aloft. "Did Vv. Byrrhis make any difficulty about letting you off?"

"Nothing to speak of. I told him that I wanted to take a friend out to Black Cliff Inn, and that was that."

Axistil and its environs became a set of unlikely patterns on the heave and fall of the downs. Hetzel brought a map to the navigation screen and established a course due north. "I want to investigate the Great Kykh-Kych Swamp," said Hetzel in response to Janika's questioning glance. "I don't know what I'll find—in fact, I don't know what I'm looking for. But if I don't go, I'll never know."

"You are a mysterious man, and mysteries are exasperating," said Janika. "I myself have no secrets whatever."

Hetzel wondered how much credence could be placed in this remark. Today she wore a short-sleeved blouse of soft-gray cloth trimmed with black piping, black trousers, and jaunty ankle boots—a costume that made the most of her supple figure. She wore no ornaments except a black ribbon binding her hair. An exceedingly attractive young woman, thought Hetzel, fresh and clean-looking, with an air of simplicity that was both charming and suspect.

"Why are you looking at me so intently?" she asked. "Is my nose red?"

"I marvel at your confidence. After all, I'm a stranger to you, and out here beyond the Reach, a stranger is usually a depraved murderer, or a sadistic fiend, or worse."

Janika laughed, perhaps a trifle uneasily. "Inside or outside the Reach—what's the difference?"

"You don't have too much to fear," said Hetzel. "I'm far too gallant for my own good, although only an Olefract could fail to notice that you are extremely pretty. You make a stimulating companion for a trip like this one."

"What kind of a trip is a trip like this one? We intend to prove the innocence of one of your former lovers, and save him from the Exhibitory."

"You astonish me! My 'former lovers' are all far away, living the most torpid lives imaginable. I wonder which of them you refer to, and how he managed to get into such mischief."

"This one is a certain Gidion Dirby."

Janika frowned. "Gidion Dirby?"

"Yes. A blond young man, obstinate, wrongheaded, seething with emotion. So he is now. Three months ago he might have been a different person entirely."

"I remember Gidion Dirby, but our acquaintance was . . . well, almost casual. Certainly so, from my point of view."

Hetzel looked down across the landscape—a savanna carpeted with green-black furze and clots of spike trees. In the far-eastern distance a glimmer of sea was visible, then a blur of atmospheric murk. Hetzel asked, "How did you happen to meet Gidion Dirby?"

"First," said Janika, "tell me what he's done, and also why you're so mysterious."

"Gidion Dirby is suspected of assassinating two Triarchs. I am not so much mysterious as confused and suspicious."

"Confused about what? And who are you suspicious of? Me? I haven't done anything."

"I'm confused about Istagam . . . and why there is so much secrecy involved. Presumably the reason is money. I'm suspicious because effectuators are paid to be suspicious, and I'm an effectuator. A high-class and expensive effectuator, needless to say. I'm suspicious of you because you were associated with Gidion Dirby on Tamar, and here you are on Maz."

"Sheer coincidence," said Janika.

"Possibly. Why were you on Tamar?"

"Tamar was where my money took me when I left Varsilla. I worked for a week in the Central Market at Twisselbane, and I worked another week in what they call their Pageant of the Foam, because it paid quite well. I had to dance and pose with not too many clothes on—occasionally none at all. While we were rehearsing, I met Gidion Dirby, who told me he was a spaceman, and lonely."

"Like all spacemen."

"I saw him a few times, and he became . . . well . . . possessive. Apparently he had fallen in love with me, and I was having trouble enough with one of the directors of the pageant. So I stopped seeing Gidion Dirby. I worked a week at the pageant, and some friends introduced me to Vv. Byrrhis, who mentioned that the Maz Tourist Agency needed a receptionist. I was only too pleased to leave the pageant and Director Swince. Vv. Byrrhis made me sign a six-month contract and gave me a ticket to Maz, and here I am."

"You never saw Gidion Dirby again?"

"I'd almost forgotten him until just now."

"Very odd." They flew over an arm of the sea, a leaden expanse glistening with a green luster. "You've been here how long?"

"About three months."

"With another three months to go on your contract. Then what?"

"I'm not sure. I'll have enough money to go almost anywhere. I'd like to visit Earth."

"You might be disappointed. Earth is a most subtle world. Very few outworlders feel at ease on Old Earth, unless they have friends there."

Janika turned him an arch side glance. "Will you be there?"

"I couldn't tell you where I'll be a week from now."

"Don't you ever want to settle down somewhere?"

"I've thought about it. Gidion Dirby has invited me to his father's loquat orchard."

Janika made a sound of scornful amusement. "Gidion Dirby. You came to Maz on his account?"

"No. I came to learn something about Istagam. But the two matters might be connected."

Janika said, "Perhaps I'll become an effectuator. It seems like fun. One always stays in the best hotels and meets interesting people like myself, and there's always a Sir Ivon Hacaway to pay the bills."

"It's not always like this."

"And what takes us out toward the Great Kykh-Kych Swamp? Gidion Dirby business or Istagam?"

"Both. And then there's another most peculiar element to the case, by the name of Casimir Wuldfache."

The name seemed to mean nothing to Janika. For a period they rode in silence over a sprawling range of ancient basalt mountains, black crags protruding like rotten stumps from maroon detritus. Janika pointed. "Look yonder—the castle of the Viszt." She took up binoculars. "Warriors are returning from a campaign, probably against the Shimrod, and the tourists have been cheated again." She passed the binoculars to Hetzel and showed him where to look.

White skull faces bobbed and blinked under crested helmets of cast iron; aprons of black leather swung to the motion of the legs. To the rear rolled six wagons pulled by ten-legged reptiles, loaded with objects Hetzel could not identify.

"The Viszts are flyers," said Janika. "The wagons carry their wings. They climb the mountains, put on their wings, and glide on the updrafts. Then, when they locate their enemies—I can't think of a better word—they swoop down and attack."

"Curious creatures."

"You know how they breed, or mate?"

"Sir Estevan gave me a pamphlet. In fact, you did too. I know that they are ambisexual, and that they go out to war in order to breed."

"It seems a dreary life," Janika reflected. "They kill for love, and they die for love—all in a frenzy."

"They probably consider our love life rather dull," said Hetzel.

"My love life *is* rather dull," said Janika. "Vv. Swince, Gidion Dirby, Vv. Byrrhis."

"Have patience. Somewhere among the twenty-eight trillion folk of the Gaean Reach is Vv. Right."

"Half of them are women, luckily. That cuts down the search by half." Janika took up the binoculars. "I might as well take a look out over the swamp right now. There might be some kind of a fugitive or a divorcé out there."

"What do you see?" asked Hetzel.

"Nothing. Not even a Gomaz, whom I wouldn't consider anyway."

They flew above a land of rolling moors with tarns of dark water in the hollows. Ahead, the course of the Dz River lay in languid curves and loops; beyond spread the Great Kykh-Kych Swamp. Hetzel examined the chart with attention.

Janika asked, "What are you looking for?"

"An island five miles or so from the north shore, where Gidion Dirby was marooned by a man named Banghart. Have you ever heard that name, incidentally?"

"Not to my knowledge."

"Three islands are possible. This one to the east"—Hetzel indicated the chart—"this one in the center, and this to the west. The center island is closest to the black circle on the chart."

"That's the castle of the old Kanitze sept, which was wiped out by the Ubaikh two hundred years ago, and Kykh-Kych Inn, which is now closed down."

"We're coming in over the east island. Look for a path leading to the mainland."

Hetzel circled the island—a hummock of twenty acres, crowned with a copse of iron trees and the tall rattling canes known as "galangal." There was no area suitable for discharge of cargo; no path led away to the mainland.

The central island lay twenty miles north—an area somewhat larger, with a level meadow marked and scarred as if by the arrival and departure of vehicles.

Hetzel hovered over the meadow. "This is the place." He pointed. "That iron tree yonder—there Dirby passed the night. . . . And there—the path leading to the shore! Here we pick up the thread of Dirby's adventures. Shall we land?"

"We're not supposed to land except in authorized locations," said Janika. "That's the rule, but it's not always obeyed."

Hetzel glanced at his watch. "We don't have all that much time if we want to meet the Ubaikh at transport depot. So . . . we'd better fly on."

Janika looked at him in astonishment. "We're to meet whom?"

"The Ubaikh who witnessed the assassinations. If we want to learn the identity of the killer, he's the obvious person to ask."

"Suppose he says it was Gidion Dirby?"

"I don't think he will. But I intend to ask him, no matter what he says."

"You seem very zealous all of a sudden."

"Yes, the mood strikes me once in a while."

Janika looked down at the swamp, now only a few hundred feet below: an expanse of black slime; various tufts of reeds, lung-plant, white whisker; wandering rivulets of dark water. The path slanted this way and that, following a series of slanted quartzite outcrops. "If I knew what you were looking for, I could look too."

Hetzel pointed to the dun-colored loom of mainland ahead. "Look for a stone wall. Gidion Dirby found a stone wall and a gate and Sir Estevan Tristo waiting for him. Except it probably wasn't Sir Estevan. More likely Casimir Wuldfache."

Janika looked through the binoculars. "I see the wall and the gate. I don't see either Sir Estevan or Casimir Wolf-face, whatever his name is. Now I can see the old Kanitze castle."

"This is where Gidion Dirby passed several memorable months, or so I suspect. He described some of his adventures to me. His chair ejected him to the floor. Sir Estevan emptied a chamber pot over his head. He observed you dancing upon the surface of his brain without any clothes on."

"One thing you can take as certain," said Janika. "I have never danced upon Gidion Dirby's brain."

"No question about this. You were evidently filmed at the Pageant of Foam on Tamar and the sequences adapted to the circumstances here. Almost certainly, Casimir Wuldfache turned the pot over Dirby's head, since Sir Estevan denies doing so. All in all a curious set of experiences."

"Unless Dirby is a madman, as I once suspected."

They approached the cyclopean bulk of the ruined Kanitze castle. The roof across the vast central keep had long since rotted away; the seven peripheral towers had tumbled to broken stubs surrounded by detritus. The tower at the far western edge of the complex had been fitted with a new roof and structurally refurbished—evidently the disused tourist inn.

Hetzel allowed the air car to drift quietly above the castle while he looked down through binoculars. He stared so long and so intently that Janika at last inquired, "What do you see?"

"Nothing very definite," said Hetzel. He put the binoculars in the rack and looked down at the ruined castle. In the shadows of the central keep he had observed a stack of crates, protected from the weather by a shroud of transparent membrane. Up from the castle rose a fume of danger, quivering like hot air.

"I don't dare to land," Hetzel muttered. "In fact, I feel the urgent desire to leave, before someone or something destroys us." He jerked the air car into motion; they skidded away to the west.

Janika looked back at the receding ruins. "This isn't quite the placid excursion I had expected."

"Perhaps I shouldn't have brought you."

"I'm not complaining. . . . So long as I escape with my life."

The castle of the extinct Kanitze became a dark smudge and disappeared into the murk.

"The rest of the trip should be relatively uneventful. The Ubaikh depot is safe ground, or so I'm told."

"The Olefract or the Liss patrol might think you're trying to sell weapons, and kill you."

"I've got Sir Estevan's translator. If necessary, I can explain."

"Not to the Liss. They believe what they see, and they're most suspicious."

"Well . . . they probably won't see us."

"I hope not."

The depot stood on a pebbly plain beside a white-and-orange target a hundred yards in diameter. Mountain shadows loomed above the north horizon; to west and east the plain extended into the blur of the sky. To the south, two miles from the depot, stood the castle of the Ubaikh sept—like the Kanitze ruins, a bulk of awesome proportions. Parapets surrounded the central keep; an inner tower rose another hundred feet to a squat roof of sullen maroon tiles. Seven barbicans, taller and more slender than those of the Kanitze ruins, guarded the keep, each joined to the parapets by an arched buttress. The area under the castle flickered with motion—Gomaz, and Gomaz bantlings at their routines and drills. Wagons rolled along an east road and a west road, loaded with what Hetzel took to be provender. There seemed to be flapping black forms in the air surrounding the outer towers. Down, down the figures drifted, darting, wheeling, diving, and swooping, occasionally, by dint of furious effort, gaining altitude before once more gliding.

Hetzel dropped the air car to the ground beside the depot. "We've got something less than an hour to wait, if the carrier is on schedule."

Half an hour passed. Across the sky came the carrier—an ellipsoidal compartment supported on four pulsor pods. It dropped to a landing at the exact center of the orange-and-white target. The entry port slid open; steps unfolded; a single figure disembarked. The carrier paused a moment, like a resting insect, then swept off at a slant to the south. Hetzel meanwhile had approached the Ubaikh with the language translator.

The Ubaikh paused to assess the situation, wattles distended but uncolored. He wore an iron collar, which appeared to indicate status, and carried a sword of pounded iron in a harness over his back. Hetzel halted ten feet from the Ubaikh—as close as he dared approach.

The Ubaikh's wattles remained a pallid white, with a network of pulsing green veins, indicating simple antagonism.

Hetzel spoke into the translator. "You have just now returned from Axistil." The instrument produced a set of hisses and squeaks, fluting up into inaudibility and down again.

The Ubaikh stood rigid, the white bone of his face immobile, the eyes glowing like black gems. Hetzel wondered whether it might be taking telepathic counsel with its fellows in the castle.

The Ubaikh hissed, clicked, squeaked; the translator printed out on the tape: "I have visited Axistil."

"What did you do there?"

"I yield no information."

Hetzel grimaced in frustration. "I have come far to talk to you, a noble and notable Ubaikh warrior."

The translator evidently failed to reproduce the exact implications of Hetzel's remark, for the Ubaikh emitted a hiss which the tape merely identified in red italics as "anger." The Ubaikh said, "My rank is high, and more than high: I am a chieftain. Did you come to traduce me in the very shadow of my castle?"

"Not at all," said Hetzel hastily. "There has been a misunderstanding. I came respectfully to request information of you."

"I yield no information."

"I will express my appreciation with a metal tool."

"Your bargains are worthless, like all Gaean bargains." Words appeared on the tape faster than Hetzel could read them. "The Gomaz were defeated by metal and energy, not by courage. It indicates weakness that the Gaeans and Olefract and Liss hide in metal cells and send forth mechanical objects to fight for them. The Gomaz are strong warriors, the Ubaikh are supreme. They often defeat the Kzyk, whom the Gaeans choose to favor. The Gaeans are deceitful. The Ubaikh demand equal access to the secrets of metal and energy. Since we are denied, the Kzyk must suffer a Class III 'Rivalry' war, to the detriment of our long ages of love and war love and war esteem. The Liss and the Olefract are intractable cowards. The Gaeans are cowards, traitors, and lie mongers. The Kzyk will never profit from the scandal of their activities. Bantlings and striplings must be tested and trained. The Kzyk will become a race of diseased monsters, sapped of strength, unworthy of love, but the Ubaikh will destroy the sept. We too are anxious for the secrets of metal and energy, but we will never become suppliants."

The spate of words ended abruptly. Hetzel made what he thought might be a conciliatory statement: "The Triarchy intends justice for the noble Ubaikh sept."

The Ubaikh's wattles became mottled with green patches. Hetzel watched in fascination. The Ubaikh produced sounds, and the translator printed out a new storm of words. "The remark is empty of meaning. The Gomaz are constrained by strength of metal and bite of energy. Otherwise we would bring a Class III war upon our enemies. The Triarchy is a monument to pusillanimity. Will the Triarchs dare to fight any of us? They sit in fear."

"The Triarchs were killed before they could deal with your business. Two of your companions were killed as well."

The Ubaikh stood silently.

Hetzel said, "The killer of these individuals has wronged us all. Will you return to Axistil and help to apprehend the criminal?"

"I will never return to Axistil. The Triarchs are excellently killed. The Gomaz are an oppressed folk; their current status is a tragedy. Let the Gaeans teach all Gomaz the secrets of fire and metal, rather than just the Kzyk, then all will join to defeat the mutual enemy. Be off with you; this is the vicinity of the superlative Ubaikh sept. I would grind you to a powder if I did not fear your weapons." The creature turned and stalked away.

The Gomaz were an obstinate race, thought Hetzel. He returned to the air car.

Janika asked, "Well, who killed the Triarchs?"

"He wouldn't tell me anything except that he approved of the whole affair." Hetzel took the air car aloft.

"Now where?"

"Where are the Kzyk territories?"

"A hundred miles north, more or less. Beyond the Shimkish Mountains yonder."

Hetzel studied the chart, then considered the sun, which hung halfway down the western sky. He turned the car toward the Black Cliff Inn, and Janika relaxed into her seat.

"What do you want with the Kzyk?"

Hetzel passed her the translator tape. "It's more or less a tirade on the sins of the Gaeans."

Janika read the tape. "It sounds as if he went to Axistil to protest favors to the Kzyk."

"And why should the Kzyk get special treatment?"

"I don't know," said Janika.

"I don't know either. But it might be Istagam."

CHAPTER 10

The Black Cliff Inn hung half over the brink of a mighty basalt scarp, under a complex of titanic ruins. Below spread a landscape that might have been contrived by a mad poet: a sodden moor clotted with turf of an unreal magenta, clumped with black water willow and an occasional eruption of extravagantly tall and frail galangal reeds glistening like silver threads.

Hetzel came out upon the terrace, to find a dozen other guests taking refreshment and enjoying the smoky-green sunset. He seated himself at a table and ordered a beaker of pomegranate punch with two stone-and-silver goblets. The perquisites of his occupation were occasionally most pleasant, thought Hetzel. The air drifting up from the plain brought a musky reek of moss and galangal and a dozen unnamable balsams. From far across the moor, thin, high-pitched calls shivered the quiet, and once a distant ululation evoked so much mystery and solitude that the hair rose at the back of Hetzel's neck.

Janika slipped into the chair beside him. She wore a soft white frock and had combed her hair into lustrous loose curls. A most appealing creature, thought Hetzel, and quite probably as careless and candid as she appeared. He poured her a goblet of punch. "Sunset at the Black Cliff Inn is a remarkable occasion, and Vv. Byrrhis is a remarkable man for having created all this."

"No doubt about that," said Janika in an even voice. "Vv. Byrrhis is a remarkable man."

"These inns—how many are there? Six? Seven? . . . They represent considerable capital. I wonder how Byrrhis financed such an operation."

Janika gave her fingers a flick to indicate her lack of interest in the matter. "I'm not supposed to know anything about it—and actually, I don't. But . . . it's well known that Sir Estevan Tristo is very wealthy."

"It seems a chancy investment," said Hetzel. "There's no possibility of firm title to the real estate."

"Vv. Byrrhis has as good title as anyone else. The Gomaz don't object; ruined castles are taboo. Black Cliff is famous for sunsets," said Janika. "And tonight we'll see ghosts."

"Ghosts? Are you serious?"

"Of course. The Gomaz call the plain yonder the Place of Wandering Dreams."

"Do persons other than the Gomaz see the ghosts?"

"Certainly. A few dull souls see only wisps of marsh gas, or white-veiled night crakes, but no one believes such drab nonsense."

Other guests came out on the terrace. "The inn must be almost full," said Hetzel. "I suspect that Vv. Byrrhis is coining money."

"I don't know. He seems harried and anxious most of the time. I suspect that he isn't as prosperous as he would like to be, but who is?"

"Certainly not I."

"Suppose you solved this case brilliantly and Gidion Dirby gave you a million-SLU bonus—what would you do with it?"

"More likely a million loquats from Gidion Dirby. From Sir Ivon Hacaway . . ." Hetzel gave his head a rueful shake. "First I have to solve the case." He brought forth the translator tape and studied it a moment. "The tirade includes a few scintillas of information, no doubt by mistake. Someone is teaching the Kzyk 'secrets of fire and metal.' Who? Why? Istagam naturally comes to mind. The Kzyk provide labor and are paid off in technology, which I presume to be illegal. The Ubaikh object. The Liss and the Olefract are also certain to object, so their Triarchs are killed off for this reason. Just speculation, of course."

"A rather frightening speculation." Janika looked uneasily up and down the terrace.

Hetzel put away the tape. "Tomorrow we'll visit the Kzyk, or at least look them over. But now let's talk of something more interesting. Lljiano Reyes of Varsilla, for instance."

"I don't want to talk about me. . . . Though, for a fact . . . well, I'd better not say it."

"You've aroused my curiosity."

"It's not all that interesting. When I wanted to leave Palestria, everyone said I was foolish and perverse, which may be true. But tonight at the Black Cliff Inn is what I wanted to find." She made an exasperated gesture. "I know I'm not making myself clear. But look, up there hangs the green moon, and here we sit looking out over the Place of Wandering Dreams, waiting for ghosts and drinking pomegranate punch. At home I'd be doing something ordinary. No green moon, no pomegranate punch, no ghosts."

Hetzel had no comment to make; for a period they sat in silence.

Across the moon floated a gaunt black shape on slow-beating wings. "There's a ghost now," said Hetzel.

"I don't think so. Ghosts don't fly like that. . . . It's too long and frail for a gargoyle. . . . It's probably a black angel."

"And what's a black angel?"

"If I'm right, it's the thing we just saw."

Hetzel rose to his feet. "Hunger is confusing both of us. I suggest that we have our dinner."

Within the ruins of the central tower, six iron legs supported a stone disk forty feet in diameter—the adjunct to some ancient Gomaz rite. At the center a post of twisted black iron rose twelve feet, to fracture into several black iron branches tipped with small clusters of yellow flames—luminous fruits on a grotesque tree. Hetzel and Janika mounted iron steps; a steward in green-and-black livery conducted them to a table spread with white linen, laid with silver and crystal.

Hetzel looked up to see open sky, with wan moonlight slanting in against the northern wall. "And in bad weather, what then?"

"In the rainy season we send people south to the Andantinai Desert, where they can see the volcanoes and carrier kites and the Great Cairn. Vv. Byrrhis has thought of everything."

"Vv. Byrrhis is a very resourceful man, and no doubt very stimulating to work with."

Janika laughed. "He wanted to take me out to Golgath Inn on the Plain of Skulls, but I thought better of it, and he hasn't been stimulating since. If he knew I were here with you, he'd be furious. Or so I suppose. Even on so innocent an occasion."

Vv. Byrrhis' emotional problems seemed remote and inconsequential. "Whom does he think you're here with?"

"He didn't ask. I didn't specify."

The steward served a salad of native herbs, which Hetzel found pleasantly tart; a ragout of ingredients beyond conjecture; thin cakes of crisp bread; two flasks of imported Zenc wine, the first yellow, the second dark amber swimming with an oily violet luster.

Janika performed the conventional Zenc wine ceremony, pouring half a goblet of dark, wiping away the luster with a square of soft fabric, and immediately filling the goblet with yellow.

"Except for the wine, everything is Maz produce," Janika said. "When I first arrived, I thought everything tasted of moss and hardly ate anything; now I'm much more tolerant. But I still think of Varsilla sea bakes and pepper pots and yams stuffed with mulberries . . . Let's take our dessert out on the terrace and look for ghosts."

The dessert, a pale-green sherbet, was served with goblets of a pungent hot brew steeped from the bark of a desert shrub. For an hour they stood on the terrace over the plain. They heard far wistful calls and soft secret hooting, but saw no ghosts. Janika presently went off to bed. Hetzel drank another cup of tea, and once more considered the translator tape.

A most complicated situation, he reflected, with the parts not merely contradictory but apparently unrelated. High stakes were obviously involved; no one would go to such lengths to motivate Gidion Dirby for trivial reasons. And how strange that Casimir Wuldfache, whom he had traced to Twisselbane on Tamar for Madame X, should now play a role in the Dirby-Istagam affair. Coincidence? Hetzel gave his head a dubious shake. The unmistakable reek of danger hung in the air; persons who had evolved such elaborate schemes would hardly balk at a life or two; perhaps they had already killed a Liss, an Olefract, and two Ubaikh Gomaz. Double vigilance was necessary; he must guard Janika as well as himself.

During the night Hetzel was aroused by the muted whine of an energy converter. He went to the window and looked out through the night. Across the sky, dim in the light of the low green moon, drifted the shape of a receding air car. Odd, thought Hetzel. Odd indeed.

In the pale light of morning, Hetzel and Janika breakfasted on the terrace. Janika seemed wan and thoughtful, and Hetzel wondered at her somber face. He asked, "Did you sleep well?"

"Well enough."

"You seem very pensive this morning."

"I don't want to go back to Dogtown and the tourist agency."

"We've got to go back to Dogtown," said Hetzel. "But you don't have to go back to the tourist agency."

"I signed a six-month contract. I'd lose half of what I've got coming if I quit now."

Hetzel sipped his tea. "Since you don't like Dogtown, where do you want to go?"

"I don't know."

"Varsilla?"

"Oh . . . sooner or later. But not just now. I don't know what I want to do. I guess I'm just in a bad mood."

Hetzel thought a few moments. "Vv. Byrrhis might let you break the contract."

"I don't think so. He's made jocular remarks that weren't really funny. But maybe I'll quit anyway."

"Vv. Byrrhis might be more cooperative than you expect. He'd get

no benefit from a sulky or apathetic receptionist. In the second place
. . . But why anticipate events?"

Janika took Hetzel's hand and squeezed it. "I feel more cheerful
already."

Hetzel settled the account. Janika made a tentative effort to pay
half of the bill, which Hetzel refused to allow, citing the generosity of
his client, Sir Ivon Hacaway. They went out to the landing stage and
climbed into the Hemus Cloudhopper. "Good-bye, Black Cliff Inn,"
said Hetzel. He looked at Janika. "Why the long face?"

"I don't like to say good-bye to anything."

"You're as sentimental as Gidion Dirby," said Hetzel. He took the
air car aloft. "Now to Axistil by way of Kzyk castle. If we're lucky,
we'll catch a glimpse of Istagam."

Janika showed no enthusiasm for the detour. "There won't be
much to see from the air, and it's worth our lives to land."

"We won't take chances, especially since a visit to the Triskelion
will probably clear things up."

"Oh? What will you find there?"

"The agenda, or the calendar, whatever it's called, of the Triarchs.
I want to learn how long ago the Ubaikh scheduled their visit."

"That doesn't seem too important."

"There you're wrong. It's the critical element in the entire case, or
so I believe." Hetzel examined the chart. "We fly north across the
Ubaikh domain, over the Shimkish Mountains, and down across this
. . . what is it called? The Steppe of Long Bones?"

"Because of a great battle a thousand years ago. The Ubaikh, the
Kzyk, and the Aqzh fought the Hissau. It was a 'Hate' war, because
the Hissau are nomads and pariahs who waylay bantlings of other
septs while they're trying to reach their home castles after being
born. . . . If burrowing out of a corpse could be called 'birth.'"

"How do the bantlings find their way home?"

"Telepathy. Only about a third survive the trip."

"It seems a harsh system," Hetzel reflected. "And the Gomaz
would seem cruel and harsh, at least in human terms."

"Because we're not fused telepathically into a single entity."

"Exactly. They probaby consider us strange and cruel too, for
reasons equally irrational. . . . There's the Ubaikh castle, over to
the west."

Janika looked through the binoculars. "Troops are leaving the castle. They're marching off somewhere—perhaps against the Kzyks. Or
the Kaikash, or the Aqzh."

The Ubaikh castle disappeared astern; ahead loomed the Shimkish Mountains—black shards above a tumble of pale-green and brown velvet. Beyond lay a plain of featureless gray-blue murk—the Steppe of Long Bones, which slowly expanded to fill half the horizon. . . . A sound from the engines attracted Hetzel's attention. The pulsors had become audible, whirring at the highest level of audibility, then gradually sighing down the scale. Hetzel stared in consternation at the energy gauge.

Janika noticed his expression. "What's the trouble?"

"No more energy. The batteries are dead."

"But the gauge shows half a charge!"

"Either it's broken or somebody disconnected the conduit and then killed the batteries. In either case, we're going down."

"But we're miles away from anywhere!"

"We've got the radio." Hetzel manipulated the dial. "We don't seem to have a radio, after all."

"But what could have happened? These cars are supposed to be carefully serviced!"

Hetzel recalled the air car he had glimpsed the night before. "Someone has decided that we've lived long enough. He left us just enough charge to get well away from the inn."

The air car floated down upon the wind-scoured pebbles of the Steppe of Long Bones. The two sat in silence. Hetzel studied the chart. "We're about here. Ubaikh castle is forty miles across the mountains. Kzyk castle is sixty miles northwest. Our best chance would seem to be the Ubaikh transport station on the other side of the mountains. The mountains are harder, but we should find water. There's no water on the steppe."

Janika chewed her lip. "The radio can't be fixed?"

Hetzel removed the case. One glance at the broken plates was enough. "The radio is done. If you like, you can stay with the car while I go for help. It might be easier for you."

"I'd rather come with you."

"I'd rather you did too." Hetzel scowled down at the chart. "If we had flown south from Black Cliff Inn, back toward Axistil, we'd have come down in the middle of the Kykh-Kych Swamp, with no chance whatever."

"We don't have much chance out here."

"Forty miles isn't all that bad—two or three days' hike, depending upon the terrain. What kind of wild beasts might we find?"

Janika looked around the sky. "Gargoyles live in the mountains.

They prey on baby Gomaz, but if they're hungry, they'll attack anything. At night the lalu come out. Last night you could hear them out on the plain. And we might see ixxen—the white foxes of Maz. They're blind, but they run in packs of two or three hundred. They're dreadful creatures; they capture baby Gomaz and raise them to be ixxen, so sometimes you'll look out on the plain and see naked Gomaz running on all fours, and they're the eyes for the pack until the pack decides to tear them apart. If we meet any Gomaz, they could consider us field prey and kill us."

Hetzel rummaged through the various storage compartments in hopes of locating a spare power cell, but vainly; he found nothing. Descending to the ground, he searched the horizons. Solitude everywhere. He checked the charts once more, then pointed toward the mountains. "There's a pass directly under that double-pronged peak. From there we should see a ridge that runs a few miles south of the Ubaikh castle. We won't get lost. With luck we'll make forty miles in two days, provided we're not killed; I'm carrying two pistols, a knife, and ten grenades. We've got a good chance for survival. I'll bring the translator in case we encounter any stray Gomaz. Since there's no point in delay, we might as well get started. If you've got spare boots, you'd better bring them. Also your cloak."

"I'm ready."

They set out to the south, across a spongy turf of black lichen. Puffs of dark dust rose behind them; their footprints were clearly defined.

"Ixxen will follow if they come on the tracks. It's said that they sense the warmth even after days."

Hetzel took her hand; her fingers closed on his. "I'm certain that we'll reach Axistil safely, and you can be sure that the folk on Varsilla would marvel to see you now—tramping across the Steppe of Long Bones in company with a vagabond like myself."

"I don't think I'm fated to die just yet. . . . Who would do such a thing to us?"

"Can't you guess?"

"No. Gidion Dirby? Unlikely. The Ubaikh? He would never think of such an exploit, and he knows nothing of air cars."

"What of Vv. Byrrhis?"

Janika's mouth fell open. "Why should he bear us malice? Because of me?"

"Perhaps."

"I can't believe it. And never forget, the air car belongs to the tourist agency, which is to say, Vv. Byrrhis, and he loves his SLU."

"In due course all will be made known. Meanwhile, if you see anything edible, by all means point it out."

"I'm hardly an authority on such things. I've heard that just about everything is poisonous."

"We can travel two days, or three or four, if necessary, without food."

Janika said nothing. They walked on in silence. Hetzel reflected that all his residual oddments of suspicion in regard to the girl might be dismissed; she would hardly subject herself to hardship of such magnitude. On the other hand, if she were the accomplice of Vv. Byrrhis, he might well elect to rid himself of her as well as Hetzel.

The sun rose toward the zenith; by insensible degrees the Shimkish peaks and ridges came to dominate the sky. Meanwhile, terrain grew ever more difficult: from pebbles and sand and fields of black lichen, to low slopes grown with prickle bush and black waxweed, and the outlying spurs of the foothills.

Three hours of climbing brought them to the crest of a ridge, where they rested and looked back the way they had come. Janika leaned against Hetzel; he put his arm around her. "Are you tired?"

"It's something I've decided not to think about."

"Very sensible. We've come a good distance." He looked through the binoculars northward over the steppe. "I can't see the air car anymore."

Janika pointed off across the distance. "Look over there. Something is moving; I can't make out what it is."

"Gomaz—marching in a column with four wagons. They're heading in our general direction, but to the west."

"They'd be Kzyks," said Janika. "Out patrolling, or maybe off to raid the Ubaikh, or one of the septs west of the Ubaikh; I forget what they call themselves. How many do you see?"

"Too many to count. Several hundred, at a guess. . . . We'd better get moving."

For a period the way was easy, up the ridge, then across a narrow plateau. Beyond rose the main bulk of the Shimkish Mountains, with the landmark crag prominent.

At a freshet of water they drank, then continued to climb, now resting frequently.

"It'll be easier coming down the other side," said Hetzel, "and a lot faster."

"If we ever reach the top. I'm starting to worry about the next ten steps."

"We'd better go on before our muscles stiffen. Like you, I'm not accustomed to this mountain climbing."

The sun moved around the sky. Two hours before sunset, Hetzel and Janika toiled up from a vine-choked ravine and out on an upland meadow, watered by a small stream. Gasping, sweating, smarting from scratches, stings, and bites, they sank down upon a flat rock. A sward of small heart-shaped leaves carpeted the meadow. A hundred yards east stood a forest of growths that for the most part Hetzel could not name: a few bloodwoods, with trunks dark red, and clotted black foliage; purple tree ferns; clumps of giant galangal reeds. A quarter-mile west stood an even denser forest of bloodwoods. Certain areas of the meadow had been trampled, and an odd reek hung in the air—an odor musky and foul, which Hetzel associated with organic decay, although nothing dead was immediately visible.

From time to time on their way up the mountainside they had glimpsed wild creatures: bounding black weasels, all eyes, hair, and fangs; a long, low creature like a headless armadillo, creeping on a hundred short legs; white grasshopperlike rodents, with heads uncomfortably similar to the crested white skulls of the Gomaz. A torpid reptile twenty feet long had watched them pass with an uncanny semblance of intelligence. In the ravine they had disturbed a shoal of flying snakes—pale, fragile creatures sliding through the air on long lateral frills. They had seen neither ixxen nor bantlings, and nothing but thorns and insects had caused them discomfort. Hetzel now noticed a dozen square-winged shapes wheeling through the air, with heads drooping on long muscular necks—gargoyles. They had glided down from a high crag, to swoop and circle a hundred feet above the eastward forest. Most unpleasant creatures, thought Hetzel. Their flight, so he noted, seemed to be bringing them closer to the meadow.

Hetzel now became aware of a strange strident sound, shrilling up and down, in and out of audibility, to a complex cadence that Hetzel could not quite grasp. He knew at once what the sound portended.

"Gomaz!" whispered Janika. "They're coming toward us!"

Hetzel leaped to his feet; he looked this way and that for a covert. The ravine from which they had only just emerged would serve; more appealing was a tooth of rock a few yards north, a little crag of rotten basalt, luxuriantly grown over with iron plant. He took Janika's hand;

they scrambled up the crag and threw themselves flat on the crest under the massive black leaves.

At the same instant, the Gomaz emerged from the east forest—a column four abreast, marching to a skew-legged goose step. At the east bank of the stream the Gomaz halted; the ululating whine of their song diminished into inaudibility. They broke ranks and went to wade in the stream.

Janika whispered in Hetzel's ear, "They're Ubaikh—a war party."

Hetzel peered down at the Gomaz. "How do you know they're Ubaikh?"

"By the helmets. Look! See that one standing off to the side? Isn't he the one who just returned from Axistil?"

"I don't know. They all look alike to me."

"He's the same one. He's still wearing that iron collar and carrying a steel sword."

The Gomaz climbed from the water and reformed ranks, but made no move to proceed. Overhead soared the gargoyles, long necks bent low.

Hetzel pointed to the forest of bloodwoods at the western end of the meadow. "More gargoyles!"

A second band of Gomaz marched into view, singing their own wavering, whining polyphony, followed by a train of four wagons. "The Kzyk," Janika whispered. "The same band we saw this morning!"

The Kzyk marched forward as if the Ubaikh were invisible. At the edge of the stream they broke ranks, as the Ubaikh had done, and waded into the water. The Ubaikh stood rigid and motionless, and presently the Kzyk returned to the west bank of the stream and reformed ranks; they too stood stiff and stern.

Three minutes passed, during which, so far as Hetzel could see, neither Ubaikh nor Kzyk twitched a muscle. Then from the Kzyk ranks a warrior stepped forth. He paced up and down along the west bank of the stream with an odd strutting motion, raising high a leg, extending and placing it upon the ground with exaggerated delicacy.

From the Ubaikh ranks came a warrior, who strutted in similar fashion along the east bank of the stream.

Three more Kzyk came forth, to perform a set of bizarre postures, of a significance totally incomprehensible to Hetzel. Three Ubaikh performed in similar postures on the east bank. "It must be a kind of war dance," Hetzel whispered.

"War dance or love dance."

On each side of the stream, while the white sequin of sun sank down the darkening green sky and the wind sighed through the bloodwood trees, the Gomaz warriors strutted and postured, swayed, dipped, and jerked. They began to sing—at first a whisper, then a fluting louder and more intense, then a throbbing wail, which sent chills up and down Hetzel's skin. Janika shuddered and closed her eyes and pressed close against Hetzel.

The song vibrated up and out of audibility, then stopped short. The silence creaked with tension. The striders and dancers wheeled quietly back to their ranks.

The engagement began. Warriors leaped the stream, their jaws clattering together, to confront an opponent. Each feinted, ducked, dodged, attempting to grip his adversary on the neck, with the mandibles now protruding from his jaw sockets.

Hetzel turned away his eyes; the spectacle was awful and wonderful; screams of passionate woe, wails of exaltation, tore at his brain. Janika lay shuddering; he put his arm around her and kissed her face, then drew away aghast; had he been swept away on a telepathic torrent? He lay stiff, clenching his mind against the tides of murderous erotic fervor.

Victors began to appear—those who had gripped their opponents' necks, either to cut a nerve or inject a hormone, for suddenly the defeated warrior became submissive, while the victor implanted its spawn into the victim's thorax, then ate the nubbin at the back of the limp creature's throat.

The battle ended; from the meadow came a new sound, half-moan, half-sigh. Of the original combatants, half remained alive. Originally there had been more Kzyk than Ubaikh, as was now the case, but the Kzyk showed no disposition to attack the survivors, who included—so Hetzel was pleased to see—the chieftain who had witnessed the assassinations at the Triskelion. Overhead, the gargoyles circled, then one by one wheeled off and flapped away to the crags. "When the war is fought for hate," said Janika, "there are no survivors among the losers, and the gargoyles carry off the corpses. But the Ubaikh and the Kzyk will leave guards until the infants break out into the air." She looked at Hetzel in consternation. "What about us? How will we get away?"

"If necessary, I have my gun," said Hetzel. "We'll have to spend the night up here. There's probably no better place, in any event."

A moment or two went by. Janika looked sidewise toward Hetzel. "A little while ago you kissed me."

"So I did."

"Then you stopped."

"I was afraid that the Gomaz telepathy was getting to me. It didn't seem dignified. There's no telepathy now, of course." Hetzel kissed her again.

"I'm tired and dirty and miserable," said Janika. "I undoubtedly look awful."

"The formality in our relationship seems to be breaking down," said Hetzel. "What would they say in Varsilla if they could see you now?"

"I can't imagine. . . . I don't want to imagine. . . ."

CHAPTER 11

The night was long and dreary. Hetzel and Janika, wrapped in their cloaks, slept the sleep of exhaustion. At dawn they awoke cramped and sore and chilled. Hetzel peered out over the meadow. The Ubaikh huddled east of the stream; the Kzyk had formed a similar group to the west. With the coming of daylight, they brought forward their wagons and unloaded caldrons of food. The Ubaikh crossed the stream, and ate on even terms with the Kzyks, then returned to where they had passed the night. For a few minutes they wandered the meadow, examining the corpses of the previous evening's battle; then they began a colloquy, half telepathic, half through the medium of whistles and trills. The Ubaikh chieftain seemed to present a fervent exhortation. The Kzyks also deliberated together, then began to whistle derisively at the Ubaikh, who became stiff and haughty. The chieftain began strutting and stalking, but to a quicker pulse than on the evening previously. No longer did the warriors seem to preen; they moved curtly; their gestures were harsh and emphatic. The singing started—staccato phrases, shrill and domineering. Down from the crags came the gargoyles, to soar with drooping necks, peering intently at the events below.

The singing halted; the warriors formed ranks as before. Hetzel suddenly jerked to his feet.

"They'll see you!" said Janika.

"I can't let that Ubaikh get killed. He's the only dependable witness. Also, I like the look of those wagons. Come on down; hurry, before they start to fight."

They scrambled down the back side of the crag. Hetzel stepped out upon the meadow. "Halt!" He spoke into the translator, with the volume at full. "The battle must cease. Break your ranks. Obey me, because I have weapons to kill all here and leave all corpses for the gargoyles." Hetzel raised his hand to the sky; one, two, three gargoyles exploded in gouts of purple flame and black smoke. A few charred fragments fell to the ground.

Hetzel pointed to the Ubaikh chieftain. "You must come with me. I will tolerate no more of your unrealistic arrogance. We will ride in the Kzyk wagons. They will take us to the Kzyk transport depot. Kzyk, prepare to march. Ubaikh, disperse; return to your castle. But both sides may leave guards to protect the bantlings." Hetzel turned and signaled to Janika. "Come."

The Gomaz had stood rigid as stone statues. Hetzel pointed to the chief. "You must come with me. Cross the stream and stand by the wagons."

The Ubaikh chieftain made a set of shrill, furious sounds, which the translator was unable to paraphrase. Hetzel took a step forward. "I am impatient. Ubaikh, disperse! Return to your castle! And you" —he pointed to the Ubaikh chieftain—"cross the stream!"

The air was full of resentful whistles. A Kzyk chieftain emitted an angry scream. The translator tape printed: "Who are you to give such orders?"

"I am a Gaean overlord! I have come to investigate the problems of the Gomaz. I need this Ubaikh chieftain as my witness; I cannot allow his death at this time."

"I would not have been killed," declared the chieftain. "I intended to slaughter two dozen Kzyk and void upon their carcasses."

"You must postpone this exploit," said Hetzel. "To the wagons; smartly, now!"

The Ubaikh and the Kzyk stared at each other, indecisive and crestfallen. Hetzel said, "Who does not wish to obey me? Let him step forward!"

Neither Ubaikh nor Kzyk moved. Hetzel pointed his gun and destroyed two corpses—a Ubaikh and a Kzyk. A wail of awe and horror arose from the Gomaz. "To the wagons," said Hetzel.

The Ubaikh chieftain trudged ungraciously to the Kzyk wagon. The remaining Ubaikh moved across the meadow and stood in a restless group. The Kzyk, without hesitation, formed ranks and marched westward. Hetzel, Janika, and the Ubaikh chieftain climbed upon a wagon, which lurched off after the warriors. "This is somewhat better than walking," said Hetzel.

"I agree," said Janika.

The wagon rolled down from the heights, with the Ubaikh crouched in surly silence. Suddenly it hissed forth a set of emphatic polysyllables. Hetzel looked at the translator printout, which read: "Since alien creatures came to Maz, events go topsy-turvy. In the old days, conditions were better."

"Events still go well enough for the Gomaz," said Hetzel. "If they had not gone forth on a mission of conquest, they would not now be subject to control."

"Easy for you to say," was the response. "We conquer because this is our style of life. We do as we must."

"We defend ourselves for the same reason. You can be thankful that we have not destroyed the Gomaz race, as the Liss would prefer. The Gaeans are not callous murderers; hence, I ask your aid in fixing guilt upon the Triskelion assassin."

"It is a trivial matter."

"Who, then, was the assassin."

"A Gaean."

"But which Gaean?"

"I do not know."

"Then how do you know it's a Gaean?"

"I can show the fact, and then my duty to you is complete; no more need be said."

The Kzyk warriors uttered sudden screams of excitement. Hetzel stood up in the wagon, but saw only the Shimkish slopes and the stony gray steppe. The Kzyk goaded the draft worms; the wagons rumbled and bounded along the trail, the worms humping and collapsing; humping, collapsing; humping, collapsing.

Hetzel spoke a question into the translator: "Why the sudden excitement?"

"They have now discovered the Ubaikh plot."

"What plot?"

"Last night we feinted a raid in force over the Shimkish, to entice their most"—here the translator underlined the word "virile" in red—"away from the castle, while our greatest forces raided the traitors' castle. The Kzyk have now divined the plan. They hurry to defend their castle; this is a Class III war, to the extinction."

The worms became tired and slackened their pace; the Kzyk warriors loped ahead, kicking up puffs of dust behind their thrusting feet, and presently were lost to view among the moss hummocks, which here gave variety to the bleak landscape.

At noon the wagon stopped at an oasis, a pond of muddy water surrounded by a copse of rag trees and a few stunted galangals. A wind blew from the south, flogging the black rag shreds; the galangals snapped and clattered. Hetzel and Janika descended from the wagon and walked down to the pond. The surrounding mud showed hundreds of small spiked footprints, where ixxen had swarmed the previous evening.

Hetzel and Janika fastidiously skirted the pond, both thirsty but loath to drink, for the pond exhaled a sweet-foul odor. The Kzyk teamsters showed no restraint; they plunged into the water, wallowed, soaked, and drank without compunction, and further soiled the water. They were joined by the Ubaikh chieftain. Hetzel looked at Janika. "How thirsty are you?"

"Not that thirsty."

"I guess I'm not either."

The wagons proceeded into the northeast. The Shimkish Mountains were gone; the steppe extended bare and featureless in all directions until it joined the sky.

Hetzel went to confer with the Kzyk teamster. "Where is the transport depot that served the Kzyk?"

"It is near the castle."

"Take us to the transport depot."

"Your command is understood."

"Do you travel by night?"

"Naturally; but slowly. The worms will wish to rest."

"How long before we arrive?"

"Midmorning tomorrow. I fear that we shall miss the fighting."

"There will, no doubt, be another occasion."

"So I would presume."

Hetzel returned to Janika. "We spend tonight in the wagon. No doubt you're hungry."

"When I think of what there is to eat—not too hungry."

"When we return to Axistil, we will dine at the Beyranion, and order all the things you like the best."

"That will be nice."

Hetzel appraised the Ubaikh, speculating whether he might choose to attack during the darkness in the hope of possessing himself of Hetzel's weapons. From the human standpoint, this would seem a strong possibility, but such an act might be alien to the Gomaz psychology. In any event, wariness was certainly warranted.

Shortly before sunset, the wagon arrived at another water hole, and this time Hetzel and Janika abandoned all compunction and drank.

The sun sank; the sky displayed a few muted colors—lilac and apple green, a band of purple; then came the long dim dusk, then night. Hetzel drew his gun and held it pointed at the Ubaikh, who never so much as shifted his position. Janika dozed, then slept until moonrise, when she awoke with a jerk, perplexed to find herself in a wagon rolling across the Steppe of Long Bones. For an hour she kept watch while Hetzel slept, and when the wagons halted, he awoke. Something huge and manlike stood off in the moonlight, a being twenty feet high with the bony white head and carapace of a Gomaz. It uttered a chattering whinny, then lumbered off to the south. "An ogre!" whispered Janika. "I've heard about them; I never thought I'd see one. They're supposed to be ferocious."

The wagons continued once more. The great green moon lifted into the sky, making the steppe a place of eerie beauty. Hetzel dozed again; he awoke to find Janika asleep, her head in his lap, and the Ubaikh as before.

Nighttime waned; a streak of submarine light appeared in the east; the sun appeared, rising behind a range of distant hills.

The Kzyk set the worms into a more rapid motion; the wagons rumbled across the steppe and presently entered an area cultivated with pod plants and fruit bushes. The wagons turned upon a gravel road, which slanted up the hillside. At the crest, the Kzyk castle came into view—a magnificent quatrefoil keep surrounded by a ring of slender spires, joined to the keep by high walkways. The Ubaikh attack had already been launched; the areas to the south and west of the castle seethed with activity.

In the middle distance, four tall gantries rose indistinct in the murk. Hetzel was unable to divine their purpose. Siege machines? They seemed too frail, too tall, too top-heavy for any such use. Between the gantries and the castle, a mass of warriors eddied and swirled in movement too complex for any immediate comprehension.

At the foot of the slope stood the transport station, a structure identical to that beside the Ubaikh castle.

The wagons rolled down the hill, suddenly silent and easy on the heavy lichenlike turf. The Kzyk teamsters paid no heed to the Ubaikh army, nor did the Ubaikh chieftain; they exercised to the full that Gomaz attribute transliterated as *kxis'sh*—a lordly and contemptuous disregard for circumstances below one's dignity to notice.

Hetzel began to apprehend the evolutions of the army, as whole platoons performed the strutting display of ostentatious challenge and aggressive sexuality that Hetzel had observed on the Shimkish meadow. Every element of the army, in turn, so displayed itself, then returned to the rear. Meanwhile, the great wooden gantries moved closer to Kzyk castle, sliding on timber rollers.

The wagon halted by the transport station; Hetzel, Janika, and the Ubaikh chieftain alighted. The wagons proceeded toward the Kzyk castle, passing within fifty yards of the posturing Ubaikh warriors. Each party ignored the others.

The front of the depot displayed a placard printed in those red-and-black ideograms developed by men to communicate with the Gomaz. Janika puzzled out the significance of the marks. "We're in luck—I think. The carrier arrives at middle afternoon on alternate days, and unless I've miscalculated, today is the day. What time is it now?"

"Just about noon."

"I feel as if we've been gone months. I won't say that I've regretted this adventure, but I'll be glad to see civilization again. I'll enjoy a bath."

"I'll enjoy arriving alive," said Hetzel. "To the dismay of our enemies."

"Enemies?"

"There must be at least two, one of whom is almost certainly Vv. Byrrhis, or—as Gidion Dirby knew him—Banghart. Then, there is Casimir Wuldfache."

"Yes. This mysterious Casimir Wuldfache. Who is he?"

"He is a component of one of the strangest coincidences in human history. With trillions upon trillions of persons across the Gaean Reach, why should Casimir Wuldfache appear in two successive cases? I will enjoy talking to him. . . . Another matter occurs to me. If the Ubaikh destroy the Kzyk and their castle, then Istagam will also be destroyed—whereupon my responsibilities on Maz are dissolved."

"And then you'd be leaving? With poor Dirby in the Exhibitory?"

"Naturally, that matter would have to be clarified. . . . I can't understand the purpose of those wooden towers. They must be offensive machines of some sort."

The great gantries were brought forward and ranged in a half-circle fifty yards from the Kzyk castle, and it could now be seen that they stood as tall as or taller than the outer towers. The strutting bands of Ubaikh formed themselves into rigid formations. On the castle parapets, the Kzyk stood quiet.

Janika hunched her shoulders. "I don't think I'm telepathic . . . but something is happening that I can almost feel, or hear. . . . It's as if they're singing, or reciting some terrible ode."

"There go the Ubaikh up the towers."

"They're the flyers. On the top platform they'll strap on their wings. The Kzyk are waiting."

The Kzyk flew first. Over the parapets, launched by some invisible device, came a dark shape soaring on wings of black membrane. The flyer convulsed his legs, kicked; the wings twisted and flapped; the flyer swung in an arc, to gain altitude where the west wind was deflected upward by the castle wall and a curving ramp below.

Another Kzyk flyer darted into the sky, and another and another; seven flyers soared in the air current hurled aloft by the ramp.

One of these now laid back his wings and darted down upon a Ubaikh captain. From the Ubaikh ranks came a rising scream. The captain swung around, apprised himself of his peril. He seized a lance, butted it into the soil, and pointed it toward the Kzyk, who wheeled away and soared off into the upflow of air and presently regained his altitude.

The Ubaikh flyers launched themselves from their towers and entered the updraft; in the air over the parapets occurred a dozen small battles, each flyer hacking at the body or the head of his adversary, but never at the vulnerable wings. Occasionally a pair grappled, tearing and stabbing at each other, to topple slowly head-over-heels toward the ground in a fluttering, flapping confusion of arms, legs, and wings, disengaging at the last possible instant, and sometimes not at all.

Ubaikh flyers landed upon the parapets to do battle with the Kzyk defenders; others settled upon the buttresses joining the outer towers to the keep, where the Kzyk struggled to thrust them off.

For an hour the air battle raged; the Kzyk defenders repelling the Ubaikh attackers, and the sward became littered with corpses. The wind was rising; the flyers soared and wheeled, rising to great heights, then lunging upon their opponents.

Tattered clouds began to fleet across the sky; in the west a bank of black clouds flared with lightning. The flyers were hurled downwind, toppling head-over-heels, and no more flyers were launched. The Ubaikh pushed the gantries closer to the castle and tilted them to lean upon the buttresses, where they served as great ladders. The Ubaikh warriors clambered up, swarmed across the buttresses, leaped down upon the parapets. From the towers, the Kzyk counterattacked, toppling the gantries to the ground. Battles raged along the parapets, then all the Ubaikh were torn apart, and their corpses thrown to the ground.

From a cloud overhead, a spout of white light struck the Kzyk castle; another, then a third; three smoking holes gaped into the structure, and Kzyk came swarming forth like frantic insects.

Janika gasped. "What terrible lightning!"

Hetzel stared in wonder up at the cloud that had discharged such awesome bolts of energy. From the corner of his eye he glimpsed motion; he looked to where a black air car floated over the crest of the hill. It spat a projectile into the cloud, then darted aside and away.

The cloud flickered to a blast of internal orange fire; down like a dead bird dropped a black hull, twisted and burned. The design was strange to Hetzel. He looked at Janika.

"The Liss patrol boat."

Within the Liss craft, backup mechanisms took effect; the boat slid out of its fall and swerved off to the west. From its bow came another spout of white dazzle; the air car was outlined in coruscations, and fell behind the hill. The Liss ship limped off to the west. It jerked ahead, stopped short, then turned up its stern and jerked down at great speed, to bury itself into the hillside.

The Ubaikh and Kzyk were now fighting a desperate war, from which all gallantry and punctilio had disappeared. Out from the castle swarmed hundreds of Kzyk, outnumbering the Ubaikh by two to one; the Ubaikh fell back.

"Here comes the transport from Axistil," said Janika in a faint voice.

The carrier descended from the sky to the landing. A pair of Kzyk disembarked, to examine the combat and the ravaged castle with calm and critical gazes.

Hetzel, Janika, and the Ubaikh chieftain boarded the carrier. Hetzel went to speak to the pilot. The carrier rose from the depot, and at Hetzel's direction slid low over the hill. The air car lay smoldering on the turf. Hetzel and the pilot jumped to the ground and went to inspect the wreck. Inside the cage of twisted metal could be seen a body: contorted, burned, but still recognizable—a man Hetzel had never seen but knew very well. "So much for Casimir Wuldfache," said Hetzel. "He died for Istagam."

CHAPTER 12

The carrier flew north along the shore of the Frigid Ocean, then swung southwest, flying through the night, while Hetzel and Janika dozed and the Ubaikh chieftain sat sternly erect. At dawn the carrier arrived at the Axistil depot, at the far corner of the Plaza. Four Gomaz passengers alighted, then the Ubaikh, finally Hetzel and Janika, limping with fatigue. "Civilization," said Hetzel. "Axistil is the end of nowhere, but right now it looks like home. Are you coming to the Beyranion for breakfast? Your old friend Gidion Dirby will be on hand."

Janika made a wry grimace. "I don't want to see Gidion Dirby. Roseland Residential is just yonder. First I'm going to take a hot bath, then I'll resign from the tourist agency, and then I'm going to bed for the rest of the day. I hope Zaressa hasn't used all the hot water."

"Tonight, then, at the Beyranion."

"Thank you for the wonderful time. And I'll see you tonight."

Hetzel watched her until she turned down the Avenue of Lost Souls. The Ubaikh stamped and hissed, a formidable spectacle in his five-pronged cast-iron helmet, black vest studded with iron bosses, and dangling black iron sword. Hetzel spoke into the translator. "Today should see the finish of this unpleasant affair, which will gratify all of us except the assassins."

The Ubaikh replied; the printout read: "Aliens are overtimorous. They fear death. They lack patriotism." The word "patriotism" was printed in red and underlined, to indicate approximation. "Why waste so much anguish over a few killings, especially since those expunged were not your own kind?"

"The situation is more complex than you imagine," said Hetzel. "In any event, your part in this matter will soon be accomplished, and you will be at liberty to return to your castle."

"The sooner the better. Let us proceed."

"We must wait an hour or two."

"Another example of Gaean frivolity! All night we hurtle through the air at great speed in order to arrive at Axistil; now you delay. The Gomaz are direct and precise."

"Delay is sometimes unavoidable. I will take you to the famous

Beyranion Hotel, a lavish castle of the Gaeans, where I intend to honor you with a gift or two." He set off across the Plaza. The Ubaikh uttered a peevish hiss and strode after him, irons clanking, and so purposefully that Hetzel cringed back in alarm; then, recovering his poise, he turned and led the way to the Beyranion, where, to his relief, no one was yet astir.

Making sounds of reluctance and distaste, the Ubaikh entered Hetzel's rooms. Gidion Dirby was nowhere to be seen; Hetzel was hardly surprised. Dirby, in his present frame of mind, must be considered unpredictable.

Hetzel motioned to the couch. "Rest upon this piece of furniture. I have decided to offer you several gifts, to compensate for your inconvenience." He went to his luggage and brought forth a hand lamp and an assault knife with a proteum edge. Hetzel explained the operation of the lamp and gave a warning in regard to the knife: "Take great care! The edge is invisible; it will cut anything it touches. You can slice your iron sword as if it were a withe!"

The Ubaikh uttered sibilant sounds. The printout read: "This is an act of appeasement, which has been noted with approval."

Gomaz for "thanks," thought Hetzel. He said, "I now plan to bathe and change my garments. As soon as possible thereafter, we will transact our business."

"I am impatient to depart without delay."

"There will be as little delay as possible. Rest yourself. Please do not test the knife upon the furnishings of this room. Do you want to look at a picture book?"

"Negative."

Hetzel, clean and in fresh garments, returned to the sitting room. The Ubaikh apparently had not shifted position. Hetzel asked, "Do you require food or refreshment?"

"Negative."

Hetzel dropped into a chair. The hot water had worked to soporific effect; his eyelids drooped. He looked at his watch: At least an hour until he could expect to find Sir Estevan at the Triskelion. He spoke into the translator. "Why did the Ubaikh attack the Kzyk in a 'war of hate'?"

"The Kzyk have allied themselves with the Gaeans. They have agreed to an ignoble collaboration, in return for supplies of 'manstuff'—printed in red, to indicate paraphrase of an untranslatable word—"and the Gaeans teach them to construct energy weapons. In five years the Kzyk will roam Maz in overpowering hordes; their bantlings will carry guns and fly like gargoyles and destroy our bantlings; the Kzyk will dominate the world, unless the Ubaikh destroy them now, alone, or in coalition with other loyal septs."

"And what is 'man-stuff'?"

"I have spoken enough to the Gaean enemy. I will say no more."

Hetzel sat back in the chair. Where was Gidion Dirby? If the Liss or the Olefract were aware of his identity—and according to Sir Estevan, they knew everything that transpired both at the Triskelion and at the Beyranion Hotel—then Gidion Dirby might well encounter unpleasantness in Dogtown. Or even at the Beyranion itself, which was by no means invulnerable to intrusion, as Hetzel himself could testify. Dirby might have been sleep-gassed and taken away, never to be seen again.

The telephone chimed. Hetzel jerked up from the chair. He touched buttons; Janika looked forth from the screen. Her face was haggard with fatigue and horror. She spoke in a husky voice. "Vv. Byrrhis is dead! There have been thieves!"

"Where are you calling from?"

"I'm at the agency."

"What are you doing there?"

"I came down to quit my job; I want to leave Axistil. I don't care about the money, and Vv. Byrrhis is lying dead on the floor." Her voice rose a quavering octave.

Hetzel thought a moment. "How was he killed?"

"I don't know."

"How do you know thieves were responsible?"

"The safe is open; his wallet is on the floor."

"And there's no money left?"

"Nothing, so far as I can see. What should I do?"

"I suppose you'd better call the Dogtown marshal. There's not much else you can do."

"I don't want to be involved; I don't want to answer questions; I just want to run away and leave."

"The old man in the curio shop undoubtedly saw you arrive, and if you don't make a report, they'll think you're involved. Call the marshal and tell the truth. You have nothing to hide."

"That's true. Very well. I wish you were here representing me instead of Gidion Dirby."

"I'll finish with Dirby today, and Istagam as well, or so I hope. Then I can devote my full attention to you."

"Unless I'm in the Dogtown jail."

"I'll telephone you as soon as I finish at the Triskelion. If I can't get you at home or the agency, I'll try the jail. You'd better call the marshal right now."

Janika gave a wan assent, and the screen went blank. Hetzel turned around, to see Gidion Dirby coming in through the door. He stopped short, looking in bemusement from Hetzel to the Ubaikh. "Who's this?" asked Dirby. "A new client?"

Hetzel made no reply. Dirby came farther into the room. Hetzel thought that he seemed flushed and excited, tumescent with some unidentifiable emotion. Pride? Triumph? Hetzel asked sourly, "How much did you take from him?"

Dirby jerked back a bit, as if he had encountered an invisible wall. He attempted carelessness. "From whom?"

"Byrrhis."

Dirby's mouth sagged a trifle, then curved into a tight smile. "You mean Banghart."

"Whatever his name is."

"Worried about your fee?"

"Not at all."

"Perhaps you should be worried. You haven't done much."

"First of all," said Hetzel, "I listened to you. Second, I prevented Aeolus Shult from turning you over to Captain Baw. Third, I've found a witness to the assassinations." He nodded toward the Ubaikh. "If you're innocent, he'll testify as much. So, once again: how much did you take from Byrrhis, or Banghart?"

"It's not really your affair," said Dirby. "Whatever I took, he owes me."

"Two thousand SLU is the receptionist's salary. A thousand is my fee. The rest of the money, I'm not concerned about."

Dirby's face became sullen. "The rest doesn't amount to very much. What do I get out of all this? Don't forget, I have a claim too!"

"Need I remind you," said Hetzel, "that this 'claim' is what you hoped to earn from your smuggling activities? And that you've just murdered a man to gain control of the money?"

"I murdered no one," snapped Dirby. "I was walking down the street; I looked into the tourist agency, and there was Banghart, big as life. I went in, and one word led to another. He went for his gun, and I twisted his neck. I won and took the money he was carrying."

Hetzel waited.

Reluctantly Dirby said, "It was a bit more than five thousand." Hetzel waited.

Dirby growled under his breath and brought forth his wallet. He counted out notes, tossed them on the table. "There's three thousand. Pay off the receptionist; the rest is your fee."

"Thank you," said Hetzel. "By now Sir Estevan will be at the Triskelion, and we will undertake to clarify the circumstances of the assassinations."

Hetzel went to the telephone, punched buttons. The screen became decorated with the flower-petal face of Zaressa Lurling. Hetzel heard Gidion Dirby mutter in amazement.

"Connect me, please, with Sir Estevan."

Zaressa's face became professionally blank. "Sir Estevan is occupied; he won't be able to see you today."

"Tell him Vv. Hetzel wants to speak to him; tell him that I have urgent information in regard to the recent assassinations."

"I'm sorry, Vv. Hetzel. Sir Estevan definitely does not wish to be disturbed."

"Regardless, you must intrude upon his relaxation. He gave me instructions to communicate with him as soon as possible. Tell him that the Ubaikh who witnessed the assassinations is on hand and has agreed to provide information."

Zaressa's mouth quavered in uncertainty. "I'm not supposed to bother Sir Estevan; why not discuss the matter later in the day with Captain Baw?"

"Young woman," said Hetzel, "I am calling at Sir Estevan's own express request! Connect me at once!"

"I can't interrupt him now. He's busy with Captain Baw."

"You must interrupt him because I'm now on my way to the Triskelion, with Gidion Dirby and the Ubaikh. We will arrive in five minutes, and Sir Estevan is anxious to see us." Hetzel flicked off the screen and blew out his breath. "I've never seen such obduracy! Is she a machine? Does Sir Estevan beat her when she makes a mistake? Is she determined to insulate Sir Estevan from the realities of life? Is she simply stupid?"

"I've seen that girl before," said Gidion Dirby in a thick voice. "Sometimes, when I was a captive, I'd wake up to find a girl crawling around the room on her hands and knees. This was the girl."

"Really!" said Hetzel. "How can you be sure? The girl wore a domino, I thought you said."

"I still recognize her."

Hetzel made a sound of annoyance. "We want fewer complications, not more."

"It's not necessarily a complication."

"Perhaps not. After all, Sir Estevan was filmed in the corridor of his private villa, no doubt by Byrrhis. . . . Well, let's get on with our principal business."

Dirby rubbed his chin thoughtfully. "Perhaps I'd better wait here until matters are settled. I don't care to risk Captain Baw."

"If you're innocent, you don't need to worry."

"Oh, I'm innocent, no fear of that."

"Then you must come. I want to set up conditions exactly as they were—"

"A reenactment."

"A reenactment, precisely."

Dirby shrugged. "Just as you say. If Captain Baw claps me into the Exhibitory, you've got to get me out." He walked toward the door. Hetzel stepped forward, grappled Dirby with one arm, felt in Dirby's pouch with the other, and withdrew a gun. Dirby wrenched himself free, face contorted. He started to fling himself upon Hetzel; then, seeing Hetzel's face—the arrogant, down-drooping mouth, the cold gray gaze—and noting the gun held negligently ready, he backed away.

Hetzel said politely, "I merely want to make sure that I, not you, control the situation. Come along, then."

CHAPTER 13

The three walked across the vast gray-silver Plaza. The sun hung halfway up the green sky; the day seemed clearer than usual, and the eccentric architecture of the Triskelion was manifest.

Vvs. Felius and Vv. Kylo stood on duty behind the Gaean desk. Vvs. Felius, observing Gidion Dirby and the Ubaikh, leaned back with bulging eyes and a trembling jaw. Hetzel went directly to Sir Estevan's office. Vvs. Felius called out indignantly, but Hetzel paid no attention.

Sir Estevan himself stood in the outer office, standing by Zaressa's desk with his hand on her shoulder. Zaressa's face was pink and her eyes were wet. Sir Estevan appeared to be consoling her. He looked at Hetzel with unsympathetic eyes. "I can't quite condone your hectoring of my secretary."

"She has exaggerated my offense," said Hetzel. "I did no more than insist upon seeing you. I have here the Ubaikh who witnessed the assassinations, and here is Gidion Dirby, who was also present. Hopefully, we will be able to discover the truth of the situation."

Sir Estevan seemed uninterested in Hetzel's remarks. "Quite frankly, I'm bored with the whole matter. So far as I'm concerned, the matter can rest in abeyance."

Gidion Dirby uttered a caw of savage laughter. "I don't want to let the matter rest! You accused me and sent your pet porpoise out to arrest me; let's hear what the witness has to say."

Sir Estevan gazed at Dirby without expression, then turned to Hetzel. "I have just received news that Vv. Byrrhis has been murdered. What do you know of this?"

"I am an effectuator," said Hetzel. "If you want me to perform an investigation, I may or may not be able to help you, depending upon the fee. Vv. Dirby hired me to bring the facts of the Triskelion assassinations to light, and this is my single concern. I suggest that you summon Captain Baw. We can then step into the chamber and allow the Ubaikh to indicate the source of the shots."

Sir Estevan gave a stony shrug. "I don't care to participate in any such demonstration. The Liss and the Olefract are the aggrieved parties. Perform your demonstrations before them."

"In that case," cried Dirby, "why did you send Baw to arrest me?"

"Captain Baw undertook the arrest on his own initiative."

"As I see the situation," said Hetzel, "the Liss and the Olefract Triarchs were killed because they were about to hear a complaint against Istagam, which they would have been only too glad to act upon. Given the circumstances of Gidion Dirby's detention and your unwillingness to investigate this matter, I believe that Gidion Dirby has grounds for legal action. Unless you cooperate now, it will appear that you are attempting to cover up for Istagam, presumably because you are profiting from the operation."

"Totally false," said Sir Estevan. "As I remarked to you, Istagam is an altruistic enterprise organized by Vv. Byrrhis. The Gomaz work productively instead of killing each other; they learn the rudiments of civilized knowledge in return. Istagam profits have built the magnificent tourist-agency inns. Neither I nor Vv. Byrrhis have cause for shame."

Dirby said brassily, "Don't be too sure of that. Who turned the chamber pot over my head? Do you think I've forgotten? Not much! Give me the opportunity, and I'll do the same for you."

Sir Estevan gave a snort of chilly humor. "I suggest that you keep a civil tongue in your head. You're now in the jurisdiction of the Triarchy; I can easily turn you over to the Liss and the Olefract, and you can vent your impudence upon them."

"You would certainly be exceeding your authority," said Hetzel. "Either you, as the Gaean Triarch, are aggrieved, or you are not aggrieved. You can't have it both ways. If you are not aggrieved, you have no right to inconvenience Vv. Dirby."

"If nothing else," said Sir Estevan, "the Gaeans have suffered embarrassment and ruinous loss of face. At the minimum, I am justified in believing that Dirby attempted murder upon me."

"This is sheer speculation."

"Captain Baw was witness to the circumstance."

"Suppose, for the sake of argument, that Captain Baw shot the Triarchs himself. He would then be certain to blame the crime upon Gidion Dirby; do you agree?"

"Ridiculous," said Sir Estevan. "Why should Baw kill the Triarchs?"

"The same question applies to Dirby. Why should he kill the Triarchs?"

"I couldn't say. Perhaps he is deranged."

"So you want to arrest a crazy man and turn him over to the Liss and the Olefract?"

Sir Estevan showed signs of boredom. "Criminality is a kind of insanity; criminals are punished under Gaean law; hence, under Gaean law, insane persons suffer punishment. How crazy is Dirby? I have no idea. He looks sane enough now."

"So does Captain Baw. So do you. No doubt the Ubaikh appears sane."

"Exactly what are you suggesting?" demanded Sir Estevan.

"I suggest that you look before you leap. Have you spoken to Vv. Dirby; have you heard his account?"

"No; it is really irrelevant. The facts are as they are."

"Vv. Dirby," said Hetzel, "be good enough to repeat to Sir Estevan what you told me."

Dirby gave his head a mulish shake. "Let him put me under arrest; I'll tell my tale in court, and let him squirm."

"If you don't tell him," said Hetzel, "I will."

"Do as you like; it's the same to me."

Hetzel said, "As accurately as I can recall, these are the circumstances." He presented a brief outline of Dirby's experiences. "It is clear that Vv. Dirby is a victim rather than a criminal. The question becomes: who in actual fact is the assassin? We can resolve the mystery in ten minutes, and it seems important to do so."

"Important to whom?" inquired Sir Estevan in a cool voice. "As I say, the grievance is not mine."

"The grievance is mine!" snarled Dirby. "For all I know, you're the murderer yourself. I'll get the Gaean marshal in and turn all the facts over to him!"

Sir Estevan threw up his arms in a fatalistic gesture. "Very well, let's make an end to it." He stepped into the lobby and signaled Captain Baw, who stood in glowering colloquy with Vvs. Felius. All marched into the Chamber of Triarchs. Sir Estevan went to the chair of the Gaean Triarch. "Captain Baw, please dispose these people as before."

"Very well. The Ubaikh stood here. Over here . . . come stand here, there's a good lad! I'd just come in through the side door with Dirby. He was about here, and I'd started across the room. I was about here when I heard the sound of shots." He addressed Sir Estevan. "Would this accord with your recollection, sir?"

"Yes." Sir Estevan seemed limp and dispirited. "Close enough."

"Close enough," said Dirby.

Hetzel spoke to the Ubaikh through the translator. "This is approximately the state of affairs when the shots were fired. Do you agree?"

The printout read: "I agree."

"Very well, then—who fired the shots?"

Hetzel read the printout. "He says he doesn't know."

"'He doesn't know'! I thought you said that he would testify!"

Hetzel spoke to the Ubaikh. "Explain your remark, if you will. You heard the shots; you saw where they came from—but you can't specify the individual who fired them?"

"The shots came from here." The Ubaikh indicated the door leading into Sir Estevan's private office. "The door opened; the shots were fired; the door was shut. I have told you what I know, and I will now return to the Ubaikh domain." He stalked from the chamber.

Dirby uttered a shout of vindictive glee. He took a step toward Captain Baw, but Hetzel interposed himself. "You are now exculpated," said Hetzel. "You are free to come and go. Why not return to Thrope and rest for a period? You have had a harrowing experience."

Dirby grinned. "Quite correct, and no doubt I'll do just that." He darted a final glance toward Sir Estevan, then turned on his heel and left the chamber.

"And now—from sheer curiosity—who was in your office?"

"When I left, the office was empty."

"In that case, Zaressa Lurling would seem to be the guilty individual."

"Impossible! Can you imagine her aiming and firing a gun?"

Hetzel shrugged. "Stranger things have happened. You had no inkling of this?"

Sir Estevan made no response. He looked toward his office. "I suppose now we must pursue the matter to its bitter limit." He went to the door, thrust it aside. Zaressa Lurling was nowhere to be seen. Vvs. Felius sat at the reception desk. "Zaressa became ill," said Vvs. Felius. "She asked me to take her place and went home."

Sir Estevan stood stiff and rigid. Hetzel asked, "Vvs. Felius, do you recall the events just prior to the assassination?"

"I certainly do."

"Did Vv. Byrrhis, or anyone else, go into Sir Estevan's office?"

"Absolutely not. No one came but yourself and that Dirby fellow."

"Thank you. I don't think you need remain any longer."

Vvs. Felius gave Hetzel a glare and looked at Sir Estevan. "Do you need me, Sir Estevan?"

"No, thank you, Vvs. Felius. You may go."

Vvs. Felius haughtily left the room. Sir Estevan sat heavily down in a chair.

"So, then . . . Zaressa either fired the shots, or else she admitted the assassin through your private entrance. As to her motives we can only speculate. In any event, she shares the guilt of the murderer, either Wuldfache or Byrrhis. His identity is irrelevant; both are dead. I suspect Wuldfache, and I assume that Zaressa was enamored of him."

"Yes," groaned Sir Estevan. "No doubt. . . . I admit that I suspected her guilt . . . and I did not care to learn the truth."

"You apparently take a more than casual interest in Zaressa Lurling."

"This is nothing that concerns you."

"As you say, the matter is irrelevant. Byrrhis was the architect of the affair. He understood the enormous profits latent in Istagam, even over a relatively short period. He also knew that opposition was sure to materialize from you, from the Liss and Olefract Triarchs, or from all three. He prepared to neutralize the opposition, and brought

Dirby to Maz. In order for Dirby to appear a convincing assassin, he must be supplied with motivation, hence his processing, which Byrrhis no doubt found amusing. He was aided by Casimir Wuld-fache, whose adventures are a saga in themselves.

"At the old Kanitze castle, Dirby was conditioned, and his mind loaded with a whole catalog of insane events. But Dirby himself was *not* insane and could emphatically affirm the reality of these events. The more he asserted, the more insane he would seem; any alienist would declare him hyperparanoid. Even better, his ravings would be corroborated by mind search, which, after all, gauges only subjective authenticity.

"So, then: Byrrhis has contrived a subtle, complex, but flexible plan. If and when complaints are made in regard to Istagam, the Liss and Olefract Triarchs will be killed, and Istagam is given another year, perhaps longer; and Sir Estevan becomes a person who by a hair's breadth has escaped assassination at the hands of a paranoid wanderer.

"But what of Sir Estevan? He must also be induced to ignore the activities of Istagam. Sir Estevan is a proud and obstinate man. How can he be so persuaded? He must be subjected to blackmail. Conditions have now been created whereby Sir Estevan can convincingly appear to be nefarious, base, and foolish. If he jibs or balks, Byrrhis, safely in Dogtown or off-planet, makes public the circumstances surrounding the assassinations and claims Sir Estevan to be his collaborator. Dirby's hallucinations are certified as reality. *You,* Sir Estevan, have performed these absurd tricks, *you* have turned the chamber pot over Dirby's head, and *you* become a figure of contempt and ridicule across the Gaean Reach; your dignity and reputation are lost forever. Hence, you are in no position to thwart Vv. Byrrhis' schemes."

For a moment Sir Estevan's face remained still—a mask, classically handsome, the golden hair curling down upon his ears, the chin strong and set. What transpired behind the mask, Hetzel could only guess. Sir Estevan might be possessed of a honed and intricate intelligence, or he might be blank and dull.

"Remarkable," said Sir Estevan coldly. "But I am not so concerned with public 'contempt and ridicule' as you suppose. Secondly, the Kzyk have lost their zest for knowledge. They are not interested in orthography and double-entry bookkeeping; they want guns and pulsors and machinery to level their enemies' castles, which Byrrhis, for all his cleverness, dared not supply."

"Byrrhis was ready to supply a commodity equally valuable," said

Hetzel. "Virility hormone—*chir*. He brought down a cargo of chemical, which now is stored in Kanitze castle, unless I am much mistaken. The Kzyk would work without cessation for this material; *chir* is the stuff they value most. Indeed, Byrrhis imported such a remarkable quantity of the material, I suspect that he planned to establish a whole chain of Istagams across the various continents. A year or two of such enterprise, and Vv. Byrrhis could retire a very wealthy man indeed."

Sir Estevan turned away. "I don't care to hear any more."

"From sheer curiosity—what will you do with Zaressa Lurling?"

"I will ask her to leave Maz on the next ship and never return. The crime was not committed against a Gaean, and I can do no more, even if I wanted to do so."

Chapter 14

Hetzel returned across the glimmering gray Plaza to the Beyranion Hotel. He had achieved his goals; he had earned an adequate fee, but the circumstances provided him no great satisfaction. For the hundredth time he wondered about the quality of his profession. Were greed, hate, lust, and cruelty to disappear, there would be little work for effectuators. . . . Maz was by no means a cheerful world. He would be relieved to see it dwindle astern.

In the Beyranion dining room he took an early lunch, then went to his rooms and telephoned the spaceport. The *Xanthine,* a packet of the Argo Navis Line, departed Axistil on the morrow; Hetzel made reservations for passage.

He poured himself a goblet of Baltranck cordial, added a splash of soda. Dirby, so he noted, had made valiant inroads upon the flask during his sojourn. Well, why not? A surly fellow, Gidion Dirby, who had learned neither wisdom nor tolerance nor generosity from his vicissitudes: the usual order of things. Tragedy was not necessarily ennobling; travail weakened the soul more often than it gave strength. On the whole, Dirby might be considered an average human being. Hetzel decided that he bore Dirby no ill will. Casimir Wuldfache? Byrrhis? Hetzel felt emotion neither one way nor the other. His mood, he thought, was extraordinarily flat. Since the confrontation at the Triskelion he had done nothing but brood. The explanation, of course, was obvious: fatigue and numbness after the events at Black Cliff Inn, in the Shimkish Mountains, on the Steppe of Long

Bones. As he sat sipping the cordial, the circumstances seemed fragile and unreal, dreams.

A chime at the door announced a visitor. Hetzel slid to the sideboard, took up his weapon, and looked around at the windows. Visits in the aftermath of cases often presaged dire happenings. He went sidling and wary to the door, touched the viewplate, to reveal the face of Sir Estevan Tristo.

Hetzel slid the door aside. Sir Estevan came slowly into the room. He presented, thought Hetzel, a most untypical and dispirited appearance. His skin showed the color of putty; his yellow hair seemed wilted. Without waiting for an invitation, Sir Estevan lowered himself into a chair. Hetzel poured a second goblet of Baltranck and soda and handed it to Sir Estevan.

"Thank you." Sir Estevan swirled the liquid around the glass and stared down into the cusps of reflected light. He looked up at Hetzel. "You wonder why I am here."

"Not at all. You want to talk to me."

Sir Estevan showed a wan smile and tasted the cordial. "Quite true. As you divined, I took an extraordinary interest in Zaressa, and now I find myself in a rather maudlin state. Life now seems very grim, very grim indeed."

"I can appreciate this," said Hetzel. "Zaressa was a most charming creature."

Sir Estevan set the goblet upon the table. "Byrrhis encountered her at Twisselbane on Tamar, apparently under rather sordid circumstances. He sent her out here and recommended that I give her a job. I became enamored; I transferred Vvs. Felius to the reception desk and installed Zaressa as my secretary, and she quickly made herself indispensable. Meanwhile, of course, she was plotting with the unspeakable Byrrhis." Sir Estevan picked up the goblet and drank. "But now, poor thing, I forgive her everything; she is paying very dearly for her offense."

"Indeed? I thought you had merely instructed her to leave Maz."

"So I did; this was her intention. I mentioned to you that Liss and Olefract both are able to eavesdrop on my offices. They knew as soon as we that Zaressa was involved in the assassinations. Zaressa went to her rooms to pack. She was accosted by two men, taken to a vehicle, and delivered to the Liss. Her roommate communicated with me; I made an urgent protest, but to no avail. They sent her away in a Liss ship. She'll never see another human being in whatever span of life remains to her."

Hetzel made a small grimace. Both men sat quiet, watching colors shift and change in their goblets.

Sir Estevan had departed. Hetzel sat for a period in silent reflection. Then he telephoned the Roseland Residence. Janika was not in her rooms. Hetzel wondered as to where she might be.

Five minutes later she rang the chime at his door. Hetzel let her in. Her eyes were red, her face was swollen with tears. "Have you heard what happened to Zaressa?"

Hetzel put his arm around her shoulder and stroked her hair. "Sir Estevan told me."

"I want to leave Maz; I never want to come back."

"There's a packet leaving tomorrow. I reserved passage for you."

"Thank you. Where does it take us?"

"Where do you want to go?"

"I don't know. Anywhere."

"That can easily be arranged." Hetzel lifted the flask that once had contained Baltranck and that now was dry. "Do you care for an aperitif? We can sit out in the garden and have the waiter bring us something refreshing."

"That sounds pleasant. Let me go wash my face. I'm sure I look ridiculous. But when I think of Zaressa, I go to pieces."

They sat at a table where they could watch the glittering flakelet of a sun drift down the sky. Across the Plaza the Triskelion loomed through the murk. "This is a terrible world," said Janika. "I'll never forget it; I'll never be gay and careless again. Do you know, it might as easily have been me as Zaressa; I might easily have done just what she did. How would she know that Casimir Wuldfache planned to shoot the Triarchs?"

"So . . . Vv. Byrrhis wasn't guilty after all."

Janika gave a scornful laugh. "He'd never have taken the risk. And Zaressa would never have opened the door for him. For Casimir Wuldfache she'd do anything. Even in Twisselbane she yearned for him. He preferred me; I couldn't tolerate him, and so both Casimir and Zaressa hated me."

"Casimir Wuldfache, oddly enough, is responsible for my being here now."

"Oh? How so?"

"At first I thought it a coincidence, but now—"

Footsteps sounded; Gidion Dirby sauntered up the path. He gave an astounded gasp and stopped short, staring at Janika with eyes bulging from his face. "What are you doing here?"

CHAPTER 15

As before, Sir Ivon Hacaway received Hetzel on the terrace of Harth Manor. Hetzel had already presented a brief report by telephone, and Sir Ivon's manner was far more affable than on the previous occasion.

Hetzel described his activities in detail and rendered his expense account, in regard to which Sir Ivon gave a rueful smile. "My honor, but you do yourself well!"

"I saw no need to stint," said Hetzel. "I do high-quality work under high-quality conditions. There remains a single matter to discuss—the bonus that you offered for decisive effectuation. Istagam is no longer in existence, and nothing could be more definite than this."

Sir Ivon's face clouded. "I hardly see the need for any larger outlay."

"As you wish. I can earn a rather smaller sum by writing an article for the micronics trade journal, describing the possibilities for a new, better-organized Istagam. After all, it never was and is not now illegal to employ Gomaz labor, and *chir* is cheap."

Sir Ivon gave a weary sigh and brought out his checkbook. "A thousand SLU will be sufficient, and I will make it my business to see that *chir* is declared contraband."

"Two thousand would better convey your appreciation. However, I'll settle for fifteen hundred, and I believe that Sir Estevan Tristo has already placed an embargo on *chir*. Still . . ."

Sir Ivon glumly wrote the check. Hetzel expressed gratitude, wished Sir Ivon good health, and took his leave. He went to the front of the manor, rang the chime, and when the footman opened the door, requested a word with Lady Bonvenuta. He was conducted into the library, where Lady Bonvenuta shortly appeared. At the sight of Hetzel she halted, raised her eyebrows. "Yes?"

"I am Miro Hetzel, to whom a friend of yours, a certain Madame X, entrusted a trifle of confidential business."

Lady Bonvenuta touched her lips with the tip of her tongue. "I'm afraid I know of no such Madame X."

"She was anxious to locate a gentleman by the name of Casimir

Wuldfache, and I am pleased to report that I have details on his present whereabouts."

"Indeed?" Her voice was more frosty than ever.

"First, I must inform you that Casimir Wuldfache took advantage of Madame X and her friendship with you and rifled Sir Ivon's file of private papers. This will come as a great shock to you."

"Why, yes. Of course. But, then . . . well, I think I know the Madame X to whom you refer. She will want to learn where this Casimir Wuldfache can be found."

"The information reached me as an incidental to another effectuation, and I will not require payment, especially as Casimir Wuldfache is dead."

"Dead!" Lady Bonvenuta blinked and clutched at a chair with bejeweled fingers.

"Dead as a doornail. I myself saw his corpse on the Steppe of Long Bones, north of Axistil, on the planet Maz, where he had been engaged in business. May I ask you a question?"

"This is shocking news! What is your question?"

"A rather trivial matter. Did you recommend me to Sir Ivon, or did he remark to you that I was an efficient and dependable effectuator?"

"I heard him discuss you with one of his friends, and I passed the recommendation on to Madame X."

"Thank you," said Hetzel. "The chain of circumstances is now complete. My best regards to Madame X, and I hope that the news regarding Vv. Wuldfache will not distress her."

"I hardly think so. It was a matter of business. I will telephone her at this minute. Good day, Vv. Hetzel."

"Good day, Lady Bonvenuta. It has been a pleasure to meet you."

Jack Vance writes:

This is the first tale concerned with the adventures of Miro Hetzel, the effectuator, the second being "Freitzke's Turn," also destined for Bob Silverberg. There will probably be others; in fact among my notes I discover the following: "Miro Hetzel receives a commission to locate an unidentified man on an unknown world before he com-

mits an undefined act." No doubt a modus operandi will suggest itself; if not, Miro Hetzel must suffer his first failure.

In regard to "The Dogtown Tourist Agency," I have no particular comments to make. The less a writer discusses his work—and himself —the better. The master chef slaughters no chickens in the dining room; the doctor writes prescriptions in Latin; the magician hides his hinges, mirrors, and trapdoors with the utmost care. Recently I read of a surgeon who, after performing a complicated abortion, displayed to the ex-mother the fetus in a jar of formaldehyde. The woman went into hysterics and sued him, and I believe collected. No writer has yet been haled into court on similar grounds, but the day may arrive.